Great Circle

Great Circle

Maggie Shipstead

RANDOM HOUSE
LARGE PRINT

Copyright © 2021 by Maggie Shipstead

All rights reserved.
Published in the United States of America by Random House Large Print in association with Alfred A. Knopf, a division of Penguin Random House LLC, New York, and distributed in Canada by Penguin Random House Canada Limited, Toronto.

Cover image: **Spiral Descent** (detail) by Christopher Richard Wynne Nevinson. Photo © Peter Nahum at The Leicester Galleries, London / Bridgeman Images
Cover design by Kelly Blair

Maps by Joe LeMonnier
Title page photo © Maciej Radecki | Dreamstime.com

The Library of Congress has established a Cataloging-in-Publication record for this title.

ISBN: 978-0-593-45941-6

www.penguinrandomhouse.com/large-print-format-books

FIRST LARGE PRINT EDITION

Printed in the United States of America

10 9 8 7 6 5 4 3 2 1

This Large Print edition published in accord with the standards of the N.A.V.H.

For my brother

I live my life in widening circles
that reach out across the world.
I may not complete this last one
but I give myself to it.

I circle around God, around the
primordial tower.
I've been circling for thousands of years
and I still don't know: am I a falcon,
a storm, or a great song?

—RAINER MARIA RILKE,
The Book of Hours

Great Circle

I f you were to put a blade through any sphere and divide it into two perfect halves, the circumference of the cut side of each half would be a great circle: that is, the largest circle that can be drawn on a sphere.

The equator is a great circle. So is every line of longitude. On the surface of a sphere such as the earth, the shortest distance between any two points will follow an arc that is a segment of a great circle.

Points directly opposite each other, like the North and South Poles, are intersected by an infinite number of great circles.

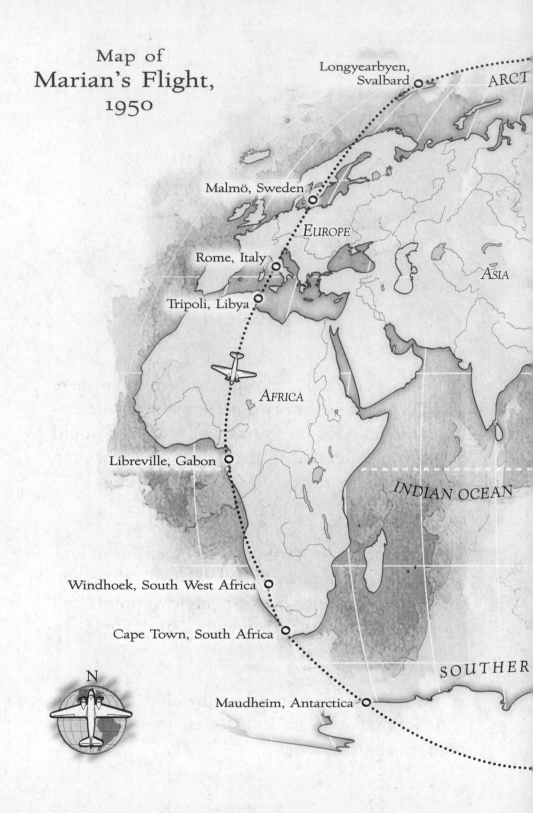

Map of
Marian's Flight,
1950

Longyearbyen,
Svalbard

ARCT

Malmö, Sweden

EUROPE

ASIA

Rome, Italy

Tripoli, Libya

AFRICA

Libreville, Gabon

INDIAN OCEAN

Windhoek, South West Africa

Cape Town, South Africa

SOUTHER

Maudheim, Antarctica

N

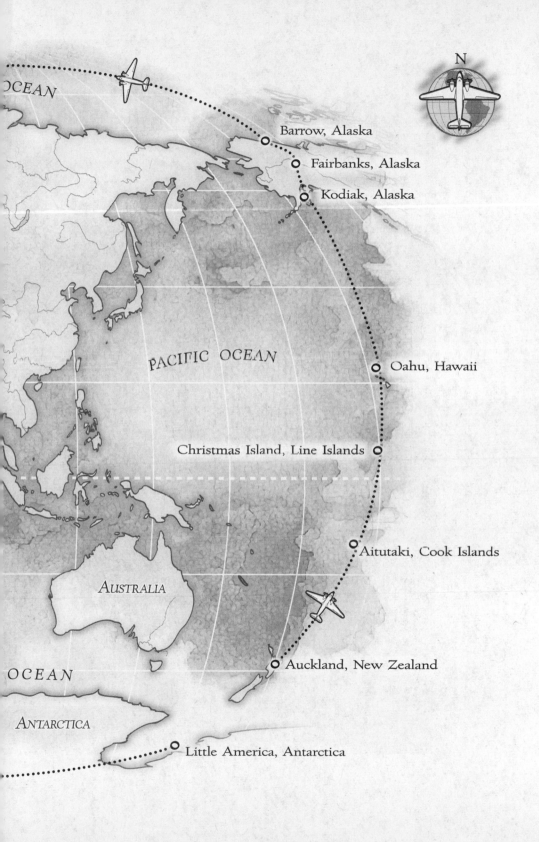

Little America III, Ross Ice Shelf, Antarctica
March 4, 1950

I was born to be a wanderer. I was shaped to the earth like a seabird to a wave. Some birds fly until they die. I have made a promise to myself: My last descent won't be the tumbling helpless kind but a sharp gannet plunge—a dive with intent, aimed at something deep in the sea.

I'm about to depart. I will try to pull the circle up from below, bringing the end to meet the beginning. I wish the line were a smooth meridian, a perfect, taut hoop, but our course was distorted by necessity: the indifferent distribution of islands and airfields, the plane's need for fuel.

Final entry from **The Sea, the Sky, the Birds Between: The Lost Logbook of Marian Graves.** Published by D. Wenceslas & Sons, New York, 1959.

I don't regret anything, but I will if I let myself. I can think only about the plane, the wind, and the shore, so far away, where land begins again. The weather is improving. We've fixed the leak as best we can. I will go soon. I hate the never-ending day. The sun circles me like a vulture. I want a respite of stars.

Circles are wondrous because they are endless. Anything endless is wondrous. But endlessness is torture, too. I knew the horizon could never be caught but still chased it. What I have done is foolish; I had no choice but to do it.

It isn't how I thought it would be, now that the circle is almost closed, the beginning and end held apart by one last fearsome piece of water. I thought I would believe I'd seen the world, but there is too much of the world and too little of life. I thought I would believe I'd completed something, but now I doubt anything can be completed. I thought I would not be afraid. I thought I would become more than I am, but instead I know I am less than I thought.

No one should ever read this. My life is my one possession.

And yet, and yet, and yet.

Los Angeles
December 2014

I only knew about Marian Graves because one of my uncle's girlfriends liked to dump me at the library when I was a kid, and one time I picked up a random book called something like **Brave Ladies of the Sky.** My parents had gone up in a plane and never come back, and it turned out a decent percentage of the brave ladies had met the same fate. That got my attention. I think I might have been looking for someone to tell me a plane crash wasn't such a bad way to go—though if anyone actually ever had, I would have thought they were full of shit. Marian's chapter said she'd been raised by her uncle, and when I read that, I got goose bumps because **I** was being raised (kind of) by **my** uncle.

A nice librarian dug up Marian's book for

me—**The Sea, the Sky,** etc.—and I pored over it like an astrologist consulting a star chart, hopeful that Marian's life would somehow explain my own, tell me what to do and how to be. Most of what she wrote went over my head, though I did come away with a vague aspiration to turn my loneliness into adventure. On the first page of my diary, I wrote "I WAS BORN TO BE A WANDERER" in big block letters. Then I didn't write anything else because how do you follow that up when you're ten years old and spend all your time either at your uncle's house in Van Nuys or auditioning for television commercials? After I returned the book, I pretty much forgot about Marian. Almost all of the brave ladies of the sky are forgotten, really. There was the occasional spooky TV special about Marian in the '80s, and a handful of die-hard Marian enthusiasts are still out there spinning theories on the internet, but she didn't stick the way Amelia Earhart did. People at least **think** they know about Amelia Earhart, even though they don't. It's not really possible.

The fact that I got ditched at the library so often turned out to be a good thing because while other kids were at school, I was sitting in a succession of folding chairs in a succession of hallways at every casting call in the greater Los Angeles area for little white girls (or little race-unspecified girls, which also means white), chaperoned by a succession of nannies and girlfriends of my uncle Mitch, two categories that sometimes overlapped. I think the girlfriends sometimes offered to take care of me because they wanted him to see them as maternal, which they thought would make them seem like wife material, but that wasn't actually a great strategy for keeping the flame alive with ol' Mitch.

When I was two, my parents' Cessna crashed into Lake Superior. Or that's the assumption. No trace was ever found. My dad, Mitch's brother, was flying, and they were on their way to a romantic getaway at some friend's middle-of-nowhere backwoods cabin to, as Mitch put it, reconnect. Even when I was little, he told me that my mother wouldn't quit fucking around. His words. I'm not sure Mitch believed in childhood. "But they wouldn't quit each other, either," he'd say. Mitch definitely believed in taglines. He'd started out directing cheesy TV movies with titles like **Love Takes a Toll** (that was about a toll collector) and **Murder for Valentine's Day** (take a wild guess).

My parents had left me with a neighbor in Chicago, but their last will and testament left me to Mitch. There wasn't really anyone else. No other aunts or uncles, and my grandparents were a combination of dead, estranged, absent, and untrustworthy. Mitch wasn't a bad guy, but his instincts were of the opportunistic, Hollywoodian variety, so after he'd had me a few months, he called in a favor to get me cast in an applesauce commercial. Then he found my agent, Siobhan, and I got consistent-enough work in commercials and guest spots and TV movies (I played the daughter in **Murder for Valentine's Day**) that I can't remember a time I wasn't acting or trying to. It seemed like normal life: putting a plastic pony in a plastic stable over and over while cameras rolled and some grown-up stranger told you how to smile.

When I was eleven, after Mitch had stepping-stoned from movies of the week to music videos and was white-knuckle climbing into the indie film world, I got my proverbial big break: the role of Katie McGee in a time-travel cable sitcom for kids called **The Big-Time Life of Katie McGee.**

On set, my life was squeaky-clean and candy-colored, all puns and tidy plotlines and three-walled rooms under a hot sky of klieg lights. I hammed it up to a braying laugh track while wearing outfits so extravagantly trendy I looked like a manifestation of the tween zeitgeist. When I wasn't working, I did pretty much whatever I wanted, thanks to Mitch's negligence. In her book, Marian Graves wrote: **As a child, my brother and I were largely left to our own devices. I believed—and no one told me otherwise for some years—that I was free to do as I liked, that I had the right to go any place I could find my way to.** I was probably more of an impetuous little brat than Marian, but I felt the same way. The world was my oyster, and freedom was my mignonette. Life gives you lemons, you carve off their skins and garnish your martinis.

When I was thirteen, after the **Katie McGee** merch had started selling like crazy and after Mitch had directed **Tourniquet** and was rolling around in success like a pill-popping pig in shit, he moved us to Beverly Hills on our shared dime. Once I wasn't stuck out in the Valley anymore, the kid who played Katie McGee's big brother introduced me to his rich dirtbag high-schooler friends, and they drove me around and took me to parties and got in my pants. Mitch probably didn't notice how much I was gone because he was usually out, too. Sometimes we'd bump into each other coming home at two or three in the morning, both messed up, and we'd just exchange nods like two people passing in a hotel corridor, attendees at the same rowdy conference.

But here's a good thing: The on-set tutors for **Katie McGee** were decent, and they told me I should go to college, and since I liked the sound of that, I weaseled my way into NYU after the show ended, with substantial extra credit for being a B-list TV star. I was already packed and ready to move when Mitch overdosed, and if I hadn't been, I probably would have just stayed in L.A. and partied myself to death, too.

Here's something that might have been good or bad: After one semester, I got cast in the first **Archangel** movie. Sometimes I wonder what would have happened if, instead, I'd finished college and stopped acting and been forgotten about, but it's not like I possibly could have turned down the colossal amount of money that came with playing Katerina. So everything else is irrelevant.

In my blip of higher education, I had time to take Intro to Philosophy and learn about the panopticon, the hypothetical prison Jeremy Bentham came up with, where there would be one itty-bitty guardhouse at the center of a giant ring of cells. One guard was all you needed because he **might** be watching at any time, and the idea of being watched matters way more than actually being watched. Then Foucault turned the whole thing into a metaphor about how all you need to discipline and dominate a person or a population is to make them think it's **possible** they're being watched. You could tell the professor wanted us all to think the panopticon was scary and awful, but later, after **Archangel** made me way too famous, I wanted to take Katie McGee's preposterous time machine back to that lecture hall and ask him to consider the opposite. Like instead of one guard in the middle, you're in the middle, and thousands, maybe millions, of guards are watching you—or might be—all the time, no matter where you go.

Not that I would have had the nerve to ask a professor anything. At NYU everyone was always staring at me because I'd been Katie McGee, but it felt like they were staring at me because they knew I didn't deserve to be there. And maybe I didn't, but you can't measure fairness in a lab. You can't know if you **deserve** something. Probably you don't. So it was a relief, too, when I quit school for **Archangel,** to go back to having a million obligations I had no choice about and a daily schedule I didn't decide for myself. At college I'd flipped through the course catalog, as fat as a dictionary, in complete bafflement. I'd drifted through the cafeteria, looking at all the different foods, at the salad bars and the mountains of bagels and the bins of cereal and the soft-serve machine, and I'd felt like I was being asked to solve some monumental, life-or-death riddle.

After I'd wrecked everything and Sir Hugo Woolsey (**the** Sir Hugo, who happens to be my neighbor) started talking to me about some biopic he was producing and pulled Marian's book from his tote bag—a book I hadn't thought about in fifteen years—suddenly I was in a library again, looking at a slender hardback that might hold all the answers. Answers sounded nice. They sounded like something I wanted, not that I could ever quite unravel what I wanted. Not that I even really knew what wanting meant. I mostly experienced desire as a tangle of impossible, contradictory impulses. I wanted to vanish like Marian; I wanted to be more famous than ever; I wanted to say something important about courage and freedom; I wanted to **be** courageous and free, but I didn't know what that meant—I only knew how to pretend to know, which I guess is acting.

Today is my last day of filming for **Peregrine.** I'm sitting in a mock-up of Marian's plane that's hanging from a pulley system and is about to be swung out over a giant tank of water and dropped. I'm wearing a reindeer-fur parka that weighs a thousand pounds and will weigh a million once it gets wet, and I'm trying not to let on that I'm afraid. Bart Olofsson, the director, took me aside earlier, asked if I really wanted to do this stunt myself, given, you know, what happened to my parents. **I think I want to confront that,** I said. **I think I could use the closure.** He'd put his hand on my shoulder, done his best guru face. **You are a strong woman,** he'd said.

Closure doesn't really exist, though. That's why we're always looking for it.

The actor who's playing Eddie Bloom, my navigator, is also wearing a reindeer-fur parka and has waterproof blood makeup on his forehead because he's supposed to be knocked out by the impact. In real life, Eddie usually sat at a desk behind Marian's seat, but the screenwriters, two aggressively cheerful brothers with Hitler Youth haircuts and Hitler Youth faces, thought it would be better if Eddie came up front for the death dive. Sure, fine, whatever.

The story we're telling isn't what really happened,

anyway. I know that much. But I wouldn't say I know the truth about Marian Graves. Only she knew.

Eight cameras will record my plunge: six fixed, two operated by divers. The plan is to do it once. Twice, at most. It's an expensive shot, and our budget was never enormous and has now been exhausted and then some, but when you've come this far, the only way out is through. Best-case scenario, it takes all day. Worst-case scenario, I drown, wind up **In Memoriam,** wind up like my parents except in a fake plane and a fake ocean, not even trying to get anywhere.

"You're sure you want to do this?"

The stunt coordinator is checking my harness, all business as he digs around my crotch, feeling for the straps and clips among bristly reindeer hair. True to type, he's got a leathery face, a leathery wardrobe, and a stop-action way of walking from a few imperfect repair jobs.

"Totally," I say.

When he's done, the crane lifts us up, swings us out. There's a scrim at the end of the tank that makes a kind of horizon with the water, and I'm her, Marian Graves, flying over the Southern Ocean with my fuel gauge on empty, and I know I can't get anywhere other than where I am, which is nowhere. I wonder how cold the water will be, how long before I'm dead. I think through my options. I think about what I've promised myself. **A gannet plunge.**

"Action," says a voice in my earpiece, and I push on the fake plane's yoke as though I'm going to fly us down into the center of the earth. The pulleys tip the nose, and we dive.

The **Josephina Eterna**

Glasgow, Scotland
April 1909

An unfinished ship. A hull without funnels, caged in her slipway by a steel gantry above and a timber cradle below. Beyond her stern, under the four impotent blossoms of her exposed propellers, the River Clyde flowed green in unexpected sunshine.

From keel to waterline she was rust red, and above that, specially painted for the launch, she was white as a bride. (White made for better newspaper pictures.) After the flashbulbs have popped, after she has been moored lonely in the river for her fitting-out, men will stand on planks hung down her sides on thick ropes and paint the plates and rivets of her hull glossy black.

Her two funnels will be hoisted up, bolted down, lashed in place. Her decks will be planked in teak, her corridors and salons paneled in mahogany and walnut and oak. There will be sofas and settees and chaises, beds and bathtubs, seascapes in gilded frames, gods and goddesses in bronze and alabaster. The first-class china will be gilt-edged, patterned with gold anchors (the emblem of L&O Lines). For second class: blue anchors, blue edging (blue, the line's color). Third class will make do with plain white crockery and the crew with tin. Boxcars will arrive full of crystal and silver and porcelain, damask and velvet. Cranes will hoist aboard three pianos, dangling in nets like stiff-legged beasts. A grove of potted palms will be wheeled up the gangway. Chandeliers will be hung. Deck chairs hinged like alligator jaws will be stacked. Eventually the first load of coal will be poured in through apertures low in the hull, down into bunkers below the waterline, far from the finery. The first fire will be lit deep in her furnaces.

But on the day of her launch she was still only a shell, a bare and comfortless wedge of steel. A crowd jostled in her shadow: ship workers in rowdy clumps, Glaswegian families out for the spectacle, urchin boys peddling newspapers and sandwiches. A brilliantly blue sky flew overhead like a pennant. In this city of fog and soot, such a sky could only be a good omen. A brass band played.

Mrs. Lloyd Feiffer, Matilda, wife of the ship's new American owner, stood on a platform edged with blue-and-white bunting, a bottle of Scotch tucked under her arm. "Shouldn't it be champagne?" she had asked her husband.

"Not in Glasgow," he'd said.

Matilda was to break the bottle against the ship, christening it with the name she could scarcely bear to think of. She was impatient for the cathartic shattering of glass, for her task to be done, but now she could only wait. There was some kind of delay. Lloyd fidgeted, making occasional comments to the naval architect, who appeared rigid with anxiety. A few unhappy Englishmen in bowler hats milled around the platform, and a pair of Scotsmen from the shipbuilding firm, and several other men she couldn't identify.

This ship had already been half built when L&O Lines, founded in New York by Lloyd's father, Ernst, in 1857 and inherited by Lloyd in 1906, acquired the failing English line that had commissioned it. (Commissioned **her,** Lloyd was always correcting. But, to Matilda, ships would always be its.) The sheathing had been under way when money ran out and was resumed once Lloyd's dollars were converted to sterling, then steel. The men in bowler hats, up from London, remarking morosely among themselves about the glorious weather, had conceived of the ship, argued over its blueprints, chosen a sensible name that Lloyd had disregarded. All that, only to have ended up obsolete: cuckolds in carefully brushed hats on a bunting-swagged platform, the brass band's rousing march bubbling around their feet. Tallow had been smeared on the slipway to grease the ship's path, and Matilda could feel its thick animal odor permeating her clothes, coating her skin.

Lloyd had wanted a new liner to reinvigorate L&O. When Ernst died, the fleet had been tired and outdated, mostly tramp steamers plying the coastwise trade, plus some passenger-cargo ships chugging across the Atlantic and a few tired wind-jammers still running the Pacific grain and guano routes. This ship would not be the largest or fastest or most opulent liner crossing from Europe—no threat to the White Star Line monsters being built in Belfast—but Lloyd had told Matilda it would be a respectable ante at the fat cats' table.

"What's the news?" Lloyd barked, startling her. The question was addressed to Addison Graves, **Captain** Graves, who was standing nearby—looming, really, though his habitual hunch seemed intended as a preemptive apology for his height. He was thin, almost gaunt, but with bones as massive and heavy as cudgels.

"It's a problem with the trigger," he told Lloyd. "Shouldn't be much longer."

Lloyd frowned at the ship. "It's like she's in shackles. She's meant to be at sea. Don't you think, Graves?" He turned suddenly ebullient. "Don't you think she's absolutely magnificent?"

The bow towered over them, sharp as a blade. "She'll be a fine ship," Graves said mildly.

He was to be the ship's first captain, had come across for the launch with Lloyd and Matilda and the four young Feiffer sons—Henry, the eldest at seven, and Leander, the baby not even a year old, with Clifford and Robert in between, all being cared for somewhere out of the way by their two nannies. Matilda had hoped to warm up to Graves on the voyage. He was not unkind, never impolite, but his reserve seemed unbreachable. Even her boldest attempts to discover something of his inner workings had yielded nothing. **What drew you to the sea, Captain Graves?** she'd asked one night at dinner. He'd said, **Go far enough in any direction, and you'll find the sea, Mrs. Feiffer,** and she'd felt reproached. To her, he'd come to represent the basic impenetrability of male life. Lloyd loved him with a wholeheartedness he didn't seem to lavish on anyone else, certainly not Matilda. **I owe him my life,** Lloyd had said many times. **Your life can't be a debt,** she'd countered once, **or then it's not really yours, and nothing has been saved.** But Lloyd had only laughed, asked if she had considered becoming a philosopher.

They had crewed on a barque together as young men, Graves and Lloyd. Graves had been a working sailor and Lloyd, just graduated from Yale, was half pretending to be. Ernst, Lloyd's father, had said he needed to learn the ropes (literally) if he was to inherit L&O. When hapless Lloyd fell overboard off Chile, Graves was quick and accurate enough to throw him a line and haul him back aboard. Since then, Lloyd had always venerated Graves as a savior. (**But you're the one who** caught **the line,** Matilda said. **You're the one who hung on.**) After Chile, as Lloyd ascended through the firm, so, too, did Graves.

The platform was no longer in the shade. Sweat was making Matilda's corset stick and chafe. Lloyd seemed to think she'd been born knowing how to christen a ship. "Just break the bottle on the bow, Tildy," he'd said. "It's very simple."

Would she know when the moment came? Would they remember to tell her? All she knew was that she'd apparently be signaled (by whom, she wasn't sure) at the moment the ship began to slide, and she was to crack the whiskey against the bow, christening it **Josephina Eterna,** after her husband's mistress.

When, months before, at the breakfast table, she'd asked Lloyd what the ship would be called, he had told her without lowering his newspaper.

Matilda's cup had not rattled when she returned it to its saucer. At least she could be proud of that.

She had been young but not too young when Lloyd married her, twenty-one to his thirty-six, old enough to know she was being chosen for her fortune and breeding potential, not love. All she asked was that Lloyd behave with respectful discretion. She had explained this to him before their engagement, and he had listened kindly and agreed there was much to be said for individual privacy within marriage, especially since bachelor life had suited him so well for so long. "We understand each other, then," she had said and offered him her hand. Solemnly, he had shaken her hand and then kissed her, full on the mouth, for quite some time, and she had begun, in spite of herself, to fall in love. Bad luck.

But she would not go back on her word. As best she could, she made peace with Lloyd's wanderings, directing her passions toward her children and the maintenance of her wardrobe and person. Lloyd regarded her affectionately, she knew, and was more tender in bed than she gathered some husbands were, though she also knew she was fundamentally not to his taste. He preferred temperamental, unappeasable women, usually older than Matilda, often older than even himself, older certainly than the ship's namesake, this Jo, who was only nineteen, dark and flighty. But Matilda knew enough to know it was often the lover who went against type who undid people.

The ship's name had seemed a poor repayment of her tolerance and generosity, and as soon as she'd found a moment alone, away from rattling china and servants' eyes, she had shed a few tears. Then she'd pulled herself together and soldiered on, as always.

On the platform, Lloyd turned to her, wrought up. "It's almost time."

She tried to ready herself. The bottle's neck was too short for her to get a good grip, especially not through her silk gloves, and it slipped from her grasp, landed with a thud perilously close to the platform's edge. As she picked it up, someone touched her shoulder. Addison Graves. Gently, he took the bottle. "You'd better remove your gloves," he said. When she had, he wrapped one of her hands around the neck and set the other palm flat against the cork. "Like this," he said, demonstrating a sideways arcing motion. "Don't be afraid to take a good swing because it's bad luck if the bottle doesn't break."

"Thank you," she murmured.

At the platform's edge, she waited for her signal, but nothing happened. The bow stayed where it was, the immense upturned nose of a proud and haughty thing. The men were talking urgently among themselves. The naval architect went rushing off. She waited. The bottle grew heavier. Her fingers ached. Down in the crowd, two men were shoving each other, causing a commotion. As she watched, one struck the other in the face.

"Tildy, for God's sake!" Lloyd was tugging at her arm. The bow was sliding away. So quickly. She had not expected something so large would go so quickly.

She leaned out and hurled the bottle after the retreating wall of steel. Awkwardly, overhand. It thudded against the hull but did not break, only bounced off and dropped to the slipway, shattering on the concrete in a splat of glass and amber liquid. The **Josephina** receded. The river rose up behind the stern in a green bulge, collapsed into foam.

North Atlantic
January 1914
Four years and nine months later

Josephina Eterna, eastbound in the night. A jeweled brooch on black satin. A solitary crystal on the wall of a dark cave. A stately comet in an empty sky.

Below her lights and honeycombed cabins, below the men toiling in red heat and black dust, below her barnacled keel, a school of cod passed, a dense pack of flexing bodies in the darkness, eyes bulging wide though there was nothing to see. Below the fish: cold and pressure, empty black miles, a few strange, luminescent creatures drifting after flecks of food. Then the sandy bottom, blank except for faint trails left by hardy shrimp, blind worms, creatures who would never know such a thing as light existed.

The night Addison Graves came to dinner and

found Annabel seated beside him was the second out of New York. He had descended without enthusiasm from the masculine quiet of the bridge into the dining room's trilling, sparkling cacophony. The air felt hot and moist, smelled of food and perfume. The ocean cold clinging to his wool uniform evaporated; immediately he prickled with sweat. At his table, he stooped in a bow, cap under his arm. The passengers' faces radiated a predatory eagerness for his attention. "Good evening," he said as he sat, shaking out his napkin. He rarely gleaned pleasure from conversation, certainly not from the self-congratulatory chitchat demanded by passengers wealthy or important enough to wrangle seats at the captain's table. At first he registered nothing beyond the pale green of Annabel's dress. On his other side sat an older woman in brown. The first of a long series of fussy dishes arrived, borne from the kitchen by tailcoated waiters.

Lloyd Feiffer had promoted Addison to captain as soon as he'd inherited L&O, when the turned earth was still fresh on his father's grave. Over a steak dinner at Delmonico's, Lloyd had given him charge of a ship, and Addison had only nodded, not wanting to betray his elation. Captain Graves! The miserable boy he'd been long ago on that farm in Illinois would finally be gone forever, ground to nothing under the heel of his polished boot, tossed overboard.

But Lloyd had raised one small concern. "You'll

have to be **genial,** Graves. You'll have to **converse.** It's part of what they pay for. Don't look like that. It won't be so bad." He paused, looking anxious. "Do you think you can manage?"

"Yes," Addison had said, his ambition outweighing the dread in his heart. "Of course."

Waiters swirled around delivering bowls of consommé. On Addison's right, Mrs. Somebody-or-Other in the brown dress was relating her sons' life histories in great detail and with such slow and deliberate enunciation that she might have been reading out the terms of a treaty. Lamb with mint jelly appeared and was eaten. Then roast chicken. Over the salad, during a brief intermission in his neighbor's recitation, Addison turned, finally, to the woman in the pale green dress. Annabel, she'd said her name was. She appeared quite young. He asked if it would be her first time in Britain.

"No," she said. "I've been several times."

"Then you enjoy it?"

At first she did not reply. Then, when she spoke, her tone was matter-of-fact. "Not particularly, but my father and I decided it would be best if I left New York for a while."

A curious admission. He studied her more closely. Her head was lowered; she seemed intent on her meal. She was older than he had initially thought, in her late twenties, and extremely fair, though the careless application of her rouge and lipstick gave her a blurred, feverish appearance. She had cream-colored hair like the mane of a palomino horse and eyelashes and eyebrows so pale as to be almost invisible. Abruptly, she looked up and met his gaze.

Her irises were light blue, filigreed with bright, pale interlocking rings like sun dapples. In them he recognized a proposition, brazen and unmistakable. He knew the look from women in the South Pacific lounging bare-breasted in the shade, from whores half hidden in the gloom of port city alleys, from **karayuki-san** ushering him into lantern-lit rooms. He glanced at her father across the table, a florid, wiry man talking boisterously, seemingly oblivious to his daughter.

"You despise this," Annabel said in a low voice. "Talking to these people. I can tell because I do, too."

Addison begged off dessert. Something needed his attention, do forgive him. He made his way out of the dining room and up two flights of stairs, clanged out through a door—CREW ONLY—onto a patch of open deck behind the bridge.

He rested his elbows on the railing. No one was around. The sea was lightly chopped. The marbled seam of the Milky Way arced through the clear, moonless sky.

He had politely denied despising anything, had turned away from the young woman and asked his other neighbor if she had any more amusing stories about her children. But Annabel had continued to burn at his periphery. Green dress, pale eyelashes. That look. So unexpected. A blue flame, unwavering and alien.

There was some relief in the workmanlike atmosphere of the bridge and, later, in the midnight pot of coffee brought to his cabin, but still she burned. In his bath, his bony knees poking out of the water, he had let his hand drift to his groin, thinking of her flushed cheeks, the loose wisps of pale hair at her nape.

It was well past midnight when she knocked at his door. She was still in the green dress, an apparition. He didn't know how she had found his cabin, but she stepped briskly inside as though she had been to see him many times before. She was smaller than he'd thought, her head only reaching the middle of his chest, and she was shivering violently. Her skin was bluish and very cold, and for the first few minutes he could barely stand to touch her for the chill.

New York City
September 1914
Nine months later

The babies were crying.

Annabel did not move. She was standing at her bedroom window in Addison's redbrick townhouse (black trim, black door with a brass knocker, near the river) and looking across the street at a black cat sleeping in a third-floor window. Often it was there. Sometimes, tail flicking, it watched pigeons pecking in the gutters below. When the cat flicked its tail, Annabel was compelled to wag one finger. When the cat stopped, she stopped. At night, lying sleepless, she would wag her finger until the digit was painfully tight and sore. A scold's gesture. Tick-tock.

In overlapping bursts, the crying built to a furious peak.

Better not to move from the window than risk the visions that bubbled up, smelling of brimstone, when she went near the twins. She should not go in the kitchen where there were knives. She should not venture near down pillows or basins of water. She should not hold the babies in her arms because she might bring them up to this window and drop them from it. **Wicked,** came her mother's voice. **Wicked, wicked, wicked.**

During one of her stints at boarding school, the morning after an ice storm, she had taken cautious gliding steps off her dormitory's porch and into a blinding, brittle, splintery world. Each maple in the school's central green was locked in its own close-fitting glass case, toothed with icicles. When the babies cried, she became like those trees: first rooted, then frozen. Their wails seemed as remote and unanswerable as the cries of birds circling their ice-filled nests.

Addison had been on the **Josephina** when they were born. Annabel had begun labor on September 4, three weeks early, and the twins were finally expelled more than a day later, an eternity later, before dawn on the sixth, the first day of the Battle of the Marne. No names had occurred to her, and she had waved a hand in acquiescence when the midwife suggested Marian and the doctor offered James, to be called Jamie.

For Annabel, the horror of the birth had merged

with the horror of the war, now that she knew what it was to scream, to bleed. The birth had become the new trouble to which her mind returned when she let her guard down. The basin of red water reappeared, the doctor's knives and forceps and sewing needles. She saw again the purple infants smeared with blood and something like custard, as small as puppies, and she was revisited by her first horror at the sight of them, her fleeting, addled belief that the doctor was holding her organs in his hands, that she had been eviscerated. The midwife had told her the birth would be a trial, but, afterward, joy would overwhelm her. Either the woman had been lying, or, more likely, Annabel was an unnatural mother.

When the babies were five days old, Addison had returned. He had stood looking into their bassinet with a puzzled expression and then at Annabel where she lay, rank with sweat, her hair matted. She'd been refusing to bathe because the doctor said warm water would encourage milk production, and she was determined for hers to dry up.

"Cool water, then," the day nurse said. "To soothe your parts."

Annabel had told her she would rather die than take a cold bath. "Your business is with the babies, not with me," she said. "Leave me be."

She had matched Addison's silence, and the next day he left again.

"Only a touch of the melancholies," the day nurse said. "I've seen it before. You'll be yourself again soon."

Yourself.

A memory from the murk of her first years. Moonlight bluing the nursery curtains; her father beside her, holding her. No one ever held her. The warmth of another body was intoxicating. Instinctively, she had clutched the silk front of his robe and felt him trembling. There the memory ended.

Age seven. She was standing in the pantry in the house in Murray Hill with her dress lifted while the cook's son, a boy of about eleven, crouched in front of her. A jagged cry from the doorway and a great, flapping rushing-in. Bosomy, bustled, black-skirted Nanny overfilled the small space like a crow jammed in a house for sparrows. The cook's boy yelped at being trampled. Nanny gave only that one cry, then nothing but agitated nose-breathing as she dragged Annabel upstairs and locked her in a closet.

Dark in there, but with a keyhole view across the hallway to the nursery, her yellow quilt on the bed and a doll abandoned facedown on the floor. "Was I bad?" she had asked Nanny through the door.

"You know you were," Nanny said. "You are the worst kind of girl. You ought to be more than ashamed."

What lay beyond shame? Annabel wondered,

crouching among dustpans and tins of furniture polish. If what she had done was so abominable, why was it permissible for her father, the god of the household, vastly more powerful than even her mother or Nanny, to touch the part of her that the cook's son had offered her a piece of lemon candy only to look at, the part that Nanny called her cabbage? This is our secret, her father said about his visits, and Mother must not know because she would be jealous of how much he loved Annabel and how much Annabel loved him and how they were warm together.

The day she showed her cabbage to the cook's boy, her mother beat her on her bare legs and back-side and called her **wicked, wicked, wicked.**

The first doctor prescribed daily baths in cold water, a vegetarian diet.

Nanny refused to answer any questions about the nature of wickedness. "That sort of talk will only encourage you."

Although, once, when Annabel had asked if boys' cabbages were bad, too, Nanny had burst out with, "Stupid child, boys don't have cabbages. They have carrots."

Wickedness, it seemed, had to do with vegetables.

Uneasily, guiltily, for reasons she could not have begun to explain, Annabel began, during unsuper-vised moments in the nursery or the bath, to touch her cabbage. The sensation dulled her mind in a pleasant way, built to an absorbing comfort, even had the power to drive off unwelcome thoughts: the skinned lamb, for example, that she had seen in the kitchen with its tongue hanging out or her mother calling her wicked. It even muffled thoughts of her father. Her father said he was trying to do something nice. That his visits filled her with dread must mean there was something wrong with her. She would try to be better.

Age nine. She woke to a gust of cold air, morning light, her yellow quilt being snatched away. Her mother stood over her, clutching the quilt like a matador's cape. Too late, Annabel realized her hands had, in her sleep, migrated under her nightgown. **Wicked,** said her mother, rearing over her like an ax about to drop. The next night Nanny bound Annabel's wrists, and she slept with her fingers interlaced as though in prayer.

"Your mother is a good woman," her father told her, patting the cords on her wrists but not untying them. "But she doesn't understand how we want to be warm together."

"Am I wicked?" Annabel asked.

"We're all a **little** wicked," said her father.

The second doctor was old and houndish, with pouchy eyes and speckled skin and long earlobes. With tongs he extracted a solitary leech from a glass jar. He nudged her legs apart.

A ringing pressed in her ears. An obscuring white light swirled in like a snowstorm, was rent apart by a bright jolt of smelling salts. The doctor went out to speak to her mother, leaving the door open.

Overexcitement, he said. **Very serious . . . not cause for despair yet.**

More cold baths and a Borax solution to be applied weekly. She was to be kept away from spices, bright colors, quick-tempoed music, anything lively or stimulating. Before bed, she was to be given a spoonful of syrup from an amber bottle that sent her into a bottomless sleep. Some mornings she thought she detected the faint smell of tobacco on her pillow, but she remembered nothing.

The day she woke, twelve years old, terrified in bloody sheets, her mother told her that she would not die but the blood would come every month as a reminder to be always on her guard against, yes, again, always: wickedness.

Around then, two other events: First, she noticed she had not smelled tobacco on her pillow for some time, and, second, she was sent away to school. The sunny chatter of the other girls, their books and bedtime prayers and homesickness and letters to their mothers, the cheerful dances they practiced with one another, their fussing over their hair and pinching of their cheeks for color—all of it made her feel like a small dark spider scuttling among their merry shoes. In a rush of fury, she understood she knew nothing of the world. She had been kept from it.

How to remedy her appalling ignorance?

Be attentive. Eavesdrop. Sift and strain for clues. Choose books at random from the library, steal more books from other girls, especially the forbidden ones they have kept hidden. Read **Wuthering Heights** and **Treasure Island** and **Twenty Thousand Leagues Under the Sea** and **The Moonstone.** Read **Dracula** and have nightmares about the zoophagous madman in the asylum, Renfield, who feeds flies to spiders and spiders to birds and eats the birds and wishes to consume as many lives as possible. Steal **The Awakening** and dream about walking into the sea, though you have never been in any water but the bathtub. (Even at school, her baths are cold.) From these books, gradually piece together jumbled theories about how other notions of shame and wickedness exist besides your mother's. Intuit that some women wish to be touched by men. (The girls sighed over certain books, lying back on their pillows. **So romantic,** they remarked, though not to Annabel, whom they found strange.) When she was sure everyone else was asleep, she returned to touching what she no longer thought of as her cabbage but as her thing, not greenly inert but alive and animal. The sensation became sharper, a piquant fishhook that snagged on her nerves as though on a net, pulling her along. She found a flickering and thrumming, a pulse and flash.

Once a week a young man came to the school to

instruct the girls in piano. He leaned over Annabel while she sat on the bench and with his long fingers sounded low, tolling notes. He was almost as blond as she, with arched, surprised eyebrows and comb marks in his hair. She took his hand one day and put it on her dress, over her thing. The terror in his face baffled her.

In disgrace, she was sent to another, lesser school, but within a month she was called home because her mother was dead. Her father treated her with distant, bewildered politeness, seemed not to remember that once he had wanted to be warm with her. Nanny was gone, and, when she asked, her father said Annabel was too big for a nanny, wasn't she? Annabel took a bath so hot she emerged looking cooked.

(Only later, overhearing gossip at the funeral, did she learn her mother had drunk a whole bottle of sleeping draught.)

A third school, the one with the maple trees, the ice storm. Her history teacher was older than the piano tutor and not afraid of her. He found reasons to summon her to his office. "Like a fish to water," he said after he had relieved her of her virginity on a sagging sofa. "I could see it in you. I could see you would be this way."

"What do you mean?"

"It's in your gaze. Didn't you mean to seduce me?"

"I suppose so," she said, though she had not **quite** known what she meant to do. She had simply returned his glances, allowed him to proceed, felt a dull, sawing pressure while both of them remained mostly clothed. Afterward, as she crossed the school green, the sadness that seemed to be the aftermath of any human contact settled on her, but the experience had not been unpleasant, and she returned to his office willingly when he next summoned her. He turned away and fumbled with himself beforehand, which he said had to do with avoiding a child. With practice, she could draw the flickering and thrumming from his ministrations, occasionally even the pulse and flash, though the sadness afterward remained.

"Let's run away together," he said, and she had gazed at him from the sofa, confused he would think there was anywhere they could go.

She was not expelled from that school but graduated at sixteen and returned to New York. As best she could, she adopted a life of outward respectability as spinster consort to her father, his companion to dinners and parties and on his travels. She tried to be good, to ward off her wicked need. But she could no sooner chase it away than she could chop off her own head and continue living. She found lovers. Their discretion varied.

"Maybe you should consider marrying," her father said.

They both knew no one in New York would dream of marrying her, despite his wealth.

Lovemaking brought relief, yes, but also shame,

rumors, scorn. She wished to be different, to be someone who did not go with men, who was not oppressed by blackness or possessed by wanting. But she failed. She failed in New York, she failed in London ("Perhaps an **English** husband," her father had said), in Copenhagen ("Perhaps a **Danish** husband") and Paris ("Perhaps?") and Rome (no talk of an Italian husband). She failed on the **Josephina.** She had not thought she could possibly have a child, had been certain her womb was rotten with wickedness.

"Addison Graves," she said to her father after she was certain of her pregnancy.

"Who?"

"The captain. The ship captain."

On the night she met Addison, her father had gone to the smoking room after dinner, entrusting Annabel to the ladies' parlor, which was easily escaped. She had stood at the **Josephina**'s stern, studying the black water, the silver clouds of bubbles welling up from the propellers. Fear had coursed through her, binding her hands to the railing. She imagined the rush of wind, the shock of the cold, the huge, slicing blades, the retreating lights of the ship.

Would she have time to watch the ship disappear over the horizon? Would she be left alone at the center of a starry black sphere, to have as her last sight infinite quiet points of light? Nothing could be lonelier. Or, she thought, more truthful. In her experience, proximity to other humans did not actually diminish solitude. She imagined herself drifting down, down, settling on the ocean floor. One final cold bath to extinguish what burned.

The wind cut through her dress. She could never predict when her willpower would give way, but on that night wickedness saved her, pulled her away from the ship's wake and drew her to Addison's cabin instead. At dinner, he had seen her for what she was. She'd felt the force of his recognition like a slap.

Perhaps, the day nurse suggested, if she held her babies, she would be reminded how beautiful they were. She was lucky to have two healthy children when some lost their babies at birth, poor souls. "God made women to be mothers," the nurse said.

"If you have any sense, if you love your God, you will keep them away from me," Annabel said, and the nurse, frightened, had taken the babies and gone, shutting the bedroom door behind her.

Against her doctor's advice, she had placed ads for wet nurses in the newspapers before the twins were born and hired the first two women who applied. They both claimed to be married. Neither offered an explanation of how her breasts had come to be full of expendable milk, and Annabel did not ask. "In my opinion the practice is not far from prostitution," the doctor had said. "Often they place their own babies under the most appalling conditions so they may sell their milk. They are not likely to be good women." But goodness did not interest Annabel.

When she had left Addison's cabin and returned to her own at dawn, her father had been sitting awake in his room beside an empty tumbler and full ashtray, still in his tie and tails, waiting, the communicating door left open. "Annabel," he said. He looked old and tired, resigned. "What should I have done differently for you?"

"You should have let me sleep," she said, and shut the door.

New York City
October 1914
One month later

Lloyd Feiffer in mourning was outwardly no different from Lloyd Feiffer in the bloom of happiness. His coat and hat were impeccable. His collar was the ideal of whiteness and stiffness, his tie knot without flaw. He walked at a clip.

But, for a month, the Lloyd Feiffer enacting Lloyd Feiffer's life and habits had been no more than an animated carapace, a hollow effigy. Inside was a shadow, a twist of smoke, a dark spirit peering out as he perused manifests and negotiated coal prices and lunched on crab Newburg and screwed his mistress. What was there before, the jovial but ruthless man, full of scornful intelligence and restless energy, seemed to have drifted away with his son Leander's last breath.

Diphtheria. Age six.

Matilda had still not emerged from her bedroom (separated from Lloyd's by their dressing rooms and a shared sitting room) and had eaten almost nothing. The surviving boys—Henry, Clifford, Robert—were kept out of the way by their nanny, and Lloyd didn't know if they spent their time in morose sniffling or if they hollered and brawled. He had never been interested in his children's daily affairs, and he would not have anticipated that, upon losing one, such pain would rise, black and primitive as oil, from his particular bedrock.

Henry, who was twelve, had come to him in his study one night and politely asked to be sent away to school. Lloyd had demurred, saying his mother needed him close.

"But she doesn't even want to see me," Henry had said. "She never answers when I knock."

"Women," Lloyd had said, "resort to theater when they wish to demonstrate the depth and superiority of their emotions. Indulgence will only prolong the spectacle. She'll emerge when she perceives no advantage to continuing."

The boy had gone away, stung and downcast. In the small hours, tired of lying awake, Lloyd had thrown off his blankets and gone striding through the intervening rooms and into Matilda's bedroom intending to scold her for her torpor, to command her to rouse herself. But Tildy, in her bed, had wordlessly lifted her arms before he could speak, and he had fallen into them and wept onto her chest. This was the first time he had cried for Leander except for the day the boy died, when he had curled forward to submerge his face in his bath and wailed into the water. Nor had he embraced Tildy since . . . he could not remember. She smoothed his hair while he cried, and he cried until he slept.

In the morning, he left her room without a word. But the next night he returned to her, and the warmth of her thawed him. The night after that he had pushed up her nightgown and made love to her.

Since then, a week had passed, the days and nights taking on an inverted quality. The dark spirit ruled in the day, and at night his wife's body exorcised it. What Tildy thought about his visits he didn't know, but on this morning, as he left the house, she had been sitting at the breakfast table with the boys, wan and silent but upright, among the living.

Lloyd's chauffeur drove him down almost to the end of Broadway, not far from where Manhattan dipped its toe into the sea. After the birth of Robert, their third son, Lloyd and Matilda had sold their Gramercy Park house and joined the northward migration of fashionable souls to a new house at Fifty-Second Street, lengthening his commute.

He'd thought about relocating L&O's offices at least a bit uptown—some of their business was already being conducted at the Chelsea Piers—but the idea of separating himself from the entrenched and collusive downtown herd of shipping offices and ticketing halls made him uneasy.

But then he worried he was becoming pigheaded like his father. Even as Ernst's wealth had begun to accumulate, he had refused to move the family from their cramped apartment on Pearl Street. Having endured the upheaval of one child, he refused to give his wife another. He yielded from sail to steam power too slowly, without imagination. He only ever spoke German at home, took only German-language newspapers, seemed to have no interest in the country where he had settled beyond its capacity as an enormous machine that manufactured money.

On the stroke of eight, the chauffeur stopped in front of a stately limestone building, and Lloyd let himself out. He ignored the doorman's flourish of welcome, walked swiftly across the columned lobby to the elevators. The ninth floor was deserted at this early hour. On the walls hung immense maps, marked with routes and studded here and there with pushpins designating ships' locations, adjusted daily. What little space was left was occupied by framed paintings of the L&O fleet, most prominently the **Josephina Eterna** and her newer sister ship the **Maria Fortuna,** named upon her launch for an aging soprano Lloyd had been enamored with at the time.

In Lloyd's office, the early editions had already been arrayed on his desk by his assistant, a marvelously unobtrusive young man. Ordinarily Lloyd would call for a cup of tea and page efficiently through the newspapers, but on this day he sat motionless, gazing at the war headlines. Germans marauding through Belgium. Trenches dug as graves for the living. The war sinking into the soil of the Continent.

A sudden red burst of rage, as though from poked-at coals. He wished for Germany to lose the war, to be humiliated, for his father to return from the dead to see it happen. He wished for everyone to learn what it was to lose a son. He wished for a black slick of grief to spread across the planet.

Thousands had left New York, eagerly returning to their birth countries to participate in the bloodshed. Immigration in reverse. The wave of enthusiasm had passed, though, and L&O's ships were running eastbound at less than half capacity. Lloyd wondered if Ernst would have gone back to Germany, taken up a rifle in his bony old hands. Perhaps. Or he might have found some covert way of aiding the fatherland. By spying, maybe, or by smuggling supplies and munitions. Or he might have been too stubborn, too slow to do anything, even to profit.

He swiveled to look out the window. To the

west he had a slot view of the Hudson between the buildings. He hoped to glimpse the **Josephina** when she passed by later on her way to the Chelsea Piers. He thought he would like to have a drink with Addison Graves.

It was a bother, Lloyd's Germanness. His middle name, Wilhelm, now seemed incriminating, an act of corporate sabotage on the part of his father. But this war might offer new opportunities. There might be a role for him, a part to play. He was not his father.

Here the memory of Henry quietly closing the study door behind him intruded and was pushed away.

"How is your wife?" Lloyd asked Addison. He couldn't bear to inquire about the new babies, who had arrived only a few weeks before Leander's death, an unjust windfall of life.

Addison studied his whiskey. "Only God knows, to tell the truth. She seems to spend all her time in bed. The day nurse told me she takes no interest at all in the babies, doesn't wash or feed them. The nurse said sometimes new mothers have difficulties but none have ever frightened her like Annabel. She called it a 'terrible gloom.'"

"The gloom's in our house, too. They should mark the doors, like for the plague."

"I'm sorry. Did you receive my condolences?"

"Oh, probably. I don't know." Lloyd preferred gin to whiskey. He took a gulp. "None of that matters, I'm afraid, condolences and so on, but thanks all the same. What has Annabel got to be down about? Is something wrong with the twins?"

"No, they're perfectly healthy."

"Is she ill?"

"She won't see a doctor. She hates doctors. But I don't think illness is the problem, at least not of the body. She seems to be almost mourning the birth, as though . . . well. I don't understand it."

"Make her see a doctor."

"Yes, maybe I should."

"You've been at sea too much."

"On the ship I know what to do."

The bones in Addison's face seemed more pronounced than ever, the skin hanging hollow between his cheekbones and jaw, his brow shadowing his eyes. The dark spirit stirred in Lloyd, spiteful toward Annabel, who lolled in bed, burdening her husband, neglecting her infants, surely unable to imagine the suffering endured by himself and Matilda. He yearned suddenly to be home, to feel Matilda stroking his hair. He had never told Addison, but, before they married, Lloyd had encountered Annabel a few times at society dinners, had heard rumors about her so seamy as to seem implausible.

"You're too patient," he said to Addison. "Tell her to get up, make herself useful. Women like to be useful. Remind her how lucky she is. Give her a change of scene. Remind her she's alive." He felt himself going red in the face. His voice grew harsh. "Scrape her out of that bed with a shovel if you have to."

Addison looked up, something unreadable in his expression. Reproach? Concern? Quietly, he said, "Maybe you're right."

North Atlantic
December 1914
Six weeks later

The **Josephina Eterna** burned. A floating pyre, a raft of flames. It listed to starboard—slowly, slowly—as though easing over to douse itself in the sea.

Smooth black water. A dense blue dawn fog, diffusing the fire's glow.

Under the surface: a frill of ragged steel and busted rivets, water in the boiler rooms, extinguishing the furnaces and drowning the stokers, flooding the forward holds, rising through the plumbing and pouring from sinks and tubs and toilets, running down passageways and up elevator shafts, water that—slowly, slowly—pulled the ship onto her side, tugged her bow down. Her engines were dead, her propellers still. Smoke billowed from the stairwells, and passengers in white nightclothes billowed with it, already ghosts.

Addison intended to drown. He would stand stoically on deck, wait for the water to rise up the buttons of his coat, submerge his gold epaulettes, sweep him away. When he'd imagined such a moment, he had always known he would take the honorable course, but he'd never contemplated having a wife on board, certainly not two infants. He had been the one to insist Annabel come on the voyage. He'd almost needed to scrape her out of bed with the shovel Lloyd had suggested, but something had to be done. "You can't be this miserable forever," he'd told her.

"I don't see why not," she'd replied.

Fresh sea air would do her good, he'd said confidently, feeling no confidence. He'd issued his orders: the ship, the air. She had yielded. No nurses, he'd said. She must care for the children herself. She had yielded. She had come aboard like a piece of baggage, silent and passively unwieldy.

On some level, the experiment had appeared successful. Before the voyage, Annabel had not taken care of the babies for even a single day, but, once forced, she had somehow known how to swaddle them and change their diapers and plug their small mouths with bottles of a warm mixture of cow's milk, sugar, and cod liver oil made according to the night nurse's written formula and brought at all hours from the ship's kitchen. Addison might have felt vindicated if there hadn't been something not quite right about how Annabel went about her maternal tasks: blank-faced, mechanical as a mill worker. One night, he had found her standing at the stern, looking down into the dark water.

They were five days out when the explosion occurred, still a full day from Liverpool, slowed by the fog, entering a region of the sea bristling with periscopes and studded with mines.

Only five hundred and twenty-three passengers were on board, with room for three times that. The crew outnumbered them.

Addison had been awake when the blast came, before dawn. Driven mad by the wailing of one twin while Annabel fed the other, he had snatched up bottle and baby and brought both into bed with him.

As soon as the rubber nipple was in its mouth, the child had quieted, its pale eyes intent on his face. Addison loosened the swaddling, and a pair of mottled pink hands emerged. "Which one is this?" he said.

Where she sat, Annabel's face was in shadow. "I don't know," she said. "It doesn't matter."

The baby's body pulsed in his lap. Its small fingers flared and curled.

He felt the change of pressure in his ears before he heard the blast. The sound came from everywhere, permeating the air. The ship shuddered and seemed to twist. A whoosh, a second of suspended silence, then water raining down. Grinding vibration followed by quiet.

"What was that?" Annabel said. Sharp, not fearful.

He dressed hastily.

A section of the starboard railing was mangled and twisted; smoke and steam drove him back when he went to look over. A fire alarm rang shrilly, maddeningly. On the bridge, he ordered the engine room be telegraphed STOP, though the engines had already gone dead. He sent the third officer below to investigate. Already, the list to starboard was noticeable. He stood motionless, looking at his boots, calculating. Fog pressed flat against the bridge windows like a blindfold. "Ready the boats," he said. "Sound the general alarm."

In the radio room, the operators tapped out distress calls. Dots and dashes. The nearest ship, a merchant vessel, was thirty nautical miles away and COMING FULL SPEED. But it would not arrive for two hours.

He considered the fire, the starboard list, the blue fog, the black water. "Abandon ship," he said to the first mate, who shouted it to the other officers, who shouted it in return. A strange echo, growing louder instead of fading.

The boat deck was in chaos. Crew members with megaphones yelled instructions over the passengers' commotion, the cranking davits, the hiss of steam. Addison strode the length of the ship, trying to impose order. He told himself he would only duck away for a moment, only ensure that Annabel was on her way to the boats with the babies and bid them a brief, stoic farewell.

He made his way through the smoke and clamor.

The simple fact that Annabel was not in the cabin dawned on him with dreamlike slowness. The two swaddled infants screamed in their basket. Annabel was not in the armchair or in the bed. She was not in the bathroom, where seawater was pouring from the fixtures. The babies' faces were purple and contorted with outrage, their spongy pink tongues curling in their shrieking mouths. He opened the wardrobe, but of course Annabel was not inside. He stepped out into the corridor, called her name, then shouted it.

Long ago Addison had trained himself not to hesitate. If he had hesitated before throwing that line to Lloyd, his friend would have drowned, would never have been his friend. But now he hesitated, standing in the middle of the cabin, waiting for something to change, for some solution to emerge. Finally, still hesitantly, he went to the wardrobe and removed his pistol from its case, loaded it, and dropped it in the pocket of his greatcoat. He lifted the babies from their basket, one in each arm.

Down the tilting stairs, out a heavy tilted steel door by pressing the latch with an elbow, pushing with a shoulder. He found the twins' flopping heads alarming, their larval bodies cumbersome.

On the boat deck, pressing aft through a panicked mob, he craned and swiveled, looking for Annabel. Where was she? The question rang in his mind, deafening and relentless. A quiet voice, speaking from some silent inner part of him, answered **You won't find her.** If she had planned to return, she would not have left.

Deep scrums had formed around the boats not yet launched or on fire or beached on the sloping portside hull. A dangerous gap was opening between the starboard boats and the ship's edge.

As Addison passed, a lowering boat wobbled on its ropes, tipped and overturned, dumping people into a sea already teeming with them. Addison felt little for them. People were dying, but soon he would die, too.

At Boat 12, he stopped. The gap was widening. This boat would be among the last launched. With one arm, he clamped the babies against his body. With the other, he drew his pistol and shot into the air.

The passengers screamed and fell away, half flattened, like tall grass in a gust of wind.

He pushed through to the edge of the deck, brandishing the gun. **Back,** he told them, **get back!** He cleared a half-moon of space so those going in the boat would have room for a few steps' running start before leaping over the gap, the strip of far-below black water. The crewmen at the davits, probably doomed themselves, tried to hold the boat steady with hooked poles. The babies cried, but Addison barely heard them.

One by one he selected those who would go in the boat, pulling them out of the crowd, signaling with a flick of the pistol when it was their turn to leap over the gap. Women and children. The women gathered their skirts and jumped. None fell. He began to look for which woman he would hand his children to, who could be trusted to survive.

When the boat was full, he still couldn't see a face he liked. They were all just strangers, just women with fearful eyes and mouths that jabbered or trembled. In his arms were babies about to be orphaned. He stepped close to the edge, grasping the swaddling of one infant, preparing to hand it across. He didn't know which twin it was. He was eager to shed his burden, to feel the rising water.

His mistake was to look at the baby's face, a knot of helpless outrage. One glance dizzied him like an uppercut to the jaw. The water receded, spat him out. How could he entrust his children to unknown women in a small, tippy boat? How could he send them off across a sea full of drowning people who would reach up to grasp at the oars and gunwales like monsters from the deep? He saw the lifeboat capsizing, the babies' white swaddling fading into the depths like the canvas shrouds he had, in his sailing days, helped wrap around the dead before sliding them overboard. No, he needed to know if they lived, to see them to land or to death himself.

He gathered both twins to his chest, took two long steps and leapt across into the boat. The close-packed women drew back, and he half fell, half stepped among them, his body curving to protect the babies. Regaining his balance, he drew himself up to his full height and roared into the crewmen's astonished faces, "Lower away!"

Trained to obey, remembering the pistol, they worked the squeaking pulleys. Boat 12 with its cargo of women and children and one man dropped away from the crowd and the smoke, descended past flames poking around the edges of portholes like the fingers of trapped demons. Slowly, jerkily, it made its way down to the water, where it settled with a gentle splash.

New York City
July 1915
Seven months later

A new Feiffer son, born in the night after a short labor. The baby was severed from his mother, knotted off into his own self-hood, bathed and wrapped and fed from the breast. George, named after the king, a fifth son, though the five Feiffer boys would never be all together on this earth.

Lloyd collapsed beside Matilda, dressed but collar undone, tiny George between them. "How do you feel?" he said.

"Tired," she said, with a note of incredulity that she must say so. "But happy. And relieved to be happy. That surge of feeling—I had it with the others, but I didn't know if it was still possible."

He rested a finger against the infant's cheek.

Since Matilda had discovered she was pregnant, not long before the loss of the **Josephina,** Lloyd had been, as a gesture of atonement and superstition, faithful. He'd found, these eight months, a monkish peacefulness in a life with only one woman. (Though there was nothing monkish about how his new fortune was accruing thanks to the war, raining merrily down on top of his old one.)

He had been sloppy with the **Josephina,** eager and amateurish, driven by anger at his father and grief for Leander, and he had paid a terrible price. Of course, the hundreds burned and drowned had paid a worse one. And Addison Graves had been sent to Sing Sing.

Lloyd had only wanted to contribute to the effort against the Germans, to **do something,** and when his friend Sir Gerald de Redvers had suggested he might smuggle armaments to England on his ships, he'd leapt at the idea. In his haste, he hadn't sought enough advice, hadn't taken enough precautions. He hadn't even told Addison what was in the crates, only asked him—told him, really—to overlook their absence on the manifest.

But, he now understood, you couldn't put armaments on a ship as casually as if they were bolts of cotton, though he still didn't know what had triggered the explosion. The crates should have been safe enough. He had been assured they were properly packed; he'd assumed they were properly stowed. Something else must have gone wrong, but there was no way to know what. Some freak thing. Something that could not quite have been his own fault, not directly.

"It happened because I didn't break the bottle," Matilda had said in the days after. "I cursed the ship."

"It had nothing to do with you."

"You shouldn't have named it after that girl."

"You're right," he'd said. "I **am** sorry."

He could not remember ever apologizing to her before. Her pregnancy had been a buoy to which they'd clung during the first shock of the **Josephina,** the horror brought by the ringing of the telephone before dawn, the telegrammed counts of the rescued and the lost, the lists of names, the painful revisions to the counts and the lists, the photographs from the crowded decks of the freighters that had picked up survivors, including one of Addison Graves, alive, with his two babies.

Lloyd had known at once that Addison would absorb the worst of the public's rage ("Captain Cowardice," the press had dubbed him) and also that he would never tell anyone about the mysterious crates left off the manifest at Lloyd's request. Again Addison would save him. He was sorry—so sorry—for his friend, but what could he do? Surely Addison would not want L&O to fail, would understand that Lloyd himself must not go to prison. Matilda didn't know, of course, about the crates bound for Gerald de Redvers. She had forgiven

Lloyd so much already. He could not expect her to forgive this.

When the **Lusitania** sank five months after the **Josephina,** it had been a terrible tragedy, yes, but also, Lloyd could not deny, a help to his own situation. Who was to say the Germans hadn't also torpedoed the **Josephina,** perhaps even by mistake in the fog, and not acknowledged it? (Lloyd had suggested this theory to a few reporters, added tempting incentives for those willing to write it up.) The **Lusitania** had also been rumored to be carrying munitions of some kind. People loved a conspiracy, and they weren't wrong that the holds of ships were good places to store secrets.

Since the wreck, Lloyd had avoided transporting weapons. There was no need, anyhow. The L&O fleet was being put to work carrying steel, lumber, rubber, wheat, beef, medical supplies, wool, horses, whatever was needed. He'd acquired a few tanker ships, which in turn had led him to develop enough of an interest in the petroleum industry that he'd quietly started up a little subsidiary in Texas, just a modest experimental outpost with a couple of geologists, a few wildcatters, an agent who negotiated leases on patches of wasteland. Liberty Oil, Lloyd was calling the venture.

The **Maria Fortuna** had gone to work as a troopship for the Canadian Expeditionary Force after he'd offered the British government an exceptionally generous rate. (Not pure altruism, as he retained control of the cargo holds.) Her tidy paint job disappeared under a chaos of razzle-dazzle: wild stripes and checkers and false bow waves designed to confuse range finders. Quite possibly at some point the United States would enter the war, and when it did, more ships would be needed. Lloyd would be ready.

Some of his vessels would be lost, but he had become less afraid of loss, inoculated against it. The dark spirit had left him, or perhaps he'd absorbed it into himself without noticing. Sadness still weighed on him, but his heart beat on; his lungs swelled and contracted. His collar was impeccably white; he walked at a clip. He had no time for mistresses, for soft afternoons playing at love. He required all his dignity. (Despite his best intentions, this bout of fidelity would last the duration of the war but no longer.) What appetite he had for variety, he channeled into business. He would be a titan. He was in the midst of a beginning. The sleeping baby, feeling his first night breeze, was the son of a new Lloyd Feiffer.

Near Missoula, Montana
May 1923
**Eight years and five months after
   the sinking of the** Josephina

Marian and Jamie Graves walked along a track above a creek, Marian in front, Jamie behind, tall for their age, nearly identical except for the girl's braid. Blond, skinny children flickering through the trees, through slants of sunlight thick with dust and pollen. Both wore flannel shirts and bib overalls tucked into rubber boots bought for them by Berit, their uncle's Norwegian housekeeper. The boots made a particular flapping sound against their shins. **Gup gup gup.**

Downstream, their uncle Wallace sat with his watercolors and a pad of stiff, thick paper onto which he was transferring the creek, the trees, the mountains. Where the sun glinted off water and rocks, he left tiny voids of white. He was conscious of nothing but the movement of his eyes and brush. When he painted, he had no memory of ever having received two small wards, of having released them into the wilderness like a pair of dogs trusted to return eventually. If he worried about the children, he could not paint, and so he didn't worry.

Still farther downstream, in the ancient glacial lake bed where Missoula sat, near the lower reaches of this creek, the Rattlesnake, was a gabled Queen Anne house with a screened porch and a round turret. Its inhabitants were Wallace and the twins and, most days, Berit, doing her best to stave off squalor. Though the exterior was shabbily kept, with flaking paint and missing shingles, and the furniture was old and threadbare, she made sure everything was at least well dusted, well scoured, well polished. Out back, a gray gelding called Fiddler had a one-stall barn and small paddock, and there was a cottage Wallace offered to his friends when they fought with their wives or ran short of money.

Past the house, the Rattlesnake flowed under the railway bridge to join the Clark Fork River as it swept through town and away to the northwest. By the time the Clark Fork ended in Lake Pend Oreille, the Blackfoot and Bitterroot and Thompson rivers had all joined, too, and from the lake they became the Columbia River, and from the Columbia, the Pacific.

Water was always on its way somewhere bigger, according to Wallace.

"Nothing's bigger than the ocean, though," Marian told him.

"The sky is," said Wallace.

The twins knew if they kept going upstream they would find an old shack, then a stretch of white water, and then, best of all, a wrecked and rusted open-top Model T, which, depending on how high the creek was running, was sometimes on the shore and sometimes half submerged.

How the car had come to be in the creek was a mystery. The track the children followed was narrow and rutted, suitable only for travel by foot or horseback. Wallace didn't know. Berit didn't know. Wallace's bohemian friends from the university made fanciful guesses but, in the end, didn't know.

After Marian and Jamie passed the shack, they began to hurry, though both tried not to let on. Their hands stayed in their pockets, their postures suggested a leisurely stroll, but their legs moved faster. Each wanted to sit behind the Ford's cracked wheel and pretend to drive. Whoever was not driving played at mechanic or bandit or servant, all fine roles but not as good as driver. Sometimes, for variety, the car was a ship, and they took turns pretending to be their father at the helm. Sometimes the ship sank, and they went with it.

They knew what people said about their father, and they were angry at him for making them contend with life as children of a famous coward. Their mother never figured into their games.

They rounded the last bend and took off running, swiping with skinny arms, shoving each other toward ruts and rocks (**GUP GUP GUP**). But when they burst out of the trees, instead of throwing themselves into the final sprint, both stopped.

The creek was high with snowmelt, and the car had been pulled deeper into the water, submerging the wheels and what was left of the floorboards. The remains of its front wheels had caught in the rocks, though not very securely; the body was swaying with the creek's flow.

"It'll be more like really driving the way it's moving," Marian said.

"Don't you think it might get loose?" said Jamie. "Scared?"

"No, but I don't want to drown, neither."

"You couldn't drown. It's just a creek."

Jamie studied the water doubtfully. The creek's slick brown middle was lumpy and choppy and whitecapped from submerged rocks and cold whip ends of currents snapping up underneath.

"We could go play in the shack instead," he said.

"You're scared," said Marian.

For an answer, he splashed in. Water poured into his boots, but he pressed ahead, straining like a man dragging a boulder behind him. Ordinarily they swam naked, but the car was unfriendly to skin, all jagged metal and flaking rust, stiff shreds of leather and wisps of dank wool clinging to rusty springs. So: swamped boots, wet overalls. He lifted one heavy leg to the running board and clambered into the driver's seat. The brake lever stuck up from the water like a reed.

Marian did not like the way the car shifted under Jamie's slight weight, how white water was shouldering at the bumper the way Wallace did when his Cadillac got stuck in mud.

"You don't have to come in," Jamie called. "I won't say you're yellow."

But Marian stepped into the creek. The current was fast, the creek bed uneven, and she held out her arms for balance. Icy water splashed into her boots.

"Move over," she told Jamie when she reached the car.

"You always drive. Go around."

"It's too deep over there."

"Climb over, then."

As Marian grabbed at the edge of the ruined backseat, the car tipped, and its right front wheel came loose from the rocks. She let go, dropping back down into the creek. The car's body slewed around so the current hit it broadside, rushing up over the floor. Jamie gaped at her as his chariot swayed and then slid toward the deeper water, the freer current. Floating now, the Ford pivoted languidly and plowed forward, the radiator disappearing little by little under the water.

It didn't go far. Once the wheels caught in the

rocks again, water poured in over Jamie. Marian, trotting along the bank, called to him. His pale head disappeared and resurfaced in the current, sleek and small, swept along. Stumbling on the rocky shore, Marian couldn't keep up and for a moment lost sight of him entirely. Panting, ducking under branches, she rounded a bend. There he was, sitting on a sandbar. Drenched and breathing heavily, his overalls dark and heavy, his boots gone, Jamie got to his feet. Then he let out the kind of wild, exultant whoop she'd only heard grown men make. He stomped his feet, picked up a rock and hurled it into the creek, raised his knobby arms. She was filled with a terrible envy. She wanted to be the one who had survived.

Ossining, New York
August 1924
One year and three months later

When Addison emerged from the gates of Sing Sing, his lawyer, Chester Fine, was there waiting, his three-piece suit characteristically rumpled, engrossed in a book he held in one hand. Chester had taken the train up from the city, and he rode back down again with Addison, the two of them watching the passing Hudson in silence. For years, Chester had been Addison's only visitor. Lloyd Feiffer had shown up one Sunday early on, but Addison had declined to see him. Later, the clerk in the canteen said Lloyd had added forty dollars to his account, but Addison was careful not to spend it. Lloyd had also sent a few letters that Addison threw away unopened, and he'd offered to buy Addison's house for an inflated price that Chester relayed one Sunday.

"Mr. Feiffer asked me to tell you it's the least he can do," Chester had said in the crowded visiting room. Both men were perched on wooden stools and separated by a waist-high divider, Chester in his wrinkled suit, Addison in his gray uniform. "He says he wants to do something for the twins."

"The twins don't need his money."

"They might someday. And Feiffer's never criticized you or scapegoated you, at least not publicly. That's a loud silence."

"I hauled him out of the sea once when we were young. He took it to heart." Addison rubbed his eyes with the heels of his hands. "No, sell the house to someone who's not Feiffer. Sell everything in the house that can be sold and throw the rest away."

"Everything? There's nothing of sentimental value? Nothing of their mother's to be kept for the twins?"

"Nothing."

When Addison was released (six months early, thanks to Chester Fine's persistent efforts), the forty-three dollars and sixty-six cents left in his canteen account was handed to him in an envelope that he slid into his inside pocket. Otherwise he carried only a slender cardboard portfolio, tied closed with string.

In Grand Central, Chester Fine shook his hand,

bid him good luck and goodbye, handed him a train ticket, and was gone with a doff of his hat. Addison looked around. Pale light descended from the high windows at a stately angle. Higher still, noble gold zodiac figures and a smattering of stars occupied a tranquil, blue-green heaven. It had been more than nine years since he'd stood under the real stars.

All around, people scattered across the grand marble floor and rattled away down tunnels like dropped ball bearings. They were disorienting, even frightening in their numbers, their hurry, their prosperity, their freedom. He had grown accustomed to being watched at all times, and he had, without realizing, assumed that when he returned to the world, he would still be famous as the cowardly captain of the **Josephina Eterna.** He had foreseen jeering crowds at the gates of Sing Sing, recognition and revilement everywhere he went. Instead he found bustling, indifferent strangers. Under painted stars, with a dismal burst of pleasure, he understood he had been forgotten.

He bought a ham sandwich, dropped Lloyd Fciffer's forty dollars in a beggar's cap, descended a tunnel, and boarded the 20th Century Limited to Chicago. After waiting around for most of a day, not venturing out of the station, he caught a train to Missoula.

. . .

A clear, warm night with a bright, nearly full moon. Wallace Graves waited at the depot. He had brought one of the household dogs, a leggy black-and-white thing, and they looked down the tracks together as the train's headlight grew larger and its huffing louder. The locomotive passed in a burst of heat and screeching brakes. Framed by sliding, slowing yellow rectangles of light, people were standing, putting on hats, gathering possessions. Doors opened and figures descended; porters heaved trunks from the baggage car. Wallace picked out Addison's stooped and looming silhouette on the platform. He held up a hand, and Addison nodded as though greeting an acquaintance and not a brother, not ending a separation of nearly two decades. When Wallace embraced him, he felt as though he were clutching an oversize skeleton to his bosom.

"Where's your luggage?" he said.

Addison bent to greet the dog. "I don't have any."

"You have that." Wallace indicated the slim cardboard parcel under Addison's arm. "What's in it?"

Addison cleared his throat. "Your letters and the photographs you sent. And your drawings of the children."

Addison had never acknowledged any of the dozens of portraits Wallace had sent, and for years Wallace had imagined them vanishing into the prison garbage. They were only little jots, sketches in ink and watercolor, easily done, but still the thought of any of his work being destroyed gave him a helpless, horrified feeling. Now the slender cardboard portfolio, carefully tied, brought a tightness to his throat.

When Addison left home for the sea, Wallace had been a small boy, separated from his brother by ten years and a little crop of nameless gravestones out under a walnut tree. Stillbirths. When, eleven years later, he'd made his own escape from their silent parents and the hardscrabble family farm, he'd set his course for the address scrawled in the upper left corner of Addison's brief annual letters.

A redbrick house near the Hudson. Even as a young man, Addison had been taciturn and inscrutable, but he let Wallace live with him, among his paltry furnishings and bewildering souvenirs from far-flung places. He had even paid for Wallace to go to art school.

Wallace gestured toward the depot. "Come. This way."

His long gray Cadillac touring car, his special joy, was parked out front. It had originally come to him in a card game during his Great Winning Streak of 1913, a month when he'd gambled his way through a succession of mining towns and won not only the car but enough gold dust to visit every brothel he happened past and then to buy himself a house, too. (A wise decision, it turned out, to sink his assets into the house before the Great Losing Streak of 1915.) He had taken care to park the car under a streetlamp so Addison would be better able to admire it—the black trim still gleaming, the top folded back, the thick, deep-treaded tires helpful for getting out **en plein air,** the front and rear seats in black leather, extravagantly scratched by dog nails.

"Marian is enamored with it," he told Addison. "She's a funny one. I'm always finding her outside polishing it or poking around the engine. When I take it to a mechanic I drop her off, too, so she can watch."

"You said so in a letter."

"It's just that you never reply." Wallace opened the passenger door with a flourish, gesturing his brother inside. The dog snaked in first and bounced into the backseat. "You must be desperate to see the twins. They wanted to come along, but I told them we shouldn't mob you. It's late anyway. They'll be asleep, but you can peek in at them. They sleep out on the porch when it's not cold. Well, when it's not **dangerously** cold."

"I know," Addison said, pulling the door shut. "I **read** the letters."

"But you don't **reply.**" Wallace went around, settled in the driver's seat. "Thank you, though, for the, ah, the financial support. It's been very welcome." He started the engine. "Home's not far." Pulling away from the curb, he went on, "I've put the fear of god into Jamie and Marian not to wake you in the morning. They get up horribly early.

They're practiced at entertaining themselves until a decent hour. They go up the creek, up the mountains. I don't know where they go. I hope that doesn't sound neglectful—I couldn't stop them if I tried. They take the horse, usually. Do you know how to drive?"

"No."

"Not much call to at sea."

"Nor in prison."

"I suppose not, no. You'll pick it up right away. I'll teach you. Marian can already do everything except reach the pedals and see over the steering wheel at the same time. It's still one or the other. Jamie is less interested in learning—less **insistent** about learning, I should say. Generally he gives Marian's passions a wide berth. He's not one to jostle. He's . . . well, he's quite tender. You'll see. Driving, though—once you've got the hang of it, you'll be able to get around on your own. We might even think about finding you a car. I think you'd like—"

"Wallace," Addison interrupted, "is there somewhere we could go to swim?"

"Swim?"

"Yes."

"Let me think." Wallace slowed the car, wanting to please. Not the Clark Fork or the Bitterroot, not at night. An idea came. "There might be somewhere." He turned west, presently steered onto a gravel track that became a dirt lane. Trees grew

alongside, though not densely, and the air was cool.
A leaping deer, caught in the headlights, seemed to
float over the rutted track and was gone. Addison
winced as they jounced and rattled, and Wallace
had to fight the urge to apologize. As though this
expedition had been his idea, as though any of it
were his idea.

He had never wanted children, never wanted
to be anything other than a bachelor, and yet he
had not hesitated to respond in the affirmative to
Chester Fine's telegrammed question, to take in
two babies who would grow into two children who
would occupy his house, his time, some portion of
his attention. He had swept his seedier appetites to
the edges of his life, mostly out of sight. Willingly,
he had done all this. He had studied Jamie and
Marian for clues about the character of his own
brother, whom he had never known well. He wondered if Marian's obstinacy was from her father or
from the mythical Annabel, wondered who had
bequeathed Jamie his almost debilitating horror
of animal suffering. The boy was undone by birds
fallen from the nest, injured rabbits, stray dogs,
whipped horses. Cruelty was inextricable from life,
Wallace tried to explain, but Jamie was not easily
persuaded or consoled. No mystery why there were
seldom fewer than five dogs in the house.

Though Wallace was eager to have Addison take
a share of responsibility for the children, he'd also
been surprised by his pleasure that Addison had

(tersely) accepted his offer to stay in the cottage after his release and by his relief that Addison did not plan to take Jamie and Marian away immediately. He hadn't realized he was afraid of losing them.

The lane ended at a shallow grassy rise, the headlights angling up off the top into nothing. "There's a little pond down there," Wallace said, turning off the engine. An insect cacophony welled up.

Addison got out and folded his jacket on the seat, set his hat on top, walked toward the water. Wallace followed. It was only a little oxbow pond, a silty crescent left behind when the river had changed course. The moon floated in its fat middle. Addison began to jerk at his tie, tugging at the knot and yanking it off over his head as though escaping a hangman's noose. He shed his shirt with the same feverishness. In the moonlight Wallace could see the knobs of his spine, the shadows under his shoulder blades. Addison pried off his shoes, peeled off his socks, fumbled with his belt and the buttons at his waist until his trousers and drawers dropped around his ankles, revealing pale buttocks. He waded in on knobby heron's legs. As the water rose around his calves, something seemed to break in him, and he charged like a maddened beast, splashing and galloping, diving under. The dog chased after him, barking.

Wallace shed his clothes and followed more deliberately, the pond bottom sucking at his feet. He took a breath and sank under the surface. Surfacing, he found he could stand on his toes, but only just. Addison was floating with his arms out, his chest breaking the surface, looking at the sky. The dog's V-shaped wake disturbed the moon.

"Is this all right? Is it what you wanted?" Wallace asked.

"I haven't wanted anything for years," Addison said. "But then I wanted to swim."

Over the more than nine years he had spent in Sing Sing, Addison had slept very little. His cell, seven feet by three feet, made from limestone quarried by prisoners long since dead, was a tomb in which, after lights-out, he lay perfectly still, perfectly awake, listening to the snores and murmurs and masturbatory rhythms of the eight hundred men stacked six high in cells identical to his. On ships, he had always been able to sleep, no matter how rough the seas or uncomfortable his berth. In prison, the persistence of his consciousness had seemed a particularly severe aspect of his punishment, meted out not by the court but by his soul.

Addison did not sleep in the cottage either, did not wrinkle the white sheets or the blue-and-white quilt on the narrow bed made up by the famous Berit. He'd found a number of crates and boxes stacked inside. Wallace said they were for him, had arrived by freight a year or two after he had entered Sing Sing. Chester Fine's name was on the shipping labels. After closing the curtains, Addison pried open a crate at random. It was full of books—his books—from the house in New York. Others held the things he had collected on his journeys: masks and carvings, animal horns, weavings, a tortoise shell, a serving tray from Brazil with butterfly wings arranged in iridescent wheels under glass. Elsewhere, carefully wrapped and padded, Addison found the paintings Wallace had made in New York and given him in lieu of rent. Docked ships. Crowded streets. The Hudson. The redbrick townhouse.

The prosecutors had conceded that Captain Graves had not, strictly speaking, broken any law by surviving, but they pointed out that the International Convention for the Safety of Life at Sea required the captain to stay aboard until all passengers had been safely seen to, otherwise he was guilty of gross negligence. Furthermore, Graves had brandished a deadly weapon to prevent passengers—women, even—from boarding the lifeboat, which could be construed as second degree murder. Five hundred and eight people had died, passengers and crew, burned or drowned or floating dead from cold in their life jackets. The leading theory was that a fire smoldering in a coal bunker had ignited the coal dust that floated and drifted everywhere belowdecks, triggering a violent blast in one of the boilers, which had blown out the starboard hull.

At most, Chester Fine countered, Captain Graves took the place of one person in the boat, and he was, after all, carrying his own infant twins, a son and daughter. Who among us could judge a man for saving his own children?

Who then, said the prosecutors, ultimately, was responsible for the explosion? And who was responsible for the competence of the crew? Who was responsible for the safety and soundness of the ship? Who?

I alone was responsible, Addison told Chester Fine. He asked him to plead guilty to everything, not to bargain against his atonement. But Chester, in his quiet, resolute way, ignored him. He said they must disregard public passions, which would fade. He said Addison would one day regret making a martyr of himself. And why save the twins only to abandon them again? A plea of manslaughter, everyone eventually agreed. Ten years up the Hudson.

So Addison had disappeared into Sing Sing with something like relief.

Wallace had sent a studio photograph taken on the twins' first birthday: two babies in white dresses sitting gravely in a wingback chair, their wispy pale hair carefully combed. Sketched portraits came, too, washed with watercolor. Addison had never arrived at a settled conclusion about which twin was which and felt too foolish to ask. Every year on their birthday, another photo was sent, and slowly the babies morphed into long-limbed, extremely blond children. Marian, with her skeptical gaze and small, reluctant smile, bore a resemblance to Annabel that, coupled with Wallace's stories of her willfulness, disturbed Addison. Jamie radiated earnest sweetness.

Some buried, occult part of him believed if he had not brought Annabel and the twins on board the **Josephina,** the explosion would not have occurred, though, really, he had little doubt Lloyd's crates were to blame. Or that he himself was to blame for not demanding to know what they contained, for allowing Lloyd to wave a hand and say they would be too complicated to declare.

As the night faded to pewter, he inched open the curtain. The stars bowed out one by one in a way that seemed gracious, even courtly, and a memory swallowed him: dawn on the **Josephina** as a few stragglers in evening wear lingered on deck or receded down corridors, tipping, stumbling, sparkling. He felt the deck vibrating under his feet. He smelled the sea.

No, it was pond water he smelled. In his hair, on his skin. Clay, not brine.

When the light turned lavender, two small figures emerged from the screened-in sleeping porch, three dogs tumbling out after. The children wore identical blue pajamas and, except for Marian's long hair, were nearly indistinguishable in their blondness and skinniness. They watched the cottage like cautious deer. Addison held very still. After a moment, Jamie turned sideways, fiddled with his pajamas, sent out an arc of urine. Marian turned the other way, dropped her pants, squatted in the grass. The dogs sniffed around and joined in, lifting legs. When they were done, they all went off toward where the horse was kept.

The engine in Addison's chest drove pistons through his limbs. At Wallace's urging, he had peered through the sleeping porch's screen in the night and seen the twins' pale heads on pillows. He'd nodded with a furrowed brow the way people did when shown a prized object that was meant to be admired but only baffled.

He crept to a different window. Marian was sitting bareback on the gray horse in her pajamas, holding the reins as Jamie climbed the paddock fence and slid on behind her, bare feet dangling. They turned toward the creek and were gone, the horse's haunches disappearing among the trees, the dogs trotting after.

Addison had never quite known whether he should believe the twins were his but had not been willing to insult Annabel in such a way. Now he believed. He could see it in their arms and legs, the shape of their feet, and in some less tangible way, too—the way the morning air arranged itself around them. He believed, also, resolutely, that he had nothing to offer them. He would never know what to say to them or how to be fatherly and warm. He could only disappoint and wound.

All was quiet outside. He washed at the basin before he slipped out and strode quickly down the road, back the way Wallace had driven him. Less than three dollars were left in his pocket, but he had more in the bank in New York. Not a fortune but enough for now.

Not long after the sun came up, he boarded a westbound train.

Los Angeles, 2014

One

If it weren't for the thing with Jones Cohen, I wouldn't have ended up playing Marian Graves. It's not like I could have predicted that at the time, though. All I knew was I had that tight feeling in my chest, like I wanted to kick over someone's sandcastle. As a kid, I'd had that feeling a lot. I'd be on set and want to go berserk and stomp the plastic stable with the plastic pony into plastic bits, but I never acted on it until I got older, not until I was Katie McGee and weaving down the 405 in the backseat of someone's Range Rover at 110 miles per hour, not doing anything more than laughing and shrieking but still feeling like I was pulverizing something.

Anyway, I don't know why I went home with Jones. At the time I would have said it was because

I wanted to, but I didn't, not really. I was bored and restless and pissed off, but none of that was new, none of that made me take Jones's hand and walk out into the light. I was tired of the light, but of course all I did was bring more on myself.

I don't remember everything. I remember sitting with Jones at the club, on a weird love seat cordoned off in its own little VIP alcove, a funereal, Victorian-looking thing with a tall black back that curved over us like a beetle's wing. I remember the tattoo of Johnny Cash on his forearm and his leather cuffs and turquoise rings. Sources said we were **cozy** and **flirty,** that I was being **seductive,** that I was **all over** the **notorious ladies' man,** but I don't remember if I suggested we leave or if he did. I don't remember exactly what I said to him, but I know I would have teased him, pressing for details about the famous women he'd slept with. I would have been earnest, then tough, then soft and vulnerable. I have a vague recollection of him telling me that his next album would be **stripped-down as fuck,** just him and his guitar. And I'd told him that sounded **amazing** and **absolutely what you should be doing,** which I sort of stand by because even though Jones's persona is douchey, he is a legitimately great guitarist. The floor was slick, and I remember slipping on our way out, one precarious shoe glissing sideways under me as we passed the shadowy coat-check guy tending his hoard of unnecessary L.A. coats in his red-lit cave. That might have been when I took Jones's hand. The hostess told us to enjoy our evening—pretty girl, hungry, giving me the usurper's eye—and the door opened, and the night exploded.

Even drunk, with everything looming and pivoting around me, I knew they would be waiting, my rookery in their black leather and their stupid Kangol hats, shit-talking and smoking while they waited, vigilant, their motorcycles and Vespas stacked around the block. The door opened, and their cameras went up like long black snouts. Shutters chattered; the flashes crowded in. They pressed closer until I almost choked on the light. Jones's guys elbowed them back, making a tunnel for us to the car. **Hadley! Jones! Hadley! Are you together? Hadley, where's Oliver? Did you split up?** In the pictures, my dress is too short. I am bleary, half smiling, sly, clinging to Jones's hand. At least I kept my legs together getting in the car.

They followed us to Jones's house in a celebratory swarm, flying along, popping white light against my window even though it was tinted the glossy, opaque black of Japanese enamel. In the car I remember Jones working my earring free with his tongue, pushing the hook through my lobe until the flimsy tangle of diamonds was hanging from his smile—a party trick, like tying a cherry stem into a knot. I remember his cavernous house with the usual huge abstract canvases and everything else white as heaven in a joke about heaven. I remember a tattoo high on his inner thigh that said, in tiny, earnest capitals, LOVE ME.

Oliver was married when I met him, when we were testing for the first **Archangel** movie. He was twenty and his wife was forty-two, a theater director from London who strode around in studded boots and asymmetrical jackets by avant-garde Japanese designers, as noble as a Roman senator. He didn't leave her for me. He didn't leave her at all. According to Oliver, after their second anniversary she announced that her passion for him had burst like an overfull balloon, destroying itself.

I didn't know about light, not really, until Oliver and I first held hands in public. It was at the premiere for the second film. We'd been secretly sleeping together for three months, but we were sick of all the spy craft and rumor-quashing. He got out of the car first, and the thousands of crazy bitches behind the barriers screamed like they were being burned alive. When he reached back and pulled me out and didn't let go of my hand, the noise and the light seared me. I thought I would be vaporized, nothing left except my shadow burned onto the red carpet. In the pictures, I'm glaring like a war criminal facing a tribunal. Oliver smiles, waves. Light is the medium of his beauty. In person, he is excessively handsome, obviously, but on film he transfixes. Between the projector and the screen he is changed into something almost unbearable to look at.

The sound and the light on the red carpet wasn't for us, though, not really. By getting together, we were making the story seem real, and the crazy bitches wanted the story to be real so badly they lost themselves. An especially radicalized splinter sect were the ones who wrote the hard-core erotic fan fiction. They tunneled through the internet, digging a labyrinth where they could pile up their desires and nurse them like larvae.

They were ruining it for themselves, and they didn't even know. They didn't realize they wouldn't like the books if the story gave them exactly what they wanted. People like stories that leave them a little frustrated, that have an itch. The bitches wanted **Archangel** to be tailored to all their most secret kinks, but they wanted it to be inviolate, too. Whenever we changed any tiny thing in the movies, they got in touch. **Lizveth's house is sky blue, not blue-green, you morons.** Or, **Gabriel is wearing an Arctibear hat when he and Katerina kiss for the first time, which should be WHITE not GRAY, which you should KNOW because it SAYS in the BOOK.**

Not that Oliver and I didn't get greedy, too. The characters lingered in us. We thought we could ride all the longing and passion we'd been acting like an updraft. We felt magnanimous when we got together, like we were fulfilling an obligation to the story. But the crazy bitches wrote about us, too. Us, the people, Hadley Baxter and Oliver Trappman, the actors in L.A., not Katerina and Gabriel, the figments of Gwendolyn's imagination who live in the nonexistent empire of Archangel.

Oliver and I once read some fan fiction about ourselves, just to see. At first we laughed at the typos, and then we got quiet, me sitting on his lap while we read a clammy-palmed fantasy about us fucking for the first time. "I only want you," Oliver said to me in that story, like Gabriel says to Katerina a thousand times. "Forever." But then, in a move that would have scandalized dear polite Gabriel, fan-fiction Oliver pulled up my "expensive couture designer gown" and got me with his "throbbing cock." **Give it to me, moaned Hadley. Oh ya. You are such a hot and famous movie star and I live you so so much.**

Oliver closed the computer. Out the window, a hummingbird appeared, attracted by the morning glory that grew on that wall of my house. It hovered and looked in at us quizzically, its iridescent chest hanging still in space, its wings nearly invisible with speed. We were sitting at a busy intersection of realities. We could feel the celestial wind.

"I live you so much," we started saying to each other.

We is safer than **I** when you're inside it, but it's a tippy thing, unreliable, ready at any moment to toss you away and leave you exposed as an **I** after all. Once you are a **we,** you are also a **them,** a target to be spotted and photographed. A prize. A quarry, by which I mean something to be stalked and also a pit mine. We were spotted and photographed together in New York, Paris, Saint Petersburg, Cabo, Kauai, on a yacht off Ibiza, partying après-ski in Gstaad, at the grocery store, at the gas station, hungover at Umami Burger. They mined us for stories, tidbits, truths and lies, lies and truths, fashion tips, fitness tips, diet tips, hair tips, relationship tips, c'mon, baby, just the tips. They rated our outfits, scored our beach bodies, announced I was pregnant with twins, announced, sorry, correction, I **wanted** to be pregnant with twins, announced I was going to rehab, announced we were engaged, announced our engagement was off. They wanted to know what was in my purse, in my closet, on my list of beauty must-haves. They scraped away at us, made us into something ransacked and empty.

When I walked out of that club with Jones, I think it was the crazy bitches I wanted to wound. In my drunken grandiosity, I imagined I had the power to bring their worlds crashing down. But like any idiot could have predicted, the bitches weathered the trauma just fine. It was my own sandcastle I was kicking over, of course, stomping it into nice, hard, flat, empty beach.

The tagline for the first film was **Love once, love forever.** For the fourth film, my last, it was **Fall**

once, fall forever. On the poster, a photoshopped, brooding Oliver and a photoshopped, pouty me were superimposed on a beautiful but ominous digital city, its skyline of gold onion domes dusted with snow. What will be the tagline for the sixth film? The tenth? **Die already, for the love of god, die forever?**

Gwendolyn keeps writing. There are seven books now. But even before I got fired, Oliver and I were aging faster than our characters. We couldn't be them forever. Or, I couldn't keep being Katerina. Everyone knows men don't get old, at least not in a way that matters. They're filming the fifth one now. The girl who replaced me is a teenager.

The creepy thing is, Oliver and I **had** first fucked in a car. But it was after the Kids' Choice Awards, not a premiere. The first **Archangel** movie won everything the kids could choose to award it. Has there ever been a bigger lie than **I only want you**? Or **forever**? Who was the first person to say that nothing lasts forever? Who was the first to notice that nothing does?

Two

The morning after I went home with Jones, Oliver's stuff was gone from my house. My bodyguard and assistant said that his bodyguard and assistant had come over in the middle of the night to collect everything after the first pictures showed up online. I'd been home for five minutes when my agent, Siobhan, called to check in and politely inquire what I could possibly have been thinking. In the afternoon she called back to relay a partial list of people who were upset with me. She herself was on it—that was implied, although she didn't yell at me the way she would have back in the early days, when we were both psyched out of our minds if I landed a commercial for microwaveable pizza dumplings. Last year I made $32 million, and she gets ten percent. When you're as famous as I am, you're like an immense, gliding sea creature, an ecosystem of your own, feeding a colony of small fry on whatever's left over in your teeth.

Alexei Young, Oliver's agent, whom I'd had sex with twice, secretly, and might still be in love with, told Siobhan that Oliver was heartbroken and devastated, which Siobhan relayed to me. The general entity of The Studio was upset and specifically the head of The Studio, Gavin du Pré, to whom I've given one blow job and not because I wanted to. The investors were upset, as was Gwendolyn-the-author-of-the-**Archangel**-books and also the director who'd done the fourth movie, which was in postproduction, and the guy who was slated to direct the fifth.

"The studio," Siobhan said, "is concerned that people—the fans—are taking this news very personally. The studio is worried you've punctured the romantic illusion. Obviously this whole franchise hinges on this idea of perfect love and the thinking is—"

I interrupted. "It's really not my fault if people are too stupid to tell the difference between reality and a story."

"Yes, I agree, in theory, but I do think an argument could be made that we all have a responsibility to protect the brand. I can't really claim to anyone that you **haven't** pulled focus from the movie."

I didn't say anything.

She said, "Have you talked to Oliver yet?"

"No. But, by the way, he cheated, too. I told you about that."

"But it never really leaked. If a tree cheats in the woods and nobody takes its picture . . . listen, I'm not judging, but you could have been more discreet. Let me rephrase. You couldn't have been less discreet. This was the PR equivalent of a suicide bombing." She paused. "Was it just a rogue impulse?"

"Isn't everything?"

She didn't say anything.

"You want to know why," I said. "I don't know why. Jones is a douche."

"Don't say that to anyone in the press. Okay. Look, what's done is done. Everyone just wants an update, some clue about which way you guys are leaning so we can start to spin things."

"You mean are Oliver and I getting back together?"

"Yes."

A guffaw flew from my mouth as though someone had Heimliched it out.

"Okay," she said. "Well. One last thing. Gwendolyn is upset enough that the studio is getting even more upset on her behalf."

"Fuck Gwendolyn. Seriously."

"She's very protective of her creation—"

"I am not her creation. She's not God."

"No, but her franchise has made you and me and a lot of other people a lot of money. All she wants is to meet. Gavin du Pré personally requested that you meet with her and smooth her feathers."

"I'm busy this week."

"No, you're not."

I hung up on Siobhan. This lacked gravitas on a smartphone, jabbing at a picture of a button. For a while I lay in bed smoking weed and watching a reality show where face-lifts in Hervé Léger bandage dresses slop martinis around and talk shit on each other. Some of these women have had so much work done their words come out all mushy because they can't move their lips. With their spooky round eyes and stubby little snouts, they look like cats transformed into humans by an incompetent wizard.

I wondered if I could spend the rest of my life lying around this house, watching TV. I wondered how long it would take for the morning glory to grow over the windows, sealing me in.

I'd been on the verge of being cast in **Archangel** when Gavin du Pré set down his coffee cup at our breakfast meeting and very quietly and politely asked me to stand up and take off my clothes.

I was surprised for half a second and embarrassed about being dumb enough to have been surprised ever after. We were alone in a hotel suite in Beverly Hills, facing each other across a little white-draped table laden with a silver coffee service and a multi-tiered stand of miniature quiches and tarts and croissants that Gavin had kept telling me to eat before he asked me to get naked. "I promise you won't get fat from one little croissant," he'd said. "Look how tiny it is. Just have a taste. A taste won't hurt you."

It wasn't like I hadn't encountered creeps before. They're on every set and in every executive hierarchy like they're mandated by some sort of local creeps union. But the stakes had never been so high, not even close. **This is a game changer,** Siobhan and I had said to each other when the meeting got scheduled. I've never figured out if she knew what she was sending me into. She'd gone out of her way to mention Gavin was married and had daughters around my age—eighteen, then.

Gavin was an inoffensive-looking, beigey, fifty-ish guy with full, pale lips and wire-rimmed glasses and pocket squares that artfully complimented his ties. "I need to get a look at you," he said, and I decided to understand that as a professional need, not a personal one.

I never told Siobhan because I didn't want her to know I'd actually done it. My uncle Mitch had been dead for a couple of months then, and even though he'd never exactly been "involved" or "protective," I had a new, hard feeling of aloneness. I hadn't even hesitated. I'd stood there naked in front of Gavin, and I turned in a little circle when he asked me to, and when he took out his dick and asked me to please suck it, I did.

. . .

The day after the day after Jones Cohen, I was lying by my pool watching a vulture circle. The sky in L.A. is full of vultures, sometimes great big spiraling tornadoes of them towering up into the clouds, only people usually don't look. I was a little surprised, almost insulted, that there weren't any helicopters spying on me. Were the paparazzi allowed to use those little hobbyist drones? Maybe not, because they would if they could. That should be inscribed over their coat of arms: **We Would if We Could.**

The doorbell startled me. I thought the paps must have climbed my gate, decided to storm the house. It rang again. I waited for my assistant, Augustina, to deal with it until I remembered I'd sent her home, urgently pressing a packet of edibles into her hand even though she doesn't like weed. My bodyguard, M.G., was patrolling the perimeter. I heaved myself up, went and looked at the security screen. My neighbor, **the** venerable Sir Hugo Woolsey (**Venerable, venal, venereal,** he says), was leaning close to the camera, waving a bottle of Scotch and shouting "Chicken soup for the philanderer's soul!" into the intercom like he didn't trust it to actually transmit or amplify his voice. Hugo dresses like a hipster Nebuchadnezzar and lives with his young and beautiful boyfriend, so it always surprises me when he does old-person stuff with technology.

"Hey," I said, opening the door. "How'd you get past the gate?"

"You gave Rudy the code ages ago. Don't you remember? He was making a little delivery." He mimed pulling on a joint. Hugo's boyfriend Rudy's principal responsibilities in life were to keep it tight and to stay current on the best weed available city-wide, medical or otherwise. "It's mayhem down there," he said, sweeping into the kitchen. "M.G. ought to have a bullwhip to crack at them."

He was wearing huaraches and drawstring pants in blue-and-white ikat and an orange linen shirt unbuttoned to show a bear-claw necklace nestled in his thick white chest hair. Hugo is tall and im-pressively burly for someone over seventy and has a sonorous, plummy voice and the world's most impressive stage pedigree.

He poured us each a tumbler of Scotch. "Cin cin." We clinked. "Rudy says the internet is burn-ing. He says you set it on **fire.**"

"It deserved it," I said, following him into the largest of my living rooms.

He sat on the couch and gestured me imperi-ously into one of my own chairs. "Oh, I **agree.**"

I raised my glass. "Thanks for this. It's really good."

"Truly exceptional, you mean, and you're wel-come. It wasn't like I was going to drink it with **Rudy.** It would be wasted on **that** palate. Might as well give it to a **child.** I wanted to be sure you were dulling your pain in style."

"I'm focusing more on opiates."

"Please don't have a meltdown. That would be dreadfully dull of you. And a terrible waste of talent, of course."

"I was kidding," I said. "But obviously I'm already in the middle of a meltdown."

"No, no, **no.** Jones **was** the meltdown. Now you're rebounding."

"It's been"—I calculated—"thirty-nine hours."

"This, my dear, is a golden opportunity to—I hate the word, but in this case it's apt—reinvent yourself. If you can't see how you might seize this particular moment, then you have no imagination at all, and I am extremely disappointed in you."

"I don't really see how to capitalize on everyone hating me."

The crazy bitches had tweeted at me that I was a slut, a whore, a cunt. I deserved to die, they said, to be alone forever, to rot in hell. Thank God Oliver was free of me, they said. Men jumped in to tell me I was ugly and unfuckable but also that I deserved to be raped, that I was going to choke to death on their dicks. They didn't even care about **Archangel.** They just couldn't pass up an opportunity to tell a woman that (a) they'd never fuck her and also (b) they were going to fuck her until she died. I'd scrolled. I was hanging in the stocks so the village could come by and jeer at me. I had committed an act of terrorism as far as the crazy bitches were concerned. I had attacked their way of life. The bitches said IN ALL CAPS that they wanted me to suffer, to be obliterated. But really they wanted me to fix it, to undo what I'd done, to return them to the way they were before.

Every once in a while, someone would be like, hey, stay strong, girl, and that was enough to make me tear up. Then someone else would say it was my fault Mitch had overdosed or that my parents were lucky they were dead so they wouldn't have to be ashamed of me.

"Not everyone hates you," Hugo said, "just the—what do you call them? The crazy bitches? Most people don't care at all about **Archangel** and therefore don't care **at all** about you. Don't look like that—it's a good thing. The worthwhile people probably think you just got more interesting, showed a little backbone. Not that Oliver isn't a nice boy, a gorgeous boy, but he's too vacuous for you. Of course I **understand** the appeal of the beautiful, vacuous boy. Rudy isn't what you would call complicated, but, you know, I'm old. I want someone young and frivolous whose most profound and complicated desire is for fun, specifically fun that is purchasable with money. That's an important distinction. Do you know how few people can actually be made genuinely happy by money? It's really quite rare. Rudy is what suits me now, but when I was your age I wanted something fraught and epic that could"—he bared his teeth and mimed ripping something in half—"tear me apart." His famous voice echoed off the ceiling.

I wanted to tell him about Alexei, but Hugo gossips.

I said, "I haven't heard a peep from Oliver. He hasn't called to scream at me or anything. Just silence. My agent says his agent says he's devastated. But he cheated on me with at least one actress and at least one model and God knows who else, and I got over it. This whole heartbroken act is a bit much."

He waved a hand in dismissal then leveled his most piercing gaze at me and asked, "What drew you to Oliver in the first place?"

"Have you **seen** Oliver?" Hugo pierced harder. I said, "He was the only one who understood what it was like to live through the whole **Archangel** thing. You know how people say you should choose someone you'd want to be in a foxhole with? But this was like, what if you're in a foxhole already, and someone else happens to be in there, too? Then you have the foxhole in common, which is not nothing." I drained my glass. Hugo went to the kitchen and came back with the bottle.

"And then?" he said, pouring. "Did the foxhole lose its luster?"

"He became part of the claustrophobia."

Hugo draped one arm elegantly along the back

of the sofa, his drink dangling from his finger-tips. "Forget love. My dear, I'm a self-absorbed old narcissist, not your nanny, so I don't care **all** that much what you do. Mostly I'm here because I can't resist meddling. But as someone who's made many rather impressive messes over the years, if I do say so myself, I believe I am uniquely well qualified to advise."

"This is different."

"I beg your pardon. How so?"

"You're a man, for starters, and there wasn't an internet when you were being chaotic."

"You're right. It's been a very simple thing being me." He glowered. "I almost married a woman once. A woman!"

"Disgusting."

"Let me ask you, what is the worst possible out-come of all this?"

"Endless public shaming. I get fired from **Archangel** and never work again."

"It wouldn't be endless. People will move on sooner than you think. They don't **really** care. And you don't need to work again. You're extremely rich. You could quit and go buy a winery somewhere. A goat farm. An island. Simplify. Live in peace. What do you **want**?"

My mind went blank, scrabbly and darting like a panicked animal. All I could think was that I didn't want to keep feeling the way I felt. I wanted to feel good. An image came to me of myself holding an

Oscar aloft, an auditorium of people on their feet, applauding me. "I want more," I said. "Not less. I want to work."

He narrowed his eyes, said in a low growl, "Good **girl.** There's no reason you shouldn't have more."

"Well," I said, "there are actually a few. No one in Hollywood cares I was unfaithful to Oliver, but they'll care I was unfaithful to the brand."

He groaned extravagantly. "You need to get outside this idea of **brands.** It's **so** tiresome. Even if this hadn't happened, I would have told you to quit. What's the alternative? You keep doing **Archangel** until you're too old and they quietly shunt you aside for someone younger? At least now you've established yourself as interesting and unpredictable, not some comely young automaton. Everyone will be looking to see what you do next. You're not their pawn anymore. And people **love** a comeback."

Three

When I was a teenager wreaking havoc, my uncle Mitch offered to take me on a trip, just us, anywhere I wanted. He thought it would be good for me to get away; he was between projects anyway. I chose Lake Superior, where my parents' plane had vanished.

"Isn't that a little morbid?" Mitch said.

I told him I just wanted to see it. And I did—I always had—but I also wanted to go somewhere where we wouldn't do our usual stuff. Some fancy tropical resort wouldn't have been a vacation because we would have just run around getting drunk and finding people to hook up with. Decadence was what I needed a break from.

We started in Sault Sainte Marie and drove clockwise all the way around, thirteen hundred miles in a rented soft-top Jeep Wrangler, the noisy discomfort of which was a just punishment for us being too cool for an economy sedan. I swam every day even though the water nearly strangled me with cold. I kept thinking about the sunken Cessna out there somewhere, wondering if infinitesimal particles of my parents were floating around me like fireflies.

"Would they just be bones now?" I asked Mitch, shouting over the Jeep's flapping top and Pearl Jam on Canadian radio.

"Probably," he shouted back. "I don't know how long any of that stuff takes."

"Why did he learn to fly?"

"What?"

"My dad. Why did he learn to fly?"

"I don't know. I never asked."

"Why didn't you ask?"

"I don't know!" He seemed irritated, then softened. "He wasn't someone who liked being asked to explain himself. Runs in the family."

Also, Mitch wasn't great at remembering to be interested in other people. It's not fair to blame him for anything, but the way some parents always repeat a mantra to their kids like "Treat others how you want to be treated" or "Actions speak louder than words," Mitch would say "You only live once." He would say it when he cracked a beer after three months sober or bet too much on a long shot at Santa Anita. He was the original YOLO guy. When I was little, I made casting agents laugh by solemnly parroting him whenever they asked me if I wanted to show them my biggest smile or be in a commercial for a water park. With my dirt-bag Katie McGee–era friends, I didn't even bother saying it. They knew.

Mitch would never have called himself a parent anyway.

On the lake's northern shore, I learned from informational placards that mountains as big or bigger than the Himalayas had once stood there, maybe the highest mountains that ever existed, but they'd eroded away to nothing, time kicking down that particular sandcastle, glaciers scraping the rock bare and then disappearing, too. I asked Mitch other questions about my parents, but mostly he didn't know or couldn't come up with anything interesting.

One night when we'd stopped at a diner, I said, "What if they didn't die?"

Mitch was smacking the side of a ketchup bottle. "What do you mean?"

"What if they just went off somewhere and never came back?"

He put down the ketchup and fixed me with a grave expression, not easy to pull off under the David Beckham faux-hawk he'd had at the time. "Hadley, they wouldn't have done that to you."

"Or to you?"

"They died. That's what happened. You need to believe that."

"Yeah," I said. I knew what I needed to believe, but knowing and believing weren't the same.

Where I was sitting, there'd once been mountains higher than Everest. Anything was possible.

An Incomplete History of
Missoula, Montana

~

c. 13,000 B.C.–February 1927

Fifteen thousand years ago.

An ice sheet advances from the north. A long glacial finger reaches down and plugs the Clark Fork River west of where Missoula will be. A lake forms, grows massive and spidery, three thousand miles square, two thousand feet deep, reflects the shadowed undersides of clouds. Mountaintops turn to islands.

Icebergs calve into the lake, float and drift. Sometimes boulders are locked inside them, carried south from far away: a journey of hundreds of years, maybe a thousand. When the bergs melt, the rocks plummet to the lake bed.

The lake gets too big, too deep, paws and digs at the ice dam until it turns buoyant and cracks apart, releasing the water. Collapsing, the lake churns over what will be Idaho, Oregon, Washington. The whole thing drains in three days, emptying at ten times the combined power of all the rivers in our world, though no statistic can get at its marauding violence, its deluvianness. Like gleeful strongmen, the currents toss giant rocks and huge chunks of ice into the air. Canyons are dug, herds swept away. Mastodons and mammoths are caught up and drowned and washed into the slack water. Saber-toothed cats, too, and beavers the size of grizzlies and dire wolves and giant ground sloths and all that lost, oversize menagerie.

From the north, the glaciers creep back down the mountains until the river is blocked again. Again, the lake fills. Again, the dam breaks. For two or three thousand years the cycle repeats, until something changes and the ice recedes. On the empty lake bed, where five mountain valleys come together like the twisted limbs of a sea star, where the peaked and porched and turreted Queen Anne house belonging to Wallace Graves will one day stand, grass grows. Saplings bend in the wind.

At some point: people. Hunters with stone tools, walking from Siberia, leaving behind carvings and paintings on the rocks. (What do they make of this endlessly unspooling land? Who could imagine a blue sphere suspended in black infinity?) Leaves rustle, rivers bend through valleys. More hunters pass through with better tools, subtler languages, myths about a great flood. Tipis and sturgeon-nosed canoes. Dogs and horses.

In 1805, white people make the scene: Lewis and Clark heading west, then back the other way ten months later, having seen the Pacific.

A narrow and wooded canyon, good for ambushes, leads east out of the valley to plains coursing with bison. Hunters coming from the west are attacked there sometimes by plains people, Blackfeet possessive of the herds, and the bones of the dead are left behind.

White people sidle in again. Porte de l'Enfer, French trappers call the canyon because of the bones. Hell Gate.

In 1855, a treaty is signed between Isaac Stevens, the governor of Washington Territory, and the local tribes (Bitterroot Salish, Pend d'Oreilles, Kootenai). The document is a fine example of its pernicious genre, full of tricks and mutual incomprehension, implied promises of death and loss. At night Stevens dreams of scraping shovels and clanking hammers, of seams stitched with timber and iron.

The grand metropolis of Hell Gate, population twenty, becomes the seat of Washington Territory's new Missoula County (**Missoula** from a Salish word for cold, chilling waters). Before long there are tents and sod-roof cabins, a few rinky-dink farms, a saloon, a post office, thieves strung up by vigilantes. In 1864 Missoula County is made part of the new Montana Territory. A lumber mill and a flour mill are built upstream, and Hell Gate turns into a ghost town in a flash, everyone gone to Missoula Mills.

More houses, stores, streets. Banks. A newspaper. A fort to protect the good people of Missoula from the Indians who have not yet been swept away. In August 1877, more than seven hundred Nez Perce cross the mountains from Idaho with their horses and livestock and dogs, retreating from the U.S. Army, looking for a place where they will be left alone, a place that no longer exists.

They camp on a riverbank, are awakened by soldiers shooting into their tipis. The soldiers try to burn the tipis, have trouble getting the fires going, keep trying. Though most of the band scatters, some children have been hidden inside, under blankets, and are burned alive. The warriors regroup, attack. The soldiers retreat. In the night, the band moves on, toward what will be Yellowstone. They will try to reach Canada, Sitting Bull's camp there, but most won't make it. Most are sent to Fort Leavenworth.

In 1883, the bleeding end of the Northern Pacific Railroad arrives in Missoula from the west, has to be pushed and pulled sixty more miles to meet tracks en route from the Great Lakes, not the first transcontinental line but still pretty good, still pretty epic, still pretty helpful as far as settling the wilderness. Ulysses S. Grant binds the continent to itself with a golden spike.

More men arrive in Missoula, rough men, lonely men, thirsty men. Want a drink, boys? Want a girl? Try West Front Street, follow the red light. Madam Mary Gleim, fat and fearsome, owns half the place, maybe more. She'll get you a girl from Chicago, a girl from China, a girl from France (ask for French Emma). She can get you Chinamen, too, if it's workers you need. If your workers want opium, she'll get that.

Missoula gets a telephone exchange and electricity, becomes a new official city in a new official state (Montana, b. 1889). A farmer in his field scratches his head over the lonely boulder that seems to have fallen from the sky.

A train crosses the plains. Wallace Graves, hungry for mountains he's never seen, is heading west from New York. He gets off in Butte, tries Butte for a while, a bronco of a town, a Babel town, where men from far-flung places go into the copper mines together, come out, take their wages to the saloon or to the girls of Venus Alley. Fights in the streets every day, every night: miner versus miner, drunk versus drunk, Irish versus Italian versus Bohunk versus Swede, union men versus scabs.

Wallace paints the jumbled structures of the mines, the gray figures walking with their tin pails, the headframe and machine buildings of the Neversweat mine and its seven slender smokestacks like cigarillos stuck in the ground. But it is not quite right for Wallace, this city. He boards a west-bound train, disembarks in Missoula, stays.

In 1911, Wallace goes with most everyone in town to a field near the fort to watch a pilot named Eugene Ely swoop up out of the bowl of mountains in his Curtiss biplane, breaching the ghostly surface of the forgotten ancient lake. Ely buzzes the crowd, dips his wings. A group of Cree have pitched their tipis nearby. They sit on horseback, watching the machine.

"What a world," Wallace Graves remarks to his lady friend, holding his hat to his head as he looks up.

A train crosses the plains. Addison Graves looks through the portraits of his children once again, holding them carefully by the corners so as not to smudge.

Wallace goes out to fetch his brother for breakfast and finds the cottage empty, nothing changed inside except the crates pried open. He finds his old paintings, sees they are not as good as he remembered. He chastises his younger self for his florid brushwork, his trite composition. The children are in the main house, back from the dawn ride he doesn't know they'd taken because he does not trouble himself with how they spend their time. They are washed and combed (combed! of their own doing!) and sitting upright at Berit's breakfast table, waiting to meet their father.

"He's gone," Wallace says without preamble, coming inside. "No note or anything."

Berit, at the stove, says, "What do you mean he is gone? Gone where?"

"Just gone."

"And his things? They are gone?"

"He didn't have any things." Wallace remembers the cardboard portfolio. Addison had taken that, at least.

Jamie bolts from the table, pounds up the stairs.

"Is he coming back?" Marian asks, rigid with seriousness.

"I don't know."

"Maybe he went for a walk."

"To be honest I think probably not. Are you upset?"

She considers. "I thought he'd want to meet us. But it would have been worse if he'd met us and then left."

"I don't know about worse."

"But he might come back."

"He might."

"I wouldn't want him to stay if he didn't want to."

"I suppose not," says Wallace. Then with some venom: "Heaven forbid he should do something he doesn't want to do."

"So things will stay the same?"

"I suppose they will."

"That's all right."

"You can be sad. You won't offend me."

She looks out the window, says, "Where do you think he went?"

"I don't know."

"I think I would be more sad if I knew where he went."

Wallace nods. Better only to wonder what he'd chosen instead of them. "I know what you mean."

For some time, some weeks, it seems possible Addison will return. But the leaves turn orange and the nights cold, and he doesn't come back.

"Why do you think he didn't stay?" Jamie is sitting on a footstool in Wallace's studio up in the house's turret. With charcoal on scrap paper the boy is drawing minnows hovering over a rocky river bottom. "Why did he come here at all?"

"I don't know." Wallace is at his easel, oils pungent on a palette, sketches pinned up around him. "I don't know him very well. We were never close like you and Marian. I think he meant to stay, but he got spooked." He leans to look at Jamie's drawing. "That's very good. I have a sense of water moving around the fish—it's clever how you did that."

"Spooked by what?"

Wallace's brush nibbles at the canvas. **By you. By the fact of you.** "It's only a guess, but I think he might not have liked the idea of owing us anything."

"Why would he think he owed us?"

Wallace puts down his brush. "You are a very dear boy."

"Why?"

"It's a forgiving question, that's all."

Quietly, to the charcoal fish, Jamie says, "I don't think I **do** forgive him, though."

Life proceeds as before. Berit struggles to keep order. She tries and fails to get Marian to wear dresses. There is never quite enough money. Wallace is paid well by the university but likes to bet on cards. Sleeping dogs lie strewn through the house.

In their bedrooms where they seldom sleep, preferring the porch, the twins hoard clattery jumbles of antlers and moose paddles and foraged troves of bones and teeth. Crumbling birds' nests line their windowsills in the company of pinecones and interesting rocks. Feathers are pinned to the walls. The twins pick up human artifacts, too: arrowheads, bits of broken crockery, bullets, nails. Jamie makes drawings of what he finds, arranges still lifes and draws them, adding color with pastels or watercolors Wallace filches for him from the university. "Here come the naturalists," Wallace says when they return to the house in the evenings, extravagantly dirty and with full pockets. "Here come the archaeologists back from the dig."

They do not always go to school. If it is a splendidly sunny day or an enticingly snowy one, they might wander away somewhere else. They have a friend who cuts with them, Caleb, wilder even than they are, a couple of years older, the son of a whore who lives in a sagging old cabin just down the Rattlesnake. (Gilda, Caleb's mother, had chosen as

a surname for herself and her son the name of the
river that flows up from the south and joins the
Clark Fork on the far side of town: Bitterroot.)

Caleb is a graceful, feline child with long black
hair loose down his back, so straight and glossy
that people say his father must have been either an
Indian or a Chinese. He picks pockets. He steals
moonshine from his mother and sweets and fish-
hooks from the shops downtown. He hates the
men who come to his cabin, hates what his mother
does with them, but will brook no insult to her.
He'll sock Marian in the gut or arm as soon as he
will Jamie, and in summer all three swim naked in
creeks and rivers.

Though Marian and Jamie have both gone at
different times to watch through a gap in the curtains when Gilda is at work, they have not dis-
cussed what they saw. Jamie was troubled by how
much bigger the man was than Gilda, the way he
threw his body at hers with the mindless force of a
pile driver. Gilda's small feet in their dirty stockings
bobbled. Helplessness upsets Jamie. He rescues
drowning bees from the creek, brings home stray
dogs, feeds abandoned baby birds with an eyedrop-
per, then with worms he gets Marian to chop up.
The birds look like angry old men with their wrinkled necks and open mouths. Some live, some die.
Wallace offers little resistance to the dogs, the other
creatures. "Poor soul," he says, looking over a raven
chick too weak to lift its head.

"No more," Berit says after every new addition, but she saves scraps for the dogs. Jamie has a recurring nightmare in which he is made to choose between shooting Marian and shooting a dog. He will not eat meat. "You will **die** with no meat," Berit says, and yet Jamie lives on.

He'd been reassured when, in the midst of all the ruckus, Gilda had reached up and coolly smoothed her hair back into place.

Marian, during her turn at Gilda's window, had been transfixed by how the man (a different man from Jamie's) had become a wild beast, how his face had twisted and his back arched, how he'd shoved Gilda up the bed and gobbled blindly between her legs. Eventually, after he had mounted her the way a dog or elk would, he went still. The beast vanished, and he became a man again, a friendly-looking man straightening his clothes. Marian began to study men after that—shopkeepers, neighbors, Wallace's friends, Wallace, the milkman, the postman— peering too intently into faces, looking for beasts.

Wallace knows Marian and Jamie slip off on adventures. He chooses not to go past the vaguest knowing, not to worry they might not return. He has adventures of his own. Sometimes he goes off after dark to find a poker game, a drink in a speakeasy or roadhouse, a woman. He is a quiet drunk but an ardent one.

A check arrives from a bank in Seattle, a decent sum. A letter with it explains that Mr. Addison

Graves wishes money to be sent periodically for the upkeep of the children. Wallace goes out and loses most of it right away in a roadhouse cardroom. (A larger check had come once, when the children were very small—their settlement from the estate of their maternal grandfather. He'd used it to settle a debt.) On his way home, at dawn, he stops and immerses himself in the oxbow pond where he'd taken Addison, but the water is cold and tea-brown and he does not feel cleansed, only scummy and sodden. Sullenly, floating, he mulls over whether the money from Addison was newly earned or from some reserve of his savings. He thinks his brother should have known better than to send him so much money at once, but then he remembers Addison knows nothing of his gambling.

The cottage that was meant for Addison glows at night like a sturdy, neighborly moon because Marian has made it her place. After her father's brief visit, she'd unpacked all the crates herself. Such wonders to be sorted through: Wallace's paintings, books of all thicknesses and dimensions, and then the glorious, bewildering array of exotic souvenirs. Some were self-explanatory (rugs, vases) and others were mysterious, such as the seven-foot-long, sharp-ended, spiraled animal horn wrapped in burlap and packed in a long tube all its own. She'd propped the horn in a corner behind the stove, left it leaning there like the neglected staff of a sorcerer. She wishes she could imagine her father buying, say, a particular red-and-black wooden bowl, but she doesn't know what sort of scene to visualize. A bustling city? A lonely fishing village? A hot place? A cold place? Why had he chosen this bowl of all the bowls in the world?

She'd stacked the books in teetering columns against one wall. She would read them, she decided, one after the other, in the order they were stacked, and she begins to do this shortly after her tenth birthday. Here and there, after she's been working on Wallace's car or mending bicycles for other children, she leaves some streaks of grease on the pages, but she decides her father is the kind of man who wouldn't mind. During the day, she carries a book with her, to school or into the hills. In the evenings, she goes to the cottage and reads in the armchair by the stove. Had her father sat in it even once? Before this windfall of books, she had not been a reader and is unpracticed at sitting still for so long.

The first volume on the first stack, not quite by chance, is **Dracula,** and, like her mother, she has distressing dreams about Renfield, the lunatic who feeds flies to spiders and spiders to birds and, when he can't obtain a cat to eat the birds, eats them himself, alive. She dreams about the beast with Gilda, and in the dream she knows the beast is Renfield, the devourer. There is no one, of course, who can tell her that her mother also had been frightened by the idea of such an appetite. No one had ever known.

Among the books are novels and some collections of verse and quite a few volumes of illustrations of plants and birds and animals labeled in Latin that she tells Jamie he may come and look at but may not take anywhere. There is a collection of Shakespeare and a fat dictionary that she keeps nearby for words she doesn't know. But mostly there are accounts of journeys. She reads about storms and wrecks, pirates and armadas, crews forced to eat their comrades. (Renfield reappears in her dreams.) She reads about Tahitian mountains rising from warm seas, their emerald summits wreathed with cloud, about the forbidding Himalayas and the high pastures of the Alps where cowbells toll. She reads about James Cook and Charles Darwin and Mary Kingsley and Richard Henry Dana and about Lewis and Clark walking through the very same valley where she lives. She reads about the winds in the Strait of Magellan that can push a ship backward at such speeds its prow leaves a wake, winds that blow Arabian sand hundreds of miles out to sea in choking orange clouds. She reads about the Congo and the Nile and the Yangtze and the Amazon. She reads about wild, naked children in hot climates who play games of looking and touching not unlike those Caleb sometimes devises when Jamie isn't around. She reads about waves towering like mountains, about maddening calms, circling sharks, whales that leap free of the ocean, volcanoes that ooze fire. There are no books among them about little girls like herself, but she does not notice.

So her father, besides making journeys of his own, liked to read about those made by others. Presumably he approved of people who had adventures. She likes Joshua Slocum's account of sailing around in the world alone in his little oyster sloop, the **Spray,** feeling like a planet unto himself. She would like to feel that way.

Her very favorites, though, are the accounts of the far north and the far south, where ships' rigging sags heavy with frost and blue icebergs drift freely, arched and spired like frozen cathedrals. She reads accounts by Fridtjof Nansen and Roald Amundsen and about the vanished Sir John Franklin but is not satisfied and brings back more books from the library, gorging herself on the deprivations suffered by Ernest Shackleton and Apsley Cherry-Garrard. Bravery at the poles seems appealingly simple. If you go there, or try to, you are brave. She comes across an etching of narwhals crowding a patch of open water amid Arctic pack ice, tusks clashing in the air like sabers in a battlefield melee. From the corner behind the stove, she retrieves the long horn and goes out across the snowy yard to the main house.

Wallace is up in his studio, Beethoven on the phonograph. He takes the book into his lap and studies the image. "Yes, I see," he says. "I think you're right."

"A narwhal tusk," Marian says. "Here in Missoula, Montana."

He looks at the etching again. "Are they fighting?"

"It says they're breathing. You don't think my father killed the one this came from, do you?"

"I think he probably bought it."

"Why is it," she asks Wallace, leaning on the spiraled tusk, her long pale braid pulled forward over her shoulder, "that both the north and the south are so cold? Why are their seasons flip-flopped, and why is it sometimes always dark and sometimes always light?"

"I don't know," he says. He flips through the book, passing images of Eskimos and dogsleds and icebergs and grimacing whales flapping their tails. He wonders if his brother had seen all those things. Marian does not seem like a child to him, nor like an adult. She has an avidity that unnerves him.

She goes back out across the snow, toward the cottage suspended in the dark like a lantern hanging from a bowsprit. More than two years have passed since her father's brief stay in it. She hopes more of his belongings will be explained by the books, that by the time she has read them all, she will know what he knew. In a way, then, she will know him. And later, when she is grown, she will go to the places she has read about, see things for herself.

Nights and days, summers and winters.

Barnstormers

———

Missoula
May 1927
Three months later

T he morning was cold, but Fiddler's barrel warmed Marian's legs. She rode bareback, reins loose, ducking under pine boughs that swept through the early gloom. When Fiddler paused to snatch wisps of grass, she pressed his ribs with her bare heels.

Most mornings since last September, when she'd turned twelve, she'd risen before dawn and bridled the horse. Jamie seldom came along anymore, maybe because he sensed she preferred to go alone. Depending on her whim, she and Fiddler might follow the banks of the Clark Fork or Bitterroot, or they might wander through town, watching the plodding circuit of the milkman's wagon, the lonely homeward transits of night workers and wandering drunks. If there wasn't too much snow, she might ride up one of the mountains or canyons.

This day, she had turned away from the Rattlesnake, ascending Mount Jumbo as the last stars winked out and the sky blued and glowed. Fiddler swung into a trot up the steep rise to the summit, where he stopped and immediately began to graze. Low silver fog lay on the valley floor, pierced by roofs and treetops. From behind her, the rising sun's rays played over the ranks of mountains across the valley, tilted slowly down onto Missoula, dispersing the fog until ordinary tidy daylight glinted off the river.

Thrusting her feet forward to hook the reins, she lay back on the horse, hands behind her head on Fiddler's haunches. She was almost dozing when she heard the distant sound of an engine. She took it for one of the local aircraft, rickety surplus Jennies and Standards sold cheap after the war and flown mostly by hobbyists. The sound was coming from the east. Louder. Louder still. She pushed herself up just as a red-and-black biplane roared over, as abrupt and magnificent as an announcing angel, passing so low it seemed she could have touched the wheels.

The Flying Brayfogles. So it said in looping white script on the tails of their Curtiss Jennies. They were Felix and Trixie, refugees from Wilton Wolf's

Flying Circus, which had gone defunct after the government decided the festive local air shows that had sprung up everywhere after the war involved too many people plunging festively to their deaths and tightened regulations. The Brayfogles were heading west, to Hollywood, to find stunt work in the pictures.

Other barnstormers had come through town before, selling rides and doing aerobatics and parachute jumps, but Marian had never really noticed them, never considered how an airplane could pass over the mountains, over the horizon, carry people **elsewhere.** Maybe she had needed the dangerous proximity of the plane, its roar and the red flash of its wings to jolt her from obliviousness. Or maybe the moment was simply right. She was at an age when the future adult rattles the child's bones like the bars of a cage.

Wallace drove her, later that day, to the airstrip at the base of Mount Sentinel that was nothing fancier than a reasonably level field marked with lime and pocked with badger holes. He'd barely stopped the car before she bolted like a rambunctious colt, galloping away across the grass toward the parked planes.

The cowling doors were open on the nearer plane's engine, and a figure in a mechanic's overall was standing on a stepladder and digging among the valves and cylinders. Another figure, in breeches and boots, lay in the shaded grass under the far plane's wing, face covered by a wide-brimmed cattle-man's hat, apparently asleep. The person on the stepladder straightened up and turned, and Marian was surprised to realize it was a woman. A blue bandanna covered her hair; her face was streaked with grease. A spanner dangled from one hand.

"Hello," the woman said, looking down at the girl and then back across the field at Wallace. "Who might you be?"

"I'm Marian Graves."

"Did you come to see the planes? Our mighty squadron of two?" Her way of speaking was sing-songy and mannered. She pulled a second ban-danna from her pocket and wiped her face, further smudging the grease.

"I saw them already. This morning I was on my horse and one flew right over me." Fiddler had spooked and she had nearly fallen off. Just as she'd recovered herself, the other plane had passed over, higher but still loud enough to upset Fiddler all over again.

"They do seem quite low sometimes, don't they? But really we're much higher than you think. Safety first, I always—" She stopped. "Oh. You mean up the mountain? That was you, dearheart? You poor thing, you must have been **awfully** frightened. Felix can be very silly."

"I wasn't scared."

"I'm glad you came by so Felix could apologize in person. I can absolutely promise you it was an accident. Just a silly mistake. You're all right, I'm glad to see."

Marian gathered her courage to say what had been consuming her all morning: "I'd like to go up in one."

The woman tilted her head, screwed up her face in an expression Marian supposed was meant to suggest sympathy. "I'm afraid we won't be giving any rides until tomorrow, and the fact is they cost money. Five dollars. We have to pay for fuel and so on—it's how we make a living. I'm sorry Felix frightened you, but we can't start taking up anyone who wants to go, much as we'd like to. Maybe we could give you a small discount as a friendly gesture, but you'll have to ask your father there if he'll pay. Unless you've been saving up?" This last quite hopefully.

"He's my uncle."

"You'll have to ask your uncle, then."

Wallace, arriving, shaded his eyes with one hand and smiled up at the woman. "What will she have to ask me?"

"This brave young lady wants to go up in a plane." Again the bandanna swabbed at the grease, this time more effectively, and a long, narrow greyhound face emerged.

"Can I?" Marian demanded of Wallace, boisterous from the embarrassment of having to ask. She and Jamie weren't given pocket money in any sort of regular way. It did not seem to occur to Wallace that there might be things they wanted to buy, and so, under Caleb's tutelage, they'd turned to petty thievery, pinching candy and fishing tackle and various bits and bobs from the stores downtown. Caleb in an hour on a busy street could unobtrusively dip enough coins from passersby for three movie tickets and lunch at a beanery. When they had any money, they spent it, and so, in what now seemed a terrible oversight, Marian had nothing saved.

"How much does it cost?" Wallace asked the woman.

"Five dollars for fifteen minutes—four fifty for you, since we're all friends now. And that's a bargain."

Wallace smiled at Marian, the same appreciative but noncommittal smile he'd directed at the fine blue sky, the grease-smeared stranger. To the woman, he said, "I hope we're not bothering you. Marian had a close encounter with one of your planes this morning. It made an impression."

"Poor dear. It must have been **so** frightening."

"It **wasn't,**" Marian insisted. "I **liked** it. Are you having engine trouble?"

"Not more than usual."

"I know about engines. I take care of Wallace's car—don't I, Wallace?"

"She does," he told the woman. "Marian is a born mechanic."

"How **charming.**"

The sleeping figure under the other plane stirred.

A sun-browned arm curled up to unhat the face, and a man came out from under the wing, stretched his back. He was trim, compact, densely mustachioed, and, crossing the grass, had a leisurely, bowlegged stride and an insouciance to the way he set his hat far back on his head with one hand while brushing grass off his seat with the other.

"Felix," said the woman, "this is the poor little girl you almost mowed down on her horse."

"You!" He stopped short with hands on hips. "An unmarked obstacle, you are."

"I'm sorry."

"It's all right. I could use a reminder not to showboat, if you can call it that when no one's even watching. What were you doing up there so early?"

Wallace regarded Marian with interest, as though he'd never considered asking her himself.

"I just go up to look around sometimes."

"Fair enough." The man shook hands with Wallace. "Felix Brayfogle." He jerked a thumb at the stepladder. "My wife, Trixie. The Flying Brayfogles." Felix shook Marian's hand next but didn't let go when she expected. He fixed her with a stern look. "No dead fish allowed. Go on. Firm grip. You won't break me."

She squeezed as hard as she could, pumped his wrist.

"Better. Cracked a bone or two. You like engines? Want to see this one?"

"Dearheart," Trixie cut in, "I'm afraid I'm busy up here, and we only have the one ladder."

"For every problem there is a solution," Felix said. He led Marian to the wing, boosted her up onto the varnished canvas. "Hop on my shoulders."

"Felix, really," Trixie trilled.

"Go on," he said to Marian. She sat on the wing's edge and scooted onto Felix's shoulders. Not knowing where to put her hands, she clutched the top of his head.

"Aren't I too big?"

"You're a slip of a thing." He walked her a few steps to the plane's nose. "There, have a good look. Easy on my hair, though. I want to keep it."

What she saw was like a car's engine but even more wonderful. She studied the paths of fuel and water, noted the valves and rods and bolts while studiously avoiding Trixie's gaze, baleful across the knot of metal. The glossy wooden propeller blades were elegantly angled to grasp and guide the air.

"It's an OX-5," Felix said from between her knees. "Looks nice but leaks like a sieve and guzzles oil. Had a good enough look?"

"Yes, thanks," she said, though she hadn't.

Felix sat her on the wing again, turned to grasp her waist and lift her down. "Say," he said to Wallace, "you wouldn't know a place near here that won't cheat us on gasoline, would you?"

Marian edged closer to the cowling, reaching up

to pet the metal as though it were a horse, and Wallace, watching her, told Felix he would drive him to a good garage if he liked and then back with the gas. While they were at it, he said, he'd show him a few spots in town to pin up notices advertising their air show and rides. "And, only a thought, so feel free to decline, but if you're looking for a place to stay, I'd be happy to put you up for the night."

"Why, that'd be terrific," said Felix.

"And you'd take Marian and her brother for rides tomorrow?"

"Certainly."

"And you, Uncle Wallace?" Trixie sang out from above. "Don't you want a ride?"

To Marian, the presence of the barnstormers transformed their house. On the one hand, she felt newly mortified by its shabbiness because she assumed pilots must be used to the finest things in life. On the other, now that the house contained Felix, it seemed infused with radiant possibility. Did he have a beast in him? Did he grab at Trixie and growl and scowl? She'd clutched his hair in her fingers, felt his shoulders under her thighs. **A slip of a thing.** Was that what she was? The thought of him made her jumpy, nervy. Already she'd dragged him out to show him Wallace's car, lifted the hood to reveal the patches and fixes she'd contrived in the engine. He was kind to her in a twinkling way and had seemed genuinely impressed by her knowledge of the car. She liked his mustache and his neat waist in belted breeches. While he bathed, she passed by the bathroom more than she needed, pausing once to press her ear against the door, listening for the occasional laconic splash.

Naturally, Trixie happened by just then. She was wearing a tired-looking, sacklike blue day dress that must have emerged from the tiny valise that was her only luggage. She caught sight of Marian and stopped, her smile wincing and curdled. Her hair, free of its bandanna and damp from her bath, was bobbed in a style that was fashionable but did not suit her long face. She wore dark red lipstick, almost purple, and had lined her eyes and penciled her eyebrows. None of it suited her. She was spoiled by being taken out of her mechanic's garb.

"If I didn't know better, I'd think you were snooping," Trixie said.

"I wasn't sure if anyone was in there."

The eyebrows lifted; the purple mouth contracted. "Curiosity killed the cat."

Neither could have explained the hostility between them. Marian endured its prickly onslaught without flinching, standing with her back against the bathroom door (a faint splash, a low cough) until Trixie flicked her bob and went on her way.

·   ·   ·

Except for Jamie, who ate a baked potato, they had Berit's venison stew for dinner.

"You don't like stew?" Trixie asked Jamie.

"He doesn't eat meat," said Marian.

"He don't have teeth, neither," said Caleb, who'd shown up unannounced and uninvited, as he often did. "There's just gums in there. It's why he only eats potatoes. He gums them up." Caleb's mother often spent all her money on drink, and when he wasn't in the mood to fend for himself, he appeared at the Graves table. Berit clucked over him, fed him sugar cubes, peeled fruit, spoonfuls of jam. She stroked his long hair when she thought no one was looking, its obsidian gloss calling to something unexpected in her orderly Scandinavian soul.

"Doesn't have teeth," Wallace corrected. His one unexpected strictness was about correct language.

"He doesn't?" Trixie asked.

"Jamie has perfectly good teeth," Wallace said. "Caleb has an odd sense of humor."

Trixie cast a dirty look at Caleb and turned back to Jamie. "No meat? Why not?"

Jamie said, "It doesn't agree with me."

"He means it doesn't agree with him spiritually," Wallace said. "Killing animals for food."

"Why does everyone speak for the dear boy? He seems to have a tongue, as well as teeth." To

Jamie, she said, "What a dear you are. What a gentle lamb."

Jamie, mortified, kept his eyes on his potato. Caleb laughed.

Wallace said he'd heard on the radio that the young pilot Charles Lindbergh had left New York in the morning and had been spotted passing over Newfoundland in the afternoon, attempting to be the first to fly the Atlantic. "He's over the ocean somewhere now, they say."

"Over it if he's lucky," said Trixie. "In it if he's not." She smirked as though she'd made a witticism.

"If he were older," Felix said, "I'd say he was suicidal, but he's a kid, so he's just damn foolish. I'd put his odds at a thousand to one."

Marian tried and failed to imagine the sea. She thought of the blue in the atlas, the stories in her father's books, but its immensity eluded her.

The dining room had flocked wallpaper and an oblong table with mismatched chairs. A glass-front cabinet of the kind that would usually display silver or crystal instead held overflow from Marian and Jamie's collections of rocks and bones. From a plain pint bottle, Wallace poured out something amber for Felix and Trixie (moonshine tinted with brown sugar, though if they wanted to think it was whiskey, they were free to).

"How'd you learn to fly?" Marian asked Felix, whose hair was still damp from his bath. He was wearing too-big clothes that belonged to Wallace because his had been washed by Berit and hung out on the line along with Trixie's.

"In France," he said. "In the war. I wanted to fly, and the French were willing to take American volunteers and train them."

"I'd want to see a war," Caleb said.

Felix looked at Caleb, and a distance passed through him, as though he were sliding back away from the table, receding to somewhere else.

"Felix doesn't like to talk about the war," Trixie said.

Felix seemed to snap back into focus. "I'll decide what I talk about, thanks." He'd been trained in the south, he said, near the city of Pau. When he was ready, he was sent to join a squadron of other Americans at Luxeuil, where they were put up in a villa near a spa. When the weather was bad they soaked in the hot baths or played cards and drank. When the skies were clear, they went buzzing off to do reconnaissance or go after observation balloons, great gray hydrogen behemoths bobbing over the front. "The best way to bust them was to fly up close and shoot an incendiary round from your pistol," he said, "but they were likely to take you with them when they blew up."

He'd seen men blown to bits, shot to pieces, hung up in barbed wire with rats eating them. Wounded men crawling. Where did they think they were going? They were trying to drag themselves away from the pain. Men could die in more ways than he'd thought.

Once a riderless horse had run into the hangar at their aerodrome from God knows where, dreadfully burned, perhaps mistaking the structure for a barn. They'd shot the poor thing to put it out of its misery.

"One time," Felix said, "I was shooting at a German and his engine caught fire, so he climbed out onto the wing and jumped. He was wearing a huge brown fur coat and looked like a bear falling through the sky. He had no parachute. He'd decided he'd rather fall than burn. I might have done the same. His plane flew on for a bit without him, burning, then broke apart." Unobtrusively, Wallace refilled Felix's glass. "Still," Felix said, raising it, "I'd take all that over what Lindbergh's gotten himself into."

The Brayfogles chose the cottage and its single bed over the sleeping porch. After dinner, Caleb went off into the night, and Jamie and Marian were sent upstairs to make themselves scarce. They knelt together on Marian's bed, a russet-colored coonhound asleep at the foot, and watched out the window as Felix sat on Fiddler's fence and smoked in the twilight. When the gelding strolled over, the man extended a hand, stroked the old horse's cheek.

"Imagine having an airplane and being able to go wherever you want," she said.

"Why did he have to tell us about that burned horse?" Jamie said.

Usually Jamie's presence gave Marian a sense of symmetry and rightness, of having been properly balanced. Without him she was like a too-light canoe, at the mercy of the current. He was the calmer one, less impulsive. Ballast. He was not exactly part of her, but he was not entirely other, either, not like Wallace or Caleb or Berit or anyone else.

But in this moment, she wished him impatiently away. She didn't want to think about the burned horse, only about Felix.

"There's nothing you can do for it now. Don't think about it."

"Do you know," he said with vehemence, "that sometimes I wish people didn't exist? I really do."

"People died, too," Marian said. She stroked the sleeping dog, who stirred and uncurled onto her side, lifting a leg to show her belly. "Millions of them, wasn't it?"

"But the horses didn't understand what any of it was for."

For Jamie, there was little solace in watching his own horse stand outside in the pleasant evening, leading a comfortable life, because he could imagine all too clearly Fiddler's panic and confusion if he were to be set on fire, if he ran from the pain but could not escape it.

Marian, still gazing at Felix, said, "I wonder why he married her, though. She's not very nice."

"I don't care," Jamie said. "We'll never see them again."

The world out the window—the tidy barn and cottage, the opalescent sky—struck Jamie as an illusion, a perfidious veil beneath which roiled suffering and death. That Marian did not see as he saw, that she only rested her chin on her fist on the sill and stared moonily down at a stranger and dreamed of flying away from their house where they were safe together, made him feel terribly alone.

He said good night and went to his room, the coonhound following. The dog jumped up onto his bed, circled, and settled. Everything in the shape of the animal commanded love: her long soft ears, the black hairs mingled with the red on her flanks, the way she slung the tip of her tail cozily over her nose. He could not make peace with the magnitude of suffering in the world. It registered in him as a wave of heat and tingling, an acceleration in his heart and a lightness in his head—a sensation both puny and unbearable. The only way to live was to shut it out, but even when he turned his thoughts away, he was still aware of it, as one who lives alongside a levee is aware of the deluge waiting on the other side.

To soothe himself, he took his sketchbook from under his pillow, sat cross-legged, and began to draw the dog.

. . .

Marian lay down in bed but wasn't ready to sleep. She thought of Felix, turned over her collection of memories from the day: his tan forearms and calloused hands, his soapy smell after his bath, his shoulders under her thighs. There was a pressure between her legs. She ground the heel of her hand there, was startled by the way a ball of sparks burst loose inside her like a blown dandelion puff.

Faint voices downstairs. She slid out from under the covers, eased around the door, monkeyed down along the banister to avoid the squeaky spots in the stairs. Wallace and Trixie were sitting on the porch, beyond the yellow splash of light from the kitchen. Marian crouched near an open window.

"Where'd all the stuff in that cottage come from?" Trixie was asking. "Felix was quite intrigued."

"Those were my brother's things," Wallace said.

"Should I conclude he was some kind of explorer?"

"In a way."

"Is he dead?"

"I don't know. I don't think so. Marian likes to go out there to read."

"She's sweet on Felix," Trixie said. "Dear thing. It's cute, really. Although I'm afraid she thinks we're rivals."

"It's that she doesn't have a mother. She doesn't know how to be around women."

"Women love Felix—your girl isn't the exception. I get weary, trying to fight them off."

"He seems devoted enough, not that I know any-thing about it."

"He is, I suppose. **Enough.**" The rasp of a match. A whiff of smoke. "Say, it must have been strange to have kids dumped on you out of the blue. How long have you had them?"

"Since they were babies."

"You're good for taking them."

"No. Dutiful. If I were good, I would have— I don't know. I don't know what I would have done. Paid more attention. Been better."

"I'd have left them on the church steps. In a reed basket like Moses."

"Ah," said Wallace. "I think Moses was left in a basket **among** the reeds."

"Either way, I would have found some reeds."

Marian's skin prickled as though with sunburn. She went stealthily back up the stairs, heaping re-criminations on herself for never before having con-sidered the magnitude of her father's imposition on Wallace. How could she have been so stupid? How could she not have realized Wallace didn't want her and Jamie? Only because Wallace was too kind to let on. She got into bed and looked out at the lit window of the cottage. Tears came, but she blinked them back. For as long as she could remember, she had planned to leave Missoula as soon as she got big enough, but now her resolve was tugged into trim, made taut like a sail.

· · ·

In the morning Wallace drove them all to the field, and after the Brayfogles pumped air into the planes' tires and topped up the water in their radiators, the three Graveses watched Felix's Jenny bump across the badger-holed grass, Felix flying from the rear cockpit and Trixie riding in front. As they flew low over downtown, Trixie climbed onto the bottom wing and leaned out, gripping the rigging wires and shouting down through a megaphone in her best carnival barker's voice about the **Flying Brayfogles! Today only! Lindbergh special only $4.00 a ride! Come on up! Aerobatics at two! Parachute jump at two-thirty!**

After they came back and landed, Trixie told Marian to get in the front cockpit of her plane for a ride. "Couple of gals aloft together," she said, more to Wallace than to Marian, who was doing a poor job concealing her disappointment over not going up with Felix. Trixie wore a leather cap and goggles, but Marian was bareheaded, fully exposed, as she wished to be.

By the time Lindbergh landed, he had spent thirty hours and thirty minutes in the air and been awake for fifty-five. To keep from falling asleep, he'd flown low enough over the ocean to feel the salt spray.

The waves had risen out of the dark like furrows plowing themselves up from a black field.

He had circled, confused, over the airport at Le Bourget. Bright winding tributaries of light flowed out from the yellow lake of Paris, surrounded what should have been a deserted patch of grass, shut up for the night. Cars, of course. A hundred thousand people had driven out to Le Bourget to see him land.

Just after Felix and Trixie concluded their show with Felix's daring parachute jump, word of Lindbergh's safe arrival reached Missoula. Felix had landed and was gathering his parachute when church bells rang and sirens sounded. The crowd at the airfield stirred, murmured about Lindbergh, but no one knew for sure until a man tore up in a runabout, sounding his horn and shouting, "He's landed! He's landed in Paris!"

People embraced; they threw hats and handkerchiefs. In France, the crowd at the aerodrome had nearly pulled Lindbergh and his plane apart in their mad adulation, thousands of people all reaching for the tall man, the salt-crusted wings.

In Missoula, the road to the airfield filled with cars and bicycles and people on foot. So many wanted rides in the Jennies that the gasoline man had to be summoned with his truck to keep the Brayfogles in fuel until sunset. Everyone wanted to be closer to the planes, to the sky, to look down on the town and pretend to be Lindbergh (Lindbergh, who was permitted to sleep, finally, at the ambassador's residence in Paris, his strange future already pulling him along).

But, before, back in the morning, back when Marian was about to go up with Trixie for her ride, Lindbergh had still been somewhere over England.

"Switch off," Felix had called, standing in front of the plane.

"Switch off," Trixie answered from the rear cockpit.

Felix grabbed the propeller and pulled it around a couple times. He took a firm hold and braced his feet. "Contact!"

"Contact!"

Felix swung the blade. There were a few short blasts of clipped sound, like cards being shuffled, as the engine roused itself. A few puffs of smoke, an acrid smell. Then a rhythmic churn: the turning crankshaft, the snare tattoo of the prop. Marian watched through the windshield as the blades blurred to invisibility. A wind came up in the cockpit. The plane jostled in place, wanting to fly. She tugged tight the wide seat belt across her thighs.

They rolled forward, picked up speed, bounced across ruts and mounds until the nose dropped and there was no more bouncing but skimming, the grass a blur. Upward pressure from below the wings. They rose. The stick and throttle and rudder pedals in Marian's cockpit (which Trixie had cautioned her not to touch) moved as though manipulated by a ghost. The earth fell away.

People and cars moved along Missoula's streets like pieces in an inscrutable game. Over the river, an osprey flew briefly alongside, clutching a fish in its talons. Heading down the valley, Trixie pulled abruptly up and without warning executed first a roll and then a loop. She swooped high above the mountains, put the plane into a spin. The valley rotated around them; the engine changed pitch; the wires hummed; droplets of hot water from the radiator stung Marian's face. Trixie pulled out and flew up again, going high before nosing into a dive. Marian knew she was supposed to be frightened, that Trixie was trying to make her recant her wish to fly, but while the earth rushed up from below and her guts pressed into her ribs and her body into the seat, she felt only lightness.

Missoula
October 1927
Five months after the Brayfogles
   came and went

"Jamie," Marian said, "I need you to cut my hair."

Jamie was lying on his bed with a volume of Audubon prints Marian had forbidden him from taking out of the cottage. From the doorway, she eyed the book but didn't remark on it. In one hand she held Berit's long scissors. She pointed the blades at him. "Please?"

"Cut it how?"

She pulled her braid around over her shoulder, with two fingers mimed cutting it off at the base. "Like that."

Jamie looked appalled. "Berit would kill us."

"But she couldn't glue it back on. I'll cut it myself if I have to."

"So do it."

"You'll do it better." Also, she wanted company in her decision, the reassurance of an accomplice.

"I've never cut anyone's hair."

"You know how things should look."

"Not hair."

"Please?"

"No!"

She pulled her braid taut with one hand and raised the scissors behind her head with the other.

"You wouldn't," Jamie said.

The tendons in her wrist stood out as the blades gnawed, coming together with a grinding sound. The pale braid flopped over in her hand like a dead bouquet. She touched her mangled nape, felt a close-cropped patch in back with long bits sprouting around it like weeds. The rest fell forward around her ears in hunks. She'd wanted sleekness, lightness, not this. Amusement fought with horror on Jamie's face. "Now you've done it," he said.

Temper flashed through her. "You wouldn't help me! You should have helped me!"

She ran downstairs and out to the cottage, fuming helplessly. It seemed to her that Jamie had an obligation to go along with her whims. He should have recognized her determination as immovable and done as she'd asked. She'd closed the scissors partly to punish him for his doubt she would follow through.

In the cottage, she sat in the armchair and

tenderly stroked the back of her head. She cried rarely and only if she knew no one would see (the morning her father left, she had only cried after she'd ridden Fiddler far up the Rattlesnake), but now she chanced a few tears before she passed a hand under her nose and got up to light the wood-stove. She knew Jamie would come soon to console her, and everything would be all right again.

From the ceiling of the cottage dangled a squadron of cardboard-and-tissue-paper airplanes. After the Brayfogles left, she had read whatever she could find about pilots and flying in Missoula's handsome brick Carnegie library. Since Lindbergh, the whole country had caught aviation fever, and besides the columns of coverage in the papers every day, new periodicals kept springing up. In the back of one magazine promising "Daring Tales of Flight and Flying," she had found instructions and stencils for making a model of a Standard biplane. That first one hadn't turned out well—its wings were crooked and dotted with gluey fingerprints; the struts were buckled—but she made another and another, lavishing them with the attention she longed to expend on real aircraft, and eventually they were perfect.

At some point in the first weeks post-Brayfogles, as she lay earthbound and pining in the cottage, lost in heady memories of the valley spinning below, of the high harmonic of the plane's rigging, the obvious fact had dawned on her that she could not become a pilot right away. She needed to be older. Not much older, she didn't think, just not thirteen. Maybe fourteen or fifteen—she believed then she would be old enough that her intentions would not seem comical. She would also need a flying teacher and an airplane, but she did not doubt those would materialize.

Another undeniable truth had occurred to her: If she hadn't been able to pay Trixie for a ride, she certainly wouldn't be able to pay for proper lessons, and so she had begun to look for income more dependable than petty thievery. Sixteen was the age for real work; fourteen if you had a school-leaving certificate, which she didn't. The librarians would pay her a dime for every cart of books she shelved, but there were not enough carts. Farmers would not hire a girl to pick apples or milk cows when there were boys after the same jobs. Opportunities were limited, but she would find a way because she **must** be a pilot. She couldn't fathom that others did not see her for what she would become, that she did not wear the fact of her future like some eye-catching garment. Her belief that she would fly saturated her world, presented an appearance of absolute truth.

It was Caleb who came to the cottage, not Jamie. She had fallen asleep in the armchair and woke to him standing over her, purloined Audubon under his arm. His hair was bound back in a braid thicker than the one she'd cut off. He laughed—high and wheezy, almost a neigh—while peering at the back of her head. "What've you done?"

"I wanted it short."

She dreaded him asking why. To explain would be impossible. Because tender lumps had recently begun deforming her chest? Because she had read something in one of her father's books about nuns shaving their heads as they entered their novitiate and wanted to mark herself with the seriousness of her intention to fly? Because she wanted to strip everything extra away, be streamlined and clean and swift?

Caleb didn't ask why. He set the book down and said, "Were you crying because your hair's gone or because you did such a bad job of it?"

"I'm **not** crying."

He smiled, patronizing.

She ran her hand over her naked neck, said, "Because I did a bad job." She was relieved to recognize this as the truth. "Can you help, maybe?"

"I don't see how I could make it any worse. Jamie was too scared to come try."

They spread newspaper on the floor, and she sat in the middle. Carefully, slowly, using a comb and just the points of the scissors, he snipped. "I cut Gilda's hair sometimes," he said.

"You do?"

"I just trim the ends. She's never given me such a mess to start with. How short do you want it?"

"Like a boy's."

"I'm a boy, and mine's longer than yours ever was."

"You know what I mean. Real short."

"All right." Snipping. "You know since you already dress like a boy people will take you for one after this."

"That's fine."

"Don't you want to be a girl?"

"Would you want to be a girl?"

"Of course not."

"Well then."

"But sometimes I wish I were fully white."

She felt cold metal against her neck, the scratch of the comb, the unhurried touch of his fingertips. "Why don't you cut off your braid, then?"

"Short hair won't make me white."

"No, but having long hair makes you seem more different than you are."

"I ain't never—I'm **not** ever going to be fully white, so there's no point. I don't care what people think, and they should know that."

"So you do care what people think."

"No."

"You care that they know you don't care what they think."

"All right, maybe a little."

After a minute, she said, "Maybe I cut my hair for the same reason you don't cut yours."

"Maybe."

Silence except for the blades.

He said, "I heard a story once about a woman who really turned into a man."

"What do you mean really turned into a man?"

"She was Kootenai. An old guy in Shacktown told me. He said a hundred years ago there'd been a woman who married a white man in one of the traders' parties but acted too wild and got sent away. She went back to her people and told them the white men had turned her into a man. After that she was a man."

"You can't just **be** a man."

"She even took a wife. She gave herself different names, too. The only one I remember is Sitting-in-the-Water-Grizzly."

"Then what?"

"She told people she was a prophet. She rubbed everyone the wrong way, and eventually someone killed her and cut out her heart." He set down the scissors, said, "You're not going to win no beauty pageant, but it's better than it was."

She ran a hand over the back of her head. It felt smoother than before. "There's no mirror in here."

"Don't you trust me?"

"I'd trust a mirror more." She stood and tried to look at her reflection in the window. All she could make out was a small head, round and pale. "But anything would be better than it was."

Suddenly agitated, he scooped up the newspaper and crunched it into a ball that he tossed into the stove. "Don't you want to know what I charge for haircuts?"

Nervousness down low in her. It had been a couple of years since they played any of his games, but he'd taken on that needling jumpiness he used to get before he proposed one. Games of captivity, games where the rules involved taking off clothes, touching. "Don't you ever just do a friend a favor?"

"Sure," he said. "Sometimes. I've done you lots of favors."

An acrid smell emanated from the stove.

"Caleb!" she said. "Why did you throw that in there with all the hair in it? It stinks."

"Listen, the price is a kiss."

Kissing was never a part of any of their games. She laughed, more shocked than if he'd suggested she strip naked.

"It's not that I'm sweet on you," he said. "I want to practice for when I have a real girl."

"Thanks a lot."

"You're welcome. Pay up." When she made no move, he gave an exaggerated sigh and came to her, looking into her face, sardonic and unafraid. It seemed impossible they would press their mouths together, but then they did. Or he pressed his to hers, hard. She sealed her lips tight together, pulled away. He smirked. "Next time you want a haircut, you'll have to kiss better than that."

"Next time I want a haircut, I'll go to a barber."

"Someone's got to teach you how to kiss."

"No, they don't."

"Don't be chicken."

"I'm not."

"Sure you are. You're shaking. I can see it."

She willed herself to stop. "Maybe I just don't want to kiss you."

The smirk came back. "That's not it."

After he'd gone, she sat stroking her head. A pressure built between her legs. She put her fist there. Sparks like dandelion fluff. **Was** she chicken? She wasn't sure if she'd felt fear or only embarrassment. If she had returned Caleb's kiss, let his tongue into her mouth, she would have been admitting she wanted to be kissed, that she **wanted** in general. Did she want? Pressure again. Some intuition: She was more afraid of the admitting than of the doing.

She ran her hand over her shorn head again, felt a stirring of pride mixed up with the pressure that was tightening in her like a bolt being turned into place. Her hair was a declaration, not an admission. All things should be declarations, not admissions. She pressed forward onto her fist as though riding a horse uphill, swayed on it. Soon she couldn't get enough leverage and moved to sit astride the arm of the chair, thought of the beastly man with his face between Gilda's legs, devouring, of Felix Brayfogle holding her shins, of Caleb's mouth, urged herself on until she was emptied of all thoughts.

An Incomplete History of
Sitting-in-the-Water-Grizzly

~

c. 1790–1837

She is born at the end of the eighteenth century, in what will be Idaho, just outside a Kootenai winter camp. She falls from her mother, who has walked and squatted, walked and squatted all night, and the frosty dawn air slaps her into a scream. An ordinary girl from the look of her.

The story is patchy, contradictory, a mixture of gossip from both white men and native people, fermented almost into myth.

When the time comes to marry, she is thirteen and big-boned, quick-tempered. She knows how to collect and prepare food, how to weave rush mats, how to do a hundred other things. But no man wants her for a wife. Spurned, she bores holes in the sturgeon-nosed canoe of the man she likes best.

A group of white men pass nearby, the retinue of the trader and mapmaker David Thompson, and in the night she leaves camp, makes her way through the forest.

In the morning, Thompson's servant, called Boisverd, emerges from his tent and finds a native girl staring at him. At first, he's afraid she might be a ghost, but she drops to her knees, crawls to him across the rocks and dirt. Boisverd has been waiting his whole life for a woman to do exactly this.

Boisverd's new wife, the girl who came out of the woods, is no trouble in the beginning. She is eager to help in the camp, eager in Boisverd's bed, never tires. When the men can barely keep trudging forward, she races high-spiritedly through the trees. She learns English quickly and some French. She laughs when the men shoot at animals and miss. When they have to cross a river, she strips off her clothing without shame and wades in, brazenly meeting the men's eyes.

Plenty of Thompson's men lack wives, and Madame Boisverd proves to be generous and obliging, strong and tireless. Her raucous laugh comes from a different tent every night, even though Boisverd beats her for it, or tries to. She fights back, gives him black eyes and swollen lips to match her own.

She has to go, David Thompson says. He fears Boisverd might kill her and doesn't want the hassle. She must return to her own people.

Again she walks through the forest. She doesn't know where her people are, exactly. They take a bit of finding. With a gun she took from the white men, she hunts for food. Prowling among the trees, she imagines herself a warrior, and an idea presents itself. More than an idea—a truth, unnoticed before.

It turns out, she announces when she has rejoined the Kootenai, that white men have supernatural powers, and they have used those powers to change her into a man.

She starts dressing as a man. This man gives himself a new name: Gone-to-the-Spirits. He hunts and fishes, refuses to do women's work. He gets a horse to go with his gun, invites himself along on a raid. The warriors tell him to go away, but he follows, camps in the darkness just outside their circle. In battle, he takes three horses and two scalps. Not bad at all.

A man wants a wife. Gone-to-the-Spirits starts approaching girls who know how to collect and prepare food, how to weave, but they don't want him. He rants and rages. He claims that the white men's supernatural powers have rubbed off on him, that everyone should think carefully before crossing him because who knows what punishments he might call down.

There is a word: **berdache.** Not a perfect word, not even close: French for catamite, meaning a young boy kept by an older man, derived through muddled Spanish and Italian from an old Persian word for slave. White trappers and traders and explorers, from the time of their earliest forays among the natives, had encountered people who weren't quite men and weren't quite women. What to call them? Some forgotten soul shrugged and offered a half-remembered insult his mother back in Montreal had spat at his older brother. The word spread, took hold.

Gone-to-the-Spirits flits in and out of the diaries of traders and explorers. He bestows prophecies on the native people. It starts as simple boasting. He tells them that not only did he change himself from a woman into a man, he has other supernatural powers, too. Like prophecy.

Then give us a prophecy.

Well, for example, some giants are coming. Soon. They will overturn the earth and bury all the tribes. Smallpox is coming, too. Again. White men are bringing it. Again. But, fortunately for you, Gone-to-the-Spirits can perform rites of protection. For the right price.

Warily, people give him gifts in exchange for his rites, but since they don't like his prophecies, they don't like him, either.

He becomes more popular when he starts foretelling a great white chief who is angry at the other, lesser white men, the ones they've met, because he'd told the white men to give away his treasures, not trade for them. He will soon be sending riches and gifts as an apology and will punish the others for their greed. Soon.

When he meets her, his wife is sitting beside a lake. She isn't doing work of any kind, and the strange sight of a woman who is not busy makes him think she doesn't have a man. He skips stones into the water as they talk. Her husband has abandoned her. She is deciding what to do.

He asks, Do you want a new husband?

He has already made a buffalo-leather phallus he thinks might fool a wife, but his wife is no fool. She is, like him, a loud laugher, a brawler. Their first night, she grabs the counterfeit cock from his grasp, laughs at its wishful size. Before he can stop her, she's pulled up his shirt to laugh at his breasts. He holds her down and finds a way to press and rub against her that gives them both pleasure.

She joins him, traveling and prophesying. She tells someone about the buffalo-hide phallus and soon everyone knows. Gone-to-the-Spirits suspects her of sleeping with other men and beats her, though she denies straying. She doesn't want anything to do with a cock, she insists. Hasn't she made that clear?

They wind up at Astoria, on the Oregon coast.

In their journals, the Astorian traders note the arrival of a husband and wife, dressed like Plains

Indians in leather robes and moccasins and leggings. The husband speaks English and French, a little Cree and a little Algonquin, other native languages too, but none of the coastal dialects. He dazzles the Astorians by drawing an accurate map of the rivers and mountains to the east. If any man comes near his wife, he grows menacing, will even draw his knife. He gambles. He can't hold his drink. He learns the coastal dialects.

David Thompson shows up at some point. Bless my boots, he says. If it isn't Madame Boisverd.

The Astorians scratch their heads, wonder how they hadn't seen it. Gone-to-the-Spirits twitches his hand toward his knife, but really he is pleased to have met this white man again, to have the chance to show him he is no longer in his power.

July 1811. They all decide to go up the Columbia River. Thompson is making his way back to Canada; the Astorians plan to erect a trading post in the interior; Gone-to-the-Spirits offers his services as a guide.

One day, as the party travels up the river, they find four men waiting for them with seven huge salmon to trade. The lower jaws of the fish have been run through with poles that rest on the men's shoulders; their tails brush the ground. Is it true, these men ask David Thompson, casting dark looks at Gone-to-the-Spirits, that you are bringing smallpox? And also giants to bury our camps and villages?

No, says Thompson. No, no, no. Certainly not.

In his journal, Thompson writes: **I told them not to be alarmed, for the white Men who had arrived had not brought the Small Pox, and the Natives were strong to live, and . . . such as it was in the day of your grandfathers it is now, and will continue the same for your grandsons.**

But nothing will be the same for their grandsons.

At some point, the party splits. Thompson heads north, telling the story of the berdache as he goes—a surefire anecdote, always a hit. The Astorians continue east, Gone-to-the-Spirits and Mrs. Gone-to-the-Spirits accompanying them. Thanks to optimistic prophecies, the Gone-to-the-Spirits household has grown to include twenty-six horses heaped with goods. One evening the Gone-to-the-Spiritses ride off without a word of farewell and, for a time, go unremarked upon by white men.

When he reemerges, Gone-to-the-Spirits has acquired a new wife but lost the twenty-six horses, starts showing up around the Flathead trading post near Missoula. He appears in the journals of the white men there as Bundosh. Or Bowdash. He comes with groups of Kootenai to trade furs and get liquor, which makes him noisy. For pay, he'll translate the Flathead and Blackfoot languages.

There's a story: Gone-to-the-Spirits was traveling

with a band of warriors. At river crossings, he always dallied behind, and another man grew suspicious and hid in the trees to watch him undress, saw Gone-to-the-Spirits had breasts and no cock, though he claimed to have been fully transformed into a man. Gone-to-the-Spirits, naked in the water, caught sight of the spy and crouched down, concealing himself. Later, when they came to Lake Pend Oreille, the chief said the warriors could pick new names if they wanted, since their raids had been unsuccessful and they needed something to shake off the malaise.

I will be Sitting-in-the-Water-Grizzly, said Gone-to-the-Spirits, trying to make the best of a bad situation.

You sit, but you're no grizzly, said the spy. Sitting-in-the-Water-Grizzly drew his knife but was driven off before any blood was spilled.

He becomes an unlikely peace messenger, running among the tribes, translating. Berdaches are natural go-betweens, not too much any one thing. (Two-spirits, they're sometimes called now.)

In 1837, a band of Flathead is surrounded by Blackfeet. Sitting-in-the-Water-Grizzly brings a misleading message to the Blackfeet to stall them while the Flathead escape.

When the Blackfoot warriors understand they have been deceived, they stab him in the gut.

Another story: Sitting-in-the-Water-Grizzly's wounds keep closing as though by magic until one warrior has the idea to make a deep gouge and reach in and cut off a piece of his beating heart. After that, when his heart is no longer whole, his wounds stop sealing themselves, and Sitting-in-the-Water-Grizzly dies.

So he didn't have powers, some people say when they hear. He died like anyone else would. So we can disregard all he said, because he didn't know any more than we do.

But, others say, I've heard his body lay in the forest for a long time without decaying, and no animals or birds touched it. That's odd, isn't it? Maybe it means something.

Maybe, people say. It might. It could.

Grace Kelly

～

Four

Not long before we broke up, Oliver and I had put on hats and sunglasses and gone out in the middle of the day to a superhero movie, the ninth one in a series. He'd seen all the others; I hadn't seen any. I sat in the dark tugging on leathery Red Vines until there was dull pain in my incisors, watching a violent fever dream of huge, luminous faces, caroming bodies, buildings toppling and machines crashing and bursts of fire. Somewhere in a dark and gleaming room was a locked briefcase, and in that briefcase was a vial of mysterious white light, and whoever possessed the vial could either save or destroy the world.

The fantasy, I said to Oliver afterward, is that you—you, Joe Moviegoer—might also possess extraordinary powers and not even know it, or you might at any moment be transformed into someone who does. But the fantasy is also about containment. Ungovernable forces come to roost inside heroic human bodies or are shrunk down and carted around in vials and briefcases. The end of everything is held inside a tiny ball of light.

"Yeah, I guess," Oliver said. "But mostly I like how the story keeps getting bigger. Like it's not even just a universe anymore. It's an **extended** universe. Like you don't even know how much more there might be."

I said there was no such thing as an extended universe. A universe either was or wasn't. Something couldn't be **more** than infinity.

"It's just an expression," Oliver said.

I was hauled in for a shaming session with some studio executives and sentenced to lunch with Gwendolyn, the author of **Archangel,** and tasked with appeasing her. Then we'll see, they said. They kept alluding ominously to decisions to be made going forward, and Siobhan did her best to defend my right to a personal life, but nobody was buying it. I sat there sullenly, not saying anything until, when prompted, I said, no, I **didn't** know what I'd been thinking with Jones, and, no, I **didn't** think Oliver and I would get back together, and, no, it **hadn't** been my **best** idea to leave the club by the front door.

· · · ·

In Hollywood, lunch is where dreams are made and broken; anything can happen at lunch; lunch is the alpha and omega. Behind every film is a mountain of spicy tuna, an ocean of San Pellegrino. No dessert for me, but do you have cold brew? With almond milk. Thanks.

When I arrived, Gwendolyn had already been seated. Her fluffy little white dog was under her chair, surveilling everyone's feet. Because she took her dog everywhere, Gwendolyn always chose restaurants with patios, and this particular patio was in a hotel's jungly courtyard under angular maroon sunshade things that looked like the sails of a pirate ship. She watched me approach without smiling, her hands folded in her lap, her platform heels barely touching the floor. She's five feet tall at most, and I felt like a courtier granted an audience with a malevolent child queen.

The ripple of excitement that followed me across the patio must have bugged the hell out of Gwendolyn, even if everyone was only talking about what a slut I am and plotting how to surreptitiously take my picture. "Heyyy, Gwendolyn," I said in a slow, cracking stoner voice. "Hey, poochie," I said to the dog, its black button eyes burning with anxious outrage.

Usually Gwendolyn would make a big show of standing up and wrapping her dinky arms around my shoulders and holding her hips a mile away while I stooped awkwardly over her, and usually she would say something like "There's my gorgeous girl." She was only in her late forties, so I don't know why she always talked like she was my grandmother. This time, though, she just sat there and stared like she was trying to turn me to stone with her mind. Or maybe she couldn't move her face. She's starting to have work done. In twenty years she'll be a skin balloon with eyeholes.

"I know, right?" I said in response to her silence as I flopped into my chair. "Totally." The waiter was all over me, draping my napkin across my lap, handing me the wine list, running through all the water options.

Gwendolyn's dog yapped, and she dragged the little peabrain into her lap, saying, "He thinks he's big." Literally every person with a small dog makes that exact same joke literally every day.

"Must be hard being that dumb," I said. I ordered a vodka soda.

"Someone's been busy," Gwendolyn said when the waiter was gone.

"Me?" I frowned and considered, like, what **has** been going on with me? "Not really. I'm basically under house arrest. Oliver always said I should put in an underground bowling alley, and now I wish I had."

"I hope you don't expect me to feel sorry for you."

Here's a key fact about Gwendolyn: Gwendolyn

wrote the **Archangel** books because she dreamed up Gabriel as a dorky sex fantasy and fell in love with him. She was working the night shift at some resort where people have conferences about medical devices and accounting software, and she was spending most of her time sitting behind the desk reading fat paperbacks about dragons and sexy wizards, and she came up with this magical pseudo-Russian dystopian world and told herself stories about forbidden teen love. Then one day she was like, fuck it, and started writing it all down. A good decision, financially.

Here's another key fact: Gwendolyn got confused like all the other crazy bitches and mistook Oliver-the-actor for Gabriel-the-character and fell in love with him. She'd light up like a Roman candle every time he was around, all fizzing and erratic and scary, and flirt relentlessly in a creepy, motherly way. I think she thought because Oliver once married an older woman she had a chance, but Oliver's ex-wife was cool to a galactic degree, like David Bowie or Charlotte Gainsbourg, and therefore ungoverned by age. Plus, Oliver was a teenager when he met his ex, romantic and susceptible, and now he's a movie star who hangs out with other movie stars and cheats on movie stars with models and singers and probably random normals, too.

"I'm going to be honest," Gwendolyn said. "I'm deeply concerned about the way you're representing **Archangel.**"

"I'm not sure what you mean."

"Spare me, Hadley." It came out in a deep, ragged voice I'd never heard before, like she'd started to transform into a monster.

"I just—" Suddenly I was too tired to keep messing with Gwendolyn. "I was eighteen when I signed on for this," I told her. "I didn't know what I was getting into."

"Right, how could you ever have anticipated becoming very rich and famous when you auditioned for a series of movies based on wildly bestselling books? What possible precedents could there have been?"

"I know, but this isn't even like normal famous. It's a fame tsunami."

"I don't think you should make light of tsunamis," she said.

The waiter materialized with my vodka soda, all chipper and professional like he didn't notice how tense we were, like he hadn't waited for the most awkward possible moment to pop in. "Are we ready to order?"

"Cheeseburger, no bun," I said.

"Fries or salad?"

"If I were going to eat fries, I would eat the bun, dude."

He pursed his lips and scribbled on his pad.

"The ahi salad with no wontons and dressing on the side," Gwendolyn said, thrusting her menu at him. When he was gone, she said, "You think I don't know fame's complicated? I have a full-time security guard at my house. People keep coming out of the woodwork, asking me for money. I'm under a **lot** of pressure to write."

"It's not the same as for me and Oliver. People don't buy magazines because you're on the cover. Nobody takes your picture when you put gas in your car. No one cares enough what you look like naked to hack your phone. Anyway, you're not under **that** much pressure to write. Just stop. Wrap it up."

"My readers want more. I do it for them."

"Oh, please."

"You'd be nothing without me." Her dog, whose head she was stroking so hard the whites of its eyes showed, started whining. "A face on a lunch box nobody buys at a garage sale. A dead girl on **CSI.** A loser trading blow jobs for new headshots. I created an entire **universe.** I made up a story that's worth billions of dollars. What have you ever done? What have you ever **made**?"

Before then, I hadn't decided what I was going to do, if I was going to smooth things over or blow things up, but now I had clarity. I leaned forward. "Whenever someone reads your books or even mentions your books, you know who they picture? Me."

I didn't know someone so small could emanate so much anger. It was palpable. Heat and vibration. She was like a space capsule reentering the atmosphere.

"Okay," the waiter said, swanning up, "an ahi salad and the cheeseburger. No wontons no dressing no bun no fries." He set down the plates. "Is there anything else I can bring you before you enjoy your lunches?"

"No, thank you." I gave him my most gracious Star-Being-Gracious smile. When he was gone, I stood up. "This has been a pleasant and professional interaction," I said to Gwendolyn, "but I'm afraid I really must be going." She looked up at me, at a loss for how to best communicate her hatred. I dug in my pocket and slapped a flash drive down on the table. "A memento," I said.

Five

It looks about like what you'd think. We made it on Oliver's phone, so there's lots of blurry jostling and shots of nostrils and armpits and double chins, and at one point the phone falls off the bed. Not the best production values in our extended universe. Oliver kept calling time outs during which I would sit there twiddling my thumbs while he got another close-up of his dick all by itself, like he was Hitchcock and his dick was Grace Kelly. I wanted to delete the video as soon as we'd finished, but Oliver wouldn't let me. "I'm sentimental," he said. So we both kept copies on USB drives that we locked up, nothing hackable.

"Mutually assured destruction," I said, though of course it wasn't.

The night before my lunch with Gwendolyn, I'd watched the video before I made the copy. I may have been a little drunk, and afterward I called Oliver, but he didn't answer. I thought I should go somewhere, but I couldn't think of anywhere. I thought I should fuck someone, but the only person I wanted to fuck was Alexei, and that wasn't happening. "This isn't who I am," he'd said when he broke off our stubby little affair. "I don't do this."

"Well," I said, "I can't help but notice that you do."

I knew Alexei was a ruthlessly good agent, a shark that only eats money, but he was also a **family man.** He chose her, his wife, and them, his son and two daughters. I say that like it was some big surprise. We'd only hooked up twice. Once on location in New Zealand and once back in L.A. What did I expect? That he would give up his whole life for me? Sign on for a big scandal? Hitch himself to some girl who hadn't finished college? Did I even want him to?

"You don't understand," Alexei said. "I don't have the benefit of the doubt. Ever. If this got out—you can't imagine the shitstorm for me. It would be way worse than if I were white."

"You're worried what other people think?" I said.

He looked at me like I'd started speaking in tongues. "Yeah," he said.

When our thing started, I was filming the second **Archangel** in New Zealand, which was standing in for Archangel's less icebound colony, Murjansk. Alexei had come to check on Oliver, but Oliver told him to go enjoy himself instead of hanging around set. Oliver told me I should go, too, since I had the day off. Make the most of it, he said. Alexei suggested we visit a system of caves where you put on a wetsuit and float through on an inner tube, and it's totally dark except for glowworms. They live on the cave ceilings and walls, and their tails shine like stars and attract flies and mosquitoes as they hatch. The poor bugs think they're flying into the night sky when really they're just flapping up to get eaten.

In the dark, my tube bumped against Alexei's, and I grabbed his cold neoprene arm like one boat tying up to another. The only sounds were dripping and lapping, the glassy rustle of water, us breathing, all of it quietly echoing. The black water reflected a thousand points of wormlight. We rotated slowly. I closed my eyes, and when I opened them, I felt as though I were staring into the heart of the universe. My eyes hurt and my skin was tight across my face from looking so hard.

"Didn't you feel," Alexei said later, in the car when we were about to drive back to the hotel, "like being in that cave and being out in space could have been the same thing? Like the difference didn't really matter?"

I turned to him, excited, worried my excitement would make me seem childlike. But his face reflected back my own enthusiasm, my own self-consciousness about being so thrilled by a tourist trap. (Our wetsuits and tubes and the polo shirts of the employees were all emblazoned with "Worm Cave Adventure!") Our wormlight filled the car. "Exactly," I said. "That's exactly how I felt. It **was** the sky, even though it wasn't."

I told him how when I was little, I'd thought the stars were perforations in the sky, little pinpricks into some other, surrounding universe that was only light.

He told me that his dad liked to say the stars were lanterns hung out by the past so the lost could find their way. "He thought he was so deep," Alexei said.

That night we were late to dinner with Oliver because we'd been in bed. But we weren't having sex when we lost track of time. I mean, we'd had sex, but we were lying there talking, making those first big careless, gleeful excavations when everything about someone is new and unknown, before you have to get out your little picks and brushes, work tediously around the fragile, buried stuff. I wanted to know everything. I wanted to tell everything. We didn't even notice the daylight fading in the room because the glow between us was so bright.

"You guys seem to get along," Oliver said later, in a different bed in the same hotel, stroking my stomach, trying to get me interested in sex, which worked because I was still all keyed up.

"He's a nice guy," I said. "We had a good day."

When I got back to L.A., Alexei asked if he could

come to my house, bring me lunch, and I shaved and fussed and obsessed over what to wear (cutoffs, old button-down) and changed my sheets and gave Augustina the afternoon off, and while we sat by the pool eating the grain bowls he'd brought from a pretentious salad place, he told me we had to stop. This isn't who I am, he said. I don't do this. I have a family.

I asked why he'd done it in the first place.

"I'm weak," he said.

I looked at the avocado and amaranth in my bowl, at the papery bougainvillea blossoms sailing along the surface of my pool like little magenta boats. In retrospect, I think Alexei found weakness easier to admit to than the wormlight. Maybe he was already thinking about what version of the story his wife would find simplest to forgive if she ever found out: A momentary lapse in judgment or a powerful infatuation? Maybe he was thinking about which version he'd rather live with. Or maybe he was telling the plain truth, and meanwhile I'd been laboring eagerly up toward a bunch of fake stars.

I made a helpless gesture. "If that's how you feel."

"It's not how I feel. It's how it is."

In the moment, I had to do anything I could to change the way I was feeling, so I went to stand in front of Alexei, between his legs. "Hadley," he said in a resigned voice, but he held the backs of my thighs and rested his forehead on my stomach. He'd taken off his suit jacket, and his dreadlocks were bound in a neat bundle down his back, against his crisp white shirt. "I think it's the illicitness, to be honest," he murmured, almost to himself. "You're coated in it like sugar. Without that—"

I said, "I'd be dull and disgusting instead of sparkly and delicious." I stared off at the far corner of my yard, where my landscaper, an expert in drought-resistant plants, had planted rows of spiked and serrated yucca and agave and palms, ranks of them, like marching soldiers waving their weapons.

"I just mean, how much of this is the thrill?" His hands were moving on my legs.

"I guess we'll never know."

So, yeah, that was the second time. Probably Alexei was the one I was really sticking it to when I made a spectacle of myself with Jones.

House of Virtue

⌐

Missoula
March 1929
A year and a half after Marian's haircut

The day had been warm, and a sense (not quite a sound) of buried melting had prevailed, of subterranean trickling beneath the snow. The river, open at its middle, flowed black and narrow between broad white banks.

But in the evening the city had contracted and hardened again. Clouds came over the mountains, promising more snow.

A delivery truck rattled across the railroad tracks, away from downtown, its side panels advertising STANLEY'S BREAD AND CAKE. At the wheel, Marian kept to the low gears, followed frozen ruts packed by earlier wheels, calmly countering slips and slides. She must not get stuck in snow or mud, must generally avoid drawing attention to what an unusual

delivery driver she made, a girl of fourteen, tall now
as some men but skinny in overalls and a sheepskin jacket and a brown muffler knitted by Berit,
cap pulled low over her cropped hair. The police
got their cut to leave her alone, but no good came
from indiscretion. She delivered bread and cakes,
yes, but also, tucked under Mr. Stanley's signature
calico covers in the delivery baskets, were bottles.

Bottles had been the answer.

After she'd cut off her hair and could be taken
for a boy (voice kept to a mumble, face turned
to her shoes), farmers sometimes hired her as a
cheap hand, but picking apples and sawing pump-
kin stems brought little income. Shelving books
brought less. Her only ideas for making the kind of
money she needed (opening up an auto mechanic's
shop, for example) were not the kinds of things a
fourteen-year-old girl, no matter how audacious,
could do.

As she lay on the sleeping porch after a day of
farmwork, sunburned and with aching arms, a wisp
of recollection had come to her. Caleb had once
sold empty bottles to a moonshiner up the valley. He'd earned enough to keep himself in candy
for weeks, but the work had struck him as drudg-
ery. **I'm not digging around in the garbage for
that old coot,** Caleb had said. But Marian didn't
mind digging.

Potshot Norman, the moonshiner was called.
She knew his cabin and the shed where he kept his

still. Walking in the woods, she'd smelled the hot mash. So she had gathered her nerve and knocked on his door, which cracked open to reveal a profusion of wild white hair and beard around startled, darting eyes.

"Eh?" he said as though she'd already spoken and he'd misheard.

"Need any bottles, mister? I can bring you bottles if you need them."

He nodded, chewing his lips. "Always need bottles, don't I."

Dimes for gallons, nickels for quarts, two and a half cents for pints. She rustled in the alleys behind the speakeasies and soda shops and pharmacies, around the city dump, in the chaotic backyards of drunks. She filled sacks with empties, green and amber and clear. Some had labels stuck on them. Premium Canadian whiskey. Premium English gin. Most were probably counterfeit printed by bootleggers, but some were likely authentic, even if the booze would have been cut with water and grain alcohol. Potshot, scrupulous in his way, boiled off the labels before he poured in his white lightning. Marian traded her sacks for bills and coins. Eventually Potshot told her he didn't need any more bottles for a while and sent her to see Mr. Stanley, the baker, who bought what she had, amused.

One day Mr. Stanley stood smoking in the back door of his bakery while she pulled her clattering sacks from Wallace's car. (Baking bread, cooking mash—smells that might reasonably be confused, though Stanley had other stills squirreled away around the valley.) Stanley said, "How'd you like to expand your business, boyo?"

"I'm always looking for business," she said. A small crisis of conscience: "But you know I'm not a boy."

"It's a girl under there?" He bent to peer beneath her cap brim. Narrowed eyes, a cloud of smoke, flour dust on hairy forearms. She was sure he was putting her on, indulging her disguise. "All right, well, how'd you like to expand your business, girly?"

By the time she crossed the railroad tracks, Marian had visited six houses, a veterans' club, two doctors' offices, and four restaurants. The dusk sky sagged with unfallen snow. At each stop she delivered baskets, some with only baked goods, some only liquor, some both. She knocked on doors; she descended into cellars; she took money from inside certain birdhouses and certain hollow trees and left bottles behind. Stanley didn't let her make the big deliveries to speakeasies and roadhouses, which required more stealth and odder hours and ran the risk of hijacking. He kept her to the small orders. A pouch strung on a cord around her neck slowly filled with bills and coins, and after each round she handed the cash to Stanley, who peeled off a few bills for her, which she took home and deposited in one of her hiding places in the cottage (hollowed-out books, a pouch buttoned to the underside of the armchair). Stanley didn't mind she was a girl. His other bottle men had stolen booze, tried to steal business. She didn't.

The previous summer, she'd told Wallace she intended to leave school after her fourteenth birthday.

He'd been in his studio. He set down his brush, wiped his hands with a rag. "But why, Marian?" he said. "There is so much to learn."

"I want to work. I've already started driving Mr. Stanley's delivery truck."

Wallace settled into an armchair, gesturing her into the other. "I'd heard."

He wouldn't interrogate her about what she delivered. He wouldn't want to know; he'd already know anyway. She said, "The law says I only have to finish eighth grade, and it's not fair you're still having to take care of us when you didn't want us. I'll pay you good money for room and board."

He blinked as though she had clapped her hands in front of his face, waking him from a hypnotized state. "What do you mean I didn't want you?"

"You've been doing a good deed. You didn't choose to live this way."

"But it's not true. Marian, you are wanted."

"You didn't want the responsibility."

He gazed around at his unfinished paintings, his mess of brushes and paint tubes. Unconsciously, he checked his watch as though in hopes of remembering a conflicting appointment. "And what do you imagine doing without an education? Driving Stanley's truck forever?"

She'd told him a thousand times already. "I'm going to bc a pilot."

He drooped. "Still this?"

"I have to save up for flying lessons, but I'll pay you five dollars a week for room and board. If I don't, if I come up short even once, I'll go back to school." She didn't tell him she'd already asked all the pilots in town if they would give her lessons and none would. There was a real airfield now, out by the fairgrounds, with a few small hangars and offices and a fuel pump.

Her teacher had not arrived yet, but he would. She knew he would.

She could see the promise of five dollars a week had snagged Wallace's interest, but he only echoed, "A pilot." He thought for a minute, his paint-flecked hands resting on his knees. "I know you like planes, but, Marian—I don't mean to be unkind, but even if you learn to fly . . . to what end? You want to be like that Brayfogle woman, living hand to mouth? Getting old with no house, no children, nothing settled? That swell of a husband of hers—if they were even married, and I doubt it—will run off at some point, and then where will she be? What do you think becomes of a woman like that?"

"I have to be a pilot. I'll do it whether I go to school or not."

"Then go to school."

"You ran away to be an artist even though it wasn't practical."

"It was different for me."

"Why should it be?"

"Don't be obtuse, Marian. Because I'm a man."

"Don't worry about me. You never have. Why start now?"

He was looking at one of his canvases: a hillside of flaxen grass, a band of cloud. "If you and Jamie hadn't come . . ." He trailed off, started again. "Maybe sometimes I wished I were completely unencumbered, but I would have been worse off if I were. I'm trying to say I think it was a good thing you came, that I had to be responsible for someone, even if I wasn't always . . . attentive." He sighed and pinched the bridge of his nose, closing his eyes. "Marian, the truth is, I'm ashamed, but I don't have it in me to make you go to school next year if you're set against it."

"You don't?"

"No."

She jumped up, bent to embrace him, kiss his cheek. "Thank you, Wallace. Thank you so much."

"Don't thank me, child. I'm failing you."

In Stanley's truck she was on her way to Miss Dolly's parlor house. The first few lazy snowflakes sifted through the headlights.

Miss Dolly, a glum, melted candle of a woman, had dug in and kept her bordello running on West Front Street after the cleanup of 1916 shut down almost all the others, her soiled dovecote cooing discreetly for some years on a block otherwise gone dark and quiet. Girls from the other houses, houses that closed, had to work out of sooty, lightless basement cribs, poking their heads up into the alleys like lascivious gophers. Miss Dolly's girls would have done anything to avoid going to cribs and worked hard, though they resented the debt Dolly kept them in for rent and meals, even for laundry and bathwater and heating their curling irons on the stove and every other thing she could think of.

Miss Dolly held on downtown even after the Chinese left and took with them their noodle shops and laundries and the herbalists who kept buns out of the girls' ovens. She held on after mechanics and upholsterers and the Salvation Army moved in down the block, after the once-fine parlor house next door was bought by a sausage maker. She kept her girls out of the front windows where they'd been accustomed to sit and rap on the glass at passersby with knitting needles or thimbles. (In the good old days, what a marvelous rattle went up on payday nights, as loud as miners' hammers and even more profitable. Miss Dolly could get misty-eyed just at the sound of glasses clinking or dice in a cup.) A fire, for which she at times darkly blamed the police and at times a bankrupted rival and at times the anti-liquor, anti-vice women, finally brought about her relocation to an unobtrusive brick house on the north side of the tracks. There was no sign out front to advertise female boarding, let alone female companionship. Customers knew to come in the back.

Near as she could get to Miss Dolly's, Marian parked the truck and unloaded a runnered sled from the back that she piled with the two baskets containing the weekly order. Down the darkening street she trudged, pulling the sled behind her.

One of the girls, Belle, opened the kitchen door. "You!" she said to Marian. "Come in!" She was not done up for callers but wore a plain blue drop-waisted dress with wool stockings and a gray shawl, her hair pulled into a low knot. Only her heavy rouge and kohl gave any suggestion of her profession.

Marian had one of the baskets in her arms. "There's another one on the sled." Belle scooted outside in her slippers, came chasing back in with the second basket, herding Marian into the kitchen.

"Good thing you came. We'd almost run out," Belle said. She said this every time, apparently oblivious to the precision with which Miss Dolly doled out each week's supply. Miss Dolly also bought imported booze from a real legger, actual premium Scotch and gin for the big spenders, but most of her customers were happy enough to drink Mr. Stanley's cheap moon. "Sit and visit for a while. Dolly's not here."

Marian should have been on her way, but she was always flattered by the attentions of Miss Dolly's girls. She took off her coat and hat and sat at the table. "Did Dolly leave money for the order?"

"I'm sure I don't know." Belle peeked into one of the baskets and squealed, flinging back the calico cover. A custard tart rested on top of the bottles. In the other basket, with even greater delight, she discovered half a dozen cream puffs, each sealed in its own envelope of waxed paper. Presents for the girls from Mr. Stanley, who came around from time to time. "Let's have one," Belle said. "Just one, we'll split it." She was already up, fetching a knife. Once she'd sliced the puff in two, she pushed her half greedily into her mouth with manicured fingers. Marian took a bite of hers. Both the pastry and the cream, cold from the truck, were firm and delicious.

Belle, still chewing, squinted at her. Miss Dolly's girls were so accustomed to done-up faces and curled hair that Marian's boyishness struck them as improper and troubling. Belle reached out and brushed at Marian's hair, trying to part it with her fingertips. "I've told you, you ought to quit chopping this so short," she said. "It looks funny."

"I like it."

"Your uncle doesn't mind you cutting it?" Wallace was known at Miss Dolly's.

"He doesn't try to stop me. Our housekeeper does. She hides the scissors."

"You cut it yourself?"

"No, my friend Caleb does."

Belle hitched one shoulder flirtatiously. "Must be a good friend if you let him cut your hair. I don't let anyone touch mine except Cora. She has a way. I keep telling her she should quit and become a hairdresser."

Marian thought of her last haircut, of Caleb looking at her naked torso afterward while her neck and shoulders were still itchy with trimmings.

Around Miss Dolly's girls, she was all sharp curiosity. She observed how they fussed with their cobbled-together little frilly outfits, how they switched in a blink from coquettish posing and vamping to bored slumping and lounging. The pull, the density of their femaleness intrigued her, even if she preferred pretending, more or less, to be a boy. Dolly's girls were gossipy and lazy and hard, but something about them seemed **important.** They were a clue to a mystery she had not quite identified.

For a time, Caleb's price had been only to kiss her. She had let in his tongue, the odd muscular wetness of it. After her most recent haircut, he had calmly unbuttoned her shirt and pushed it off her shoulders, gazed at her naked chest. She'd felt like those paintings of Jesus where he was flayed open, his heart exposed and radiating light. When Caleb had reached out and brushed her nipple with his thumb, though, she'd shoved him away, and he'd laughed the way he did after he'd picked a pocket.

Belle got up and went to the kitchen sink, wetted her hands before working more forcefully at Marian's hair, parting and smoothing. "It's no good," she said. "I need a comb and some brilliantine. Wait a minute."

Alone in the kitchen, Marian listened to Belle's footsteps retreat up the stairs. She heard a distant murmur of voices. A pot on the stove gave off oniony steam. Beside the stove, a door led to the basement stairs, and this opened. Mrs. Wu came in. She was very thin with a small, round face and hair shot through with gray. She glanced at Marian without surprise, crossed to the stove, and stirred the stew with a wooden spoon. Then she drew a few bills from the pocket of her apron and handed them over, saying, "From Miss Dolly," before she disappeared back down to the basement.

Footsteps tumbled chaotically from above. Belle burst into the kitchen. "Come upstairs. No one's here but a couple girls. We'll do you over, dress you up, just for fun. What do you say? Say yes."

"Yes," Marian said. Stanley's truck could wait. She only had a few more stops to make.

"Good!" Belle dug a bottle out from under the custard tart. Two inches of moon went into a tumbler. She topped off the bottle with water, corked it, nestled it back in place.

Upstairs, Belle pulled Marian along a dark hallway. She shoved open a door into a cramped box of rosy light: a pink scarf over a lamp, pink wallpaper spun through with roses and lilies. Cora lay on her stomach on an unmade bed in a robe, reading a book with her ankles up and crossed. A girl who called herself Desirée was sitting at a vanity in her step-ins, tiny but plump, her face puckered tight like a bud, black hair loose down her back as she brushed it. There was barely room for all of them. Bits of lace and silk dangled like vines from the drawers of a small dresser.

"Whatever **shall** we do with her?" Belle said about Marian.

They set upon her, had her clothes off in a heartbeat. They were used to nakedness and were not bothered, so neither was she, though they laughed at her for wearing boys' drawers. Belle took a gulp of moon and handed the tumbler to Desirée, who drank and handed it to Cora, who passed the dregs to Marian, who swallowed them. When she was younger, before Caleb started cutting her hair, she'd often swum naked with him and Jamie, but while that'd had a prelapsarian purity, this felt like a ritual stripping down, an assumption of blankness. She clutched her money pouch against her bare chest. "You think we're after your money?" said Desirée. "Pardon me while I laugh."

"I can't lose it, that's all."

"We make our own money."

"How much?"

"Depends. More than you, I bet."

Theirs was a form of income Marian had never considered. Gilda, Caleb's mother, always seemed dirt poor, but who knew how she'd fare without the booze.

"Getting diddies, aren't you finally?" said Cora. Irish accent.

"Where?" said Desirée. "I don't see any."

"They're there," said Cora. "Fetch your magnifying glass." To Marian, she said, "Are you bleeding yet?"

Marian, for all her reading, had no idea what the girl meant, and so it was from a prostitute in a room pink as a block of rose quartz that she learned about the monthly curse, which sounded like a curse indeed, the way Cora told it, her explanation tinged with the horror of lost income. Garbed in a black slip of Desirée's and an ivory peignoir, in stockings and garters and shoes with a strap and heel, Marian stared at herself in the vanity while the girls brilliantined her hair and powdered her face and kohled her eyes and rubbed in rouge with their thumbs.

"Does it hurt?"

"Not really," said Belle. "Some girls get terrible bellyaches. And you have to watch out because once you get it, you can get knocked up. You know what that means, don't you?" Marian knew. "But if it happens, you come see us, and Mrs. Wu will sort you out."

"Sort me out how?"

"A little too much dragon smoke," said Desirée, "and a bit of a scrape." She perched on the vanity, grasped Marian's chin. "Mrs. Wu used to be one of Miss Dolly's girls. She started a sideline in keeping everyone out of trouble."

"But then she got married?" Marian asked, wondering about Mr. Wu. The girls laughed.

Desirée said, "Open your mouth just a bit." A red lipstick made the circuit of Marian's lips. Desirée leaned back to inspect her. "Could be worse."

Marian's reflection showed a vaguely familiar person. The whites of her eyes seemed unnaturally bright within their kohl moats. Her freckles were lost under paint and powder. Her face seemed both soft and hard, its planes sharp but not yet set all the way. "What do I do now?"

"Now we sell you to the highest bidder," said Cora, squeezing the bulb of a perfume bottle, sending a fragrant mist onto Marian's sternum. "Lots of gents out there looking for someone just like you. How old are you anyway?"

"Fourteen and a half."

"That's older than I was when I started. You're a virgin still?"

"How much would I get?"

"You oughtn't," Belle said. "Not you."

"There's money in it," said Cora.

"You're setting yourself as inspiration?" Desirée said.

Cora looked peeved. "I'm not sharing a room with eight brothers and sisters anymore, am I? Not living next to a stockyard that smells of shit."

"Now," Belle said to Marian, "put your hand on your hip like this and say, 'Hiya, mister, need a date?'"

"Hiya, mister," Marian said solemnly. "Need a date?" The girls fell all over themselves laughing.

"Date to a funeral, maybe, you ask like that," said Desirée.

"Sit like this," Cora said, arching her back and looking over her shoulder, "and say, 'No twat like this one.'" Marian obeyed, blushing, goaded by their laughter, the dirty word, the glimpses of herself in the mirror.

The doorbell. Loud and resounding, startling them into silence.

"Just when we're having a laugh," Cora said.

Belle said, "No one had an appointment."

"They don't **need** an appointment," said Cora. They heard the muffled sounds of Mrs. Wu letting someone in.

"Damn." Desirée had sprung to her feet, begun to root through a drawer. "It's for me. I forgot."

"Cora can go," said Belle.

"No, it's Barclay Macqueen. He's choosy."

"Why, thanks very much," said Cora.

"Not like that, just—he likes everything just so. Go down there, Belle, and stall for a minute. Cora, help me put my hair up."

"It's Barclay Macqueen?" said Marian.

Cora was already twisting Desirée's hair back from her face. "Know him?"

"I know who he is."

"Take the kid," Desirée said to Belle, screwing a red bullet of lipstick up out of its tube.

Marian grabbed her clothes off the floor. "Come on," Belle said, trying to tug her along. "I have to get down there. Dolly will be furious if he leaves."

"I feel strange going down like this."

Belle eyed her. "Let's see what he does when he sees you."

"I can't," Marian said, dragging backward.

Belle pulled her by the arm. "Just as a lark. It'll be funny—you'll see. They can't help themselves. Say the bit about your twat. I dare you. I'll give you a whole cream puff."

Downstairs Belle grabbed Marian's clothes out of her hands and tossed them into the dark front parlor before she passed briskly through a swinging door to the back parlor. Marian hung behind, leaning against the wainscoting in the hall. Through the door, she glimpsed the crossed legs of a seated man, a polished black shoe tipping at the end of an elegant ankle. A shoe, not a boot, despite the snow. The door closed. The hallway was dark except for one electric wall sconce. Belle said, rather grandly, "Terrrrrrribly sorry to have kept you waiting, Mr. Macqueen. Desirée will be just one more minute."

A low voice, a hint of an accent not unlike the Scottish miners' but cleaner, softer: "I'm told patience is a virtue, and this **is** a house of virtue, isn't it?"

Marian had known Barclay Macqueen's name since she'd started driving for Stanley. A rancher, in theory. From up north. His father, a Scotsman, had made himself one of the first cattle barons in the state, back before there was even need of fences. His mother was Flathead Salish. When misfortune put local moonshiners or bootleggers out of business, a raid or an explosion or an intercepted shipment, it was Barclay Macqueen's name they whispered. The feds had busted Old Potshot not long before, destroyed his still and a dozen other rinky-dink stills around Missoula, and rumor was they'd been tipped off as part of their bargain with Barclay Macqueen. Mr. Stanley didn't know how much longer he could hope to be spared. They said Barclay Macqueen knew every trick in the book. He brought booze over the line by automobile, rail, mule, horse, backpack, canoe; he had operations in every town in Montana and more in Washington and Idaho and the Dakotas; he owned more speakeasies and cordial shops and roadhouses than you could count; his payroll was crowded with cops, lawyers, feds, train crews, councilmen, congressmen, judges, all their bookkeepers; he had liquor warehoused everywhere from mine shafts to church cellars to actual warehouses. They said his thousands of cattle and his massive landholdings weren't more than a hobby. They said most of the people who worked for Barclay Macqueen didn't even know it.

"If virtue's what you're after, we'll find it," Belle said, overly vivacious. "Anything for you, Mr. Macqueen."

"Maybe another day. Will Desirée be ready soon?"

"I'll just go check." Belle burst out of the room and bustled past Marian, giving an exaggerated shrug.

"Belle," Marian whispered. "What am I supposed to do?"

Belle stopped halfway up the stairs, leaned over the banister to whisper back, "Say hello. Tell him you're thinking of going on the game."

Belle was only mocking, but Marian, nettled, thought, why not? Why shouldn't she fund her flying off men's lust? She thought again of Gilda, remembered the beast. A grandfather clock at the end of the hall marked the seconds with a sound like a tongue clicking in disapproval. Marian could have ducked into the front parlor, put her overalls back on, and left, but curiosity immobilized her. She heard an impatient rustle, shoes hitting the floor. A few footsteps, and the door was pulled open.

What did Barclay see?

A long thin creature caught in the spill of light.

Pale blue eyes ringed black, a fragile neck, stockings bagging slightly where there wasn't enough leg to fill them, black patent shoes like hooves below narrow ankles. A gleaming ivory cap of hair wrapped around a small head. Slender wrists, long fingers. He saw her startle. He saw fear and then a flare of something—something in her gaze like bared teeth. Defiance. He did not recognize her as a child. Why should he have expected to see a child here? He had been thinking of Desirée, had knots and heat inside him.

What did Marian see?

An elegant man in a black suit, cuffs white and starched, gold watch chain across a black waistcoat, black hair barbered precisely and glossy with oil. He had a broad Salish nose, full lips, firmly rounded cheeks pinpricked with freckles. His complexion was olive, his eyes dark blue. He was not quite handsome. His eyes were too low in his face, his jaw heavy like a fighting dog's. She saw him see her, sensed how the sight of her arrested him.

"Who are you?" he said.

Belle was coming back down the stairs with Desirée, who had on a modest cream-colored dress over whatever arrangement of straps and frills were underneath. Marian slid away, along the wall, and Barclay followed. She had been foolish to think she could ever do what Belle and the others did. A silly child, all dressed up.

"Who are you?" he said again.

Helplessly, she looked at Belle, who appeared to be trying to squelch the giggles. She could not say she was herself, Marian Graves, not when she was done up like this, not when he was looking at her that way. There was no answer.

"She's just a kid," Desirée said, taking Barclay's arm. "She's not one of ours."

He didn't shake her off, but he didn't respond to her touch, either. He was still looking at Marian. Belle was looking at her, too, biting her lip, eyes teary with mirth. Desirée looked furious. Their faces cornered her like hounds around a fox.

"Shall we?" Desirée said, her voice rising.

He yielded, followed. Marian pressed back against the wall, turned her face away as he passed, caught the smell of his hair oil and some other fragrance, slightly bitter. She was not used to per-fumed men. His step slowed. She knew he was willing her to look up into his face, but she would not. "She's just a kid," Desirée said again. "Marian, you go home."

"Marian," he repeated.

Still she did not look up, not until Barclay and Desirée had finally climbed the stairs and a door had closed. Belle was doubled over with laughter. "You're in trouble," she said, gasping. "Oh, lord." Marian darted into the front parlor, feverishly shed the robe and slip, the stockings and shoes. **What trouble?** She pulled her shirt and overalls back on, stepped into her boots but didn't bother tying them, bolted past Belle into the kitchen to retrieve her coat and muffler and the empty baskets.

Mrs. Wu turned from the stove, took in Marian's painted face first with surprise, then with dismay. "No," she said, shaking her head. "No good."

Marian was home before the snow started in earnest. She went upstairs to wash her face. The soap stung her eyes, but no matter how she scrubbed, she couldn't get rid of the last traces of kohl.

Berit had made a chicken pie that Marian ate in silent agitation. For Jamie, there were boiled carrots and onions, as Berit was still trying to punish him into eating meat. Wallace was out somewhere. Jamie was telling her about going up Mount Jumbo that afternoon. "I didn't see any elk. All I did was this." He opened his sketchbook to a drawing of a squirrel scaling a tree trunk. The charcoal lines were spare but sure, and Marian felt the roughness of the bark, the splay of the tiny claws, the shimmy of the scrabbling body.

Through a mouthful of pie, she said, "Do you know anything about Barclay Macqueen?"

"You'd know more than I would," he said. Marian knew he worried about her job, though he liked that they now had money to buy treats and movie tickets. For Christmas she had given him a pair of field glasses and a watercolor set. "Why?"

"I met him. Sort of. I ran into him." She wanted

to explain how some disturbance had moved through the air between them, rolling off him, breaking against her, but she knew in describing it she would make the encounter seem like nothing, or like too much.

"Where?"

"Miss Dolly's."

He flushed. "It doesn't look right, you going into places like that."

"No one sees me. Not unless they're already there, in which case, they shouldn't be on any high horses."

"People talk."

She looked up. "What do they say?"

"That you work for a moonshiner."

"That's true, anyway."

"What is that around your eyes? You look like a raccoon."

Savagely, she scraped up the last of her chicken pie. He wouldn't have understood even if she could have explained. She said, "I don't care what they say."

Great white flakes big as moths were swooping and fluttering when she went out to the cottage. She tried to read, but she kept floating out of herself, back to Miss Dolly's. Sitting in the armchair, she was perfectly still, but the memory of Barclay Macqueen wound through her like a serpent. She put on her coat and went out again into the night, the snow. As she made her way toward

Caleb's cabin, wading through the snow, her heart was beating so hard she could feel her pulse jumping in her neck. A blurred thrumming surrounded her, invisible hummingbird wings. But his window was dark, and when she tapped on the glass, he didn't come.

Missoula
May–July 1929
Two months after Marian met Barclay
  Macqueen

One Sunday morning, Jamie was dozing in his cot, enjoying the cool early breeze in his hair and the sunshine slanting onto his blanketed legs when the dogs sprang up barking and pushed out through the screen door, bustling to greet Wallace, who was walking up the driveway. Jamie watched Wallace stagger through the swirl of animals without seeming to notice them, as a man intent on drowning himself might plow heedlessly through the waves. His collar was open; his hat was pushed back on his head. He'd gone out the night before in the car, so he must have run out of gas somewhere or driven into a ditch. On such mornings, he was unpredictable. He might wordlessly retreat to bed and not emerge until dinner, or he might regale Jamie with lengthy, jolly, disjointed tales, or he might complain bitterly about some small injustice at the card table, or he might beg forgiveness for some obscure offense, or some combination. There was no telling.

Wallace yanked open the screen door and collapsed on Marian's cot, releasing a stale gust of sweat and booze. One dog slipped through with him, but the others were trapped outside and milled around whining until Jamie got up to let them in. "Where's your sister?" Wallace asked.

He didn't sound as drunk as he looked. "Driving for Stanley," Jamie said, getting back under his covers.

"I know it's for Stanley," Wallace said morosely. "She couldn't very well be driving my car."

"Did it break down somewhere?"

Wallace waved the question away. "Do you know Lena? The trapper?"

"Lena?"

"She's as burly as a man and wears men's clothes. She smokes a cigar."

Jamie knew who he meant, although he had not known her name. "I've seen her."

"She's ugly as sin."

Jamie remembered her face well enough: heavy and jowly, thickly browed, her nose mottled like pink granite. She **was** ugly, but saying so seemed cruel. Wallace went on: "There's something so

offensive about an ugly woman. An ugly man—
that's unfortunate, but there still could be aesthetic
interest there. An ugly woman is disturbing." One
latecoming dog was still wagging outside the screen
door. "Oh, for Christ's sake." Wallace flung himself to his feet and let it in. "There, happy?" He
lay back down. "Last night Lena was saying she's
out with the rifle now, not traps. Spokane Fred
was at the table—this was that boxcar place near
Lolo. You know it?" Jamie nodded, understanding
Wallace meant a certain roadhouse to the south,
cobbled together from two boxcars. "You know
Spokane Fred?" Jamie nodded again. He had a
passing familiarity with most of the dissolute gam-
blers around Missoula. They'd replaced Wallace's
old friends from the university, the ones who used
to come over and argue when Jamie and Marian
were little but had, at some unnoticed moment,
stopped visiting.

"Fred asked why, and Lena said because she
doesn't like to get nursing mothers by mistake in
the spring. Then this stranger who was in the game
said, 'Must be expensive to have a heart.' And Lena
said if the babies die now she can't trap them later."

Jamie was too puzzled by the line of conversation even to feel his usual burst of aversion to trap-
ping. "Seems like more foresight than most people
have. Is that where the car is? Lolo?"

Wallace stared up at the porch's ceiling, hands

behind his head. "Do you think if Marian were to become a pilot she'd end up like Lena?"

"You mean ugly?"

"Yes, I suppose. Tough and alone, with a cigar stuck in her face. I imagine Lena's raw material was rougher stuff than Marian's, but Marian . . . I already have trouble picturing her in a dress. Can you imagine Marian as a bride?" His laugh stumbled over itself, became a cough.

"We're only fourteen," Jamie pointed out.

"I know," Wallace said. "I know. It's not too late." He propped himself on his elbow, looked at Jamie. "Maybe you could have a word with her?"

"She'd punch me."

"Mmm." Wallace subsided onto his back. "You're probably right. I wish Berit were still around."

He'd been late paying Berit so many times she'd finally taken a job for a professor's wife in a big house south of the Clark Fork, though not without shedding a few rare Norwegian tears when she embraced the twins goodbye. Before she left, she'd taught Jamie to cook a few things. He refused to cook meat, of course, but he didn't mind frying up fish if someone else did the catching and gutting. So Caleb brought trout sometimes, or Marian did. She got bread from Stanley's, too, and when the housekeeping money Jamie extracted from Wallace wasn't enough, she made up the rest. Jamie tended a vegetable garden modeled on the one Caleb kept.

Sometimes a gift shop in a hotel downtown sold one of his drawings, though that money he put away for himself. He tried to keep the house clean, but because neither Marian nor Wallace seemed to notice or mind the creeping grime and disarray, he was gradually surrendering.

"Berit was always trying to get Marian to wear dresses," Jamie said. "It's impossible."

Wallace didn't say anything but covered his face with his hands.

"Wallace?"

"I need you to do something," Wallace said, his voice hollow against his palms. "I need you to tell Marian when she comes home. I can't do it."

"Tell her what?"

"I lost the car."

"What do you mean lost it? Where?"

"I **lost** it. I bet it in the card game last night."

Jamie couldn't help himself. **"Why?"** he burst out. "Of all the things to bet!"

Wallace sat up, swung his legs to the floor. His hands dangled between his knees. "I was winning—well, first I was losing." Then he'd felt his luck turn, like wind knocking a weather vane. He'd won a small pot on three of a kind. Then he won again, kings, a bigger pot, and **again,** on a flush. Besides Lena and Spokane Fred, there'd been a stranger at the table, a red-haired fellow in a swank over-coat with a fur collar. The stranger had pulled out a bottle of Canadian whiskey—"The real stuff,"

Wallace said—and poured a toast. A lightness had come into Wallace. "I wasn't likely to win the next hand, but I knew I would. And I did. I knew I should lose a couple of times for form and get out of there, but I couldn't even lose when I **tried.**" The chips, flocking around the table like wayward birds, had homed for him. "Then this stranger said, wasn't I the uncle of the girl who delivered booze for Stanley? I said I didn't know what he was talking about. He said, you're Wallace Graves, aren't you? He knew Marian's name."

Wallace paused. "He got under my skin. I started thinking about Marian, about how when you were little I only cared that you came home eventually and with all your limbs but now I'm supposed to worry about her **reputation.** I should have left. I knew my luck was gone."

But he'd stayed and lost, and lost, and lost. Spitefully, sullenly, determinedly. He lost all his chips, and several IOUs, and then he'd lost the gray Cadillac. The red-haired stranger in the fur-collared coat won it. The car was ancient now, the last remnant besides the house of the Great Winning Streak of 1913, kept running only by Marian's devoted ministrations, and maybe that was why he'd allowed himself to bet it: out of vindictiveness, because the car was the loss Marian would feel most acutely. Bad luck, Wallace believed, was no more than a kind of gloomy mood that welled from an internal spring, and Marian—the way Lena had reminded him of her, the stranger's unsettling mention—was the cause of his mood and therefore of his losing streak, too. "There's no money for another," he said. He wiped his nose with his cuff. "Will you tell her? I need to go to bed now, but you'll tell her?"

When Marian came home, Jamie dutifully told her about Wallace losing the car, absorbed her initial fury, stopped her from rousting their wretched uncle out of bed to be excoriated. She demanded why he wasn't angry, and he said they couldn't both rage. "So if I weren't angry, you would be?" she asked.

"Maybe," he said. "I don't know."

It was true they'd always been like two adjacent locks in a canal, one opening into the other, pouring off excess feeling, seeking equilibrium, though she was usually the lock in danger of overflowing and he the one who absorbed excess, rose up as she sank down. People thought being twins made them the same, but it was balance, not sameness, she felt with him.

That night in their cots on the sleeping porch, she asked, "Why do you think he gambles? We'd be fine for money if only he wouldn't."

"I don't think he means to," came Jamie's voice in the dark. "I don't think he can help it."

"You wouldn't think it'd be so hard to stop throwing your money away."

"I think he's after the thrill."

"What thrill? He never wins."

"And if he quits he never will, either. I think he likes to hope."

"Hope shouldn't be so expensive."

"You know he's sorry."

Marian's cot creaked as she turned over.

"Yes," she said. "He even cried a little when he finally stopped hiding from me. He kept saying he'd gotten into a tough spot. That's all he'd say. He wouldn't tell me who'd won the car, just said a stranger."

"Doesn't matter, does it? Better not to know. Maybe you'll see it around."

"Probably not, because no one but me would take the trouble to keep it running."

After a hesitation, Jamie said, "The car **was** Wallace's, though. He owned it. He could bet it if he wanted to."

"But he bet it for nothing. For no good reason. He was just losing something for the sake of losing it."

The next day from her hiding spots in the cottage she collected most of her flying money, earned bottle by bottle, basket by basket, and went into town and bought a used Ford from a mechanic she knew.

He was a customer of Stanley's. His wife was a lush, and he gave her a good deal. People treated her differently now she knew their secrets.

She informed Wallace that he could drive the Ford to the U, but if he was going out gambling or drinking he'd have to walk or find a ride or buy his own damn car. If he lied, they both knew she'd find out. And she told him she would only pay three dollars a week in room and board now. The rest would be his rent on her car.

The sadness of the cottage, an emptied treasure box, outweighed the pleasure of the jaunty black Ford, her own wheeled and engined thing. On the bright side, her debt to Wallace seemed eased slightly, made bearable. She and Jamie might have been foisted on him, but Wallace had a way of acquiring burdens for himself, too. Without the twins around, he might have ruined himself long ago. Perhaps they had kept him just far enough from the precipice.

The model airplanes hanging in the cottage had come to seem forlorn: the tender relics of a child's fantasy. Flight, the reason for all her labor, was almost forgotten as she worked to make back what had been spent. The money was slow in returning. Mr. Stanley's business had stagnated. The feds, desperate to make Prohibition something other than a dismal failure, were cracking down. Stanley was being edged out, he hinted, by Barclay Macqueen.

Ever since the night of Barclay Macqueen, Marian

had made her deliveries to Miss Dolly's as swiftly as possible, never venturing beyond the kitchen.

"What're you so sore about?" Belle wanted to know when Marian refused to be dressed up again. "We only had a bit of fun. No one touched your pure self."

"I'm not sore," Marian said. "I've got a lot of stops to make, that's all."

She wasn't sure what she was, but it was bigger than sore. When she thought about Barclay Macqueen, her skin tickled; her pulse accelerated; her guts felt pulled in different directions. At night on the sleeping porch, sometimes she thought about Caleb kissing her, pushing her shirt off her shoulders, but lately her mind had been veering away to Macqueen, how he'd pinned her against the wainscoting with his gaze, how he'd asked, **Who are you?**

She took a second job, making deliveries for restaurants in the Ford. Berit's son Sigge, who'd become a Prohi, came by the house once and warned her that Mr. Stanley was going to get raided. She tried to give him what money she had, but he brushed her off. "I'm not crooked," Sigge said. "I just know you haven't always had it easy."

The feds found only bread and cake at Stanley's.

A hot day in June. Caleb showed up when she was outside tinkering with the Ford's engine. "I'm going for a swim," he told her, leaning against the car. "You can come if you want." He put on his most charming smile. "You can even give me a ride if you ask nice."

"Jamie will be home in an hour," she said. "He'd want to come, too."

Caleb was looking at her the way he did before he named the price of a haircut. "I don't feel like waiting an hour."

She thought about lying, saying she had to work, but she knew she would just sit around being regretful after he left, ashamed for not having dared. He was watching her, waiting. He took out a silver case full of hand-rolled cigarettes and lit one for each of them.

"Fancy," she said about the case.

"I took a rich guy hunting," he said. His eyes were still on her. He knew she was scared.

"Fine," she said. "Let's go."

She drove them west out of town, turned south where the Bitterroot wound in tight bends through flatland. Caleb whistled as they rattled along. He took a flask from his pocket and offered it to her. The moonshine burned her throat. She winced, handed it back.

"You need a haircut," he said, reaching to touch her neck with one finger.

"I'm fine for a while," she said, tipping her head away.

She parked among the trees, lemony sunlight

in the branches. As they walked toward the water, Caleb said, "Is Jamie going on with school next year?"

"Why don't you ask him?"

"I haven't seen him lately. I'm always gone." Caleb had been spending more time in the mountains, sometimes alone, often as a hunting guide for men who paid him to find the game, to take the shot if they missed and pretend he hadn't. Marian had bought him a good rifle, and he had paid her back even more quickly than promised. People talked about him, the seventeen-year-old kid who knew where the animals would be. They talked about the serene deadliness with which he shot. It helped his business, he'd admitted, that Wallace had always been after him about his grammar. He spoke well.

"Then we should have waited," Marian said. When Caleb didn't reply, she asked, "Do you think Jamie's soft for not hunting?"

Caleb thought before he answered. "Last time we went fishing," he said, "we met some kids who'd covered a dog with a blanket and were throwing stones at it. I had to stop Jamie from killing the kid who didn't run fast enough. So, no, I don't think he's soft."

Marian remembered. The dog lived with them now, creeping after Jamie like a temple slave, watching him from beneath tables and beds. The boy had needed to go to the hospital. Jamie was lucky the kid's father had a grimy past and no interest in involving the police. Otherwise Jamie might have been sent to the correctional school at Miles City.

I think I was levitating, Jamie had said. **I was so mad I could have killed that kid, and I wouldn't have felt bad at all. I** wanted **to kill him.**

You taught him a lesson, Marian had said.

No, I didn't. Some people are rotten inside, and the rottenness will never go away.

They came to the river's edge, to a pool sheltered from the current. Caleb shed his clothes out in the open, but Marian went behind some trees. Privacy lay only in speed. Naked, she sprinted for the water, trying to cover herself with her hands. A whoop burst from her as she splashed in. Stones bruised her feet. She crouched, breathless from cold and anticipation, her teeth chattering. Caleb was standing in water up to his chest, his arms moving in broad arcs under the surface as though he were smoothing the sheets on a bed. He came toward her. He'd been holding the flask underwater and offered it to her now, dripping. She unscrewed the top, coughed from the cold moonshine.

Caleb tipped his head back, submerging his long hair. His clavicle strained against his skin. "You know I went to see one of Miss Dolly's girls. I saved up."

She tried to hide her urge to recoil. "Why would I know that?"

"I thought they might have told you. Why are you mad?"

"I'm not **mad.** Which girl?"

"Belle."

Marian didn't mean to make a face but did.

"What?" Caleb said. "She's the prettiest one."

"She's just—" She wanted to say **common,** as though she were a snobbish character in a novel. But what authority did she have? Here she was naked in a river with a boy.

"She's just what?"

"Nothing. Did you tell her you know me?"

"Yeah. She asked if I was the one who cut your hair, and I said I was."

Marian was outraged. "Why did you tell her that?"

"Why shouldn't I?"

She didn't know, exactly. She said, "I'd think you wouldn't want to go to whores."

"Why not?"

"You know why. I wouldn't have thought you'd want to drink, either."

"Don't talk about my mother."

They stared fiercely at each other, chins in the water, lips purpling with cold.

"Sorry," she said.

She saw him decide not to be angry. He turned sly, said, "Belle taught me things."

"What things?"

"She said it was good to know how to make a girl happy, but if I want to be happy myself, I'm better off just going to see her. She said other girls will just worry about being proper and won't be any fun."

"**I'm** not worried about being proper," she said before she'd thought.

He smiled his pocket-picking smile. "You want to make me happy?"

"No." Marian had no real word for the part of her that had come alive, was tugging at her attention. **Twat,** Miss Dolly's girls said. **Twitchet,** they said. **Peach, bits, clam.** None of these seemed quite right. She said, "What things?"

"You mean what did she teach me?"

Marian nodded. He moved closer, backing her into shallower water. He leaned down and took one of her breasts into his mouth. The sensation was more strong than pleasant, the completion of a circuit. They were standing together, their torsos out of the water, him bending to his task. She felt his erection. She watched, fascinated, the place where her flesh disappeared into his mouth. He did not quite devour like the beast with Gilda, was gentler, deliberate. He was the one to pull away.

"Did you like it?"

"I don't know." She couldn't admit she had.

He kept moving toward her, and she kept moving away, so they traced a circle in the water. "Belle told me Barclay Macqueen liked you, and Desirée got jealous. Is that true?"

"What if it is?"

"Do you know who he is?"

"Of course I do."

"Are you going to let him do things with you?"

"I'll probably never see him again."

"So you would let him."

The idea of Barclay Macqueen touching her seemed absurd, fantastical. "It's a silly question."

"So you **would.**" They were standing still now. He looked serious, worried, like he was going to ask another question, but instead he said, "I don't want you to be my girl or anything."

Was he telling the truth? "Good, because I don't want to be your girl."

"Just fun, then," he said. Underwater, his hand swam toward her, but she stepped away.

"I'm cold," she said and got out, feeling his eyes on her backside but not caring. She dressed without drying off, went back through the trees, drove away. She didn't worry about leaving him alone so far from town. One place was as good as any other to Caleb.

At night in the bath she studied her breasts, one now so much more experienced than the other, tiny red pinpricks visible around the nipple where his mouth had left a bruise.

A July afternoon flaring and fading into evening. Marian knocked on the back door of a house near Pattee Canyon, up at the end of a long narrow track cut through forest. The house was handsome but not large, freshly painted green with white trim. It had no close neighbors. She had not made a delivery there before.

Barclay Macqueen opened the door. She could only gape at him. He wore a white shirt and black waistcoat. One corner of his mouth turned up. He said, "Hello. Who are you?"

She couldn't read his tone, whether he thought he was asking her for the first time or whether he was alluding to Miss Dolly's hallway. "I'm Marian Graves."

"So this time you have an answer."

He remembered. Of course he did.

"I've got a delivery."

"Let me." He took the basket from her. Four bottles of moon. He'd only ordered them so she would be sent to him, that much was clear. It was herself she'd delivered. "Come in and I'll pay you."

"I'm fine to wait here." Through the open door she saw a red-haired man sitting at a kitchen table, reading a newspaper. He glanced up, went back to reading. She had seen him before, around town.

"Come in," Barclay said again, amused. "Or I'll complain to Stanley about his bottle man's favoritism, paying visits to Dolly's girls but not to me."

Confounded, she stood where she was.

"This is Sadler," Barclay said of the red-haired man. "He doesn't bite. Are you sure you won't come in? Don't you want to see my house?"

Sadler was watching her, smiling faintly, coolly. She said, "What's so special about it?"

"Only that it's mine."

"Seems like it'd be a lot of work to see everything that's yours."

"You've been listening to gossip. Fine, wait here." He disappeared briefly, came back with the empty basket. Shutting the door on Sadler and his newspaper, he said, "I've been spending more time in Missoula, and I don't like hotels, so I thought I should have a place." He drew a gold cigarette case and lighter from his pocket, and sat on the edge of the porch, black shoes splayed in the grass. He patted the planks beside him. "Sit for a minute. Do you smoke?"

She sat. "Sometimes." He lit a cigarette for her—ready-made, not hand-rolled—then his own. She noticed his hands were lightly freckled, the nails clean and carefully trimmed. She thought of Caleb's cigarette case, Caleb at her breast. Caleb was not so unlike this man but less controlled, less formed. Caleb's nails were bitten to the quick.

"I've just come back from Chicago," Barclay said. "Have you ever been there?"

"Only on a train when I was a baby."

"Have you ever been outside Missoula? Excluding infancy."

"I've been to Seeley Lake, and my uncle took me to Helena, once."

"But not outside Montana." She shook her head. He said, "Well, Montana's a good place. As good as any I've seen."

"I want to see other places."

"Elsewhere is overrated, in my experience."

"What places have you been?"

"Oh, lots."

"Outside America?"

"Yes."

"Have you ever been to the Arctic?"

"No, thank god. It sounds terrible." He saw her reaction. "You'd like to go? You don't think it sounds lonely?"

"I wouldn't mind."

He had a crooked smile, higher on one side. "I've had enough of being lonely, I think."

She nodded, at a loss for what to say.

"Aren't you going to ask why I'm lonely?"

"All right."

"So ask."

"Why are you lonely?"

"It's a chronic condition. My father sent me away to Scotland, where he came from, when I was very small. To a cold, dark, dismal school run by cold, dark, dismal people. Dark in terms of their souls, not their skins, which were extremely white. I've always been considered a curiosity. Brown for a Scotsman, ghostly for a Salish. My mother is Salish. Did you know that?" Underneath his careful ease she caught an almost imperceptible quiver of nerves, like fishing line gone taut after a bite.

"Yes."

"You've been asking about me?"

"No," she said too forcefully. "I heard it somewhere."

He seemed amused. "That must mean you know my name, even though, rudely, I haven't introduced myself."

"You're Barclay Macqueen."

"What else do you know about me?"

"You have cattle up north."

"What else?"

"You're a businessman."

"What kind of business?"

She looked him full in the face, dragged on her cigarette. The tobacco was milder than anything she'd smoked before but also richer. "Cattle. Like I said."

"What else do you know?"

"Not one thing."

"You understand discretion. That must serve you well in your business." A sidelong glance. "The bakery business." She smiled, looked away to hide it. He said, "What do the girls at Miss Dolly's say about me?"

Frightened but bold, she said, "They say you like everything just so."

He had a rough, barking sort of laugh. "That's

true. I do. Why shouldn't I? Everybody should know what they want." His eyes moved over her face. "Marian Graves. What is it you want most?"

No one had ever asked her such a question. To be a pilot. To be a pilot. To be a pilot. Telling him would be so simple, would require only four words. But she said, "I don't know."

"Sometimes too much discretion becomes a hindrance." When she didn't reply, he said, "If you won't tell me what you want, then I can't help you get it. And I do want to help you."

"Why?"

"I like your face." He tossed his cigarette to the ground and pressed it out under a polished black shoe. "Would you like to know what I know about you?"

Almost in a whisper: "Yes."

"Your father was the captain of the **Josephina Eterna** and was sent to prison. Your mother was lost. You and your brother were sent here to live with your uncle, Wallace Graves, who is an excellent painter, in my opinion, but a drunk and a very bad gambler. Are you impressed? I know you aren't yet fifteen. I know you're a good driver and mechanic and that you're Stanley's bottle man. Bottle girl. Stanley seems to enjoy the novelty—you're a sort of flourish for him. He has style, for a small-timer. And you don't steal, and you don't talk. As to why you haven't run into more trouble with feds or the like, that's partly down to luck and partly down to lawmen being lazy and corrupt. And, for the last few months, it's been partly down to me."

She tried not to show how startled she was.

"All because I like your face," he said. "Even now, when you're disguised as a boy, however unconvincingly, I like it very much. There's something Shakespearean about your appeal. You won't know what I mean."

"You mean **Twelfth Night.**"

"And **As You Like It.** And **The Merchant of Venice.** I thought you didn't go to school."

"There are other ways to learn things."

"That's true."

She stubbed out her cigarette on the sole of her boot, tossed the butt away. Her nervousness had given way to a gathered, deliberate feeling. She knew, without knowing how she knew, how he wanted her to be. Amused, aloof, a little tough. She was aware of the sharp edge of the porch against her fingers, the way he watched when she stretched out her legs.

He went on. "What I couldn't entirely understand at first was **why** you would drive for Stanley. For money, yes, but most girls your age aren't so compelled by money that they leave school and indenture themselves to moonshiners. And since your brother is still in school, the impetus can't have come from your uncle, or else he would have made your brother leave, too, and go to work. How am I doing?"

"All right."

"All right. Good enough. So I'll give you some of my hypotheses and tell you my conclusion, and you can correct me if I'm wrong." Watching her, he said, "I thought maybe you'd taken it upon yourself to help your uncle with his debts, of which he has many, and more all the time. But I never heard about you trying to pay anyone. So then I thought maybe you're after thrills. Otherwise, why would you have let Dolly's girls dress you up like that? You like being disguised. As a whore, as a boy."

"This isn't a disguise. It's practical."

He smiled briefly, indulgently. "Or I thought you might be saving up to run away. But then you bought a car and didn't go anywhere. So I concluded the car wasn't it. There was something else you wanted to buy. And then it came to my attention that you'd been haunting the airfield. I made a few discreet inquiries and discovered that, yes, you'd been hanging around and pestering the pilots for lessons ever since Lindbergh's flight, which makes it two years. But no one will teach you."

She hadn't expected him to be so methodical in uncovering her deepest wish. She hadn't known it was something that could, with enough patience and persistence, be excavated.

"That must be frustrating," he said, so gently, "for someone who wants more than anything to be a pilot."

She was afraid. This fear wasn't her earlier keyed-up nervousness or the jitters she'd felt in the river with Caleb, not ordinary anxiety but an inarticulate dread, some primal resistance to the thing that roiled between them. "I don't want to be a pilot," she said. "It was only something that got into my head for a while. I thought it would be a lark to learn to fly."

"I wish you would trust me, Marian."

"A bootlegger I met in a brothel?"

She meant it as a joke, a leavening, but she had misjudged. His face closed. "I'm a rancher," he said quietly. "That's important to remember."

An owl glided overhead. It flapped in among the trees and disappeared. Barclay watched it, scowling.

His shift in mood made her uneasy. She wanted to be back in his good graces. She said, "I was tired of school and wanted to make some money. Wallace never wanted kids of his own, but he took us in because he's good-hearted. There was no one else. I wanted to pay him back, that's all. Help out."

"But what do you want for yourself? Beyond this ambition to 'help out'?"

"I don't know. Nothing. The usual things."

He leaned toward her. "I don't believe you one bit."

She was aware of his maleness, the breadth of him, the sureness with which his black shoes were planted on the ground, that scent she'd noticed at

Dolly's, some kind of hair oil or perfume, bitter and musky. She wondered how old he was, couldn't guess. (Twenty-eight.)

His crooked smile swung up again. "In your research, did you learn I was only nineteen when my father died? I came home after one year of university in Scotland. He left everything to me. The ranch, but also the responsibility of taking care of my mother and my sister and, very much to my surprise, quite a lot of debt. I thought there must be some mistake. One of the largest landholders in the state, a man who made a performance out of being pious, temperate, living well but not extravagantly. I couldn't understand how he could have been in debt until I started going through his papers. Mismanagement, that's all it was. The simplest thing in the world. Trusting the wrong people. Bad investments. He dug in deeper and deeper until he'd dug himself into a nice, deep, black pit. Fortunately, he relocated to a literal pit before he could dig us under any further. I couldn't bear to tell my mother. In the end I didn't have to. It turned out I had a knack for identifying opportunities, and this was eight, nine years ago—a time of great opportunity."

The early days of Prohibition. He looked at her to be sure she was following.

"I got us out of the hole, and then I kept working. I wanted to be sure I'd never be back in it. I found the men who'd ruined my father, and I ruined them." The crooked smile. "Not that they knew it was me. I prefer an indirect approach." He grew abruptly somber. "I'm saying this because I want you to know I understand what it's like to be burdened by someone else's mistakes when you're young. I know what it's like to be underestimated. But being underestimated can be an opportunity, Marian, if you know how to take advantage. Do you see?"

In her experience, being underestimated hadn't gotten her anywhere, certainly not behind the controls of an airplane, but she said, "I think so."

"When I first saw you—I don't know how to put it. I recognized you as someone I needed to know. You fascinated me. Otherwise I wouldn't have—" He broke off, scraped moodily at the grass with one heel. "I meet girls all the time. Ordinarily I forget about them right away. If you were just another one, I would have forgotten about you already, too. I thought I would. I waited for you to go away. Instead, you're always here." He tapped his temple with a finger. "Just from that one glimpse. Do you ever think about me?"

At the memory of when she thought about him, how she thought about him, she flushed. "I have to go." She stood, took the basket.

He reached out, grabbed her leg just below the knee through her trousers. His grip was strong, like the jaw of an animal. "Marian. All I want is to get to know you. To be your friend." He recovered himself and let go, looked up into her face. "Here's a piece of advice, now that we're friends. If you're giving Wallace money, you might as well throw it in the river. I've looked into what he owes. He won't ever be able to pay it off, and at some point it'll all come due. But I could help."

She longed to ask exactly what Wallace owed and to whom. His debts seemed to her like a dark well she was forever peering into, listening for the splash of a dropped pebble. She said, "Just because I was dressed up like a whore doesn't mean I am one."

His expression did not change. "Remember you can always come to me."

She'd had no reason to be curious about the house when she arrived, but on her way out she paused, contemplating its separate green-and-white garage alongside which she'd parked Stanley's truck. The structure resembled a miniature barn, wide enough for two cars, with sliding doors padlocked shut. There were two small square windows on each long side, and she thought if she found something to stand on, she could see in. She was curious what Barclay drove. She'd seen bootleggers' cars around, here and there, powerful Packards or Cadillacs or Studebakers, Whiskey Sixes, and she'd heard stories about souped-up engines, false floors and hollowed-out seats, armored gas tanks, flanged wheels for driving on railroad tracks and across trestle bridges.

A bucket and a wooden crate had been left beside the garage, and she stacked them and climbed up, cupping her hands against the window. Inside was a car she'd seen in magazines but never in person, a gleaming black Pierce-Arrow brougham, long and low with wide running boards, swooping fenders, whitewall tires. A silver archer on the hood pointed its arrow at the oncoming world. All her confusion about Barclay was, for the moment, supplanted by a longing to lift that hood and look at the eight (eight!) cylinder engine underneath. A wild impulse seized her to go knock at the door again and ask if she could see the car. She knew Barclay would comply, would maybe, perhaps, even let her drive it, but then she would already have begun to owe him.

She was so enraptured that at first she didn't notice the second automobile on the far side of the Pierce-Arrow, in the shadows, mostly covered except where the tarp had gotten hitched up in front, showing a bit of gray paint and a bumper she knew well.

"I don't want to make deliveries to that house anymore," she told Stanley. "Someone else can do it."

Stanley looked weary, his hair white with flour dust, his big hands clasped over his apron. He'd been making money hand over fist since the Volstead Act passed, but Marian had no idea what

he spent it on. He lived in the same house as before, worked every day in the bakery. His wife wore
ordinary clothes. He must be stashing it all away.
"You gotta," he said. "He asked for you specially.
He didn't try anything funny, did he? Because if he
didn't, you gotta. Do it for me, all right? I've taken
a lot of chances for you, put a lot of trust in you.
He'd ruin me in a heartbeat if he wanted, and he
asked for you specially. Okay?"

What could she say?

She could only remember one other night when
she hadn't been able to sleep. The night her father
came home, she had lain awake on the porch while
Jamie slumbered on the other cot. He'd been as
anxious as she was, maybe more so, but somehow
he'd managed to drop off, so only she had heard
their father's voice, low and indistinct. Only she
had seen his shape in the cottage window when he
closed the curtains. In the moonlight, the tall grass
between the house and the cottage had looked
tipped with silver, like the fur of a wolf.

For the almost five years since then she'd slept
easily every single night—**You're a genius for
sleep,** Wallace said—but now she lay awake again,
thinking about Barclay Macqueen, listening to
Jamie's breathing. An odd longing for her brother
came into her. How was it possible to miss someone who was asleep just there, on a cot across a

narrow gap, almost close enough to touch? But at the same time he seemed impervious, irretrievable, like something glimpsed from a moving train, already receding into the distance.

Barclay Macqueen. When she closed her eyes, she found herself looking through Gilda's window at the beast, through the window of Barclay's garage at that bit of gray hood. Why did he have the car? To worsen her lot? To take something from her? Or would he offer to return it as part of some future bargain? Jamie would say she should have nothing to do with Barclay. He would say he had a bad feeling, and she would struggle to explain that she had a bad feeling, too, like she was in a river being pulled toward a waterfall, panicked but also violently, recklessly curious. In her cot she pressed her heel against the bruise Barclay had left when he clutched her calf, felt a dull pain and sharper pleasure.

She threw off her blanket, pulled on her boots, slipped from the porch. There was a moon, nearly full. She walked surefooted in the dark to Gilda's cabin. Nothing happened when she tapped on the window of the tiny closet where Caleb slept, only a ripple in the reflected moon. He must be in the mountains. No light at Gilda's window, either, but when Marian turned to retreat home, she saw a shadow on the grass. Caleb was sleeping outside on a bedroll.

No fear in her, only a daring indistinguishable

from necessity. She dropped beside him with the urgency of a soldier entering a foxhole. He startled awake, but she put her mouth on his before he could speak. He relaxed. He understood. She stripped off her pajamas, and he made himself naked in a single motion. He had always seemed like a person on the verge of nakedness. He rolled her onto her back. She felt his penis poking against her, nosing around, wayward, and then hard pressure, heat, a dull sawing. She observed the pain and strangeness with detachment, observed the way his black hair slid over his shoulders, the rise and fall of his hips between her knees. She imagined Barclay's hips, Barclay's shoulders, Barclay's breath against her neck. She didn't know what to do with her hands, so she pressed them to the grass.

It was over quickly. She had not felt pleasure, but she did feel relief. She stood and dressed. "I still don't want to be your girl," she said, looking down at him, stretched out in the moonlight like a slender basking cat. She knew this was the truth; Barclay had made it true.

His teeth glowed. "Don't flatter yourself."

She poked his ribs with her foot. "Ass," she said and started for home, drowsier with each step.

In the morning, for the first time: her monthly blood.

**Missoula
September 1929
Two months later**

A t the airfield?" Marian said, looking at the
delivery list Mr. Stanley had given her.

"Special order. Gent called Marx,"
Stanley said.

"I know everyone at the airfield, and no one's
called Marx."

"He's been vouched for."

"By who?"

"By someone who's good enough for me and so's
good enough for you."

When she arrived, a couple of pilots were sitting on oil drums outside the general office, leaning against its corrugated side, drowsing in the
sun. The afternoon sky was deep blue, undiluted

by cloud. If she were them, she would be up flying. She called out the truck window, "I'm looking for Marx?"

They stirred. "Yeah, the new guy," one said. "Try the hangar down at the end."

The other one said, "Got any free samples today, Marian?"

"I've got some day-old buns."

"What about something that comes in a bottle?"

"Depends—you want to take me up?"

"Depends."

She drummed her fingers on the steering wheel. "I've got to go see this Marx first."

The pilot shrugged. "I might've gone home by then."

She drove down to the newest and largest hangar. Inside was airy coolness, grids of smoked-glass windows. At the far end, big sliding doors had been rolled open onto the field, and the bright rectangle of light was sliced across by the long orange wings of an aircraft, nose pointing out, black fuselage sloping down to an orange tail.

"Hiya." A man was sitting in a camp chair under the portside wing reading a newspaper, his feet propped up on the bottom rung of a stepladder. "You must be Stanley's famous delivery girl."

"Who wants to know?"

Letting the newspaper flop across his lap, still with his feet propped up, he regally held out a dirty hand, large for his skinny arm, with broad fingertips like a frog's. "Tough guy, huh? I'm Trout Marx."

"Marian." She balanced the basket on her left hip and leaned down to grasp his hand, gripping firmly, thinking wistfully of Felix Brayfogle. This man was remarkably ugly. No mystery about the derivation of his nickname. His mouth was downward-bent and almost impossibly wide, more like a grouper's than a trout's, really. When he spoke, he revealed a yellow saw of crooked teeth. The rest of his face offered little compensation. His eyelids were droopy, though one more than the other; his ears were short, scooped tabs stuck to the sides of his big, round head, and he was entirely bald. But he had a calm, cheerful way and a goblinish charm. Marian said, "Nice ship."

"You like planes?"

"Yes."

"Been up in one?"

"A few times."

"Ever been at the controls?"

"No one's ever given me the chance."

"No? Why not?"

No need to explain the obvious. She set down the basket and walked under the wing, looking up at the smoothly varnished fabric. The plane was new enough to still smell faintly of bananas, a chemical joke played by one of the solvents in the doping. She closed her eyes, inhaled.

"You look like you're smelling a bunch of roses," Trout said.

"Better than roses."

She circled around to inspect the silver propeller and grease-blacked sunburst of engine cylinders. Her gut feeling was that if she played her cards right, he might take her up; she had to be careful not to say anything to make him brush her off as just a kid, just a girl. "What's the make on this?"

"That's an upgrade. Pratt and Whitney Wasp. Four hundred fifty horsepower."

"Top speed?"

"They say a hundred and forty, about, but I've done faster and it didn't catch fire or nothing. Those lights were custom. Good for landing at night."

"Do you do a lot of night landings?"

"Some. You seem to know a thing or two about planes, don't you?"

"I read a lot."

"That so? What do you read?"

"All the flying magazines. What's in the news-papers. Books." She was particularly sharp-eyed for mentions of women pilots, studying their ex-ploits as though reading tea leaves. She didn't idol-ize them, the way she did male pilots, but envied them with a rawness that sometimes curdled into dislike. The obligatory photos of them powdering their noses in the cockpit disgusted her, and the fuss around Amelia Earhart, who was given credit for being the first woman to cross the Atlantic by air even though she'd merely been a passenger on the **Friendship,** baffled and annoyed her. You might as well celebrate a sack of ballast.

She preferred Elinor Smith, who'd gotten her license at sixteen and, at seventeen, flew a Waco 10 under the Queensboro, Williamsburg, Manhattan, and Brooklyn Bridges on a dare. (There she was in all the newspapers afterward, powdering her goddamn nose.) Next, Elinor had set a record for solo endurance flying—nearly thirteen and a half hours—and after someone broke it, she set a new one. Twenty-six and a half hours in a big Bellanca Pacemaker. After that she set a women's speed record: 190.8 miles per hour.

"What kind of books?" Trout said.

"You know. By pilots. About pilots." Proudly: "I read one about the theory of flight."

"What'd that one say?"

"It was about Isaac Newton and lift and Bernoulli's principle, that sort of thing."

"Ber-who-lli's principle?" Trout said. "Never heard of it. What's it say?"

Marian, who had intended only to make a breezily knowing allusion, climbed up on the landing-gear strut and peered through the side window into the cockpit. The long fuselage was empty except for two wicker seats bolted to the floor side by side at the controls. "It's hard to explain, but it has to do with how the air pulls the plane upward." She hoped he wouldn't press.

"Well, I've been flying a long time, and I never heard of it." He set aside the newspaper and got to his feet as she hopped off the strut. He only came to her shoulders, but he looked strong. Sturdy. He said, "You want to go up or just stand around drooling? It's a good day for it."

For a moment, she stared fiercely at the plane. Then she said, "I have money. If you'd be willing to teach me a few things, I can pay you for a lesson."

Hands in his pockets, he grinned, showing all his frightful yellow teeth. "Good for you. Money's a useful thing. But this'll be free of charge. She's already fueled up. I just need you to help me roll her out."

For such a large machine, the plane moved easily. They each took a side and pushed a wing strut as though leaning into a plow, emerging into the bright day. Marian's body coursed with so much adrenaline she felt translucent. Here was her teacher. He had arrived, as she'd known he would.

"You know how to do a walkaround?" he said, shading his eyes and looking up at her.

"Only in theory."

"Like Ber-whatzit's theory? This one's pretty simple. You give the plane a good looking over and make sure there's no holes in it and no oil's leaking out nowhere. You check the tires. That's about it."

The Travel Air proved to have no obvious holes or leaks, so Trout opened the cabin door, down near the tail, and told Marian to go sit in the seat on the right. "Starboard," she said.

"Oh-ho! We've got a regular Ber-whoozit on our hands!"

She had to stoop as she walked up the cabin's sloping floor. The inside smelled of gasoline. Bolt holes on the floor showed where more seats could go, but there were only canvas straps and metal hooks. "You fly a lot of cargo?"

"Some," he said, climbing in after her.

Once they had settled in—an elbow-to-elbow squeeze, even for a small man and a skinny girl—he pointed out instruments set into the dash: "There's your fuel gauge, your compass, your altimeter, your tachometer, your oil pressure, your clock—"

"I know what a clock is."

"You're a damn genius. There's your air-speed indicator, your rate-of-climb indicator . . ." He showed her the levers, the pedals, the twin steering wheels yoked together, the crank up above their heads that adjusted the horizontal stabilizer, the brakes that could only be operated from his side. "You don't have to remember everything right this minute," he said.

But she did remember.

Never before had she ridden in a plane that didn't require someone to swing the propeller. An electric motor got the flywheel spinning, the engine caught, a cloud of smoke billowed and dissolved. A few spluttering bursts became the uneven rattle of pebbles shaken in a can, then the impatient waltz beat of a galloping horse, then a steady metallic panting. The propeller blurred.

"It would be better to learn in a biplane to get the basics," Trout shouted over the noise, "but I don't have one at the moment. Anyway, the idea's the same."

He had her operate the rudder as they taxied, feel the awkward yaw of the plane on the ground.

At the end of the field, Trout paused to check the gauges and stick a wad of tobacco in his lip before he pushed the throttle forward. They jolted and rolled, picked up speed. Marian sensed the buoyancy in the plane, the way the tires dug less and less deeply into the grass. The fuselage tipped level as the tail wheel lifted. Trout pulled back on the yoke, and the plane parted from the ground.

"All right, now I'm easing off," he said. He pushed his wheel slowly forward. "She can get off steeper than that, but there's no need here. In the mountains you've got to be sharper, but here we've got nothing but room." Below on the valley floor were the hangars, the cruciform shapes of a few biplanes moored on the grass, the fairgrounds' long barns and oval racetrack.

Trout adjusted the throttle, cranked the stabilizer.

A new fear struck her: What if she had no aptitude for flying? Her vision of herself as a pilot had been so convincing, she'd forgotten she didn't actually know how to fly, that she would have to learn. For the first time, the magnitude of her decision to leave school worried her.

"Okay," Trout said. "Take over."

"What do I do?"

"Just try to stay straight and level."

This proved more difficult than it sounded, and she had to keep adjusting the controls according to Trout's instructions. There was a pervasive strangeness to being in the air, worked upon by invisible forces, struggling always for levelness. The plane was alive, the air was alive. Below, her city was alive, too, but in the incomprehensible way an anthill is alive: full of minuscule, pointless activity.

"Want to try a turn?" Trout said. "You take the wheel, and I'll manage the rudder."

"I can do both."

"It's tricky."

"I know what a coordinated turn is."

"Knowing and doing are two different things, but if you say so. Go right ahead."

Her fear was gone. There was no room for it. She pressed with her right foot, turned the wheel slowly to the right, felt for balance. The plane banked and turned. Of course it did—it was made to be flown; the controls **controlled**—but still the fact that she had told an airplane what to do and it had obeyed seemed momentous. Her side window filled with the dark coils of the Bitterroot, the tops of trees. From the ground, the pattern of it all was invisible:

how the river fell along the valley in casual bends like a tossed fishing line, how the water always fused back together after being split and spliced by sandbars. Vantage brought obscurity, too, though. Detail was lost, the world reduced to patchwork. All trees were the same. Fields looked uniformly flat and green.

"A little more rudder," Trout said. "You feel it slipping?" He spat tobacco juice into a coffee can.

As soon as she had the plane zipping along level, mountains would loom up, and she would have to turn again, flying around the valley like a marble riding the inner surface of a bowl.

When they were back on the ground, engine off and propeller stopped, just shy of the hangar, Trout said, "You're a natural."

Joy. Only joy. He could not have known he was saying the words she most wished to hear.

"I am?" she said, hoping he would elaborate.

"I've taught worse." He motioned her out.

Now that she had flown it, the Travel Air looked different. She knew the feel of the wheel and the pedals, the rhythmic kick of the engine as the sparks fired, the look of an orange wingtip pointing down at the river as she pivoted around it. She'd been concentrating too hard to fully absorb the miraculous fact that she—she, Marian Graves—was piloting a plane, but now, remembering, she got light-headed.

"The thing about flying," Trout said, "is that it's **un**natural. You've got to train yourself not to follow your instincts but to build up new instincts instead. For example—the simplest example—say the plane stalls and you're losing altitude, what do you do?"

"Push the stick forward, dive to get speed back."

He nodded. "You've read about it in a book, but it's different up there. When it happens, the last place you want to go is down, but you've **got** to do it. You have to aim the nose just where you don't want to go and go there. Getting a pilot's mind takes a long time. You've got to be patient. And you've got to have nerve. When you're up there, you can't get flustered and stop flying."

"I know."

"No, you don't. You can't, not really."

Was he about to tell her she should give up? Even though he'd just called her a natural? Had he identified some fundamental inadequacy in her? The whole valley seemed silent. No wind. No birdsong.

Finally he said, "So what do you say?"

Her mouth was dry. "About what?"

"You want to keep flying?"

For a moment she wasn't sure she could answer. "If you'd just tell me what you charge, I'll find a way of paying it."

Trout beamed up at her, his droopy eyes scrunched almost closed by the upward curve of his long mouth. "I have good news for you. Great news. So good you won't even believe it." He paused dramatically.

"Believe what?"

"There's someone who wants to pay for your lessons. You won't have to pay a dime."

For a moment her disorientation was complete, but just as quickly it cleared, replaced by certainty. "No," she said.

The big fish mouth arced downward. "What do you mean no?"

"No."

"Marian!" He reached for her shoulder, gave her a gentle shake. "This is **good** news. You've got a benefactor."

"Who is it?"

"As a matter of fact, this person would rather stay anonymous."

"Barclay Macqueen."

Trout's face locked up tight. "I don't know that name."

"There's no one else it could be. No. I have to pay my own way."

"I'm afraid that's not possible." Trout looked genuinely regretful.

"Isn't my money as good as Barclay's?" Of course it wasn't.

"I don't know who you mean."

"He can't have thought I wouldn't guess. There's

not a whole crowd of people fighting to pay for things for me. Only one's been offering lately."

"Why not just enjoy the gift, then?"

She turned away. "Nice meeting you. Thanks for the lesson."

Trout put up his hands. "All right. He said you might not accept his offer at first, but he also said you'd come around."

Marian thought for a minute. "He owns the plane, doesn't he?"

"Technically, Mr. Sadler does. So, I'm afraid I can't let you pay for your own lessons. If it were my plane, I would. If I had a plane like this, I'd do a lot of things." He seemed to be getting even smaller as he spoke, hunching into himself. Abruptly he went striding off toward the hangar, short legs working furiously.

Marian didn't follow. She wanted to be alone with the plane. The engine was still giving off heat and the smell of oil. She bowed her head, rested one hand on the propeller as though it were the lid of a coffin. If Barclay had really wanted to be generous, he would have put his plane in her path and allowed her to pay Trout something reasonable for instruction and to become a pilot under a blissful illusion of self-sufficiency. But no, he wanted her to know she was beholden. Why, exactly, she didn't know, but she knew enough to be wary.

"They're not cold," Trout said from behind her.

He was holding two beer bottles from the basket she'd delivered. "But after a first flight, you need something to celebrate."

She took one. "Thanks."

"Pull up some grass," he said, sitting down. She sat cross-legged beside him. The beer was warm and malty. "I remember what it was like," he said, "wanting to be a pilot."

The low sun glinted off the plane. "All along," she said, "when no one would give me lessons, I was sure it was because my teacher hadn't come yet. I thought he'd just show up one day, fly into town the way the first pilot I ever knew did. So when you said you'd take me up . . ." She took a morose swig.

"Why not just let things happen the way he wants? I get paid. You get to learn. He gets to be your patron. Everybody's happy."

"He's not doing this out of the goodness of his heart."

The band of reflected sunlight on the plane narrowed and disappeared. The air began to cool.

"Maybe this is like what I was saying about flying," Trout said quietly, picking at the grass. "Maybe you have to go against your instincts. You want to pull away, but you'll only get through if you do the opposite."

"I should do the opposite of pulling away from Barclay?" She looked at him hard.

He couldn't hold her gaze, lifted his hands again.

"None of this is any of my business, but I think he means well." He glanced back at her. "Don't you?"

"I really have no idea."

"Can I level with you, Marian?"

"Sure."

Trout cleared his throat, stretched his mouth in a wide grimace. "You'd be doing me a big favor. He's gotten it into his head that I should teach you to fly. I'm a good teacher. I promise. And I do other flying for him. Transport flying. Up north. You follow?"

Of course. No wonder there were no seats for passengers. The plane was for bringing liquor from Canada. She shook her head at her own slowness.

"No?" he said.

"No, I follow. I just . . . feel stupid."

He pointed the butt of his bottle at the plane. "You can put skis on it, handy for winter. You can put on floats and land on water. What I bring back is only a drop in the bucket, but your friend is smart enough to know that you get enough drops and pretty soon you've got a full bucket."

Skis! She momentarily forgot her crisis, so thrilling was this idea. "You land on skis?"

"Learn to fly with me and you will, too."

Here was a new image to ponder and burnish. Herself swooping the Travel Air low over a smooth white plain, sending up rooster tails of powder as she landed.

"I've got a wife and kids. I'd owe you a big one."
He offered a sad twist of his long lips. From inside
his jacket he pulled a notebook and a pencil and
handed them to her. "Here. You keep track of your
flights in it."

The logbook's pages were ruled, and there were
headings for Date, Aircraft, Aircraft Number,
Engine Type, Weather, Duration, and Notes.
Trout handed her the pen. "Go on and fill out
the first line." When she paused at Duration, he
said, "Thirty-seven minutes. Then put 'instruction'
under Notes. Geez, you have terrible handwriting."

She tried to hand the logbook back to him, but
he said, "No, it's yours. Keep it. And I almost forgot. I'm supposed to tell you happy birthday."

"It was yesterday," she said.

She and Jamie were fifteen.

Marian drove from the airfield to the green-and-
white house. She knocked at the front door, kept
knocking until Sadler opened it. "He's not here,"
he said.

"You tell him," Marian said, "I have a condition."

"Oh?"

"When I'm qualified I'll go to work for him flying across the line. I don't need charity."

"He won't agree."

"That's fine," Marian said, "because, like I told
him, I never wanted to fly anyway."

They stared at each other, and she intuited how much Sadler disliked her for complicating his duties. None of it was her fault, she wanted to say. Barclay could have just left her alone. "You'll tell him?"

Sadler rubbed his cheek as though testing his shave. "You want my advice?"

The question exhausted Marian. "How should I know if I do without getting it?"

He studied her for a long moment, said, "I'll tell him." He shut the door.

As she drove back to Stanley's, she pressed on the accelerator. The boxy old delivery truck swayed around the turns. Giddily she imagined pulling back on the steering wheel, feeling the tires part from the road. Barclay would agree. She knew in her gut he would. He wouldn't mean it, would have some plan for going back on his word, but she wouldn't let him. She was going to learn to fly, and then she was going to go to work as a pilot. A force was pressing up from under her. Lift. It was lift.

Manifest, Manifest

Six

Once, when I was fifteen and on hiatus from **Katie McGee,** my dirtbag friend Wesley and I liberated Mitch's Porsche in the middle of the night so we could drive out to the desert to drop acid and watch the sunrise. We'd had visions of lying on boulders under the starry sky, but it was freezing and windy, and we ended up sitting in the car with the heater on. Once the drugs kicked in, I didn't like how his face looked. I kept trying to focus on anything except him, but his horrible face kept looming closer and closer, gray and papery and blank, as though someone were shoving a wasp nest at me. Dawn had been a red slit, night sliced open with a scalpel, with the bristly silhouettes of Joshua trees raising their clubbed arms against it.

When I came back, Mitch, who was in one of

his periods of sobriety, was lying out by our pool with the newspaper. "Where's my car been?" he asked when I flopped onto the chaise next to him.

"The desert," I said. "Wesley and I wanted to watch the sunrise. It's not a big deal."

"How old is Wesley?"

I didn't answer. I didn't actually know. Mitch turned a page of the paper. After a while, he said, quietly, "Do you think you might be getting a little out of control?"

Ordinarily I would have bristled at his hypocrisy, but because he asked with what seemed like genuine curiosity, like he didn't already know the answer, and because I'd never expected him to ask at all, and because I'd gone to the desert looking for awe and come away with terror, I said, "I don't know. Maybe."

He turned another page. "You don't need to do this wild phase, you know. You could just skip it."

But I did need to. I didn't see another way. I needed to spring-jab out into my life like a switchblade. "You only live once," I said.

Gwendolyn didn't leak it, the sex tape, but I still got fired. I got fired so quickly I couldn't help but be impressed by the swiftness of her vengeance.

Gavin du Pré called me himself.

"Do you know who this is?" he said.

"Yes," I said.

"Do you know why I'm calling?" His voice was quiet, ratcheted so tight it was a miracle any sound was escaping him at all.

"I have a guess."

"Gwendolyn is threatening to leak a sex tape of you and Oliver unless I fire you. Do you know where she says she got it?"

"From me."

"That's right. From you. So you see I'm in a difficult situation here, Hadley. What would you do if you were in my position? If you'd given an actress the chance of a lifetime, and she'd repaid you by being **staggeringly** ungrateful and disrespectful?"

"If I were **you,**" I said, "and I can't pretend to know you all that well, but from what I **do** know, I would probably offer some kind of bargain that involved sucking my dick again."

He was silent. I recognized it as the horror-movie silence that precedes someone jumping out of the shadows and stabbing you to death.

Finally, he said, "I don't know what you're talking about, and if you were to make any such slanderous insinuations publicly, you would find yourself on the receiving end of a very damaging and protracted lawsuit that would expose everything—and every**one**—you've ever done. But, yes, you are fired, and I will make sure your career is over. You're finished."

I turned off my phone and went into a windowless room downstairs in my house, a sort of

Moroccan-themed screening room, and I lay on a big tasseled pillow and watched a show about a woman who fixed up decrepit old houses. She was tiny and strong and used a nail gun a lot. The houses always ended up with claw-foot tubs and wainscoting and subway tile. From the pictures I've seen from when I was a baby, my parents' house outside Chicago looked like one of her projects if she'd abandoned it halfway through. There's a photo of my mother bathing me in a claw-foot tub, but you can see the linoleum floor is peeling and discolored. In another you can see nice wood floors but also a sad-looking futon covered with a rumpled sheet. I don't know why they didn't fix it up nicer. They had some money, enough for the Cessna that killed them. I don't know if they wanted to live that way or just didn't want badly enough to change.

Eventually I fell asleep.

By the next morning, the news was everywhere, spreading from **The Hollywood Reporter** to celeb gossip sites to CNN, glee dolloped all over it like whipped cream. I had three thousand Twitter notifications. "News flash," I tweeted. "Nothing lasts forever. Get over it." Then I deleted my account and turned off my phone.

Of course I'd meant to piss off Gwendolyn, to flaunt that I'd not only had what she most wanted but had tossed it away. I'd known this was the probable outcome, but still I reeled like a charred and tottering cartoon knight who'd just been flambéed in dragon's breath.

I was lying on the couch watching a different real estate show, one where unreasonable people shop for cheap houses in boring places, getting little endorphin rushes from random strangers making decisions, when Augustina reminded me I'd scheduled a session with my trainer. I was supposed to be getting into shape for the fifth movie, eating nothing but fish and kale, thinking only of my triceps, but that was irrelevant now.

"You could cancel," Augustina said. "He'd understand."

But I had to get out. I said I'd drive myself. M.G. rode shotgun. At the bottom of my driveway I crept slowly, carefully, mindful of lawsuits, through my rookery. They filled my windows with their lenses. Their hands suctioned to the glass like starfish. "You want me to get them to move back?" M.G. said. He only speaks when absolutely necessary, generally just hovers stone-faced in my vicinity. But I said no, it was okay. One photographer belly flopped across the hood, shooting into my face. I made a big sideways sweeping motion at him, shouted, "Get the fuck off!" Even with the windows up, the shutters made a din. A swarm of robot insects. Playing cards in bicycle spokes. A hundred old film projectors running at the same time.

Manifest, my trainer said. **Manifest.** I was

supposed to look in the mirror and manifest, in my mind, the body I wanted. Holding weights, I leaned forward, bent my knees, opened my arms out and up. My trainer called it the butterfly. I tried to imagine the body I wanted, but all I saw was a butterfly struggling slowly through heavy, swampy air. "Engage your core," my trainer said.

A while ago I had a shrink, briefly, who told me to imagine a glowing tiger every time I doubted myself, to imagine the tiger was my source of strength, my essence. I was supposed to imagine the tiger glowing brighter and brighter and a thick layer of dust settling on everything else until the whole world was gray except for my tiger. The tiger was like the vial of white light in that superhero movie. The tiger was preposterous. The tiger was me. The tiger was everything but me.

Everyone knows Los Angeles is a city of deniers. Everyone knows this is a city of silicone and Restylane, of charismatic stationary-bike preachers and kettlebell gurus, of healing crystals and singing bowls, of probiotics and juice cleanses and colonics and jade eggs you stick up your vag and exorbitantly expensive snake-oil powder you sprinkle on your coconut chia pudding. We purify ourselves for life as though it were the grave. This is a city that's more afraid of death than any other. I said that to Oliver once, and he told me I was being a little negative. I said it to Siobhan, and she gave me the name of a shrink. I said it to the shrink, and he asked me if I thought people were wrong to fear death. I said I didn't think the fear was the problem as much as the struggle. I said I thought the struggle should be to accept death, not to defy it.

"Hmmm," he said. "Imagine a tiger," he said.

Seven

I floated on a raft in my pool. I felt stunned, like a critter picked up by a bird of prey and then dropped, a beating heart inside an inert, sprawled body. The insides of my eyelids glowed blood-orange.

I must have fallen asleep, or almost, because when a very English voice called out, "You really shouldn't sleep in a swimming pool," I startled and tipped off the raft into a blue blur. The water stung and fizzed in my nose.

"I didn't think you were **actually** asleep," Sir Hugo said when I surfaced. He was holding the half-empty bottle of Scotch and two glasses and had a canvas tote bag over his shoulder. "Augustina let me in."

I hauled myself out at the edge. "Are they still down there?"

"The photogs? Oh, yes."

I wrapped a towel around myself, and we sat at the table where I'd once eaten ancient-grain bowls with Alexei.

Hugo poured the Scotch. He held up his glass. "To an ending."

I clinked.

"Now, my girl," he said in a gentle growl. "What do you want to do? Will you take time off?"

I imagined what I would do with time off. I would float in the pool, smoke weed, manifest the body I wanted, imagine my tiger, watch people renovate houses, wait for something to happen. It wasn't **un**appealing. But, in rebuttal, the vision of myself holding an Oscar came back to me again, obliterating those laconic half thoughts like a cartoon safe crushing a cartoon cat. I was onstage, raising the statue above my head, living out the default dream of everyone in Hollywood. My arm and shoulder looked perfectly toned. A theater of people was on its feet, even Gavin du Pré. Alexei was there too, looking wistful.

"I'd rather move forward," I said.

"Good." He paused for a second and breathed in so hard his nose flattened, signaling he was about to quote something. " 'Men at some time are masters of their own fates; the fault, dear Brutus, is not in our stars, but in ourselves, that we are underlings.' "

"**Men** are masters of their own fates."

"Women didn't fit the meter."

"They never do, man."

"I have something for you. It's out of print, so don't be careless with it." He pulled a book out of his tote bag and handed it over. An old, slender hardback, with a mustard-colored dust jacket crumbling at the edges. On the front cover was an illustration of an airplane flying over the ocean, the sun behind it and a few stretched-out shallow **M**'s scattered around to suggest birds. The title was in elegant italics: **The Sea, the Sky, the Birds Between: The Lost Logbook of Marian Graves.** The smell of the Van Nuys public library came back to me, and I could almost feel the sweaty vinyl embrace of the beanbag chair in the children's reading corner.

"I've read this book."

Hugo's box-hedge eyebrows flew up. "You **have**?"

"Don't look so stunned. I read."

"You **do**?"

"Ha ha. It made a big impression on me when I was a kid. Orphan solidarity, you know. Team Raised-by-Uncles. I thought it would be full of hidden messages, like tarot cards or something."

"Ah." Hugo nodded. "I can imagine it. Wee Hadley the bibliomancer, consulting the text for signs and omens. It's the perfect sort of book for that, isn't it? Mostly cryptic bits and pieces. What did it tell you?"

"Nothing."

"Yes, well, that's not surprising. Really I'm most intrigued by the question of whether or not she intended it to be read at all. I think the fact that she left it behind at least **suggests** she couldn't bear to destroy it. What do you think?"

I considered bluffing but instead admitted, "I don't remember it very well. I think I was ten or eleven when I read it."

"Reread it. And then read this." He took another book from the bag, a paperback. On the cover was a soft-focus photo of the back of a woman's head as she gazed toward a silver airplane parked on a flat expanse of white. A fur collar stood up against her neck. Apparently **People** magazine had used the words **Irresistible . . . dazzling . . . high-wire** in relation to it somehow.

I read aloud, "**Wings of Peregrine: A Novel.** By Carol Feiffer."

"To be honest, it's"—Hugo teetered his hand— "not the best. It doesn't have the depth one wishes for, and the prose is sometimes quite dreadful. But it's the basis for **this.**" From the tote bag he took a sheaf of paper clamped together with a binder clip and tossed it onto the table. A script. Its title page was stamped diagonally with the name of Hugo's production company. "The Day brothers brought it to me with Bart Olofsson already attached to direct," he said. "They've done something quite un-expected, gone for almost a Coen brothers vibe, a little antic but not as dark. Just the tiniest bit camp but still quite affecting, I think."

"So many brothers. You don't have anything else in that bag, do you? No more homework?"

He turned the empty bag upside down and shook it. "Not a page."

I pulled the script closer.

PEREGRINE
written by
The Day Brothers

based on the novel Wings of Peregrine
by Carol Feiffer

I knew about the Day brothers. Kyle and Travis, blond twins with Nazi haircuts who vaped on the red carpet. They weren't even thirty but had created a quirky, violent limited series for HBO set in Reno. They were having a moment. And Bart Olofsson had made one talky indie movie that was the darling of Sundance and then like three superhero movies, so he was probably ready to do the reverse sellout. These people were considered cool, and working with them might make me seem cool. "Whose idea was this?"

Hugo grimaced. "It gets a little complicated. The Days were commissioned by the son of the woman who wrote the book."

"That couldn't have been cheap."

"No, but they wouldn't have done it if they didn't like the project. Which they do. The guy's name is Redwood Feiffer. He wants to be a producer. And he already knew the Days from being young and hip and extremely rich. He's a Feiffer Feiffer."

"What's a Feiffer Feiffer?"

"Like the Feiffer Foundation. Like the Feiffer Museum of Art. The father died—Redwood's father; his parents have been divorced for ages—anyway, he died, and Redwood came into a major share of the family fortune. It's from oil, I think? Chemicals? Something ghastly. His mother, Carol, wrote this novel, and—here's the really interesting part—his paternal grandmother not only published Marian's book in the fifties but **paid for her flight.** The family's all knotted up with this story. And Redwood's a do-gooder-slash-creative-type. Very enthusiastic."

I got it then, what the racket was. "So he's looking to be something other than rich and idle, and he thinks he's going to reinvent Hollywood."

"That's likely his basic plan, yes."

There was no real inflection to his words. Like how a general planning an air strike might give an estimate of civilian casualties. A bit of businesslike hardness to forestall pity. There are always a bunch of these rich kids floating around L.A., riding on fortunes they didn't earn as though on litters born aloft by the ghosts of their ancestors. They want to make **good** movies, they all say: projects chosen for quality writing, compelling vision, original voice, etc., and **not** for their prospects in the Asian market. They want to reinvent something that doesn't want to be reinvented, to **disrupt** a system that's orders of magnitude more complex and predatory and fortified than they think. That's their plan. Hollywood's plan is to strip the flesh from their bones so slowly they won't notice at first. Tiny little bites, and then big ones at the end.

But, to be fair, Hugo wanted to make good movies, too. He just needed other people's money to do it.

"He's putting up all the money?" I asked.

"Ah, no. But a good chunk. Frankly with the locations and the airplanes and the CGI and all, it's a bit rich for our blood, so we took it to Sun God." Sun God Entertainment was backed by hedge funds and had ambitions to make movies that were too expensive to be indies but not expensive enough to be worth the studios' time. "They signed on, and now perhaps there is just the slightest overabundance of cooks in the kitchen, but I think it could work. With the right star, of course." He winked. "We couldn't pay you much."

"How not much?"

"Scale. And something on the back end."

"Siobhan's going to **love** that."

"Screw Siobhan. You don't need the money. This is your moment to show the naysayers what you're capable of." He was making his voice extra sonorous, booming at me like I was a medieval army he was trying to rally to wipe out another medieval army advancing over some moor.

What was I capable of? I didn't actually know. I pictured myself with the Oscar again. Did I deserve an Oscar? No, but who did, really? **Manifest.**

Hugo clapped his hands on his thighs and stood up. "Think about it."

I walked him through the house. As he stepped out the front door, I said, "I should tell you, Gavin du Pré has a grudge against me. It might be inconvenient."

"He's not involved."

"But still. He can do things."

"How do you know he has a grudge?"

"Oh, I got that feeling yesterday when he told me he'd kill my career. His exact words were"—I put on the raspy growl of a comic book villain and clenched one hand into a fist—" 'you're finished.' "

To my surprise, Hugo only laughed. "Do you know who the head of Sun God is?"

"Ted Lazarus, isn't it?"

"Do you know that Ted Lazarus and Gavin du Pré hate each other?"

"Vaguely."

"Do you know why?"

"No."

"Gavin fucked Ted's wife. So it's fine. Everything's fine. Everyone's already out to ruin each other." He reached for my hand. "This will be a **very** good role for you, my dear. This will **elevate** you." He kissed my hand with a loud smack and went striding off. While he waited for my gate to open, he squared himself up, then, between the parting panels, swept a low bow to the paparazzi, who cheered.

Eight

After Hugo left, I got in the bathtub and opened Marian's book.

EDITOR'S NOTE
The document contained in the following pages, reader, has taken a most unlikely journey before settling, as it has, in your hands.

Very true, I thought.

In 1950, Marian Graves, an accomplished pilot and the author of this short tome, vanished along with her navigator, Eddie Bloom, while attempting to circumnavigate the globe longitudinally, by way of both the North and South Poles. They were last seen in Queen Maud Land, East Antarctica, when they refueled at Maudheim, the encampment of the Norwegian-British-Swedish Antarctic Expedition. From Maudheim they were to have flown across the continent, passing over the South Pole, to the Ross Ice Shelf, where lay the remains of the various bases built and used during Admiral Richard E. Byrd's Antarctic expeditions, all dubbed "Little America." Though the bases were abandoned, more than enough cached gasoline would have been available to refuel the plane, the **Peregrine,** before Marian and Eddie embarked on their journey's final leg, bound for New Zealand. Tragically, after departing Maudheim, neither pilot nor navigator nor aircraft were ever seen again. For almost a decade, nothing was known of their fate. Most assumed the **Peregrine** had crashed somewhere in the pitiless Antarctic interior.

Now, thanks to a remarkably fortuitous discovery, we know that Marian and Eddie indeed reached the Ross Ice Shelf. Last year, while conducting research as part of the collaborative International Geophysical Year, scientists exploring the buried remnants of Little America III found not only the expected artifacts of Byrd's 1939–1941 expedition but also an odd bundle of yellow rubber. They determined, to their great surprise, that it was the kind of aviation life preserver known as a Mae West, and it was wrapped carefully around Marian's handwritten journal containing her elliptical, fragmented musings from the flight: the manuscript of this very book.

I'm afraid I cannot elucidate her reasons for leaving behind her journal (and, ominously, one of their two life preservers). Perhaps she weighed the odds of reaching New Zealand versus the odds of future visitors to Little America finding the book and, disturbing to contemplate, found the latter more likely. It can be counted as a stroke of luck that the base was still in existence at all. Icebergs are continually breaking, or calving, from the Ross Ice Shelf, and half of Little America IV, a more recent encampment from 1946–47, has already been carried out to sea.

As exciting as we may find the news that Marian's flight extended far beyond what was previously known, bringing her only 2,600 nautical miles short of a completed north–south circumnavigation, this revelation also carries with it a sad truth: Marian Graves and Eddie Bloom took off from Antarctica and were lost. Despite the fanciful theories some have put forward, we can be certain they lie together deep under cold and stormy waters, in a tomb without walls, a place that remains lonely beyond imagination despite the thousands upon thousands who have made their final rest there.

The offices of D. Wenceslas & Sons have lately been the site of impassioned debates over whether or not Marian would have wished for this manuscript to be published without having a chance to edit and consider its text. Was the manuscript intended as a posthumous message in a bottle? Or was she turning her back on her own words? Admittedly, both in conversation before her flight and in the pages themselves, Marian expressed ambivalence to me about the idea of a readership, but, as I have argued to my colleagues, if she truly did not wish these pages to be read, why did she then not simply destroy them, as she could have so easily? We reached no consensus, and she left no instructions, only the journal itself, abandoned in a frozen, hostile place. What she left resembles less a book than a scaffolding for a future book, but I felt she would prefer it be published as is rather than having it shaped and prettified. Beyond simple corrections of spelling and grammar, I have left her writing unedited, as the risk of distorting her thoughts and intentions seemed to out-weigh my own impulses toward tidiness.

I am glad to have known Marian. I wish she were still with us, but I am grateful for her decision, long ago now in that desolate place, to leave behind a record of her final flight. While the record, like the flight itself, remains incomplete, at least it has brought us closer to the end.

Though, as Marian points out in this text, a circle has no end.

Godspeed.

Matilda Feiffer
Publisher

1959

An Incomplete History of Marian's Fifteenth and Sixteenth Years

September 1929–August 1931

The same month Marian turns fifteen and goes up with Trout for the first time, a test pilot takes off from an airfield in Garden City, New York. He is already known for speed records and stunting and long-distance flying, and in less than thirteen years he'll become much more famous after he leads sixteen bombers in a bold daylight raid over Japan.

Jimmy Doolittle makes one circle and lands. It's a brief flight, only fifteen minutes, mundane except for the opaque hood over his cockpit, cutting him off from everything except the instruments. Flying blind, it's called. Some of his instruments are experimental, among them the Sperry gyroscopic artificial horizon. In its later form, a fixed airplane (you) is superimposed on a gimbaled sphere. The sphere is black below its middle and blue above (the earth, the sky) and orients you to the planet. This object will make the future possible. Before, you didn't fly in bad weather, so there could be no scheduled flights. Not really. No reliable airlines, certainly. Mail pilots took their chances; lots of them died. Before, if you lost sight of the ground for long enough, you were probably toast. Fly into cloud, and you'd likely end up in a spiral, though you might not even realize what was happening until too late. Up, down, left, right, north, south—all of it a terrible tangle, dragging you out of the sky. Survivors described a state of terminal confusion.

When Doolittle goes up with Sperry's invention, plenty of pilots, despite their many brethren who'd corkscrewed down to their deaths, don't believe such an instrument is necessary, take offense even at the suggestion. The more cautious sorts keep a close eye on their indicators to make sure they aren't inadvertently turning, but if you get distracted and start a spiral, those indicators won't be much help. The lucky living (Trout among them) tell one another that dead pilots are dead because they didn't have the elusive, magical "it."

You have to fly by the seat of your pants, they say. Meaning: A real pilot feels the plane's every movement in his ass.

But it's your inner ear, not your ass, that's the problem. And your inner ear is a liar.

A man, blindfolded and spun slowly in a rotating chair, will think when the chair slows that it has stopped. When it has stopped, he will think it has begun to spin the other way. The mistake happens deep in his ear, among the tiny hair cells and drifting fluid inside the semicircular canals of the bony labyrinth. These are the minute, impossibly fragile internal instruments that detect the yaw, pitch, and roll of the human head—wondrous little gizmos to be sure but poorly evolved for flight.

Imagine a biplane. Left to its own devices, the plane will naturally begin to bank, slowly entering a balanced, insidious turn that a pilot can't always detect if the real horizon is obscured by darkness or cloud. Neither your ass nor your inner ear will bother to tell you about a balanced turn if you're in it long enough, and without help from the right instruments, you'll think you're flying along straight and level. But the airplane's nose will drop toward the earth; its path will tighten, begin to describe a funnel. Presently, you will become aware that your airspeed has increased and altitude decreased, that the engine is whining and the guy wires singing, that the dials are moving and you're being pressed into your seat, and without an artificial horizon you will conclude the plane is in a dive (speed going up, altitude going down), not a turn. At this point the airplane might be banked to vertical or beyond, might even be upside down, and when you pull back on the stick to bring up the nose, you will only tighten the turn further.

It's called a graveyard spiral.

Now one of three things will happen. You will pop out the bottom of the cloud with enough time to make sense of where the ground is and to level the wings and pull out. Or the airplane will break apart under the stress. Or you will spin directly into the earth or ocean or whatever's there.

With the right instruments, you have a fighting chance of leveling out even if the cloud goes all the way down and brushes the earth like the marabou hem of a diaphanous white robe worn by God. But getting right with the horizon isn't easy. The sky is full of traps and temptation. Pilots report that their instruments went haywire in cloud, though of course they didn't—the pilots' own bodies are lying, not the dials. Your inner ear gets comfortable in a spiral. Even after you've extricated yourself, when the instruments say you are flying straight and level again because **you are,** your ear begs to differ. You're the blindfolded man in the rotating chair. The fluid inside that labyrinth is still spiraling, and the tiny little sensory hairs insist you are, too. Your ear begs you to throw the controls over, to make the spinning stop. Sometimes pilots listen, put themselves right back into a spiral. An oblivion of mist hides the earth, the truth.

It's difficult to believe the gauges, that array of soulless little dashboard windows, over the insistence of the body, which is as sure as you live and breathe that you are funneling down into death.

But you're not. You're dizzy inside a cloud. That's all.

The second month of Marian's fifteenth year, October, the stock market crashes. Black Thursday. Black Tuesday. All of it spiraling. Things breaking apart.

But Marian barely notices. Wall Street seems far away, and, anyway, she is flying.

From high enough up, the mountains in their blazing autumn dapple resemble lichen-covered rocks, bright and nubbly, and she imagines they are in fact only rocks, that she has been shrunk to the size of a gnat. What is the difference between her and a gnat, really? Relative to the distance between the planets? To the size of the sun?

No, you can't go up every day, Trout says when she asks. Not too much too soon. You've got to give things time to sink in.

Trout can't teach her every day anyway. He has to fly to Canada, pick up booze in some hamlet, fly it back over the line, land on some stubby landing strip hidden in the mountains. Men in fast cars will be waiting there to distribute his cargo to points unknown. The nation is thirsty. The nation wants to drink away its cares. If he's landing after dusk, the leggers will light up the strip with their headlights, make a small glowing green rectangle in the great shadowed nothing of the mountains.

Marian keeps driving for Stanley. She nearly causes an accident when she steps hard on the brake while going around a corner, daydreaming it into a rudder.

Practice is all she needs to be competent, Trout says. As far as being good, well, that comes down to a lot more practice, some natural ability, and a bucket of patience. To be great? Trout shrugs. Not everybody has it in them.

She doesn't tell him she is determined to be the best. Probably he'd say there's no such thing, that she might as well be determined to be an actual bird, and even birds get lost or caught in bad weather, fly into things, misjudge their way into that last smashup.

After six lessons of an hour each, she solos. Trout believes it's better to solo sooner rather than later so she won't build it up too much in her head. "Just fly the same as always," he says. She goes up and is alone in the sky, but she is concentrating too hard to exalt. Trout's voice has lodged in her ear, pointing out her mistakes, keeping her company. She bounces her landing, and Trout waves her up again. She circles around, lines up, touches down a little long. The earth below, so dependable and stationary when she is standing on it, turns into a wobbly, tippy thing on final approach. He waves. Again. Go again.

"If you're going to do real mountain flying," Trout says, "you have to be able to land on half a dime. Otherwise you'll roll off a cliff or plow into the trees."

"**When** am I going to do real mountain flying?" she asks, feigning impatience though she knows she isn't remotely ready to land anywhere except on a flat runway with plenty of open space.

"Not real soon," he says.

He chalks a line on the Missoula strip. She'll have to land short to hit it. Mountain flyers have to know how to land short, he says. He wants her within fifty feet of that chalked line nine times out of ten. Her ambitions for herself are all about accuracy, precision, steel nerves, the seat of her pants.

And there is Barclay Macqueen.

"Trout says I need to get rid of my old instincts and replace them with new ones," she tells him on his porch, delivery basket forgotten at her feet. "Because if you do what feels natural, you'll get yourself killed."

"I don't follow."

"Like if you're long on approach, you can't just point the nose at the ground because that'll increase the speed and you'll balloon up and away. Or if you didn't turn tightly enough to line up, you can't just add rudder or you'll skid into a spin. Trout says then you might as well aim for the cemetery and save everybody some trouble."

"Sounds dangerous."

"Of course it's dangerous."

When she'd returned for her second lesson with Trout, she had known she was accepting Barclay's patronage and therefore his presence and also the unanswered question of what he would eventually ask for in return. But, she told herself, even if she hadn't gone back to the airfield, he would have insinuated himself into her life some other way.

"You're not afraid?" Barclay says.

"No." Then: "Maybe a little sometimes, but it's worth it."

"Frankly, I'd prefer you to stay on the ground."

She is afraid he'll say what would seem to follow: He'd prefer her to stay on the ground, and so he will keep her there. But he bites into one of the cream puffs Stanley has sent. A shower of confectioners' sugar speckles his black waistcoat.

They have never acknowledged he is paying for her flying. He has never mentioned the message she'd given to Sadler, her plan to pay him back, which she has chosen to take as tacit agreement. She has never told him she knows Wallace's car is in his garage. They have not spoken again of Miss Dolly's. They pretend they have simply struck up a friendship, the delivery girl and the well-heeled cattle rancher. This can't last, this state of congenial denial. The suspense of it weighs on her.

She waits, but he only goes on eating the pastry. More sugar clings to his chin, and as she realizes he isn't going to cut off her lessons, she goes giddy with tenderness. She reaches to brush at his chin, but he catches her wrist, stays her hand.

Aloft, life is more relentlessly three-dimensional than on the ground. She has to be aware of the plane's three axes, where it is in space, where it will be in another second, another minute. Trout makes her take off and land, take off and land until the regular rise and fall of the horizon, the surge and easing of the engine, begin to feel like functions of her own body. She learns to wallow just shy of a stall, slowing her glide enough that the controls go slack but not so much that the buoyancy falls out from under her. She learns how to sideslip in a crosswind. (Helpful for short landings, though she's still not close enough to the chalk line, most times.)

She no longer marvels at Missoula's miniature streets and buildings. The city is no more noteworthy than the pattern of a familiar rug.

"Enough circles," Trout says one day. "Let's go somewhere."

They fly up to Flathead Lake and back. Not far

but somewhere. In her logbook, for the first time, she writes in the notes column "x-country."

"X-country" makes regular appearances. Trout instructs her in navigating by train tracks, roads, and rivers, by the compass and the clock. She keeps a map pinned to one knee, a notepad strapped to the other for jotting calculations. She learns the air is smoothest at dawn and dusk. She learns to always be looking for where she can land if the engine quits.

She had not understood the emptiness of Montana, had never quite lost the fanciful idea that once she got up high enough she would find a magnificent vista onto the rest of the world. So far she's only found valleys and mountains, trees and trees and trees, the sun's fading stain. She longs for something different.

They could be at the ocean in one day's flying, she tells Trout.

All in good time, he says.

One day, somewhere between Kalispell and Whitefish, he points down at a roof in a valley. "That's Bannockburn."

"What's Bannockburn?"

"I'd have thought you would know. It's the Macqueen ranch."

A big house with chimneys. Forest and mountains and grassy valleys all around it. "How far does the land go?" she asks.

"Oh, I don't know. All this and then some."

Bannockburn, Jamie tells her later, is the name of a poem about a battle the Scots won against the English. He'd read it in school. He finds it for her in a book. Robert Burns.

At Bannockburn the English lay,—
The Scots they were na far away
But waited for the break o' day . . .

What happened after the battle? she asks Jamie. They were independent, he says. For a while.

Now's the day, and now's the hour is the line that lodges in her mind.

She stays aloft longer than planned one evening, solo, flies west toward the setting sun. Darkness comes up from behind her, spreads over the dome until only a band of deep rusty red is ahead of her. When she turns back, the stars have crowded in from behind. Trout gets some of the airfield guys to light up the runway with their headlights so she can land. He's too relieved to be angry, too angry to be relieved. "If you got killed, who do you think he would blame?" he asks her.

October leans into November. The trees are tipped with gold, the cottonwoods bright as apricot flesh. The landscape flares and shimmers.

Some money goes missing from her nooks and crannies in the cottage. Wallace, of course. She puts the rest in the bank, though it feels strange to deposit her ill-gotten gains in so law-abiding a place. A few of her father's older and more richly illustrated books disappear next, and some of the more obviously valuable knickknacks. A jade horse. A string of ivory beads carved to filigree.

"Where are they?" she demands of Wallace in his studio. "Who'd you sell them to?" She is certain the answer will be Barclay Macqueen. There are no canvases on the easels. He hasn't been painting. As far as she can tell, he hasn't been going to the U, either, but she doesn't know if he's been fired or has just stopped showing up. Dust coats the craggy patches of dried paint on his palettes.

Wallace is wearing his bathrobe over a collarless shirt, open at the neck, and he is barefoot and hungover and slumped sorrowfully in an armchair, his head resting between thumb and index finger on a propping arm. She stands over him. Jamie skulks in the doorway. "I sent them to a curiosity dealer in New York," Wallace says, "someone I knew when I lived there. The horse was very valuable."

"I'll buy it back. How much did you get for it?"

He quotes an astronomical sum. She can't buy it back.

"It wasn't yours to sell."

"Marian," says Jamie. "It wasn't really ours, either."

She looms over Wallace. "Why don't you make

more paintings and sell **those**? You're **supposed** to be a painter."

Wallace shrivels into the chair. "I've lost the ability."

"No," says Jamie. "You just need to go out into the mountains like you used to."

Wallace shakes his head. "I've tried. I try, and there's nothing. It's like my painting arm has been amputated."

"That can't be," says Jamie. "It's in your head."

"Of course it's in my head," says Wallace. "**You** do it then if it's so simple. I see your little sketches. Go ahead and make paintings people want to buy."

"People do buy Jamie's watercolors," Marian says. "He sells them in town."

Wallace, even in his shame and dishevelment, summons a dismissive grimace. Now that Jamie's drawings and watercolors have become very good, at least to Marian's eye, Wallace ignores them.

"At least I'm trying," Jamie says. "At least Marian's trying."

"I'm trying, too," Wallace says. "I'm sorry if my efforts don't impress you. Did you have a use for that jade horse? Please tell me what it was."

"Enough," Marian says. "It's done. What did you do with the money?"

"I needed to settle a few debts. Urgently." Wallace's cheek is mashed against his palm now as though his head is growing heavier and heavier.

"A few," Marian says. "But not all."

"No. Not all."

She puts a lock on the cottage door.

November leans into December.

Commander Richard E. Byrd, a navigator famous for flying over the North Pole with pilot
Floyd Bennett in 1926, flies over the South Pole.
Eventually, after he's dead, a consensus will emerge
that he and Bennett probably hadn't actually made
it to the North Pole (erased sextant sights in Byrd's
diary, unanswerable questions about the plane's
maximum speed, the time elapsed). But Byrd and
his crew really do fly over the gleaming white disk
of the polar plateau all the way to the South Pole
in a plane named for Bennett, who's dead by then.

In Missoula, a browning and dulling, the earth
waiting sullenly for snow. A dusting falls, then a
thick smooth skin of white. Trees and rocks show
through like abrasions.

If the cloud ceiling is too low, Trout will shake
his head, send Marian away. Sometimes cloud
comes when they're already aloft, layers closing in
or walls rising up, blocking the way.

"Inside there's just gray nothing," she tells Jamie.
"Sometimes you feel like you don't even exist, or
like the world doesn't."

"That sounds awful," he says.

"But when you come out the other side,

everything seems brighter, like a blindfold's been taken off."

Sometimes when they emerge, even when she's been concentrating on staying level, the wings are disconcertingly tilted.

"I'd know if we banked enough to matter," Trout tells her. "You've got to learn the feel of it. Seat of your pants."

But the wings tilt when he is at the controls, too. It seems to her that a malevolent force lives in the clouds, something that tips them askew just to prove it can. Also, if Trout is so confident in the seat of his pants, she wonders why, when the cloud is serious, he turns them back, lands as soon as they can.

Sometimes—irregularly and not often—she wakes on the sleeping porch to a dark figure standing over her, touching her shoulder. She never startles, always knows before she is even awake that it is Caleb. Does Jamie stir when she gets up and they go together to the cottage? If he does, he doesn't let on.

"Do you do this with Barclay Macqueen?" Caleb asks in the cottage's narrow bed. They are crowded in shoulder to shoulder, on their backs. Near the ceiling, the wings of her model airplanes are chalky with moonlight.

"I don't do anything with him."

"You go see him."

"How do you know that?"

"People know."

"I'm delivering what he orders from Stanley."

"What does **he** need from Stanley? He has all the booze in the world."

"He doesn't even drink."

"He's a bootlegger who doesn't drink?"

"He acts like its impolite to mention he's a legger. We pretend he's not. And we pretend he doesn't pay for my flying."

He puts his hand between her legs. "What would he say about this?"

Her imagination reels, returns an ominous red wash of feeling, like the glow of a forest fire over the horizon. "I'd never tell him, not for anything."

"Do you like him?"

"What do you care?" she says. He is touching her more purposefully. He reaches for the envelope he has put on the windowsill that contains rubbers. They use them when they have them, or else he pulls out. The prospect of a baby makes them laugh with horror.

"Of course you like him. He's the one who let you fly."

"It's more than that."

"So you do like him."

"Shhhh."

"You like this, too, though."

"Shhhh."

. . . .

In the winter, she learns to land on skis. It's not so difficult, though judging altitude is tricky, as a snowfield looks the same from ten feet as it does from a hundred. Sometimes the moment of contact catches her by surprise. Then there is the trick of reversing the engine to stop, as the skis have no brakes.

"Sit and visit," Barclay says. In the cold months, they sit inside at the kitchen table. She is never sure whether Sadler is somewhere in the house, though once in a while a creaking floorboard might give him away. Barclay is careful not to touch her, but, near him, her whole body is a receptor. His presence saturates her. She feels she has just emerged from cloud into a vibrant, revelatory world.

"Tell me about the flying," he says.

She tells him in minute detail, pleased to have the chance. Jamie frets about the dangers, about Barclay. Caleb has no patience for technical details. Talking to Wallace is like talking to a mop soaked in gin. But Barclay listens to even her most involved technical treatises.

He's never been up in an airplane. He doesn't like the idea of it.

She's told him that someday she'll take him up. You'll like it, she says. You won't believe how much you can see.

He says he's content with the view from a car.

He asks broader questions about her life. He is polite but persistent, like a newspaper reporter.

"So this barnstormer," he says, "with the ridiculous name—"

"Felix Brayfogle. It's not ridiculous."

"So this Frederick Boarsnoggle flies over you, and you almost fall off your horse, and after that, you just know you need to fly airplanes."

"Yes. Deep down and without a doubt."

"My word. But why?"

"I don't know."

"You must have some idea."

She says, "You know how you said I was someone you needed to know right from the start? Even when you had no idea who I was?" He nods. "It's the same." Love, she means. Love sprung from nothing.

"It can't be quite the same thing."

"Maybe not. But I wanted to see other places, too, and I realized an airplane would get me there."

"I keep telling you, you'll find Montana's as good a place as any."

She gropes for how to make him see it her way. "And I get tired of worrying about Wallace. I used to feel so guilty he'd been saddled with us, but lately I can't trust him to take care of himself."

"What about Jamie?"

"I'd feel bad leaving it all on his shoulders."

"I mean—wouldn't you miss him?"

"Awfully."

Barclay is solemn. "I told you I have a sister? Kate? I wish I could hold her life in my hands like an egg, make everything good for her. It's a burden—the wish itself, and the fact it's impossible."

"That's what I mean. Things might be better without anyone to worry about."

He leans forward, his folded arms sliding on the table. "That's not true. That would be the most terrible loneliness."

In the spring, she learns to land at night. Lights have been installed at the airfield.

Trout teaches her to step hard on the rudder and whip around in a ground loop to avoid onrushing obstacles. She is usually close to the chalk line now, sometimes right on it.

May 1930: Amy Johnson, age twenty-six, daughter of a Yorkshire fish merchant, flies solo from Croydon Aerodrome just south of London to Darwin, Australia, in a de Havilland Gipsy Moth. Ten thousand miles in an open biplane at eighty miles per hour, always too hot or too cold, sunburned and reeking of gasoline. When she takes off she has only eighty-five hours of flying experience and no knack for landings. But she has a ground engineer's license, knows about engines. Near Baghdad, a sandstorm forces her down, and she sits on the plane's tail with her revolver, goggles caked with sand, listening to what might be the howling of wild dogs, might only be the wind. She breaks the speed record to Karachi but smashes a wing. Repairs take time. In Rangoon, she smashes another wing, the undercarriage, and the propeller. More repairs. The whole trip takes nineteen and a half days, the last spent fighting headwinds for five hundred miles across the Timor Sea, worrying about fuel. Then Darwin, and fame, but not the speed record she'd wanted.

As Marian's sixteenth birthday approaches, Trout says it's time for real mountain flying. Finally. They follow canyons, ride updrafts over ridges. Treetops whip by just under the wheels. She learns there is another landscape above the rocks and trees, an invisible topography made of wind. She learns if she flies straight at the lee side of a ridge and doesn't rack off in time, the air will turn to quicksand, sucking her down.

To practice landings, they go to some of the wilderness strips where Trout hands off cargo to the bootleggers. She has to land short, real short.

Trout bemoans that he can't teach her more advanced aerobatics. "The big girl's no good for it," he says about the Travel Air, "but you ought to have some practice. When things go wrong, you'd be calmer in your head if you were used to being turned every which way."

"Trout says you've got to practice spins so you know how to get out of them," she tells Barclay.

"He says a pilot needs to learn not to panic. He says your reactions get faster."

She knows what she is doing, what she is asking for, what will happen. In a few weeks, she arrives at the airfield and there beside the Travel Air is a brand-new bright yellow Stearman biplane. Trout's smile hangs between his ears like a ragged hammock, but while they walk around the plane to admire its gleaming sleekness, the dashing set of its wings, he says in an undertone, "You sure about this, kid?"

She is beginning to understand how Wallace built his debts. Just this one last thing, she tells herself. Then she will be ready to start flying across the line, paying down her debt. "At least this way I'll learn some stunts," she tells Trout.

Trout sits in the front cockpit and Marian behind, both in helmets and goggles and parachutes, harnessed in over the shoulders. The Stearman has a stick instead of a wheel, and at first she's awkward with it. ("From the elbow, not the shoulder or you'll pull at an angle," Trout said on the ground. "You have to learn the feel of it." The great unifying thesis of his instruction.) She likes the way the open cockpit fits snugly around her, how her legs extend out to meet the rudder pedals. She likes her face in the wind.

Their third time up, the stick jerks in her hand— Trout signaling he wants to take over. He climbs high, starts a dive. As Trixie Brayfogle had, he pulls up into a loop, but this time Marian is not watching the tumbling sky and ground. She watches the gauges. They level out again. Without turning to look at her, Trout raises both hands to tell her she is back in control. He'd already talked her through it: the necessary altitude and airspeed, the RPMs, the limits of all these things, the lightness and slowness she would feel at the top, the dive back toward the earth. "A loop is just another turn," Trout says. "Only it's flipped up on its side."

She climbs, begins her dive.

"I flew a loop," she tells Jamie on the sleeping porch. "Three, actually." Her heart races as though she were confessing a secret, though she won't tell him how she had gone to see Barclay afterward, how, when he opened the door, she had grasped him around the neck and kissed him.

A heavy pause, then, grudgingly, Jamie asks, "What was it like?"

"Promise not to laugh—"

"I might laugh."

"—but I felt like I was a fixed point, and I was using the controls to make the rest of the world turn around me. I was literally the center of the universe."

He laughs. "You feel that way all the time, though."

She laughs, too. "Maybe I **am** the center of the universe. Did you ever think of that?"

"Aren't you worried about what he wants?"

"Yes, but mostly because I don't know what exactly that is."

"Seems obvious to me."

"If I thought all he wanted was to take me to bed, I'd be relieved. That would be simpler." But she does know what he wants, or thinks she does.

You have to learn the feel of it. The dive had made her heavy; then, at the top of the loop, she had floated free in her harness.

Barclay had clutched her to him, lifting her boots off the ground. With her mouth covered by his and her body clamped against his and not even the reassurance of the porch under her feet, the determined impulse that had propelled her to kiss him collapsed into alarm and claustrophobia. He seemed to have gone blind and dumb, like a salmon beating muscularly upstream, driven by instinct. She writhed to get free, and for a second or two it seemed he would not let her go. She twisted, arching her back, and the movement seemed to wake him. He dropped her so abruptly she stumbled.

"I'm sorry," he said, breathless, holding up his hands as though to prove he was unarmed. "You surprised me. My guard wasn't up."

She tried to steady herself. "It's all right."

They looked anywhere but at each other. Marian

went to sit on the edge of the porch, and he followed, sat beside her.

She said, "I came to tell you I flew a loop today."

"I heard Trout got a new plane. One that's good for aerobatics." A kingly smile.

"He said Mr. Sadler wanted another for his collection." This was the closest allusion she had made to Barclay's patronage, the boldest of her darting forays toward the truth.

"Sadler's quite an aviation enthusiast," Barclay said.

"He's got terrific taste in biplanes."

"He says he has a promising pilot."

Her pleasure at hearing another person affirm her destiny bordered on ecstasy. Barclay had given her Trout; he'd given her a plane, and now he was offering his belief.

She asked, "Is your guard up now?"

"Enough. Why?"

This kiss was not a straitjacket like the last one but a gathering in. She was aware of his slow breathing, of how, when he leaned just a little bit away, she followed without meaning to. Something bound her to him, a rough pull, strong and coarse as rope.

He pulled away. "I can't play at this, Marian," he said. "We can't start down this road. You'd better go, and next time you come, we'll go back to being how we were before."

That would have been the moment to ask what he wanted from her. But she didn't need to.

"He wants to marry me," she says to Jamie.

"He said so?"

"I just know. Does that make you feel any better?"

"No."

"Me neither."

"Why does he want to?"

"Thanks a lot!"

"Come on. Why? You're just a kid."

"I'm not."

"Of course you are."

I recognized you as someone I needed to know.

She says, "I happened to catch his attention in a certain way, and once he has an idea in his head he doesn't let go."

"So you have one thing in common, at least. Are you **going** to marry him?"

The elation of the loop is gone; only the plunging sensation of the dive remains. She wishes Jamie would tell her not to, that she doesn't have to. She wishes he would imply Barclay is buying her so she could rage at the idea, drive it away. She wishes he would ask if she loves Barclay, and she could say she thinks she might. And she does love Barclay, perhaps, or at least strongly desires him, but she also senses she is inside a trap, the dimensions and mechanism of which remain concealed.

But Jamie knows better than to do any of these

things. In the light from the moon, she can see him watching her with the melancholy of someone who has cared for and released a wild animal, hoping it will find its way on its own.

"Probably I'd better," is all she says.

September again. She is sixteen, flying every day now. When she can't fly because of weather, she trails after the mechanics, learns to make repairs.

"Like a fish to water," Trout says about her knack for stunts. That is how she feels, too, doing aerobatics: like she has been delivered to her natural element after a cruel separation. No thoughts of Barclay intrude, or of Caleb, or Wallace, or Jamie. In the biplane, she is always the fixed center of the universe, wheeling it around herself with stick and rudder.

Vrille: Get up high, throttle back almost to a stall. Kick the right rudder, yank the stick back and to the right. Spin down, engine hollering, tail up, violence in the fall, earth revolving below like the dome of a twirling umbrella.

Slow roll: Keep the nose aimed at a fixed point, push the stick to the right. When the wings have gone vertical, start cross-controlling with the left rudder. Come off the left rudder, push the stick forward. You'll be hanging in the straps as the plane inverts; your feet will want to fall away from the rudder pedals, but you can't let them. Then all of it in mirror image, quickly, as the engine can't be trusted while upside down. It's like riding a bicycle in one direction with your hands and another bicycle in the opposite direction with your feet.

Stall turn: Trout doesn't want to teach her this one, so she reads up and tries it out solo. Bank up vertical until the airspeed falls away to nothing, then just before gravity catches you, left full rudder to cartwheel over the wingtip, feed it right stick then forward, pivot until you're zooming nose down toward the earth, pull out level.

Trout is angry, says he's seen good pilots crack up that way. He won't let her fly for a week, not until she brings him a few bottles of moon and promises not to do it again. They both know she's lying, but a truce is made.

There is more, of course. Immelmann turns and bunts and barrel rolls and chandelles and all of them strung together, one leading into the next as she ties gigantic, elaborate knots over Missoula, plunging in and out of the lost glacial lake.

The flying-service pilots and local hobbyists forget they'd refused to teach her. They call her the Red Baroness and Lindy Girl. They want her to go to Spokane to compete at an air show, but she has no license and Barclay would not like her to draw attention to herself.

When the weather cools, a shearling coat and heavy boots appear for her so she can keep flying the open Stearman.

Another winter. More ski landings. More real mountain flying. A few close scrapes in the cloud: treetops brushing the skis, rocky escarpments narrowly missed.

In March, Elinor Smith, who'd flown the East River bridges, climbs to twenty-five thousand feet over New York City in a supercharged Bellanca, attempting to reclaim an altitude record. Frost forms on her breathing tube. Something goes wrong, something comes uncoupled or the air bottle cracks. Blackness drops over her like a hood. With an unconscious pilot, the plane descends more than four miles. At two thousand feet, Elinor woozes back into consciousness, manages to sideslip the plane down onto a bit of open land, noses over, walks away.

"That," says Trout, "is nerve."

A week later Elinor goes up again, hits thirty-two thousand feet.

Marian, sick with envy, circles the Travel Air up to fifteen thousand feet. A little higher. Its ceiling is sixteen thousand, but she thinks the specs are probably conservative. The engine splutters and skips and pops. She adjusts the mix but can't get it to smooth out. It runs like a three-legged horse. Spooked, she eases down.

"Lucky," Trout says when she confesses. "Go too high and you get drunk. There's a kind of crazy up there. You'll start seeing things. You'll think someone's in the plane with you. You'll see another ship out the corner of your eye, just off your wing, when none's there."

She needs something to **do,** she tells Trout, she tells Caleb, she tells Jamie, she cautiously intimates to Barclay. She can really fly now. Trout has drilled her and drilled her, made her land on the tiniest patches of scrub grass and mountain gravel. She could probably land on a fence post like a hawk and take off from it, too.

"I could fly over the line," she insists to Trout. "I want to be **useful.**"

"I'm all trained up," she says to Caleb, "but for what? They won't let me help run the booze. I can't compete at stunts without a license. I can't **go** anywhere. What's the point?"

"And we're still acting out this charade," she says to Jamie, "where Barclay has nothing to do with any of it. He's a kindly cattle rancher, and I'm the delivery girl who stops by to chat. What's the point?"

"You said he likes things his way," says Jamie. "If he didn't want you to be in the charade, you wouldn't be."

In February, Amelia Earhart had married George Palmer Putnam, her publisher and promoter, some say her Svengali. He'd proposed six times. On their wedding day, she wrote him a letter saying neither should expect fidelity and that sometimes she would need to be apart from him and from the confinements of marriage. She asked him to promise to let her go in a year if they weren't happy together.

Marian knew nothing of this, of course, could not dream of such a bargain.

Before her seventeenth birthday, three important flights.

First.

Weather comes in. Trout, flying the Travel Air, spirals out of cloud, can't regain control. At least that seems the most likely explanation. There isn't much left of him.

Marian spends a long night in the cottage drinking real Scotch, doing her best to harden herself. Hadn't Trout told her all pilots had dead friends? Hadn't he said she could end up being a dead friend herself? At his funeral, she barely looks at his wife and children, all of them short and froggy and miserable. (Barclay promises he'll do right by them.) She tells herself Trout had gone out the way he'd wanted. The final crack-up. Probably he wasn't even afraid, was too focused on trying to fix what was wrong. Probably it had happened too fast for him to feel any pain.

His body had been badly burned. His front teeth had been embedded so far in the dash they'd stayed there when they pulled the rest of him out.

Barclay had sent her a black dress to wear to the funeral, fine soft wool trimmed with black grosgrain ribbon, small shiny black buttons. She wears her flying clothes instead. Jamie sits beside her. Barclay, in the next pew forward, ignores them until the very end, when he turns around and offers his hand to Jamie, says, "Peace be with you."

Jamie says with a dueler's grim resolve, "And also with you."

Afterward she goes to the green-and-white house with the dress still in its box.

"You can have this back," she tells Barclay. "I didn't wear it."

"I noticed," he says, ushering her into the kitchen. "You didn't like it?"

"Trout would have laughed at me from heaven." She drops the box on the table.

"You believe in heaven?"

"No."

"So? What do you think happens?"

"I think nothing happens. Is Sadler here?"

"Mr. Sadler has business in Spokane."

"It's time for me to start flying over the line. I know where the landing strips are. I've practiced on them. Without Trout, I'm the only one who can do it."

He leans against the sink and lights a cigarette. "That's not true. The country's lousy with pilots."

"It was my condition from the beginning. You know it was."

"Marian, I never agreed to your so-called condition."

She gapes at him. "You did. You let me keep taking lessons."

"You can't assume you have a deal with someone just because you issue a decree."

"I said I didn't want lessons unless I knew I had a way to work off what I owe you. It's not fair otherwise."

Amused: "Not fair you should have what you most wanted?"

"Not fair you won't give me a way to pay you back."

"Isn't it a little unseemly to try to leverage Trout's death into a flying opportunity the very day of his funeral?"

"His number came up," she says, defiant. "He always said it could."

He smokes, watching her. "Are you really this hard?"

"Trout would have said I was ready. I know the mountains. You know you can trust me. If not this, then let me drive for you. Let me do **something.** I'll go back to collecting bottles. Anything. I feel like some rich man's daughter, or like I've been taught to fly just because it's funny to see a girl in an airplane, like a dog walking on its hind legs."

A long silence. He offers his gaze as a kind of challenge; she holds it. Finally, he says, "I don't think of you as a daughter, or a dog." He shifts, stubs out his cigarette in an ashtray. "But the biplane can't hold much cargo anyway. I don't think it's worth the risk."

Like that, without fanfare, the charade is over. "It holds thirty cases," she says. "Maybe a few more. Trout told me. That's not nothing if it's premium brands. And you'd keep your air routes open in case you wanted to get a bigger plane again."

"It's not enough to justify putting you on the wrong side of the law."

"I've been on the wrong side of the law for years," she says, feeling blustering, silly.

"But not on my account." She tries to interrupt; he cuts her off. "Just this one little time, Marian, I won't give you what you want. Not right now."

"But soon?"

Hesitantly, he rests one hand on her shoulder, squeezes gently, as though testing fruit. "If a pilot with Trout's experience died, how can you know it won't happen to you?"

"I can't, but I have to do it anyway."

"If anything were to happen to you, I would never forgive myself."

"It wouldn't be your fault." She steps so close her left foot is between his feet. "Let me jump the line. Please."

He seems almost as though he will agree but recovers himself, moves away. "Don't do that."

"Do what?"

"Don't **offer** yourself."

"You're the one trying to buy me."

"I'm not trying to buy you, I'm trying to **help** you."

"Then **help** me by letting me be **useful.**" She storms off, out the door. He doesn't follow.

That night in the cottage with Caleb, she does what she has not done before: She **fucks** him. She has never before associated that word with what they do, but now it fills her head. She sits atop him, furious, gouging with her hips.

At first he responds in kind but then turns passive and watchful. At the end, he pushes her off, comes into an old washing flannel. She has struck the wall—not hard—but she shouts at him. He covers her mouth with a hand, and she bites. Part of her wishes he would slug her like he did when they were kids, but even as he yanks his hand back, grimacing in pain, she knows he won't. Instead, he pulls her roughly to his chest, holds tight until she quits fighting. She thinks he is waiting for her to cry. She will not. She can't. Eventually, they fall asleep.

At dawn, after he has dressed, he sits on the edge of the bed, his hair loose down his back. "We have to stop this," he says. "Whatever you have with him, you have to sort it out. I can't help you with it."

"No," she says. "No one can."

· · ·

Second.

The plan is not a reaction to Trout's death. She had been mulling it over for months, but she'd hesitated because of how worried Trout would be and because she'd feared Barclay would blame him. Now the consequences are only hers.

On a clear June morning, she takes off in the biplane, fuel tank only half full, nothing out of the ordinary, nothing to draw attention. She purls up a lazy loop. When she's leveled off again, she turns northwest, following the railroad.

Jamie has disappeared for the summer. A few weeks before, at the end of May, Wallace had found a note from him on the kitchen table that said he was going away but would come back in time for the start of school. They shouldn't worry. Marian was hurt he had left without telling her, then envious. She might have gone with him if she'd known. Then she was hurt afresh by the thought that he hadn't told her for exactly that reason.

A map is pinned to her knee, the route already plotted. She'd left a note of her own in the hangar: **Gone x-country, back tomorrow.** She knows Barclay has spies who will find it when she doesn't come back. After that, lickety-split, he'll have his people calling every airfield for three states in all directions, promising an irresistible reward for any information about any lone girls in Stearman biplanes. She'd left the note only because otherwise he'd have filled the sky with search and rescuers.

She turns north again, follows the Clark Fork up to Lake Pend Oreille. She sets down outside a nothing town where she's been before, not far from a gas station she's scouted. The owner has a fuel truck, comes out to fill her tank. A risk, but unavoidable. Off she goes. West, then north, following the Pend Oreille River. When it bends to meet the Columbia, she knows she is over Canada.

She carves her way west, low among the mountains, her wings paring air off the slopes. The weather mostly holds. For a while there is a thick, low mat of cloud, and she stays above it, tobogganing the airplane's belly along the top, the prop half buried in the mist. This is what she has always wanted: choose a point on a map and fly to it. She thinks Jamie probably also went west, toward the sea.

Before he left, she'd woken one night to him gently shaking her.

"You were having a nightmare," he'd said.

She'd been dreaming about Trout. She'd been with him in the Travel Air, spiraling down, and Trout was pleading with her to help him, but her controls didn't seem to be attached to anything.

"I was dreaming about Trout."

"I figured. You were talking."

The spring night was rustling and chilly, and she scooted over so Jamie would slide in, head to toe with her.

She said, "Do you think Trout was afraid?"

"Wouldn't you be?"

"I want to think he wouldn't have been. But I don't think it works that way."

"It would have been quick, at least."

"Even if he'd known for certain what was going to happen, I don't think he would have stopped flying."

"Not for his kids?"

She shook her head. "I hope he at least knew Barclay would make sure his family was all right." They were quiet. She added, "Whatever he felt, it's done now."

But Jamie was asleep.

More snowcaps appear as she flies on. The country's emptiness pleases her—she is less likely to be spotted. After some hours, she descends into a long open valley checkered with farmland. Mountains to the north. The city of Vancouver standing up to the west. Beyond, water blues the horizon. The Strait of Georgia. She wants to fly out over it, over Vancouver Island to the open ocean, but she doesn't have enough fuel or daylight.

She chances an airfield north across the harbor from the city. When the pilots hanging around ask where she's come from, she says Oregon. She asks where she should leave the plane for the night, where there is a cheap hotel. They look at her funny, but she stares back hard. She can't pass for a boy anymore and has no choice but to be an odd, tall, dusty, freckled girl, racoonishly suntanned from her goggles, with short-cropped hair. A man takes a grease pencil and a notepad from the pocket of his overalls and writes down directions to a rooming house a couple of miles away. "Tell Geraldine that Sawyer sent you," he says, tearing off the page. "She's a nice lady. I'll keep an eye on your plane. What's your name?"

"Funny, my name's Geraldine, too," Marian says. She points to the north and the bigger mountains. "Do you ever fly up in there?"

He shakes his head. "Not much there for me."

Geraldine's is halfway up a steep hill. Be in by midnight, Geraldine says, no guests, and no drinking in the house. In Marian's room, a window frames fading twilight, a line of dark blue sea cutting across the gaps between the houses. Restless, she sits on the bed, stands at the window, sits again. A knock at the door. She opens it to Geraldine holding out a folded nightgown. "I noticed you didn't have any luggage. I thought you might need something to sleep in."

The gesture is simple, but Marian is not used to being cared for. "Thank you," she says, clasping the garment to her chest. Her voice betrays her by shaking.

"It's really nothing." Geraldine is younger than Marian had expected, almost as blond and freckled as herself but soft and bosomy. "You all right?"

For a moment, Marian wants to tell her everything, to pour out the tale of her parents and her uncle and Barclay Macqueen and Trout. She would tell Geraldine she is only sixteen and has flown here from Montana by herself, and tomorrow she is going to fly out over the ocean just to look around, to **see** something. Geraldine will say she wished she were half as brave.

But instead Marian just says she's fine, that she hadn't been expecting to spend the night. Engine trouble is all.

In the morning, she fuels the plane and takes off, circles the field to get her nerve up. Then she follows the harbor out, passes over the strait, over Vancouver Island, and is finally, finally over the sea. Wind draws a delicate pattern on the water like the weave of linen, overlaid by shadows of clouds. Well out from shore, she longs to fly on even though the horizon will only ever recede, but she knows she has to turn around, to go home and face what must be faced. She tells herself at least she's seen the ocean. Flying back, she turns up an inlet toward the mountains, tells herself she's just following a whim, though it's more like a dare.

At the end of the sound, the water is bright and milky from a river disgorging glacial meltwater, braided with pale sand. She follows it north. The mountains are more rugged than any she's seen. All the other "x-country" entries in her logbook were only puny feints against the great immensity of the planet, but this—**this**—is real mountain flying. She should turn around, be on her way back to Montana, but, gunning the engine, pulling her scarf up over her mouth and nose, she ascends. Twelve thousand feet. She flies at a snow-covered saddle, crosses over it into a high bowl. Rock and blue ice loom up, hemming her in. Below, crevasses fissure an ice field. The widest looks big enough to swallow the plane whole. In places, the snow has broken through, and there is blackness underneath.

The engine catches, sputters with disapproval.

She tries to circle up and out, but the plane is sluggish, heavy. She adjusts the mix, but still the engine protests, begins to miss. Her heartbeat seems to miss, too. A stiffness creeps into her limbs. Her armpits prickle.

She circles and circles. The cold wind on her face feels as sharp and violent as glass shards. Her arms are so heavy; she can barely work her feet on the rudder. No one will ever find her. No one will even know where to look. The blackness at the bottom of the crevasse will swallow her. Snow will shroud her. But, on the other hand, then no one will know how foolish she'd been to come into these mountains. She will not give them her broken body, will not leave her teeth stuck in the dashboard of the plane. Barclay will have no recourse but to wonder. In his mind, a phantom version of herself will go on living a thousand different imagined lives in a thousand different places. He won't be able to consign her to the past, to the ranks of the dead. The engine misses badly; the plane dips woozily.

Jamie will never know what a lonely, needless death she's contrived for herself.

The thought of Jamie strikes her like a slapping hand. The buzzing in her head clears. No. No, she will not leave him alone in the world, will not punish him for his summer escape by vanishing forever. Willing movement into her leaden arms and legs, pressing into her own body as though shifting a heavy weight, she pushes the stick forward and dives, following the curvature of the bowl. When she is barely skimming over the ice, she pulls up. Rattling and sputtering, just barely, she clears the opposite ridge.

Descending, her face and hands thaw. Terror comes alive in her. She trembles hard enough on the controls to make the plane bobble. She turns south.

The pilots in Missoula are relieved, want to know where she'd gone. "To Vancouver and back," she tells them, wooden. She'd had to spend another night out, sleeping in the plane in a field.

"Any good?" one asks, perplexed by her flatness.

"It was all right." Why hadn't Trout told her about the blackness that lived in the depths of ice?

"Macqueen is fit to be tied," another says. "He was around all morning, looking up at the sky like he was about to go up there and tear down the whole damn thing."

· · ·

She's only been home an hour before Barclay shows up, driven in his long black Pierce-Arrow by Sadler. At the door, Wallace asks feebly what he wants.

"I want a word with Marian."

Marian is listening from the stairs. "It's all right, Wallace," she says, coming down. Without protest, her uncle shrinks back into the house. Marian leads Barclay to the cottage.

He shuts the door behind them. His anger makes his freckles stand out; his eyes are almost black. In a quiet voice, he asks how she could have betrayed him so spitefully. She is stupid, foolish, selfish, and he never should have trusted her. Of course it had been a mistake to allow her to fly. "I should have known," he says, "that you'd take everything I've given you and throw it back in my face."

Marian stands and listens without flinching, and when he is done, all she can do is cry. She bends like a willow in the gusts of her own sorrow. He will think guilt is what wracks her, won't guess it is grief—grief for Trout, but also for the idea she'd had of herself as fearless in the air, of the sky as an ally rather than an indifferent immensity full of ungovernable forces.

The fury goes out of him. "Don't cry," he says. "Please, Marian. I was only angry because I was afraid I'd lost you." He gathers her against himself. "Why did you do it?" he asks in a fervent murmur. "Why would you run away like that?"

"I wasn't running. I wanted to **go** somewhere.

Like I've been telling you." When she feels him start to pull away, she holds on, says, "I wanted to see the ocean."

"And did you?"

"Only the edge."

"It all looks the same."

She wants to explain the crevasse to him, how she had not crashed into it but had been swallowed nonetheless, but she only says, "I had a fright in the mountains." Hurriedly, she adds, "I went up a little too high, that's all. I learned a lesson."

His arms tighten around her. "Sometimes you seem so wise and sometimes very foolish." The warmth of his body intervenes between her and the ice, the blackness. She would have told Jamie about the crevasse if she could have, if he were there, and then she would have been fortified in her dealings with Barclay. But Jamie had left her behind. And Caleb had cut her loose.

She presses her face into Barclay's neck. He goes very still. She says, "I've been having nightmares about Trout."

Again she thinks he will tell her not to fly, even forbid it, but he says, "Don't expect yourself not to be troubled, Marian. Something would be wrong if you weren't."

His kindness, as Geraldine's had, makes her cry. But her tears are gentler now, a slow seep from under her lids, a fluttering in her abdomen. He kisses her just under her ear.

Does she regret the flight? She decides she doesn't. She would have peered out of the cockpit and into something bottomless and unfathomable sooner or later. At some point she would have found the edge of her own courage. There is nothing for it but to adjust, be humbled. So she is not exactly who she had thought. So what. She will be someone different.

Barclay has one hand around her shoulders and the other lifting underneath her backside, hoisting her against him. Barclay is pressing her backward like a dance partner, guiding her toward the narrow bed. They are lying down. He has her trousers undone, his hand inside. She pushes back against him, slides her hips. His eyes are glassy, his expression slack. She keeps moving, holding his gaze.

Outside, Sadler coughs.

The sound is so clear, as though Sadler were sitting in the armchair a few feet away. Barclay snaps out of his reverie, removes his hand. Immediately it seems impossible that they had, seconds before, been doing what they'd been doing.

He stands up quickly. "I'm sorry."

She fastens her trousers. "For starting or for stopping?"

"Starting," he says as though it should be obvious.

"Didn't you like it?"

"Too much."

"Then why did you stop?"

"I have no right to compromise you like that." She

turns her head to the wall, waiting for him to leave, but he sits on the edge of the bed. "You're upset."

Outrage pours out of her. Yes, she tells him. She is. Why didn't he ever consider whether or not **she** liked it? Whether **she** wanted to stop? Why must she always be **protected**? He can't keep her safe against the dangers that matter: the darkness, the possibility of falling. His attempts are insulting. And it's outrageous for him to say he shouldn't compromise her. What had he done with his patronage and his airplanes except compromise her? What had he done except use her own dreams against her? And even when they both want the same thing—

She stops, suddenly shy about admitting she wants him, wants to see his body and to be touched, that she is not a virgin anyway. (This last she must never say.) Fucking would be more truthful, at least.

"You want to . . ." He hesitates.

"I want to fly across the line."

"That's all?" His disappointment is plain.

"And I want to go to bed with you."

Shrewdness and thrill, stubbornness and lust, worry and smugness play over his face. "All right," he says, putting on his hat and opening the door. "All right, fine. To both. Not today, but soon enough."

Third.

Barclay agrees to be taken up. His first flight.

On a hot July day he arrives at the field and strides around nervously, scowling at the planes. He and Marian have not been to bed yet, but sex now seems like a trapdoor that may open under them at any moment. She has begun flying over the line.

Sadler has taught her the code used for arranging pickups and shown her how to read a special map printed all over with tiny numbered dots. Most are just decoy nonsense, but some are real caches and landing strips.

"You disapprove," she'd said to Sadler.

His eyes on the map, voice lilting like a man relating an item of mild interest from a newspaper, he said, "It's not my place."

Her first run had been to an anonymous farmer's field in British Columbia. The farmer had driven a tractor out to meet her, pulling a wagon stacked with cases of whiskey.

The sun had been low when she took off again. The weight of the cargo made the fuel go quickly, shifting the plane's balance, and she'd had to keep a close eye on the trim. Briefly the leadenness had come into her again, the blank, heavy buzzing feeling, but it had passed quickly, never quite taking root. Only two cars were waiting for her small delivery, their headlights pinpricks in the dusk. They'd backed up close to the plane when she'd landed and opened their trunks and also hidden compartments under the backseats. Brisk and businesslike, they'd hauled the cases out. In a few days, a message had come directing her next pickup.

As Marian takes off and circles up, Barclay sinks low in the front cockpit until the top of the flying helmet she'd given him is barely visible. She banks steeply around the city, trying to tip him into looking down, but the little leather dome of him, glossy as a bullfrog's back, doesn't move. She can't even be sure his eyes are open. Her plan had been to go easy on him, take him on a pleasant aerial tour of the valley, but she's nettled by the idea that he might spend the whole flight hunkered down, stubbornly fearful. She pulls the stick back and punches it to the side, kicks the rudder. The plane turns tidily upside down. Barclay's head dangles out of the cockpit, and he clutches the edges as though he thinks he'd be able to hang on like a crab were his harness to break. Another kick, and Missoula swings back down.

He twists to look at her, shouts something into the wind, jabs his gloved finger down at the ground. She smiles, turns the nose to the northeast.

When he understands she is flying him out of town, he turns again, shouts again, but what can he do? He is at her mercy, and she has a full tank of fuel.

After half an hour, Barclay, bored with being angry and afraid, is sitting up and looking out. He peers over one side, then the other. Eventually the sawtooth ramparts of Glacier National Park come into view, overlapping rough blue ridges fading with distance. The sun catches the rock layers in the mountainsides. In some places they lie in a flat stack, in others are folded and wrapped like taffy on the mixing hook. Glaciers cling to the slopes, smaller than the ones she'd seen in Canada. Below are bright blue-green lakes of meltwater, opaque as enamel.

She wonders if the fear will return, but she feels only a tightness in her throat that might just be anxiety about what will happen after they land. Before she flipped the plane, she had not considered how he might perceive the maneuver as another rebellion or betrayal, even mockery. Hopefully Glacier's grandeur will soothe his temper. What would she do if, in punishment, he forbade her from flying the plane? She would leave Missoula, of course. For the first time, she wonders if he could stop her from leaving, if he would.

The fuel needle drops lower, and she steers back toward Kalispell. Barclay has not turned around again, has not acknowledged the wonders she has shown him. As they pass into the ordinary greatness of lesser mountains, she feels peevish and depleted, as though she'd stayed too long at a fair or picnic.

Clouds are coming in, getting denser and lower. By the time they land in late afternoon, it is overcast.

"We'll have to wait out the weather," she says

to Barclay as he climbs out of his cockpit. She is casual, pretending she has not just kidnapped him and turned him upside down.

He looks at the sky. Calmly, he says, "I have a place here. An office. We'll go there."

As they walk into town, Barclay takes a ring of keys from an inner pocket of his jacket. "It's a good thing," he says, "this didn't fall out and land on someone's head back in Missoula."

Anticipation hangs between them, making them awkward. The air is humid, thick with imminent rain. A man smoking in a doorway greets Barclay, and they exchange pleasantries while Marian stands off to one side, unacknowledged by Barclay. The stranger's gaze flicks curiously over her.

The office is actually a small house on a side street. Only two rooms, close and warm. The first contains two desks with telephones and type-writers and lamps, a block of wooden filing cabinets, and a stove and sink. Everything is perfectly tidy. Barclay goes into the next room, a bedroom, and pulls the curtains shut with a brisk snap. She follows, tentative.

"Does someone live here?"

"No." He indicates a closed door. "You can go in there to clean up."

The bathroom is floored in white octagonal tiles. There is a claw-foot tub, a sink, a toilet with a pull chain. In the mirror she sees a wind-blasted urchin, face grimy except where her goggles had been, hair plastered to her head as tightly as a bathing cap. **Clean up.** She eyes the bathtub. Ought she to take a bath? Would that be strange? Would it be strange not to? She can smell oil and gasoline on her hands. They are, of course, about to go to bed together. How will she avoid starting a baby? He must have thought of that—he couldn't want a baby.

She turns the tub's hot-water tap, pees under cover of the noise. When the water is a few inches deep, she gets in, splashes and dips like a bird in a puddle, tries to settle her heart. She puts her head under the faucet and does the best she can with the small cake of soap left beside the sink. She has the feeling of readying herself for a rite, a sacrifice. After she gets out, she hesitates, wrapped in a towel, debating, then puts her dirty flying clothes back on except her socks and boots, which she carries with her.

He is sitting on the edge of the bed, but when she draws near, he gets up and goes into the bathroom, brushing past without a glance. She stands, bewildered, in the middle of the room, listening to him urinating. She goes to the window and peers through the gap in the drapes, holding her boots in front of her like an old woman with a handbag. She wants to lift the sash, let in some air, but feels she can't. The light outside has gone gray, and the street is quiet. Now the sink runs and splashes. A black Ford trundles by. Water from her hair drips down her collar.

Barclay's footsteps behind her. His chest is against her back, and he is reaching around and taking her boots from her and dropping them, unbuttoning her trousers, pushing them down, turning her. He unbuttons her shirt with shaking fingers. So speedily unveiled, she covers her breasts with one arm, but he pulls her arm away and tugs down her drawers. He steps back, looking at her. The ferocity of his interest makes him appear almost scornful. **Who are you?** She is not the girl she'd been at Miss Dolly's. She'd felt more exposed wearing those flimsy borrowed clothes than she does now, naked.

On the bed, it is strange to be naked while he is still fully clothed. She feels the roughness of his wool trousers against the insides of her legs, his belt buckle scraping her belly, the buttons of his shirt against her sternum. She tries to undo them, but he pushes her hands away. He seems to want her to lie still. When she caresses his neck or back, he seems almost to flinch, and so she leaves her hands at her sides until he lifts one and uses it to squeeze his penis through his trousers. He puts a finger inside her as he had before, but when she rocks against it, he glowers, flattens his other hand hard on her stomach, holding her in place. She wants to ask how they will stop a pregnancy, but his stormy expression forbids it.

Finally, in one abrupt chrysalis, he sheds all his clothes. His body is nearly hairless, though there are sparse dark nests in his groin and armpits.

When he stands to get something from a pocket of his jacket, his penis stands out from his body like a spigot.

With relief she sees the thing he's fetched is a rubber. Miss Dolly's girls had told her the most difficult part about rubbers was getting anyone to wear them. The girls preferred pessaries, which they said were not always easy to come by. Barclay crawls onto the bed, nudges her legs apart with his knee. He pauses briefly, meeting her eyes, giving her a last chance to change her mind. The first sensation is one of adjustment: her groin muscles absorbing the strain of his weight, much greater than Caleb's, her internal architecture shifting. The feeling of him is obscure and distant, some message from a subterranean city, yet as he moves she begins to feel a gathering, a quickening, as though what they are doing is urgent and necessary, as though something important hangs in the balance.

Maybe she had known this would be the consequence of turning the plane upside down.

"Are you all right?" he says.

"Yes."

"Does it hurt?"

"A bit."

"You haven't done this before, have you?"

"No."

He stares at her. She can't tell if he believes her. Brusquely, he pulls out, turns her over so her face is engulfed in pillows and pushes into her unceremoniously from behind. After a moment he rolls over, pulling her on top of him. Then he is pressing her onto her back again, pushing her knees up against her shoulders.

As he arranges her limbs first one way and then another, he radiates itchy dissatisfaction, and she surrenders to the role of startled, silent bystander. What does he want from her? He doesn't quite seem to know. She wonders if all his encounters are like this, if all his girls feel like dolls in the hands of an impatient, tyrannical little boy.

He turns her over restlessly, puzzling at her body as though it contains the key to something he wants but is not itself that thing. To her surprise, she finds his impersonal manipulations exciting, but he, fussing over the position of her arms, is beginning to have difficulty maintaining an erection, a possibility she hadn't ever considered. Placing her arms above her head and pushing them firmly into the mattress as though telling them to stay put, he takes his softening member in hand and attempts to stuff it into her.

"Shit," he says, rolling off. He hunches on the edge of the bed, trying to chafe himself back into hardness.

"Did I do something wrong?" she says.

The movement of his arm ceases. "I don't know how to trust you," he says.

"What should I do?"

"Promise not to be with anyone else."

"I have. But what should I do **now**?"

He turns and looks at her until he seems to reach a decision. Drawing a long breath through his nose, he swivels to lie beside her. Holding her gaze, he fits his hand carefully around her throat. He does not squeeze, but her pulse flutters like a trapped butterfly.

What follows is not entirely different from what had come before, but he is more decided. He holds her by the head, the hips, the wrists. He puts his penis in her mouth, something Caleb had never done. She is lost in a state of perpetual transition: exhilarated then nauseated, fearful then reckless, debased then venerated. He seems to **want** so profoundly. She thinks he might destroy her, break her like some small animal and not even notice because what he wants is not actually in her but beyond her, somewhere else, or perhaps doesn't exist.

When he comes, it is with a terrible grimace.

At some unnoticed point it had begun to rain. He gets up to open the window, letting in the dusty smell of a summer storm.

"Are you all right?" he says, returning to bed.

"Yes."

"I meant to be gentle. I'm sorry."

She doesn't know whether or not he wants her to say it was fine.

"There's no blood anyway," he says, uneasy.

"I spent a lot of time on horseback," she says.

He seems to accept this. He asks, "Do you know what a rubber does?"

"It's so I don't get pregnant." She pauses. "You thought to bring one along."

"I've been carrying it around, just in case. How did you know about rubbers?"

"From Dolly's girls. Lucky **that** didn't fall out of your pocket and land on someone's head."

He is on his side, close to her. He rests his fingertips on her clavicle. "Someday, of course, we'll want a baby."

Marian is taken aback. "I've never thought about it." This is the unadorned truth—never once has she imagined herself cradling an infant.

"All girls want babies."

"How would I fly if I had a baby?"

He looks confused. "You wouldn't."

She is equally confused. For months he'd listened to her talk about what she wanted. She'd never said anything about babies. "I have to, though," she says.

They look at each other in dismay. He puts one hand on her belly. "Not yet. Someday."

"I don't want to stop. Not ever."

"You're young," he says in a patient tone. "What makes you happy now is different from what will make you happy later. You must know that I love you. I'll take care of you. I'll marry you." These last are not posed as questions.

So he had never believed her. He had been indulging a child's make-believe. A long blade of rage cuts through her, but she stops herself from reacting by remembering flipping him upside down, making him afraid. He'd thought he was reclaiming something when he put her face in the pillows, turned her body over and over like a pebble he was worrying in his pocket, but really he was only accepting what she'd offered. He'd needed her to give him the imperative of reclaiming his dominance, and she had. Could there be power in submission? She will probably have to marry him, she knows; he will win their game of push-pull, but if she agrees now, she will lose too much.

She says, "Not yet."

She flies to Canadian farms and brings back cases of premium brands, learns more about the business. Barclay's interests and supply chains are diffuse and diverse. He buys from middlemen who buy legally from boozoriums scattered around Saskatchewan, Alberta, British Columbia, Manitoba. He has relationships with whiskey exporters in Scotland, with importers in Canada, with lawmakers and law enforcers. He has lawyers in Helena and Spokane and Seattle and Boise who cover his tracks and help out the little guys when they get caught.

One afternoon when they are in bed in the

green-and-white house, he says, "I don't feel right about this."

"You seemed to enjoy yourself."

"That's not the point." Petulantly: "I wish you'd just agree. If you're going to eventually, why wait?"

A pessary snugly cups her cervix. She thinks of the device as her small but stalwart ally. Cora from Miss Dolly's had gotten it for her at a steep price, of which Marian assumed a good chunk was commission. "Like this," Cora had said, pinching it between her fingers. "Then you shove it up yourself and let go. It'll pop into place."

To Barclay, Marian says, "Only if you promise I can keep flying forever and never have any babies." She speaks lightly, but he doesn't smile. She tries again: "Why can't we go on as we are? Eventually you'll get tired of me, and you'll be glad I'm just your pilot."

He is serious, almost grim. "I have to hide almost everything I do. I want this to be on the up-and-up, respectable and official, and I want you to be respectable, too."

"I'm not respectable?" The sting surprises her.

"I want you to be more secure, to have some kind of status in the world." He touches her cheek. "I don't want anyone ever to see you the way I first saw you."

"I thought you said I fascinated you."

"You did. You **do.** But that was something private

between us. If anyone else had seen you like that at Miss Dolly's, there would have been a simple, sordid misunderstanding, but I saw through your little outfit." He props himself on an elbow. "It had to be **me** who saw you. I know it. I saw someone out of place, who needed me but didn't know it yet. At first I was relieved you were a whore because I thought I could have you, but then I was so much more relieved when I realized you weren't. I didn't want anyone else to have you." He rolls onto his back, pulls her against him with her arm over his chest, her leg over his thigh. "And what did you see? When you first saw me?"

"A stranger."

"That's all?"

"Not quite." She doesn't want to talk about Miss Dolly's anymore. She wishes the memory didn't loom quite so large for him. Her hand moves to his groin, and his breathing deepens.

"What else?" he says.

"I saw a man who would let me fly his biplane as much as I wanted forever and ever."

"Yes," he says, but he means the motion of her hand.

She had thought he might lose interest in her once she was plucked, no longer a figure of fantasy, but he hasn't. If anything, her enthusiasm for sex has made him more fixated on marriage. He seems jealous of the act itself. The first time she'd clenched and pulsed around him, when they were in their second day of being trapped by rain and cloud in the Kalispell house and had gotten the hang of each other, he had stared at her in frank astonishment. He'd asked how she'd known how to do that, and she'd lied and feigned surprise and said it had simply happened. He'd told her not all women were capable of climax and, more important, not all men were capable of inspiring such phenomena. She was fortunate on both counts, he'd said.

He'd asked her again if she'd been with anyone else, told her it was all right if she had, he only wanted to know the truth. **No,** she'd said. **Only you.** There could be no other answer.

His arm is around her; he is gripping her backside. "You saw the man you'd marry," he says, his eyes half closed.

"But only maybe," she says, "and not for a very, very long time."

From there, the negotiations continue silently and are understood differently by each of them.

Sometimes she thinks she should accept Barclay and have done with it. There are worse lots than a husband who excites her body, a husband with money, a husband who is the reason she can fly an airplane. But the question of children makes her balk—that, and a more general disquiet.

He goes away for a few weeks in August. When

he returns, he asks how her considerations are going. She says well enough. He asks how much longer she will need. She says she doesn't know.

She has come to be grateful for Jamie's absence. Without him around to worry and disapprove and with Caleb making himself scarce, she can more easily tell herself there is nothing to worry about, nothing to disapprove of. Wallace seems oblivious to the nights she is away from home. He spends most of his time in his studio, drinking and listening to the phonograph.

She wishes Jamie would come home but also that he would stay away.

Yes and No

～

Nine

It took me three days to read Marian's book, Carol Feiffer's book, the Day brothers' screenplay, and Marian's book again. I didn't have a lot else to do, and I was tired of reality TV. Mostly I read in bed, though I took a bath each morning and another each night and read in the tub, too, ignoring my guilt about the drought. Being swallowed up by something—by Marian's thoughts, by Carol's breathless prose, by bathwater—was pleasant and primal, amniotic. One way or another I would need to emerge from this particular moment, but the question was into what? Limbo was comfortable as long as I could convince myself it never had to end, as long as I could hide in the unknown, be the Schrödinger's cat of casting decisions, both Marian and not Marian.

Hugo came by on the second afternoon on the

pretense of wanting to "discuss" the books and the script, but I knew he was there to persuade, and he knew I knew, and he probably also knew how flattered I was and how hungry for flattery. "The character is an actor's dream," he said about Marian, casually, as though this observation were unrelated to any business between us. "There's a foundation of fact but still an abundance of freedom." Hugo had excellent intuition, so he surely knew I would balk if he applied too much direct pressure. But he also knew that, deep down, I was desperate to be told what to do. I'm not sure why he bothered. There were better actresses, more reliable actresses, actresses who looked more like Marian Graves. I think he got a kick out of getting people to do what he wanted while simultaneously doing exactly as **he** pleased, staging little subversions like hiring the recently disgraced.

Siobhan called on the third afternoon, having gotten wind of what was brewing and having decided she was opposed. "I don't want us to rush into any decisions," she said. "I think we should let the dust settle a little more."

"It seems like a good project, though, doesn't it? And a good part?" I said, wheedling. It wasn't so much that I felt confident it **was** a good project, just that I didn't want to have to weigh Siobhan's opinion against Hugo's. I wanted a consensus. I wanted a voice from on high.

"My hesitation has more to do with the timing," she said. "I don't want us to leap at the first opportunity and then end up being stunt casted. I don't want you to be a spectacle."

"Hugo says we're always spectacles. He says the point is to be a spectacle. Are you against it because I'd barely get paid?"

"No." The word popped out too quickly. She paused, and I sensed her recentering herself. "It just feels—to me, from what I know—like maybe too many people already want too many things from this project. The **vision** of it feels scattered."

"So you think I shouldn't do it."

"I think you should ask yourself what you want from this. Why **this** project?"

I saw myself flying a plane over the ocean. I saw myself gazing out over a wasteland of ice. The version of **Peregrine** I imagined was good, even great, but I could only conjure fragments, only flashes of myself with swelling music in the background like the clips they edit together in movie trailers to make any crappy, pretentious drama look Big and Important. I saw myself raising my Oscar. But if that actually happened, what would be left for me to want? Or what if Siobhan was right and I was just being needy, letting myself be taken advantage of, throwing away my one chance at redemption? The future felt like a blindfold.

I'd asked the shrink if the glowing tiger was

supposed to be scary, and he'd said that the self could, at times, feel dangerous. I said, "So I'm the tiger."

He said, "Yes." Then he said, "And no."

In the end I said yes to Marian because yes is easier than no. Yes is an accelerant, a rush. You only live once. I called up Hugo myself, and he said this was wonderful news, he was **thrilled,** and he would get in touch pronto about scheduling the audition, and I tried to pretend I hadn't assumed I wouldn't have to audition.

Before my callback for Katie McGee, I'd stayed in character for days, like I was Daniel Day-Lewis in a training bra, as though Katie McGee were really a character and not just a marketable alloy of precocity and sass. Mitch chaperoned me to the studio himself, marking the gravity of the occasion. No one had yet told me to manifest anything back then, but I manifested the living fuck out of Katie McGee. I walked into that room radiating more Katie McGee–ness than I ever did again for the run of the show. I was pure, unadulterated spunky charm, and when I saw the studio people light up and exchange glances while I said my lines, I felt a white-hot pleasure in my core like the fusion at the center of the sun, radiating outward, warming the faces of the adults behind their table. For the first time in my life, I felt a sense of perfect belonging, of doing something just right, of certainty that I would get what I wanted.

I'd given up hoping ever to feel that way again, but once I realized getting to be Marian wasn't a given, I suddenly wanted to be her a thousand times more badly than I had. I submerged myself in her. I strode around my house the way I imagined she would. I barely glanced in the mirror because I imagined she disdained vanity. I slouched and sprawled in chairs. I started speaking deliberately and not like a SoCal bubblehead, which had the unintended consequence of making Augustina worry I was mad at her. I tried to do everything the way I thought Marian would, to be confident and self-contained. I googled my brains out, looked at every photo of her I could find and watched the only stray bit of film that seemed to exist: Marian and Eddie Bloom, the navigator, climb out of the plane after a test flight in New Zealand; he grins; she puts her hands in her pockets; they look at each other; she looks at the plane. There's a close-up of her, her eyes sliding away from the camera, and a close-up of him, looking sturdy and pleasant. In Carol Feiffer's novel, Eddie is in unrequited love with Marian, while she's hung up on her childhood friend, Caleb, and I scrutinized the clip for fraughtness between them. Her smile was more reluctant than his, but when they glanced at each other, I could identify only the basic presence of inscrutable silent communication, not its nature.

They were saying something to each other, but it was encrypted, accessible only to them.

There was one other thing. Hugo had suggested I take a flying lesson (gingerly, given my family history), and I said no and then okay and then no again. Then maybe. He said I could think about it, but just in case, he would have one set up and get the instructor to sign an NDA. That way the option was there. I tried to think about the lesson the way Marian would, to inhabit a person who actually wanted to fly a plane. I wasn't afraid of flying itself, of being aloft. I didn't get nervous on commercial flights. I didn't connect that experience, the white noise of it, with my parents plunging into a vast and freezing lake. I didn't need to recite statistics in my mind or engage in soothing meditations or remind myself of the trustworthy physics of the whole enterprise. But when I imagined flying a plane myself, I could only think of falling.

Hugo's people had arranged the lesson for very early morning to avoid the press and humans in general, and in the dark predawn, pacing my kitchen, dressed and ready to go, I clutched my phone, desperate to cancel yet never dialing. I'd barely slept. Then M.G. was bringing the car around, headlights on, and I got in and sat paralyzed inside the runaway forward momentum of a yes I'd never quite uttered.

The instructor pilot had thick salt-and-pepper hair the texture of a badger's and a fat gold wedding band and aviator sunglasses in his front shirt pocket for when the sun came up. He didn't seem flustered by me. He walked around the plane, explaining what all the different parts did. The Cessna was chunky and earnest-looking, cream-colored with two brown stripes and a single propeller. The morning was overcast. The long strips of grass between the little airport's runways were gray with dew.

"So what happens on an introductory flight like this," the pilot said, "is we'll take off and get up over the marine layer and fly around a bit, and I'll explain what I'm doing, and then you can have a turn at the controls. Sound good?"

"Sure," I said.

I must not have sounded convincing because he said, "You nervous?"

"A little." I could tell he hadn't bothered to google me, didn't know about my parents. He thought my misgivings could be cajoled away.

"Don't be. I do this every day. I'll talk you through every step, and you don't have to do anything you don't feel comfortable with. Deal?"

Ordinarily I would have found his teacher-coach vibe irritating, but now it reassured me. "Deal," I said, and he beamed, close-lipped.

The seats in the cockpit were bourbon-colored leather, cracked with use. The doors locked with levers that seemed too flimsy to keep out the sky, and the seat belts were floppy nylon straps that didn't retract. We put on green plastic headsets, the cups bulbous like flies' eyes, and the pilot's voice came pinched and tinny through them over the noise of the engine as it warmed up. He was telling me about the instruments, pointing at the dashboard, but I wasn't really listening because I had no plans to ever become a pilot. What caught my attention was the slight sideways jostle of the plane caused by the turning propeller. I knew the plane didn't have a mind or feelings, wasn't capable of eagerness, but it was an eager, ready feeling, like a racehorse in a starting gate or a boxer just before the bell, the movement of something constrained that knew it was about to be free.

The pilot taxied out and throttled forward, peeled us up off the runway into pulsing gray cloud. The propeller droned; my armpits prickled. I held perfectly still, as though the plane were a frightened animal I didn't want to startle. The pilot was talking, but I couldn't focus on his words. When we surfaced into the sky, pulling the sun up with a flash, he said, "There she is!"

A mat of plush gray lay over the ocean and the coast. Mountaintops poked up like islands. "That's Catalina," the pilot said, pointing. So some were actually islands.

He made the plane go slowly up and down, turned it to the right and then to the left, explaining about balanced turns, about how you didn't just steer with your hands but also controlled the rudder with your feet. Eventually he asked if I wanted to try. "Put your hands on the yoke," he said. "Don't turn, just try to fly straight and level."

I put my hands on the yoke. I felt overwhelmed by precariousness.

"Good," said the pilot. "Now, Hadley, if you want, you can gently pull back, and the plane will go up."

At first I pulled so tentatively I wasn't pulling at all, and nothing happened. I pulled harder. The windshield angled incrementally toward the sky, and I felt the earth falling away behind me, sucking me down.

I snatched my hands away. "I don't want to do it," I said.

"Okay," the pilot said, calmly taking over, clearly no stranger to freak-outs. "Okay, but you did just fine. You asked the plane to go up, and it went up."

I said, "I don't like the feeling."

He shook his head. "Best feeling in the world," he said.

Ten

When I went in to audition, Sir Hugo was there, sitting at a table with Ted Lazarus, the boss of Sun God Entertainment whose wife got banged by Gavin du Pré, and Bart Olofsson, the director, and a casting director who shall remain nameless but is much-feared and looks like someone's kooky aunt with her pink Keds and spiky red hair. "How are you, Hadley?" she said, and I could tell from her grave intonation she was asking about **Archangel,** about Oliver.

"Great," I said. "Really excited to read for you guys."

An assistant tended a camera on a tripod. Off to the side in overflow seating (a wheeled desk chair) was an enthused-looking hipster guy with a dark beard, retro gold-framed glasses, and hair just long enough to tuck behind his ears. "This is Redwood Feiffer," Hugo said. "I mentioned he will be producing as well."

"Fantastic to meet you," Redwood said, jumping up to shake my hand. "I'm a massive fan."

At some point, Sir Hugo had set about wooing Siobhan, and since wooing is one of his strong suits, she'd come around. The information that a rich young dupe was involved in the project had helped her warm up to the whole thing. "These obscure historical footnotes **do** make for good content," she'd conceded to me. "And the Day brothers **are** having a moment." It could be an interesting angle for publicity, she'd said, this whole family affair, Redwood and his novelist mother and publisher grandmother. Just like Sir Hugo had, she'd called them **Feiffer** Feiffers. "And your own history—" She cut herself off.

"Yeah," I said.

"The lost parents. It's a helluva coincidence. I don't mean to sound callous."

"It's not really a coincidence," I said. "It's a reason."

"A reason?"

"For why I should do this. Hugo says it's destiny."

"He would say that," Siobhan said.

After my utter failure to fly a plane, I'd only become more determined to be Marian. I needed the relief of being someone who wasn't afraid. It helped that she wasn't completely alien, that we were both products of vanishment and orphanhood and negligence and airplanes and uncles. She was like me but wasn't. She was uncanny, unknowable except for a few constellations I recognized from my own sky.

I responded to Redwood Feiffer with the kind of smile you give the money guy. Not explicitly flirtatious but on the road to it. "Yeah?" I asked him. "Big into **Archangel**?"

"One **hundred** percent." I assumed he was kidding, but he leaned forward in his swivel chair, said earnestly, "Those movies are beautifully made and really romantic. Also, I'm always fascinated by things that turn into phenomenons. Like, **why,** you know? What is it that strikes a chord in so many people? When it happens, it seems so intuitive in retrospect, like you can clearly see the void that was filled, but the real trick is identifying the void when it's still a void."

"The billion-dollar void," Hugo said. "Let's hope there's a vanished-lady-pilot void."

"Okay," said Ted Lazarus, "should we get started?"

When you're a movie star, you're basically a good-looking dingbat running around with headshots, but people don't see the dingbat. They see the sum of the characters you've played: someone who's time-traveled, who's saved civilization, who's been chosen by a beautiful, powerful man as the object of his undying devotion, who's been rescued from terrorists by her father, Russell Crowe. You take on weight and consequence. It's like the dance of a thousand veils except with every role you're putting **on** another veil, concealing yourself. Still, the effect is more seductive than a striptease.

"Ready when you are," Hugo said. He was going to read the other parts.

"Good to go," I said.

I looked at the floor, the blue-gray institutional carpet, and when I looked up, the conference room seemed to become less tangible, blurred as though frames of it were alternating with frames of another life. **Manifest, manifest.** The memory of the Cessna flickered and went out. I didn't look at the people at the table, but I felt my glow reflecting off their faces. I was hunkered down in a tent in Antarctica while a blizzard raged, and Hugo was Eddie Bloom, and we were talking about what would happen when we got home, describing what we would eat. I told him I loved him even though I didn't really, not the way he loved me. It didn't matter, though, because neither of us thought we'd survive.

"No one will ever find us," he said.

"We're not just going to disappear," I told him. I knew that was a lie, even if I didn't want it to be.

Millionaire's Row

Seattle
May 1931
Two months before Marian flew Barclay over Glacier National Park

Inside a tunnel, Jamie clung to the side of a boxcar, hot darkness pressing in, clanking and sulfurous. The glow of the headlight seemed far away, pulling the train along behind like a comet's tail. When you think the train is slowing, the tramps in Spokane had told him, reach down with your foot and start tapping the cinders to gauge the speed. Best to make your leap before you get to Union Station. The bulls there aren't pleasant. You'll end up in jail or beaten or both.

Back in Idaho, Jamie had been awakened in a rail yard by a bull's nightstick across his shins, had little interest in another encounter.

He'd heard it was possible to suffocate in the long tunnels, but the tramps thought he'd be all right.

The clacking and huffing slowed. He lowered himself until his toe clattered through the cinders. Too fast still. A screeching he thought must be the brakes, and he tried again. This time the ground seemed to grab at his foot, wrenching loose his grip. He fell, landed hard, and rolled away. At least his knapsack cushioned him a little.

Walk along the tunnel, the tramps had said. You'll find a way out eventually.

One hand on the wall, he limped and stumbled through the darkness until his fingers found a steel door. Behind it, a ladder. After a hatch and another tunnel, he emerged into cool air and, under a gray sky, the biggest city he'd ever seen. Grand buildings wore corbels and pilasters like medals on their puffed-out chests, cornices like epaulets. The wide streets teemed with cars and trolleys. Signs clamored about lunchrooms, tailors, mattresses, Coca-Cola, cigars, canned crab, everything else anyone could sell. A passing man in a suit pointed to his own temple and said, "You're bleeding, you know."

Jamie spat on his handkerchief and dabbed at his scalp and cheek as he walked. The already dingy cotton came away smeared with soot and blood.

Ranks of apartments and offices and houses and churches marched up the hills, but he turned down toward the waterfront. When he'd decided to leave

Missoula for the summer, the Pacific had drawn him irresistibly, and finally here it was, oily gray, hectored by gulls. Ships and boats crowded the piers. On a semblance of a beach, crunchy with broken shells and ripe with rotting seaweed, he wet the handkerchief and wiped at his face, wincing at the sting of salt. He'd wanted no part of what was happening with Marian and Barclay Macqueen, and he'd gotten so tired of worrying about Wallace, so fed up with his way of trying to conceal his drunkenness by speaking and moving with a careful, childish hauteur.

Jamie couldn't even escape into his friendship with Caleb. Marian had changed that, too. Neither she nor Caleb had ever made any allusion to their trysts, but Jamie knew they'd happened, knew they'd stopped. In some ways, he had always been the least necessary vertex of their triangle, but, in at least one way, he'd been essential: Marian and Caleb needed a buffer to convince themselves they weren't a pair. Not that he thought they were— or should be—a proper couple. No. But the wildness that had rooted in all of them as children had grown thickety and riotous between Marian and Caleb, as barbed as blackberry shrubs, hopelessly entangling. They were a pair, as some things naturally and undeniably were, and once a pair was established, everything outside it (himself, for example) became inevitably and inherently extraneous. He and Marian were a pair, too, of course, but the bond of their twinness was so fundamental it could almost be disregarded. Or at least Marian seemed to think so.

Turning uphill (everywhere seemed to be uphill), he walked for hours, stopping men in work clothes to ask if they knew of any boardinghouses, knocking at doors until he found somewhere cheap enough that would have him, dried blood and all.

"Do you know where I could find work?" he asked the proprietress after she'd shown him his closet-like room, its small window almost opaque with dirt.

"Not much work for the finding."

This turned out to be unequivocally true. There were simply too many people looking for work, droves of grim men with grim stories about lost homes and farms, usually with families to support. He'd had an idea he could get hired at the docks or on the fishing boats that was underlaid with the queasy, barely acknowledged hope he might turn up a clue about his father, might even, by some miracle, stumble upon him. But although he was tall and strong for his age, he was not as tall and strong as most men haunting the waterfront and not as desperate, certainly not aggressive enough to push to the front of the crowd when a boss came looking for hands.

He looked into the faces of men coming off ships, waiting for some burst of recognition. (Had the ocean's gravity really been what pulled him west? Or had it been the tidal pull of his father?) He bought a coffee in a dockside café and asked tentatively if anyone knew Addison Graves. No one did, though one meat-faced man wondered aloud why he knew the name, then snapped his fingers and said, "Captain Cowardice!"

After a few days Jamie gave up the docks. His fantasy of finding his father seemed foolish once he'd absorbed the scale of the city, the multitude of ships. There was no reason to assume he would recognize Addison or that Addison was even alive. And if he was, why shouldn't he be living in Tahiti or Cape Town? Or even Tacoma, which was only thirty miles away but might as well be the moon?

One day Jamie took the ferry north to Port Angeles. From the railing, he watched the prow peel back the water to its white pith. What if he were to sign on to a ship, write to Marian and Wallace from China or Australia? Had his father felt the same sense of possibility? Or was it temptation? The temptation of becoming an absence. On a ship, he could do nothing to keep Marian from Barclay, nothing to stop Wallace from running up debts. On land, he couldn't do much, either, but he was dogged by the obligation to try. At sea, perhaps his sense of obligation would stretch thin enough to snap.

But, on the return journey, the wind was cold and the water choppy and dark, and he imagined being lost at sea somewhere far away, how Marian would never know what had happened. He couldn't abandon her. True, she would likely abandon him one day soon, but he would rather endure that loss than inflict it.

He tried several canneries, but there were no jobs. He tried a steelworks, a lumberyard, a produce market. Nothing. Every night he counted his dwindling money, saved from the sales of his watercolors and stolen, just a little bit, from Marian. Every night he calculated how much longer he could stay.

After ten days of gloomy skies, one Saturday dawned clear and fine. Out the circle he'd rubbed clean in his little window, Mount Rainier's gigantic, snowy crown hovered in the blue.

Such a day seemed too precious to spend begging in vain for work, so he took the few cents he usually would have paid for a day's food and spent it on a streetcar up to Woodland Park, where there were amusements. He meandered by a Ferris wheel, a small zoo, a row of carnival games. Under a tree, he reclined in the grass and watched people enjoy themselves. Not everyone had lost everything. Not everyone spent their days hoping to cram sardines into cans. Some carefree people still dawdled and laughed in the sunshine, and rather than resenting them, he was pleased to know such lives were possible.

Presently a man set up two chairs and a little easel near the entrance to the zoo. He bought a balloon from a passing vendor and tied it to his easel, pinned up a sign that said CARICATURES 25 CENTS. Within minutes, a young father approached with his little girl, who sat squirming in the chair until the artist, with a flourish, presented her with his drawing. The father handed over a coin. Over an hour, the man sold three more portraits. A dollar! Jamie walked casually behind the artist's easel when the next customer came. The subject's face was recognizable but exaggerated, with giant eyes and a wild grin.

That same day, with almost the last of his money, Jamie bought a large pad of thick drawing paper and a box of charcoal pencils. A necessary gamble. For chairs he scavenged two apple crates. That night he recruited a few fellow boarders as models for his samples, and the next morning he went back to Woodland Park. He chose a spot beside Green Lake, far from the amusements so as not to impinge on the other artist's territory. He weighted down his samples with rocks and propped a piece of cardboard against his crate on which he'd written PORTRAITS in big letters, embellished with sketched figures out for a day in the park: a mother pushing a baby buggy, children with balloons, a hatted man strolling, some leafy trees, a family of ducks. He hadn't drawn many portraits before, but he thought he could do well enough.

Before long: his first customer, his first quarter.

Some sunny weekend days he made four or five dollars. Some gray days, he didn't make anything. He experimented with different locations, different parks: Playland and the swimming beach on Lake Washington and Alki Beach on Puget Sound, where there were saltwater pools. When it drizzled, he sheltered near the Pike Place Market. In lulls, he drew general scenes—bathers lounging, children on a carousel, fruit peddlers at the market—and tried to sell those.

Jamie found he liked how the people he drew gave him permission to look closely and without hurry at their faces. He liked how people became vulnerable when they were about to be drawn, revealed more than they intended with their little adjustments. They sat up straighter or slouched, met his eye or evaded it. They seemed to become more themselves under his scrutiny, to radiate their most essential qualities. His special talent, he discovered, lay in his ability not only to see his subjects accurately but also to intuit how they **wanted** to be seen and to draw the overlap. His portraits were less flattering to the face than to the soul.

People seemed pleased.

One fine afternoon in July, as he waited beside Green Lake in Woodland Park, a group of three girls about his age sauntered by. All wore summer dresses and hats and ankle-strap pumps and radiated prosperity. A blonde led the way, plump and busty, striding forward with the confidence of someone who assumed she would be followed. The other two trailed after, both dark, one quite short and one quite tall. The short one was talking a blue streak and at the same time gnawing on a stick of rock candy. The tall one moved her long limbs tentatively, sliding along as though on ice she didn't quite trust. She nearly stopped Jamie's heart, that tall girl. She was leaning to one side, bending her ear toward her short, candy-eating companion. Her long, lowered eyelashes gave her a serene, enigmatic look.

The three glided on, a little flotilla of elegance, passing through the crowd, the park, the hard times as though none of it were of any consequence. Jamie watched the tall girl's retreating back with the bereft feeling of having dropped something precious and irreplaceable into a deep lake.

"Hey, kid," somebody said. "How much to draw my girl?"

Jamie turned, startled. A sturdy young man hitched his thumb at a sour-faced young woman, her arms folded across her chest.

"A quarter."

The man's face tensed, then sagged. "Nah, she don't need it that much."

"Actually," Jamie said, "I could use the practice. Call it a nickel." Really what he could use was the nickel.

"Deal," the man said, tough and smug again.

He fumbled in his pocket, tossed a coin to Jamie. "First price is never real," he told his girlfriend.

"Business not exactly booming?" she asked as she sat down.

He smiled. "At least I'm outside on a nice day."

"Yeah." She seemed unconvinced. About her boyfriend, she said, "I thought he was taking me to Playland, but he's too cheap."

Jamie would have to be careful not to let his instinctive dislike for these people and his sorrow over the lost tall girl creep into his drawing. In fact, he resolved to make an especially good portrait, to think of nothing but the face in front of him until he got the best version of this unpleasant girl down on paper.

With his pencils, he turned the corners of her mouth up ever so slightly, made her uneven eyes almost but not quite the same size (make someone too perfect, and the likeness becomes a critique), left out the faint pockmarks on her cheeks. What he wanted to capture was a certain brassiness that showed through her sourness in glimpses, maybe a hint of humor.

He was well into his work when the three girls came strolling back in the opposite direction. His eyes darted away too many times, and his subject turned to look.

"If you don't mind holding still," he said, but her movement had already attracted the girls' attention. They halted, looking at him, whispering.

"Oh, I see," his subject said. She gave him a big, saucy wink, though he saw something wounded and scornful underneath it. She beckoned to the girls. "You're distracting my artist," she called. "Come over here."

The blonde, the leader, pursed her lips in a why-not way and ambled in their direction, the other two in her wake. The short one, her rock candy worn down to its last nubs, circled behind Jamie and looked over his shoulder. To his model, she said, "It's good. You'll like it." She put the wooden candy stick sideways in her mouth and crunched.

"I doubt it," said the sour girl. "I never like pictures of myself."

"How much longer?" said her boyfriend.

"Only a minute," said Jamie.

The blond girl came around to look. "We should get ours done," she said in a general way. The tall girl, Jamie's girl, hung back.

"Almost finished," Jamie said. Finally he tore the page from his pad and handed it to his subject.

She brightened. "That's not half bad."

Her boyfriend leaned over her shoulder. "Hey, he made you look really nice."

"How much are they?" the rock candy girl asked Jamie.

"A quarter," said the guy as his girlfriend stood and replaced her hat.

"My treat, girls," the blond girl said. To Jamie,

she directed, "Start with Sarah." She pointed at the tall girl.

So he started with Sarah.

Sarah Fahey, he learned soon enough, was the youngest of five children, one boy and four girls, though the girls with her in the park were her friends, not sisters. She lived on Millionaire's Row near Volunteer Park, in her family's large house that looked to Jamie like something out of a storybook with its timbers and herringbone brick and abundance of chimneys. An expansive, luminously green lawn was trimmed as close as baize. The house even had a name: Hereford House. Jamie had not known that houses **could** have names. Nor did he know, at first, that Hereford was a variety of cattle.

Sarah's brother had gone away to Harvard and was still in Boston even though he'd graduated. Everyone assumed he would come back to work for their father, though Sarah said she suspected he didn't want to. Her eldest sister was married and lived nearby with her husband and baby. The next sister was studying art history at the University of Washington and lived at home but was away for the summer in Europe, and the sister after that, Alice, would start UW in the fall. "Mother's big on education," Sarah said. She herself had one more year at a private girls' school.

Sarah's mother was tall and willowy and had a languid grace that Jamie supposed would one day be the final form of Sarah's gawkiness. She had been a suffragist and then devoted herself to the Women's Christian Temperance Union. After the passage of Volstead, however, she had not protested when her husband filled their cellar with a robust stockpile of wine and liquor that, more than ten years on, was diminished but far from exhausted. It was mostly the drinking done by other people's husbands that Mrs. Fahey had objected to, and, anyway, trying to oppose the decisions of Mr. Fahey tended to be a futile provocation that improved the happiness of no one.

But first, that warm July day when she was still a stranger, Jamie drew Sarah's portrait. Her friends fell all over themselves when he was done. "It's **you,** Sarah," said the rock-candy eater, whose name turned out to be Hazel. "It's your absolute essence. The Madonna of Woodland Park."

"It's almost spooky," the blonde, Gloria, said. She looked sharply, almost accusingly, at Jamie. "How'd you do that?"

"I had a good model," Jamie said, blushing furiously.

"Oh, **did** you?" said Gloria.

So thrilling was the experience of sitting and looking at Sarah that he hadn't wanted to finish the drawing. Sarah hadn't said much while she sat, though from time to time she'd responded to her friends' banter. When he handed her the torn-off page, she'd held it in her lap, regarding it with frank interest. "You're talented," she said. Her gaze was direct, her voice lower than he'd expected and more authoritative. He'd taken her quietness for shyness—a silly assumption, given that he, too, was quiet but not shy. He wished he could amend the drawing, which suddenly seemed sentimental and idealized. Hazel had chosen the right word: **Madonna.** Docile, venerated.

"It's not quite right," he said.

"It might be a little too kind. But it's very good."

His blush deepened with dismal regret. He had wanted her to find the portrait uncanny, to think him astute.

"Sarah's father collects art," Hazel put in, "so she's well informed. And one of her sisters is studying art at UW—"

"Art history," Sarah corrected.

"—and, also, what you should know about our Sarah is that she never gives empty praise. Sometimes you can feel almost neglected. But then when she tells you something nice, you can take it as unvarnished honesty."

Sarah said, "Why would anyone want empty praise?"

"Because it's pleasant!" said Hazel.

The other two were anxious to have their turn under Jamie's magic pencils, and though they exclaimed with pleasure and admiration over the finished products, Sarah's was his best effort by far. "You should sign them for us," Gloria said. "So when you're famous we'll be able to prove we own early works. And so Sarah knows your name."

He obliged, blushing again.

"Jamie Graves," read Gloria. "Are you often in this spot? If our other friends are jealous and demand portraits of their own?"

"Sometimes," he said. Then, with a little burst of hope, though he had planned to try Playland the next day: "I'll be here tomorrow."

Hazel pumped his hand goodbye. "Very nice to meet you," she said. The other two followed suit. He wanted to cling to Sarah's cool, slender hand forever.

Only after they were gone did he realize they hadn't paid.

What a despondent night he spent lying awake on the lumpy mattress in his cheerless cell, listening to his fellow boarders growing raucous downstairs. At some point there would be a fight, he knew, and the landlady, in her nightgown and brandishing a fire iron, would break it up, and only after that, sometime around sunrise, would there be quiet. He would never see Sarah again because theirs were not the kind of lives that would intersect, and though that was far worse than being shorted seventy-five cents, a little money would have been some consolation. Even though the park was still busy, he'd packed up, humiliated and furious with himself.

If only he were the kind of boy who could have asked Sarah to ride the Ferris wheel with him or take a stroll along the water. Had the girls deliberately skipped out? Had they gone off and laughed at him, tossing their portraits into the nearest trash can? Even if he'd remembered the money in time, he wasn't sure he would have had the nerve to ask for it or the will to lower himself.

As the rowdiness downstairs built to a garbled crescendo, he decided he would go to Union Station at first light. He had enough money for a ticket home. He didn't have the heart to hop another freight train. The spirit of adventure had left him. He'd proved nothing but his own haplessness.

Earlier than usual, his landlady entered the fray, and it was still dark when quiet fell. Jamie slid irresistibly into sleep. When he woke, the day was bright and blue again. Mount Rainier's summit gleamed above the horizon. Perhaps, he thought, he should go back to Woodland Park, as he had told the girls he would. Perhaps they would have realized their mistake. He could always catch a train later, that very night even.

He stopped at a bright and expensive bakery he'd always eyed but never entered and bought a glossy chocolate pastry on his way to the streetcar. If this was to be his last day, he might as well enjoy himself. In the park, his first customer was a mother with twins, a boy and a girl, age five. The children sat very still, stern as two miniature titans of industry. He considered telling the mother he had a twin sister but decided he didn't have the heart for the inevitable follow-up questions. Were they dear friends? They used to be. Weren't they exceptionally close, though? He hadn't written home once. He had no idea what Marian was doing, what dark bargains she had struck with Barclay Macqueen.

After several hours, just when he was about to give up on Seattle entirely, when he had almost started to relish the idea of a long, self-pitying rail journey, Sarah Fahey came hurrying along the path beside the lake. "I am so, so, **so** sorry we didn't pay," she said, breathless. "Gloria sometimes forgets the offers she makes, and we were all so in love with our own images that we couldn't think of anything else. We didn't realize until later, and we were absolutely horrified. Here." She held out a folded dollar bill.

He hesitated. "I don't want to take it."

"Why not? Of course you have to take it."

"But I'd like to ask you to take a walk with me, and if you've just given me a dollar, you might feel strange about it."

She lowered her arm a little. "A walk?"

"Just along the lake. If we have nothing to say, you can turn back."

They walked up the shore of Green Lake, falling into a comfortable stride. She asked how old he was. She was three months older, already seventeen. He asked how she knew Gloria and Hazel, and she said she'd always known them. Their mothers had been friends first. "Don't you have friends like that?" she asked. "Ones you played with when you were in diapers?"

"Maybe you'd count my friend Caleb, though I doubt he ever wore diapers. He lives nearby, and we just sort of came across each other, him and me and my sister. His mother didn't know my mother. I didn't even know my mother."

"What do you mean? What happened to her? Oh." She stopped, appalled, covering her mouth with a hand. "I'm sorry. I am so horribly nosy. You don't have to tell me if you don't want."

"No, it's all right." He tried, as best he could, to explain his family. He wasn't accustomed to talking about himself, but when he tried to skip ahead or gloss over details, she interrupted, prompted him to expand. He realized, as he talked, how little he'd said to anyone since he'd left Missoula. In a new city, anonymity fostered silence.

She listened with her head tipped toward him and her eyelashes lowered like when he'd first seen her. She had heard of the **Josephina Eterna,** and she said she thought it had been the right thing for his father to get in the lifeboat but cruel of him to come to Montana at all if he was only going to run off. She asked what it was like to have a twin, and what Marian was like (he told her about the flying but made no mention of Barclay Macqueen). She wanted him to describe his school and his dogs and Wallace. So Wallace had taught him to be an artist? No, he said. Not really. When Jamie was little, Wallace used to seem amused by his drawings, to praise them, but he'd become discouraging, even disdainful.

"Maybe he's started to see you as a rival," Sarah said, and Jamie felt a righteous gratitude to her for articulating a suspicion he had long tried to suppress. But all he could say, without getting into the drinking and gambling or acknowledging the resentment that had saturated Wallace along with the liquor, was, "I don't see why he should be. He's a very good painter."

He told her about the evening he'd decided to leave, how he'd sat on the kitchen floor with the dogs milling around him, saying goodbye to each in turn before he slipped out the kitchen door and walked in the dark to the tracks. He'd run alongside the first westbound train and grabbed onto the irons, feeling the fearsome heaviness of the train, the irresistible pull of it. For a while he'd lain on the coal-blacked bottom of an empty gondola car, his rucksack serving as a pillow, looking at the stars and shivering with exhilaration and terror. Periodically a tunnel enveloped him with a smoky whoosh, as though he'd been inhaled by a dragon.

"Weren't you afraid?" said Sarah.

"Very."

At dawn, somewhere in Idaho, he'd been woken by a sharp pain across his shins, the thwack of the rail-yard bull's billy stick. "You're lucky," the bull said. "Sometimes they don't look before they dump in the coal." He'd gone through Jamie's rucksack, taken five dollars from his paltry roll of bills, sent him walking along the tracks out of town, told him he should be grateful, and he was. Jamie had hidden in the bushes until nightfall, hopped a train that took him to Spokane. The tramps had pointed out a Seattle train, advised him about the tunnel, about tapping the cinders.

"Did you know someone here?" Sarah asked. "Is that why you came?"

They had already circled the lake and were back sitting in the shade on his apple crates. Embarrassed, he told her about his vague plan of haunting the dock in search of his father.

"What would you do if you found him?"

"That's a good question. I don't actually know."

"Are you sure you **want** to find him?"

"I think so. It must mean something that I keep thinking about it." Though he's never sure what to imagine after the first flash of recognition.

"Even though he's given no sign he wants to be found?" Her voice was friendly, curious, firm, a bit teacherly.

He said, "I think he owes me . . ." He couldn't think how to finish the sentence. "A conversation."

"What if he's awful? Or insane?"

"I'd try to help him, I think."

"Maybe it's less that you want to know where he is and more that you don't want to **not** know."

Mulishly, he said, "I don't see how those are so different."

She smiled, a trace of pity on her long face. He wanted to draw her again. Not a Madonna this time but someone disguised as a Madonna. "Then I hope you find him. I can't imagine life without my father. He looms large. Gloria and Hazel and I think we're so wild, going around the city by ourselves, but we're just as coddled as anything. The only reason I'm allowed my bit of freedom is that I'm the youngest, so my parents have had to relax some, if only out of exhaustion."

"Youngest of how many?"

"Five."

He realized he had been so pleased by her attention, so happy to be known again by someone even in some small way, that he'd failed to learn anything at all about her. "You tricked me into talking about myself this whole time," he said. "Now you. Start at the beginning, please."

"Tricked you?" she repeated. She looked at her delicate silver wristwatch. "Unfortunately, I have to go home. I'll be in big trouble if I stay to tell you my life's story, although it will seem very dull after yours." She stood. "Can we meet again?"

Trying to conceal his euphoria, he said, "We

have to. Otherwise I won't forgive myself for rambling on."

She promised she would come again the next day.

He spent the night in a fever. He ached to kiss Sarah, to feel her slender torso against his. He thought he might actually trade his life to see her naked. He wanted, with an uneasy undertow of shame, to do to her what he had seen that unknown man do to Gilda so long ago, to press her under his weight, to dredge and rut and dig at her. Most of all, he wanted her to want him to do this.

As muddy dawn lightened the window, he took up his drawing pad and started sketching in a frenzy. Sarah from the waist up, bare-breasted. Sarah lying naked with her arms behind her head, her legs demurely crossed. Then Sarah with her legs apart, a shadow between them to disguise his uncertainty.

Their second meeting, he had to keep fighting off erotic reveries as they walked around the lake. Her nearness, her bare forearms, her lavender aroma overwhelmed him, but he made himself try to listen, to repay the attention she'd given him.

She told him about her sisters and brother, her parents, her English sheepdog, Jasper. Her mother was passionate and political but, in Sarah's opinion, also too submissive to her father, a businessman, who was alternately jovial and overbearing and tolerated his wife's causes as long as she didn't bore him with talk of them. She said she would go to UW like her sisters, though if it were up to her she'd go somewhere farther away, like Wellesley or Radcliffe. ("Isn't it up to you?" Jamie said, and she laughed and said nothing was up to her.) She mentioned she had shown his portrait of her to her father, who was, as Hazel had said, an art collector.

"I think Father's self-conscious about his origins," she said. "Art is one way for him to show how cultured he's become. I don't mean to make him sound superficial. He loves it genuinely and is very knowledgeable. I asked him if he'd heard of your uncle, and he had. He thinks he might even own one of his paintings."

"That seems unlikely." But, after he'd spoken, Jamie realized he had no idea how far Wallace's paintings might have traveled.

"He's fairly certain. He said I should invite you over to see it. He'll have it brought out of storage. He wants to meet you. 'The Portraitist,' he calls you."

"All right," Jamie said. In a fit of daring, he took her hand and squeezed it.

She squeezed back, said, "My father likes people who make their own way."

She wrote directions to Hereford House on a page of his drawing pad and told him to come on Sunday, after lunch, when Mr. Fahey would be home.

. . .

The house was bigger than even the grandest residences in Missoula, its equally imposing neighbors kept at a polite distance by walls and wide lawns.

A brass ring dangled from a brass bull's nose in the middle of the front door, and, after some hesitation, Jamie lifted it and rapped once. Immediately a girl who resembled (but was not) Sarah flung open the door, and an enormous barking haystack of gray-and-white fur came hurtling out from behind her. "Jasper!" the girl scolded, swatting at the animal's bearlike haunches. Jamie offered his palm, and when the dog paused to sniff, the girl caught him by his collar and heaved him back. She was tall, though not as tall as Sarah, with the same long neck and a longer, cannier face. "I assume you're Jamie," she said. "I'm Alice, the next one up. Come in, please. Sarah is here somewhere. Aren't you **tall,** though? You're really only sixteen? No wonder Sarah likes you. No boys are ever as tall as Sarah."

She ushered him into a square entryway paneled in wood with the golden translucence of honey. A tasseled Persian rug was underfoot, and Jasper lolloped around, panting and peering out from under his disheveled white fringe. A wide doorway with a leaded transom window led into a larger space, also paneled, also with a rug. From there a staircase led up to a balustraded gallery. Though dazed by the opulence, Jamie hadn't missed the import of Alice's words. Sarah liked him. He longed to interrogate her about how exactly she knew Sarah liked him, and what form, exactly, Sarah's liking took.

From the center of the high, coffered ceiling dangled a cascade of prisms and bulbs. Paintings and drawings of all shapes and sizes crowded the walls, some in elaborate frames. Alice pressed a switch, and the chandelier flared to life. "Daddy likes art," she said.

"God," Jamie said, gazing around. "Seems like it."

Alice tittered. "Daddy likes God, too," she said, "so you'll want to watch what you say."

Jamie, thanks to Wallace and to the public library, knew a good amount about art, enough to recognize, among Mr. Fahey's eclectic collection, a Remington cavalry scene and an O'Keeffe iris. "You see this one?" Alice tapped the frame of a head-and-shoulders portrait of a woman against a dark background. "That's Mother. John Singer Sargent painted her. Do you know who that is?"

"Was." Jamie moved to get a better look. The painting was exquisite. "He's dead. That's your mother?"

Again she tittered. "Yes. You'll meet her."

The woman in the painting had the same small chin and long lashes as Sarah. Her eyebrows were raised and her lips parted as though she were about to offer a retort.

"Father has gobs more in storage, but honestly

once you've seen this room, you've seen the best of it. Patience is **not** his strong suit. He wants the good stuff to hit you right when you come through the door."

"I can't quite take it all in."

"You're here!" said a voice from above. Sarah came hurrying down the stairs. "Alice, why didn't you come get me?"

"I called you," Alice lied. "You must not have heard. He's just been here a few minutes. We were talking about portraits. Jamie has promised to draw mine, haven't you, Jamie?" She looped her arm through his.

"Don't let her boss you," Sarah said to Jamie. "Alice is the bossiest sister."

"I'd love to," he told Alice.

She released him. "Good. After you finish talking with Father, I'll sit for you."

Jamie nodded, then stopped. "Oh—I don't have my pencils."

"Then you'll have to come back," Alice said. "You should do one of Jasper as well." She seized the dog's mop of a face and said to him, "Don't you think so, Jasper? Haven't you always wanted to be a muse?"

"Father's waiting," said Sarah. She beckoned to Jamie. "Come on."

She led him deeper into the house. Everywhere were paintings and drawings, far more than he could take in. He found the house in general to be gloomy, cluttered, and close, with not enough windows. The density of artwork added to the oppressiveness, but Sarah seemed perfectly at ease, keeping up a narration as she walked. "This is the sitting room, and this is a room we only use for parties, that's the music room, that's the dining room. This clock is very old." They came to a dark, heavy door, and Sarah whispered, "Just be confident." She knocked with the back of one hand. In the dimness, as she listened and knocked again, Jamie saw her face in quarter profile, her jaw set with tension.

"Come in," commanded a booming voice.

Sarah pushed open the door, saying, "Daddy, this is Jamie, the Portraitist."

"The Portraitist!" repeated a man standing behind a desk. He was shorter than both Jamie and Sarah and very stout, as pink as a pencil eraser but much shinier, with a prodigious salt-and-pepper mustache. The room, as all the other rooms had been, was crowded with art. "Come in, Portraitist!" Sarah's father reached across his desk to shake hands. He gestured at the jumbled paper on its surface. "I never mean to work on the Sabbath, and then I always do. Hopefully God will forgive me."

"I'm sure he will, sir."

"Are you? That's reassuring." He looked searchingly up into Jamie's face. "Who taught you to draw, boy?"

"No one, really."

"But Sarah told me Wallace Graves is your uncle. He must have taught you."

Jamie started to say something agreeable, then stopped. Had Wallace taught him? Jamie couldn't remember any actual instruction, only scattered praise from long ago. All of the puzzling and experimenting, the criticism and despair, the leaps forward and moments of exultation—all of that had come from himself. But of course he **had** learned from watching Wallace. What would be simplest to say? "I suppose so."

"Do you paint?"

"Watercolors sometimes. I've never tried oils."

"It's my opinion that oils prove the artist," Mr. Fahey said. "You ought to enter the arena sooner rather than later. See what you're made of."

Sarah made a small sighing sound, the faintest of protests.

"I don't have anything against oils," Jamie said. "Just that they're expensive."

"I saw your picture of Sarah," Mr. Fahey said. "Impressive, although not everyone who can draw can paint." Getting up from his desk, he gestured to an unframed canvas propped facing the wall. "Let's have a look at this. I believe it's one of your uncle's." He picked up the painting and turned it around.

Homesickness punctured Jamie. There was the Rattlesnake, well upstream from Wallace's house but unmistakable, on a day bright with summer haze.

"Yes, sir," he said. He cleared his throat. "That's his." He leaned closer. Surrounded his whole life by Wallace's paintings, Jamie had ceased to notice them. He thought Wallace might have chosen a more interesting composition, but he had captured the **feeling** of the landscape, its balance of harshness and softness.

"Nice little scene." Mr. Fahey swung the painting around and held it at arm's length, studying it. "What's your uncle doing now?"

He drinks. He stews in his own grime. He scrapes together a few cents to lose at cards. "He still paints." A lie. "He teaches drawing and painting at the University of Montana, in Missoula." Another lie.

Mr. Fahey set down the canvas. "Stroke of luck to have an artist for an uncle, and one who took an interest in you. Not everyone gets that kind of help."

Jamie didn't know how to explain without appearing to argue or seeming ungrateful. He remembered he was supposed to seem confident. "True," he said. "Not everyone."

"Jamie lives in Missoula, too," Sarah said. "He's only here for the summer. He's staying with relatives."

"That so?"

Jamie stopped himself from glancing at Sarah, surprised at how easily she'd lied. "That's right. With cousins."

Mr. Fahey didn't appear overly interested in Jamie's relations. "Here's the thing. I didn't want Sarah to say anything until after I'd met you myself, but I have a job that needs doing, if you'd be interested in some extra employment. Are you?"

Hope strong enough to lift him like a wind. "Yes, sir."

"You don't even know what it is, but you know you're interested."

Jamie dipped his head. "I am, sir."

"Fair enough, hard times. Everyone's got to start somewhere. I started from nothing, myself." He cleared his throat. "What I need is for someone to help me catalog all this." He gestured at the walls, the patchwork of art. "Everything on the walls, everything in the attic, everything in the basement. It's a lot, and there's another storage room full at my office. Most of it's not labeled, to be honest. I have boxes of receipts and old auction catalogs and some of those might help you match things up. I'll warn you, it's a real mess." He gestured at his desk. "As you can see, I don't have a knack for organization. All I want's a big list, but it's still a task for Hercules. I just want to know what I have. Take stock. I don't care how you go about organizing things except someone from UW might come take a look, so keep out anything you come across you think might be worthwhile. Sarah's sister Nora is studying art history—I would have thought she might be interested in sorting through everything, but she was more interested in spending the summer in Europe. I'll pay you three dollars a day, five days a week. Nine to five. The cook will see you have lunch. How's that?"

"Sounds terrific, sir. Thank you."

Mr. Fahey waved them toward the door. "Go on, then. Don't look so happy. It's an impossible job."

"See you tomorrow, sir."

"No, you won't. I'll be at work. I'm leaving you in the clutches of the women." When Jamie had pulled open the door for Sarah, Mr. Fahey called, "Portraitist!"

Jamie turned.

The man was standing in front of his desk, hands in his pockets. "What do you think of my collection? It's something, isn't it?"

"It's magnificent," Jamie said truthfully.

"Magnificent." Mr. Fahey nodded. "That's right. Amazing what a little beef will buy." He grinned and waved them out again.

Slaughterhouses, Sarah explained as they went back through the house. Half a dozen of them. Cattle and hogs. Processing plants and tanneries, too, or shares of them. Places that made fertilizer and glue and candles and oils and cosmetics. The Depression had hit the business but not as hard as it might have. Her father sold a lot of things people needed, even if they were finding ways to need less of everything.

At the front door, she smiled more freely than before and told him how glad she was he'd taken the job. Alice came running downstairs to see him off, too, full of reminders to bring his drawing materials when he came back. And he promised and smiled and waved and made his way back past the topiaries to the street and then back to his boardinghouse, downhill and up again, the neighborhoods contracting around him into ordinariness and then squalor.

He thought that when he and Sarah had walked around the lake he **must** have conveyed his feelings about animals, the burden of his anguish for them. Even if he hadn't, he thought she ought to have intuited something. Or, really, he thought she ought to feel the same way he did.

Though he barely wanted to admit it, he'd already begun entertaining fantasies of finding a way to study at UW with Sarah, to become a real artist in Seattle, to be a young husband who came home to a pleasant, sunny house and kissed his wife and infant. The idea of a family of his own making had been more exotic and beguiling than anything he'd ever considered, and now . . . ? Tainted, ruined.

He wondered if some primal memory of the sinking of the **Josephina** had lodged in him and, over time, morphed into an outsize horror of fear and helplessness, of mass death. Though he didn't think his horror **could** be outsize, really. How could it ever be big enough? And yet it must be somehow disproportionate because most people seemed untroubled by the origins of the meat they ate, by the scrawny dogs everywhere, abandoned in hard times, likely to starve or be picked up by the dog-catcher and killed. Why couldn't he make peace? The world was not going to change. He would be happier if he could simply forget.

He skipped dinner and lay on his bed in the boardinghouse as evening purpled the window.

He loved Caleb, and Caleb killed animals. But hunting pained Jamie less than slaughter. Hunting was an intersection of two lives, not a corralling, an extermination.

But Sarah wasn't the one cutting throats. To condemn her would be unfair. He hated that her father would be paying him in blood money, but maybe there was some good in relieving such a man of a tiny bit of his surplus fortune. (A very tiny bit.) He would also promise himself to do something good with some of the money. To buy food for stray dogs. Yes, that was what he would do. And otherwise he would try to put the slaughterhouses out of his mind.

That he found himself enjoying his time at Hereford House was both a relief and reason for self-recrimination. First and foremost, there was Sarah, who appeared unexpectedly and irregularly, climbing up to the attic (he had chosen to begin in the attic) to help sift through dusty files, matching scribbled receipts to miscellaneous drawings and paintings. The infatuation he'd felt after their first walks had been deflated a bit by the mounting evidence that she saw nothing wrong with her father's business, but his attraction was undiminished. Not that she was flirtatious. She was sharp and attentive and meticulous. She seemed to relish setting things in order. He didn't dare try to kiss her.

Alice had been waiting for him that first Monday morning, determined he would not do anything before he'd drawn her portrait. "We'll go outside for the light," she'd announced.

He drew her sitting under a cherry tree behind the house, her arms wrapped around one knee, seeming to suppress a smile. As he was working, another tall female figure came striding across the lawn in a skirt and cardigan, Jasper lumbering in her wake.

"The Portraitist at work!" Mrs. Fahey said in a voice even lower and richer than Sarah's.

Jamie scrambled to his feet. She offered her hand. Sargent's portrait was apt, though she'd aged. Her hair was cut in a blunt bob, and her face was bare of makeup and full of amused intelligence.

"Let's see it," she said, holding a hand out for the drawing pad, which he had lifted, out of protective instinct, toward his chest. "Oh!" she said, when he handed it over. "But it's wonderful. I shouldn't be surprised. What you did of Sarah was marvelous, but this is . . . it's a whole scene. I'm going to have both of them framed."

"Don't you think he should do one of Jasper, Mother?" said Alice.

"Certainly. And one of Penelope and the baby." She gave the drawing pad back to Jamie. "Penelope is my eldest daughter. She has a new baby. I'd want you to draw my son and my other daughter, too, so I could have a complete set, but they're away."

"And you," said Alice, still under the tree.

"What about me?"

"He should draw you, too. See how it stacks up against the Sargent."

Jamie said, "I think the comparison would be depressing."

Mrs. Fahey raised an eyebrow. "For you? Or me?"

"Me!" he said. "Of course. I mean—I would be happy to try, if you want."

"Good, then," she said, amused. "So you shall."

July turned to August.

He made progress cataloging the art, but the job was too big for half a summer. Still, he persisted, sorting and describing as best he could. Examining so many drawings and paintings was an education. He looked carefully at each piece, considered what the artist had achieved versus what might have been intended. Much of the work seemed mediocre at best. ("My husband's greatest pleasure is in the hoarding of his treasures," Mrs. Fahey said one day. "He takes pleasure in their number and in their being **his**.") But the collection also included many fine pieces and more than a few extraordinary ones. As instructed, Jamie set aside any that struck a chord in him, including a set of a dozen unidentified small watercolors he found in a shallow box tied closed with ribbon. They were washes of color: gyres of gray and blue, or bands of brilliant orange and green, and though they could not be said to be clearly **of** anything, Jamie was certain their subject was the sea. Something illegible was scribbled on their backs—a signature, maybe. If the expert from UW came, Jamie almost hoped he would say the watercolors were junk because then he might be bold enough to ask if he could keep them.

In the evenings, on his way home, he bought cans of tongue or hash, loaves of day-old bread, whatever was cheap, and fed stray dogs. Sometimes he sketched them, a few quick lines. He hated when they snarled and snapped among themselves or when they followed him back to the boardinghouse.

If Mr. Fahey was not expected home early, Sarah might go for a walk with Jamie after he'd finished cataloging for the day. He'd finally gotten his nerve up to kiss her. The first time had been unexpectedly simple. She'd come with him to feed the strays. At their feet, a dog was devouring a mound of canned meat, and he had leaned forward and put his mouth on Sarah's. They'd both stood perfectly still, lips together, until Sarah pulled softly away. The next time, beside the waterfront, was not simple. Her long pliant body had bowed against his, and in his excitement he grasped her too roughly, startling her. With a little practice, though, they found an equilibrium that, while not quite satisfying, was sustainable enough. He could hold her in his arms if no one was around to see but not squeeze her too hard or push her against a wall, not feel her breasts. Sometimes, though, she forgot herself and pulled him closer, one of her long thighs sliding between his. This never lasted long. She would snap back to propriety and extricate herself, as disorientated as an awakened dreamer, her cheeks flushed.

"Tell me more about your adventures," she would say sometimes, and he told her about how he and Marian and Caleb had hitchhiked to Seeley Lake and then hiked the fifty miles back through the mountains, or how they'd once found a human skeleton in the woods with a hatchet lodged in its moss-speckled skull, or about the rail-yard bull smacking his shins. "I don't know if those are really adventures," he said.

"They are!" she exclaimed. "I'll never get to do anything exciting. I wish I could meet Marian and Caleb," she said. "And Wallace."

"Maybe you will someday."

A melancholy Madonna smile. "I don't think they'd be very impressed by me."

They would find her alien, daunting, prim. They wouldn't know how to be around her. It didn't matter. This—what was between him and Sarah—was his. "They don't know anyone like you."

"I don't know anyone like them. I wish I were more like them."

This was the moment to tell her everything he'd left out. Wallace's drinking. Barclay Macqueen. The creak of the porch's screen door in the night, when Caleb came for Marian. But instead he kissed her again.

When he could, he made drawings of her, sometimes from life, sometimes from memory. Some he gave to her, some he kept. "I love these because I love thinking about you looking at me," she said. "It's a very particular kind of vanity."

Occasionally, when Sarah and Alice were both out, Mrs. Fahey invited him for afternoon coffee in a small glassed-in conservatory that was her particular domain. To get to it, he passed through a parlor that also seemed to be her own. There was no art in these rooms. The walls of her parlor were clean and white, sparsely hung with photographs of her family. Her conservatory held potted ferns, a dog cushion, and a round marble table with wicker chairs where they sat. She asked him many of the same questions Sarah had about his life, but since he was not consumed with romantic anxiety and carnal longings, he could relax more into his account of himself, find opinions he hadn't quite known he possessed.

"I wish my sister were more ladylike," he surprised himself by saying one day.

Mrs. Fahey smiled with a deeper melancholy than Sarah's. "Why? Does she want that, too?"

"No, she doesn't," he said frankly. "But her life seems so much more difficult than it needs to be. If she had a girl's haircut and wore girls' clothes, and if she'd kept going to school and didn't care so much about airplanes, everything would be simpler." At Trout's funeral, when Barclay Macqueen had turned around to shake Jamie's hand, there had been something sneering and triumphant in his face, as though Jamie were a bested rival. **Peace be with you.**

"Yes," Mrs. Fahey agreed. "It probably would be."

"If she'd had a mother, would she have turned out this way? Do you think?"

"Maybe, maybe not. Mothers don't control everything, though sometimes we'd like to. I've learned—too slowly, but I have learned—that attempts to control others are likely to backfire. I worked for the passage of Prohibition because I earnestly believed women's lives would be better—easier, as you say—if their husbands couldn't go out and drink their paychecks away and come home and do the vile things drunk men sometimes do. But I was naïve. People's wishes for their own lives tend to outweigh others' ideas about how they should behave." She paused. "We must bend in the wind sometimes, Jamie. So much is beyond our control."

Jamie quashed a tremor of impatience that he couldn't explain things better, not to this woman sitting in her glass room, serene in her belief that his doting uncle had sent him to Seattle for a summer with his cousins. "Marian doesn't always see the problems she's creating for herself."

"Is it that you think if she were more ladylike you wouldn't have to worry about her?"

"I don't know."

She leaned forward. "Would you draw her for me? Your sister? I'd like to see what she looks like."

So he summoned Marian from a blank page. He forced himself to draw her as she was, with her cropped hair and her sharp, almost insolent gaze. As he drew, he felt a tug deep in his guts, like he'd swallowed a hook and the reel was back in Montana.

Mrs. Fahey looked at the drawing for a long time. "Yes, I see. She's formidable." She sighed and patted his forearm. "You've had to take care of each other more than most children and grow up quickly. It must have been very hard sometimes."

When he was safely in the attic, he sat on the floor and wept. He had not known how badly he had wanted someone to say exactly that.

During a spell of unusual heat in the third week of August, the art expert from UW came, a sprightly man in a bow tie who proceeded rapidly along Hereford House's walls, stooping one moment and stretching on tiptoe the next, peering through his spectacles as though his whole body were a kind of specially designed art-evaluating scope. From time to time he jotted in a notebook. Jamie followed along, offering what insight he could, all of which the expert greeted either with irritable **mm-hmm**s or silence.

Twice Jamie mentioned he had set aside some works that seemed noteworthy. "I doubt that was necessary," the man said, pulling a small nautical painting from the wall and turning it over.

"Mr. Fahey asked me to. So we could get your opinion."

"Oh, yes?" He hung the painting back on its nail. "What are your qualifications exactly?"

"I've been cataloging the work."

"Mm-hmm."

Mr. Fahey came home in midafternoon, when the two of them were surveying the music room. He pumped the expert's hand, boomed pleasantries at him, demanded to know what he thought. "Your honest opinion," he said.

"It's a very, very interesting collection," the expert said. "You have many first-rate pieces, as you know. The Sargent, for example. Truly remarkable." He took a handkerchief from his pocket and mopped his brow. The house's gloom made the heat especially stifling.

"My wife is the subject," Mr. Fahey said with pride.

"Is it really?" said the expert, even though Jamie had already told him. "Remarkable!"

"There's been talk of a museum," Mr. Fahey said. "The Fahey Museum. I like the sound of that, I have to say."

The expert swabbed his face again. "It's an intriguing idea. Perhaps—just as a preliminary impression—this collection might not be quite enough on its own, judging only what I've seen thus far, but certainly you've laid an excellent foundation." Delicately: "You do know they've begun building an art museum in Volunteer Park? To house the Fuller collection?"

Mr. Fahey's face clouded. "Of course I know," he said. "I can practically see it from my bedroom."

The expert winced but pressed ahead. "Have you considered perhaps joining forces?"

Mr. Fahey eyed him suspiciously. "I have."

The expert became conciliatory. "A first step,

I think, would be to have someone come in and start sorting through everything, cataloging it. I assume you have records of purchases? Attributions? Provenances?"

"That's what Jamie's been doing." Mr. Fahey fixed Jamie with a perplexed stare. "Didn't you tell him?"

"I'm sure this young man's been doing his best," the expert said, "but it's a job for someone with real expertise."

Mr. Fahey appeared embarrassed. "The boy's a gifted artist," he said. "I wanted to give him a helping hand. No harm in him rummaging through the lot."

"I sincerely hope not," the expert said primly.

Jamie's face flamed. The man hadn't even looked at his notes, his meticulous lists, his assembled clues and theories about what exactly Mr. Fahey had bought for himself. Certainly Jamie hadn't uncovered all the answers—that would be impossible—but he was confident he'd been useful. Nor had the expert deigned to look at the pieces he'd brought down from the attic and set aside; he **knew** those were worth at least a glance.

"Jamie," said Mr. Fahey, "go get one of your portraits to show him."

Now his humiliation would be compounded by being treated like a child, made to present his own work as though begging to be indulged with praise. Stiffly, he said, "I wouldn't want to impose."

"Go on now," Mr. Fahey said as though sending away a dog hovering too close to the dinner table.

Jamie trudged through the hot, dark house to Mrs. Fahey's parlor. The four portraits—Sarah's, Alice's, her own, and that of Penelope, the eldest sister, who had come over one afternoon to sit for him with her baby—were hanging, framed, in a row. He yanked down Alice's and trudged back, offered it with his head down.

The expert scrutinized the drawing, then peered at Jamie through his spectacles as though he were another artwork to be evaluated. "Who taught you to draw?"

"His uncle," said Mr. Fahey at the same time Jamie said, firmly, "No one."

"You said your uncle did," Mr. Fahey told Jamie. To the expert, he added, "His uncle is the painter Wallace Graves. I own a landscape of his, actually."

"I taught myself," Jamie said, digging his hands into his pockets.

"Mm-hmm," said the expert. He looked over the portrait again, then back at Jamie. "You said you'd selected some works you especially liked?"

There would be a celebratory dinner, and Jamie must stay. Mr. Fahey insisted; everyone insisted. The watercolor sketches he'd found in the ribbon-tied box, the washes of color that suggested the moods of the ocean, were by J. M. W. Turner. The expert was almost certain. They were valuable, important, **remarkable,** and might so easily have gone overlooked. For his part, Jamie was both vindicated and disappointed, as he had decided that if the expert would not look at the works he'd picked out, he was going to take the watercolors back to the boardinghouse that very night and then, soon enough, to Missoula. He still wished, just a little, that he had taken them when he first found them, told no one.

"Well done," Mr. Fahey had said to Jamie at least half a dozen times. "I knew I saw something in you."

Even with the windows open, the dining room was sweltering. Sweat dampened the women's temples. Mr. Fahey kept mopping his brow with his napkin. The second-eldest Fahey sister, Nora, the art history student, had just returned from Europe, and Penelope had come over with her husband and infant and nanny. There was talk that Jamie must draw Nora after dinner to complete the pantheon in Mrs. Fahey's parlor.

"Don't forget Daddy!" Alice said.

"I wouldn't dream of inflicting this mug on Jamie after such a parade of beauties," Mr. Fahey said. He was in high spirits, pinker and shinier than ever.

The first course was oysters, then cold consommé, then poached salmon.

Nora was full of observations about Europe.

"On the crossing there was always a breeze. One gets used to the cooling effect."

"**Does** one?" Alice asked, putting on a queenly accent and looking down her nose.

Jamie had eaten the oysters and, despite misgivings, the salmon, had vainly hoped by some miracle the meal would not involve beef. When the inevitable steak was placed in front of him, a thin, crimson liquid pooling around it, he looked surreptitiously for Jasper, but the dog must have been shut away somewhere.

"I'm interested in this young man's plan for the future," said the art expert, turning to him.

Everyone looked at Jamie. "I have another year of high school," he said, "and then I'll probably go to the University of Montana."

"To study art," said the expert.

"I'm not sure," Jamie said.

Mr. Fahey leaned back in his chair, chewing. "How is the art department at Montana?"

"I think it's good enough," Jamie said. "My uncle taught"—he caught himself—"teaches in it."

Mr. Fahey pushed more steak into his mouth, took a gulp of wine, and said, "I think you ought to come to Seattle. Either to UW or Cornish College. Talent like yours, you shouldn't be stuck in a backwater."

Jamie almost laughed at the idea that he could afford such a thing.

"Furthermore—" said Mr. Fahey

"Some would say Seattle is the definition of a backwater," Nora observed. "Compared to Europe."

"Nora," said Alice, "don't be stupid."

Sarah said, "It's snobbery, not stupidity."

"Furthermore," said Mr. Fahey again, raising his voice, "I would like to help you." The Fahey women looked at one another.

"I don't think I understand," Jamie said.

"I'm saying I'll pay for your schooling and expenses, boy! You'd continue working for me, of course, in one way or another. Maybe with the art, depending on how things shape up with this museum idea, or maybe with my business." He pointed his knife at Jamie. "I'm a self-made man myself." This in a tone of light interest, as though he had not already said so many times already. "I like to give others a leg up when I can."

Jamie, flabbergasted, didn't know what to say. He longed to accept, to fall back into the Faheys as though into a feather bed. If he did, incredible as it seemed, his vision of himself as a husband to Sarah, the father of her children, a prosperous citizen of a Pacific city, might plausibly come to pass. But ambivalence stopped him. There were the slaughterhouses, and, yes, he liked to draw, and over the summer he'd grown vain about his talent. But what if there was a latent Wallace in him? What if, by becoming an artist, he would create the right conditions for dissolution and anarchy to spread through him like a fungus?

He needed to think more, and not in this hot room, at this table full of Faheys and their plates of bleeding beef.

"You've left him speechless, Daddy," said Penelope.

Mr. Fahey said, "Finish up your steak, and we'll have some champagne to celebrate." Then he looked more closely at Jamie's plate. "Why, you've barely eaten anything. Are you ill, boy?"

Jamie glanced at Sarah, who looked back with perplexity. "Aren't you hungry?" she said.

It didn't matter, he realized, whether or not he wanted to be an artist. He said, "I don't eat meat."

"What?" Mr. Fahey appeared genuinely confounded.

"I don't eat meat."

"No **meat**?"

"No."

"Is it some kind of religious belief?"

"No, sir. I just can't abide the idea of it."

"I don't follow."

"You feel sorry for the poor animals!" Nora exclaimed. "That's it, isn't it?"

Mr. Fahey sat back. His face was turning burgundy. "You can't abide the idea of my business? The business that built this house? That bought this art? That's paid you all summer?"

"I couldn't accept your offer," Jamie said, "though I appreciate your generosity."

"You couldn't—" Mr. Fahey cut himself off with a small sputter. "The offer is rescinded. I couldn't trust a man who doesn't eat like one." He narrowed his eyes. "And you're not to hang around my daughter anymore. Don't think I don't see you trailing after her."

Desperately, Jamie searched Sarah's face for understanding, but he saw only confusion and worry. She looked at her mother, who gazed steadily back, gave the smallest of nods. Sarah gathered herself, said to her father, "He doesn't trail after me."

"You're not to see him anymore!"

Again she looked to her mother, but this time Mrs. Fahey was studying her plate. Tears overflowed onto Sarah's cheeks, but Jamie saw she would not go against her father.

"Son." Mr. Fahey was pointing a thick finger at him. "Son, God put animals on this earth for food. Animals kill and eat each other. We're animals, too. We're just smart enough to have figured out a better way to get meat than wandering around with bows and arrows. We've bred these animals to eat them. Cattle and pigs and chickens wouldn't **exist** if they weren't food." He opened his mouth, pointed to his canines. "These?" he said. "God gave us these to show us what He wants us to eat. And that is the steak on your plate!"

Jamie put his napkin on the table, rose from his chair. "Goodbye," he said. "Thank you."

As he walked down the hall, he could hear Mr. Fahey shouting after him that he was an apostate and a fairy and that he should get out, **get out** of his house.

He did not feed the dogs that night. He went to Union Station and bought a ticket on a night train to Spokane and then on to Missoula.

Lonely and righteous, Jamie went home and learned his sister was engaged to Barclay Macqueen.

Missoula
August 1931
Two weeks before Jamie came home

A pale evening sky, deep rivers of shadow between the mountains. Marian circled until the drivers switched on their headlights, landed on the strip of flat land they'd illuminated. While they were unloading the cases, Caleb came walking out of the forest, his rifle across his back. The drivers' hands went to their holsters.

"It's all right!" Marian cried. "He's my friend!" She jogged to meet Caleb, threw her arms around him in a way she would not have if they'd met in Missoula. Out here, there was a sense of occasion. "How did you find me?"

He was brown from the sun. His hair was braided down his back. "A little bird told me. How about a lift home?" Caleb had built himself a small cabin up the Rattlesnake from Wallace's house.

She glanced at the men, who were making no secret of watching them. "You won't be scared?"

"What's there to be scared of? Aren't you a good pilot?"

She'd been late arriving, and now they were late taking off. Darkness had fallen entirely by the time they reached Missoula, and the city's lights shone gold among the mountains.

After she'd put the plane to bed, Marian drove Caleb back through town, up the creek past Gilda's house, past Wallace's house. After the road had dwindled to a rutted track in the forest, he told her to stop where a trail led off through the trees. "Come have a drink," he said. "You saved me two days' walking."

The cabin was not far. As they walked in the dark, Marian said, "Why don't you get a car?"

"I don't want the responsibility. I don't really like ownership in general."

"Sometimes it's worth it on balance, isn't it?" she said. "Not that I have much experience."

"I'd rather keep things simple."

His cabin stood in a circular clearing and was small but expertly constructed, with tightly notched corners and each log hewn to sit flat on the next, smooth strips of mud daubing sealing the gaps. He took a key from his pocket.

"You lock your door," she observed.

"So?"

"So you want to keep owning some things, at least."

"Sure, but I resent the worry of it." He ushered her in, and she stood in darkness as he lit a kerosene lamp and then another, revealing a squatting black stove, a rocking chair, a cot, a bearskin on the floor, antlers on the walls. "Take off your boots, would you?"

The cabin's interior was perfectly, painstakingly tidy. The blanket on the cot was tucked smoothly around the thin mattress; another was folded across the foot. His few dishes were stacked on a shelf above the sink. He hung his rifle on a rack that held three others, their stocks and barrels gleaming.

"Did you cut the logs yourself?" she said.

He was pouring whiskey into tin mugs. "I did. But I bought milled lumber for the roof and rafters." Handing her a mug and indicating the rocking chair, he said, "Sit there." He busied himself lighting a fire in the stove. When he sat on the cot, their knees were almost touching.

"You keep your place very tidy."

"I had enough mess for a lifetime with Gilda."

"You were so savage when you were little. And now look at you—sweeping and folding. Everything in its proper place."

"Everything savage stays outside now. In its proper place."

"Do you have a girl, Caleb?"

"Can't I keep my cabin clean without you seeing a woman's touch?"

"It's not that. I've just wondered ever since we stopped . . ." She didn't need to finish the sentence. They'd never put a word to it, anyway. It had always been a kind of ellipsis.

He leaned back against the wall, his legs crossed. "There are girls," he said, "but there's no girl." He watched her. She saw a languid stirring of his old slyness. She thought he would make a joke or a proposition, but he said, "I've been on Barclay Macqueen's ranch before."

"Bannockburn."

Caleb nodded. "Some associates of his hired me for a hunt. We had permission. Nice country. The house is something."

"Good or bad?"

He shrugged. "Depends on your taste in houses."

"I've only seen it from the air. Even though I might—" She stopped.

He finished for her: "Go to live there."

She nodded. Her chest was tight. Why was she afraid? Caleb got up to pour more whiskey into her mug. He stood beside her, his hand on her nape. His touch was cool. She'd forgotten the coolness of him.

"Who cuts your hair now?"

"Someone who charges in money."

He tugged her out of the chair and onto the

floor with him, sideways into the triangular space between his legs, loose in his arms. For a long time, he held her in silence. He kissed her mouth, but the kiss was innocent, led no further. Everything that had ever happened with Caleb seemed innocent now, compared with Barclay. "Your heartbeat is coming through your whole body," he said.

"I'm telling it to stop."

"Not stop."

"To slow down. It's not listening."

"I could help you go away. There are places where he wouldn't find you."

She resented Barclay horribly; her gratitude to Barclay was bottomless. She wished she could vanish and never return; she couldn't bear leaving him. **Who are you?**

"The funny thing is I think I love Barclay. I've never admitted that before."

His cheek was against the top of her head. "You have a strange way of showing it."

She knew she should leave; she wished they could crawl into his cot together. "It's a strange kind of . . ." She trailed off. She could not say the word **love** again. "It's a strange thing."

Barclay knew she had flown a man from the mountain strip back to Missoula, and he knew that man was Caleb, and he knew she'd driven him to his cabin and stayed inside for three hours. "Three hours," he said. They were standing in the kitchen of the green-and-white house, the table between them. "Tell me, what could possibly have kept you busy for three hours?"

"If you sent a spy after me," she said, furious, "he probably looked through the window. So what did I do?"

"You screwed him."

His certainty drew her up short. "But I didn't."

"Don't lie." Black eyes, stark freckles.

"I'm not. You're lying. I know because I'm telling the truth."

A silent standoff, both incredulous.

"He's my friend," Marian said. "He's always been my friend. Am I not allowed to have friends?" Her voice rose. "Do you want me to be completely alone except for you?"

He sat down heavily, the anger going out of him. "Yes," he said. "If I'm being honest."

"You want to know what we did—we talked." She gathered herself, said as though making an accusation, "I told Caleb I loved you."

He looked up. "You did?"

"When did you start having me followed?"

"Say it again. Tell me what you told him."

He was radiating thrilled pleasure. She felt only hopelessness. "Not now."

"Tell me you love me."

Louder, she said, "When did you start having me followed?"

"After you flew to Vancouver. Only because I was so afraid of losing you."

Thank god Caleb had stopped their trysts when he had.

"I thought you would do something foolish and get yourself into another bad situation," Barclay said. "It was for your protection. I wasn't looking to trap you, only to keep you safe."

"We don't trust each other. We should admit it."

"I'll stop if we're married." Vehemently: "Because when we're married, I'll take your vows as your promise not to run away. Because I know you're honorable." He stood again, came around the table, and knelt at her feet. "Say it now. Please. Tell me what you told him. It should be between us, not you and him."

She did as he asked. As the words left her, they caused a strange sensation, as though a knife had been in her gut and pulling it out was both a relief and a new wound, a fatal breach. She had known she would have to admit, eventually, that she loved him, and now she had, and now she could let it be true. He pressed his face into her thighs. She touched his head. He looked up and said, "I love you so much, Marian, but I have to tell you something. And before I tell you, you have to know that I'm sorry. I wouldn't have done it if I'd known— I should have waited."

She was frozen. She was in the cockpit over the crevasse.

"There's something—I set something in motion when I was angry, but I can undo it." His eyes were full of tears. "Marian, I've done a terrible thing. But you have to understand—you made me wait too long."

The Cosmic Whoosh
of the Expanding Universe

Eleven

I'd once heard a costume designer say the best actresses didn't even look in the mirror; they **felt** a costume. At fittings for Marian, I kept my face turned away from my reflection as though it would turn me to stone. I walked around in a heavy coverall flight suit thing and sheepskin boots feeling as burdened and out of my element as an astronaut marooned on earth. On one wall, a patchwork of photos of female pilots and random era-appropriate people had been pinned up along with costume sketches and pretty much every photo of Marian in existence, and I wallowed slowly over to look.

I'd seen her wedding photo before, online, where she and the gangster Barclay Macqueen are standing outside a handsome courthouse, leaves blowing around their feet. Marian is holding her hat on her head and smiling wanly, as though at an unfunny joke. Her new husband looks elated.

Next to it was a printout of a portrait in charcoal I hadn't seen before. Marian was very young in it, almost but not quite a child, her hair cut very short, a look on her face like she was about to contradict whatever you'd just said. "What's this?" I asked.

The costume designer had followed me across the room and was fussing with a strap at my waist. "Her brother drew it. It's in a private collection somewhere. Isn't it lovely? So much personality." She was tugging me backward, turning me to face her assistants. They studied me.

"She looks like a flying squirrel," one said. He held up an arm and gestured to the space under it. "All webbed in here."

"It's authentic," the designer said defensively, "a real-deal Sidcot suit, but I think we can tailor it so her shape isn't quite so lost."

My resolve cracked. I glanced in the mirror. They'd already cut my hair down to a severe sort of pixie and bleached it. I was a small pale head atop a huge brown body, puffy and fungus-like.

"Don't worry," the designer said. "We'll make it more flattering."

"I don't care about that," I lied.

"I promise," she said, as though she hadn't heard. "You'll look great."

. . .

Siobhan called to say Redwood Feiffer wanted to have me over to his house for lunch. Always with the fucking lunches.

"Just me and him?" I considered informing her that I would not be giving this guy a blow job. My career was no longer a blow job–based barter economy.

"It's a little unusual, but I don't think he **knows** that. I think he's so rich he's used to hanging out with anyone he wants. You should think of it as a friendly thing. He seems like an okay guy." **He's the money,** her tone said.

Redwood's house was only two miles west of mine as the crow flies, though crow flight is a less than useless measurement in the hills, where the streets are as kinked and looped as Silly String. I left M.G. behind and drove myself, thinking it might be offensive to bring a bodyguard to lunch. I was twenty minutes late by the time I pressed the buzzer on Redwood's security box and followed the driveway's nautilus curve to a hunkered-down house that was all sharp edges and raw concrete, like the bunker of an impossibly chic warlord. Redwood was waiting on his Brutalist doorstep in Adidas sneakers and a rumpled tan linen suit over a T-shirt with the jacket sleeves rolled up.

"Buenos días!" he said as I walked toward

him. "Wow, I like your haircut. Très Marian." Confidently, he opened his arms for a hug. "What's the good word?" Just a moment too late, he saw my hesitation, my slight affront at his presumption, and switched smoothly to handshake mode.

"I never know how to answer that," I said, shaking hands. "Do you say fine? Like, the good word is **fine**?"

"Now that you mention it, I don't actually know. Maybe you just say a word you like." He was leading me into a gigantic room that was fully open to the outdoors on one side. I'd seen houses like this before. They're suspicious slit-eye pillboxes on one side and, on the other, nothing but openness and innocence, letting in the whole city-encrusted valley, the whole sky. Enormous sliding glass doors were recessed back into the walls so Redwood didn't have to deal with anything as gauche and disruptive as windows.

"**Tart,**" I said. "That can be my good word." Augustina had used it that morning to describe a certain PR person's tone, and I'd felt a little trill of pleasure.

"But which meaning?"

"All of them. That's why it's a good word. The meanings speak to each other."

"Ah! Yes. I get it. The tempting dessert, the seductive woman, the sharp, sour taste. Very nice."

"What's yours?"

He considered. "I'll go with **perchance.**"

"Why?"

"It's funny, and it expresses ambivalence, which is my go-to emotion. Either that or **mayhaps.**"

We walked through a room with low couches and a huge flat-screen, past a gleaming black grand piano, and out onto the patio. There were four chaises lined up next to a pool, and, beyond, the big flat circuit board of Los Angeles planing off into pale haze.

"Cool house," I said.

"Thanks. It's a rental while I decide if I want to move here. None of this stuff is mine." He gazed off at the indistinct horizon. "I know this is a really obvious observation, but I feel the need to make it anyway—the sprawl of this place is legit mind-blowing. Especially when you fly in. Do you look out the window on planes?"

"Sometimes."

"You can see the **most** amazing things. Like, once I was on a flight to Europe, and the pilot came on and said the northern lights were going **off** out the left side, and basically no one bothered to lift up their shade! There's something damning about that, how people didn't look."

"I've never seen them."

"But wouldn't you **look**? They're **wild.** Sheets of green, like you'd expect, but it's the scale that blew my mind, how they're moving crazy fast but somehow you can't even really see them moving. I read a poem once that described the aurora as the moon hanging up her silken laundry. And another that called it glowworm light. I like that."

His earnestness had me off-balance. Who talks about poems? I said, "I went in a glowworm cave once."

"What's a glowworm cave?"

"What it sounds like. A cave with glowworms living on the ceiling. It's pitch-dark, and the worms really look like stars, even though they're just larvae. The one I went in had water—maybe there has to be water, I'm not sure—and the worms were reflected, so you felt surrounded by all these little points of white light."

What even is **this?** Alexei had said while we floated through the cave. **Could we be dead? Would we even know?**

I don't think we'd know anything, I'd said. **In general.**

Yeah, he'd said, **it's just wishful thinking that life and death would be interchangeable. This is nice, though. It's very nice.**

The whole thing had been impossible from the beginning, of course, but I still felt a stupid sense of loss whenever I thought about him. Other people get to have infatuations that last long enough to become real love and then disappointment and boredom. I only got the cold, extraterrestrial luminescence of an afternoon and evening spent staring into someone's face and saying, **Yes,** exactly, **I know** exactly **what you mean.**

"I'd like to see that someday," Redwood said about the glowworms. "Here—come into the kitchen. I have a couple more things to do and then we can eat."

"You cooked?"

"It's a salad. I assembled."

The kitchen's big sliding doors were open to the patio, and he'd set two places at a table under a pergola grown over with wisteria. While he whisked vinaigrette, he said, "Sorry, I'm realizing now that I didn't really think through how much like a date this would feel. I hope it's not awkward for you. I just wanted a chance to talk without any minders around."

"Will it feel more or less like a date if we have a glass of wine?" I said.

"Who cares?" He opened the refrigerator, its stainless steel door as large and heavy as a bank vault's, and retrieved a bottle, poured two glasses. His hands were unexpectedly elegant, his fingers long and deft. We clinked. "Cheers. You read Marian's book, right? Don't break my heart and tell me you only read the script."

"Of course I read it," I said, as though I would ever think of not reading the book, as though I'd read all the **Archangel** books and not, as was the truth, only the first one. "I'd actually read it before, as a kid, basically by accident." I realized I was wading into a conversation about my parents, so I said, "I read your mom's book, too."

"What'd you think?" Before I could answer with some vague flattery, he said, "I know it's not the best thing ever written. I thought I should say that. I didn't want you to think I thought it was some masterpiece."

"It's good," I said.

"**So** noncommittal. But what?"

I looked at him over the rim of my glass. "But nothing."

"Come on. Say it. I'm not defensive about her book. She is, fair warning, but I'm not."

I suspected he was setting a trap, but I still answered. I said I thought the voice of the book, Marian's voice, the **I** his mother had given her, didn't line up with the voice in the actual book Marian had written, as herself, for real.

All I knew, Carol Feiffer had written, as Marian, **all I'd ever known, was that I belonged to the sky.**

All I knew, she'd written in the next chapter, **all I'd ever known, was that no man would ever own me.**

In her journal, in what's now Namibia, Marian had written: **I'd like to think I will remember this particular moon, seen from the particular angle of this balcony on this night, but if I forget, I will never know that I've forgotten, as is the**

nature of forgetting. I've forgotten so much—
almost all I've seen. Experience washes over us in
great waves. Memory is a drop caught in a flask,
concentrated and briny, nothing like the fresh
abundance from which it came.

I told Redwood I thought Carol had missed the
point of Marian a little bit. I said the book felt
wishful, like it was trying to force Marian to be
something—someone—more familiar and reassuring than she actually was.

Redwood nodded almost sorrowfully and said,
yes, he knew what I meant. "It's trying to bend
Marian to make her more—I hate this word—
relatable, but in the end it distorts her."

"Exactly," I said. More than once, while reading
Carol's book, I'd thought of the fan fiction Oliver
and I had read about ourselves, the dollhouse feeling of it, the author gripping us so tightly we might
have snapped in half. **I live you so much.**

Redwood blew out a long breath. "My mother
has strong impulses toward tidiness. She's not religious, but she still thinks everything happens for
a reason. In the middle of a nuclear war, she'd be
the one saying everything was going to be fine, and
it's nice she's an optimist but annoying she's not
more of a realist. I'm not sure she actually remembers anymore what parts of the book she invented.
Anyway, I made a decision to be purely supportive. Grab the wine, would you?" He picked up the
salad. I followed him outside.

"It sounds like you guys are close."

"She's my non-evil parent. She and my dad got divorced when I was six, and we were always kind of a team. He's dead now."

"I'm sorry." We sat. He'd put out cloth napkins, a bowl of flaky salt with a little spoon in it, a carafe of ice water.

"It's okay. I hated him, insofar as anyone actually manages to hate a parent."

"I'm still sorry."

"Thanks. I hate him less now that I don't have to interact with him."

"That sounds complicated."

"I don't know. Sometimes things are simple." Redwood told me that his father had been chief counsel for a chemical company that was an off-shoot of Liberty Oil and had spent his days fighting lawsuits brought by tumor-ridden plant workers, towns with contaminated groundwater, chemists whose discoveries had been stolen, environmental groups concerned about air and water and frogs and birds. Then, in one of those instances of random, abrupt mortality that create the illusion of cosmic justice, he'd dropped dead of a brain aneurysm at sixty-four.

"My parents died when I was two," I said. "Small-plane crash."

"I know. Google."

"Right."

"I'm sorry, too."

"It's okay. I didn't know them."

"That's what I'm sorry for."

"We're getting right into the dead-parents convo. Wow."

He smiled, chewing, a little squinty, and there was something about the way he was looking at me, something skeptical and amused, that made me think he might not be as much of a dupe as we all thought. He said, "By dessert we'll have worked around to small talk. Hey, was it hard cutting off all your hair?"

I'd stared into the mirror at the salon like an arsonist watching a house burn down. I ran a hand over my head. "It was a relief. I feel lighter."

"Maybe I should cut mine."

I tilted my head and studied him. "Not yet," I said. He smiled. I said, "So, if you're—perchance—sort of ambivalent about your mom's book, why didn't you just commission the Day brothers to adapt Marian's?"

He made a face. "I mean, all things being equal, I would have, but I didn't want to hurt my mom's feelings." Marian was a shared obsession of theirs, he said. Carol had read Marian's book aloud to him when he was a child. His father had given her the book when they were dating, and Redwood thought she might have married him partly because of it, because she fell in love with the idea of Matilda Feiffer and the family connection, the family legend. "I think she wanted to be part of the story," he said. "Like of the **Josephina Eterna** and Marian and all the titans-of-industry stuff. But that story's over, so she just ended up in a really different, really not great one."

He said the Day brothers had surprised him by being unexpectedly fired up about his mother's book. All the overwrought conjecture gave them something to work with, tonally. Redwood said he'd imagined a more conceptual film, something about the ambiguity of disappearance, maybe like a spiritual/metaphysical Terrence Malick take (of course he had), but what the Days had written would be cool and high-concept in a different way. Like a tiny bit camp.

"Right," I said. "Hundred percent." And I needed to believe him, even though what he was describing wasn't quite what I'd imagined.

We worked on our salads.

He said, "How does the process work, figuring out how to play a part?"

I wanted to say that I just put the plastic pony in the plastic stable and smiled the way they told me to. But I said, "I imagine myself as someone else. That's pretty much it."

"I asked Sir Hugo the same question, and he talked for an hour."

Fucking Hugo, so sure people would want to listen to him talk. Of course, people **did** want to listen to him talk, to that voice, all smoke and whiskey and the north wind. Just try to find a nature documentary Hugo hasn't narrated. Just try to find an animated villain he hasn't voiced.

"I'll sound ridiculous if I try to explain it," I said.

"Like me with the northern lights."

"Like me with the stupid glowworms."

He pinged his glass lightly against mine. "To mystery. May we not ruin it."

Twelve

After lunch, Redwood and I moved to the chaises by his pool, kept going with the wine, gossiped about people in Hollywood, trotted out our best anecdotes, ventured small confidences. The pool tiles were tiny and square and cobalt blue, and the water was perfectly smooth, dense-looking like gelatin.

I didn't feel the way with Redwood I'd felt with Alexei, but I felt something, some zing or zip. Was the lack of wormlight reason enough **not** to embark on something? What if I never had the wormlight ever again? I didn't think the answer was becoming a nun, married to the memory of a brief affair with a married dude. Was it stupid to sleep with The Money? Was it stupid not to?

Maybe I wanted him to kiss me just so I could confirm he wanted to. Maybe I wanted him to fall in love with me so I could decide whether or not I wanted to be in love with him. You get used to people falling in love with the idea of being with you. You think you should always have their feelings in hand like a down payment.

"How are things with Oliver?" he asked from behind his sunglasses.

"I haven't heard from him."

"Nothing."

"Nada."

"And how do you feel about that?"

"I guess I'm surprised he could walk away without needing to yell at me. Most people want you to witness how much you've hurt them, but not him, apparently. I don't know if that means I didn't really hurt him or that he has more dignity than I thought." I made my face a study in neutrality. "And you? Anyone special?"

"No one at all."

When I'd googled Redwood, I'd clicked through watermarked society shots of him with an array of beautiful, serious-seeming women. "I'm not sure I believe you."

"It's the truth."

A pause. I said, "I have a question."

"Shoot."

"Why do you have a grand piano?"

"It came with the house, but I do play. The piano is part of the reason I picked this place."

"Will you play for me?"

"Yes."

"Most people at least pretend to be reluctant."

"I like to show off. But stay out here."

I don't know what he played. It was slow and sad. The notes drifted out the open mouth of his bunker house, settled on my skin. I looked over the valley through the sound as though through mist. Then he stopped, and I was myself again.

"Could have been worse," I told him, but he heard what I was really saying.

"It's my party trick."

I thought of Jones Cohen removing my earring with his tongue, diamonds hanging from his lips.

In the evening, pink light submerged the city. I said I wanted to swim, thinking of skinny-dipping, but Redwood went into the house and came back with a one-piece bathing suit for me that smelled faintly of chlorine. I didn't ask whose it was. The cool water felt sharp and shivery on my sunburned skin. I leaned back against the infinity edge, and Redwood waded toward me, rosy light reflected in the droplets on his beard. I thought he was going to kiss me, but he just leaned against the edge, too, facing the other way, looking out.

After dark, when the city was lit up orange as a flat field of poppies and we were back on the chaises, wrapped in towels, he asked if I felt like eating some 'shrooms.

I said sure.

He went inside and came out with a foil-wrapped bar of chocolate.

"Sir Hugo's boyfriend gave this to me. I have no idea how strong it is."

"If it's from Rudy, probably really strong."

We each ate a square.

Redwood got to his feet. "I'm going to turn off those lights."

He went inside. The lights in the pool went off, and then the indoor lights. Piano music emanated from the house again, something dissonant and tattered-sounding, full of holes and gaps. I didn't know if it was supposed to sound that way or if this was now a song in the key of 'shroom. The mauve light of the city pulsed in the sky and on the pool's surface. The music started to draw together, to become something that made sense, and I felt like I could pull it toward me, shape it into a mass I would hurl out over the valley like a storm.

Marian had written: **The world unfurls and unfurls, and there is always more. A line, a circle, is insufficient. I look forward, and there is the horizon. I look back. Horizon. What's past is lost. I am already lost to my future.**

Listening to Redwood play, I thought about how the medium of music is time, how if time stopped, a painting would exist unchanged but music would vanish, like a wave without an ocean. I wanted to tell him this, but when he came back, I got distracted by how his aura was gray and wispy like smoke. "I can see your aura," I said.

"What does it look like?"

"Like smoke."

The city sparkled and revolved like a galaxy.

They call it the City of Angels, he said, but the name actually just means The Angels. And, like, **what** angels?

All of them, I said. I guess.

It's really exciting, he said. We're making something out of nothing.

I thought he was talking about us. I wanted to say, that's what all relationships are, but then he said, well, not nothing. Marian was real, obviously, but people's lives don't get preserved like fossils. The best you can hope for is that time will have hardened around someone's memory, preserving a void in their shape.

Or he said something like that, and I realized he was talking about the movie, not us.

You might find out some things, he said, but it'll never be enough, never be anything like the Whole Truth. You're better off just deciding what kind of story you want to tell and telling it.

I think that's sort of what he said.

I said, But where do we begin? Where's the beginning?

. . .

He forgot to answer, or maybe I'd only asked in-side my head, and for some unmeasurable period of time we sat there looking at the view, think-ing about whatever, and then he was like, what **is** this place?

It's The Angels, I told him.

I know, he said, but what **is** it?

I could hear wind chimes coming from a neigh-bor's house, so I was like, it's wind chimes.

What else?

A helicopter went blinking by.

It's helicopters.

What else?

It's wind chimes and helicopters, I said. And it's muscle cars and leaf blowers and trash trucks pick-ing up everyone's bins and tossing them back like tequila shots. It's coyotes yipping like delinquents who've just left lit firecrackers in a mailbox, and it's mourning doves sitting on power lines practic-ing the same sad four-note riff. It's the thrum of hummingbird wings and the silent gliding gyres of vultures and the long-legged stepping of white egrets through shallow green water in the concrete channel that's the river. It's dance music pound-ing in a dark room full of people pedaling bicycles going nowhere. It's gongs and oms and whale songs soothing in the dim inner sancta of spas. It's a Norteño song bouncing out of a passing El Camino and schoolkids singing **o beautiful for spacious skies** in a classroom with the windows open and the rasp of a beat from somebody's earbuds you pass on the sidewalk. It's pit bulls barking through chain-link and Chihuahuas yapping behind screen doors and poodles snoozing on terra-cotta tiles. It's blenders and grinders and juicers and hissing steel espresso machines the size of submarines and waiters who talk too much—**Any special plans for the weekend? Do anything special over the weekend?**—and water, so precious, splashing into fountains and pools and hot tubs and tall glasses on shaded patios, burbling from hoses and geysering from broken pipes. And underneath, there's the hum of traffic, always there, like the ocean that lives in seashells, like the cosmic whoosh of the expanding universe.

At least that's what I tried to tell him. I don't know what I actually said.

Then he said something about how L.A. is dust and exhaust and the hot, dry wind that sets your nerves on edge and pushes fire up the hillsides in ragged lines like tears in the paper that separates us from hell, and it's towering clouds of smoke, and it's sunshine that won't let up and cool ocean fog that gets unrolled at night over the whole basin like a clean white hospital sheet and peeled back again in the morning. It's a crescent moon in a sky bruised green after the sunset has beaten the shit out of it. It's a lazy hammock moon rising over power lines, over the skeletal silhouettes of pylons, over shaggy cypress trees and the spiky black lionfish shapes of palm-tree crowns on too-skinny trunks. It's the Big One that's coming to turn the city to rubble and set the rubble on fire but not today, hopefully not today. It's the obviousness of pointing out that the freeway looks like a ruby bracelet stretched alongside a diamond one, looks like a river of lava flowing counter to a river of champagne bubbles. People talk about the sprawl, and, yeah, the city is a drunk, laughing bitch sprawled across the flats in a spangled dress, legs kicked up the canyons, skirt spread over the hills, and she's shimmering, vibrating, ticklish with light. Don't buy a star map. Don't go driving around gawking because you're already there, man. You're in it. It's **all** one big map of the stars.

At least that's what I heard him saying.

And I was like, you know what? It's mostly just houses. And when you think about houses, really think, aren't they **so weird**? They're boxes where we keep ourselves and our stuff, boxes shaped like Tudor manors and chic cement warlord bunkers like this one and glassy mod spaceships and geodesic domes and sleek vitrines. L.A. is mysterious crumbling old hilltop piles, and it's haciendas wrapped in bougainvillea and Craftsman bungalows neat as a pin and little flat-roofed adobe things with bars on the windows, and it's surf shacks and drug shacks and grumpy-old-man-no-solicitors shacks and patchouli shacks strung with prayer flags, windows glowing red through printed Indian cotton as though inside is the beating heart of everything. It's the tents of the homeless crowded under an overpass; it's the spherical mud nests of swallows high up under an overpass; it's vines hanging from an overpass like a beaded curtain. It's trash blowing around in the hot, dry wind, nesting in ice plant by the freeway. It's the teasing, skipping, arcing fan dance of lawn sprinklers. It's the snip snip of pruning shears and the plunk of lemons falling from laden branches to split open and rot on the sidewalk under hovering bees, and it's the placid blue gliding pool net maneuvered by a gardener in a broad straw hat, graceful as a gondolier.

It's grass dying of thirst and tall berms of oleander running down the middle of the freeway, blooming and poisonous and hardy as fuck, dividing northbound from southbound, lava from champagne, and it's cacti and yuccas and aloes and agaves and water-hoarding succulents with names like blue chalk fingers and blue horizon and queen of the night and burro's tail and purple emperor and firesticks and cobweb houseleek and zebra haworthia and campfire jade and ghost plant and flamingo glow and string of pearls and painted lady. I want Redwood to know all this. (Seriously, though, he said again, like **all** the angels?) I want him to know that L.A. is a desert wind blowing through the garden of paradise. I need him to understand that I am a purple emperor, and I am a painted lady, and it is: all. so. succulent.

I told him, and he said yes. Yes, exactly. And I thought I saw a cold point of light, like a star but not a star, coming from him, coming from nowhere.

Marriage

~

North Atlantic
October 1931
Two months after Jamie came home
  from Seattle

arian Macqueen, seventeen years old and newly married, stood at the stern of an ocean liner, the chill of the railing seeping through her gloves as light drained from the murky sky. Barclay was bringing her to Scotland for a honeymoon. She'd been told she would meet his father's people and his acquaintances from school and see castles and highlands. They'd gone by train from Missoula to New York City. "I don't know what you're looking at," Barclay had said somewhere in the plains while Marian stared hungrily out the window. "There's nothing out there."

The gust of the train washed through golden

prairie grass, tossed blackbirds into flight. "I want to see it anyway," she said.

After a week in New York, they had boarded this ship (Cunard, not L&O) bound for Liverpool, from where they would take another train north. The first three days had been stormy enough that the decks were closed to passengers except for the glassed-in parts of the promenade, and Marian had roamed impatiently, peering out the rain-streaked windows at the shifting, whitecapped water. Barclay was seasick, but she was untouched. Quickly she'd developed the knack for inclining her body with the roll of the ship, penduluming from side to side as she walked down the corridors. Other passengers staggered drunkenly or clung to the railings while she only grazed her fingertips along the walls.

"Very good, madam!" said a passing steward. "You have your sea legs."

She imagined her father would be proud to see how unaffected she was. She imagined explaining to Addison that she was accustomed to motion, describing her aerobatics, how the plane felt like an extension of her own body, except **more** responsive, **more** coordinated than her limbs ever would be. She could spin and loop and always know exactly where she was. He would be proud of that, too, she thought. An undertow of self-pity caught her. It would be nice if **somebody** were proud of her. Wallace wasn't capable. She and Jamie were barely speaking, and who could ever tell what

Caleb thought. Barclay was proud of having married her, but he saw her flying as a rival.

On deck, damp blew around her, scouring her cheeks. As best she could figure, at some point during this night they would pass not far from where the **Josephina** had gone down, where she, Marian, had been set on a course that had taken turn after turn until returning her to this patch of ocean as a rich man's bride, the wife of a criminal.

She was wearing clothes selected for her by women at Henri Bendel in New York to replace the clothes that, after their engagement, had been selected for her by women at the Missoula Mercantile to replace her shirts and trousers: a silk dress and stockings, T-strap shoes, onyx-and-diamond danglers clamped to her ears, a rope of pearls slung twice around her neck, a mink coat and a navy cloche. She had three trunks full of such things. Barclay had insisted on all of it. The responsibility of owning so many fine and delicate possessions, so many sparkling bits and bobs that served no real purpose but must not be forgotten or lost or broken, worked on her like a kind of drag, slowing her. She was unused to shoes that should not be gotten wet and gossamer fabrics that snagged or stretched unless she remembered to move cautiously at all times. If the three trunks had gone up in a bonfire, she would have felt only relief, but since Barclay knew far more about how women should look than she did, she deferred.

Her hair had been cut in the Plaza Hotel salon by a woman whose own hair was a miracle of sharp angles and avian sleekness, like Mercury's helmet. "It's so short already I don't know if I can do much with it," the woman had said, fingering Marian's pale crop, but somehow she had snipped it into something that might be taken as daring and gamine.

Another woman had taught her how to make up her face, sold her an assortment of mirrored compacts and a fistful of brushes and pencils. Her skin had been powdered and rouged until her freckles vanished; her eyes were ringed in black, her lips painted red. When she caught sight of her reflection, she had the same uncanny feeling she'd had at Miss Dolly's, of glimpsing a stranger who turned out to be herself.

What would have happened if, when they'd first met, Barclay had simply set his mind on seducing her? She would have gone willingly enough. Why all the fuss? He'd needed to break the feral pull between them, tame and subdue it. Since the wedding, though, she had sensed some buried, unacknowledgeable regret in him. He could neither tolerate wildness nor reconcile himself to its loss.

In the salon, a girl getting her hair set had told Marian about a party she was going to—"Well, it's the kind of party that happens every night"—with her brother and his friends in midtown. In a certain alley, she explained, there was a certain steel door that was plain except for a small plaque that read

NO ENTRY. "That's what they call the club, see? No Entry. So it has a sign out front after all. Inside it's classy as anything—you just need to say the password. Even now there's always a big cheery crowd. And there's a full band playing, and dancing and cocktails and all of it. I'll give you the address. The password this week"—she lowered her voice—"is 'rodent.' Don't ask me why, and don't worry, there aren't any. I'm telling you honestly, it's as swank a place as you've ever been."

Marian did not let on that, indeed, such a place was guaranteed to be far more swank than anywhere she had ever been.

"I like your dress," the girl added. "Where are you from?"

"I was born in New York," Marian said.

"Were you?" The other's round, benign face was full of interest. For a terrible moment, Marian thought the girl was about to unleash a cascade of follow-up questions. All she knew was the address of the house in which she had been born, given to her by Wallace. Barclay had promised they would go by it in a taxi if there was time. But the girl only said, in a confiding voice, "Lucky you. I'm from Pittsburgh. Could you tell?"

"No," said Marian.

Over dinner she suggested to Barclay they might investigate No Entry, just to see what it was like.

"Those places are all the same. Lots of talk, lots of drinking."

She picked at a piece of fish. "It might be nice to hear some music."

"There's not much to do in those places for us," Barclay said, "since we don't drink."

That Marian would turn teetotaler after their marriage was a decision he'd made without consulting her, a rule she'd awoken to find hammered into place. She would have liked to try a cocktail in a jazz club but didn't wish to argue. She hadn't anticipated how much of her behavior after marriage would be motivated by a wish not to argue.

The night she'd gone to Caleb's cabin and then to the green-and-white house, after she'd told Barclay she loved him, he'd confessed he had been carefully and quietly buying up Wallace's debts, consolidating them. He'd grown tired of waiting for her, had been worn down by the prolonged uncertainty. He'd been maddened by jealousy when he learned she'd gone to Caleb's cabin, he said. He told her he felt nothing but disgust for Wallace, for all debtors; he wished someone had punished his own father for his waste and foolishness. He believed he was serving justice when he sent his emissaries (his goons, Marian thought) to inform Wallace of what had come due. A huge sum, unpayable. Despair in a number.

I've done a terrible thing, Barclay had said. **But you made me wait too long.**

Seeing his confession detonate in her, he had become frantic, told her he could undo it. She must forgive him, she must forget he'd tried to ransom her uncle because everything was fine, he would make everything fine always. Wallace's debts were forgotten! Forgiven! Pretend this never happened! Please!

She had bolted from the green-and-white house.

At Wallace's, she had eased in through the dark kitchen, shushing the dogs. She was suddenly angry at Jamie for being off on his summer adventure, leaving her alone with this mess, even if she bore more than a little responsibility for it. Though the house was silent, she'd sensed Wallace's presence somewhere, a cloud of suffering. She passed through the sitting room, turning on lamps, calling softly for her uncle until she found him upstairs in his dark studio, sitting in his armchair with a pistol on the small round table beside him. When she appeared in the doorway, he snatched up the gun and brandished it wildly, like a man trying to take aim at a bee. "Don't come in here!" he cried.

Light fell into the room from the hall, illuminating his gaunt praying mantis figure, his ragged bathrobe, his bright, frantic eyes. A mostly empty bottle stood beside the chair. She'd expected a scene like this, though not the gun, which she hadn't known he owned. "It's all right, Wallace," she said. "Everything's fixed now. What the men told you isn't true. You don't need to worry."

"You don't understand." His voice cracked. "It's too much. It's impossible." He pressed the muzzle of the pistol to his temple and began gasping for breath like a drowning man.

"Wallace," Marian said. "Listen to me. Your debts are paid off. They're gone. You don't have to worry about them anymore. I've fixed it."

He didn't seem to hear. He'd stopped gasping, maybe stopped breathing altogether. His eyes were closed. His lips were moving soundlessly.

"Wallace," she said. "Wallace. I'm paying them off. I've paid them off."

He opened his eyes, seemed to focus on her.

"They're gone," she said. "Wiped clean."

"All of them?"

"Yes, all of them. Everything."

His arm slackened, fell into his lap. He didn't seem to be paying attention to the weapon still in his hand. "How?"

"Someone helped me. Put that aside now."

He set the gun on the table and curled sideways in the chair, a hand over his eyes. "Who?"

She moved closer, took the gun. "Barclay."

He nodded. Tears caught in his beard. The thought came to her that if he had killed himself, she would have been free.

She didn't know if he could think clearly enough to realize that Barclay had also been the one to call in his debts in the first place.

Barclay came looking for her later that night, found her in the cottage. She told him she couldn't marry a man who would do such a thing. She couldn't love such a man. She'd been about to come to him freely, but now she could not, could **never** feel anything for him. All she asked for was time to pay him back. She didn't care if it took the rest of her life.

He had tried to embrace her, had begged, claimed madness, blamed her for the madness. When she would not yield, he'd finally said, coldly, "What you don't understand is that I've bought your uncle and he isn't for sale. Not to you or anyone. It's done."

In the Plaza dining room, Barclay said, "I wouldn't have thought a nightclub would be your idea of a good time, the way you talk about wanting to see empty, unspoiled places."

"I don't know what all I like," she said. "I've never been anywhere."

In the morning, they took a taxi to the house where she'd been born, in a neighborhood that seemed quiet, a little grimy. The house's flat brick face triggered no emotion in her, certainly no epiphany. A gaunt man in a cap and overcoat was sitting on the stoop next door. When Marian called to him, he hurried over, cap in hand, filling the window with his thin face and eager eyes. "Do you know who lives in this house?" she asked.

"It's a boardinghouse, ma'am. Nice enough if you can afford it. Not for me. I can't even afford lunch, can I?"

Marian started to apologize, but Barclay was

already reaching across, thrusting a coin at the man. "Let's go," he said to the driver. Marian looked out the back window at the receding brick house, the tall figure flipping the coin in one hand.

Since the ship hadn't been at capacity to begin with and most people chose (or were obligated) to lie low through the storm, Marian found herself in splendid isolation. In the mornings, she might drink coffee under the amber glass skylights of one lounge, and later she might read a book amid the Chinoiserie latticework of another. When a waiter offered her champagne—"Complimentary, madam"—she accepted, and then she ordered another glass and perhaps a third, counting on Barclay to be too wretched to notice her flouting of his ban on drinking. The ship pressed up from below, dropped abruptly away. Crashing sounds came at random intervals, and at times the long steel body corkscrewed or juddered violently as though passing over a washboard road. In the nights, Barclay groaned and cursed while Marian dropped effortlessly into oblivion. In the mornings, Barclay made it clear he regarded her peaceful slumber as selfish and disloyal.

"Better stay here and get some more rest, then," she said, and went off to her coffee, her book.

By the fourth morning, the sea had mostly settled, though the clouds had not lifted. In the afternoon, she found a seat at a small table in the ladies' lounge to avoid Barclay, who had mostly recovered from his seasickness but not his wounded pride. She had a pen and several sheets of the ship's stationery and was planning to write to Jamie. **Dear Jamie,** she wrote and stopped. She'd never written him a letter before. There had never been any need.

When he'd finally come back to Missoula, he'd seemed older, melancholy about something but also more assured, more firmly himself. He appeared at the airfield one day in late August, fresh off the train. As she drove them home, he told her he'd gone to Seattle, drawn portraits in parks, found a job with a rich family. "I met a girl," he said. "It was her family."

"Oh? And?"

"It turned out we didn't understand each other."

"In what way?"

"We were just too different. It doesn't matter— maybe it was only puppy love."

She had smiled grimly. He didn't know about her betrothal. "I'm glad you're back."

At the house, Wallace had been sitting on the porch, wrapped in a blanket. At first Jamie was occupied in greeting the dogs, but Marian saw his shock when Wallace rose and came unsteadily toward him.

"Are you ill, Wallace? You're too thin."

"I am ill," Wallace said. "But it's been my own

making. Too much drink for too long, Jamie. I've made a mess of things, but Marian and Mr. Macqueen have found a doctor who will help me. I'm going to Denver soon to stay with him."

Jamie stiffened. "What does Barclay Macqueen have to do with it?"

To Marian, Wallace said, "You haven't told him."

"Told me what?"

Marian couldn't summon the words.

"Your sister is getting married," Wallace said.

Jamie looked at Marian. "To Barclay Macqueen?"

She lifted her chin. "That's right."

"Why? What did he **buy** for you?"

She had turned and gone into the cottage, slamming the door.

Some time later, Jamie knocked. "Do you have anything to drink in here?" he asked.

"Whiskey or gin?"

"Whiskey."

She took a bottle from a cupboard, poured two glasses.

"The real stuff," he observed. "Not easy to come by."

"I've been flying to Canada for Barclay."

"Glad he's willing to let you get arrested."

"He'd rather I didn't fly at all."

"Why did he buy you an airplane, then?"

"Because he knew I wanted one."

They sat, Jamie in the armchair and Marian on

the bed. Jamie said, "Wallace told me Barclay paid off his debts. Is that why you're marrying him?"

Marian had expected the question, but still it wearied her. What could she say? That she had been outmaneuvered into a state of exhaustion. That Barclay was more determined to marry her than she was to avoid marrying him. That there was nothing to do now but go forward. "Not entirely," she said.

"Marian." He leaned forward, elbows on his knees, and peered at her searchingly. "No amount of money is worth marrying a man like him. We'll find another way. There has to be one."

Looking at Jamie was like seeing a vision of herself as a man, full of certainty that things could be set right, full of faith that new possibilities would always arise. "There's no other way," she said. "Believe me."

"There **is.** There must be. I can't stand to see you give up so easily."

Easily. The weariness grew heavier. "You don't know anything about it."

"Tell me, then. Tell me everything so we can sort out a solution."

How she wished there were a solution. Speaking each word slowly and clearly, she said, "Did Wallace tell you how much he owed? We could sell the house—sell everything—and still not have enough to pay it and no way **ever** to pay it."

"So you're selling yourself instead."

She was so tired. Her voice creaked as though she were on the verge of sleep. "It's more of a trade. Me for Wallace. And for you. If I had turned my back on Wallace, you would have been next. He wasn't going to give up. You'd think one of you would thank me sometime."

"No one's asking you to be a martyr, Marian. It's lunacy."

"All he wants is for me to love him. He'll be happy if he thinks I do."

"You believe that?"

"I have to."

"And you think you'll be able to pretend to love him for the rest of your life?"

"I did love him. I might be able to again, despite this."

"How can you?"

"It doesn't matter. I'll tell him that I do. He wants to believe I do."

"No. **No.** A person like that has no limits. He'll never be satisfied. He'll always want more from you." Something seemed to coalesce in Jamie, some idea or resolve. "He belongs in jail. That's the answer. Everyone knows what he does. There must be some lawman somewhere he hasn't paid off."

"Please just leave it alone." This possibility that Jamie would try, in some feeble way, to avenge her honor, frightened her. "Please. You'll only make things worse."

Jamie's cheeks were flushed, his eyes bright. "You think he's dangerous. I can see it. You're afraid of him. This isn't love."

She felt heavy as lead, too heavy to argue anymore. She told him there was nothing else to say.

Jamie hadn't come to the wedding, and Wallace had already left to go dry out in Denver. Marian and Barclay stood in front of a judge in the Kalispell courthouse with Sadler and Barclay's sister, Kate, as witnesses. Afterward, they'd taken a photo outside on the steps while a gusty wind blew leaves around their feet. They'd had lunch in a restaurant, and Sadler had driven them directly to Missoula to catch an eastbound train.

The fourth night at sea, Barclay managed to appear for dinner. Instead of going to smoke cigars after, he joined her for a turn on deck. He held her arm and made her walk on the inside, away from the railing, as though she were the unsteady one. Beyond the ship lay blowing darkness, an absolute void. "It's not pleasant to imagine falling in," Barclay said.

"It reminds me of flying through cloud at night. Sometimes you feel as though you don't even exist at all."

"That's terrible."

"Or liberating. You realize how little you matter."

He gathered her under his arm. "You matter."

"Not really. No one does." They were strolling beneath the long line of davit-hung lifeboats, a procession of keels passing overhead. She said, "We must be close to where the **Josephina** went down."

"I don't like to think about it," he said.

"Sometimes," she said, "I wonder what my life would have been like if I'd known my parents. Wallace has said, or not quite said, that they weren't happy together. They married hastily." But who was she to judge anyone's reasons for marrying? Her parents might have known full well they would be unhappy and had bound themselves together anyway for reasons long lost. "Jamie and I would have been children in that house in New York. I can't imagine it. If you change one thing, you change everything."

"It would have been terrible," Barclay said, kissing the back of her glove, "because I wouldn't have met you."

What would Wallace's life have been like if the twins had never been sent to him? She had called the doctor in Denver long distance before they left New York. Wallace seemed committed to his treatment, he said, though the process was not easy, especially not in the early stages. Wallace, when he came to the phone, sounded shaky but lucid. He said he was beginning to hope he would be able to paint again.

"I wonder if I would have learned to fly," she said to Barclay.

They had reached the stern. "I'm sure of it."

"Why?"

"Because flying is in your bones." She peered at his shadowed face above the faint white glow of his shirtfront, surprised. She wanted to say that she, too, believed this, but before she could, he added, "That's how I felt when I saw you. You were in my bones."

He was always busy choosing bits and pieces of their lives to weave into the story he was constructing around them like a bird building a nest, like a prisoner building a prison. But when he leaned close to her, her body responded, as it always did. At least there was that. She held him tightly, using him as a shield against the void that pressed in around the ship.

Edinburgh, Scotland
November 1931
One month later

A clever puzzle of a city, assembled from blocks of pale, sooty stone. Marian, out walking, often found herself above or below where she wanted to be, as the cobbled streets made a complex lattice wedged in among the abrupt rises and falls of the underlying landscape, navigable only via tunnels and narrow passageways, bridges and steep, hidden stairways. Glimpses of the sea came and went. The castle lay curled like a sleeping dragon at the top of the main street, while, on the other side of town, a massive rough outcropping of rock, the Salisbury Crags, stood up higher than all the spires and domes and chimneys as though in primitive rebuke to human ambition.

Many days—most—were uncompromisingly gray, but sometimes in the afternoons a cold, clear yellow light slanted down, bringing every stone and slate and chimney pot into almost unbearably sharp focus. Marian had heard someone—one of Barclay's acquaintances—describe Edinburgh as being like a shabby tuxedo. She didn't think the comparison held. Yes, Edinburgh was both elegant and well used, but it was too solid and too ancient to be likened to a garment, too hewn and heavy. Missoula seemed like an Indian camp in comparison, something you could roll up and carry away on your back.

Barclay often left her alone during the day while he went off on business. To her shame, she found she was not quite the intrepid traveler she had imagined. She worried about making etiquette missteps, understanding Scottish accents, being conspicuous. Mostly she drifted through the streets without speaking to anyone, or she read in the hotel's library. Without Barclay, she felt timid, but with him she felt squashed and crowded. He chose what they did and when. He ordered for her in restaurants without asking what she wanted. They went into the Highlands to visit friends of his, to a frigid lodge set on the edge of a black lake. At the long, candlelit dinner table in a cavernous room where the walls bristled with antlers, Barclay became an unfamiliar iteration of himself, at ease in formal wear and able to chatter blandly about hunting and land rights. This malleability unsettled Marian. Who was he, this man? Since the wedding, she'd felt frozen, like a rabbit in a hawk's shadow, uncertain how to respond, torn between hating him for Wallace's sake and wanting to love him for her own.

One morning, alone, after nearly half an hour spent examining the timetables in Waverley Station and gathering her nerve, she took a train to Glasgow. If Edinburgh was a shabby tuxedo, Glasgow was a tuxedo worn by a chimney sweep. She walked along the River Clyde, trying to catch a glimpse of the shipyards where the **Josephina** had been built, but the day was chill and foggy, and she didn't know where to go. The poor neighborhoods near the water spooked her, the way people's eyes lingered on her fine coat, her glossy handbag. If she'd been in her old clothes she wouldn't have worried, but her coat and bag and little clip-clopping shoes advertised her as rich and helpless.

On the return train, she'd blinked back tears of frustration. Here she was, away from Missoula, finally on an actual **journey,** and yet she was more confined than ever. The bulk of Britain to the south and the greater mass of Europe below it were so near, just over the horizon. But she could go nowhere at all.

Edinburgh
November 13, 1931

Dear Jamie,

I meant to write you from the ship, not that
I could have posted a letter except maybe in a
bottle. I have no excuse for why I haven't written
since then, seeing as we arrived in Edinburgh
nearly a month ago. Do you know I've never
written you a letter? There was never any need.

What I want to say is that it pains me to be
on the outs with you. I haven't forgotten you
warned me early on to be cautious of Barclay
and I didn't listen. Or not well enough. I
thought I could manage. By the time you came
back from Seattle, there was nothing to do but
yield—please trust me—though that doesn't
mean there weren't other solutions, earlier, that I
didn't see or ignored. I was blinded by my desire
to fly, and maybe it explains some small part
of things to admit I did feel drawn to Barclay,
always, from the beginning. That pull seems to
justify so much. Maybe you know what I mean.
You never really told me about the girl in Seattle.
I wish we'd had a better chance to talk. I know
I have a tendency to hog the spotlight, and I'm
afraid I did it again.

In any event, here I am. A wife. I'm told girls

dream of being wives, but wifedom seems an awful lot like defeat dressed up as victory. We're celebrated for marrying, but after that we must cede all territory and answer to a new authority like a vanquished nation. The central danger now is of Barclay getting his way yet again—he wants a baby, and a baby is what I dread most. It seems an awful snare. I've told him I can scarcely imagine ever having one and absolutely not anytime soon, and I thought he understood, but—no, he does understand. It's that he doesn't care. He wants me snared.

It's strange to think of you all alone in Wallace's house. Do you drive the Ford? I hope so. Do you see Caleb? Have you been drawing? What do you hear from Wallace? If you see Mr. Stanley, will you give him my regards?

At least this hotel has a library. I feel like I'm a child again, with all these hours I've had to myself to read. Over my life I've had so much time to myself. But, Jamie, I never felt lonely before now because I was never on the outs with you. I'm ashamed to say I hadn't realized how much I've relied on you. I feel I've lost a wing and am now just a useless ball of junk, falling. I hope you will write back and say you are still there, unseen but intact.

I'll go out now and mail this myself so there's no chance of Barclay intercepting it. A wife can

have no expectation of privacy. A sister sends
only love.

Your Marian

P.S.—We will be here for almost three more
weeks, so if this letter is not delayed and you
write back promptly—and if I've ever begged
you for anything, it is that you would—I'll have
a good chance of getting it before we start the
journey home.

Missoula
December 1, 1931

Dear Marian,

I'll take the easy way and answer your questions
first. I hadn't been driving your car, but once I
got your letter I decided I would. Thank you
very much. It makes a nice change from creaky
old Fiddler or my bicycle. You asked about
Caleb. I see him the way you might spot a wolf
in the woods—only from time to time and
always with a thrill. Last week he came over to
the house and we had a drink and listened to
Wallace's phonograph. He is still himself, though
I'd say a little too aware of the mountain man

role his customers expect him to play. Sadly Gilda is not well at all. I asked Caleb if he could afford to send her to the doctor in Denver, but he said she would never go and I believe he's right. At least she has stopped having men in since Caleb now gives her plenty of money to drink away.

You asked if I have been drawing, and I have. I've been trying my hand at oil paints, too, although to be honest mostly what I've been doing is moping. Maybe there's something about this house that turns men into mopers. The girl in Seattle—I don't have the patience to write down the whole story, and I wouldn't assume you'd have the patience to read it. But I will say I had hoped she would be taking up less space in my thoughts by now. One thing I learned is that you don't just love a person, you love a vision of your life with them. And then you have to mourn both. I always thought I'd go to the U and join the Forest Service, but now I'm having trouble imagining myself there. My vision of life with Sarah has made my old ideas look shabby in comparison.

I miss her, but I also have a strange, vengeful urge to <u>show</u> her, though show her what exactly I couldn't say. I suppose I want her to feel regret, to suffer as I am, even though I also want to be the one to spare her from all suffering. Does that make any sense?

Caleb says to give it time, which is all I can do for now anyway.

Wallace seems to be well enough. His letters and his doctor say so, but I still think he's on the fragile side. I called last week. It seems to me he's been squeezed out and dried like a mushroom and is now reconstituting himself with fresh life. He said the world seems almost too clear to him now that he's not drinking, too bright, like sunlight on snow. He also said he's begun to paint again. I wondered where he was getting money for supplies, but the doctor told me Wallace's "patron" had set aside an additional allowance just for that. Barclay will never be redeemed in my eyes, but I can acknowledge this one kindness. Wallace feels so guilty, by the way, and cried on the telephone and told me he feels as though he'd sold you. I assured him he hadn't, that no one sold anyone.

I am sorry for what I said. It was an odd (and small) consolation to hear there is an attraction between you and Barclay. I can understand, after my own puny, ill-fated romance, how attraction can lead us astray.

But if you don't want a baby, you must do everything in your power to avoid it. I'm no expert on the subject, but I think you were right to use the word "snare" in your letter. I know you believe Barclay loves you in his way, but he is also trying to break you. The two things might be the same for him. Nothing that has happened so far can't be escaped or undone, but if you had a baby I doubt you would find it in yourself to abandon it as we were abandoned. I hope you will leave Barclay one day and find your way back to your own life. Please, Marian. Don't give in.

I don't know if I'm as useful as a wing, but I will always do what I can for you if you ask. Even if you don't ask, I will still try my best.

Yours,
Jamie

The man at the front desk of the Edinburgh hotel from which Mr. and Mrs. Macqueen had recently departed sighed when he saw the letter. Forwarding service had been requested, and so the letter went into a pouch with a few other straggling communications and was addressed to Mr. Barclay Macqueen and sent off to America.

Montana
December 1931–January 1932

Sadler met Marian and Barclay at the Kalispell depot in the elegant black Pierce-Arrow. "You've had a long journey," he said, opening the back door for Marian, who didn't bother to concur.

Another man, a Salish who worked at Bannockburn, followed behind in a truck with their luggage. Marian slept through the drive, willfully indifferent to the conversation of the men or the first glimpse of her new home. Barclay had to shake her awake. For a moment she thought she was back in the Scottish Highlands. She saw snow, mountains, a square, dignified, symmetrical house made from gray stone, roofed in slate.

Barclay's mother and his sister, Kate, were standing on the front steps between two enormous stone urns. Kate, in riding boots and sheepskin jacket and broad-brimmed hat, shook Marian's hand. At their wedding, she'd said, "He won't be talked out of it. I've tried."

"I've tried, too," Marian had replied.

Kate had scowled, said, "I'm sure."

Barclay's mother, Mother Macqueen, as she wished to be called, wore a brown dress and heavy shawl. A silver crucifix dangled nearly to her waist. Her gray hair was bound in two thick braids looped back up on themselves, and her face was pleated with long, delicate wrinkles. She surprised Marian by embracing her and patting her back as though offering reassurance to a child. "You are very welcome here," she said in a low murmur. Her accent was an odd mix of Salish and French.

Marian had not been prepared for such a warm greeting, for warmth at all. Barclay had said little about his mother. She wondered if Mother Macqueen was remembering being a bride, being taken under the auspices of Barclay's father, encompassed by his whiteness and wealth.

Mother Macqueen was holding her hands and gazing into her face. "You are a blessing," she said.

Gently, Barclay separated them. "Come inside, Marian," he said.

Life as a wife began.

Marian had trouble finding any way to be useful. There was a landing strip on the ranch, but the Stearman was back in Missoula. She asked when she might go and get the plane, but Barclay put her off with vague admonishments about settling in, finding her place, enjoying being a newlywed. She told herself she needed to wait, to make the best of things, and eventually he would relax his vigilance. At least on the ranch she needn't wear silk dresses.

A Salish girl did the dusting and sweeping and laundry, one in a long succession of girls who had been educated, like Mother Macqueen, in a convent school where the French-speaking nuns emphasized domestic skills and the Bible's most frightening pronouncements and tried to drive the nativeness out of their charges. Mother Macqueen had graduated with an esoteric set of beliefs, partly of her own concoction, that Barclay said had both enchanted and deranged his father: She perceived life as a continuous storm of divine wrath and celestial mercy, human beings blown one way and then the other by competing gusts on which angels and devils flew like bats.

An older Scottish woman did the cooking. A gang of men worked the cattle and cared for the horses and mended the fences. Kate worked with the men, but any attempts Marian made to help were rebuffed. She had the sense Barclay had forbidden anyone to allow her to work, leaving her with nothing to do but wander aimlessly around the ranch. She suspected he was trying to bore her into having a baby.

"What are you doing today?" she asked Kate

one morning when she contrived to meet her on horseback.

Kate's cheeks were flushed with cold. "Mending fences."

"I could lend a hand."

"No, we just want to get on with it." She rode off, her horse's hoofbeats muffled by snow.

Just after the new year, the parcel of held mail arrived from the hotel in Edinburgh.

In their bedroom, Barclay read Jamie's letter aloud in a furious, tremulous voice: "'I hope you will leave Barclay one day and find your way back to your own life. Please, Marian. Don't give in.'" He waved the pages at her. "Horseshit. Meddling horseshit."

"I told you I didn't want a baby," she said feebly.

"You don't mean it."

"I **do.** What can I say to make you believe I know my own mind?"

"Don't you care what I want?"

"Is what you want for me to be miserable?"

"You won't be. You'll see—you'll love the baby. And it's your duty to give me children. You're my **wife.** Won't it make you happy to do your duty?"

"Never," she said, loudly, getting louder. "Never ever."

He clamped a hand over her mouth. His mother

and Kate were in the house. The Salish girl was somewhere. The cook was in the kitchen. "I could make you," he said. They blazed at each other. She pushed his wrist away.

"You **can't** make me," she said, quietly, but with all the force she could muster.

"I can take away your—" He formed a ring with his thumb and forefinger to signify her diaphragm. "Your thing. I have rights."

She thought of Mrs. Wu, what Dolly's girls had said: a little bit too much dragon smoke, a bit of a scrape. She thought she could walk to Missoula if she needed to, over the mountains.

"You can't make me," she repeated. "I would find a way."

He looked alarmed, then disgusted. "Who are you?" he said, so differently from how he'd ever said it before.

"Who I've always been."

He shook his head. "No. You've changed."

"Then you're the one who's changed me. Blame yourself."

Just before dawn, a car horn. Faint but insistent, growing louder. It was not the volume but the out-of-placeness that perforated Marian's dream. She stood at the window in her nightgown. The Pierce-Arrow was weaving through the early gloom up the long ranch road. Sometimes the horn keened for long, sustained seconds; sometimes it was only half a bleat.

Downstairs, Kate was already out on the porch, dressed, waiting.

"What's wrong?" Marian said, tying the belt of her wool robe. "Why is he doing that?" The car was drawing near, and she wasn't sure whether Barclay would stop at the house or go careening past.

"He's probably drunk," Kate said.

"He doesn't drink."

"Not often."

"Not ever!" When Kate didn't respond, Marian added feebly, "He told me not ever."

The car slewed to a stop. Before Barclay had even opened his door, Marian could hear him bellowing his sister's name. "Kate! Kate!" He stumbled out. "Kate!"

Kate went to meet him, and he lurched to hug her. The force of him made her stagger. He was hatless. His hair stood up in tufts and bunches. "Kate!" he said again, in a choked voice.

She steered him up the steps. He stared at Marian as he passed, leaning against Kate, reeking of booze, lips parted as though he were about to say something. He seemed less like an ordinary drunk and more like someone maddened by a terrible ordeal. Inside, his mother was knitting beside the massive stone fireplace. Without slowing her work, Mother Macqueen shot Marian a hard glare. "It's the devil that catches him."

"He catches his own self," Kate said. She was leading Barclay away from the stairs, toward the back of the house.

Marian followed. "Where are you taking him?"

"To the guest room. To sleep."

"He should be in our room."

"No, this is better. He'll be sick. It'll be easier for me if he's down here."

"I'll take care of him."

Barclay craned his head over Kate's shoulder to look uncertainly at Marian.

"**Now** you want to take care of him?" Kate said. "You choose your moments."

"He's my husband."

"Be my guest, then. Help me get him up there."

One on each side, they heaved him up the stairs. On the landing, breathlessly, Kate said, "I've never heard you call him your husband."

"Well, he is." Already Marian had begun to regret her flash of possessiveness. Barclay stank. He tripped over his own feet. She should have let him stew downstairs under his sister's ministrations. But they got him into the bedroom and flopped him facedown onto the bed, his feet hanging off the side. Marian said, "He drove from Kalispell like this?"

"From somewhere."

"It's a miracle he made it."

"He always gets home." Kate picked at the laces of one of Barclay's muddy shoes.

Marian pulled off the other shoe. "He's done this before?"

"Once a year maybe. It's always the same. I think somehow he manages not to let the drink fully hit him until he's on the ranch road."

Marian understood why Kate had been already dressed and outside. "You knew he'd gone drinking."

"I suspected. I've been wrong before, waited up all night only for him to stroll in fresh as a daisy." She caught Marian's eye. "Off whoring."

"If you're trying to shock me, remember I met him in a brothel."

"How could I forget? In that case, do you think you can manage to undress him? He'll be sick before long. You need something for it." From beside the fireplace she took a tin bucket full of kindling, dumped it out into the grate. "This'll do." She set the bucket beside the bed.

"We had an argument."

"Let's roll him over." They took Barclay by the ankles and tugged him so he lay longways on the bed, then rolled him onto his back. "Oh, there he goes. Get the bucket." Barclay had begun to retch. Kate hauled him upright by the lapels just in time for Marian to catch, with the bucket, a gush of what seemed to be unadulterated whiskey. "Oh good, he's made himself into a still," Kate said.

When Kate was gone, Marian took the bucket to the bathroom and emptied it before she tried to undress him. His trousers were easy enough, as were his socks, but he'd passed back into lumpen insensibility and she couldn't get him out of his coat. This proved a blessing a minute later when she needed to haul him up as Kate had, by the lapels, so he could vomit again. When he'd finished, she stripped off his coat, waistcoat, and shirt, leaving him in his drawers. She pushed him onto his side, folded the blankets over him, emptied the bucket, curled up beside him under a quilt.

For some hours, they dozed. He woke a few times to heave, though there seemed to be nothing left in him but pale green foam. When she woke to find him staring at her, she couldn't guess the time. The sky was gray and heavy. "I wouldn't have expected this," he said, his voice hoarse.

"Expected what?"

"That you'd tend to me."

"I didn't like that you were calling for Kate."

"I'd have thought you'd have been relieved."

"You weren't even out of the car and you were wailing for her over and over. Do you remember?"

"I was desperate."

"For Kate?"

"For comfort, I think. I get a feeling sometimes, like something terrible is chasing me, getting closer. I felt that way driving back. If I'd known you'd take care of me, I would have called for you, not Kate."

He fell quiet, and she wondered if he was asleep until he said, "You torment me, Marian. You do."

She considered for a minute, said, "I don't see how. You're the one with all the power."

"No, I'm not. I never have been."

She didn't want to spell out for him all the means he had for controlling her, all the ways she'd already yielded. "I didn't think you ever drank."

"Not often." His eyes were closed. "I drank after I first met you. That was the worst time. I went up-stairs with Desirée, but she wasn't you, so I didn't want her. She tried, but I couldn't do anything. I went out to the car—remember it was snow-ing that night? I'd driven myself, and I got stuck trying to drive away, so I got out and pushed. Of course I slipped and fell and knocked my face on the bumper. By that point I was in such a state I couldn't do anything but go off downtown and find a saloon. I was plenty cold and wet by the time I got there. I started drinking, and I sat and thought about why you'd gotten under my skin with that one look. Why you, when I see so many girls? I could have so many girls." He glanced at her, closed his eyes again. "When I saw you, I'd thought I could have you right then—I would have paid any price. But when it turned out I couldn't, I found I was . . . I suppose I was devastated. Beyond all reason. I do know I'm stubborn. I know I like having my own way too much, but knowing didn't help. So I decided the problem had to be you, specifically you.

"Usually before when I'd been drunk I'd been able to get to Kate. Or Sadler. Or someone's been around to help, but that time I was all alone and all I could think about was how I might never have you. And there were other things that show up when I get this way. Old darkness. It wasn't only you, but you'd brought it on. And there was too much snow for me to get anywhere, not out of Missoula, let alone to the ranch. I went walking around town—I don't know what I thought I was looking for, but I kept stumbling into snowdrifts. I started thinking about how people say it's not so bad to freeze to death because they say it's just like falling asleep. So I walked down to the riverbank and found a nice deep snowbank, and I dug a little grave for myself and lay down in it. I was so drunk I didn't even notice the cold, and I was so tired and so relieved to be somewhere quiet that I could easily have drifted off—I was drifting off—and then I happened to think, what if I **could** have you? Not buy you but earn you, persuade you. It wasn't so impossible. It actually seemed simple. I didn't know why I hadn't thought of it before. Obviously you were too young—I would have to wait a while—but I thought I shouldn't be hasty in killing myself. I could always do that later."

He stopped speaking. She wondered if he'd

meant his last words. She'd considered his death before, even hoped for it. She imagined she might feel relief. Or she might feel oppressive guilt. Either would be bearable; both together would not.

"You didn't wait long enough. I was still too young."

"If I had waited, would things be different?"

She pitied him for the hope in his voice, as though the past could be altered. "Yes, but I don't know if they'd be better."

He turned onto his side, facing her. "You were the one who pushed to go to bed. **You** didn't think you were too young."

"I don't mean when we went to bed. I mean when you sent Trout and the plane. I was too young to understand the bargain."

She thought he might be angry, but under the covers he took her hand. "I didn't mean it as a bargain. I meant it as a gift."

She wove her fingers through his. "No, you didn't."

"You don't think things might still change? With a baby?"

"Not the way you want them to."

"You didn't really need me. You could have run away and found some other way to fly, if you'd really wanted to."

"Would you have let me go?"

A knock at the door. Mother Macqueen came in with a teapot in a knitted cozy and one cup and saucer on a tray. She set the tray on Barclay's night-stand, bent to pour.

They sat up against the pillows. Ignoring Marian, Mother handed Barclay the cup of tea. She rested her hand on the hummock of his legs, said, "Don't give yourself to the devil."

"There's no devil, Ma," Barclay said. His voice was tender. "Why haven't you figured out those nuns were full of shit?"

"I thought she would help you." Mother nodded toward Marian. "No. She pretends she's the one who suffers, but she brings the suffering."

"Ma. Leave it alone. I won't drink anymore. I promise."

"The devil makes you lie."

"I need to rest, Ma. And, when you go, will you take the devil with you?"

"Only you can make him go," she said, but she went, closing the door.

Barclay poured more tea and handed the cup to Marian, who said, "What did she mean?"

"Drink turns man to sin. She thinks I'm playing into the hands of bootleggers, who are agents of the devil."

"She doesn't know you are one?" The tea was too sweet. Mother had put sugar in the pot.

"Of course not."

It was true his mother was cloistered on the ranch except for Sundays, when Sadler and Kate took her to church. If Barclay wished her fellow congregants to keep their mouths shut, Sadler's presence was enough to ensure they did, and, anyway, what would they dare say to her face? But still Mother Macqueen must have noticed the signs. She knew, Marian decided, but she was pretending not to. They, the three women—herself, Kate, and Mother—were living in one house with three different men, all of whom happened to be Barclay Macqueen.

"But what did she mean about me?"

"Oh." He pursed his lips, making a show of appearing reluctant to explain. "She thought a good woman would be what stopped me from drinking. Since you haven't, and since you aren't pregnant, she thinks you must not be a good woman after all. There are some holes in her logic—she could never stop my father from drinking. I'm not like him. I don't do it often." This somewhat plaintively. "But now you've dashed her hopes."

"She really thinks you're a cattle rancher?"

"But I am a cattle rancher," said Barclay. "And you are the barren wife who has driven me to drink."

Montana
Winter–Spring 1932

A week after he'd gone drinking, as though it were a perfectly ordinary request, Barclay told Marian he needed her to go pick up some cargo across the line.

Sadler drove her to Missoula to get the Stearman. From the backseat, she asked, "Has anyone else been flying my plane?"

He looked at her in the mirror. "You mean **my** plane?"

"Has anyone been flying **your** plane, then?"

"Not that I know of."

She didn't know whether to believe him, or if the truth mattered. She picked over the Stearman jealously, examining it for traces of another pilot. Once alone in the sky, though, she no longer cared.

She turned a loop, tossing the mountains up over her head.

She made a few more trips over the line in the next week and then, when she entreated, was granted an afternoon flight with no stated purpose or destination. Barclay made her promise to be back in three hours, and she was, having flown a northeasterly route, though she told him she'd gone west, toward Coeur d'Alene. The lie warmed her like an ember.

A full tank could take her six hundred miles. She fantasized about those miles, that radius. She could refuel and fly on. And on. People had flown between continents in lesser planes. But if she ran away, she knew it would only make Barclay more determined to get her back and keep her. If she stayed, eventually he might come to understand they were badly matched. Having tethered her to him, hooded her like a tame falcon, he could still cut her loose, release her. If she stayed, he still might let her go.

But their truce, their wary tenderness, began to give way as winter thawed: the inevitable collapse of goodwill between two people with intertwined yet irreconcilable wishes. Some days, especially when he told her she could not fly, she turned away from him in bed, shook off his caresses. But when she relented, there was still fire between them. Maybe she'd never loved him, had only been tricked by the reflected flicker. Barclay pinned her arms while she glowered and glittered at him.

He went away on business for a week in March and instructed her not to fly while he was gone. On the third day, she drove a ranch truck into Kalispell, speeding on the muddy, winding roads just enough to scare herself, marveling again that Barclay could survive the route drunk. She looked in the shops without seeing anything she wanted to buy. She found a place to have a drink and had three. Drunk, as she'd lost her tolerance for booze, she parked under a tree on the edge of the airfield and waited for someone to land or take off, but no one did.

"Thought you might have gone for good," Kate said when she returned after dark.

The next morning, she uncovered and untethered the Stearman, took off from Bannockburn's rugged strip, mud clinging to the wheels. Only after she was in the air, idly angling the wings this way and that, admiring the mountains' snowcaps, did she decide to fly down to Missoula and surprise Jamie.

One of the airfield boys gave her a lift up the Rattlesnake. The house was looking worse for wear. She'd thought Jamie, left to his own devices, might have spruced things up, but the paint was peeling; the roof shingles were sodden and buck-led. Winter-brown weeds grew thickly around the foundation. She was about to let herself in the side door, but a pang of unease stopped her. For the first time she could remember, she went to the front door and knocked.

The sound set off a cacophony of barking that went on and on, seemingly an army of dogs on the other side of the door. She pressed her ear against the wood, listening for footsteps. She knocked again. The barking reached a new, frantic pitch, and finally she heard the creaking of the stairs, Jamie telling the dogs to quiet down. The door was yanked open, and her brother blinked out at her. "Hello," he said as though to a stranger.

He had dark circles under his eyes, and a wispy blond beard clung to his cheeks like algae. His clothes were daubed in paint. "You look terrible," she said. "What's wrong with you?"

"Nothing." Five dogs streamed out, went to lift legs and squat in the dead grass and crumbly snow. He watched them pensively. "I must have lost track of time. They've been shut in all day. That was awful of me. What time is it?"

She looked at her wristwatch. "Just past noon."

Suddenly he seemed to shake himself free of whatever strange state he was in. "Marian!" He lurched forward to embrace her. With a pang of revulsion, she inhaled the mingled smells of his unwashed body, turpentine, and booze. She'd had enough of drunk men for a lifetime. He said, "What are you doing here?"

"Visiting you."

"Come inside." He held the door open, waved her in.

The house was cold and dark, the curtains closed. Plates and bowls were scattered on the floor and furniture, some of the bowls partially filled with water for the dogs, some of the plates bearing traces of whatever he'd been feeding them. Two dogs circled around her legs, panting and peering up as though apologizing for the state of things.

It occurred to her for the first time that it was a Wednesday. "You aren't at school."

"No, I've stopped going," he said airily. He padded toward the kitchen, barefoot despite the cold. "Do you want a drink? I'm going to have one."

The kitchen was a worse mess than the other rooms, heaped with dishes and smelling of decay. A half-empty bottle of clear moonshine was on the table. Jamie picked up a dirty glass, rubbed the rim with his shirttail, poured in two inches and handed it to her. Three inches for himself went into a glass he didn't bother to clean.

"That's awful stuff," she said, coughing after she'd sipped. "I'd forgotten."

"It's not so bad." His eyes were shining. "I needed to fortify myself. I want to show you something, but I'm very nervous about it. Should I show you?"

"Show me what?"

He went on as though she hadn't spoken, his words coming out lopsided, smeared together. "I was just imagining showing you when you arrived, which seems like a sign, doesn't it? Mostly I think about showing them to—" Turning, he hurried out of the kitchen.

She followed. "Show me what?"

"What I've been doing!" he called over his shoulder, racing up the stairs two steps at a time. The spindly shape of him, the looseness of his clothes, the manic pitch of his voice reminded her so much of Wallace. She forced herself to climb slowly, not to panic and grab him and shake him by the arms and order him to stop drinking, to bathe, to go to school. Was it the house that did this to people? Was there some curse that turned men into mad drunkards?

At the top of the stairs, she paused to compose herself before she walked the length of the dark hall toward the wedge of light spilling from Wallace's old studio. When she looked inside, sunlight pouring in from the curve of windows momentarily dazzled her eyes. She saw Jamie's dark shape darting around, and as her eyes adjusted, she saw the paintings.

They were oils, mostly landscapes, some with birds and animals unobtrusively in the scene, almost hidden. At first glance the paintings appeared rough, even primitive, with obvious brushstrokes and patches of solid color, but as she kept looking, she saw they were precise in what they represented, just in a way that was different from the delicate, glossy realism of Wallace's work, more about mood. Charcoal and pencil sketches were piled everywhere. Jars of water and turpentine crowded the windowsills. Jamie was chattering nervously. "Oils are awfully expensive, but Wallace left some behind, and I hope it's all right I spent some of your money on supplies. I'll find a way to pay for more myself, but it just seemed important that I work. It's the only thing I seem able to do right now."

Propped in Wallace's threadbare old armchair was a portrait of a girl with a long face and frank gaze. The same girl appeared on a canvas set sideways on the mantel. The remnants of a fire still smoldered in the grate, blackened scraps of torn paper among the ash. Another painting of the girl lay flat on the floor, grit and flecks of paint marring it. Marian stepped closer to a mountain scene on his easel.

"There's wind in it," she said. "I don't know how there's wind in a painting."

Jamie was hovering behind her. "It's not done. It's not quite right. I'm so nervous my mouth's dry." He drank from the glass he was still clutching. "I haven't shown anyone, not even Caleb."

She touched his shoulder, trying to calm him. "You're an artist," she said. "A real one."

His eyes filled. They looked away from each other. She said, "But even real artists need to bathe sometimes."

· · ·

In the evening, Caleb showed up. Jamie had been induced to wash and take a nap, and Marian was making headway on cleaning and airing the house. She'd fed the dogs and built a fire. Caleb came in the kitchen door with two trout in a creel. "Mrs. Macqueen," he said. "To what do we owe this honor?"

She whispered in case Jamie had woken: "Have you seen him lately? Did you know?"

"Your majesty is upset—"

"Caleb."

He set the basket on the table. "I've had enough already with Gilda. I'm not hiding bottles from anyone ever again."

She put a skillet on the stove for the fish. "You should have told me. How long has he been like this?"

Caleb leaned back against the wall, folding his arms. "I'm not sure. Maybe a month? Before that he was moping around, hung up on that girl, but he was going to school and wasn't drinking, or not as much. He insists he's working on something important. I don't think he's really like Wallace or Gilda. I think he's putting this on a little bit."

From the other room, a brassy dance tune blared from Wallace's gramophone. Jamie appeared in the doorway, a glass in hand. "Cold for fishing, isn't it?"

"You wouldn't eat anything else I could bring."

"Where do you even find trout this time of year?"

"They go deep, but they're there." Caleb took a loaf of bread and a paper bag from his knapsack. "Compliments of Mr. Stanley."

Looking inside the bag, Jamie said, "Hallelujah, he sent cream puffs."

After they'd eaten, they settled around the gramophone, Jamie reclining on the floor beside Marian's chair, Caleb lying on the settee.

"Marian," Jamie said, breaking through some idle talk about Caleb's hunting, "Sarah said she thought Wallace might not have liked that I was making drawings. Do you think that could be true?"

"Sarah?" Marian said.

"The girl in Seattle," Caleb said.

"Because I always thought he was encouraging," Jamie said, "but when I really think about it now, I wonder if he might have been the opposite."

"I don't know," Marian said. She hadn't paid much attention to the dynamic between Wallace and Jamie, had been too preoccupied with flying.

"Sarah's father offered me a job," Jamie said. "I could have gone to live in Seattle. I could have had a whole life there, but I said no. Do you know why?"

"Why?" She was afraid the answer would be that he hadn't wanted to leave her alone in Missoula.

"Because his fortune came from meatpacking." Jamie laughed, sagged sideways onto one elbow. "Of all things. What luck!" He grew solemn. "I must be a fool."

In a garbled torrent, he told the story of meeting Sarah in the park, about her mother and sisters, the big house, the art, the topiaries, the seduction of being praised. When he'd reached the ignominious end, he dramatically drained his glass. Brightly, before Marian had gathered her thoughts to speak, he said, "Say, would you dance for me?" He tapped his knee in time with the record.

"What?" Marian said.

"You and Caleb. I'd like to sketch people dancing."

"I'm a terrible dancer, Jamie."

Caleb, though, stood and pulled her up from her chair, brought her firmly into his arms.

"You don't have to give him his way on everything," she whispered.

"What's the harm in dancing?" He turned her.

Craning her neck, Marian glimpsed doodled lines in Jamie's sketchbook that did not quite add up to pictures but still resembled dancers. She found herself responding to the feel of Caleb, his familiar smell: earthy and coniferous, so different from Barclay's perfumed musk. Though her feet were clumsy and her body stiff, though Jamie was pouring more moon into his glass, she felt weepy from happiness.

When the record finally fizzed and went silent, she stepped away from Caleb, wiped her brow on her sleeve. Jamie had fallen asleep, his head flopped back against the chair, the sketch pad still in his lap.

Caleb put on a different record, drew her onto the settee beside him. "Why didn't you visit sooner?" he said.

She tried to make up an excuse, but she was too wrung out. "Barclay didn't want me to go any-where. He wasn't letting me fly for a while. He was punishing me for not wanting a baby."

"For not wanting one or not having one?"

"They're the same thing, at least for now. He shouldn't have been surprised. I always told him I didn't want one, but he has this idea that he knows me better than I know myself, when really he's ob-sessed with trying to make the real me match his imagined version of me."

Caleb's jaw was tight. "He's a bastard," he said.

"Marian." Jamie was awake. He hadn't moved but was gazing at her from the floor, his face hag-gard. "Will you take me somewhere?"

"What do you mean? Now?"

"Soon. I need to leave here."

"Where do you want to go?"

"Just somewhere else." He drew his knees up to his chest. He'd gotten so thin. "You're gone. Wallace is gone. Caleb's always off hunting. It feels like Seattle is the only thing that's ever going to happen to me."

"Can't you just finish high school?"

"You didn't."

She started to formulate some wry response about

not everyone getting to marry Barclay Macqueen, but before she could speak, he said, plaintively, "Please, Marian. I can't stay here."

Her model planes still hung from the cottage's ceiling, dusty, the glue showing yellow in places. Everything was as she'd left it. Jamie had confined his chaos to the house. It was nearly dawn, but she sat in the armchair and flipped through some books—Captain Cook in the South Pacific, Fridtjof Nansen in Greenland. She waited for them to fill her with an eager sense of nascent adventure, but they lay dead in her hands. Before, she'd been certain the world would fall open to her once she could fly. Now she knew she would never see any of those places.

"You'll leave him eventually," Caleb had said after Jamie had gone to bed, when they were saying goodbye in the kitchen.

"And then what?"

"Whatever you want."

"It's not that easy."

"I could help. We could buy a plane and take hunters out in it."

"We?"

"Why not?" He looked intently at her.

"We're not like that."

"We could be."

She shook her head.

"He'll swallow you up if you let him," Caleb said.

"It's not the end of the world, being swallowed up." But she thought of the crevasse.

"Sometimes I want to grab you and shake you until you see sense."

"Go ahead."

He put on his hat and stalked off into the night.

The day Barclay was due home, she returned to Bannockburn. She'd stayed three nights in Missoula.

From the bedroom, she watched Barclay emerge from the car and Sadler go around to pull suitcases from the trunk. Barclay stared up at her in the window, and she knew he already knew she had flown the plane.

It was late afternoon. She sat with a book but did not turn any pages. He burst through the bedroom door like a hot wind. He said, "Enjoy your trip?"

She thought she might brazen it out. "Yes," she said. "I went to see my brother. You?"

Earlier she had inserted her diaphragm in anticipation of his return, armored herself at least in that one way, and when he took her by the arm and jerked her off the window seat, put her on the bed, she was glad she had. He got her trousers down around her ankles, turned her onto her stomach. Face to the quilt, she waited, but he leaned a knee into the small of her back, grabbing her wrists with one hand. He pushed the fingers of the other between her legs, digging and scraping—purposefully, as though in an effort to unclog a drain. He was trying to pull out her diaphragm. "Don't," she said. Inadequate, but what else to say? His knee pressed harder into her back. He seemed calm and intent, as though subduing an animal. His nails scratched inside her; there was a feeling of suction when he finally pulled the cap free. He shifted so he was straddling her, his knees clamping her arms to her sides. He held the diaphragm in front of her eyes and with his thumb pushed the rubber out into an obscene protrusion, stretching it until it tore. Tossing the ruined object to the floor, he undid his belt.

When she was a child and had wrestled with Jamie and Caleb, she had fought with her whole body, all her limbs, everything down to her fingers and toes. She'd writhed like a serpent even after she'd been pinned.

Under Barclay's weight, she lay still as a corpse. She stared at a pile of logs stacked in the fireplace, noticed how the bark curled up like scraped skin, how the pale, splintery split sides had a faint sheen. She was conscious of fear, but the stronger sensation was of humiliation. To be bare-buttocked and immobilized was excruciating, but the worst of her shame was that she had not foreseen this.

There was pain, but it seemed distant, just over some horizon of herself. Barclay didn't take long.

He made intermittent gasping sounds, and she absorbed without interest that he was crying, or almost. She was waiting; that was all.

When he was done, he lay heavily on her. Eventually he climbed off, and she heard him dressing and sniffling but saw only the unburned logs in the grate. She did not move, nor did she shift after the door closed behind him. Some notion of washing twitched in her mind, but the effort seemed impossible. Where she was, her lungs continued to fill with air and her heart to beat, and so her situation was apparently endurable.

At night in bed she often imagined flying. She would choose a landscape to pass beneath her: mountains with lakes and rivers, perhaps rolling sand dunes if she was feeling adventurous, or tropical islands in a turquoise sea. Lying there with her trousers still around her ankles, she took off from the ranch, flew west over the mountains, flew until she was over the sea, fell asleep over a sheet of blue.

Her second day home in Missoula, she had driven Jamie and Caleb in her old Ford up the Bitterroot, stopped at a broad, flat stretch with no ice. Caleb had been first to plunge into the water. The cold had wrapped around Marian's ribs when she followed, squeezed her malaise from her like spent breath. She and Jamie, in their underclothes, had only jumped in once and run right out again, but Caleb, naked, had splashed and whooped.

The third night, she had woken in the cottage to

Caleb crouching beside her narrow bed. His face close to hers, his hand resting on her wrist, he had said in a low voice, "What do you think?"

"I can't," she'd whispered, and he'd waited in silence for a moment and then gone away.

As the darkness faded, she'd gotten up and walked to the airfield without saying goodbye to Jamie.

Now Caleb was beside her again, but he wasn't kissing her. He was shaking her by the shoulder. Except, as she opened her eyes, it wasn't Caleb but Kate. Marian reached to cover herself, but a blanket had already been pulled over her naked backside. Out the window, bands of pink blazed among gray clouds.

"He sent me to check on you," Kate said. "He said he lost his temper."

Marian turned her head away, looked at the logs again. She couldn't summon the energy to be embarrassed that Kate had found her lying exposed.

"Did he do this?" Kate said.

"Of course he did."

"No, this."

Marian looked. Kate was holding the mangled diaphragm on a handkerchief.

She nodded.

"I know what it is, you know."

"Good for you."

"I'm sure you think I'm just an old maid."

Ordinarily, she would have been interested in whether Kate was implying experience or just knowledge, but not now. She said, "I don't think about you." As an experiment, she rolled onto her side and curled her knees in, holding her breath to keep from gasping at the rawness between her legs. She hadn't moved in hours. She had the sensation of cracking out of a thin pane of ice.

"You don't want a baby?"

"No."

"What are you going to do?"

Marian had not considered the question in practical terms. She had so far avoided considering anything. Again some thought of washing came to her. She imagined walking into the hottest pool of the Lolo Hot Springs, sanitizing herself like Berit boiling jam jars on the stove.

"Nothing. I can't do anything."

"Aren't there . . . rinses and things? Can't you drink something?"

"Do you have those things here? Because otherwise I don't know how I'm supposed to get them." Throwing bitterness at Kate like clumps of mud.

Another long silence. "I might be able to get you another one." Kate held up the diaphragm. "If that's what you want."

Marian had already refrozen in place, but she made herself crack loose again, lift up on her elbow. "You could?" This small piece of kindness, suspect as it was, nudged her out of her stupor, toward a precipice over which could only lie the full brunt of misery. With effort, she sat up. A painful pressure came into her head; a different one settled in her groin, raw and hot.

Kate wrapped the handkerchief around the torn rubber disk, put the bundle back in her pocket. "But if I get you one, you can't let him catch you with it."

"He might feel it."

Kate looked toward the door. "Maybe it's better not even to try. It might make things worse."

"No. Please get me one—please. From where, though?"

"I have friends in England. They're legal there, but it'll take a while, so you'll have to fend him off, or just keep him from—" Averting her eyes, she made a small flicking gesture with her fingers. "I'm going to light the fire, and then I'll run you a bath."

"Why are you helping me?"

"If you have his baby, we'll never be rid of you." She crouched beside the fireplace, struck a match. The logs flared and caught.

She decided, lying in the bath, that if she simply willed herself not to be pregnant, she wouldn't be. Her body was only a vessel for her will, so why not? Other women simply hadn't been strict and forceful enough within themselves. She could seal her womb against him. She slid deeper into the tub, lay unmoving in the water. Thin rafts of bubbles drifted and broke apart like clouds.

And since it turned out she wasn't pregnant, she concluded her will had succeeded. She knew this was not true; she believed it anyway.

She resumed her aimless movements around the house and ranch.

In April, as a late snow fell, she encountered a bear in the forest, thin after the winter, humped and shaggy, its back dusted with white. The animal lifted its head. The black nose throbbed, nostrils pinching closed as it sniffed the air, examining her scent. She carried a rifle across her back but did not draw it, kept still. With its heavy shoulders the bear shoved the earth away, stood on its hind legs. Small, assessing amber eyes. Something humble in its posture to balance the immoderacy of its size, the extravagant length of its curved pale claws.

It thumped back down, sending up a cloud of fresh snow, and shuffled off into the trees. She was not worth the trouble.

She watched it go. She thought it might have been Trout, come to remind her she was still alive.

Barclay was sorry. After her bath she had returned to bed, remained there through the night and into the next day. When he came to her, he drew her out of bed and knelt at her feet, pressing his forehead to her belly, the womb she believed she had locked against him. She stood with her arms at her sides and looked down on his bent head and the upturned soles of his shoes like an indifferent god.

"When can I fly again?" she'd said.

He gazed up at her, beseeching. "Do you forgive me?"

She thought of Jamie begging her to take him away from Missoula. Still, she shook her head.

"You can fly when you forgive me," he said.

Red Herrings

Thirteen

The assistant director shushed everyone—the whole cast sitting at the big U-shaped table with our scripts and our sharp new pencils like kids on the first day of school, the surrounding scrum of bagel-eating, coffee-drinking production people and studio people and investors—and then Bart Olofsson stood up and peered down into his first-edition hardback copy of Marian's book (not Carol's, which he clearly disdained) and read the opening aloud in his faint Icelandic accent.

"'Where to begin?'" he intoned. "'At the beginning, of course. But where is the beginning? I don't know where in the past to insert a marker that says: here. Here is where the flight began. Because the beginning is in memory, not on a map.'"

He looked up and stared into our faces with grave intensity, almost accusingly, like a priest reminding us that we were sinners. I glanced at Redwood in the scrum. He looked solemn, earnest. It had been a week since the night of the 'shrooms, and I hadn't heard from him except for when I'd sent him a GIF of two sloths floating in outer space with the text **Us on shrooms talking about LA.**

He'd responded, **Ha!**

"Here we find ourselves at a beginning, too," Bart told us. "We are about to make a movie. But this is not a big bang out of nothing. That moment Marian can't identify, when her flight began its trajectory toward reality? That was **our** beginning, too. In life, beginnings are not fixed but ambient. They are happening all the time, without us noticing." He tapped the book. "In here, Marian wrote, 'I am already lost to my future.' Strange words, yes?"

The first line of Carol Feiffer's novel is, **I don't know it, but I am about to be swallowed by either fire or water.** It's supposed to be Marian narrating as a baby on the sinking ship. Then the story runs straight forward in time until she crashes into the ocean. **The cold brings the darkness, and I am lost. But I am not afraid.** That last sentence felt tacked-on to me, a wishful, spluttering little protest. After Redwood told me his mother always wanted things to be fine, it made sense. She was trying to reassure herself.

The movie, though, starts at the end, in the airplane, when they're running out of fuel and there's nowhere to go. Then it jumps back to the shipwreck and runs forward, with the round-the-world flight broken into parts and slotted in every once in a while, so finally we wind up back in the plane again at the end, when they crash.

"I think about it like this," Bart said. "We are confined to the present, but this moment we're living now has, for all of history, been the future. And now, forever more, it will be past. Everything we do sets off unforeseeable, irreversible chain reactions. We are acting within the constraints of an impossibly complex system." He paused and stared around again. "That system is **the past,**" he said.

I caught Sir Hugo's eye. He winked.

Bart says everything like it's the aha moment of a TED talk, I'd said to Hugo once. **It hypnotizes people into thinking he's a genius.**

But his grandiosity lends everything a lovely sense of occasion, don't you think? Hugo said.

"But," Bart said, "sometimes, beginnings can be simple. In a film, for example, the beginning is a single frame. Today, let us give ourselves the relief of containment, of limits. Let us begin on page one."

He gestured to the assistant director, who had clearly been waiting for this cue and leaned into his microphone. "Exterior. Day," he read from the script. "A two-engine silver plane is flying over whitecapped ocean, no land in sight. A faint trail of leaking fuel streams from under its wing. Marian, voiceover."

"I was born to be a wanderer," I said, the amplified twin of my voice following a millisecond behind. "I was shaped to the earth like a seabird to a wave."

That 'shroomy night by the pool, what chain reactions had Redwood and I set off? Not the ones I expected. I'd slept in his bed, but he never even kissed me. He'd said I should just **crash here** because we were **too messed up to go anywhere** and **some company would be nice.** He gave me the choice between his bed and a guest room, and I thought he was giving me the choice between hooking up or not, and I thought I was choosing to hook up. But when I emerged sexily from the bathroom in one of his T-shirts, he was already asleep. Around dawn, I think I woke up, and I think he was spooning me, but that might have been a dream because when I woke up for real, he was in the kitchen making breakfast tacos.

"I think you're great," he told me when I left, and kissed me below my ear, and who the fuck knows what that's supposed to mean.

Maybe the problem was that we hadn't actually been in a beginning, not starting a chain reaction but still riding out an old one. I was still trying to escape my feelings for Alexei, my guilt about Oliver, hoping Redwood would turn out to be the key that freed me. Maybe he was hoping I was something equally improbable. We think each new romantic prospect, each new lover, is a fresh start, but really we're just tacking into the wind, each new trajectory determined by the last, plotting a jagged yet unbroken line of reactions through our lives. That was part of the problem: I was always just **reacting,** always just getting buffeted along, never setting a destination.

After I'd gotten home from Redwood's, I'd taken a green juice into the office, where Augustina was working on the computer. She always seemed to be getting jerked around by men, so I thought she might have some wisdom.

"What does it mean," I said, leaning in the doorway, "when you spend the night with a guy in the same bed but nothing happens, and as you're leaving, he kisses you here"—I tapped my neck—"and says he thinks you're great?"

She grimaced—she couldn't help herself—then rearranged her expression into thoughtful neutrality. "He probably thinks you're great," she said.

"Yeah," I said, thumping the doorframe twice, like I was dismissing a taxi. "Thanks."

"Remember your interview tomorrow," she called after me.

I got in bed and looked at Alexei's Instagram, then Alexei's wife's, then Oliver's, then Oliver's ex-wife's, then Jones Cohen's, then basically everyone's

I'd ever slept with. I don't know what I was looking for. Not the selfies or beaches or children or sandwiches I got. I was laboring away, pulling up a huge heavy net full of red herrings. Maybe I was looking for the answer to what I should be looking for.

I already knew I was going to text this guy Mark by the time I got around to his profile. I'd known him since my **Katie McGee** days. Once Santa Monica High School's premier drug dealer, he'd become an entertainment lawyer, handsome and discreet, never romantically attached or possibly just never constrained by his attachments, not very interesting but nevertheless an absolute pillar of self-assurance. I'd turned to him in times of need before. People say **fuck buddy** like the concept is so edgy and clever, but I thought of Mark more as a human placebo. If I believed he would make me feel better, he did.

No one was staking out my gate anymore. The paparazzi had lost interest. Abandonment stings, even when it means freedom. I sent Augustina home, and Mark glided up the driveway in his BMW and drank the fancy mezcal I poured for him and complimented my Marian haircut and took me to bed in his practiced, luxuriously confident way, and when he moved to leave, I asked him to spend the night.

So, when the writer from **Vanity Fair** showed up the next morning, Mark was still there, sunning himself on a raft in the pool, as conspicuous as one of those huge flamingo-shaped inflatables I'd seen in everyone's Instagrams.

The article wouldn't come out for a few months, but when I saw the writer's gaze alight on him out the window, I could almost have dictated the eventual lede:

There's a man in Hadley Baxter's pool. A gorgeous man, in sunglasses and itty-bitty trunks, floating on a raft. "Just a friend," she says with a sly smile, leading the way through her Spanish-style home. "We've known each other since we were naughty little kids." In other words, Hadley doesn't need your pity. Hadley Baxter isn't back. Hadley Baxter never left.

Of course, though, what I wanted was for Redwood to read that right then, right now, not in a few months. I wanted him to know his rejection—if that's even what it was—hadn't hurt.

"What would you say drew you to this role of Marian Graves?" the writer asked when we were ensconced in my living room with canned seltzers and half glasses of white wine (**"Just a cheeky one, as my friend Hugo would say," Hadley says, referring to Sir Hugo Woolsey, her neighbor and a producer of** Peregrine). I splayed sideways in an armchair. She was perched on the couch, her recorder on the coffee table.

"I'm sure you've done your research and know about my parents," I said. "I've always been interested in disappearance. A lot of the time—maybe most of the time—when people disappear it's actually, literally death, but it's not perceived that way. There's an escape hatch built into disappearance. It **is** an escape hatch. Marian gets framed in the context of what **really** happened, like her never coming back is some unsolved mystery, but even if she turned into a yeti and roamed Antarctica for fifty years, there's really only one upshot at this point. She'd be a hundred years old now. Disappearance comes for us all, you know? I used to wonder if my parents might be alive, like if somehow they'd faked their own deaths. You can't help picking at things. A couple of years ago I even hired an investigator, but he didn't find anything. He said he didn't think there was anything **to** find. Just a really big lake. Anyway, if they were alive, that would have meant they went to great lengths to abandon me."

The writer blinked. She said, "What do you think now?"

"Now it seems like they never existed at all."

She nodded slowly, leaned even farther forward, asked, "Are you a searcher, Hadley?"

"What do you mean?"

"Let me put it this way. I think of a seeker as someone looking for enlightenment. I mean searcher as something more open-ended, someone who's actively trying to find their way."

I looked out the window at Mark trailing his hand in the water. "Maybe I am," I said, "but not a good one because I always seem to be a little bit lost." That was a nice pull quote for her, **I always seem to be a little bit lost,** something to superimpose in big italics over a photo of me styled to look rebellious but also waify: leather jacket with no shirt underneath, heavy eyeliner, forlorn expression.

She said, "And what about love? Are you searching for that, too?"

"I'm probably more likely to find enlightenment."

"Is it possible they're the same thing?"

"No," I said, "I think they're opposites."

After the table read was over, after the assistant director had read "Fade to black" into the mic as Marian sank into the depths, when everyone was milling around congratulating each other, I sought out Redwood while pretending I wasn't.

"Hey," I said, feigning surprise when we came face-to-face. "You do exist. I thought maybe I'd hallucinated you."

He laughed nervously and tucked his hair behind his ears. "FYI, all those pink elephants were real, too," he said.

"We could just pretend it was a normal business lunch and not an intergalactic journey, if you want."

Quietly, glancing around, he said, "After you get

drunk or high with someone, do you ever wonder if you made a total idiot out of yourself?"

"No," I said. "I assume I did."

He smiled, relieved. "You didn't at all. But maybe I did?"

"To be honest, I don't totally remember what we said."

"Yeah, to me, that always feels like part of the problem."

"Just assume everything you said was brilliant."

"What if I have a nagging feeling most of it was ridiculous?"

"Maybe we could do it again," I ventured, "and just stick to wine?"

"Yeah," he said. "For sure." And he was about to say something else, but someone called him away.

Lodgings

———

British Columbia
June 1932
Three months after Marian visited Missoula

The Stearman crossed into Canada. Below, the world was green with new growth, and the wind blew easterly through the bright morning, rutting the sky and bouncing the plane. Marian banked west.

Jamie was hunkered down in the front cockpit with his valise and his box of paints and brushes. Cases of whiskey would occupy that space on the way back; Marian would blame engine trouble for her delayed return, say she'd had to put down in the wilderness, fix the plane herself. Barclay might not believe her, but at least by then her task will be done.

Caleb had written to tell her that Jamie had not improved, that he kept talking about her taking him somewhere as though his departure was imminent. Might it be worth a try? Caleb thought he knew someone to rent the house, care for the dogs and Fiddler.

Caleb never wrote unless it was important.

Marian had told Barclay she forgave him, let him fuck her, willed her womb closed. She started flying across the line again, mailed two letters from a nowhere town. One was to Jamie, telling him to be ready, that she would come get him soon and without warning. The other was a query, though an unanswerable one because she instructed the recipient not to write back. She didn't want Barclay to see any letters coming from Vancouver.

The only clouds were sparse and stringy, like shreds of sheep's wool caught on barbed wire. The propeller was a circular smudge, a transparent disturbance. Barclay had known what the price of forgiveness (even feigned) would be. Flight, of course. He gave it grudgingly, suspiciously, knew each trip she made over the line was a pantomime of escape.

In the front cockpit, Jamie gazed blearily down. He'd gulped a good amount of moon before they left, a last drink, he'd told himself, proud about recognizing his need to take a break from booze, smug about resisting the urge to smuggle a bottle along for the flight. If only Sarah could be in the plane, too. He imagined her interest, her delight in the landscape below. When he'd first returned to Missoula, after Wallace left for Denver and Marian for Barclay, he'd missed Sarah so badly and so persistently that the sensation had scared him, and he'd fled into his work and into booze like a panicked elk fleeing into a lake to escape swarming flies. With his painting, he could summon her image. With his painting, he could **show her,** though he still didn't know what exactly. After nearly a year, thoughts of her no longer distressed him but offered something like companionship, especially when he drank. He imagined long, rambling conversations with her, peppered her with questions she never answered.

Marian descended into a long valley. Raw country turned into farmland that turned into neighborhoods, a city sprawled out under transiting cloud shadows, ending at the sea. As she bore to the north, across the harbor from downtown, Jamie picked out the small airfield that was the center of the circle around which they had begun revolving, drawing closer and closer as though a tether were being reeled in.

"If you'd have let me write back, I would have warned you I only have my smallest room free."

Geraldine was for the most part as Marian

remembered, fair and soft and bosomy in a way that seemed maternal, reassuring, though her manner was more brisk and her gaze more skeptical.

"That's fine," Marian said.

"Is it fine with you?" Geraldine said to Jamie. "You're the one staying."

"I'm sure it is."

"You might want to look first."

He'd been quiet in the taxi from the airfield. Marian imagined he'd been feeling the beginnings of a hangover months in the making, or maybe absorbing the unfamiliarity of the place, the difficulty of starting over. "Go look," she told him, though she knew he would not refuse the room.

While Geraldine took him upstairs, she waited at the kitchen table. She had last sat there only a year ago, the morning of the day she flew over the crevasse. Jamie and Geraldine were gone longer than she expected. The house seemed quiet; the other boarders must be out. She looked at her watch, thinking about how far she could get from Vancouver before sunset, where she might manage to spend the night without word getting back to Barclay.

Laughter and footsteps. Creaking stairs. When they came back into the kitchen, both of them seemed lighter and brighter than before, pinker. "Is it all right?" she asked Jamie.

"A palace," he said cheerfully.

"No guests," Geraldine said, suddenly stern, her

brightness snuffed out. "Be in by midnight. And no drinking in the house."

"All right," Jamie said.

"Go unpack, then," Marian said. "I'll wait here."

When he was gone, Marian stood. "Will you tell him I said goodbye?" she said to Geraldine.

"You won't stay the night?"

"I can't. My husband is expecting me."

"Not even a cup of tea?"

"I can't."

Geraldine looked at her with concern that was more practical than sentimental. "Why couldn't I write back to your letter? Is your brother in some kind of trouble? You ought to tell me if he is."

"No. Or, nothing a change of scene won't fix."

"Are **you** in some kind of trouble?"

"It's a long story."

"About what?"

Marian had been moving toward the door, with Geraldine following. "My husband, mostly."

"Ah." The woman nodded, her mouth in a twist that suggested she knew a thing or two about husbands.

"I don't like goodbyes," Marian said at the door. "Jamie knows that. He won't be surprised."

"I don't mind goodbyes," Geraldine said. "I'll pass along yours."

An Incomplete History of the Graves Family

~

1932–1935

In May 1932, Amelia Earhart flies a Lockheed Vega from Newfoundland to Northern Ireland, alone. The first solo Atlantic crossing since Lindbergh. A difficult flight, stormy and almost fifteen hours long. Ice builds up on the wings. The plane spins down three thousand feet. When she regains control, she is low over the whitecaps. She might have disappeared then, in a cold place without islands or atolls, where people couldn't dream her back to life, make her a castaway. They would have looked for her and found only water, as they did anyway, later. Probably she would have become just another dead pilot, briefly famous, lost in pursuit of a dream, now forgotten.

Night in Hopewell, New Jersey. A baby's empty

crib. A ransom note on the windowsill. Charles Lindbergh's first child, a son, twenty months old, is gone.

Chaos. Uproar. Headlines as big as they go. Everyone's a sleuth. Everyone wants a piece of the action. From prison, even Al Capone offers to help.

After ten weeks and a thousand false leads, after Lindbergh pays ransom to a man who promises his son is safe on a boat that turns out not to exist, the baby is found four miles from the Lindbergh house, skull fractured, badly decomposed, dead since the night he was taken. Lindbergh has always been quiet, truthfully pretty weird. (Once, as a prank, he filled a friend's water pitcher with kerosene, watched him drink. Lindberg laughed until he cried; the friend went to the hospital.) He turns further inward, peers out of himself through a narrow chink, a gap in the curtains. His wife, Anne, never sees him cry.

Amy Johnson of Britain-to-Australia fame flies from London to Cape Town in a de Havilland Puss Moth named **Desert Cloud,** beating the solo record set by her own husband—Jim Mollison, a drunken lout and relentless philanderer but a good pilot. The Saharan dunes ripple silver under a full moon.

In August, Barclay finds Marian's replacement diaphragm. Lately he's been penetrating her without fanfare, like an animal obligated to breed, but one night, trying to elicit pleasure, to make her respond to him as she used to, he puts his fingers in her, feels the rubber rim. He strikes her across the face with an open hand, and she hits him back, fist closed. "If you go up in that plane again," he says, one hand over his watering eye, "I'll pour gasoline on it and light a match."

"Then I'll do the same to myself."

"You wouldn't."

"Are you sure?"

"Where did you get it?"

She won't say. His sister is no ally, but Marian won't betray her. He throws the diaphragm on the fire.

After that she is kept to the ground, where the air feels thick and heavy, her movements sluggish. Barclay mates with her grimly, daily. She doesn't think he makes her suffer out of hate. She thinks he believes pregnancy will come as a kind of cure, convert her entirely and immediately into the woman he thinks she should be, prove he's been right all along. He believes she will love him for his rightness. Sometimes he rages at her for **lying there like a corpse, trying to make me feel wrong about it.** He insists she has been with other men, makes insinuations about Caleb, about lovers scattered as widely across Canada as his caches of booze. He gets better at catching her wrists, dodging her blows. Her self, her interior habitat, once full of purpose, has become hollow and inert and uncanny, as though she is a hermit crab who has somehow mistakenly shed the inner animal instead of the shell. Her body grows hard, bony, thinner than she's ever been. He is heavy on her; the air is heavy on her; weight and oppression are constant, uniform.

Still she is not pregnant.

"I'm a witch," she tells him when he demands to know her trick. She sees he almost believes her, in spite of himself.

When she took him to Vancouver, she had told Jamie to send letters to the post office of a town she could visit between deliveries. But now, since she can't fly, she can't pick up her letters, and she doesn't dare write to him. She doesn't want Barclay to know where he is.

One day in the fall, she walks far from the house. Clouds of round gold leaves shimmer on the aspen trees like a suspended rain of coins. A whistle, high and sharp. Caleb comes striding through the forest, the shimmer. He is as he always is: hair braided down his back, barrel of his rifle sticking up over his shoulder. He glints with humor, with the presumption of her love. In a rush, she realizes how lonely she's been.

She wraps her arms around his waist. He curves a hand over her nape. She knows he is noticing, as her former barber, the raggedness of her hair. Barclay had wanted her to grow it long, so instead she'd cut it herself, badly, with Mother Macqueen's sewing scissors.

She is talking into Caleb's chest: **What** are you doing here? **How** are you here? **Why** are you here?

"Jamie said he hadn't heard from you."

"I haven't written. I couldn't. How is he?"

"He seems better. He's painting. I think he's bedding his landlady. Here. See for yourself." He pulls an envelope from inside his jacket. "I'm just the messenger."

"You didn't walk all the way from Missoula, did you?"

"Not **all** the way, but maybe you and Jamie could look into more efficient ways to correspond. I've heard there's a postal service."

"You have to be careful not to be seen. Really, Caleb. Not by anyone. Barclay won't like it. He's already taken away my plane."

"He's locked you up."

"Do you see me in chains?" She doesn't know why she has the impulse to defend Barclay. "It's not forever."

"It is unless you leave him."

"He'll cool off."

Gently, he says, "I used to think my mother would get better."

"That's different." She looks away, scanning the trees for spies. "I'm sorry you had to come all this way just to deliver a letter."

"It wasn't just for the letter. I wanted to see you. I was worried." He studies her. "You're too thin."

She bristles, then subsides, feeling he has broken

a promise to her by worrying, insulted her judgment and competence, but knowing, too, that she has given him good cause.

He adds, "I'm always out wandering around. It's not a hardship to wander in this direction."

"I envy your wandering."

"Come with me, then. Leave."

There is no reason for her not to go except the impossibility of it. "If I slink off, I'll feel like a coward."

"Marian."

"I need him to let me go."

"He'll never do it."

"Or else nothing will ever be resolved. I need a real **end** to it, an agreement of some kind. I can't feel as though I owe him anything."

"You think he doesn't know how to make you always think you owe something? Your marriage is a contest to him, and if he lets you go, he'll lose."

Heat rises in her. She can't tell fear from anger anymore. "Don't argue, please. I can't bear it."

He yields. "At least read the letter. I brought a pencil and paper so you can write back." A twist of a smile. "You'd think I don't have anything better to do than be your personal courier."

In his letter, Jamie had thanked Marian for bringing him to Vancouver. He'd tried to reassure her that he was better, that the dark enchantment of

Wallace's house had been broken. He expressed mortification for how low he'd sunk, for the state in which she'd seen him. **I let myself lose track of things.** He told her he'd gone to meetings of a local group of artists, the Boar Bristle Club, named for the hog hairs used to make certain paint-brushes. They'd included a few of his paintings in one of their exhibitions, and he'd sold one, not for much. On the weekends he peddled portraits in the city parks like he had in Seattle, and he'd got-ten a job in an art supply store, and he'd placed an ad in the newspaper offering drawing lessons. **The only fly in the ointment is that I don't hear from you and don't know how you are.** And, he added, he and Geraldine had become good friends.

The truth: Jamie is in love. Or—not quite. He **wants** to be in love, because without question he is in lust, and not to love the first woman he sleeps with strikes him as impolite, even seedy. And why shouldn't he love the soft, welcoming body he is permitted to touch with his hands and his mouth, to rest his weight on, to venture inside? Why shouldn't he love the good woman who in-habits it, who has, through sheer carnal force, fi-nally displaced Sarah Fahey from the center of his thoughts? There is no reason not to love Geraldine, and yet he doesn't. Not quite. But he feels affection for her and, whenever he is not in her bed, an ea-gerness to return to it.

In Missoula, when he'd **lost track of things,**
he'd been tormented by the knowledge that Sarah
Fahey's life was continuing without him, that she
would go to UW and meet a boy and get married
and do all the things she was going to do anyway if
he'd never shown up at all. In bed with Geraldine,
he feels a vague sense of triumph, as though by
making love to a different woman he is taking
some abstract retribution. But this feeling is even
more impolite than the absence of love, and Jamie
tries to quash it.

What Sarah needs is forgetting.

Geraldine tells him she is thirty, and he thinks
he believes her. Somewhere around there. She'd
inherited the house from her mother. There are
three boarders besides Jamie: an older man who
is a retired teacher, a young man apprenticing with
a tailor, and a single woman around Geraldine's
age who works in an office and is always wink-
ing conspiratorially at Jamie. He is beginning to
understand he is attractive to women. **Aren't you
a tall drink of water,** said a woman in dungarees
picking up a large order of clay from the art supply
store where he works, and when he'd asked, blushing, what that meant, she'd said, **You'd be just the
thing on a hot summer day.** Later he'd seen her
again at a lecture put on by the Boar Bristle Club,
asked around a bit. Her name is Judith Wexler.
She's a sculptor.

Sometimes he worries Geraldine doesn't always remember he is just eighteen. Or, when he detects a trace of the maternal in her solicitous fussing, he worries she thinks of him only as a boy.

But unease might be part of love, he speculates.

Dear Jamie,

I'm writing this from inside a stand of yellow aspens, where I came walking with no intention or expectation of meeting anyone, in fact with the purpose of being alone, when who should appear but Caleb. He'd tracked me with the same stealth he uses on the elk but kindly didn't shoot me. Not much to report except that I'm fine. Barclay won't let me fly, but I hope that will change. I have to hope. Anyway, please don't worry about me.

Have you spoken to Wallace? I have, and he seems well enough. I'm glad you won't be following him to the doctor in Denver. Fresh starts, I suppose, are possible.

Please keep writing, even if my replies are as anemic as this one. I'm not myself right now.

It's 1933.

Elinor Smith, the teenage daredevil who flew under New York's bridges, marries at the age of twenty-two, quits flying not long after, disappears from the scene. (Quits flying, that is, until her husband dies in 1956. She will make her last flight in 2001, age eighty-nine, nine years before her death.)

The pilot Wiley Post has one eye and a Lockheed Vega named **Winnie Mae.** He flies around the world—alone, the first to do it alone—in under eight days with eleven stops. A northerly route: New York, Berlin, Moscow, a string of muddy towns in Siberia and Alaska, Edmonton, New York again, not technically a great circle but undeniably a big one. Post has two innovations on his side: a newfangled radio compass and a rudimentary Sperry autopilot. He can home in on radio beams to find his way, snatch catnaps in the cockpit. Still he is so desperately tired.

Amy Johnson and her husband, Jim Mollison, fly west across the North Atlantic against the prevailing winds, aiming for New York. They crash in Connecticut but survive. (In 1941, transporting a training plane to RAF Kidlington, Amy, thirty-seven years old, will get lost in bad weather, bale out over the frigid Thames Estuary, and either drown or get sucked into the propeller of the boat that tries to rescue her, her body never found.)

Bill Lancaster, an English pilot, crashes in the Sahara trying to break Amy's record to South Africa. His wrecked plane and dry brown twist of a body will lie undisturbed and undiscovered on the empty sand until 1962. Every day the turning earth lifts him to meet the dawn. Elsewhere, the world will destroy itself, rebuild.

Hitler bullies and bargains his way to the chancellorship. When he gives speeches, his head snaps back as though his own words are punching him in the jaw.

According to the Treaty of Versailles, Germany is never again allowed an air force, but German pilots have been training in secret in the Soviet Union. (Not Stalin's best decision, this particular helping hand.) Others are trained under the thin guise of civilian sports clubs, hearty young Aryans soaring in gliders through the fresh Alpine air.

More and more planes are built, other flying machines, too. Airships. Autogiros. Flying boats. Records are made and broken for distance, speed, endurance, altitude. (Marian hears little of this, as she seldom sees a newspaper at Bannockburn.)

More airlines spring into being. A United Airlines Boeing 247 explodes over Indiana. The first bombing of a passenger plane. No one ever figures out who did it or why.

A great blankness settles in Marian. Never has she been so idle. She has no daydreams, no ambitions. Once in a long while, Caleb comes and finds her out on the ranch, startling her, carrying her old life on him like a scent.

Dear Marian,

I have moved across the harbor to Vancouver
proper. I'm afraid Geraldine and I didn't part
on good terms. I disappointed her, but I could
not have done otherwise. I am sorry about
it, though.

Jamie lives in a rooming house on a block of Powell
Street where unruly Gastown begins to subside
into tidy Japantown. His accommodations are
not a private home like Geraldine's but a grimy
three-story building between a billiard hall and a
Japanese barbershop.

Relief in the grit and anonymity of this new iteration of life, in the rowdy city bustle, the Gastown
beer parlors and loggers' hiring halls, the clanging,
whirring streetcars and huffing freight trains, the
Japanese greengrocers and noodle counters, the inscrutable signs and chockablock window displays
just to the south in Chinatown.

Perhaps he might dip a toe into the nightlife.
Perhaps away from the dark influence of Wallace's
house he can have a few drinks and not **lose track
of things.** Being free of Geraldine makes him miss
her, but the missing feels dangerous, needs to be
dispelled. He needs to be touched, needs new
memories to lay over the old.

A few bleary nights, a quick and queasy encounter with a prostitute.

He paints street scenes, harbor scenes. Once a week he gives drawing lessons to a rich widow, arranging still lifes of fruit and flowers for her to render with timid, fussy lines. He falls in with some other members of the Boar Bristle Club, all men in their twenties, most barely scraping by. Two teach at the art school, a few have had work in traveling exhibitions or won museum purchase prizes. They critique each other's work, but mostly they drink together. He asks them about Judith Wexler and they tease him mercilessly—**She'd eat you for lunch! There be dragons, lad! Abandon all hope, ye who enter her!**—without telling him anything of use.

He writes to Marian:

I have a feeling I have reached a juncture full of consequences that can't be anticipated but will later seem inevitable. Should I embrace a bohemian life as a temporary lark or resist it as a trap? I'm afraid of being sucked under as Wallace was (as I nearly was), but to live without any fun at all seems too extreme a precaution and also discouraging to the making of art. I want love but not a wife, not yet. I want drink but not dissolution. I want momentum but not to careen. I suppose what I want is some kind of equilibrium, but I suppose I want the thrill of tipping back and forth, too. Do you know what I mean? Maybe not—you've always been one for single-minded pursuit. Maybe the answer is in painting. It's true that when I'm working is when I'm most at peace.

Happy birthday.

They are nineteen. Marian, by this time, is pregnant. Her monthly blood had been irregular for months because she has gotten so thin, but she knows even so. Her breasts throb as though the skin might rip. She manages to hide her nausea from Barclay, knows she can't keep the secret for long.

How stupid she'd been, how passive and superstitious and wishful and ridiculous: an earthbound ghost wandering among the trees, a breeding sow waiting in the bedroom. She had wondered, in spite of herself, if there might be some truth to Barclay's certainty that the moment of conception would convince her of her destiny as a mother, but instead the meeting of sperm and egg had been the formation of that first ice crystal on the surface of a lake from which a solid, unbroken pane blooms and feathers out to the encircling shore. She peers down through it into the black depths of herself and does not hate the floating mote of life suspended there but will not pity it, either.

No denying anymore that Prohibition is bound to end. Barclay's associates have been coming to

Bannockburn to discuss what to do. "Cattlemen," he tells his mother. "Come to talk cattle."

"They're bootleggers," Marian whispers to Mother Macqueen, leaning over her chair. "Your son is a criminal, as you well know." But Mother pretends not to hear, hums as she knits.

Barclay is loath to relax his surveillance of his wife and seldom leaves the ranch, but once in a while business keeps him away overnight. Marian waits. She has no real plan, only her will, which has returned to her like a wayward hawk coming to the glove.

One afternoon Barclay and Sadler drive away, not to return until morning. She waits through supper with Kate and Mother, waits beside the fire while Mother's knitting needles click away the seconds, waits in bed through midnight, beyond midnight, until the silence feels settled. She creeps down the stairs, testing every footfall, certain the tattletale house will betray her.

The September night is warm and clear, with half a moon. She wears trousers, a plain shirt, a canvas jacket. She takes a knapsack containing a wool blanket, a water canteen, some food, a flashlight, a compass, a knife, and a stash of money she'd withdrawn from the bank in Missoula on her last visit and kept buried in a tin can near the airstrip. Everything else she thinks of as her own is in the cottage behind Wallace's house. Mrs. Barclay Macqueen's fine clothes and jewelry—none of it has anything to do with her. The moon blues the ranch road as she crosses it, casts her shadow, blues the wings of the Stearman. She'd thought Barclay might have disabled it in some way, was prepared to walk over the mountains, but after she pours in oil and cleans the spark plugs, the engine turns right over. When she discovers the gas tank is still half full, she trembles with anger and shame. He'd been so certain she wouldn't disobey him.

She wishes she could go to Missoula, to Caleb, to her cottage. She wishes she could go to Miss Dolly's, to Mrs. Wu. But it is too much to hope that no one at the ranch will hear the plane take off, that anyone will be fooled by her note. In Missoula, she would be found before noon.

A trundling rush along the bumpy ground in the dark, a parting. She banks over the moonlit mass of trees, turns northwest. The sky stays clear, but even the densest clouds would not have stopped her. Passing over the dark sheen of a lake, she takes off her wedding ring and drops it.

"He doesn't know about the baby?" Jamie says after Marian has told him the story. The morning she left Bannockburn, she had landed the plane in the wilderness when it ran out of fuel, concealed it as best she could by pushing it nose-in among some trees before walking ten miles to the nearest town. There, she'd spoken to no one except the bored station clerk who'd sold her a one-way train ticket to Boise. She'd gotten off after two stations and bought a ticket to San Francisco, repeated the ruse once more, then stayed on a train to Vancouver.

"No," she tells Jamie.

"He doesn't know where you went, either?"

"I didn't tell him, and I'm almost positive he never knew I brought you here. He would have gloated and held it over my head. Still, he might show up sometime. I'm afraid he will, but I can't do anything about it. If he comes, just tell him you don't know where I went, which will be true."

"I'm not afraid of him."

"You ought to be. I'm sorry, Jamie. It's all my fault."

They are walking beside Oppenheimer Park. On a baseball diamond, a team of Japanese men is practicing. Jamie points at them. "They're the best in the city. If you stay, we'll go to a game. Everyone comes out."

"I can't stay long. Promise to be careful, will you?"

"What can Barclay take from me? I don't have anything."

"You know it's not what he'd **take.** I've always been afraid of exactly this situation."

"Well, you shouldn't have stayed with him for my sake."

"I didn't. I was paralyzed somehow."

"What made you un-paralyzed?"

"Getting pregnant."

He hesitated.

"I can't have it," she says brusquely. "I'd be tied to him forever. Even if by some miracle he never found out, he'd have gotten his way. And adoption is out of the question. I couldn't leave a baby to wonder about its parents. It's not an experience I'd recommend."

"No. Me neither." He ushers Marian into a tearoom.

As they sit, she says, changing the subject, "What did you decide about the bohemian life?" A waiter brings a ceramic pot, two handleless cups.

"I didn't so much make a decision as slide into an ongoing compromise."

"This tea is **green.** What kind of compromise?"

"Try it. It's good. The compromise is that I'm living day to day without making any sweeping decisions."

Just live each day was what Judith had told him to do when he confessed his anxieties. She'd shrugged her bare shoulders, sitting naked on her mattress, smoking a cigarette, unable to comprehend why he would worry so much. **Don't decide anything.** He has not yet told Marian about Judith, whom he is desperately in both lust and love with. Marian would not like Judith, would find her pretentious and self-absorbed, and he is not sure he wants to grapple with whether that view might be correct.

"Is that compromise?" Marian says. "It sounds a

little bit like procrastination. You don't think you'll go back to being how you were before, do you?"

"No," he says thoughtfully, "but the worry is always in the back of my mind. I think worrying acts as a kind of brake. Anyway, I've been concentrating on painting. I've sold some in the club's exhibitions. And there's a photographer here, Flavian—he's from Belgium—who's opened a gallery and wants to sell my work."

"That's good." She peers into her teacup. "This tastes like plants."

"Tea **is** plants."

"If you sell another couple paintings, could you move out of that place where you're living? It looked like a flophouse."

"It is one, basically, but I don't know where else I would want to go. That's the problem. I might as well stay where I am and save the money. This way I can afford my share in the studio, too."

"Can we go there? I want to see what you've been painting."

"We'll go this afternoon." He leans forward, lowers his voice. "But, Marian, what are you going to do?"

"I can't have it," she says again. "I would have gone to Miss Dolly's—there's someone there who could help—but Barclay would find out in no time. So I was thinking I'd ask at the brothels here until someone tells me where to go."

When he thinks of Barclay, he feels the same fury as he had years ago, when he'd almost killed the boy who'd been throwing stones at that dog. The fury, logically, exists only within the confines of his mind, his body, but it seems so much bigger and stronger than he is, elemental, something that might break him apart from the inside. He imagines Marian knocking at brothel doors, being sent to some disreputable doctor. A dark room, a tray of rusted instruments. "Barclay would kill you if he knew."

"I don't think so. But even if I knew he would, it wouldn't change anything."

What can he offer her? He knows nothing about the secret doings of women. He thinks of the prostitute he visited in Gastown, can't imagine asking her for the time of day, let alone help in procuring an abortion for his sister. Judith might know, but he wouldn't trust her to keep a secret. Then a connection shunts into place in his brain so forcefully there's an actual physical sensation. "I know someone—" He pauses. **Does** he know her? The sum of his knowledge is small but suggests she is capable and compassionate, invested in this kind of problem. What if she turns Marian away, though? Then Marian will do what she is planning to do anyway. What if she has Marian arrested? She wouldn't—he thinks he knows that much, at least.

"You should go to Seattle," he says. "I know

someone there who might be able to help you. It's better than not knowing anyone."

Marian goes to Seattle by train, in an ordinary traveling dress bought for its ordinariness, an ordinary hat to cover her short hair, plain shoes. She carries a new suitcase containing another such disguise and also her old clothes, which serve as a talisman, a promise she will soon revert into her real self. She gives a false name when she checks into her hotel: Mrs. Jane Smith springing into existence.

"You're just like your portrait," Mrs. Fahey says. They are in a downtown bistro.

"Portrait?"

"Jamie drew you for us. I still have it. I'll bring it to show you tomorrow. He did it from memory, which seemed extraordinary to me and even more so now that I see how apt it was." She puts her hand on Marian's. "I'm so pleased to meet you, even though I'm sorry the circumstances aren't happier. I don't know how Jamie knew to contact me. I've helped other girls in situations like yours, but I certainly never mentioned anything about that to him. He must have good intuition."

"He does, usually, and he adored you and your daughters."

Mrs. Fahey, perhaps hearing the exclusion of her husband, smiles and releases Marian's hand. "He and Sarah in particular had a special friendship." She stirs sugar into her coffee. "I'd like for you to meet her, but now might not be the time. How is Jamie? He didn't say anything about himself in his letter. I've been imagining him at the University of Montana, but the postmark was from Vancouver."

"He's well." Marian hesitates, wondering if this elegant woman, lifting her coffee cup so delicately by its handle, won't find Jamie's life strange or disappointing. "He's trying to be an artist."

Mrs. Fahey brightens. "Oh, I'm glad! His talent seemed unusual. I hope he's famous one day. No, I shouldn't frame it that way. I hope he's fulfilled."

"Me too."

The woman looks at her, head cocked. "The way Jamie described you, I was expecting someone more . . . unorthodox. I mean in the way you dress."

"I'm trying not to stand out."

"Why?"

"My husband will have people looking for me."

"Ah," Mrs. Fahey says. "I see."

The next morning, when Mrs. Fahey comes to Marian's hotel to escort her to the doctor, she unrolls a sheet of paper, holds it up so Marian can study her own charcoal image. "Jamie would draw me differently now," she says. "It doesn't seem possible I was ever so sure of myself."

"I don't pretend to know you well, but I think you are very brave." Mrs. Fahey rerolls the drawing, holds it out. "You take this. As a reminder."

Marian shakes her head. "I don't know if I can keep it safe. But someday I'd like to have it. Do you mind holding on to it a while longer?"

A tray of instruments rattling on wheels. A bright ceiling light. The sweetness of ether. An afternoon spent in bed in the hotel. Some blood. A dull pain. In the evening she writes a long letter, pages and pages, folds them carefully into an envelope. From the hotel's telephone book she copies the address for the Bureau of Internal Revenue, buys a stamp from the man at the front desk. The next day she wanders along the waterfront, all the way down to a Hooverville that had once been a shipyard, looks out over the broken, ramshackle geometry of the shacks, dirt packed like grout in between. The pane of ice in her is gone, as is the bit of life floating beneath it, but she has not been restored to how she was before, only feels a new loss, welcome but still felt.

On her way back to the hotel, she posts her letter.

The next day she books passage to Alaska. Jane Smith, she tells the man in the ticket window, and so he records her on the manifest.

In 1934, planes can fly farther, faster, in worse weather. More routes are opening.

Jean Batten, a New Zealander, flies from England to Australia, beating Amy Johnson's record by four days. (Today there is a statue of her at the Auckland airport.) Sir Charles Kingsford Smith crosses the Pacific from west to east. (The Sydney airport is named for him.)

The Alaska Territory is big country, rough country, country without roads, country best traveled by air. Fly an hour or walk a week, they say. Mail routes that take a dogsled nearly a month might take a plane seven hours. Alaskans are already the flyingest people, but they need more pilots. In the end it is simple for Marian to do the thing she's always longed to do: get paid to fly.

Fresh off the ship in Anchorage, she'd found a place to live, bought a truck, and gone from hangar to hangar, Jane Smith in search of work, showing her logbook as proof of her experience. Asked about a license, she'd said, "I never got one," and no one pressed her about why not. (Alaskans aren't big on bureaucracy.) The logbook is an irregular document. So many destinations recorded no more precisely than "Canada," so many flights marked simply "Cargo." Even her name, so scrupulously plain, has an air of erasure. A man with a hangdog face, scarred lip, and crumpled hat looked at the logbook, looked at her, took her up for a check ride, hired her on the spot.

She flies people and supplies where they need to go, learns to fly floatplanes, lands on water, lands on skis in the winter. She does most of her own maintenance, has to do emergency repairs so often she doesn't consider much an emergency anymore.

The small house she rents is on the outer fringe of town, where it's easy to keep to herself. Was this what her father had done after he left Missoula? Slung his skills over his shoulder and set out? Sometimes she startles awake at the sound of animals outside, thinks Barclay has come for her. She keeps a rifle by the bed.

"What are you doing messing around with planes? You're good looking enough to get a husband," a pilot says from behind her, low and turgid, standing too close as she fills a canister with water for a plane's radiator. "Especially here."

"I had one, once," she says. "He's dead." Her voice like a chipped blade. He steps back, waits for her to crank closed the tap.

On clear days, north across the Cook Inlet, Mount McKinley appears. If she flies in that direction, it grows and grows, white as the moon, seeming to rise as the moon does, seeming separate from the earth, too huge to be of it. To the east are the sawtoothed Chugach Mountains, the Wrangell Mountains beyond, the Alaska Range to the north. Mountains everywhere: monstrous, ice-choked cousins of the forested peaks that had encircled her as she looped and spun over Missoula. (She doesn't dare do aerobatics in Alaska, doesn't want word to get around of a girl with a knack for them.)

The impulse to flee persists; the horizon beckons. If she could just go farther, live nowhere, possess only an airplane, and if that airplane never needed to land, **then** maybe she would feel free.

Jamie moves out of the flophouse, finds a small apartment of his own on a quieter street in the same neighborhood, one room only but clean and tidy with pine floors and an oddly miniature bathtub he can only fit in with his knees bent nearly to his chest. "Did you answer an ad seeking a gnome?" says one of his Boar Bristle friends.

Judith has gone to Europe to, as she put it, **see what it's all about.** "You won't pine for me will you?" she'd asked him. "Because I'm going to forget all about you." And she'd smiled her crafty smile that could have meant either she was joking or she wasn't.

There is often a loose swirl of women around them, Jamie and his friends, and Jamie now takes his appeal for granted. To demonstrate that he is, in fact, not pining for Judith, he beds the cigarette girl from a billiard hall, a couple of barmaids, a girl he meets out dancing who never stops making tart little jokes out the corner of her mouth, even when she's naked. He regards his old belief that he should love the women he sleeps with as touchingly naïve.

Judith has left some of her books in his keeping, and he reads **Modern French Painters, Painters of the Modern Mind, The Artist and**

Psycho-Analysis. He worries he has strayed too far toward the picturesque, that his lines lack rhythm, his compositions originality, that he is old-fashioned. He worries he has nothing to say with his paintings and that is why Judith has gone to Europe, to find men who do.

"Thanks, love," he says to the women he buys beer and cigarettes from, not even hearing the word anymore.

Eleven days into 1935, Amelia Earhart becomes the first person to fly solo from Honolulu to Oakland. Stars hang outside the cockpit window near enough to touch, she writes. Ten thousand people surround her after she lands, and her red Lockheed Vega seems to wallow on a human sea.

"I wouldn't want to fly over that much ocean," says Marian's boss, the man with the scarred lip.

He's not one for posturing, and she likes him for it. Most of the other guys say they'd do it, too, if they had the kind of money Earhart has from her husband and from smiling for pictures and putting her name on malted milk tablets and luggage sets and whatever else. They act like her flights some-how don't count, aren't real.

Jane Smith is a real Alaska flyer now. She shut-tles between towns and what pass for cities, out to bush villages and encampments and lonely cabins, bringing mail, food, fuel, dogs, dogsleds,

newspapers, motorcycles, explosives, wallpaper, tobacco, doorknobs, you name it. She flies men out
into the backcountry who strike it rich and others who drown or freeze or get eaten by bears or
blow themselves up. She flies corpses wrapped in
canvas sacks.

Once, a corpse smells so bad she lashes it to the
wing. Once, a woman gives birth in her plane. Once,
she lands on the frozen surface of the Chukchi Sea
to rescue the passengers of a ship locked in ice.
Somewhere she picks up a Russian word, **polynya,**
for the patches of open water in the sea ice where
whales come to breathe. The landscape is secretive and harsh and impossibly immense, and she
borrows some of its inscrutability for herself, its
disinterest in human goings-on. Unfriendliness is
another form of camouflage.

In winter, the sun rises in the south. Far enough
north, it never rises at all. She wears long johns
and wool sweaters and over those a reindeer-hide
suit. At first glance you wouldn't even peg the pilot
Jane Smith as a woman, would only see a shaggy
block—she still remembers Sitting-in-the-Water-
Grizzly, signs a blank postcard to Caleb that way
and asks someone going to Oregon to mail it from
there—but she carries a knife and a pistol for when
second and third glances happen. Rough country.

Cold is murder on planes. Fuel tanks freeze; hy-
draulic pumps don't work; rubber tires and gas-
kets turn brittle and leaky; instruments quit. On

cold mornings, she lights a fire pot under the engine, puts a canvas tarp over it to keep the heat in, watches like a hawk because the gas or oil or tarp itself might ignite at any moment and sometimes does. She's put out more fires than she can remember. She's broken propellers, skis, a wing, flown with sprays of leaking gasoline fanning out behind her. Once what she thought was solid ground had turned out to be marsh and splashed up at her as the wheels touched, flipping the plane. She was all right, hanging upside down in her seat, mucky water running in under her head. A mule team had to come pull the plane out. She patches skis with flattened-out gas cans, propellers with stovepipes, struts with birch trees. She flies in weather others shake their heads at, stashes her money away as she's done since she was a child.

Once, she flies to McCarthy, only knows she's to pick up a man and bring him back to Anchorage. He's waiting beside the airstrip in handcuffs. He's a miner, she's told. He raped another miner's wife.

Fine, she says. She has them stow him in the back with some bundled furs she's picked up. They cuff him to his seat. Fifteen minutes in the air, and she rolls the old junker plane tidily upside down. She figures if it breaks apart at least she'll take him with her, but they come upright again. He's screaming, both his shoulders dislocated.

Bad weather, she says when she delivers him under a bright blue sky. Got bumped around a bit.

The story gets out, makes a man think twice before he tries to get close to her.

Come summertime, the one-eyed circumnavigator Wiley Post is touring Alaska with beloved national wit Will Rogers in a nose-heavy, cobbled-together plane: wings from one model, fuselage from another, pontoons from yet another. Marian glimpses them in August when she's up in Fairbanks, shakes her head at that plane, those fat pontoons. Near Barrow, at the northern edge of the continent, Post and Rogers crash taking off from a lagoon and die. Marian knows lots of dead pilots now. Alaska's an easy place to crack up. Bush pilots fly into mountains, vanish over the ocean.

All the more reason to keep to herself. No need to mourn.

Helen Richey, a well-known racer and aerobatics pilot, gets hired by Central Airlines to be the first American woman to fly commercial passenger aircraft. But she's rarely on the roster, isn't trusted in bad weather, is asked to give talks promoting the airline instead of actually flying. The men in the pilots' union—there are only men in the pilots' union—won't let her join. She quits. What else can she do? No American airline hires another female pilot for another thirty-eight years.

A new American plane, the DC-3, makes commercial passenger travel profitable, can take off from mud, sand, snow, whatever you want, develops a reputation for being tough, even indestructible. Two propellers, a ninety-five-foot wingspan, an engine that can be serviced quickly and easily. The wartime version will be the C-47. Ten thousand of them. Skytrains, Dakotas, Gooney Birds. They'll fly the hump from India to China, schlepping cargo through a maze of mountains too high to fly over, the passes still at fifteen thousand feet. They'll disperse D-Day paratroopers like dandelion seeds. They'll crash in jungles and deserts and mountains and cities. They'll litter the ocean floors. Of the ones that survive the war, plenty will be repainted, refitted, find new peacetime careers. One will be the **Peregrine.**

In November, a balloon called **Explorer II** is released in South Dakota, reaches 72,395 feet with two men inside, an altitude record that will stand for almost twenty years. In their photos, seen for the first time: the curvature of the earth.

Jamie happens upon the images in a magazine, goes home and slathers white gesso over a canvas, erasing a half-finished harbor scene. He begins again: a segment of his neighborhood from a high angle, almost a bird's view, slightly warped as though by the shape of the planet, with shallow bands of harbor, mountains, and sky squeezed in at the top, ever so slightly bowed. What he wants to express, he has come to realize, is infinite space.

A Mr. Ayukawa, who owns a department store in Japantown, buys the painting from Flavian's gallery. When Jamie stops in to collect the check, Flavian relays an offer of a commission. Mr. Ayukawa would like a portrait of his daughter. "He's a businessman," Flavian says, his voice heavy with significance. "You know my meaning? He is in many businesses." Jamie is reminded unpleasantly of how people had talked about Barclay Macqueen. "You are a polite person, but you should be extra polite to him. Oh—you know that Judith is back?"

"I've seen her."

Judith had swanned into a Boar Bristle lecture, her new French husband in tow—a poet, apparently. She'd kissed Jamie on both cheeks, told him he **must** go to Europe, that Vancouver was utterly provincial, that art here was barely even art. He'd wanted to ask her why she'd come back, then, though he suspected the answer was because in Europe she would not have the pleasure of lording her time in Europe over everyone else. He remembered Sarah Fahey's sister calling Seattle a backwater, how she'd made him embarrassed for believing Seattle marvelous and cosmopolitan.

He went out and got drunk after that, painfully nostalgic for the months he'd spent enchanted by Judith, the thrill of climbing the dark stairs to her studio, the way her skin was always filmed with fine gray dust from her clay. He'd really thought—fool—that when she came back she would feel more for him than before, that somehow the expansion of her world would not diminish his place in it.

The Ayukawa family lives in a fine white house on Oppenheimer Park. Miss Ayukawa—eighteen years old, a nisei born in Canada—sits for him in a large parlor furnished in a ponderous Western style with dark rugs and heavy furniture. His painting of the neighborhood has been mounted above a long walnut sideboard. The room might have been gloomy but for the large windows. It is a breezy, unusually sunny morning. As Jamie makes preliminary sketches, rafts of yellow light and leafy shadow sweep across the floor.

"We'll never have this light again," he says. "I shouldn't get used to it."

She wears a plain brown day dress; her hair is swept up in a smooth twist. Sally, she's said to call her. Her beauty doesn't escape him even in his downtrodden state. "I should remember this city as gray because it almost always is," she says, "but I think I'll remember the sunny days best."

"Remember it?" He glances at her grandmother, present as a chaperone, clad in a cotton kimono and asleep on a burgundy silk sofa. Her needlework lies abandoned in her lap; her wire-rimmed spectacles have slipped toward the tip of her nose.

"I'm going to Japan. I'm getting married."

"Oh, I see." Her tone does not invite congratulations. "And this portrait is . . . a wedding gift?"

Her upper lip flattens in anger. Her feathery eyebrows draw together. "It's for my parents to remember me by."

He doesn't know what to ask that will unearth what he wants to know. Instead he asks her to tip her head down just a bit. After two hours, a uniformed maid comes and ushers him out.

The next time he comes to the house, the day is overcast, but the scene is as it was before: Sally in the brown dress, beside the same window; her grandmother asleep on the sofa.

Sally gazes out the window, still and steady, but as Jamie works, he senses inward agitation. He has not looked at a person so carefully in a long time, is out of practice trying to depict, the way he had in Seattle, the tidal zone where a person's inner and outer selves wash together. "How do you want your parents to remember you?" he says, moving his brush rapidly over the canvas.

"As I am, I suppose."

"What I mean is, a person's thoughts show through. For example, if you want to leave behind a version of yourself that's happy, you should think about happy things."

"Happy things," she repeats, looking again out the window. "I'm going to a country I've never been, where I know no one, to marry a man I've seen one photograph of. I'm afraid an abundance of happy things doesn't spring to mind." Her voice has risen, and she and Jamie both look at her grandmother, who does not stir.

"Only one photograph," Jamie says. "Is that . . . common?"

"It used to be, coming the other way. My mother was a picture bride. My father was already here. Their families arranged the match. She didn't mind—her generation didn't expect anything better. But I'm from **here.** My father has odd ideas. He doesn't want to go back himself, but he says it's important we don't lose touch with our homeland. **His** homeland."

With a small sigh, her grandmother rouses herself. She pushes her spectacles into place. "Junko," she says, and asks a question in Japanese that Sally answers, her tone light.

"She wants to know if you're making me beautiful," she tells Jamie.

"What did you say?"

"I said I'd told you to paint me as I am."

"They're the same," he says, made reckless by his persistent, mortifying melancholy over Judith. He doesn't know if he is trying to drive away his sadness or make it worse by groveling before another unattainable woman. Sally does not translate. She settles back into her pose, but now she looks directly at him rather than out the window.

"What does junko mean?" he asks after a while.

"It's my Japanese name," she says. After a pause, she adds, "I don't like it. I'd rather just have one name."

He returns three more times. She continues to watch him while he paints. He sees—or thinks he sees—different moods sweep through her gaze the same way the leaf shadows blow across the floor. Defiance is what he chooses to paint, defiance but, as a mercy to her parents, none of the anger that comes and goes. He sees curiosity, too, when she looks at him. Judith only ever looked amused or bored. Impossible, perhaps, to spend so many hours looking into a person's eyes and not imagine an unspoken intimacy.

I love these because I love thinking about you looking at me, Sarah Fahey had said about his drawings of her. Does Sally like thinking about him looking at her? When he works on the portrait at home between sittings, he feels a tension, a winching together that tightens into urgent desire. He adds a faint warp to the portrait's background, a suggestion of curvature, of the room pulling away from behind Sally, pushing her closer to the viewer.

On the last day she sits for him, he slips her a scrap of paper with his address written on it, whispers that he'd like to see her again. She looks at the paper, slides it into her pocket. When she raises her gaze to him again, he sees contempt, and he has a terrible sense of having made a major miscalculation. None of what he'd sensed roiling in her had anything to do with him. He is just some unimportant man trying to insinuate himself into her hour of crisis. He paints falteringly for another half hour, gives it up. He will finish it in his apartment. "I've got enough from life," he tells her.

Three nights later, in the small hours, there is a knock at his door: quiet but urgent, a light, persistent rapping. He gets out of bed and pads across, wide awake, thinking she's come after all. He is filled with a vision of how she will look, how she will rush into his arms, how they will escape together.

Two men are outside the door, white men, neither as tall as Jamie but both built like steamer trunks. They push in before he can recover from his surprise, bundling him across the room by the arms, pushing him to the floor.

Through his terror, he wonders why he had ever thought Barclay would come personally. He'd always imagined being able to at least **try** to reason with the man, to appeal to his feelings for Marian, to explain that he needed to let her go.

One steamer trunk sits on him while the other closes the door, calmly turns on the bath tap.

"We just want to know where she is," the one sitting on him says. "That's all. We'll leave you be once you tell us."

"I don't know," he says. "She didn't tell me. She knew better than that. She knew he'd send you. She was going to Seattle and then on from there to somewhere else. That's all I know."

"You expect us to believe you didn't come up with a little plan together?" says the man by the tub.

"We'll see," the other man says matter-of-factly. He has a job to do, that's all. There will be no appealing, no explaining. Jamie understands this as he is hoisted up beside the bathtub, struck in the face before his head and shoulders are plunged into the cold water.

"I don't know anything else," he says when he's lifted out. Again he's held under, brought out, struck. "Please," he says until he can't summon the breath to speak.

In the morning, he finds himself still alive, lying curled on the bare pine floor. He hauls himself up, runs a hot bath. The touch of the porcelain is horrible to him, the water full of menace, but the warmth eases his pain. Lying cramped in the tub, in water tinted pink from his blood, he plans what he will do.

Everything he will take with him fits in one suitcase. Some clothes, his better paints and brushes, sketchbooks. Because he will go from the Ayukawa house to the train station, he carries the suitcase in one hand by its handle and Sally's portrait clutched carefully by a stretcher bar in the other. The paint is not quite dry.

The maid's eyes widen when she opens the door, takes in his swollen face. "No," she whispers. "Go away!" She makes a shooing gesture.

He says, "Please tell Sally—Junko—or her

grandmother or whoever is home that I'm here, and I've brought the painting, and I need to be paid."

"No," the maid says again. "Go away!"

Jamie's confusion is intensified by his general state of addledness, his pounding headache, his urgent, determined need to flee the city. Why would the maid send him away when he's brought the painting? He needs the money he's owed, no matter how rude he must be to get it. More loudly, he tries to explain again, asks for Sally. He is nearly shouting when a dapper man in a gray suit appears beside the maid. She retreats into the house with a bow.

Jamie has not met Mr. Ayukawa before. His thick bushy eyebrows are so unlike Sally's feathery ones, but Jamie recognizes her expression when he draws them together. "I am surprised you would come here," he says.

"I'm leaving town," Jamie says, uneasy, "and I wanted to be paid. For this."

He turns the canvas to face Mr. Ayukawa, and the man's eyebrows fly up. His face is full of the same mournful astonishment as the face in the moon. When he speaks, it's in a whisper: "Just tell me where she is."

Jamie stares. "What?"

The man stares back. "We found your address in her room. You must know. Where is she?"

And finally Jamie understands.

Memories Roadshow

⌒

Fourteen

A few days after the table read, even though I'd been determined to make Redwood get in touch first, I'd cracked and texted him. **Just following up to make a plan for a totally normal, earthbound hangout.**

I'd love that! Let me check my schedule and circle back.

But I hadn't heard anything for another week, until he wrote, **Hey stranger! My mother is in town and I'd love for you guys to meet. Come over for dinner?**

When I arrived, Carol Feiffer was the one to answer the door. She keeled back for a hug, arms out, fingers extended into stiff prongs. "Here she is!" she cried, her voice redolent with Long Island. At first I thought she was talking about herself. **Here I am!** Her face was sharp as a hewn arrowhead;

her hair was the ideal version of a practical bob. Under austere layers of charcoal linen, she carried herself with regal assurance, like a spiritual guru or a university president.

"I've been dying to meet you," Carol said, leading me toward the kitchen by the arm. She leaned back, looked me up and down. "I'm not disappointed. You're every inch the star."

I gave a snorty little dismissive chuckle. "I liked your book."

She turned to me, glowing. "**Thank** you, my dear. Thank you so much. I never expected **this** to come of it. I just wanted to tell a story. Leave it to my son to make a"—she waved her hands—"whole big thing. But, you know, Marian is so important to me. I had a terrible marriage, quite honestly, and in the very depths of it I found such comfort in Marian's book. She got me through the darkest part of my life. She inspired me to seize my freedom. Which is ironic because I never would have known about her if not for the connection to my ex-husband's family." She reached to squeeze my arm. "And now you're going to bring her to so many people. You'll change lives, Hadley." She nodded at me earnestly, rapidly, forestalling any skepticism. "You will."

I didn't tell her the only life I'd given much thought to changing was my own. I didn't tell her about my covetous vision of myself hoisting a golden prize. "I hope so," I said.

Redwood was in the kitchen, tending something in a pan. I hadn't known anyone else would be there, but a girl in a white sleeveless jumpsuit and no jewelry except for a small gold ring in her nostril was leaning against the counter with a glass of rosé. She had curly hair up in a bun, a tiny, beautiful, dark-eyed face. Something about her reminded me of marzipan, the little animals you're not quite sure are food or figurines.

"Look what the cat dragged in," Carol said, presenting me, and the girl put her hand on Redwood's upper arm, like, **mine,** and in a flash I decided that this—she—was why we hadn't hooked up, why he'd been AWOL. That dick had told me there wasn't anyone. **No one at all.**

"Hey stranger!" Redwood said, and it rankled just like it had in his text, as though he were subtly chiding me for being out of touch, when he was the one who'd left me hanging. He kissed my cheek and gestured to the white jumpsuit. "This is Leanne." Leanne waved from where she was, determinedly unfazed by my celebrity, and Redwood pointed out the window. "The Day brothers are here, too, and Mom brought a friend."

I turned. So it was a whole convention. Redwood wanting me to meet his mother didn't make me special. Outside, a wiry older woman with close-cropped silver hair was standing beside the pool, drinking a glass of red wine and, without visible reaction, listening to whatever one of the Day brothers was saying. She wore jeans and slip-on Vans and a big white button-up shirt. The Days were wearing dress shirts and chinos so tightly tailored they looked like superheroes' unitards.

"That's Adelaide Scott," Carol said in such a way I knew I was supposed to recognize the name.

"Ah," I said.

Leanne, seeing right through me, said, "She's a famous artist."

"A sculptor," Carol said. "And installations. She actually met Marian Graves once, when she was a child. I brought her because I thought you might be interested in picking her brain. Not that she's not excellent company in her own right."

What was I supposed to take from a child's memory at least sixty-five years old? What tidbit could this woman give me that I could possibly use? There should be an **Antiques Roadshow** for memories, and I would sit behind a desk and explain that while your memory might be lovely and have tremendous sentimental value, it was worth nothing to anyone but you.

People's thoughts about Marian were all basically the same but usually presented with an air of revelation. Bart Olofsson had stared earnestly into my face and said things like **I see her as being very strong, very brave,** as though this was some radical theory.

Absolutely, I'd said.

Someone who's so strong, so brave like

that—she was compelled **to do the flight. Otherwise she would have exploded.**

Totally, I said, even though bravery and strength aren't reasons but qualities. I don't think she had a reason, not really. Why does anyone want to do anything? You just do.

"Adelaide!" Carol called. "Come meet Hadley."

The woman and the Days all turned. The Day who'd been talking extended one arm to usher Adelaide in, and I caught a trace of disdainful amusement on her face at being herded. "Hello, Hadley," she said, shaking my hand after they'd all trooped inside and the Days had cheek-kissed me. She was tall and willowy, had a long, pale, lined face, and wore no wedding band, no makeup except for dark red lipstick. I couldn't decide if she was beautiful. "I hear you're an actress."

Carol made a show of friendly exasperation. "Hadley's a **movie star,** Adelaide."

Adelaide's tone conveyed a shrug. "I'm afraid pop culture is an area I've particularly neglected."

"But pop culture is so **fascinating,**" said one of the Days. "You just have to look at it on a deeper level. It's like contemporary art in that sometimes the actual product isn't the point as much as the context in which it's created."

Adelaide gazed at him without interest.

"I agree," Leanne jumped in. "Like take Hadley's **Archangel** movies. As a feminist, I object to their emphasis on traditional gender roles—the man as the protector, you know—but as a consumer I was still sucked into the love story, gobbling down the popcorn. It's a dog whistle only women can hear." She took a green olive from a bowl and popped it into her mouth.

I asked her, "How do you and Redwood know each other?"

"We're old friends," Redwood said.

"We deflowered each other," Leanne said, extracting the olive pit from her lips.

"Leanne!" Carol said, covering her ears.

"Don't pretend you didn't know," said Leanne.

A buzz. Redwood went to a panel on the wall. "Hello?"

"IT'S HUGO," came a roar through it.

"It was right before she left on the flight," Adelaide said. "She came to see my mother in Seattle. I would have been five."

The eight of us were sitting at the table outside, under the wisteria, eating salmon with some kind of too-sweet sauce of Redwood's invention. Redwood had set out place cards, which meant I now knew which Day was Kyle and which was Travis.

"My family collected art," Adelaide went on. "My mother was an old friend of Jamie Graves. We still own quite a few of his paintings, though most are out on loan."

Carol piped up. "That's how I found Adelaide. I knew of her work, of course, but I didn't realize there was any connection to the Graves story until I was researching my book and started looking into her family's collection. I've been thinking—wouldn't it be fabulous if there were a Jamie Graves exhibit to coincide with the release of the film?"

"At LACMA," Travis Day said. "Hundred percent yes. Or maybe a more unconventional space, somewhere—"

"Yes!" Carol interrupted. "LACMA would be fabulous!"

"Or somewhere more unconventional," Travis said again. "Like a warehouse or somewhere repurposed."

"Do you want me to talk about Marian Graves or no?" Adelaide said.

Travis looked miffed. Carol clapped a hand over her mouth. "Go ahead," she said in a muffled voice.

"Marian came to town in 1949 just to see my mother," Adelaide said. "They'd never met before, but they had Jamie in common. And also—Carol put this in the book—my grandmother had helped Marian get an abortion when she was leaving her husband, although no one told me that until I was an adult."

"That's why she came?" Hugo said. "To reminisce?"

"You'd have to ask her," Adelaide said. "Good luck with that."

I took a preparatory breath. I had a sense of ful-filling my duty, asking my prearranged question, like the littlest kid on Passover. "What was Marian like?" I said.

Scraping the sauce off her fish with a butter knife, Adelaide said, "I couldn't say, really. I told Carol I wouldn't be much help to you, as I wasn't much help to her."

"You were a tremendous help," said Carol.

Sir Hugo leaned forward and fixed Adelaide with his signature piercing stare. "But you **do** remember her."

Adelaide seemed immune to the piercing, refused to buy into the drama of her role as eyewitness. She made an inscrutable moue with her red lips, said, "Marian Graves was a very tall, very thin, very blond grown-up I was called in to greet more than sixty years ago. I don't think she was good with chil-dren. I don't think she said much to me. Honestly I'm not positive I actually remember her at all or if I just remember the memory." She looked at me. "See? Nothing you can use."

"You never know," said Carol. "It was you who told me about Caleb Bitterroot." She turned to Hadley. "There's very little out there about him, but once I realized he'd been in Marian's life from beginning to end, I saw the outline of a grand ro-mance. I'm very intuitive that way."

"What she means is that there's no proof of any

romance at all," Redwood said, and Carol made a **psssh** sound and flicked her hand at him.

"Is it different," Leanne asked Sir Hugo, "playing a real person versus a fictional character?"

He swirled his wine. "A bit. With a real person, you need to be cautious of falling back on an impression. Your task is to make the person, fictional or not, **seem** real."

"Same with writing," said Kyle Day, but no one paid him any attention.

"It's not like you can really know **that** much about anyone, anyway," I said, annoyed that Leanne had clearly intended the acting question only for Hugo. "No one sees most of what we do. No one knows more than a tiny fraction of what we think. And when we die, it all evaporates."

Adelaide looked at me with a new glint of interest, sharp but unreadable.

"My parents died in a small-plane crash when I was two," I told her. "I was raised by my uncle."

"Ah," she said. "So you understand something about Marian."

"I don't know," I said. "I can't tell if I do."

"Mitchell Baxter," said Travis, and when Adelaide, predictably, looked blank, he added, "He was Hadley's uncle. He directed **Tourniquet**."

"Ah," said Adelaide.

"He's dead now, too," I said.

Carol, trying to get us back on track, said, "I

think Jamie Graves and Adelaide's mother, Sarah, were lovers."

"Of course Carol has the spicy theory," said Leanne.

Sir Hugo hoisted his distinguished eyebrows at Adelaide. "Do you think they were? Or do you perhaps **know**?"

"They were childhood sweethearts," she said, "but in my admittedly new acquaintance with Carol, I've noticed she thinks any two people who have anything to do with each other are probably lovers."

"I'm a hopeless romantic, what can I say," Carol said.

"I'm not," said Leanne, pouring herself more wine.

"Me neither," said Sir Hugo. "I'm a hopeful hedonist. Redwood? Did you inherit the dreaded romance gene?"

"It's recessive," said Carol, "and his father did **not** have it."

"I'm open to possibilities," Redwood said. "I don't know if that's romantic or not. Maybe I'm a cautious romantic."

"When I first met Redwood," I said, avoiding Leanne's eye, "he told me his go-to emotion was ambivalence, and ambivalence isn't romantic."

"What about you?" Adelaide looked at me glintily again.

"Not a romantic," I said.

"Come on, don't say that," said Travis, who I'd begun to sense was nursing an interest in me. Ordinarily I might have flirted back, but something about his shininess, his zeal repulsed me.

"No?" Adelaide said to me. "What, then? Are you a cynic? A skeptic? A stoic?"

"I don't know what I am," I said. "Everything always seems to fall apart around me."

"You're a wrecking ball," said Sir Hugo.

"What about you?" I asked Adelaide.

"I was a romantic for a long time. Disastrously. I believe since then I've been what's known as an opportunist." Beadily, she looked me over. Her deadly confidence reminded me of a bird of prey, a hawk or a falcon. "A piece of advice for you," she said. "Knowing what you don't want is just as useful as knowing what you do. Maybe more."

Sometime after dessert, when everyone had adjourned to the living room for one more drink and to listen to Redwood play the piano, I'd gone to the bathroom. When I came out, a figure was waiting in the dark hall. Adelaide.

She moved closer, holding out her phone. "I don't mean to lurk, but would you give me your number? I might have something more for you about Marian, but I didn't want the whole gang to know." Her voice was low, unhurried.

I didn't ask why. I tapped my number into her phone. Then we walked back toward the crazy cascading sound of "Flight of the Bumblebee," saying nothing, locked in a conspiracy I didn't understand.

An Incomplete History
of the Graves Family

~

1936–1939

A German immigrant named Bruno Hauptmann is convicted of kidnapping the Lindbergh baby and executed. Charles and Anne Lindbergh, hounded beyond endurance by the press, flee to England with their second son. Someone in the American embassy cooks up the bright idea that Lindbergh should pay a friendly visit to the German Air Ministry, casually gather intelligence on the new Luftwaffe. He tours fields and factories and the air-research institute, Adlershof. He lunches at Hermann Göring's gilded and bejeweled house, attends the opening ceremonies of the Berlin Olympics.

Hitler, Lindbergh concludes, might be a bit of a fanatic, but sometimes you need a fanatic to get things done. (Lindbergh is a fan of getting things done.) The German people seem to be bubbling over with vigor; the Luftwaffe would woefully outmatch anything America could cobble together. No, the way German Jews have been stripped of their citizenship isn't ideal, but Nazism is certainly preferable to Communism, isn't it. Two sides to every coin.

In 1936, Marian is no longer Jane Smith, because Barclay is in prison. She reads about it in the newspaper. He could still send someone to find her, she supposes, but she has had enough of hiding, of vanishment. "My name is actually Marian Graves," she tells people in Alaska who have known her for more than two years, and they have less trouble making the switch than they might have because she seems like a different person now, will look you in the eye, appears capable of interest, of pleasure, unlike the gloomy and taciturn Jane Smith.

With the money she's socked away, she buys her own plane, a high-wing Bellanca, and goes into business for herself. For a while, she flies out of Nome, lives in a ramshackle cabin near the airfield. Muskoxen wander past her outhouse, ancient-seeming creatures, haloed by their own frozen breath, their thick coats swinging around their ankles like monks' robes.

The price of gold has gone up, and she flies geologists to the fields, brings engineers to build the dredges and men to work them. With the seasons, she flies cannery workers and miners in and out. She flies to the reindeer herders, passing low over the swirling brown galaxies of their animals.

People pay her in gold dust, in pelts, in firewood, in oil, in whiskey. Plenty often they try not to pay her at all.

Plenty often she goes north over the Brooks Range, up where trees don't bother trying to grow. In Barrow, at the Territory's northernmost tip, seal and polar bear skins dry on stretchers outside the houses, and staked dogs howl at her plane. Once, out of curiosity, she flies beyond the whale-rib gateway that marks the extent of the coast and out over the loose northern jigsaw of spring ice that the planet wears like a skullcap, flies far enough north to see where the jigsaw begins to fuse into one immense ice quilt, ridged high where the currents have forced the pieces together.

A dizzy feeling to being so far north.

Barclay hadn't assembled an army of lawyers when the feds came for him but pled guilty to their charge of tax evasion, took a sentence of seven years. He paid a fine to the government, but the ranch is safe, as it had long been in Kate's name. Other assets—his speakeasies and roadhouses turned legitimate businesses after the repeal of Prohibition, his hotels, his shares in mining and construction companies, the Kalispell cottage, the Missoula house, the Stearman biplane, which had eventually been found where Marian had abandoned it—all this technically belongs to Sadler. Even Barclay's bank accounts are in the names of companies registered to Sadler.

Marian flies under green auroras. She flies under the midnight sun.

The Bellanca gets wrecked and patched so many times it's a jumbled mass of **spare parts flying in formation,** as Alaskans say. **Better hope the termites keep holding hands,** they say. Still it flies well enough until a storm blows it away across a frozen lake and crashes it to bits against rocks on the other side. She gets another one with a bigger engine.

Since she is herself again, she writes to Caleb, tells him where she is, encloses a separate letter for Jamie, asks for his address since she can't imagine he's still in that flophouse in Vancouver.

Jamie has left Vancouver entirely, Caleb reports, and gone into the mountains to be, he thinks, an art hermit. **The decision was sudden and he wouldn't say why, but he seems fine. I guess all three of us were meant to live in splendid isolation.**

She considers flying to see Jamie but finds she doesn't want to leave Alaska, is frightened by the thought of crossing back into her old life. So maybe she's not quite herself again, not that she's foolish enough to think there is one fixed version of a person.

In time she heads south to Valdez, forms a loose partnership with a pilot who supplies the high-altitude lode mines in the Wrangell and Chugach Mountains. He's worked out a method for landing on glaciers. If the light is flat, he makes a low pass and drops something dark—anything, a gunny sack or a branch—onto the ice to help with depth perception. He shows Marian how to look for the undulation in the surface snow that means buried crevasses, how to slip sideways on landing so the skis are at a right angle to the slope and the plane doesn't slide away over the edge.

In Valdez, since she keeps skis on the plane all year for glacier landings, she takes off from mud-flats when the tide is out. She learns to rock side to side in her seat as she throttles up to help pry the skis free from the ooze. To the mines she delivers the usual meat and flour and tobacco but also dynamite and carbide, steel and lumber and spools of cable, barrels of oil, all manner of machine parts. Once she has a pair of prostitutes as passengers, once a member of Roosevelt's cabinet. Once she flies an orphaned grizzly cub to Anchorage, bound for a private menagerie.

People like to remind her that she is from outside. You can't become an Alaskan. It's just not possible. She is not one of them, but still, she feels she belongs.

. . .

Denver, spring of 1937. Jamie edges around the bedroom door, and Uncle Wallace, sitting propped up with pillows, squints uncertainly.

"It's Jamie," Jamie says. "I came to see you."

Wallace's face cracks open with delight. "My boy," he says. "How wonderful."

Jamie grasps Wallace's hands, sits on the edge of the bed, catching the sweet odor of morphine. "How are you?"

"At death's door." Wallace pats Jamie's cheek, the patchy blond scraggle that grows there. "But you're not a boy at all with this beard. It's been at least a year since I've seen you—is that possible?"

"I suppose it is," Jamie says. They have not seen each other in more than five years. Five years since he'd put a frail, trembling drunk on the train to Denver.

"And where is—where is—"

"Marian's in Alaska. She's a pilot."

"She's the reason I'm here, you know. Her and her husband. Is he in Alaska, too?"

"He's in prison."

Wallace seems unsurprised. "Good," he says, but mildly, as though he'd been told the weather was fine.

Wallace's housekeeper, stout and matronly, pushes the door open with her rump, backs in with a tray of coffee and sliced cake. "Thought you might like a hot drink and something to eat, Jamie, after your journey."

"This is my son, Jamie," Wallace tells her, patting Jamie's arm.

"I've met Jamie," she replies. "I let him in. He's your nephew." To Jamie, she says, "He gets confused. Especially about names, things like that. Details."

"I'm not **confused**," Wallace says bitterly, but when she holds a cup of water to his lips, he smiles and takes a docile sip. She touches his forehead, and Jamie wonders what they have been to each other.

"Tell me something," Wallace says when she's gone. "Anything. Dying is boring. Regale me with tales from outside this room."

Jamie tells Wallace about the mountain cabin where he lives, once abandoned, a half-day's walk from the nearest settlement. He'd repaired the roof and floor, recaulked the gaps between the logs. He keeps a garden and chickens for eggs; he fishes in a nearby river, has learned to can vegetables and smoke fish, to plan ahead for the winter. "You remember I wouldn't fish before?" he asks Wallace.

"Yes," Wallace says vaguely, nodding. "The worms, wasn't it?"

"I felt sorry for the fish," Jamie says, "not the worms. I still do, but I've made peace with it."

Wallace nods again. "You have to live the way you want," he says. "That's what I did. No other life seemed honorable to them because theirs was such a wretched hardship. They thought anyone who lived another way was too big for their britches and must be immoral."

Now Jamie is confused. "Who thought that?"

"Our parents, of course. You remember. You were the same way."

Wallace has him mixed up with Addison. "Was I?" Jamie says.

"Of course you were. If you hadn't left, I might never have thought of leaving. But you had to go to sea." Wallace pats his hand. "Tell me something else."

Though Jamie isn't sure whether Wallace is talking to him or Addison, he tells him, trying to make the story sound funny, about the two men who'd come to his apartment and nearly drowned him, how he'd assumed they'd been sent by Barclay Macqueen when in fact they'd been emissaries of Mr. Ayukawa, whose daughter had run away, probably with some man.

"We've all had mishaps," Wallace says. "Then what?"

In the mountains, he'd begun painting obsessively. Even before he'd had a mattress or a functional stove, he'd stood in the ruined little shack and worked.

"I'd had an idea about incorporating the curvature of the earth into my paintings, and I've been building from there. I've been making landscapes that are sort of . . . folded. Have you ever seen how the Japanese fold paper?" There is a sketch pad on Wallace's nightstand, and Jamie rips out a page, tears it carefully into a square, folds a crane.

"A bird," Wallace says, holding the delicate thing in his trembling fingertips. "Did the man pay you for the painting?"

Jamie had laughed on the Ayukawas' doorstep, laughter that stung and buzzed in his sinuses like turpentine vapors. He'd bent over with his hands on his knees, wiping away tears. "She ran away?" he'd said.

To Wallace, he says, "He paid me more than we'd agreed on. I think he felt guilty."

"Good," Wallace says. "Good."

In five days, he is dead. There is a will, leaving the house in Missoula to Jamie and Marian. He wishes to be buried in Denver.

Jamie delays writing to Marian, whom he feels obscurely estranged from, writes to Caleb instead. He does not intend for Caleb to go to Alaska to tell Marian the news, but that is what Caleb does.

"What's the closest you've ever come to dying?" Marian asks Caleb. They are lying in her bed, in her cabin outside Valdez. He has been with her for three nights; she doesn't know how long he will stay.

She had sprung for a double bed to celebrate her return to her real name, and they have never had so much space to share. Sprawled on his back, he says, "I don't know. I don't think you **can** know."

"Isn't there something in the past that chills you to think about?"

"Not one thing in particular." Facetiously: "It takes more than death to scare **me,** Marian."

"Do you remember after Trout died how I flew to Vancouver?" She tells him about the skipping engine, the crevasse, the cold. That was when death had **felt** closest, she says, but maybe she'd actually been closest when she was a baby on the sinking **Josephina.** She would have died and never known anything about it, never known what a ship was, or an ocean, or a fire. She wouldn't have known what death was.

Caleb said he thought all living things knew about death, at least enough to struggle against it.

"Or maybe I came closest some other time," she said, "and didn't even notice."

The first night, after he'd told her Wallace was dead, after they'd walked along the shore, watching the sea lions and bald eagles, she'd drawn him into bed. She hadn't been with anyone since Barclay, and memories of him came as sharp intrusions of panic and claustrophobia. She hadn't told Caleb what Barclay had done, but he seemed to have an instinct. He held her gaze when he came, offering her his helplessness. The second night had been better, and the third, and on this, the fourth, she'd almost believed she'd returned to the time back before Barclay, when she and Caleb had made love with simple urgency. Almost. She can never go back.

He is broader than she remembered, solid, a man.

A little impatiently, he says, "It's too much to think about: everything that might have happened but didn't." But, in the same brusque tone, he says to the ceiling, "There was one time when I was a kid. Gilda had a man. Usually I ignored what she did, but that night I couldn't take the sound of them. I decided to go to your house even though it was snowing hard. It didn't even occur to me to worry about finding my way, but the snow was piling up. I couldn't see the shape of the ground to get my bearings. I couldn't see anything, really. The wind was up. I'd been walking for much too long, but I didn't want to admit I was lost, not that admitting it would have changed anything. I knew I shouldn't, but I sat down to rest." He stops.

She remembers Barclay's story about the night they'd met, about collapsing drunk in the snow. "Then what?"

"Well, I didn't die."

"Go on. Tell the rest."

"You can imagine. I got too cold. I remember trying to decide if I could bear to keep living with Gilda. In the end I don't know if I really decided anything, but I stood up and walked a little way, and then I saw the lights of your house, not far away at all. I went in through the kitchen and tried to pretend I wasn't as cold as I was, but Berit wasn't fooled."

Marian props herself up. "I remember that! I'd forgotten all about it. Is that what happened?

I remember you coming in completely blue and Berit whisking you away. I listened at the bathroom door and heard you crying in the tub."

He winces. "My hands and feet were frozen. Thawing them was awful. Berit kept asking why I'd been outside, and I kept telling her I'd heard wolves around the cabin and had gone out to hunt them. Usually she didn't have any patience for my tall tales, but that time she played along. She asked if I'd gotten any. She sat beside the tub and listened to me chatter while I thawed. I was crying the whole time, it hurt so bad."

"Good old Berit."

He makes a small sound of agreement, says, "But afterward, for some reason, what Gilda did didn't matter anymore. I felt, I don't know, fortified. Like suddenly I was aware I could choose my fate."

"I think I understand."

She tells him, flatly, about the war she'd fought with Barclay over her womb, the siege she'd endured. "I needed a shock to leave—it was the pregnancy that fortified me."

He rolls over to kiss the inside of her elbow, and when he lifts his head his face is strained with anger. "I already hated him, but now I want to kill him."

"There are worse things."

"That's not the point."

"It's in the past."

"Not entirely. You're changed."

"You're not." They smile. She says, "I can't make myself understand that I'll never see Wallace again."

"Have you forgiven him?"

"I think so. Barclay would have found another way."

Caleb makes a strange grimace. "He sent me a letter for you. Everyone knows I'm your postmaster."

"Wallace did?" She doesn't understand why he has waited so long.

"No, Barclay." Caleb gets out of bed, rummages in his bag, drops a sealed envelope in her lap.

Marian—

I don't know where you are, but I will live with not knowing. Not knowing is an atonement I can make and one I know you would want from me. In case you doubt the weight of my sacrifice, I will tell you my dearest dream is to walk out of these gates a free man, find you, and beg forgiveness. Without your forgiveness, I believe I can never consider myself truly free, and so I won't be. I'm sure you think I want something more—that forgiveness, once gained, won't satisfy me and I'll try to forge onward, to take back your love, and that I will be as I was before: too passionate, throwing myself against your walls until I am battered beyond recognition to either of us. I used to think that if only you would open to me and

embrace what was between us, we would both
be happier. I was so caught up, so overwhelmed
by my own certainty, I couldn't see that you are
someone for whom being fully open is the same
as being destroyed. You kept telling me that
the version of you that seduced me in the first
place was incompatible with the version of you I
wanted for a wife. You exert such a mighty pull
on me, Marian. I was turned inside out by it; my
guts were hung out for the birds to peck. I regret
the things I did while writhing in that particular
agony. I'm not blaming you, but I'm offering
my suffering as a small token of explanation.
I deserve to suffer more, I know. I can't say I'm
glad there was no baby, but I do recognize that
maybe some larger wisdom was at work there.

I'll leave this now, Marian. I expect no reply,
though I long for one. I won't assume your
forgiveness, but I'll continue hoping to see you
again one day so I might ask for it in person.

Barclay

P.S. Perhaps you've heard somehow, but Sadler
and Kate have married. Are you surprised? I was.
I wish them more happiness than we found.

Marian sits for a moment with the letter open
in her lap. Her eye catches the word **passionate**

again, and she leaps from bed to throw the papers into the stove.

After Caleb leaves, Marian is lonely for the first time since coming to Alaska. The uninhabited ring of space she'd cultivated around herself begins to seem less like a protective barrier than scorched earth. At night, restless, she thinks of Caleb, sometimes of Barclay, of how he'd been before he turned. (A turn—that is how she thinks of what happened when he'd pried the diaphragm from her body.) She touches herself, thinking of Barclay more often than Caleb, and afterward is ashamed, troubled.

As an experiment, she goes to bed with a man and then a few others, ones she seems unlikely to run into again or can reliably avoid if she wants: no pilots, no miners, nobody in Valdez. There is a boatbuilder in Seward, a newspaperman in Anchorage, a Canadian geologist just passing through. Alaska has a glut of men. From each encounter she takes a small supply of images that she shovels like burial earth on top of her memories of Barclay: a stranger's face contorted and exposed by concentration, the grip of hands on her hips, certain murmured words. She wondered what memories they take from her, what fragments they revisit in lonely times.

Jamie finally writes:

Dear Marian,

I know Caleb has told you the sad news.
Forgive me for not writing sooner. We've had
such a long silence that breaking it felt somehow
overwhelming. I've been blue ever since burying
Wallace—bluer than blue, like the tail end
of dusk. Some of it's plain grief, but I think
I am also mourning the past. I told Wallace
that you are a pilot in Alaska, and he didn't
seem surprised at all, though to be fair he was
generally a little foggy. I've tried to throw myself
back into my painting—my one real companion
since I left Vancouver—and I've been finding
myself painting memories of Wallace's
paintings, landscapes I haven't seen in years and
remember only in the vaguest way, trying to
reproduce them and also capture some sense of
time's distortion.

From Marian's response: **It's been too long a
silence. For now let's not try to fill in everything
that we've missed but continue fresh from the
present.**

In July, Amelia Earhart and her navigator,
Fred Noonan, nearing the completion of an attempt to be the first to fly the earth's full circumference, an equatorial great circle of twenty-five
thousand miles, take off from Lae, in Papua New
Guinea, bound for Howland Island, a fleck of land

twenty-five hundred miles away. They never arrive. For decades people will believe she is still alive, that some complicated saga followed her last radio communication. But almost certainly she ran out of fuel, crashed into the ocean, and died.

In January 1938, a spectacular aurora ripples over Europe. First a green glow on the horizon, then someone is connecting the stars with a quill pen, red ink bleeding upward, arching across in crimson pulses, in orange plumes that unfurl and vanish. London must be burning, people in Britain say, gazing at the sky. Firefighters in the Alps are sent to chase flickering reflections on the snow. Across the continent, people call their local police, ask, **Is it war? Is it fire?** Not yet. It's a solar storm. Charged particles from the sun collide with gas molecules in the atmosphere. In Holland, crowds awaiting the birth of a princess's baby cheer the aurora as a good omen. Across the Atlantic, in Bermuda, people think the streaks of red mean a ship is burning at sea.

Jamie, in Canada, takes the aurora as an omen, too. He will do what he has been thinking about doing. He heaps six months of work in the snow, making a tidy cone of his paintings of his memories of Wallace's paintings, splashes them with kerosene, tosses on a match. The paint blisters and bubbles; black-edged holes spread, disintegrating the canvas. Prodding the pyre with a branch, he feels terrible regret and also relief. The paintings were halfway between one thing and another. He'd needed to make them, but only in order to experience destroying them.

The next time he goes to town, there is a telegram from Flavian. One of his landscapes has been chosen for a purchase prize by the Seattle Art Museum. Flavian, retroactively begging Jamie's pardon for his audacity, had entered it in an exhibition. Flavian would like to know if Jamie has more work for the gallery. Also, Jamie is expected in Seattle in one month for the prize ceremony.

Once, caught out overnight in Cordova by abysmal weather, Marian meets a well-dressed woman older than herself, the unmarried heiress to a cannery fortune, who offers to share her room in a hotel already overcrowded with fellow strandees. There is only one bed, of course. After a good meal with wine, after they've gotten under the covers, the woman murmurs an offer to scratch Marian's back, quietly enough that Marian could pretend not to hear. But she says all right, turns on her stomach, tugs up her shirt.

Fingertips trail down her back. A weight turns over low in Marian's belly. It has never occurred to her that a woman could summon such a feeling, yet there it is; the touch is so light, so expert, that Marian is curious to know what else might be possible. She shifts onto her back, and the gentle fingers, without hesitation, trace over her ribs. The woman's lips touch Marian's sternum as delicately as if meeting a porcelain teacup. Marian is wearing men's white cotton drawers, and she lifts her hips and pushes these down.

Through the whole encounter, she does not touch the woman, or kiss her. She remains perfectly passive, not submissive, exactly, but cool, almost regal, until her thighs clasp around the woman's head, and she shudders. After, she turns over and, removing the woman's lingering, questioning hand from her hip, goes to sleep.

When Marian returns to Valdez, a letter from Caleb containing another letter from Barclay is waiting for her. She throws this enclosure into the fire without reading it. For a while, she thinks of the woman more than anyone else at night.

Marian hears about Kristallnacht on the radio, feels dread tempered by distance. Everything seems far away except the mountains, the mines, the glaciers.

Charles Lindbergh goes to Germany, accepts a medal from Hermann Göring. A camera flashes.

When, in April 1939, he returns to the States, he is less a hero than before, rumblings in the press about how he's become a mouthpiece for the Germans, an appeaser. America, Lindbergh is very certain, must not enter the war. "We must band together," he writes in **The Reader's Digest,** "to preserve that most priceless possession, our inheritance of European blood."

He believes himself fair-minded, blessed with elevated logic. And if Lindbergh believes something, then, Lindbergh believes, it must be true. He starts making radio addresses, then public speeches, draws crowds, fills places like Madison Square Garden with thousands of people who simply don't want to go to war again but also with Nazi sympathizers, fascists, and anti-Semites (whom the others are willing to overlook).

A brief detour into the future: After Pearl Harbor, Lindbergh shuts up. He tries to go to work for PanAm or Curtiss-Wright, and his offers are at first eagerly accepted then awkwardly rescinded because the White House disapproves. Eventually he persuades the marines to send him to the South Pacific as an observer, asks to go to the front lines. He flies dawn patrols and rescue missions, fires on Japanese planes though he isn't really supposed to, figures out methods of reducing fuel consumption, which expands fighters' ranges. He's genuinely helpful. His reputation is rehabilitated somewhat, but he will never be as he was.

After the war, his marriage frays but endures. Anne writes books, chafes under his efforts to control her and the children when he is home, which is not often. He secretly takes up with three German women, has seven secret children with them. Does he want to repopulate the world with little Lindberghs? He tells his children again and again that they must be mindful of genetics when choosing mates.

In his sixties, he dedicates himself to advocating for endangered species and indigenous people. He is obsessed with the threat of nuclear war. He'd helped to shrink the world but wishes it had not shrunk.

When a Saturn V rocket rises from its launchpad, carrying the astronauts of **Apollo 11** to the moon, Lindbergh is there in Florida, craning up at the vanishing spark. The rocket burns more fuel in the first second of its launch than the **Spirit of St. Louis** did getting from New York to Paris.

In 1974, on Maui, he dies. He does not want to be embalmed, chooses wool and cotton clothes and wrappings that will decay. He wants Hawaiian hymns to be sung for him. He makes sure there is room for Anne in his grave lined with lava rocks, but, almost three decades later, she will choose to be cremated, scattered elsewhere.

Flavian had come personally to drag Jamie out of the mountains and bring him to the prize ceremony at the Seattle Art Museum, which he had endured uneasily, unused to crowds of people and nervously vigilant for any Faheys. None had appeared, but the Turner watercolors he'd discovered in their attic had been on display, arranged in a luminous row on an otherwise empty wall with a plaque beneath: ON LOAN FROM THE FAHEY COLLECTION. They are only simple washes of color on small rectangles of textured paper, and yet they seem to convey sprawling vistas of the sea and sky, infinite space.

Among the many hands he shook, one belonged to a man from the WPA. Why wasn't Jamie working for the Federal Arts Project, he wanted to know. It was meant to keep artists in work. They needed a mural for a library in Bellingham. Would Jamie do it?

Yes, he said, though Flavian was displeased, wanted him to keep painting canvases that could be sold and, please, Jamie, please, don't burn any more, at least not without showing them to Flavian first.

But Jamie had liked the idea of painting something rooted to one place, something solid. He closed up his mountain cabin, shaved his beard, returned to his home country. After he'd finished the mural in Bellingham, the WPA had sent him to Orcas Island to paint a mural in a post office. Now, in the first weeks of 1939, he is on a train, going to meet Marian in Vancouver. Their reunion is long overdue, but she didn't want to cross back into the United States proper. Not yet. He wears a black overcoat and a gray worsted suit, finds himself eager to revisit the city he'd fled in a panic.

Marian had fit two auxiliary fuel tanks into her plane's cargo hold and taken three days to fly from Valdez, with four stops. She'd kept mostly to the continent's shoreline, snowy peaks to her left. She felt mostly the simultaneous focus and boredom of an uneventful flight, though she'd had to wait out some weather and, a few times, under the steady grind of her engine, she'd thought she heard the phantom skipping and coughing of Barclay's Stearman.

When she'd arrived at the hotel, the man at reception had given her clothes a long, censorious looking-over, but she'd lifted her chin and held out her money (grease under her fingernails). She'd arranged with Jamie that he would choose a hotel but she'd pay for their rooms. She'd insisted. He has little money, and she's doing all right. In the hotel she'd taken a bath and tried to tidy herself, but there was only so much that could be done, only so much she was willing to do. Even if she'd wanted to wear a dress, she no longer owns one. She has a lipstick but no other makeup. Her face is densely freckled, her hair chopped and mangled as always. She'd put on a clean shirt and trousers, wiped her boots with a hotel towel, smoothed her hair, pinched her cheeks. She wants Jamie to look at her and see a seasoned bush pilot, to see, somehow, six years of survival in rough country and to be impressed by the fight of it but also to believe her competence is so total that every challenge has been met with ease and aplomb. So she'd armored herself in boots and trousers and shearling jacket but with some regret, as she also wants him to think his sister beautiful. She hopes she won't seem too strange.

He is standing near the fireplace in the lobby, his hands in his pockets, and he turns toward the stairs as she walks down. He doesn't seem startled, only happy. She is the one who's surprised. He is a grown man, though of course he is. Like her, he is still very blond and freckled, but his hair is expertly cut and stylishly oiled. Even in the small motion of turning to greet her, he'd given off a new self-contained ease. "Are you always so dapper?" she asks as he hugs her, patting her bearishly on the back.

"Only when I want to impress someone." He holds her at arm's length. "You're still not interested in blending in."

"Will I embarrass you?"

He offers his arm. "Never."

They walk to dinner, their long strides matching. They are a little stilted with each other at first, uncertain how best to carve into the years that have passed. They talk about Wallace, about the house and what they ought to do with it. Jamie, they eventually agree, will go to Missoula to sell it, find a place to store what should be kept (Addison's books and souvenirs, Wallace's paintings) and sell the rest. Old Fiddler has died, but he'll find homes for the dogs still around. Neither imagines ever living in Missoula again. Jamie insists war will indeed come, gets a righteous pleasure from predicting catastrophe even though, in his heart, he can't quite believe people would be so foolish. Even someone like Hitler—how can he want another war? How can anyone want it? Jamie is puzzled by the fundamental concept, the idea that people must kill one another in staggering numbers until someone somewhere somehow decides they should stop.

Marian has no answers. Her world is so uncrowded she can't fathom enough people getting together to have a war. The idea of battle seems puny and futile against the inhuman enormity of the north.

They eat at a chop suey place Jamie knows, a dim, narrow room with bottle-green booths and hanging lamps. The waitress brings beer and cups of egg soup, but Jamie leaves his spoon in the saucer. He says, "Have you heard about Barclay?"

Marian looks up. "Has he been released?"

"He was." Jamie hesitates. "But there's something else." He pauses again, clears his throat, says, "Barclay is dead."

The news thumps her like a gust of wind. A ringing in her ears. Jamie goes on, "It was in the newspapers. I thought you might have seen. Not long after his release, he was driving from the ranch to Kalispell, alone, and it seems someone knew enough to be lying in wait. It was a rifle shot from a distance."

She finds she is bracing against the table, grasping its edge. She makes herself let go, gulps from her beer. "When?"

"Just last week. Caleb said everyone thinks Sadler did it, since he and Barclay's sister had gotten used to being rulers of the realm. The police don't seem very interested in investigating, and I don't know how much there is to investigate, anyway. No one saw anything. Sadler seems to have an alibi. According to the newspaper, Barclay died a pauper. On paper anyway. You were mentioned in the article but not by name, probably Sadler's doing. It just said no one knew where his wife had gone. There was a will, but I guess you weren't in it."

Marian's hand shakes as she sinks her spoon into the soup, watches the viscous yellow liquid flow over its sides. What is this feeling? It's too strong to be identified, the way heat and cold can both burn. Shock, she supposes. She lifts the spoon, spilling some. The soup sears her mouth. Jamie pats her knee under the table, doesn't say anything. She wipes her cheeks with a napkin, shakes her head. "No more of that," she says, meaning the tears.

Barclay will never show up in Alaska. He'll never show up anywhere. She had burned his last letter unopened. But what could it have said? Should she have written back to his first letter, told him she would forgive him only if he forgot her, left her alone forever? Would that have changed anything? Did she want anything changed? Can you mourn and rejoice at the same time?

"Why would they need to kill him?" she says, her throat rough, burned from the soup. "Everything was in their names already." She wonders if Sadler and Kate loved each other. Had they always? She had never seen any signs, though maybe that's what Kate had meant when she said she wasn't just an old maid. She decides she doesn't care. They are no more consequential than characters in a book read long ago. They will not come looking for her.

"I don't know," Jamie says. "I don't know how any of it works."

"You said a rifle shot? Just one? And Barclay was driving—he hadn't stopped the car?"

"I think so."

"Sadler wasn't a good shot."

"Maybe he got lucky."

"Sadler wouldn't have wanted to plan on luck."

They stare at each other, wondering.

The waitress brings a plate of noodles with pork, a bowl of green beans in sauce. Carefully, Marian says, "When Caleb came to see me in Alaska, I told him some things about Barclay. Things I hadn't told anyone. He was angry."

They look at each other for another long moment. Jamie says, "We shouldn't think this way. We shouldn't go down this road."

"I'm not sorry he's dead. But I always thought I'd see him again. I thought there was some reckoning still to come."

"I know."

"I used to think I would never feel free of him unless he agreed to free me."

"I know."

"Sometimes I still feel that way."

"You are free. You have been for a long time. You're feeling the shock."

"I meant what I said. I **am** glad he's dead."

"I'm glad he's dead, too. Will you tell me what you told Caleb?"

"Maybe later. I need another drink first."

"In Vancouver," he says, "some men came to my apartment in the middle of the night once and roughed me up. They kept demanding I tell them where 'she' had gone. I assumed they were Barclay's goons trying to find you, but they were actually **different** goons looking for a **different** woman. It was farcical. Like something that would happen to Wallace, having so many goons after you that you lose track." He laughs.

Marian is horrified. "Is that why you left Vancouver?"

"Partly. And two women in a row had hurt my feelings."

"Tell me."

After dinner, he leads her some blocks to a bar he likes. Cold mist hangs in the air. A few of his

Boar Bristle friends will meet them later. A street-car rattles past, hats and newspaper tops filling the windows. He says, "Do you think you'll ever marry again?"

"No."

"I thought maybe you and Caleb, someday."

"No. Can you imagine? Two hawks in a box."

Through gaps in the buildings: a sliver of the harbor, the lights of ships. She imagines Caleb in the trees, waiting with his rifle, patiently watching the road below.

Fall Once, Fall Forever

―◡―

Fifteen

When someone lurks in a dark hallway waiting to ask for your number, you expect them to use it. But I heard nothing from Adelaide Scott.

I wasn't Katerina anymore, but I was still contractually obligated to go to a nerd convention in Vegas to promote my last **Archangel** movie, to sign autographs and sit on a dais with Oliver and answer questions, even though I hadn't seen or talked to him since before The Night of Jones Cohen. My contractual jet picked me up at Burbank. My contractual veggie tray was waiting with my specified bottle of Dom. M.G. fell asleep before we even took off because what could he really protect me from on a plane. Augustina played a game on her phone. The jet launched itself up into the night.

I ate half a weed gummy bear and drank some champagne. It was my first time flying since my lesson, and I'd worried the vertiginous feeling would come back, the terrible downward suction, but it didn't. I flipped through Marian's book again. Every time I opened it, I had that same feeling I'd had as a kid, like there was something hiding in it. Everyone had their own idea of what **Peregrine** the movie would be, how best to squeeze Marian's completely unknowable existence into a neat pellet of entertainment, and I thought I should have one, too. Adelaide Scott had said it was as important to know what you don't want as what you do, and at least I knew I didn't want the movie to be about either plucky girl power or the tragedy of biting off more than you can chew. A paragraph caught my eye:

My brother, an artist, said what he wished to convey in his paintings was a sense of infinite space. He knew this task to be impossible, as, even if a canvas could accommodate such a concept, our minds seem incapable of grasping it. But he said he believed, most of the time, that an unachievable intention was the worthiest kind. My flight has as its stated intention a plain and, I believe, achievable goal, but that intention has arisen from my own inherently unachievable desire to understand the scale of the planet, to see as much as can be seen. I wish to measure my life against the dimensions of the planet.

Were we doing a bad thing, compressing her? Reduction was inevitable. You have to choose a version, even if that version will be as dwarfed by reality as a life is by a planet.

Below was pure darkness with scraps of light floating in the distance and pinprick headlights strung along I-15 like dewdrops on a spiderweb. In a while we came down over a bright dense tangerine city suspended across a black desert void. I could see the Strip with its castle and pyramid and fountains and huge revolving wheel, a row of glossy hotel blocks like gigantic foil-wrapped candies.

A black SUV was waiting on the tarmac. On the way to the hotel, Augustina ran through the schedule. Interviews in the morning, a panel in the afternoon with Oliver and the director and a couple of other actors followed by the reveal of the new trailer, a VIP meet and greet afterward, then a fence-mending dinner with the director and people from the studio. Out the window, the city blinked and flashed like a spaceship disguised as a city.

"Is Oliver here yet?" I asked, fiddling with my phone.

"He is," she said. "Do you want me to—"

"No."

We went into the hotel through a secret entrance for high rollers and The Famous, up a secret elevator. Vegas is full of these hidden portals, gilded crawl spaces for golden rats.

I sat on my enormous white bed and looked out my wall of windows. I ate the rest of the weed gummy bear. I ate some smoked almonds from the minibar. I stared out at where the city's embers met desert blackness and worried about seeing Oliver, wondered if I should text him to break the ice. When he'd vanished, he'd been punishing me, but he'd also made everything easier. The thought of facing him made me squirmy. I didn't want him to be mad at me, but I needed him to be mad so I'd know I mattered.

I lay back on the pillows, texted Redwood instead. **Thanks again for dinner last week. It was fun.** Leanne had stayed when everyone left, and the memory of her waving from the doorstep with Redwood and Carol gave me a dark and discontented feeling.

A few minutes later: **Thanks for coming! My mom was excited to meet you. We need to hang out soon.**

:), I said.

I waited to see if he would add anything else. When he didn't, I wrote, **So I'm in Vegas.**

Gonna win big?

Somehow I doubt it. I typed and deleted, typed and deleted, typed, **Leanne seems cool, but I thought you said you weren't seeing anyone**

[Thinking-typing dots]

I don't know if I am

Ok?

Do you ever let things play out a little with someone just kind of to distract yourself?

That's maybe the only thing I've ever done

I think Travis Day has a thing for you

[Emoji with the flat mouth and flat, pained dashes for eyes] **Does Leanne know that's what's up?**

Unclear

Distract yourself from what?

Also unclear

I typed, deleted. Typed, deleted. **I think I miss you a little.** I sent it before I could think more.

[An eternity of the three dots, then nothing.]

I woke up early, restless and bothered, itchy for something to happen. I ate a room-service breakfast while staring at the city, the desert, all of it pale and washed-out. The days here were the nights' ashes.

Oliver was already in the greenroom when I came in with Augustina and M.G., and his beauty, so familiar, popped in my face. I could almost **hear** it. He opened his arms and said, in a small, sad voice, "Hey."

I knew everyone in the room was watching us when we hugged, but when I looked, their eyes snapped away. Oliver steered me to a couch.

"How have you been?" I said, awkward, shifting around, black leather squelching under me.

"Good." He nodded. "Yeah. Better. I had a hard time for a while."

"I'm really sorry. I wanted to tell you that. We never talked, so—"

He held up a hand in deflection. "Let's not."

"Okay." I didn't know what he wanted me to say, or not say.

"How are things with Jones?"

"I was never **with** Jones."

"I'm seeing someone."

I wasn't remotely surprised, but I said, "Really? Who?"

A young guy in a headset and lanyard hurried over and squatted beside us. "Guys, I'm **so** sorry to interrupt, but I've been asked to let you know we're running slightly behind. It's going to be a minute. Thanks **so** much for your patience."

When the guy had hustled off, Oliver said the name of the actress who was taking over as Katerina, and I laughed a high, incredulous trill. Startled faces swiveled, bounced away again. I whispered, "Isn't she seventeen? You do know that's illegal?"

Irritation and mild pity came into his eyes, as though I were some pathetic low-level bureaucrat avenging my own insignificance by clinging to arbitrary rules, and maybe I was. "She's an old soul. I was seventeen when I met my ex."

"And look how well that worked out."

"I don't regret it." He gave me a tragic look. "I never regret loving someone."

"Must be nice."

"Meeting her really helped me get over you."

Even though deep down I'd never believed he loved me, I was struggling to resist his plaintiveness. He leaned closer, emanating tender melancholy, and I understood that the best and easiest thing I could do would be to join him in his version of our story, to cut loose the tangled mass of what had really happened.

"It's really nice to see you," he said.

I pulled a veil of wistfulness over my face. "Yeah. You too."

The door opened, and Alexei came in.

"We'll always be friends," Oliver said during our panel, blasting his light out at the crowd like Moses parting the Red Sea. "I only want good things for Hadley. She's an amazing person."

We were sitting side by side at a long table in front of a backdrop of the endlessly repeating convention logo. People held up their phones, recording. I summoned a cloying smile. I said Oliver and I still cared deeply about each other. I said I would miss the franchise and the **Archangel** family, but I was looking forward to moving on. I was excited about the future. Alexei was standing just off the edge of the stage; I didn't dare look at him. I'd barely looked at him in the greenroom, either, afraid everyone would see me blazing bright for him, afraid he'd see it.

A screen rolled down. The lights dimmed, and there was Archangel, golden and frozen. There I was in chains. There was Oliver on a throne.

Light reflected back on the audience. I watched them watch my image, their faces all angled up at the screen like it was going to feed them. But Alexei, when I dared glance at him, was watching the actual me. Sometimes I imagined meeting him again for the first time but under different circumstances, if he were divorced or had never married, but then we would have been at the mercy of a different Olofssonian system of a different past, pushing us forward through a different network of chain reactions. Maybe then there wouldn't even have been a flicker. Or maybe then there would have been love, or enlightenment.

I was in a white, fur-trimmed dress being chased across a snowy plain by a man dressed all in black, carrying a black ax, his face covered with a black knight's helmet. I stopped running. Below me was a dizzyingly high cliff of blue ice, sheer and deadly. Black waves broke against it, throwing up plumes of white spray. The camera started pulling back and up, revealing that the ax man and I were alone atop an iceberg, and the iceberg was floating in an empty, stormy sea. Close-up on my face as I watched my attacker approach. Cut to black. **Fall once, fall forever** appeared in white text, faded away, was replaced by the release date. Everyone cheered.

In bed in New Zealand, Alexei had told me about his parents, who were loving and intellectual and performatively stodgy in a dust-ruffle-pipe-smoking-Bush-voter way that he'd come to think of as white-people camouflage and broke his heart because it didn't even work. He'd talked about the maddening bullshit that came with being black in Hollywood, no matter how stuffy your upbringing: how lonely it was sometimes, how awkward development people could be, how clear it was when they wished there wasn't a black dude in the room so they wouldn't have to feel uncomfortable ignoring race or making tokenist suggestions. How everyone assumed he only represented black talent or basketball players. How he still got taken for an assistant even though he was thirty-nine years old and crazy successful. How he still got pulled over so cops could express skepticism about his ownership of a Tesla. Before Oliver got **Archangel,** Alexei's boss had told him to cut off his dreads. **You want to be taken seriously, you need serious hair,** he'd said. Alexei hadn't done it, though, and now he was a partner and no one ever said anything about his hair except to compliment it too much.

He sidled up sideways during the VIP meet and greet, both of us aiming our words in the same direction like we were driving down a road somewhere.

"I didn't know you were going to be here," I said.

"Me neither until two days ago. Oliver's been after me for a boys' weekend. I ran out of excuses."

Oliver thought Alexei didn't have enough fun, Alexei told me, and had insisted on buying him lap dances and a Patek Philippe watch, insisted on losing fifty thousand bucks at poker, insisted on spraying champagne over the crowd at some club where a famous DJ occasionally pressed a button on his laptop. "I don't remember signing up for any **Entourage** reenactment society," Alexei said. "Am I supposed to have a rage attack in a Porsche now?"

This made me laugh in the faces of the VIPs on approach, some rich-looking parents and two tween girls in alarmingly sexy Katerina outfits. From the other side of the room, Oliver glanced at us. "Excuse me," Alexei said, pulling back into his shell of professionalism, drifting off toward Oliver.

More little girls showed up, and people in costume, and a lone bearded guy who unpacked a whole esoteric theory about the underlying philosophy of **Archangel.** I smiled and signed things and posed for photos, but all I could see was Alexei, even when I wasn't looking at him. Redwood had gone out of my head almost entirely. When I did think of him, it was with tenderness, even nostalgia, as though our affair that hadn't happened yet was already far in the past. When Alexei came sidling up again, I didn't look at him, but he filled my horizon like a thunderhead.

Sideways, he said, "Do you want to get a drink after this?"

It's cool, we were both projecting in the dim light of the secret bar for high rollers and The Famous. It's chill. We're friends. And what do friends do? They hang out. They catch up. We each held this fiction in front of us like a shield.

"You won't leak it, will you?" Alexei said about Oliver dating a teenager. "That's really the last thing we need right now."

"Does Gwendolyn know? Is she devastated?"

He rolled his eyes. "She suspects. Oliver's had to launch a charm offensive."

"It'll get out eventually."

"Not everything does," he said, looking at me intently. "I hope to god not everything does."

An enormous sculptural light fixture hung from the ceiling, a ball of blue glass tentacles resembling a sea anemone that cast us in a watery glow.

"No," I said, "some things are just between two people."

"But," he said, "that doesn't mean those things don't maybe scare the shit out of people. Maybe people **thought** they could just have a little fling but then the reality freaked them out."

"But," I said, "maybe other people could have been more understanding, too. I feel like people might have been impulsive and might have refused to see the big picture."

He smiled, his cheeks shining blue. "Maybe."

I sipped from my drink. "Seems possible."

"Maybe also some feelings have lingered more than one individual expected," he said.

"That might sound familiar," I said.

From there we kept on with our looping, harmless, catching-up talk, but the shields had been lowered. It's easy sometimes to feel like audacity is its own form of protection, like recklessness somehow neutralizes danger. Sitting in our purple velvet booth, I didn't ask him about the state of his marriage or what, specifically, his feelings about me were or anything I really wanted to know. I talked about Sir Hugo and Marian Graves, and I turned Redwood back into a dupe we were all bleeding dry before he was washed out of town on a wave of bewildered disappointment.

"Is it going to be good?" he said. "The film?"

I'd only ever asked myself that question and never answered it. Usually I was surrounded by people insisting it would be good, not letting in any doubt. "I don't know," I said. Suddenly everything felt as precarious as when I'd taken the Cessna's yoke. Alexei rested his hand on my knee, steadying me.

In my room, he peeled off my dais-appropriate jeans and blazer, put his face impatiently between my legs. When we were fucking, he turned me onto my stomach, and he murmured my name in my ear while my face was in hot pillow darkness, and I found I was crying. Outside, the desert faded purple and then black while someone turned up the dial on the city, lit up that tangerine net, ready to catch some unseen circus performer falling from the sky.

When Alexei left, I stood in the doorway in a hotel bathrobe and kissed him beneath the glossy black bubble that hung from the ceiling like an egg laid by a sea creature, the glossy black bubble meant to make sure no intruders reached the vestibule between the elevator and the door to my suite, the glossy black bubble that concealed a camera that recorded our kiss, a camera that sent silent, time-stamped, colorless footage of our kiss to some hotel security guy who probably hated his job and hated the assholes who stayed in these suites and maybe already knew I was a scandalous little whore and wanted everyone to know the extent of my slut-tiness. Anyway, that guy saw a chance to make a buck, and he took it.

The War

~

Valdez, Alaska
October 1941
Two years and nine months after Marian and
Jamie met in Vancouver

Marian had hoped the war would not find its way to Alaska, would not bother with such a place, but in 1940, someone somewhere had finally considered the strategic advantages of that gigantic cold fist of Pacific territory and the growing likelihood that any and all strategic advantages would soon be needed. Anchorage filled with soldiers. Frantic construction began on bases there and in Fairbanks and on a string of a dozen airfields running east-west from Whitehorse, in the Canadian Yukon, to Nome on the Bering Sea. Supplies and materials and people flooded in on ships, seeped north into the interior by truck, train, riverboat, airplane.

No one was going to give a government contract for supply hauling to a woman, but the pilots who did get contracts had more work than they could handle and, for once, a customer who could be trusted to pay up. Some threw jobs Marian's way. With her share of the money from Wallace's house she'd bought a battered twin-engine Beechcraft off a guy who was giving up and heading back to Arizona, and she rented a proper frame cottage in Fairbanks. She was known for her spooky ability to fly in bad weather, landing exactly where she intended even when the whole Territory was under one big impenetrable cloud. Some of the other pilots called her a witch. She didn't mind. She'd told Barclay she was one because she wished she were.

Finished bases sprang up among the mountains and out on the tundra, with hangars and control towers and houses with all the modern conveniences, tidy settlements made from bits and pieces she'd helped haul up, everyone as industrious as ants. The wilderness was still mostly wilderness, but Marian felt possessive of the land, worried for it. The new military pilots coming in thought they were hot shit, but they didn't have to learn the country. They'd only just learned to fly. They flew from one beacon to another, landed on actual runways, not in the bush. Yes, storms still came in like holy hell. Yes, planes still disappeared and were never recovered, but a pilot didn't have to earn Alaska like before, not in her opinion.

She took a break and flew herself down to see Jamie, who was living in a drafty clapboard house overlooking a drizzly, melancholy Oregon beach. He'd stopped working for the WPA because he didn't feel right taking employment meant as relief. Collectors had started buying his paintings; three landscapes had gone in a traveling exhibition as far as Boston and New York, one had been bought by a museum in St. Louis. He'd parted ways with Flavian—been seduced away, really, by a prominent dealer in San Francisco.

"I don't know why I think Alaska should stay as empty and difficult as it's always been," she told him as they walked on the broad, empty beach. The waves left behind gleaming skins of water on the sand, silver with reflected fog. "It's ungenerous of me, and less for the sake of the place than for my own vanity."

"You went there because you needed a place to hide," Jamie said. "It makes sense your instinct would be to keep people out."

"Maybe. I do have an idea of it as a fortress." She picked up a shell, tossed it out into the water. "You should come see it. You should paint it."

"I'd like to. I will."

His new paintings pulsed with an eerie, internal light. They retained some of the warp of the first landscapes he'd made after leaving Vancouver, and although the ocean, which has no angles, was his most common subject, the work still conveyed a sense of folding, a compacting that, paradoxically, suggested expansive openness. One large canvas was propped up across from the narrow iron-frame bed where Marian slept, as wide as the wall and nearly as tall. Looking at it, she had the feeling of flying toward the horizon.

After a few days, she left without saying good-bye, flew on to Missoula over a landscape rusted with fall. A real airport had opened west of town. Some of the same pilots were still around, incredulous at the sight of her. They told her they'd been sure she was dead, one way or another.

A history professor from the U and his family had bought Wallace's house, and when she walked past it on her way to Caleb's cabin, she saw the paint was bright and new, the roof mended, the windows clean. The barn appeared unoccupied, but the cottage had been spruced up, with fresh paint and flowers in window boxes. A little girl in a blue dress playing with a doll on the porch stopped to watch Marian. Another woman might have paused to say hello, explained that she and her brother had slept on this very porch when they were small. Another woman might have been wistful for a childhood lived in a well-kept house, in apparent safety and security, but Marian's wistfulness was only for the particular simple wildness of the years when her only concern had been how to enlarge her world. She went on her way, along the trail into the trees.

"I have a girl," Caleb said. "I thought I should mention it."

Marian felt an unpleasant jolt. They were sitting on the back step of his cabin, drinking whiskey from tin cups. "Good for you."

"I thought if I wrote and told you, you might not come."

"I would have come," she said, not knowing if that was true. She had been enjoying the nearness of his body, the cool air and the orange leaves, the pleasant anticipation of sex. But now she felt hot and furious and, to her horror, near tears. She cleared her throat. "You should have told me, though, so I could have figured out somewhere else to stay."

"Stay here. I'll sleep on the floor."

"Would your girl like that?" He didn't reply. She said, "Who is she?"

"She teaches English at the high school. She came here all alone from Kansas. You'd like her— she's gutsy. Brave, actually."

"Yes, so brave, being a schoolteacher."

He was very still. In a low voice, staring into his cup, he said, "I knew you wouldn't like it."

"But you let me come here anyway. Were you **testing** me?"

"If I had been, now I'd know that you don't care about seeing me unless we're—" He broke off. "I don't know what to call it. I don't even know what we do. Do we fuck? Make love?"

She'd never had a word, either. "What do you call it with her?"

"We don't do that."

"You **don't**?"

"She's not like that."

She seethed. "Not like me."

He stood up. "No, not like you, because with her I know where I stand. I know what she wants from me."

She stood, too, facing him. "All right. Go on. What does she want from you?"

"She wants . . . I don't know. She wants to go on walks in the mountains and have picnics. She wants to have a nice time."

"How sweet, Caleb. Good for you finding such a nice girl, finally."

His gaze might as well have been an awl. "She wants me to love her."

Marian couldn't catch her breath. She knew he was setting her up to ask if he had given this woman what she wanted. But she would not. She felt like a snarling dog. "Are you going to **marry** her?" He flinched. She said, "So you're actually just as conventional as anyone. You're going to live in a sweet little house with a sweet little woman and make a bunch of babies and read the newspaper every night with your slippers and pipe."

"I don't know!" Nearly a shout. "What do you want me to do? Stay here and be ready in case you need a letter delivered? Not that you ever say thank

you. Should I wait around in case you need someone to tell you how completely justified you are in
doing exactly what you want, when you want, even
when it's the worst possible decision you could
make? Or in case you want me to fuck you once
every five years? And then you'll just go off again
without even saying goodbye."

He spun and walked rapidly away, then dropped
into a squat, his head in his hands. She went to
him, knelt in the dirt. He sat back, pulling her with
him. His embrace was painfully tight. With one
hand, she gripped the end of his braid, tugged it.
"I'm sorry," she said into his shoulder. "And thank
you for delivering my letters."

He was quiet for a long time, his face buried in
her neck, clinging to her. Finally he said, "Next
you're going to say goodbye."

"I don't do that."

"But you're going to leave."

Against his chest, she nodded.

Seattle
December 1941
Two months later

As soon as Jamie stepped into the exhibition, wearing a borrowed, too-short tuxedo and holding a saucer of champagne, he looked for Sarah Fahey. For weeks, he had nursed a fearful hope she would attend.

In the years since he'd come to Seattle for his purchase prize, he had avoided the city, largely for fear of running into Sarah or any of the Faheys. But fear of what? What could they do to him now? In better moments, he thought: Nothing. In low moments, he had cataloged four nagging yet irrational fears. First, he worried they might conclude his entire career had been an attempt to climb his way into their echelon. Second, he was afraid they would somehow make him realize his work was ridiculous and he was an impostor. Third, he feared he would still love Sarah, and, fourth, he feared he would not.

But those last two were particularly silly because, he'd decided, really the only reason she persisted in his thoughts at all was that their separation had been so abrupt. She was like a book with the final pages torn out, leaving him at the mercy of his imagination. If he were to see her, she would no longer be an enticing mystery but a real woman, no longer a dream sylph his mind could turn to when things went awry with other women (as they always did) nor a magical solution to all the riddles and disappointments of his existence. Also, he theorized, he'd been so starved for love when he met her, so desperate for a life of his own, that he'd blown their youthful romance wildly out of proportion. It had been a summer of kisses, no more. If he could just see her, he would be cured of her.

And quite probably she would be married, which would be a resolution in itself.

In any event, enough was enough. To refuse this exhibition would have been lunacy. He'd arrived two days before the opening to supervise the installation and had spent his free hours wandering around the city, taking in a decade's worth of change. On his walks, he'd gleaned a bittersweet enjoyment from remembering the boy he'd been in this place. Thinking about Sarah felt acceptably nostalgic in Seattle, not pathetic, as it did elsewhere. In his clapboard house on the Oregon shore, he sometimes looked at the old drawings he'd kept of her, her teenage likeness still stirring him, and afterward felt gloomy and ashamed.

But then, there she was. Though they were separated by a noisy, spangled crowd, though her back was to him, he couldn't have missed her. She was looking at an Emily Carr painting, her small head with its careful upward twist of glossy brown hair silhouetted against swarming brushstrokes, trees and sunlight swirled together in a euphoric vortex. A triangle of bare back showed above the lustrous emerald dip of her evening gown. These things—the twist of hair held by a pearl-studded comb, the delicate, exposed spine—had no obvious visual connection to the girl he had known, but still he'd recognized her without hesitation or doubt.

His own painting, a six-by-ten-foot rectangle of Oregon shoreline, had a wall to itself, off to Sarah's left. She studied the Carr for another minute before stepping sideways to the next canvas. After another period of contemplation, she moved on again, drawing closer to Jamie's painting while keeping her gaze averted. Deliberately, he thought. Everything about her seemed deliberate. Lanky elegance had replaced her timid adolescent gawkiness.

He began to maneuver through the people, seeking a better vantage for when she finally looked at his painting, though part of him also wanted to leap between her and the canvas, to forestall her judgment by assuring her that he already knew it was inadequate, a failure, like all his work.

Someone grasped him by the shoulder, stopping him. "Marvelous," said a man Jamie remembered vaguely as having something to do with the museum, small and pink and curly-forelocked as a cherub. Was he a board member? The man pumped Jamie's hand. "Absolutely marvelous. My congratulations."

Jamie thanked him distractedly. Sarah was on the last canvas before his.

"I must ask you," the man said, straining onto his tiptoes, trying to catch Jamie's eye, "how did you develop this technique—style, I suppose—of creating angles? The sense of folding? Its effect is so original—you've intrigued me! Did you simply stumble upon it?"

"Origami," Jamie said shortly. He downed the last of his champagne, set the glass on a tray held aloft by a passing waiter.

"What?"

"Origami. Japanese paper folding."

"Really? **Really.** The little birds and frogs? Fascinating. I would never have made the connection, but I see. I see! Tell me—have you spent time in the Orient?"

Sarah squared her shoulders, pivoted left, and stepped in front of Jamie's painting.

Sea and sky were gray, barely differentiated except through the brushstrokes, subtle angles suggesting the billows of clouds and the rhythmic geometry of swells and currents. In the foreground loomed the huge haystack shape of the famous basalt formation on Cannon Beach. This he had rendered, in contrast to the sky and ocean, as flatly monolithic, a black void. Sarah was very still against its darkness.

"Mr. Graves?" said the cherub.

Jamie's body was dissolving into anxious effervescence. His mouth was dry. "Excuse me," he whispered, brushing past the man just as Sarah turned from the canvas.

What was her expression? He tried to fix it in his memory for later examination: cheeks flushed, eyes wide and liquid and active, neither recognizably appreciative nor obviously displeased but clearly **provoked.**

When she caught sight of Jamie, she startled and froze. Her flush deepened, spreading rapidly down her throat to her décolletage. Pressing a hand to her sternum, she smiled sheepishly, tremulously.

In a fluster, he hurried toward her, tugging at his cuffs, cursing himself for being too proud to buy his own tuxedo. He'd told himself he didn't care how he looked, that he had no wish to pretend to be a fat cat (though Jamie was no longer by any means poor), and now his comeuppance was to resemble a scarecrow. He darted to kiss her cheek.

"Sarah." He didn't dare say anything else. When he'd imagined their meeting, he'd failed to account for adrenaline, for shaking knees, trembling fingers. He jammed his hands into his pockets.

"I wondered if you would be here," she said. She touched her throat. "I'm so nervous. Why am I nervous? We're old friends."

Gratified by her admission, nettled by the word **friends,** he said, "Old sweethearts, actually."

"We were **children,**" she declared, laughingly but with a note of insistence, and chattered on before he could reply, saying, "I can hardly believe it. I see your name attached to these really truly extraordinary—really, Jamie—these paintings, not just this one but others, too, and I still picture a boy." The crowd pressed in densely, and she was pushed closer, almost against his chest. All of him was alive to her. She clasped his forearm quickly, almost covertly. "I tried to imagine you grown up and couldn't, but now that I see you, you make perfect sense."

He was studying her. "I know what you mean. You've changed but you haven't." The bones stood out more sharply in her long face than they had, but still there was an inevitability to her adult self. The long, veiling eyelashes that had given her a shy, modest affect as a girl were blackened with mascara, and as she looked up at him through them, he sensed with some disquiet a new artfulness to her.

She gestured at the canvas, said, "I look at this and I am so proud. I don't have any right to be, but I am."

"It's . . ." He trailed off, looking at the canvas. "It's not what I wanted it to be, but thank you. The truth is I would never have become an artist if not for that summer."

"That's not true."

"It is."

"It isn't. You were meant to be an artist. You didn't need some silly little romance to make you one."

Jamie's pulse of displeasure at **silly** and **little** were countered by the avidity in her gaze. He had the sense she was trying to memorize him, too. "It wasn't just that," he said. "No one had encouraged me before. You gave me a sense of possibility. Not just you. It was your mother and your father, even though . . ." He hesitated, then hurried on. "And being around all that art. It was an education, a beginning."

He was breathless, surprised by his own earnestness. She was beaming. She said, "Well then, the heartache was worth it."

Just then, a man slid from the crowd, putting his arm around Sarah's waist. He kissed her temple, drew back, and pressed his palm to her forehead. "You're burning up. Are you feeling all right?"

Flustered, she pulled away, then turned back apologetically, pressing his shoulder with hers. "Yes, just warm."

"You should get some air. I'm sorry—hello." The man offered his hand to Jamie, who, gripping it, imagined he could still feel the dampness of Sarah's brow on its palm. **Whose heartache?** he wanted to demand of her. **Yours? What did you mean?** The man said, "Lewis Scott. I interrupted. I was distracted by concern for my lovely wife."

"Lewis, this is Jamie Graves," Sarah said. "The artist and my old friend. Jamie, this is my husband, Lewis."

"Oh!" Lewis said. "I've been wanting to meet you for ages!"

Jamie had been too intent on Sarah's face to notice her wedding band. This man, her husband, was sandy-haired and genial-countenanced behind tortoiseshell glasses. A prominent, slightly humped nose did not detract from his handsomeness. His tuxedo fit perfectly.

Leaning in, Lewis gestured, as Sarah had, over his shoulder at the Cannon Beach painting and lowered his voice. "It's the best one here. I don't know a fraction of what Sarah does about art, but even I can see it's a knockout. Everyone's been saying so. Congratulations."

Miserably, Jamie thanked him.

"I can tell you're not the kind of artist who eats praise for lunch. I'll stop embarrassing you right after I tell you those old portraits you did of the Fahey girls are spot-on. Sarah's hangs in our house still, and it's one of my favorites of all our art. I'm biased, of course, but there it is. Now I'm done. No more torturing you with compliments. Down to business. How long are you in town? We'd love to have you over for dinner. You should meet the boys."

Almost apologetically, Sarah said, "We have two sons. They're four and seven."

Jamie cleared his throat, said, "You've been married awhile, then."

"Eight years," said Lewis. "Sarah wasn't even twenty. I was a medical student at UW and relentlessly persistent. Could you come tomorrow?"

"Tomorrow's Sunday," Sarah said. "We have to go to my parents'."

"Couldn't we skip it?"

She gave Lewis a look rich with the silent communication that comes from a long and intimate history. Jamie felt contorted with envy. She'd married only two years after he'd left Seattle, maybe even when he'd still been drunkenly rattling around Wallace's house, mooning over her. He said, "Don't change your plans because of me."

"I would dearly love to change our plans," Sarah said, "but my father would be difficult about it. You remember how he is."

"I didn't realize you knew the mighty patriarch," Lewis said, and Jamie understood that Sarah must have told him very little about their past. (Because it did not matter? Or because it did?)

"I've seen some of your family's pieces on loan

here," he said to Sarah a little stiffly. "Is your father still thinking about a museum of his own?"

"Oh, I never know what he's thinking. Sometimes he wants a museum, sometimes he wants to sell everything. Then when he does sell one, he immediately wants to buy it back. I've stopped trying to keep up." To Lewis, she said, "Jamie was the one who discovered those Turner watercolors. They were moldering in a box somewhere."

"If tomorrow's out, then come the next night," Lewis said. "Would you? I know it would mean the world to Sarah. We're always having boring doctors over. An artist would be a breath of fresh air."

Jamie had intended to leave the next day. To accept Lewis's invitation, he would have to add not one but two nights at his hotel. No, it would be better if he pled other commitments, departed as planned. He was about to offer his regrets when Sarah touched his arm again. She said, "Please come."

It was settled.

In the morning, Jamie went back to the museum to take in the exhibition without the obscuring crowds and the distraction of Sarah Fahey—Sarah Scott, he reminded himself. The gallery was empty. His footsteps sent up soft echoes. The canvases, all Pacific Northwest landscapes, abounded with trees and mountains, islands and ocean. The artists had taken different approaches to conveying light, had complicated or simplified their scenes in pursuit of different moods and effects, but still Jamie grew depressed looking at one after another after another. What was the purpose of painting all these branches and waves? No painting would ever definitively capture trees or the sea. But was that even his goal? Definitiveness? He longed to communicate something not about trees but about space, which could not be defined or contained. Was the pursuit in itself reason enough to persevere? He didn't know.

All the other questions he had for himself concerned Sarah Fahey. For example, why had he agreed to go to her house for dinner? There was a simple enough answer: He wanted to see her again. He wanted that so badly he was willing to endure the excruciating presence of her husband and children, to witness another man living out a dream he'd once had for himself. But why? When he examined his feelings for Sarah, he found violent confusion. There was no giddiness in his heart, no euphoria, only churning unease. If he spent more time with her, though, he supposed his present feeling might have the chance to settle into something recognizable. Perhaps a sentimental, nostalgic affection. Perhaps indifference. Perhaps love, after all. He didn't know which he was hoping for. Was love worth cultivating even if it came to nothing?

After he'd finished with the exhibition, he took a stroll through the museum to visit the Turner watercolors. By the time he emerged, it was eleven-thirty, and since he'd skipped breakfast, he ducked into the first diner he came across, sat at the counter and ordered coffee and scrambled eggs with toast. He was still waiting for his food when a cook in a soiled white jacket came out from the kitchen and switched on the radio perched on a shelf above the cash register, put the volume up so loud everyone in the room quit talking and turned to look. A clipped nasal voice was talking rapidly about Japanese envoys and the State Department, Thailand, and Manila. The president's press secretary, the voice said, had read a statement to reporters. Slowly Jamie gathered that Japan had bombed a naval base in Hawaii. A teenage girl two stools down burst into tears. When the reporter said a declaration of war was certain to follow, some people cheered. The program ended with promises of further bulletins, dropped without fanfare back into regularly scheduled programming: the New York Philharmonic playing something dismal and discordant.

Jamie didn't know where to go, so he walked toward the waterfront. Apparently others had the same idea because a crowd was already gathering, mostly men, milling around, casting baleful looks to the west, at Bainbridge Island and Japan somewhere beyond it, as though a swarm of air-planes might appear on the gray horizon at any moment and the men would . . . what exactly? Throw stones as the bombs rained down? Feeling foolish, Jamie left the crowd to its posturing, walked uphill. The city had taken on a stunned quiet, distinct from a normal languid Sunday hush. The tinny, ambient buzz of radios seeped from windows. People stood clumped on the sidewalks. To Jamie, the war so far had been like the sun, relentless and undeniable but not to be looked at directly. Distant continents were being consumed by suffering and death, and, even if the impulse was cowardly, he had avoided fully confronting the horror of it for fear that he, too, would be swallowed up. But there was to be no escape. He felt as he had as a child in the mountains when he'd found himself, more than once, trapped far from shelter as a storm approached, bristling with lightning.

From his pocket he drew Sarah's embossed card. He remembered the street. She lived near Volunteer Park, not far from her parents.

Sarah opened the door after he'd rung the bell twice. Her eyes were red-rimmed, and new tears sprang up when she saw him. She didn't seem to question why he'd come, only beckoned him inside, saying, "It's too awful." She hugged him quickly, almost roughly, then lifted the hem of her skirt to wipe her eyes, seeming for a moment like a little girl. "Anyway," she said, laughing a little, "welcome."

The Scott residence was an imposing two-story Craftsman with a deep front porch. Inside was spacious and airy and surprisingly full of houseplants. Philodendrons sent down tendrils of heart-shaped leaves from shelves and tables; potted palms stood politely in corners as though waiting to be asked to dance. Geometrically patterned rugs were scattered on walnut floorboards, and an eclectic collection of artwork adorned the walls. The sound of a radio droned from within, growing louder as Sarah led him down a hallway and past a dining room. She stepped around abandoned toys: a metal truck, a hobbyhorse, a misshapen castle built from wooden blocks. Through a doorway into a small study or library, Jamie glimpsed his old portrait of her, matted and framed, a brass lamp fixed above it.

"Is Lewis home?"

"No, he runs a clinic in one of the shacktowns on Sundays. He left before the news came, but he would have gone anyway. People count on him. He's a good man." This last was said with such obvious defensiveness it gave him a perverse hope.

"And your sons?"

"They slept over at my sister's so we could go to the opening. I haven't been to retrieve them yet. I don't want them to see me this upset. Do you remember my sister Alice? She has two boys almost the same ages as ours. Come into the sunroom."

The sunroom was bright with flat silver light and crowded with plants. Jamie was reminded of Sarah's mother's conservatory, where he had felt so adult when invited for coffee. The windows looked out onto a sloping lawn, electric green under the overcast sky. From a portable radio set amid a thicket of ferns on a side table came the information that Japanese immigrant populations on the West Coast had been put under strict surveillance. Sarah lowered the volume to a murmur, picked at the ferns. "I'm supposed to feel patriotic, I think, but mostly I'm afraid. And so angry." She gestured to a wicker chair with floral cushions. "I'm sorry. Please sit."

"I don't mean to intrude."

She sat on a love seat at right angles to him. "I'm glad you came. I've just been staring into space, envisioning what will follow from this. The powerlessness might be the worst part. And the rage! I don't know what to do with it. I'm grateful my boys are so little still, but all those other mothers . . . I can't think about it. They'll want doctors. I'm sure Lewis will go if he can. I'd go myself if I could. What will you do?"

The question hadn't occurred to him, though, yes, of course, he was an able-bodied twenty-seven-year-old man. He couldn't begin to grapple with the possibilities and so put them aside, saying, "It's hard to imagine you wanting to go to war. I think of you as being so gentle."

"Yes, well, I'd prefer a gentler world. But everybody has their limits, don't you think?"

He remembered his surge of happiness that someone had shot Barclay Macqueen. "It seems so."

"I feel like I might burst out of my skin with anger. I want Germany and Japan to be nothing but ash and rubble. I want to come down from above in a blaze of vengeance like a Valkyrie and make them pay. Is that at all what Valkyries do? I've never thought about killing anyone, ever, and yet I find myself daydreaming about putting a bullet right between Hitler's eyes. Don't you?"

"Hitler seems so abstract, like the devil."

"He isn't, though. He's a real man. Isn't it strange, that one person had the power to start this? That's an oversimplification, but you know what I mean." She closed her eyes briefly. "Let's talk about something else. I don't want to waste our time together rambling on about the war. Tell me about your life. Tell me everything that's happened."

"Everything? There's so much, but also so little."

"We need a starting point. How about—tell me where you live."

"Oregon, for now. On the coast. I lived in Canada before that."

"You're not married?" Her tone was carefully neutral.

He shook his head.

"And your sister? Is she married?"

So her mother had not told her about Marian's visit to Seattle. "Actually, Marian is already a widow."

Sarah's tears, so close to the surface already, welled up. "Oh, how terrible. I'm sorry to hear it. Are there children?"

"No. Thankfully."

"Yes, it's a mercy they don't have to grieve their father."

Jamie hesitated. "I meant something a little different. She didn't want any. Her husband was a vile man, but even if he hadn't been, she wouldn't have wanted any. She only wants to fly airplanes. She doesn't like being bound to people."

Her forehead creased with consternation. "Being **bound** to people is the heart of life. My children have lit me up, lit up the whole world. It's love like you can't imagine."

He smiled ruefully. "Be that as it may, I don't know if they're in the cards for me, either."

She slumped back into the love seat, exhaling. "I'm sorry. I don't know what good there is in my saying something like that. But you'll have them. I'm sure you will."

"Maybe, maybe not. I think I'd like them. But I also think Marian would say she knows her own mind. She wants a different kind of life."

"I shouldn't have judged. It's no business of mine how your sister lives. Or how you live."

This last remark stung. He said, "Do you know what this reminds me of?"

"No, what?"

"When we walked around the lake together, when we first met, and you extracted my whole life from me, and I didn't realize until later that I hadn't asked you anything about yours."

"I'd forgotten all about that." He must have looked crestfallen because she added hastily, "Not about that day or the walk. I'd forgotten you were so worried about having talked too much. But it was the same then as now—your life is more interesting than mine."

"No—"

"Oh—there's a bulletin. Will you turn it up?"

Jamie reached for the volume knob. Japan had declared war on the United States and Great Britain.

After a minute, she said, "That's enough."

He turned down the volume again. Tentatively, he said, "I wish there was a way I could just convey everything to you in a flash, have you know it all without having to tell you."

"I don't. I like the way you have to find out about someone little by little."

"But we don't have time. And I don't trust myself to explain things right."

She was looking at him keenly. "I've always liked how honest you are. That's all you have to be, to explain things."

"I struggle with the same thing in my paintings. Everything I want to paint is too big, and so I've started to think what I really want to paint is the too-bigness. Does that make sense?"

"Yes, I think so. It's there in the beach painting."

"I think I'm drawn to impossibility." Cautiously, slowly, he reached out and took her left hand in both of his. She let him.

"Yes," she said quietly after a pause. "Impossible."

"Your life went on as though I were never in it."

"Only outwardly."

"Isn't that what matters?"

"I don't think so. But I'm just— I have an ordinary life, Jamie. You wanted me to rebel, and I couldn't. It's not my way. Sometimes I wish I were less conventional, but the simplest explanation is I don't have the guts." She gripped his hand more tightly. "I've always only wished you the best. I want you to be happy."

"I don't like that, how you say that."

"You don't want me to wish you happiness?"

"No, it's that there's something final about it." He released her hand, hunched forward. "Was our summer just a sweet little rite of passage for you?"

A soprano's aria warbled quietly from the radio while Sarah thought for a long time, staring out at the lawn. "No," she said finally, decisively. "But, Jamie, shouldn't it have been? Wouldn't it be better if we decided now, together, that it was? I honestly don't know why it **wasn't,** why I haven't completely let go of it. But I have a **life.** I have children. Even if my feelings about you are complicated, what possible difference could it make?" Her gaze blazed on him like a searchlight, and he felt exposed, as though she could see his most pathetic, persistent hopes and desires. She said firmly, "No good can come from us going to bed."

The mention of sex, discouraging though she meant it to be, aroused him. Trying to sound jokey but fooling neither of them, he said, "You don't think it could be worthwhile in itself?"

She remained outwardly composed, but he had the sense she was struggling. There was so much he didn't know about her; he couldn't guess what all she was weighing in the balance. Finally, with resolve, she said, "I won't ever leave Lewis. I love him—it's important you understand that. So I don't see the point. It would just bring us both pain."

Sorrow settled in him, petulant disappointment floating on top. He said, "I should go."

She didn't argue but escorted him back through the house. At the front door, they paused. "Please give my apologies to Lewis for not coming to dinner tomorrow," he said.

"I will." She paused. "What will you do? Will you join up?"

"I don't know."

"You don't want to."

"Of course not."

"Didn't the idea of animals being mistreated

use to drive you to blind fury? Don't you feel the same way about people?" She stopped, placed her hand on his arm, ardent, damp-eyed. "We must be brave."

He saw she was warmed by her sense of her own goodness. Was he, in the same way, seduced by an idea of his own virtue? How could anyone see clearly through the innate haze of self-righteousness? "You wouldn't even stand up to your father."

Her hand fell away. "You'd compare that to this?"

"I'm only saying it's easy enough to tell others to be brave when you've always chosen the safest path."

"That's not fair. We're not all as free as you to choose our own way."

"**Choose,** yes. You said you wished you were less conventional—well, you could have been, but you chose over and over again to do what was expected. And that's fine, but don't pretend someone else made you this way."

"I don't!"

"Good!"

They stood glaring furiously at each other. She yanked open the door, and he strode out, donning his hat, hearing the slam behind him but looking resolutely ahead, away.

Out the door, down the street, out of the city. There—he had it, a resolution.

New York City
April 1942
Four months later

A doorman ushered Marian off Fifth Avenue and across a black marble lobby into the custodianship of a brass-buttoned elevator operator who wore a faint smirk as he looked her over. He flung the grate closed, cranked over the lever Marian thought of as a throttle, sent them upward. She wondered what the other pilots had worn when they showed up for their interviews. "Your floor, miss."

Alone in the hallway she paused to gather herself, smoothing her trousers, adjusting her logbook under her arm. She knocked, and a uniformed maid opened the door to Jacqueline Cochran's apartment.

Inside and into splendor. The foyer's floor was inset with a marble aviator's compass. Along one wall a glass table and case were crowded with flying trophies—globes and cups and spires and winged figures. A mural of famous aircraft covered the walls and ceiling. Marian craned and swiveled as though she were at an air show: the Wright Flyer, the **Spirit of St. Louis,** Amelia's Lockheed Vega, a squadron of biplanes, a stray zeppelin, and, of course, Jackie herself winning the Bendix transcontinental race.

In Alaska, in February, Marian had heard from a pilot who'd heard from his sister who flew crop dusters in California about a telegram she'd received from a woman named Cochran. She was recruiting female pilots to join the Air Transport Auxiliary in Britain, ferrying warplanes. EVERY FRONT NOW OUR FRONT, the telegram said. FOR THOSE DESIRING QUICK ACTIVE SERVICE SHORT OF ACTUAL COMBAT BUT INCLUDING FLIGHT EXPERIENCE WITH COMBAT PLANES THIS SERVICE ABROAD SEEMS IDEAL CHANCE.

Marian, panicked she would be too late, had cabled Jackie Cochran directly, giving a truncated explanation of her bush flying, a tally of her hours, a plea for consideration. Warplanes! If they took her, she would fly warplanes, the kind of aircraft she'd seen transiting through Alaska ever since Lend-Lease passed, hundreds of them bound for Russia. An answer tap-danced in along the wires the next day. Come to New York for an interview. If satisfactory, you will proceed directly to Montreal for flight check and from there to England.

The maid steered her across a grand living room where a man was talking on the telephone in clipped, businesslike tones and down a hallway, its walls frescoed with more aircraft. A smartly dressed young woman brushed by, carrying an armful of files. Marian paused to examine a framed newspaper photo of Jackie in a cockpit, holding up a small hand mirror to apply lipstick.

In a bright room with windows open over the East River, Jackie sat behind a white-and-gold desk, half submerged in a lake of papers held down against the warm breeze by paperweights of different sizes and materials: a brass eagle, a hunk of amethyst, a compass. As she stood and reached across to shake Marian's hand, Marian absorbed her careful blondness, the red silk of her belted dress. She seemed a lacquered and corrected sort of person, a flattering portrait of a woman painted atop that very woman.

After they sat down, Jackie toggled a finger at Marian. "This won't do."

Marian thought Jackie was summarily rejecting her. "I won't?"

"You need to be an ambassador. You're meant to represent American women. **Ladies.** Not grease monkeys." Her accent was carefully refined, but underneath was a disguised twang, a sharp elbow.

Marian looked down at herself. "I thought about getting a dress."

"Why on earth didn't you?"

In the morning she'd hesitated outside the glass doors of Macy's, stylish ladies sweeping past, the corners of their shopping bags bumping her imperiously. She'd glimpsed gleaming floors and counters, bottles of perfume, her own incongruous reflection. "I didn't want to get my hopes up," she told Jackie.

"That's all inside out. You must dress for your aspirations."

"I don't aspire to be anything other than a pilot."

Jackie's smile was more of a wince. "Don't be stubborn. You must know they want the contrast, the magazine pictures of the pretty girl like any other, neat as a pin, hair curled, serving coffee and cake, who happens to be the same girl flying the big plane. You can't have the pilot without the lady."

So the lipstick in the cockpit was an armoring, not an obeisance or a pandering affectation but something more like a beetle settling its wings down into a smooth shield.

An incomplete history: Jacqueline Cochran is born Bessie Lee Pittman in 1906, raised in shabby itinerancy in the humid sawmill towns of northern Florida by people who are almost certainly her biological parents, though later she'd tell everyone she was an orphan, preferring the idea of herself as separate. She is one of five children, a barefoot urchin, a crab-catcher and chicken thief. The story she tells—and it's likely true enough—is that she wore dresses made of flour sacking and slept on a straw mattress in a shack on stilts with oiled paper for windowpanes.

A leering old man tells her she'd started out as a boy but an Indian had shot her through with an arrow when she was very small, making her navel and surprising her so thoroughly that she'd sat down on an ax, becoming a girl. A girl is a boy who has sat on an ax, he says.

She wonders why boys still have navels, then. Had they not been surprised when the Indian shot them? Or was it that there weren't any axes around? The air smells of the high sharp burn of a blade through wood. A fine layer of sawdust sticks to her skin. She wanders where she will. When she is very small, she witnesses a man lynched in the woods, burned.

Bessie Lee, eight years old, has a night job pushing a cart through a cotton mill, bringing spools to the weavers. As Jackie Cochran will tell it one day, that's how she earns the money to buy her first pair of shoes. She knows to eat her lunch quickly and hide in her cart for a nap, hopefully unnoticed by the men. (She learns to punch and kick, which is sometimes enough.) Soon she gets promoted to spinner and walks until dawn between the rows of bobbins, looking for snags. Lint in her lungs, ears full of the screeching machines. The steamy hot southern night presses down on the mill's long roof, presses down on the cotton fields and the red clay earth as the child reaches into a machine and ties a broken thread back together with her small, nimble fingers, sets the bobbin spinning again.

Bright little girl. Again she is promoted. She oversees a gang of fifteen children who inspect the newly woven fabric for flaws, fifteen bent and wizened miniature people, hunched like jewelers over smooth, rippling cool cotton.

During a mill strike, ten years old, she gets a job in a beauty shop sweeping up shorn hair and mixing shampoo.

Here begins her rise.

Jackie clasped her hands on her desk, said to Marian, "If you're picked, you'll transport planes where they need to go. From factories to airfields, for example, or from airfields to repair depots or vice versa, freeing up RAF pilots for combat. No matter your experience, you'll start with trainers. Everyone does. If you're good enough, you'll upgrade from there. You'll learn a whole class of planes—twin-engines, say—and then be expected to transport types you've never flown before just by reading the specs. It's an actual, concrete contribution, but it will be difficult. Do you think you're up for it?"

Marian was so terrified of saying something that would mean she would not get to do what Jackie had described, she found she could not speak. She nodded.

"Yes?" said Jackie.

A whisper: "Yes."

"Did you fly here from Alaska?"

"Yes."

"In what?"

"A Beechcraft 18."

"How long did it take?"

"Nine days."

"Not a speed record, then."

"There was some weather, and I stopped to visit my brother in Oregon." Poor Jamie, cornered by his own goodness, trying to talk himself both into and out of joining up. **What should I do?** he'd said. She said maybe he could get a job making recruitment posters. She wanted him safe.

"In Alaska, you must be used to weather."

"I'm used to it being awful."

"Good. The Brits aren't teaching ATA pilots to fly on instruments, so you'll have a leg up. There's lots of cloud and fog over there, and it comes on you quick."

"Why aren't they teaching them instruments?"

Jackie poked at a stack of papers. "They say because they want the ferry pilots to stay within sight of the ground and not be tempted to go over the top. It's wishful thinking. The climate there is pernicious." She paused briefly to let Marian admire the word. "You get caught out, and then what?

Even if you know what you're doing, it's hazardous. You've heard of Amy Johnson? The English girl who flew to Australia? She was flying for the ATA and had plenty of experience on instruments, and she still got stuck above the cloud and baled out and drowned. I don't mean to scare you. You'd have heard about it anyway before long."

"I know lots of pilots who've died."

"Me too. By the way, if you get over there, don't tell the Brits I was complaining. They think I complain too much. But in my opinion, not teaching instruments is a waste of airplanes. And pilots. They say safety's the reason for it. I think it's more about ex— What's the word? More about being fast and cheap. What's that word?"

"Efficiency? Expediency?"

"Expediency! That's it. I'm always learning new words. I collect them. What sort of schooling did you get?"

"Only to eighth grade."

"But you know words."

"I read a lot as a kid."

For the first time, like a lighthouse newly lit, Jackie emitted a gleam of fellow feeling. "So you're like me. An **autodidact.** That means you're not afraid to work."

"I like to work."

"Do you know, I bought my own Model T when I was fourteen? With money I made doing hair."

. . .

By eleven, Bessie Lee Pittman is cutting hair, rolling and pinning and plaiting it. She has a way with beauty, with improvement. Respectable women come in through the shop's back door, embarrassed by their vanity, while the prostitutes, the fancy girls, march in the front. Bessie Lee likes the fancy girls, the stories their madam tells about distant cities.

She doesn't tell Marian, or anyone, this part of the story: Fourteen or so, she comes up pregnant, marries the father, Robert Cochran. The baby stays with the Pittmans in Florida while she moves to Montgomery, buys herself that Model T with money made from doing permanent waves. But is being a beautician enough? For her? For little Robert Jr.? She trains to become a nurse, takes a job with a doctor in a mill town. In the light of an oil lamp with a corncob wick, she extracts a baby from a woman laboring on a too-familiar straw mattress. Three other children are lying on the floor. There's no clean blanket to wrap the baby.

No, this is all wrong. This must not be her life.

Robert Jr., playing in the Pittmans' backyard, four years old, dies in an accident. A fire. He's buried under a heart-shaped headstone. Jackie erases him from her story of herself, can't bear not to.

Away, away. She must get **away.**

Twenty years old, divorced, Jacqueline Cochran arrives in New York City, gets herself hired at Antoine's beauty salon in Saks Fifth Avenue. Monsieur Antoine, Antoine de Paris, the original celebrity stylist, has a flair for the next big thing. He'd invented the shingle cut and a charmingly gamine coif as short as a boy's that he gave to Coco Chanel, Edith Piaf, Josephine Baker. He likes Jackie and her strict lipstick and resolutely powdered nose, the whiff of sawdust under her expensive perfume.

Every winter she travels from New York to Antoine's Miami outpost, driving her Chevrolet in one long go, picking up hitchhikers for company. In Miami there are speakeasies and jazz bands and casinos, swanky supper clubs, cocktails, and long white beaches. You wouldn't know there was any Great Depression from Jackie's silk stockings, her gold compacts with little round mirrors that show only her a bit of herself at a time. But none of it is enough. None of it lasts. Curls go limp. Oil seeps through the powder. Up in the Panhandle there's still that grave marked by a heart. The night sky presses on the roof of her hotel, on the palm trees in its gardens and the flamingos sleeping under them. The wish to break free persists, but break free from what? The gilded life she has so laboriously constructed around herself? Away, away, but to where?

·   ·   ·

"I bought myself a Ford, too, as a kid," Marian said. "I earned the money driving a delivery truck."

Jackie's approval shone more brightly. "Is that so? Laudable. What will you do with the Beechcraft if you go abroad?"

"Sell it, maybe. Store it. I don't know. It's had a hard run already. I've been a bush pilot."

"I know. Your telegram said." Jackie held out her hand for Marian's logbook, flipped to the last page, looked at the total hours. Her plucked and penciled eyebrows rose and flexed. "I was surprised I hadn't heard of you, if you've flown this much. I thought I had a good idea of the most experienced girls out there, but this goes to show."

Marian waited to hear what it went to show, but Jackie just kept paging through the book. "I've kept mostly to the north," she said. "And to myself."

"You've certainly flown."

Goaded by the remembered gleam of the flying trophies, the gleam of Jackie's hair, Marian said, "I have more hours than are in there. A lot more."

At once Jackie clouded over. "Why aren't they recorded?"

Marian shouldn't have said anything. She looked hard out the window, trying to think how to explain that she'd flown for a bootlegger without a license, that she'd been Jane Smith before she could be Marian Graves again. "For a while," she said finally, "I was going by a different name."

"Why?"

"I'd left my husband, and I didn't want him to find me."

"Where is he now?"

"He's dead."

"I see." Jackie followed her gaze out the window, seemed to be thinking.

In 1932, Jackie finds herself at a dinner party in Miami, seated beside a Wall Street millionaire still in his thirties, Floyd Odlum. He is from Union City, Michigan—humble roots, a Methodist minister's son who'd made himself into a financier. In 1929, he'd had a bad feeling, heebie-jeebies severe enough that he sold off most of his holdings before the crash. After, he bought up companies cheap. They say he is the only man in America to **make** money on the Depression. He'd heard there was a woman at dinner who actually worked for a living (he didn't meet many of them) and asked to be seated next to her.

Over crab cakes, he asks: What do you want?

The salt, if you wouldn't mind, Jackie says.

Ha. I meant in life.

Her own cosmetics company. But there is so much territory, so much competition, especially with everybody tightening purse strings, some people left with just strings and no purse.

Little luxuries go a long way when you're feeling downtrodden, she says.

He says, Hope in a lipstick.

That's right.

What if you learned to fly an airplane? he says. You could cover big distances faster.

She has never considered flying, but something about the idea begins to gnaw and nibble at her right then. She wonders aloud, **Could** I fly a plane?

Of course you could, he says so firmly she has no choice but to believe him. She recognizes then that he will be essential to her. He is an external font of self-belief.

To him, she is another undervalued commodity, an asset to be picked up cheap and made mighty.

He is already married, but so what.

The first time she goes up, the flying bug bites. The bug swallows her whole. This is it. This is away.

Still looking out the window, Jackie said, "Do you like New York?"

Grateful to be released from talk of her husband, Marian said, "I'm not at home in cities." Anchorage and Nome and Fairbanks had swelled with the war but were still just frontier towns. Since Pearl Harbor, there'd been blackouts at night. Everyone in the Territory was on edge.

"Is this your first time here?"

"No, I was here years ago for my honeymoon. Only for a few days."

Jackie regarded her curiously but seemed to

decide against probing further. "All right, listen, if you go to England, you'll have to sign an eighteen-month contract with the ATA. Are you prepared to do that?"

"Sure."

"Yes?"

"Yes."

"The job won't be cushy."

"I wouldn't know what to do with cushy."

"Still, I have an obligation to tell you it'll be dangerous. Long hours, bad weather, rationed food and fuel, trigger-happy antiaircraft gunners, beat-up planes that might fall apart in midair. No radio. Germans buzzing around looking for something to shoot down. Barrage balloons all over the place. Your ship could even be sunk on the way over."

Marian hadn't thought about the crossing. "Has that happened?"

"To plenty of people, but none of my girls. Yet." She peered at a page in the logbook. After more flipping, she closed the book, held it out to Marian. "Are you up for it?"

Marian reached to take back the book. "Sure."

"That's a yes?"

"Yes."

One manicured finger tapped the desk, the brown gaze lingered on her. "Clothes aside, the brass is concerned our girls be of the highest moral character."

"All right."

"They're petrified of embarrassment. Some of the men who've gone over already behaved badly. So the girls have to be impeccable. There's no room for error, none at all. When people expect you to be common, you have to work twice as hard not to be."

Floyd helps Jackie get her cosmetics business off the ground. Company motto: **Wings to Beauty.** He helps her get her physical self off the literal ground, too. She makes her debut on the air racing scene in 1934, showing up at a starting line in Suffolk, England, one of twenty flyers bound for Melbourne. A sputtering engine sets her down in Bucharest, but she reappears the next year in Burbank, California, for the start of the Bendix. Amelia Earhart is first to depart, just before five A.M. into a dangerous, thickening fog. The pilot in front of Jackie crashes on takeoff and is killed. Burned. While the wreckage is being cleared, Jackie calls Floyd, divorced now and her fiancé, and asks what she should do.

Logic would dictate the safe choice, he says, but logic shouldn't always outweigh a powerful emotional urge. It's a philosophical question. (She has not yet told him about Robert Jr., certainly not about the man burned in the woods so long ago.)

So?

So you have to decide for yourself.

The answer is away. But away **in** the plane? Or **from** the plane? She takes off, but when she circles high to escape the fog, her engine overheats and forces her down again.

In 1936, she and Floyd marry, buy the fourteen-room apartment overlooking the East River where Marian will one day come for her interview. They pick up a country house in Connecticut and a ranch outside Palm Springs. They buy a building in New York and establish an orphanage—really!—for the city's barefoot and gimlet-eyed future Jackies. They help pay for Earhart's 1937 circumnavigation attempt, the flight on which she and Fred Noonan disappear, though Jackie says she'd had doubts about Fred finding Howland Island, had warned Amelia to no avail.

In 1938, Jackie wins the Bendix. In 1939, she sets a women's record for altitude, two national records for speed, one intercity record. Prizes and trophies accumulate. She volunteers as a test pilot. In September of that year, after Germany invades Poland, she writes to Eleanor Roosevelt suggesting that, in the event of war, women pilots might be put to use domestically. Supportive flying. **Feminine** flying. For example, they could deliver trainer planes from factories to bases, freeing up men.

The first lady thanks her for the suggestion. Yes, if we go to war, we will need women to help, she writes. But exactly how women are utilized will be for men to decide.

. . .

"It's the flying I'm interested in," Marian said. "If I wanted to run around, I could have done it in Alaska. Mostly I've wanted to be left alone."

"Mostly. All right. Well. Just don't go hinting to anyone that you have more hours than are in here. Everything needs to be by the book. And in the book. Understood?"

"Sure. I mean, yes."

When she laughed, Jackie pulled her chin inward, compressing her flesh. Marian warmed to the flaw. "You're a quick study. Like me. Once you get to Montreal, the ATA will want you to get checked out before they take the trouble of shipping you over. My advice: Be nice to the check pilot. He's the sort that'd rather see you in the kitchen."

Marian said, "He'd be disappointed by what I cooked."

June 1941. Jackie wrangles her way into flying a Hudson bomber across the Atlantic from Montreal to Scotland. Male ATA pilots in Montreal don't like the idea. Not so long ago, people got parades for flying the Atlantic. When word gets out about Jackie, the pilots threaten to strike.

Okay, okay, say the bosses. She'll fly, but a man will take off and land.

When Jackie shows up for departure, the

Hudson has been drained of antifreeze and the oxygen system is set up wrong and the special wrench for turning on the oxygen has gone missing. Jackie fixes things, buys a new wrench. The life raft is gone as well, but since it probably wouldn't be much help anyway, she leaves without it. When they stop to refuel in Newfoundland, the wrench vanishes again; someone breaks a cockpit window. She buys another wrench, patches the window with duct tape. They make it across the ocean just fine, Jackie at the controls until she sets up the final approach and relinquishes her seat.

"My secretary will sort you out with the hotel in Montreal where we've put the other girls," Jackie told Marian. "And you need to get some new clothes. Today. The ATA will fit you for uniforms in London, assuming you pass, but you should have a traveling suit and a few dresses. Most of the time you can probably get by with slacks—not those you're wearing. Nice slacks. And you'll need a few blouses, and a pair of pumps and some plain oxfords." As she spoke, she jotted a list on monogrammed stationery. "Don't overdo it, though. Some of the girls have brought along steamer trunks full. Do you have money? I could send my girl with you to shop."

"I have money."

"I'll call my woman at Saks. She'll be expecting

you. Ask for Mrs. Spring. She'll take you to the hair salon, too, Antoine's. They know me there." She stood. "Good luck."

Marian stood, too, shook hands.

"I'll see you over there, if you go," Jackie said. "Behave yourself and don't crash any planes without good reason, and you'll be fine."

At the door, Marian stopped, turned back. "If you don't mind, I'd rather keep it between us that I've been married. Is that all right?"

Jackie gave her a long look, a small nod.

After Jackie returns from Britain, she dines with the Roosevelts, again pitches her idea about using women ferry pilots. Maybe we'll start looking into it, the president says.

Her staff combs through thousands of files, comes up with a hundred and fifty experienced pilots. But the generals say they have more male pilots than airplanes at the moment. And how should they be expected to house a handful of girls on air bases where there are hundreds, maybe thousands of men? Chaos would ensue. So: No. The answer is no.

For now, they say, see if the Brits want your girl pilots.

The Brits want everything and everyone they can get. In London Jackie sets herself up in luxurious digs, rents a Daimler, parades around in a mink coat. The ATA doctor, she learns, is planning to strip her girls naked during their physicals, and she says absolutely not, digs in about it—a confusing creature to her British counterparts, seemingly both crass and a prude. (Back in the cotton mill, sometimes punching and kicking hadn't been enough.)

In 1953, over a Mojave salt flat, Jacqueline Cochran will be the first woman to break the sound barrier. In 1964, in an F-104G, she will reach a speed of 1,429 miles per hour, faster than any pilot ever.

But back to 1942, when twenty-six American pilots, Jackie's girls, crossed the Atlantic from Montreal to Liverpool, and Marian Graves was among them.

Montreal
June 1942
Two months after Marian met Jackie

Marian had not known Montreal was on an island, nor had she ever been anywhere where people spoke a language other than English. The sky over Dorval Airport had a fairground atmosphere, snarled with long buzzing ropes of engine noise, crowded with aircraft coming in from factories or leaving for Europe or wavering through touch-and-gos with student pilots. B-17s passed among single-engine trainers like whales through schools of fish. The larger bombers and transports would head up to Gander and then right across to Ireland or Britain. The smaller fighters and trainers might be taken apart and loaded on ships or they might fly the ice-cube route: Newfoundland, Greenland, Iceland, Britain.

A pageant of uniforms was ongoing in the city, the significance of the different colors and insignias at first illegible to Marian.

Tiger Moths and Piper Cubs circled and circled the field, trainees at their controls. A season of mass chrysalis: men to pilots. The war demanded more of everything.

After three weeks in which she managed to snatch only five hours of flying, Marian checked out in a bright yellow Harvard trainer, its landing-gear doors hanging down like jaunty spats. The cockpit smelled of hot metal and rubber and an elusive acrid note that she had come to think of as the odor of flight itself. The check pilot, an American, was, as Jackie had warned, skeptical of women flyers. "But needs must," said one of the other girls staying at the Mount Royal Hotel. A couple of them had bought the check pilot a beer, with good results, so Marian did the same, dug out a bright smile, did her best to concoct flattering questions that got him talking about his close scrapes and heroic saves before chronic headaches had sidelined him from the Army Air Corps.

A doctor poked and prodded, weighed and measured, took her blood, asked a series of oddly detailed questions about her menstruation. "No flying," he said, "during your menstrual period, as well as three days before and three days after. It's regulation."

"Sure," Marian said. (The other girls had warned

her about this idiocy, so she'd been prepared to keep a straight face and blandly agree, as if obeying wouldn't mean being grounded half the time.)

Mostly her job was to wait. Jackie's girls had been crossing the Atlantic just four or five per ship so they couldn't all be blown to smithereens by the same torpedo. In the meantime they hung around the airport and the Mount Royal. Usually Marian drank at night in the hotel bar with the other pilots, the Atlantic ferry boys and Jackie's girls. She wasn't used to so much company, and while the others grew more boisterous as they drank, she got quieter, sat nodding along with the conversation. At some point she couldn't anticipate until it was upon her, she would get up and leave without saying good night.

She especially wasn't used to the company of women. Yes, the girls all loved to fly and wanted to take this chance to get out and do something, and most were basically all right, but they tended to have only ever lived with their parents or perhaps in a ladies' dorm at college or perhaps with a husband. She had hoped she would feel more like she belonged than she did. She told them little about herself. ("Aren't you the mysterious one," said a girl whose father had bought her a plane for her sweet sixteen.)

Thank goodness for Ruth.

Ruth Bloom. From Michigan. She'd arrived two weeks after Marian, and they'd met in the lobby of the Mount Royal, Marian pushing in through the revolving door still in flying clothes, Ruth at the front desk in a blue dress and pumps, her hem on the short side. The beat-up brown suitcases at her feet gave her away as a flyer with their patchwork of gum-backed stickers advertising aircraft manufacturers and air races. She spotted Marian at once, called out, "You must be one of Jackie's girls."

Ruth was short and busty with strong, plump calves and a small but solid waist, a shrewd sort, gregarious, mischief wrapped around her like a feather boa. Her husband was in navigator training in Texas, she said. He was hoping for heavy bombers. She and Eddie had met in a government-sponsored civilian pilot training course open to undergraduates; not enough men had signed up so there'd been room for her—at least, there was once she'd made it clear she wouldn't leave anyone alone until she was let in. Eddie had joined up right after Pearl Harbor, washed out of pilot training, got slotted as a navigator instead. Ruth said she couldn't just sit around twiddling her thumbs while he was off doing his part. She'd gotten the telegram from Jackie, and so here she was.

"Are you married?" she asked Marian.

"No."

"Ever get close?"

Marian looked away. "No."

"I'm nosy," Ruth said without apology. She studied Marian. Something about the appraisal reminded Marian of Miss Dolly's girls. She half expected Ruth to start putting lipstick on her. But Ruth's air of barely contained mirth, her confidence in Marian's friendship from the first instant of their acquaintance, reminded her of Caleb, too. "You're striking," she said, "even though you're trying hard to hide it."

Marian ran a hand over her hair, which had been tidied in the Saks salon but was flat now from the helmet she wore while flying the open Harvard. She had been instructed to grow it out at least into a bob. "I try not to stand out."

"But you draw attention by making yourself so plain. You **must** have worked out that much." A small soft hand darted up and grasped Marian by the chin. Obediently, Marian allowed her head to be turned from side to side as though she were a horse for sale. Ruth seemed to be suppressing a smile. "Bashful," she said.

"Not really," Marian said, pulling free.

Ruth's smile broke out fully. "If I buy you a drink, will you tell me everything I need to know about this place?"

They finally left Montreal in midsummer, four of them together in a cramped cabin on a small Swedish freighter: Marian and Ruth and Sylvie-from-Iowa and a girl from California who went by Zip. Marian had tried to conceal the depth of her happiness that she and Ruth would travel together and begin their training together because she wasn't sure how important any particular friendship should be in these times. But Ruth must have been pleased, too, because she'd clinked her beer against Marian's and said, "Thanking my stars we won't be wrested apart, Graves."

Marian hadn't seen Caleb or written to him for the better part of a year. Jamie hadn't heard from him, either, didn't know if he'd married the schoolteacher. Her silence wasn't out of anger; she was trying not to meddle. She'd always kept a distance from him, really, afraid of what would happen if they put more weight on their long, old love than it could bear. With Ruth, she feared overstepping, taking their friendship too seriously, but mostly she felt a pleasure in her company that was tender and heady, almost embarrassing in how much it resembled infatuation. Not only did Ruth understand, without need of explanation, how Marian felt about flying, but she understood what it meant to be a woman who flew, all the frustrations and indignities, the skepticism that buffeted like a headwind.

"I think he'd pass a centipede if it solemnly promised never to believe it could fly as well as he does," Ruth had said of their check pilot. "That's all he wants. Not to know you can fly, just to know you know your place."

"Why a centipede?" Marian had said.

"I can always pick out a leg man. I flashed him

a bit of mine, called him a hero, now I'm bound for London."

The way she spoke to Marian was sometimes maternal, sometimes jocular, sometimes flirtatious, always good-naturedly bullying and coaxing and chivvying her along, and though Marian would never have expected to enjoy being treated like a pet, it was relaxing simply to do as Ruth bid her.

In a small convoy with an old destroyer as escort, they first crossed from Montreal to St. John's, Newfoundland, to wait for a bigger convoy to assemble. Long, slow, warmish days passed at anchor. Marian had sold the Beechcraft, and as she watched planes passing over, bound for Europe, she felt sharp pangs for it. In the evenings, the pilots played cards and drank with the other passengers.

Sylvie-from-Iowa said she was joining the ATA because she'd already met all the men in her town, her county, probably in all of Iowa, and anyway she'd rather fly planes than build them. Zip said she wanted to fly a Spitfire, obviously. And she wanted to be able to say she'd seen things, out in the world. Ruth said, "If you just want to **say** you've seen them, you could stay home and make up stories."

Zip rolled her eyes. "Of course I want to really see things."

"Then say **that**," said Ruth.

Zip and Sylvie sunbathed on the prow and wrote letters. Ruth, in dungarees, enlisted Marian to help her paint the ship's railings. The crew, amused, handed over brushes and buckets of paint and then smoked and loitered and watched, commentating among themselves in Swedish until Ruth grabbed them by the arms and forcibly set them to work. On the warmest day, all four of the pilots stripped down and jumped overboard, Sylvie in a swimsuit she'd been smart enough to bring and the rest in their underwear. They held hands, but the water ripped their fingers loose. Marian, kicking up to the surface, fought back a horror she couldn't explain at the dark steel wall of the ship's hull underwater.

The convoy, sixteen ships, left without fanfare one evening, steaming east. The first night, the crewman with the best English came around to issue a reminder about the blackout. He stood in the doorway of their cabin, blushing and looking at the ceiling rather than at the women lounging in their bunks, Sylvie tying up her hair in rags, Zip painting her toenails. He pointed at the curtains over the blacked out window and said, "Always keep close. And better this"—he gestured at the cabin door—"open, always, because a torpedo comes, then the whole ship"—he made a motion with his hands like he was wringing out a towel— "and then maybe is like"—he overlapped one flat hand with the other, pressed them together.

"Gets stuck?" said Zip.

"Yes." He nodded gratefully. "Stuck. If you are inside, then—" He shook his head.

"We're probably not getting out anyway, but

thanks for the thought," Ruth said from behind her book.

The crewman nodded. "Sleep with clothes on, yes, for fast—" He whistled and sliced a hand upward, nodded again, and left.

When the others wanted to turn out the light, Marian and Ruth went out on deck. If there was a moon, it was hidden behind clouds. In the darkness they could hear the engines of other ships all around but saw nothing. A few times Marian thought she made out a hulking shadow-shape off to starboard, but always it dissolved and reappeared elsewhere, a trick of her eyes. "I don't like the idea of being stuck in the cabin," she said to Ruth. "Getting blown up would be one thing, but being trapped and living long enough to know you're trapped—I don't like it."

"Me neither," said Ruth. "But there's a sense that if you're meant to survive, you survive. And if you're not, you don't."

"Easy to say while we're nice and alive and standing next to a lifeboat."

"I think we ought to hone our fatalism. Really, what's the difference between taking your chances on a ship and flying?"

"Flying you have some control over."

"Not as much as we like to think."

The second day, fog closed in and stayed for the rest of the voyage. On the eighth night, they slept at anchor, and in the morning, they passed into

Bristol Channel. As the ship neared the harbor, Marian and Ruth stood at the rail, watching the upended prows and funnels of bombed ships loom out of the fog at strange angles, blackened and half sunk, sharpening from vague phantoms into ruined hulks and fading away again.

London was blackness against the taxi windows. On the train from Bristol a steward had come around as the evening faded and closed the curtains. The lights inside the train were dim and blue, as were the lights in the station, and once they were outside, it seemed as though Britain had disappeared entirely.

Marian was crammed in one taxi with Ruth and Sylvie and their handbags and train cases. The larger luggage rode behind with Zip in another. The driver slowed, making a turn, and something greenish white slid by outside, glowing: a conical apparition with two orbiting moons.

"What **was** that?" Sylvie said.

"A ghost!" said Ruth.

"Don't say that," said Sylvie.

"Only a copper," said the driver. "They paint their capes and gloves with phosphorescence."

Peering out, Marian began to see the blackness was less total than it had first seemed. Downward-angled slits in the covers on the taxi's headlights allowed a faint glow out onto the road, and here and there the white-painted bumpers of other cars came and went. Traffic signals, reduced to small floating crosses of red or green, hung in the dark. When they stopped at one, Marian could make out the passing shapes of pedestrians and a handsome set of steps leading to a jumble of rubble. "It's the underworld out there, isn't it?" said Ruth. "The kingdom of the shades."

"Get yourself some white gloves, that's my advice," said the driver. "Some bit of white to wave around is what you want for hailing taxis."

"Or for hailing the boatman," Ruth said. "To take us across the River Styx."

"Don't be spooky," said Sylvie. "I'm afraid of the dark."

"If you'd been here for the Blitz," the driver said, "you'd know there's worse things than dark." He stopped short behind a bus that had loomed up suddenly and cliff-like, a large white circle painted on its blunt end.

"Like what?" said Sylvie.

"Sylvie," warned Ruth.

"Like fire," said the driver.

The lobby of the hotel was a bubble of noise and light, crisscrossed by uniforms, insulated from the darkness by a shell of sandbags and heavy curtains. There was a note from Jackie Cochran, wishing them welcome and saying she would meet them for breakfast. Sylvie and Zip had a double on the fifth floor, and Ruth and Marian were on the sixth in singles with a shared bathroom.

Marian, lying fully dressed on the bed, realized she hadn't been able to close a door behind herself, to be fully alone anywhere other than in the toilet, since Montreal. She shut her eyes and pressed her hands against them. Auroras traveled across her lids. Behind the door, running water and gentle splashes signaled that Ruth was taking a bath. A memory of the woman in the hotel in Cordova came to Marian, but she pushed the thought away. She got up and turned out the light, slid in between the window and its heavy velvet curtain. In the time since they'd arrived, the thick cloud had broken apart into gliding silver rafts. A bright half-moon hung high over the blacked-out city. Beyond the ink spill she knew to be Hyde Park, roofs and chimneys and towers rambled into the distance, moonlight glinting off them as though off ice on mountaintops.

Missoula
August 1942
Not long after Marian arrived in London

Caleb was sitting on a stump he used for chopping wood. Jamie, standing behind him, lifted the same heavy scissors Caleb had used on Marian's hair long ago and cut off his braid. The long severed black weight of it flopped dead and glossy in Jamie's fist. "What should I do with this?" he said.

"Keep it as a memento."

Jamie dropped the braid in Caleb's lap. "No, thanks. It's all yours." He did his best to snip the rest short. "It's a little patchy."

Caleb ran a hand over his scalp. "I'm sure the army won't mind finishing the job."

"Poetic justice for the way Marian used to look."

"I never said I was any good at cutting hair. I was just the only one who'd do it."

"Do you hear from her?"

"No."

Something in Caleb's voice precluded further questions. Jamie said, "She's in London."

"Good for her."

Speculatively, Jamie snipped at a bit of hair behind Caleb's ear and winced at the result. He said, "Are you still seeing the teacher?"

"No. I couldn't quite get to the slippers and pipe."

Jamie thought Caleb might be using some kind of euphemism. "What does that mean?"

"It means I can't be tamed, Jamie-boy." Caleb slapped the severed braid against his thigh. When he spoke again, he was more serious. "It's better this way—no one to say goodbye to."

Caleb had written Jamie to say he was enlisting, and Jamie had come from Oregon to see him off. The paperwork was already signed; Caleb would leave when they told him to. Soon. The recruiters had been very interested in his experience as a hunting guide, he said. He'd told them he was twenty-six, not thirty.

Jamie still didn't know what he would do.

Marian had visited him in early April on her way to New York. He'd told her about seeing Sarah Fahey in Seattle. "She said she wished she could fight. Easy enough to say."

"It **is** frustrating not to be allowed to really do anything," Marian said.

"Yes, I know. I do know that. She also said we all must be brave. I'm not interested in bravery for its own sake, but this war . . ." He trailed off.

"Yes," Marian said. "I know."

"What should I do?" He looked at her fearfully.

"What **I'd** like is for you to live in peace and be safe. In the grand scheme of things, it doesn't matter what you do. You going to war won't tip the balance. Can't you get a job painting recruitment posters or something?"

"That seems like a cop-out, convincing other people to go and die."

"I doubt you'd personally convince anyone, no matter how good an artist you are."

"**You** take risks. **You're** brave."

"It's not the same," she'd said. "I really want a chance to fly those planes. Not that I don't want to pitch in—I do—but I'm not doing it purely on principle. There's something I want in it, whereas you just want to live harmlessly, and the war means abandoning that. Anyway, the ATA might not even take me."

"They'll take you," Jamie had said.

After the haircut, when he and Caleb were deep into a bottle, Jamie said, "What would happen if I couldn't do it?"

"Do what?" Caleb was lying on his back on the cot in his cabin, one arm under his head. Jamie sat in the rocking chair. The windows were open to the warm night.

"Fight."

"You'd probably die. But you'll die anyway, someday."

"Come on."

"You might not know until you're in the thick of it."

"Then it'll be too late."

"I think probably most guys can't really fight. They're just there. Adding numbers. You could get a job where you don't have to shoot at anyone, you know. There are lots of other jobs."

"Everyone keeps saying that. Marian thinks I should make propaganda."

"You could be a cook or something like that."

Besides Berit's scissors, Caleb had claimed Wallace's ancient gramophone after the house was sold, and he heaved up and went to it. Choosing a record, he set it in place, cranked the machine, dropped the needle.

Debussy. After the first few notes, Jamie remembered being a child peering through the banister while, below, Wallace and friends argued about art. "Do they let you choose?"

Caleb sat on the cot, cross-legged, and lit a cigarette. "Probably not. Have you ever killed anything? A bird, even?"

"Spiders and flies. Fish."

"What if tomorrow we went after elk? I'd take you. The rut's just starting. It's interesting out there."

In hopes that Caleb would not see how abhorrent he found the idea, Jamie studied the bottom of his cup, sluiced the whiskey around. "It seems wasteful to kill something just to prove to myself that I can."

"All these city hunters I take out there, that's what they're doing. But the truth is, there are too many elk and deer now that the wolves and grizzlies are mostly gone—"

"Thanks to you," Jamie put in.

"—and they starve."

"I'm not sure it's a good test," Jamie said. "If you don't kill the elk, it's not as though the elk will kill you."

Caleb drained his cup and set it aside. "It's easier to kill an elk than a man, Jamie. But you don't have to do either."

"Right, I could just embrace being a coward."

Caleb met his eye. "You're not a coward."

Jamie wanted to ask Caleb whether he'd killed Barclay Macqueen. But what difference did it make? And there **were** people Jamie had wanted to kill: that boy who'd been torturing the dog, Mr. Fahey, Barclay. He had it in him, the urge. "All right. Let's go tomorrow."

He didn't sleep well. The whiskey had set the

cabin and the sound of the crickets spinning slowly around him, and he lay on Caleb's floor at the center of the sickening swirl and thought yet again about Sarah Fahey's letter. It had arrived in July, long after Marian had come and gone.

Dear Jamie,

I hope you don't mind that I've written—I got your address from the museum. We parted on imperfect terms, and I feel regret about our conversation. I still believe it is not enough to do nothing, but now that more time has passed, I've come to believe it is unconscionable to persuade people who abhor violence, as I think you do, to commit it. I want no part of such a process, even though I understand this war requires numbers above all else. Which brings me to my purpose in writing: I have heard of an opportunity. All branches of the armed forces are seeking artists to document the war. A family friend who's high up in the navy told me about it, as of course we know many artists, and I mentioned you. My understanding is that you would complete the necessary training to earn your commission and be sent to combat areas but would not be expected to fight. There would be risks, of course, but, if you want, I would be happy to connect you with the relevant people.

I hope you and your sister are well. My

brother, Irving, is an officer on a destroyer in the Pacific, and Lewis has joined as a medic. I miss them both horribly.

Sarah

Jamie hadn't told Caleb about the letter or mentioned it when he wrote to Marian for fear they would tell him this **opportunity,** as Sarah had put it, was a perfect solution to his dilemma. Nor had he replied to Sarah. He could not disagree with her implication that being a military artist would nominally fulfill his duty, but still he bristled. She didn't think he could hack it. Millions of other men had simply gone off to war, but she thought he needed a special, cushy assignment. On the other hand, the assignment was something he was plainly qualified for, much more than he was to be a grunt.

He woke hot and dry-mouthed after only a few hours, his heart racing, the smell of coffee hanging oily in the air. Though night still seemed entrenched, Caleb was moving around, cracking eggs, setting a pan on a burner.

They ate in silence. Caleb instructed him to go outside to the pump and scrub with soap so the elk wouldn't catch their scent so easily. As the darkness faded to indigo, they walked into the woods. For hours, Jamie followed Caleb, a rifle on his back, his head aching and his stomach sour. He didn't ask where they were going. Clouds of blue mist shifted among the trunks and branches. He tried to step where Caleb stepped, to make as little noise as he did, but Caleb seemed to slither like a snake, with barely a rustle, while he clomped along like a cart horse. A stick cracked under his boot. Caleb glanced back.

"Sorry," Jamie whispered. Caleb held up one arm. Jamie stopped.

Caleb seemed to be listening, but Jamie, straining his ears, perceived only faint dripping and under that an ambient silence prickling with all the sounds that could not be heard: growing plants, creeping insects, drifting dust. In the war, he knew, such a silence would be tense with the possibility of unseen weapons being lifted and aimed. Caleb took a bamboo tube from his belt and blew through it, making a shrill rising note that ended in a low honk. They waited. In the distance, an elk bugled. Caleb gestured to the left, and they continued on.

By a small pond, Caleb pointed to hoof prints and to mud smeared on the trees by wallowing animals. After a while, he stopped again and knelt with his rifle across his knees. Jamie sat on a cushion of pine needles, his back against a tree trunk. There was nothing to see, only mist. Jamie allowed his eyes to droop closed.

Some time later, Caleb shook his shoulder to wake him. A hard knot of bark was digging into his back, drool slimed his cheek. Caleb pointed into a meadow that had materialized just beyond the trees. Yellow light pierced the patchy fog still hanging low over tall grass. A herd of elk was moving slowly along, grazing: females with knobby legs and mulish ears, the bull at the back, watchful, the dark fur at his neck thick and shaggy like a lion's mane.

Jamie picked up his rifle. They crept forward to the edge of the trees. "You'll have a clear shot," Caleb breathed. "Wait."

Jamie cocked the gun, bent his cheek to the stock. The bull moved closer. Through the sight, Jamie watched him lift his head, tilt it so the thick branches of his antlers tipped parallel to his back. His black nose pinched and quivered; his eyes showed white at their inner corners, urgent with the rut. "Now," Caleb whispered.

The animal was rough and heavy with life. Jamie imagined the legs crumpling, the magnificent antlers lying in the grass like discarded pitchforks. He lowered the rifle. Reflexively, Caleb lifted his, accustomed to taking the shots others missed. "Don't," Jamie said.

The bull elk looked toward them, ears swiveling. Jamie jumped up, waving his arms. He shouted. The animal turned and ran, setting the cows galloping. Dull thunder as the herd streamed down the meadow, their cream-colored haunches flashing bright until the fog swallowed them.

England
August–November 1942
Just after Marian arrived in London

First Marian and the others were sent to Luton, north of London, for ground school and flight checks. Everyone, men and women, had to begin at the beginning, regardless of experience. "You might have two thousand hours," the instructor said, "or you might have two, and you'll still have to sit here and listen, and you'll still have to pass the tests." They wore civilian clothes (their uniforms were being made in London, at Austin Reed), were issued big, amorphous Sidcot suits for flying.

Ground school Marian found very interesting as she'd never learned about aerodynamics except haphazardly and long ago in the Missoula library, and she'd never learned Morse code or studied, in a systematic way, navigation or meteorology. This was the school of her young dreams: rows of desks occupied by pilots, walls plastered with maps and charts and diagrams of engines and instruments. **Safe, not brave.** Their instructor repeated this often enough for it to be a kind of mantra. Their purpose was to safely and efficiently transport airplanes wherever they were needed, not to be heroes. The planes were to be **undamaged,** or at least not damaged further than they already were. Sometimes they'd be flying brand-new aircraft, sometimes battle-bruised ones. Sometimes they'd be taxiing each other home in tired old crates.

The ATA operated under what Marian considered a clever and audacious system. After completing flight school at Luton in light aircraft, mostly open biplanes, and logging enough cross-country flights, pilots were sent to headquarters at White Waltham, south of London, and were trained to fly single-engine fighters, known as Class II, which included Hawker Hurricanes and, after a proving period, the longed-for Spitfires. Once they'd proved themselves capable, pilots were posted to one of fourteen ferry pools: the northernmost was Lossiemouth in Scotland, the southernmost Hamble, near Southampton, where the Supermarine factory churned out Spitfires that needed clearing away before the Germans could bomb them.

Each pilot was issued a small book, bound at

its top with two metal rings, FERRY PILOTS NOTES and FOR OFFICIAL USE ONLY stamped in yellow on its blue canvas cover. This contained information on every plane they might fly; they would be expected to take off in unfamiliar models after only a quick perusal of the notes. If they did well with Class IIs, they would return to White Waltham to upgrade to Class III, light twin-engine planes, and so on up to Class V, the hulking four-engine heavy bombers. Class VI was flying boats, but women were not allowed to fly those, as they would need to be put among a male crew, an intrusion that could only result in chaos.

"Chief amongst your concerns," said the instructor, "will be flying below the weather. If you can't, stay on the ground. To avoid attracting attention, you won't be using radios, and if your aircraft has guns, they won't be loaded." He hesitated. "That is, in **theory.** If you should happen to find yourself in an armed aircraft, under no circumstances are you to fire your weapons." Here some of the pilots exchanged rebellious glances.

"You'll be completely on your own. So remember: safe—"

"—not brave," chorused the pilots.

"I'll never understand why they won't teach instruments," Marian said to Ruth as they walked back to their billets, two little brick houses on the same street, occupied by families who happened to have spare rooms. Marian's room belonged to a son gone to Canada for RAF training. A model of a Sopwith Camel biplane hung from the ceiling, and on her first night she had lain looking at the underside of the wings and wondering what had ever happened to the Brayfogles. She'd always thought more about Felix, but now she wondered about Trixie. She ought to have admired her.

"It's not as though you can help it if weather closes in on you," she continued to Ruth. "They say they don't want to waste planes and pilots, but you'd think fewer would crash if they knew how to fly in cloud."

"The bosses are cheap, plain and simple," said Ruth. "And in a big old hurry."

"Do you know how to fly on instruments?"

"Nope," Ruth said cheerily, "but I'm planning to be safe, not brave. Anyway, look at Amy Johnson. She knew what she was doing, and she still packed it in."

Marian was skeptical of this logic. They were standing at the little wrought-iron gate to Ruth's billet. "I could teach you some things," Marian said. "Just in case."

"Only if we have our lessons at the pub. I'm getting enough school."

"You won't listen there."

"Then we'll reward ourselves after with trips to the pub."

"Twist my arm," Marian said, waving goodbye.

After a few hours up with an instructor in

plodding Tiger Moths and Miles Magisters, open to the wind and rain, Marian soloed. Funny to "solo" after years of flying alone, but she refrained from smirking or complaining, dutifully entered the occasion in her new logbook. After soloing, the next step was twenty-five cross-country flights around Britain, navigating by compass and paper map, following railroads and rivers and Roman roads. Quick hops. The mosaic landscape droned by below, grouted with hedges. On good-weather days she could knock off three or four flights (she was still adjusting to the smallness of this country, which could fit in Alaska's pocket), but fine days were interspersed with more that hung low and gray, sometimes turning flyable only after the pilots had been told to clear off home. Even when the weather was passable, a dirty miasma hung over Luton, stinging Marian's eyes as she passed through in her open biplane. After Dunkirk, the Vauxhall auto factory there had been converted to produce Churchill tanks and army trucks, and the smoke from its chimneys mingled in a dense, acrid soup with smoke from houses and from the smudge pots intended to shield the factory from German bombers. Elsewhere (everywhere, it seemed) she had to worry about barrage balloons tethered on chains around airfields and factories to ensnare or at least deter German planes.

Both Marian and Ruth had Monday as their day off and adopted a routine of going to London on Sunday evenings. They usually saw a movie or a play and spent the night at the Red Cross Club, which was cheaper than a hotel and more fun. There was a penny jukebox and a good snack bar and central heat, and American soldiers and nurses were always around and sometimes pilots they knew. At the PX, they bought salted peanuts and Nestlé bars and cans of beer. Several times they were obliged to go for uniform fittings at Austin Reed. They were to have a skirt, a pair of trousers, two tunics, a jacket, and a greatcoat, all in RAF blue, cut uncomfortably tight for Marian's taste, not tight enough for Ruth's.

Some of the more sophisticated girls, ones like Zip who'd gone to fancy colleges or who were especially beautiful like Sylvie, got invited to cocktails at the embassy or for dinner at Jackie Cochran's flat in Knightsbridge, but Ruth and Marian were happy enough to spend most of their time as a solitary pair or with the transient acquaintances Ruth was always picking up.

"I'm surprised you're not Jackie's favorite," Marian said to Ruth once after they'd run into Sylvie on the street, who'd let slip that Jackie had served real blueberries the night before. "You'd think she'd want you around to charm all her impressive friends."

"No," Ruth had said, drawing on her cigarette and squinting in contemplation. "I'm too brassy. No one can say Jackie's not remarkable, but she's not really **fun,** deep down. She tries, but you can see the strain. Just as well. I'm glad not to have any more obligations."

"If you don't mind, then I don't," said Marian. "I'd be sorry to be left out if you were invited, and she'd never invite me. She probably thinks I'd show up in a burlap sack."

"No, it's the opposite. You're the one she'd have if we weren't thick as thieves. She'd like to improve you." Ruth linked her arm through Marian's and rested her head against her shoulder. "Silly goose doesn't see there's nothing that could possibly be improved."

But in September Jackie was gone, back to America, to head up an all-female domestic version of the ATA, the WASP. No more cocktails in Knightsbridge. Helen Richey, famous for being the first female commercial pilot in the United States, was put in charge of the American contingent. But by then Jackie's girls were deep into their training, with little need for a den mother.

Everyone in London seemed to drink a lot, to never sleep enough, to be ravenous for fun. The mood in the nightclubs and dance halls was deliriously defiant, and Ruth led Marian into the thick of things. Ruth was a flirt but never let any of the men even kiss her, so far as Marian knew. She always talked about her husband on nights out, more than she did other times. Marian, though, if the hour was late, might let a man kiss her in a shadowy corner of a dance floor, or she might let her knees part as someone ran his hand up her leg in a dark taxi. If there had been an opportunity, she might have done more, but always Ruth appeared and laughingly but firmly extricated her, shepherded her back to the chaste dormitory rooms of the Red Cross.

Slowly Marian had grown accustomed to the blackout and to discerning the people moving through it like benthic fish, flashing their white gloves or phosphorescent boutonnieres. She enjoyed the shock of passing from the outdoor darkness into a nightclub: loud and humid, sparkling like the inside of a geode. Here was the subterranean persistence of life. The peaceful world had been burned away, but its roots were intact, safe down in the dark, nourished by booze, smoke, and sweat.

One especially frigid night Ruth and Marian were put on fire watch together, which meant they were to sleep on cots at the Luton airfield. By eight o'clock, when it had long been dark and there was nothing to do but sleep, they lay shivering on their cots in their wool underwear and Sidcot suit liners until Ruth said, "Do you think you could bear to squeeze in with me? I'm so cold I'll never fall asleep."

"All right," Marian said, and Ruth lifted the blankets for her. Lying back to back, Marian felt acutely conscious of the slight difference in the rhythm of their breathing, but when she synchronized herself to Ruth, the feeling was even stranger, as though they had fused into a pair of lungs. She was aware, too, of the softness of Ruth's rear against her own, aligned since Ruth (much shorter than she) had scooted down and covered her whole head with the blankets. Marian knew she could sleep—she could always sleep, anywhere—but she was not sure she wanted to.

"I haven't heard from my brother in a while," she offered. "Not since we arrived."

Ruth scooted up above the covers so her voice was unmuffled. "Maybe his letter's just stuck somewhere. I got a batch yesterday and some of them were ancient."

"Maybe."

"I had a letter from Eddie. He's gotten his crew now. They sound all right. One guy gets airsick every time but no one tattles on him, not even after he decided to drop his barf bag down the flare chute and the wind blew it back up and splattered everyone. Their last training flight was over water so he thinks it won't be too much longer before they go overseas." She shifted, her shoulders pressing against Marian's. "He said they're all getting along, which is a relief."

Marian had little sense of Eddie beyond the fact that he'd washed out of pilot training. "Were you worried?"

"A bit. People don't always know what to make

of Eddie. Don't get me wrong—he's terrific. But sometimes . . . I don't know." Ruth rolled over, squeaking the cot's springs. Now the softness against Marian's back was breasts instead of rump. "You're warm," Ruth said. She snaked her arm under Marian's and held her hand in front of Marian's face. There were red, swollen patches at her knuckles. "Do you have these? Chilblains? They're awful. I have them on my feet, too."

"You need to do a better job drying your socks and boots," Marian said, and it seemed natural to take Ruth's hand in her own and draw it beneath the covers, holding it against her sternum to warm it.

"Your heart is beating fast," Ruth said after a minute.

"I don't think so."

"It is." This in a loose, sleepy voice.

Marian didn't answer. Something about the way Ruth talked about Eddie was odd. The elliptical idea came to her that if she were Ruth, she would figure it out. Ruth would get everything out of Ruth without even seeming to try. She found she wanted to go to sleep quickly, before Ruth could change position again, and so she did, falling away into herself.

England
November–December 1942
Continuing on

A letter finally came from Jamie, dated back in September. He was going to be an artist in the navy:

Who would have thought such a thing existed? I wouldn't have, but Sarah Fahey wrote to tell me. At first I thought I should just enlist anyway, but I came around to thinking maybe I should do this instead. After all, they want artists, and I am one. I leave for training in San Diego soon, and from there I don't know. I hope you won't worry, at least not as much as I worry about you.

So it was done. The war had come for Jamie, too. Worry wasn't the word for what she felt. Dread, perhaps. Anticipatory grief for what he would see, how he would be changed. Caleb was gone to the army, too, but there was nothing she could do for either of them, so she tried to set her fears aside.

As winter approached, the worsening weather made cross-country flights more and more difficult to complete, so in early November, when Marian had done only eighteen instead of twenty-five, the ATA shrugged off its own requirement and gave her her wings and four days' leave. Ruth still needed to catch a few more flights, so Marian went to London alone but found that, without Ruth, even the most familiar parts of the city made her shy and tentative. The Red Cross Club, so lively and welcoming in Ruth's company, felt daunting. She'd come to rely on Ruth to swing her into conversations like a trapeze artist tossing her partner into another's grip. When an air force captain tried to strike up a conversation in the snack bar, she managed only the most stilted chitchat and fled at the first opportunity.

She was, she abruptly understood, in love with Ruth.

This realization, in those words, came to her fully, finally, on her second day in London. She was at Austin Reed picking up her uniforms, standing and looking at herself in a cheval mirror while the tailor fussed with the cuffs of her blue jacket, and she wished Ruth were there to fill the awkward silence with chatter, and as she thought about Ruth, she saw her own face change.

She recognized her flushed and fearful expression in a way she had not been able to recognize the inward sensations from which it sprang, and the knowledge shocked her, both that the object of her love was a woman (besides the woman in Cordova, she'd never thought much about women) and that she was capable, after Barclay, after so many years up in the north trying to freeze her heart solid and let the wind erode it down to nothing, of falling for anyone at all.

But the question was what to do, and the answer was nothing. Ruth was a warm and loving friend, but surely she would find Marian's feelings strange or disgusting or frightening. Ruth was married. Marian thought she might have sensed a charge between them the night they'd slept nestled together on fire watch, but surely that had been in her imagination. Surely Ruth had only been keeping warm. Surely there was no way Ruth would ever be interested in . . . Marian didn't know how to name what she wanted. Possession, maybe. Touch, certainly. Closeness they already had, but Marian wanted something more purposefully important. She couldn't risk explaining such desires to Ruth. Ruth would want nothing more to do with her, and that consequence was unacceptable—although, even as Marian told herself this, she could not entirely believe that Ruth would banish her.

Ruth always seemed to understand. Why should she not understand this, too?

Because it was deviant; because it was offensive; because Ruth would be horrified and betrayed. In any case, even if by some miracle Ruth understood, understanding was different from reciprocation. Understanding without reciprocation would have the same result as revulsion, really: the loss of Ruth. Had Marian fallen in love right when they first met without even knowing it, when Ruth had taken her chin in her hand and studied her? She had fallen when Barclay looked at her at Miss Dolly's. Why did she respond so to being looked at?

Once, the sirens had sounded when she and Ruth were at the Red Cross Club, but rather than going down into the shelter, they'd gone up on the roof, into the calamitous night. Everyone said the sporadic raids were nothing compared to the worst of the Blitz, when huge pink mountains of smoke had seemed to dwarf the sky itself, but still there was the grinding throb of German engines, the soft burst of incendiaries, the dumb blank faces of the barrage balloons, planes caught like moths in the sweep of searchlights. Bombs thudded against the city. Antiaircraft shells flashed white in the sky. Beyond, visible in patches through the smoke and drifting cloud, the stars shone impassively.

Fires had burned, though not near the Red Cross, and Marian had wondered if there were people inside the flames. Of course there were, but still she hoped that somehow there were not. Ruth, without looking away from the spectacle, had taken Marian's hand. What disproportionate comfort Ruth's small hand had brought, her warm grip seeming to counterbalance the city lying belly-up, growing brighter and brighter as the flames spread.

As she left Austin Reed with her heavy parcel of uniforms, Marian didn't know how she would face Ruth, how she could pretend nothing had changed. The feeling of safety and ease would be gone, and Ruth's presence would bring only loneliness and longing. She should wait for her infatuation to pass. People could fall out of love. It seemed almost inevitable that they did. And if she stepped back from the giddy immediacy of her feelings, she saw mercy in the impossibility of their fulfillment: She could not be trapped by love again. She would not be.

When she returned to the Red Cross Club, it seemed like divine providence that instructions were waiting for her. She was not to go back to Luton but straight on to White Waltham to upgrade to Class II airplanes. She would not have to face Ruth, not right away.

White Waltham was in a pleasant market town called Maidenhead ("Lord, that name," Ruth had said), with timbered houses along a sedate stretch of the Thames. Marian found a room in a small hotel not far from the airfield that was only a bit more expensive than a billet. Back to the ATA classroom she went to learn about superchargers and carburetors and on and on. After two weeks of lectures, she was in the air again, in Harvards like the one she'd checked out on in Montreal, startling in their power after all her puttering cross-country flights in Tigers and Magisters.

There was a new American Club nearby, with a pool (closed for the winter) and a terrace and snack bar. She went sometimes for cocktails with other pilots but said little. No one tried to draw her out as Ruth had. Had she always been so uncertain about how to talk to people? She couldn't remember how she had been before Barclay, before Alaska.

She bought a motorbike and rode around the countryside when she had free time and enough gas coupons. She went to Henley and watched people rowing on the river. She rode past Eton College, where boys played rugby in the fields and loitered in tailcoats outside crenellated brick buildings. She rode past villages where you'd never know there was a war, past others that were little more than bomb craters, past the wreckage of a B-17 among a stand of beech trees. Mostly she rode past grass and trees, stone walls, sheep.

One afternoon, after flying circuits and bumps in a Harvard, she came into the flight office and there was Ruth, blue-uniformed and grinning. "Howdy, stranger," she said.

Marian's first response was joy, then terrified dismay, and Ruth, who had stepped forward for a hug, noticed the shift and faltered. Their hug was off-kilter, as stiff as an embrace between two mannequins.

"I was going to write and tell you I got my wings—and my togs," Ruth said. She struck a fashion model pose in her uniform. "I got seconded to Ratcliffe for a bit. Mostly I'm the taxi service." She pointed out the window at a Fairchild 24. "That's me. But then I got sent down here, and I thought I might run into you and save the postage."

"Congratulations." Marian turned to study the big map of Britain on the wall, updated daily with locations of barrage balloons and no-fly zones.

"You went off to London and then not a peep," Ruth said.

"It's been busy."

Ruth waited for more. When none came, she said, "You've probably missed me, though. Even though you haven't written."

Stricken, Marian looked from the map to her boots. Ruth stepped closer. "You're acting so peculiar. Has something happened? Did I do something wrong?"

"Nothing. I'm not feeling right. That's all." Marian swung her parachute onto her shoulder. "I have to go."

Ruth didn't call after her, didn't follow. Marian,

riding her motorbike back to her hotel, saw the Fairchild take off and disappear.

Two weeks later, on a rare clear-skied day in mid-December, Marian got her first Spit. She'd delivered a Hurricane to Salisbury, and, without fanfare, the ops officer there pushed the new chit across the counter.

The plane was waiting, its long, perforated cowling angled up at the sky. It had been camouflaged for photo reconnaissance, and, except for its black prop and its roundels and tricolor, the whole of it was cornflower blue, as though the sky had stuck to it. It had no armor and no guns so it would be light and fast, able to reach its ceiling quickly, over forty thousand feet, and carry enough fuel to get to Germany and back.

The female members of the ATA were unanimous that the Spitfire, hero of the Battle of Britain and symbol of RAF pluckiness aloft, was in fact a woman's plane. The cockpit was petite; a woman slid into it like a finger into a glove. The controls responded to the softest touch. Men, they all agreed, tried to muscle the thing too much, wanted to dominate it out of its most essential grace. One of the English girls had lost her pilot fiancé when he tried to take off in a Spit with an air traffic controller on his lap, larkily giving him a lift somewhere, and couldn't pull the stick back far enough because the cockpit was too full of male bodies. Both had been killed.

Marian climbed into the cockpit, consulted the Ferry Notes, began her checks. She had flown plenty of Hurricanes, which she liked and weren't so different from the Spit, but there was something newly thrilling about this plane, the close hug of its cockpit, how the controls seemed to press up eagerly under her hands and feet. The engine started with a harsh rattle, settled into a steady popping, a textured drone. Marian wasted no time taxiing since Spits were prone to overheating on the ground. She swung the nose from side to side, peering around to see where she was going. In no time at all the cockpit was warm enough to make her sweat. This was a plane meant to be in the air. On the runway she throttled up. The muddy field rushed alongside. A bounce over a rut, and the ground released her.

The Spit was needed in Colerne, in Wiltshire, not far. She dawdled on the way, turning a forbidden roll, a loop, carving and slicing the sky with the thin, elliptical wings, the earth swinging up and over. Under the Perspex dome, she was the hinge of it all, the swivel point. She went into a steep climb, leveled off. Ten thousand feet. Higher already than she was supposed to fly. There was a pressurization system, but the notes said to keep it off, as low-flying ferry pilots should have no call for it. She didn't know how to turn it on anyway.

She would just go a little higher. Another nudge to the throttle. Three hundred miles per hour. She wanted to smear the plane into the sky, blue on blue. Up. Fifteen thousand feet. She needed to be careful not to get carried away, but she felt well in control. Below, Britain was molded to the earth's curvature; fields and hedges slid over it like iridescence over the surface of a soap bubble. Up. Seventeen thousand feet. She must pay attention, come down soon. The air was meager in her lungs. She remembered the skipping of the Travel Air's engine when she'd flown too high over Missoula. Why did she have this impulse to throw herself at boundaries, be flung back by them? She felt the beginnings of fear, like frostbite beginning in the warm core of her instead of on her skin.

In the thin air, the plane traveled faster, nearly four hundred miles per hour. She couldn't stay long. Up, though. She needed to find out what was up there, to be away from what was below. Away from Ruth. Away from the world where Jamie was in the war. Cold now. Much too high, but only a little bit farther and she would know what she wanted to know. She was sure of it. The engine seemed to grow quiet, but still the altimeter's arrow swept to the right. The sky turned midnight blue at the edges of her vision, darkness bleeding up and inward as though she were sinking into something.

· · ·

After she landed and taxied in and switched off the engine, Marian sat in the cockpit, quite still. Cold lingered in her; her head ached. Her hand trembled when she finally opened the canopy. She walked to the ops office, handed over her chit, received a new one, a Miles Master needing transport to Wrexham.

"Everything all right?" said the officer who took her chit. "You're a bit green around the gills."

"Fine. I'll just have a coffee before I go."

She made her way to the canteen, and there sitting at a table reading a newspaper was Ruth. The world narrowed to Ruth as it had to that last point of light, flickering through the propeller, before she'd fallen unconscious.

Ruth looked up blankly at the sound of Marian's footsteps, then she was standing and coming toward her. "Are you all right?" she said. "You look completely wrung out." Only two pilots were in the canteen, both men, absorbed in their newspapers.

"Just a headache."

"When did you get so fragile? Next you'll be telling me you have the vapors."

Marian glanced at the pilots. "I thought a coffee would help."

"I'll get it," Ruth said. "Go outside. Get some fresh air. I'll meet you."

The brick of the building was cold against Marian's back, but the sun warmed her face, hurt her eyes. Squinting, she took the mug Ruth brought her. The coffee was abrasively bitter but very hot. "What's going on with you?" Ruth said. "You're acting so strange."

"What are you doing here?" Marian asked.

Ruth seemed to decide against pressing her, said, "Taxi service, what else? They must think I'm all right at it since it's all I do. Once in a blue moon I ferry a Moth—yippee. Where would the war effort be without one more decrepit biplane? But next week I'm finally going back to White Waltham. We'll be reunited." This last with forced cheer.

"I might have left by then."

Ruth dug in her pocket for cigarettes. When she'd lit one, she said, "We've gotten out of sync, haven't we?"

Marian indicated the plane parked by the hangar. "I'll probably be posted soon. I've just done my first Spit."

"The blue one? How was it?"

When she had come to, she had been in a spiraling dive, a pinwheel of fields and hedges spinning into a blur.

"Like everyone says."

"Heaven?"

"Just about."

"I'm dying of jealousy." Neither said anything for a minute. The coffee and the oxygen-rich air were helping Marian's headache, though Ruth's smoke wasn't. Ruth added, "If you'd written I would have told you Eddie's here now, in a training unit at Bovingdon."

"Really?"

"Yes, really." She was growing cool, remembering Marian's neglect.

"I'm glad for you." Marian knew she didn't sound glad at all. She'd never known jealousy like this, the sting of it.

A distant engine sang a single nasal note, crescendoed as it came closer. A Spitfire appeared, lined up, landed. "My passenger's here," Ruth said. "Time to go." She stubbed out her cigarette on the brick wall, put the butt in her pocket. "See you, Graves."

She was walking away. Marian said, "Ruth." Ruth turned. Everything Marian wanted to say was stuck in her throat. "See you."

Ruth seemed to droop. A sadness emanated from her that Marian didn't understand. "Sure," she said.

Marian was posted to the No. 6 ferry pool at Ratcliffe before Ruth arrived at White Waltham, and again she was relieved, and still she did not write.

Trust Your Lust

Sixteen

"P icture!" Bart shouted. "Lock it down! No talking, please! Settle in, please. Sound rolling. Camera. Swinging a lens, and we'll go again. Hold the work, hold the talk. Last look. First team is in."

Life is full of sound, and film sets are full of silence. We were shooting in a retro music venue in downtown L.A., a big, balconied room made up to look like a wartime London nightclub. Extras were strategically distributed to make the place seem jammed, and they mimed chatter and laughter and moved noiselessly through the dance floor's revolving spangles, sweating in their costumes because air-conditioning would make too much noise. They danced in silence while the white-jacketed swing band pretended to play, trombone slides going in and out while the bandleader conducted to music that only existed in the tiny buds in his ears.

After the Alexei kiss hit the internet, I wasn't allowed to talk. Siobhan and our emergency PR triage people said it was best to issue a statement saying I would not be commenting about my private life and let everyone scream into the void.

Outside on the hot white sidewalk, guys in black T-shirts pushed around rattling dollies piled with utilitarian bric-a-brac: rolls of tape, coils of cable, tripods, racks of lights, big squares of rubber flooring. Trucks and trailers clogged the street. Hair and makeup girls bustled around, their belts heavy with brushes and clips and spray bottles and big nylon pockets like the ones animal trainers carry treats in.

I swayed and turned with Actor Eddie in the middle of a crowd of other swaying, turning couples, who, if the real Marian Graves had danced in a club like this, would have been absorbed in their own lives but were now just props meant to plump up my world, make it look real. A camera orbited around me and a boom hung over my head like a fuzzy black moon, and I was supposed to be falling for my friend's husband.

"Ruth's my friend," I told Eddie.

"Ruth's not here," he said. "And tomorrow I'm going to fly over Germany, and I might never come back. So what do you say?"

. . .

If I ever had a real meltdown, if I ever well and truly lost my shit, at least inside my own head, it was that week after Vegas.

Alexei didn't return my texts or calls. He didn't make any public statements. Finally he emailed me that he had a lot to sort out and needed to concentrate on his family and didn't want to have any contact at least for a while.

What I wanted was to scrape my whole life away, cast aside everyone I knew because everyone I knew had disappointed me, build a new existence from scratch. I wanted to escape the system of my past, all the chain reactions. I wanted to be the big bang.

But instead I took a bottle of Scotch over to Sir Hugo's. M.G. drove me the hundred feet between our gates because the paparazzi were basically eating each other alive at the bottom of my driveway.

"My dear, you are becoming a toxic asset," Hugo said frostily. "You're lucky we can't fire you." We were standing in his kitchen, and he was filling two glasses nearly to the brim.

"Last time you said I'd made myself interesting."

"There are **limits.** We need women to see this movie, and women generally aren't enamored of homewreckers. I know it's unfair, I know it takes two to tango, but there you have it. We want people to look at you and see **Marian Graves,** not think about the chaotic tabloid strumpet who keeps getting caught shagging the wrong people." He clinked his glass against mine. "Cin cin."

I took a swallow. "This thing with Alexei didn't really feel optional." Nothing as insignificant as the dignity of his wife or the prospect of total ruin would have stopped me. I saw a bumper sticker once in L.A.: **Trust Your Lust.** This is not prudent advice.

"Is it over?"

"I hope so, but I hope not."

Hugo pierced at me. "Are you in **love** with Alexei Young?"

I set my glass down, covered my face with both hands, nodded.

"But not just since Vegas." Hugo was no fool.

I uncovered my eyes. "No."

"Well, remind yourself that you'd probably love him **much** less if you were actually with him, because that's the way it always plays out. Relish the pining and leave it at that. Spice of life." He opened a cupboard. "I wouldn't say no to something to nibble on, would you?" He came out with a box of water crackers and a jar of mustard. "What about young Mr. Feiffer? I thought there might be something there."

"I thought there was. Then I thought there wasn't. Then I thought maybe, and now I think I ruined whatever might have been."

Hugo spread mustard on a cracker. "Well, that's probably for the best. For the sake of the film."

I'd thought this movie would save me, **elevate** me, like Hugo had said, lift me up and carry me away. But I was too heavy for it. I was going to drag it down. "Do you think the movie's going to be good?" I asked.

"That depends on a lot of things, including you. But I hope so."

"What can I do?"

"Unfortunately there's not much you can do except **act,**" said Hugo, "ideally extremely well. And for god's sake, don't go to bed with anyone else. Not a soul."

"I have been acting."

"I've seen the dailies. They're adequate. But I can still see **you,** and frankly you are the last person I want to see."

"Tell me how not to be seen. Please."

He waved a hand. "I can't **tell** you. Anyway, I don't believe for a minute that's what you want. You want to be seen so very badly. You reek of it. You're terrified of what happens if no one's looking at you."

"No, I want to disappear," I said. "Really. I want the ground to swallow me up."

"No." He swallowed a mouthful of cracker. "You don't. You want people to wonder where you went."

That night, after maybe a touch too much weed, I was sure my whole house was watching me. I knew there were cameras and listening devices hidden in every light fixture, every pen, every electronic gadget, and I went outside to get away from them. But being outside in the dark by the pool was terrifying, too. The Santa Anas were up, and everything was dry and rustling and rattling.

I needed to know I wouldn't always feel the way I did, so I called Redwood. I'd seen him on set but only fleetingly. We hadn't mentioned Alexei. We hadn't mentioned what I'd texted him from Vegas. We hadn't really mentioned anything.

He sounded wary when he answered.

"I'm sorry to call so late," I said, "or maybe at all, because I know things are weird, but I'm freaking out." My words came out in a pathetic squeal. "I'm having a really hard time, and . . ." And what? What could I possibly ask of this person I barely knew? "And I don't know what's okay to say to you."

I heard him take a deep breath, in through his nose and out through his mouth, the way they teach you in yoga. "I should have replied to your text," he said. "I was going to—I just needed to think—but then the next day the Alexei story was everywhere, and I felt pretty confused. More confused. Because I was already **quite** confused."

"About what?"

He spoke quietly, as though he were trying not to be overheard. "I like you, and I don't presume to know how you feel about me or what you want, but I need to be careful . . ." He trailed off, then restarted. "Like one minute you're texting me that you miss me, and the next you're having this thing with Alexei Young. It feels a little dramatic."

"For what it's worth," I said, "there's history there." He was silent, and I went on, "I didn't know he was coming to Vegas. I thought it was over. It had been over for a long time."

When he spoke again, his tone was softer. "You don't owe me an explanation, but, on the other hand, I think knowing that does make me feel a little better."

"Okay. Good."

"What's going on with that? With you and him?"

"Nothing. It's over again."

"Because of him or you?"

I wanted to lie, but I said, "Him."

"That's honest, at least."

"Will you come over? Just to hang out?"

He hesitated. He said, "I can't. Leanne's here."

"Oh, well then, I won't take up any more of your time."

He didn't say anything for a few seconds. "She and I **are** friends."

Now I hesitated, then plunged. "How come nothing happened the night I stayed over?"

Another big gap of silence. "I'm trying this thing," he said, "where I have to know the women I sleep with."

"We'd talked all day."

"It was still just a day."

I couldn't decide if he was being ridiculous or if I was. "Are you single?"

Silence again, then: "Yes." I heard her voice in the background. "But I should go."

"Just one more thing," I said, not wanting him to hang up. It scared me how irrelevant Redwood had seemed when Alexei was around and how essential he seemed now that no one was around. "I was thinking. Adelaide Scott said it's good to know what you don't want, and I don't want to be a wrecking ball anymore. I want to hang out with someone I actually like."

"Okay," he said, quietly. "Well. We'll talk. But I really do have to go."

After we hung up, I thought about texting Travis Day, asking him to come over, but I didn't. That was something at least. Where was my medal? My prize for impulse control? And the night didn't scare me anymore. It was just wind, just leaves brushing together. My house wasn't watching me. Nothing was watching me. I was a dumbass sitting by a swimming pool in the dark, feeling unloved and sorry for myself but also, suddenly and pleasantly, invisible.

The War

~

**Alaska
February–May 1943
Six weeks later**

In the letter he received with his orders, Jamie had been informed his task was to **express if you can, realistically or symbolically, the essence or spirit of war.** What the essence or spirit of war **was,** the letter did not disclose.

He was allowed to state a preference for where he went, and he requested Alaska, not because he thought it the most likely location for the essence of war but because he was curious to see the place that had held Marian's attention. And he thought he might as well work inward from the war's edges.

On the naval transport from San Francisco to Kodiak, Jamie sketched soldiers playing cards or sunbathing on deck. He painted them stacked in their bunks, their skin nicotine yellow in the sickly glow of the hanging light fixtures that swung sickeningly with the roll of the ocean. The ship, before, had transported cattle, and Jamie thought its new purpose was not so different, still involved livestock.

He stood watch like everyone else, just as in basic training he'd marched and drilled and shot and jogged like everyone else, had sailed around San Diego harbor in a whaleboat and slept in a hammock. At night, some of the boots had cried but tried to muffle the sound, others ground their teeth so loudly it echoed.

For a week, he saw only water. Despite the spreading V of the wake, despite the shifting colors of the sky and the low passage of the winter sun, the ship seemed to be just churning in place, always at the center of the same flat disk of empty sea. The rest of the world seemed irrelevant. His father's life had been spent at the center of such disks. Over time, what did that do to a person?

He tried to paint the roar and blast of the engine room, the green-white crust of sea spray that froze to the railings, the band of pale sky at the horizon, the prow chopping down on the white-capped swells, sending up walls of spray. Titanium white. Davy's gray. Indigo. Blue black. Some guys heckled him about his sketching and painting; some seemed worried about him. They asked if he knew how to shoot his rifle. He only said yes and no more. He'd been one of the best shots in boot camp, payoff from all the tin cans he'd blasted to smithereens as a child.

In Kodiak, he was told to report to a captain. He showed his orders, explained he was the combat artist.

"Christ, what next?" said the captain. "All right, what do you need?"

"I'm not sure," said Jamie. "I'm supposed to go around painting what I see." He didn't want to explain how, really, the point was to **interpret** what he saw. The captain didn't strike him as someone who would relish being interpreted.

"Sounds great. They'll surrender in no time now you're here. Carry on."

Jamie sent off the paintings he'd made on the voyage and began new ones, working with stiff fingers and numb toes through the short, cold days. The inner parts of Kodiak's harbor were frozen in a flat pane (titanium white) that ended in a crisp edge against the open water (Mars black). Slabs of ice, padded on top with new snow, broke off and floated away. Sometimes the glossy black fins of orcas sliced up, rolled down through the water's surface like the turning cogs of submerged wheels. Bears came to forage through the garbage. Sea lions (Van Dyke brown, a little Venetian red) lay in heaps on the docks and rocks, roaring and biting. The females were smaller and tawnier than the males, bullied and put-upon, with tragic black eyes.

Jamie painted the mud and snow, the barracks and hangars and storage buildings, the jeeps and lumber piles. He painted a trawler tied up next to a submarine, a destroyer plastered with snow along its broadside after a blizzard, two P-38 Lightnings silhouetted against a snowy peak. The snow was white; sometimes the sky was white, sometimes the sea, too. He would need more white paint, more gray and blue and ocher, more Naples yellow for the tender winter light. He hadn't used watercolors much since his boyhood, but he returned to them, leaving patches of the paper dry and bare for snow, adding faint streaks and blotches of gray to suggest the dimensions of the mountains.

If he was idle, he felt guilty and conspicuous, though of course he was much more conspicuous when he was working: an eccentric figure at an easel, some **en plein air** fanatic obliviously scraping away with his brushes in the middle of a war. This was what the navy wanted him to do, he reminded himself. **We believe we are giving you the opportunity to bring back a record of great value to your country,** the letter had said. Had the letter been sincere? Sometimes he felt almost mocked by it.

He ate meat because it seemed impossible not to. He drank but not too much.

Before he learned to lash down his boards and canvases, more than one had been lifted off his easel by the wind, sent cartwheeling through the mud to lodge against the wheels of some machine or smash into the side of a building, leaving a smear of color.

The barracks' interiors were collaged with women, barrel-vaulted Quonset huts densely papered with smiling movie stars and nameless models the way some cathedral ceilings were crowded with angels and apostles. The women from home, the real women, were kept in pockets or pinned above bunks and washstands like patron saints. Men were always showing their sweethearts and wives to Jamie. Proudly, anxiously. They worried their girls wouldn't wait, not that they themselves usually turned down the chance to stray, if it arose. You just want someone to touch you, the guys said. There was no point in feeling guilty.

In the nurses' quarters were photos of men in uniform. They worried those men would die, but also that they would stray.

"Is someone waiting for you at home?" This was a nurse, Diane, who showed Jamie a photo of her parents and another of her sister in a WAAC uniform.

"No," he admitted. "No one at all."

On their first outing, he kissed her in the lee of a boulder. After their second, a dance in the Officers' Club, in the cab of a bulldozer left unlocked, he put his hand down her woolen trousers. She lifted her hips and he tugged off her pants, maneuvered around the bulldozer's various levers and knobs until he could wedge himself between her knees. She gave him a little nod, and he pushed into her.

He hadn't been with anyone in months, didn't last long, pulled out and came into his handkerchief. Then followed an awkward parting, a heavy melancholy filled with thoughts of Sarah.

The captain had decided he liked Jamie's paintings. He asked gruffly if Jamie would paint one of the harbor for him personally. When Jamie delivered it, the captain asked where he wanted to go next. To the action, Jamie said, though that word made him queasy: chipper, dishonest shorthand for violent death. The captain said he would see what he could do.

Jamie was put on the passenger manifest of a shovel-faced PBY Catalina seaplane, bound for Dutch Harbor. Five days in a row they tried to go, but the weather was terrible. Three days, they didn't even take off. The other two, they turned back. He stopped bothering to say goodbye to Diane. On the sixth day, finally on their way, over the ocean with only gray cloud in the windows, the plane jolted and bounced with awful swoops and groans, and Jamie held his paint box against his chest, closed his eyes. Almost daily, planes and crews vanished into the Bering Sea, downed by weather more often than enemy fire. He wished Marian were flying the plane.

In Dutch Harbor, bombed by the Japanese six months earlier but mostly repaired, he made more paintings, sent them off. Planes were smudges in the sky, one or two small brushstrokes each. He wasn't there long, was only waiting to go west again, following the sweep of the perforated Aleutian arm toward Attu and Kiska, tiny, muddy, storm-scoured islands far out in the chain that the Japanese had invaded in June and needed routing from.

He was lucky with his flight to Adak. Arriving at all was lucky, and at times the clouds had even broken open, revealing the islands below: steep, snow-capped, smoke-plumed volcanic cones sloping down into collars of sheer cliffs fringed by waves.

He stayed in a Quonset hut with a cohort of army journalist types. ADAK PRESS CLUB said a sign on their door.

The Seabees had filled in a lagoon with bulldozed volcanic ash and hammered down perforated steel planking to make a runway. After a storm, planes returning from bombing runs would land in standing water, their propellers driving up dense clouds of mist as they hurtled down the runway in angry white puffs, only their noses and wing edges visible.

The Japanese flew over sometimes, strafing and bombing, usually not doing much damage. The tundra swallowed their bullets and bombs. "We do better than that, don't we?" Jamie said to an army photographer after an attack.

The man gazed after the departing planes. "Yeah, their mud is probably much more shot up than ours."

Jamie was loitering outside the hospital huts when a man, wounded by a bomb, was unloaded from a jeep, part of his jaw missing, his uniform soaked with blood. The photographer came running, ducking behind his camera. The man held up a sticky red hand, warding him off. Jamie sketched the man from memory later but felt dirty about it. There had been a helpless intimacy to the destroyed body, something embarrassing about the obviousness that he would die. He'd wanted privacy.

Jamie enclosed a sketch of a row of P-40s in a letter to Marian, their cowlings painted to look like the mouths of roaring tigers.

I wish I could talk to you about Alaska, though I don't know if you ever had reason to come this far out into the islands since there was only fog and mud and muskeg out here before. Now there's a harbor and a runway. A tent city. There were some people on Attu and Kiska, missionaries I think, and people at a weather station, but no one seems to know what happened to them.

He wanted to tell her about everything the war had brought to Adak's empty shores. Endless ships disgorged all the ingredients of civilization, everything needed to feed and house and entertain ten thousand men. Huts and hangars but also cold-storage buildings and mess halls and darkrooms and torpedo shops, movie theaters and gymnasiums and surgical suites. A menagerie of machines arrived along with everything required to tend them, mountains of ammunition and ordnance, of tools and spare parts. The essence of war sometimes seemed to be the accumulation and transportation of stuff, of things. He wanted to list these things for Marian, to make her marvel at their number and variety and mundaneness (consider the journey of a single can opener), but the list could never be long enough to make his point. Maybe that was where the scale of the war lay, in the bits and pieces.

He made a watercolor of ships in the harbor and sent it to Sarah without a note.

In April, bombardment against the Japanese increased; invasion seemed imminent. The assumption was Kiska would be first because it was closer. Out by the runway, Jamie ran into the executive officer and told him he'd like to go along when the invasion happened. "You want to paint the invasion?" the man repeated, puzzled.

"I'm supposed to paint more than supply lines and air support."

"The landing force is coming from somewhere else. They won't stop here, so there's no way to get you in with them. It'll be a quick operation."

"Maybe I could go with one of the bombers."

Fog was advancing over the water, and the XO jabbed a thumb at it. "You wouldn't see much, thanks to this shit. Are you sure you don't want to go back to Kodiak? Get on your way somewhere else?"

Jamie watched the fog drift and creep toward the

shore. It was a neutral party to the war but power-ful. It shrouded and delayed, swallowed planes. "Maybe," he said. "Soon."

On May 11, word came: The invasion had begun. Attu was the target, not Kiska. They thought it would take three days. Probably only five hundred Japanese soldiers were on the island.

Days passed. The officers were grim-faced. There were more Japanese soldiers on the island than they'd thought. Multiples more. Conditions were bad, the going slow.

After a week, Jamie went up with a bomber crew, but the XO was right. He didn't see any-thing. They dropped bombs into the gray noth-ing just to conserve fuel. "Stupid motherfuckers," the navigator said, and Jamie didn't know who he meant, the Japanese or their own command-ers or the bombs themselves. The thought struck him that, up in the air, they were no different from planes that vanished. Only their eventual return to Adak distinguished them. Being aloft meant being lost to everyone but yourself, and he wondered if that appealed to Marian. Or maybe she didn't notice anymore.

An armada assembled in Tokyo Bay: carri-ers, battleships, destroyers, etc., all bound for the Aleutians to drive the Americans back to the main-land. It never sailed. Might have; didn't.

After two weeks, word came that the infantry was closing in on the harbor where the Japanese had retreated. The XO passed Jamie where he was sketching near the harbor, then turned back, boots squelching in the mud. "A ship's stopping in later today before resupplying Attu," he said. "If you still want to go, I could arrange it. You might make it in time for the last push. How about it?"

So Jamie was on a ship, and the next morning he was on a landing craft chugging through the layer of clear air between the low fog and silver water, and then he was on a dismal gray beach, cratered from shelling. A sleeping bag and food and extra socks were in his backpack; over one shoulder he had a small satchel with his pencils and notebook and watercolors, and over the other he carried a rifle and ammunition. Three tractors were waiting on the sand. He helped load them with supplies, then followed on foot with eight other men. They walked for hours. The truck and tractors outdistanced them, but the tracks were easy to follow. Once he tried to sketch, but he was told it wasn't safe to stop, better keep moving.

Eventually the rear lines came into sight: a colony of peaked tents pitched amid mud and sphagnum moss on a sloping valley floor, snow-streaked peaks above. Scattered bodies of Japanese soldiers began to appear beside the road, limbs at strange angles, sometimes just a helmet atop a crumpled mass. In the bivouac area, Jamie found a lieutenant in charge of a company of engineers and explained that he was a combat artist ("Something new every day," said the man) and wished to go to the front. He was told there wasn't really anywhere to go at the moment. The forward groups were holding their positions. "Make yourself at home," the lieutenant said, making a sweeping gesture toward the tents. "Sample the many delights of Attu."

In the evening, not far away, Japanese soldiers drank sake in gulps. They'd been on the tundra for a year and were low on supplies. For a time there was almost only night; now there was almost only day. Always there was fog, the terrible wind. The colonel in charge had decided against surrender. The Americans' defenses in the valley were light, but, beyond, they had a battery of howitzers on a hillside. If the colonel could seize those, he could turn them back on the Americans. The plan was desperate, almost impossible, but an attempt would be an honorable course.

A thousand men were left. They jumped up and down, screaming and stamping the soil. Pistols were pressed into the hands of the wounded, who, as instructed, shot themselves in the head. Those who couldn't were dispatched with injections of morphine or, when patience ran out, grenades. They drank more, everything they could find.

At dawn the colonel ordered them to break for the American lines.

Screams woke Jamie. A man near him was

bayoneted where he lay, but Jamie was overlooked. He struggled from his sleeping bag, ran uphill with his rifle, away from the chaos. Grenades sent up sprays of earth. He half fell into a foxhole already occupied by the body of a long-dead Japanese soldier.

Three Japanese, not far away, cut the guy lines of the medical tent. The canvas fell, draped over thrashing bodies on cots. The soldiers started bayoneting. Later Jamie would remember the tormented dog from so long ago, under the blanket, but he thought of nothing as he brought up his rifle and took aim. The first one he got in the back of the head. The man's body jerked forward as though yanked by a rip cord. The second he caught in the shoulder, spinning him down into a crouch. While he was kneeling, one hand over the wound, Jamie hit him in the chest. The third man was looking around, confused. Jamie saw that his only weapon was a bayonet tied to a stick, and he dropped this, stood there gazing at the mountains until Jamie's next shot pierced his forehead.

Jamie set aside his rifle. He took a small notebook and a pencil from his chest pocket. His hand shook badly.

After a time, the Japanese seemed to lose their sense of purpose and moved in short erratic bursts, like minnows, brandishing weapons at nothing. A few ate rations taken from the dead, wolfing down chocolate bars. They passed around packs of cigarettes, lit up. From uphill came the sounds of continued battle, but the men on the valley floor stood in casual clumps as though at a party. They took grenades from their belts, tapped them against their helmets to start the fuses, held them under their chins or against their stomachs. Quick blasts of gore. Smoke like a magician's screen, revealing, as it dissipated, that bodies recently whole and alive made headless and handless or scooped out at the middle.

In the foxhole, Jamie drew and drew, would only realize later that he had covered pages with garbled scribbles and blotches out of which no sense could be made.

Ratcliffe Hall, Leicestershire, England
March 1943
Two months before the Battle of Attu

One long. Two long. One short, two long.
T. M. W.
Tomorrow.

Marian, in bed, imagined Ruth in her identical bed on the other side of the wall, one finger tapping. Tomorrow . . . Lndn . . . dinnr w Ed . . . pls? Want u to . . .

No more tapping. Had Ruth fallen asleep? Or forgotten her Morse? Marian pressed her palm against the cold plaster, waited. Finally she tapped with her index finger.

To w?

A reply: To knw hm.

In January, when Marian had arrived at Ratcliffe

Hall, she had learned it was called a "great house," not a mansion or a palace. There was one other woman pilot billeted there, an English girl, and three men, two of whom were American, but Marian, daunted by the grand surroundings and the rapid chatter of the others, kept to herself. She was given one of several rooms over the garage, all of which had the luxuries of radiators and hot water. There were tennis courts and what she learned were squash courts. There was a butler who cleaned the pilots' boots, and dinner was served in a wood-paneled dining room, accompanied with wine and ale. Occasionally, illustrious friends of their host, Sir Lindsay Everard, appeared at the table without warning.

Sir Lindsay was heir to a brewing fortune and owned a nearby aerodrome he'd given over to the ATA. He was not a pilot himself but an enthusiast, a collector of pilots and airplanes, who seemed delighted the war had brought so many of each to his doorstep.

The aerodrome was crowded with a shifting assortment of most everything the RAF flew, though Marian, not yet qualified to fly all the types, mostly flew taxi planes and cleared Spitfires churned out by the factory at Castle Bromwich. Less frequently, she picked up Oxfords from Ansty and Defiants from Wolverhampton and flew to and from maintenance units in the Cotswolds.

Or at least she did these things in theory, as

the dense industrial haze that hung over the midlands grounded the pilots many—perhaps most—mornings. Sometimes three whole days might pass when they couldn't fly, even as increasingly urgent messages came from Castle Bromwich about all the shiny new Spits piling up. On the days Marian flew deliveries, if she finished before dark a taxi plane might bring her back to Ratcliffe, or she might return via train, or she might have to find lodgings wherever she was, which was not always easy or even possible. It wasn't rare for her to find herself lugging her overnight bag and parachute through closed-up unfamiliar little towns, looking for a place to sleep.

One February night, grimy from delivering a Spit to Brize Norton and another from there to Cosford, Marian returned to Ratcliffe and noticed the door to the next room standing open. She peeked in. A woman leaned over a partially unpacked suitcase. Marian stopped, elation surging up before she could tamp it down. "Ruth!" she said.

Ruth straightened, coolly unsmiling, a dress in her hand. "They said you were in the next room. I asked if there was anywhere else, but there isn't. You'll have to blame the ATA." She'd asked for Hamble, not Ratcliffe, she said. She was taking the place of the English girl, who'd gone to upgrade to twin-engines. "Don't worry. I won't get underfoot."

"I'm glad you're here," Marian said helplessly. She hadn't been aware of being unhappy, but her burst of joy at seeing Ruth felt like a relief, an antidote.

"I don't know what to say to that," Ruth said, hanging the dress in her wardrobe with a clatter. "You dropped me completely."

"I'm sorry—I really am."

"Are you? Being sorry's all well and good, but I think you owe me an explanation."

Marian hesitated. She couldn't tell Ruth the truth, but she didn't want to lie. "Could you trust me enough to forgive me even if I don't explain? You're right I've behaved badly. There's a reason, but could you trust that it doesn't matter?"

Again Ruth looked her over, gauging her sincerity. "We'll see."

They were awkward for a few days, but then they were as they'd been in the beginning, better even, more grateful for each other. Ruth had been lonely, too, she said.

The Ratcliffe dinner table was dramatically enlivened by Ruth's presence. She dove headlong into the conversation, and when, a week into her residency, ski planes came up (Marian suspected Ruth had somehow steered the conversation toward them), she said, "Marian, tell them about taking off from the mudflats."

And what could Marian do but describe herself rocking from side to side in her old Bellanca, trying to unstick the skis from the stinking muck at Valdez.

"Why did you have the skis on at all if there was no snow?" Sir Lindsay wanted to know.

She explained about bringing supplies to the high mines, landing on glaciers even in the summer, and Sir Lindsay's interest was so apparent, his questions so probing, leading her inexorably from one anecdote to the next, that she scarcely noticed she was behaving almost as a raconteur, holding the whole table rapt. Though, when she finally hit a patch of astonished silence after describing a williwaw blowing her off a glacier, she clammed up, embarrassed, sawed fixedly at her meat.

Sir Lindsay turned to Ruth. "You've unlocked our sphinx," he said. "Well done."

Marian had been avoiding meeting Eddie, had ducked other invitations from Ruth but never a direct plea until the Morse code message came through the wall. Until then, if Ruth said Eddie would be in London, Marian would beg off, ride her motorbike alone to Leicester or Nottingham or elsewhere. If Ruth said Eddie couldn't get away, Marian would go into town with her, and they would stay at the Red Cross Club, and all would be as it had been. Dinners, movies and plays, cocktails, dancing.

But Marian couldn't refuse. Bomber crews didn't have much in the way of life expectancy.

She lifted her finger, tapped OK.

Eddie met them at the Savoy. Marian gave his hand a firm shake, looked him in the eye. He was very tall and had a long rectangular head like a cart horse's and warm eyes under heavy brows. Though his teeth were long and a little crowded, he showed them unreservedly when he smiled. "I've been wanting to be friends with you for a long time," he said. "Ruth doesn't usually rave about people."

"You'll give her a swollen head," Ruth said, leaning on his arm.

"Before the war," Eddie said as he steered them to the American Bar, "I never would have dared come into this hotel because I would have been worried about looking like a hayseed, but the way I see it, if I can fly over Germany, I can drink anywhere I want." He indicated his olive jacket, his silver navigator's wings. "It helps not having to worry about what to wear."

Marian nodded. Her own blue uniform felt like armor, too, like a universal explanation.

Ruth poked her in the back. "You'll have to talk tonight, Marian, or Eddie will think I've been telling tall tales."

"I know what you mean," Marian said to Eddie, thinking of Jackie scolding her for wearing flying clothes to her interview. "It's a relief to be above reproach."

"Above reproach!" Eddie said. "That's exactly it. You know, I almost don't want to admit how much I've been enjoying London. The mood is exuberant, isn't it? I want to say **careening.** Do you know what I mean? I guess when people are being reminded all the time they might die—they **will** die—they make more of an effort to be alive. Don't you think?"

They ordered cocktails, and Eddie told a story about his ball turret gunner falling asleep as they approached a target, curled in his steel and Plexiglas bubble under the B-17's belly. "I don't know how you sleep like that, dangling in the sky, but this guy can sleep anywhere. He's famous for it."

"Marian can sleep anywhere, too," said Ruth.

Eddie raised an eyebrow. "That so? What's your secret? I'm a terrible sleeper."

"Keep going with the story," Marian said.

"Well, we didn't know he was asleep, only that he was being real quiet. He said he didn't wake up until the flak was really going, and then he"—Eddie mimicked someone lurching and blinking awake—"swiveled around and immediately, **immediately,** shot down a Messerschmitt. We got back in one piece—one slightly perforated piece—and he said he'd been having a dream about shooting down an airplane, and as soon as he woke up, it came true." He leaned forward, amused, looking between Marian and Ruth. "Isn't that strange? I'll tell you, we all thought hard about what we wanted to dream about before we went to sleep that night in case it was contagious—dreams coming true."

"I hope you dreamed about waking up at an air base in England," Ruth said.

Charming. That was the word for him. Marian had met so few charming people, at least not whose charm was of Eddie's easy, generous, affable variety. She could see, watching Ruth watch Eddie, that she loved him.

"Marian could fall asleep in a ball turret if she wanted to," Ruth said.

Eddie asked, "Where's the most unlikely place you've ever slept, Marian?"

Marian looked at Ruth, who waited expectantly, wanting her to impress, to dazzle. She felt defeated already. She could never compete with Eddie's charm. Still, she resolved not to be dull.

"Once," she said, "in Alaska, I crashed a plane into a river, deep enough that there was water in the cockpit. There was no chance of help until the next morning, so I slept on top of the plane." She hunched her shoulders, losing momentum. "It was summer. It wasn't too bad, except for the mosquitoes."

"Tell him about the bear," Ruth said.

"A bear came by," Marian said miserably. "Fishing."

"A **grizzly** bear," said Ruth.

"Were you always brave?" Eddie said. "What were you like as a child?"

Marian thought. "Naïve," she said. "Boyish. Obsessive."

Eddie smiled broadly.

They went to dinner at a Greek restaurant. "There's something shocking about the scale," Eddie said about Greenland, over which he'd navigated a brand-new B-17 when he came from the States. "All you can see is ice. White to the horizon. My maps might as well have been empty pages."

Marian was run through by deep envy. She envied him Ruth, and she envied him Greenland. She remembered the etchings of icebergs and whaling ships in her father's books.

"Once," she said, "I flew north from Barrow, at the very top of Alaska, out over the pack ice. I almost couldn't make myself turn back. There was something . . ." She trailed off. She didn't know what she wanted to say.

"Mesmerizing," he said. "I found the blankness mesmerizing."

"Yes," she said. "That's what it was."

"Marian always pushes too far," said Ruth. "She can't help herself. Anyway, all that ice sounds awful to me. There aren't even any people there."

"There are some around the edges," Eddie said. "Must be hardy folk."

"No people is part of the appeal," said Marian.

Eddie lifted his glass. "To no people."

Leaving the restaurant, they plunged into the blackout as though dropping into an underwater cave. Piccadilly deprived the eye but crowded the other senses. Bodies pushed from all around. Soldiers and women hooted and laughed, wheeling past like bats.

To Marian, tethered to Ruth by the hand, the noise and movement and hilarity seemed like another form of stillness, of waiting. They were all waiting. For the liquor to kick in. For a kiss or a touch. For dawn. For sleep. For duty to resume. For the war to go on, to end, if it ever would. For what would happen to happen.

Eddie steered them through a door and a dark velvet membrane of blackout curtains into a humid bubble of life. Massed uniforms shifted and bobbed on a dance floor like a raft of kelp on a swell, dappled with colored lights. Under the smoke the air had a sweet-and-sour funk, like the people themselves were fermenting. Onstage, horns glinted, violins dipped and parried, a singer knit his brow and clutched the microphone as though the song were being dragged out of him by an unseen claw. They went up to the balcony. Eddie was describing the view from his navigator's desk, out a bomber's Plexiglas nose. "Sometimes it's like a rose window in a cathedral," he shouted over the band as they slid into a banquette, "and sometimes it's a portal into hell."

A roundel of sky and cloud, puffs of flak bursting from nothing, like black popcorn. Hundreds of bombers in formation, planes transforming into masses of smoke and flames. Sometimes one would fall, burning, onto another. It got so cold in the planes their skin stuck to the instruments. They wore so many layers of clothes and gear they were big as boulders. Water passed below, thin beaches or marshy coast, then the geometry of human life: fields, roads, roofs. Onto these things they dropped bombs. There were real eggs for breakfast rather than powdered ones on days they flew.

Ruth, between them on the curved banquette, lolled against Marian's shoulder. Why, Marian wondered, did Ruth not lean against Eddie instead? A few times on winter days she had gone with Caleb and Jamie to the hot springs near Missoula, and the sensation of being submerged in warmth while her cheeks burned with cold and her eyes teared from wind was not unlike how she felt now, most of her basking in the pleasure of Ruth's closeness while her extremities remained exposed to Eddie's frigid band of sky.

"Enough," Eddie said, interrupting himself. "Marian, I've been wondering—how'd you get it in your head to fly?"

"I just wanted to. That's how it is for most everyone, isn't it?"

"There must have been something."

"The barnstormers," Ruth prodded her.

"Yes," she said, reluctant, "I did meet some barn-stormers when I was a kid."

"The same day Lindbergh flew the Atlantic," Ruth said. "Destiny." She signaled a waitress for another round.

"Then what?" Eddie said.

Ordinarily this was a question Marian would dodge. The facts of her life seemed too strange to tell, too steeped in shame and consequence, and she wasn't sure she could adequately explain herself. But for once she didn't want to retreat or evade. In the midst of a war, her secrets were inconsequential.

She said, "Even as a kid, I knew I needed to make money to be a pilot, so I cut my hair off and dressed as a boy so I'd get hired to do odd jobs."

"Were people fooled?"

"Some were. Some people never look closely at all, at anything. And I think some preferred not to look too closely. Also, it wasn't so unusual in Montana for people to live on the fringes."

She told them about collecting bottles, about driving for Mr. Stanley, about Wallace and his drinking and gambling. "Then a man came along who offered to pay for flying lessons."

Eddie looked puzzled. "Why?"

"It turned out, he wanted to marry me."

"How'd you get out of that one?" asked Ruth.

Marian forced herself to meet Ruth's eye. "I didn't. I married him. Eventually."

"You **married** him?" Ruth said, drawing back, outraged and transfixed. "You told me you'd never even gotten close to marrying anyone."

"I lied," Marian said. "I don't talk about him. He wasn't a very nice man." She watched the dancers below. She and Barclay had only danced once, on the crossing to England for their honeymoon. In general he had disdained dancing, but the night the storm abated, he'd led her to the ballroom after dinner. The floor had risen and fallen under their feet with the swell, like someone breathing. "He's dead now, anyway," she said.

"But who **was** he?" demanded Ruth.

Marian said nothing. How could she explain Barclay?

Eddie's warm, mournful eyes lingered on Marian. "We've interrogated Marian enough. Now we should dance." He stood and held out a hand to Marian.

"So you're both going to abandon me?" Ruth said. "The drinks haven't come yet."

"Ruthie, for as long as I've known you, you've never had a problem finding someone to dance with," Eddie said.

Out in the night again, Marian turned to say a quick goodbye to Ruth and Eddie, to flee from the sight of them going off together, but the brief flaring glow of someone's cigarette lighter caught them embracing. Not kissing but holding each other tightly. The lighter snapped closed; the murk swallowed them. Ruth called her name.

"I'm here," Marian said.

"Where?"

"Right here."

Ruth had her by the arm. "Let's go. I hate goodbyes."

"Why aren't you going with him?"

"Do you want me to?"

"I don't understand."

"I don't understand why you lied about being married."

They walked a little way down the street in the general direction of the Red Cross Club. "Don't you love him?" Marian asked. "It seems like you do."

"Of course I do. He's Eddie. What's not to love? Didn't you love **your** husband?"

Dawn was soaking through the cloud. Shapes were coalescing, different grades of shadow. "At the end I hated him."

"But in the beginning?"

"Maybe in the beginning."

"You could have just told me you were married," Ruth said. "You're not so special that everything has to be a secret."

"I don't think I'm special."

Ruth let out a derisive snort. "You do **so**. And that's why you know you can drop people, and they'll still come back. You were right, too. I came crawling as soon as you snapped your fingers."

"That's not it at all."

"Tell me, then."

"Why won't you answer me about Eddie? Don't you sleep together?"

"Why do you **care,** Marian? Oh!" In the dimness, Ruth tripped over the outstretched leg of a soldier passed out on the sidewalk and lurched down hard onto her hands and knees.

"Oh!" Marian echoed. She knelt beside Ruth. "Are you all right?"

Ruth sat up, shaking out her hands. "Yes, but it stings." The drunk hadn't moved, and Ruth poked his leg. He stirred, curling up. "Guess he's not dead," she said.

"We should move so no one does the same to you." Marian took Ruth's arm, hoisting her up. They sat in a doorway on a low granite step. Marian caught the smell of urine from somewhere and of smoke and morning damp. Ruth's palms were raw and gritty, her stockings torn at the knees and streaked with blood. Gently Marian took Ruth's hand, turned it over, and kissed her knuckles. She felt like a Spitfire held too long on the ground. She needed to **move,** to **act,** or she would boil over.

"It's not like that with Eddie and me," Ruth said. "We do love each other, but we're different. We don't—it's not romantic between us. Sometimes it's easier to be married because married people seem like everyone else. No one asks questions. Or not as many. Do you have any idea what I'm talking about?"

"I think so," Marian said, and she teetered for a final moment before she leaned over and kissed Ruth, who kissed back without hesitation. It was an ordinary kiss, in some ways—the wetness of a mouth, the blindness.

A two-note whistle broke them apart. An American airman swayed by, leering bemusedly. "Room for me?"

"Not even a little," Ruth said. "Go home."

"Come on, girls, be nice."

Marian got to her feet, pulling Ruth with her. As they hurried down the street, holding hands, Ruth gasped as though she'd suddenly remembered something.

"What?" said Marian.

Ruth lifted the hand Marian was holding, scraped from her fall. "You're hurting me."

Marian had been squeezing without realizing it. "I'm sorry." She kissed the knuckles again.

"It's getting light," Ruth said, gently reclaiming her hand. "People will see."

Ratcliffe Hall, Leicestershire, England
April 1943
One month after Marian met Eddie,
** one month before the Battle of Attu**

Have you heard about the night witches?"
Ruth asked, lying on her back in bed at
Ratcliffe Hall.

Marian shook her head. She was wedged between
Ruth and the wall, propped on an elbow, her other
hand stroking Ruth's belly under the blankets.

"Russian girls in old biplanes," Ruth said. "They
have a whole regiment of them. They fly over
German lines at night and drop bombs by hand.
They cut their engines and glide in—**whoosh**
in the dark, like a broomstick passing over. Of
course they get killed like crazy."

"At least they're doing something useful."

"So are we."

"Mostly I sit around waiting for the weather to clear."

"This is useful," Ruth said as she pushed Marian's hand downward. "Maybe we're night witches, too."

Marian smiled, pulled her hand back up. "They called me a witch in Alaska, as a joke, because I could get where I wanted even in bad weather." But she was thinking of Barclay, too, how he'd half believed her when she'd claimed to have cast a spell on her womb.

"It just means they were scared of you."

"Maybe." Her thumb brushed the underside of Ruth's breast, and Ruth lifted her ribs encouragingly. "Do you think any of the other ATA girls do this?"

"Yes. Well, I don't know. I could name a couple who'd certainly **like** to, whether they know it or not." Ruth had been smiling but turned serious. "It's so expected for girls to like men that most of them never stop to think if they really do. Wasn't that how it was for you?" She waited, beseechingly, for Marian to agree. She seemed unable to stop herself from seeking reassurances that Marian hadn't enjoyed sleeping with men, or at least that she preferred sleeping with Ruth.

"I guess," Marian said. "Sort of."

"There's always been girls like us hidden in the nooks and crannies."

"I don't exactly know what kind of girl I am,"

Marian said. She had trouble with that word, **girl,** but **woman** didn't feel quite right, either, applied to herself. Being a woman seemed to suggest a person who owned baking pans and a string of pearls.

"People make assumptions. Did I tell you the name of my high school? Our Lady of the Assumption."

"You did."

"The nuns only ever told us it was a sin to let boys touch us. They never said anything about girls." She sounded amused and spiteful.

"It seems to me you knew yourself better from the beginning than most people ever do."

"Maybe," Ruth said, "but some of that's just being headstrong."

Ruth had told Marian she'd known from childhood she preferred women. She'd been a wily little thing, canny enough to keep her mouth shut and start figuring out how to get what she wanted without being run out of her little Catholic parish in her little Michigan town with pitchforks.

"Did Eddie always know, too?" For Marian had finally come to understand the nature of Ruth's marriage.

"I wouldn't want to speak for him." A silence. "Think how much had to happen for you and me to meet."

"Well," Marian said, "there had to be a war."

"And of course this **completely** justifies that."

Ruth, full of dark laughter, had let her voice get loud, and Marian shushed her. They looked at each other, listening, but no sound came from the other rooms above the garage.

"They wouldn't think anything of me being in here, anyway," Ruth said in a whisper. "Just two gals having a late-night chat."

This was true. In the month since their first kiss, every night they'd both been at Ratcliffe they'd wound up in one or the other of their beds. The visitor had to return to her own room at some point—a maid brought tea in the mornings—but so far no one had seemed to notice anything.

Once, by a stroke of good luck, they'd been caught out together the same night in Lossiemouth and had found a pub whose dour proprietress had informed them brusquely that "You'll have to share a room. It'll be cozy, I'm afraid."

"I suppose we can manage," Ruth had said, "if we must."

There was glee to be taken from the subterfuge, from the world's lack of imagination, and Ruth showed her how to take it, though Marian knew that for Ruth there was also bitterness at the necessity of secrecy. People had begun asking them if they were sisters, even though they looked nothing alike: Ruth short and buxom and dark; Marian tall, narrow, and fair. "They're picking up on our closeness," Ruth said, "but they don't know what to make of it, so they draw the only conclusion they can think of."

Yes, Ruth always said, **we're sisters.**

Not that Marian could imagine wanting to flaunt their relationship. She didn't wish she could write to Jamie and tell him she was in love because no part of her wanted to face his surprise, his consternation. She didn't think he would berate her for being immoral—as an artist he knew all types—but she thought he would be uncomfortable in a way that would wear a groove between them. The groove would deepen and widen into a chasm bigger than the immense wedge of the planet that already separated them. He wouldn't be able to keep from imagining what she and Ruth did together, and she feared that revulsion would inevitably creep in, grow on his idea of her like mildew.

She wouldn't say she'd discovered a firm **preference** for women, but neither would she now confidently say that she preferred men. In this moment she would choose Ruth over anyone, but still she missed, a little bit, the inherent imbalance of power she'd felt with a man, the momentum toward submission, toward breaching, the demanding solidity of a cock. She tried not to let herself think about Barclay. After him, with other men, even Caleb, he'd reverberated in her like an echo, sometimes only faintly, sometimes as violently and shockingly as a gunshot in a canyon thought to be empty. With Ruth, though, no echoes intruded. With Ruth, the act was more egalitarian and, surprisingly, in some ways more carnal, driven by a grasping sort of resourcefulness, a blind determination to merge.

The first few times they were together, Marian hadn't put her mouth on Ruth, but when she finally did, she'd found saltiness, pungency, flesh inside flesh, a rawness unlike anything on a man's body. Her own clitoris, as much as she had ever confronted it, had struck her as embarrassing and extravagantly ugly, like a turkey's wattle, but Ruth was clearly pleased with her own and smitten with Marian's. She treated the little flap as important, central, even deserving of reverence. An idol in a hidden shrine.

When the stars aligned, they went out in London with Eddie. Ducking into crowded, smoky rooms, loud with jazz and yeasty with spilled liquor, Marian got the same giddy, feral thrill she'd had as a child when embarking on some adventure with Jamie and Caleb: rambunctious joy heightened by the conspiratorial nature of their triangle. Marian knew Ruth had told Eddie they'd become lovers, something Eddie acknowledged only subtly, by directing a welcoming, brotherly warmth at Marian. She imagined he must have affairs of his own. How could he watch planes just like his, flown by men he knew, burn and fall, and not seek pleasure, release, comfort, life?

"Marian saved my life, you know," Ruth said one night in May, arching a dramatic eyebrow as she sipped from her cocktail. They were celebrating Eddie's return from his fifteenth combat mission. If he survived twenty-five, he could go home.

Eddie turned to Marian with mild curiosity. People were saving each other's lives all the time. "How'd you do that?"

"Don't look at me," Marian said. "I don't know what she's talking about."

"Yesterday I was taking a Fairchild from White Waltham to Preston—" Ruth cut herself off, reached across the table to touch Eddie's arm, said in a sweet schoolteacher's voice, "You might not know this, Eddie, but to get there you have to fly through the Liverpool corridor. Do you know what that is?"

Amused, he said, "I'm sure you'll tell me."

"It's a strip of air space two and a half miles wide between the Liverpool balloon barrage and the one at Warrington. Anyway, I'd already gone in when out of nowhere, I was in cloud. Truly out of nowhere. One minute, clear sailing. The next, nothing but white. It turns out it has to do with the dew point. Some strange phenomenon."

"Did Marian change the dew point?" Eddie said. "Is she the god of weather?"

"Almost," said Ruth.

"Marian must be the sun, then. She came and burned away the cloud."

"No, but she **had** taught me a few things about flying on instruments."

"I didn't think you were listening!" Marian said. She turned to Eddie, explained, "She would only let me try to teach her in pubs and was always changing the subject. I barely told her anything."

"You told me that if I got caught in cloud, I should straighten up, get back on course, turn very slowly and shallowly around to the reciprocal, and then try to dive under."

"Anyone could have told you that."

"But no one bothered except you. So I did it, but the only problem was that I got down to five hundred feet and the mist hadn't thinned at all. So then I thought I'd go over, but the cloud went up forever. I went to seventy-five hundred feet, and I was still in it."

"You should have bailed out," said Eddie.

"I thought about it," Ruth said, "and I might have, except I'd been late to catch the taxi plane and hadn't had time to change into my trousers, so I was wearing my uniform skirt and, just between us three, I'd run out of clean undies and wasn't wearing any." She looked between them. "You see the problem."

"Ruth," Eddie said, "given the choice between death and gliding down with your unmentionables out, you should have chosen the latter. Actually, I'm almost surprised you didn't relish the opportunity to be a scandal."

"Me too," Ruth said thoughtfully. "In retrospect, I think I didn't want to be so helpless. Anyway, I just . . . flew along, hoping a hole would open up."

"I'm on the edge of my seat," Eddie said, "even though it appears you survived."

"I saw a thinning. Or, I thought I did. I might have imagined it. I had no idea where I was. When I dove, I could have been plowing right into the balloons or a hillside." She stopped talking. Eddie took her hand.

"You had the windup," Eddie said.

"I did. I really did." Ruth's voice wavered. "You know, when it's happening you're concentrating so hard you can't really feel anything, but later it hits you, and it's like you have a chill and can't get warm again."

"Give me a bit of advice, Marian," Eddie said. "Anything. For luck. What do I need to know? What will save my life?"

"It was only common sense, what I told Ruth."

"That's not advice. Come on."

Marian considered, said, "My first flying teacher told me to learn when to ignore my instincts and give in when I wanted to resist, and resist when I wanted to give in. He wasn't really talking about flying, though. And he died not long after in a crash."

Eddie laughed. "My **strong** instinct is to ignore this terrible advice, but maybe that means I should take it. You've given me a conundrum."

A week later: word that Eddie's plane had been shot down. He was classified as missing. Ruth lay on her bed, the telegram discarded on the floor. "His seventeenth mission," she said to Marian, who sat stroking her back. "How can they expect anyone to survive twenty-five? It's inhumane. You should have seen them look at me when the telegram came, like I was being **rude** for crying. Why doesn't anyone cry here?"

"People are afraid if they start they'll never stop."

A few days later, when Ruth was delivering a Spitfire, she detoured and landed at Eddie's base, feigning a mechanical problem. In the hangar and the ops room, she badgered anyone she could find for information. Crew members in other planes had reported seeing three parachutes before Eddie's plane exploded, she learned. But no one could know whose they'd been.

Pacific Ocean
June 1943
A few weeks later

A troopship slid under the Golden Gate Bridge, heading to sea. From where Jamie stood at a high railing, the decks looked mossed over with men, a carpet of khaki-and-green bodies as dense as sod. They didn't know their destination. A piercing evening brightness glanced off the whitecaps and the wheeling seabirds and the Golden Gate's orange-red towers, one of which was about to be swallowed by a bank of fog pouring down over the Presidio. The water glowed milky jade until the fog caught the ship. Jamie went below.

The ship had once been an ocean liner, but all the furnishings and fittings had been removed; in their place, bunks were stacked everywhere, tight as baker's trays. The windows and portholes had been boarded over or painted black. On the decks, where couples might once have strolled arm in arm, heaped-up sandbags encircled outdated anti-aircraft guns. It wasn't a new ship, nor fast enough to rely on speed for defense—not like the **Queen Mary** or **Queen Elizabeth**—and so a destroyer dogged along with it. The hull and superstructure had been painted gray, effacing the vessel's name on the bow and stern, and it was not until the second day, when he saw some soldiers using an old life ring to keep their dice from rolling away, that Jamie learned the ship's name. **Maria Fortuna.**

He had not thought about the **Josephina Eterna**'s sister ship since he was a child and Wallace had shown him newspaper clippings about the disaster. In photos, he and Marian had been two bundled, faceless pupae being carried down the gangway of the SS **Manaus** by their father. There had been stray mentions of L&O's other, newer liner, **Maria Fortuna,** which had only recently gone into service. He walked around the ship, trying to imagine its former splendor. Some merchant seamen had stayed on, and he waylaid an engineer in a corridor belowdecks.

"She had a sister ship that sank, didn't she?" Jamie asked. "The **Josephina**?"

"That's right. Bad thing. Before my time, of course." Soldiers and sailors were squeezing past in both directions. "Better stop holding up traffic," the engineer said and was gone, absorbed into the flow.

Jamie had been given a few days' leave between the Aleutians and his departure from San Francisco, and when the transport plane from Kodiak unexpectedly stopped in Seattle to refuel, he'd decided, on impulse, to disembark.

When he identified himself on the telephone, Sarah Fahey—Sarah Scott—had made a small, indecipherable sound. "Did you get the watercolor I sent?" he asked.

She cleared her throat. "I did."

He waited for her to say something else. When she didn't, he said, "I didn't mean to bother you. I thought of you because I'm in town, but I'll let you go."

"Yes," she said in a vague voice. "Yes, all right."

He'd gone out and had too many drinks in a bar rowdy with servicemen. The same old bewildered, clutching, yearning feeling rose up in him like something coming out of the deep, roiling the surface. Why had he called her? Why couldn't he leave well enough alone? If there was one thing he should have learned from their last meeting, it was that she was an illusion, a fantasy, and anything between them was impossible, anyway. Seeking her out yet again was the height of foolishness.

When he'd made the watercolor of Adak's harbor,

it had been one of those golden moments in between storms, the horizon deep indigo while lemony light skittered across the water. Even the ugliest
heaps of military junk along the shoreline had been
bathed in a heavenly glow, and he'd felt a pressure in
his chest—the sublime. As the colors seeped from
his brush, he'd been overwhelmed with gratitude
to Sarah. She'd goaded him into enlarging his life.

Attu hadn't driven away his gratitude but had
complicated it, shot it through with something
dark and heavy as iron ore.

In the morning, he found a message slipped
under his hotel room door. Would he please meet
Mrs. Scott for lunch? An hour was given, and an
address, just down the street. He tried to remember
if he'd told her where he was staying, was nearly
positive he hadn't.

He'd thought, right up until the appointed time,
that he wouldn't go, but of course he did. She was
waiting at a booth in the back of the dim, grubby
diner she'd chosen, out of place in her neat blue
suit and pumps, her face tense.

"Nice to see you," he said. He sat down and
began studying the menu. "Do you already know
what you want?"

She reached across the table to touch the back of
his hand. "Jamie, I'm sorry," she said.

He put down the menu. "For what?"

"To start, for the way I was on the phone. I was

shocked. And my sister was in the room. I couldn't say anything I needed to say with her there."

A waiter appeared, an older man in a paper hat with a paunch hanging over his stained apron, pen poised above his notepad. "What'll it be?"

"We might need a minute," Jamie said. The guy stuck the pen behind his ear and went away.

"Are you actually hungry? We could go somewhere else to talk," Sarah said. "To your hotel?" She blushed. "I chose this place only because it's right nearby." He slid out of the booth at once. She held out her hands. "I may need your help. My knees are shaking."

"How did you find me?" he asked as they walked out, her holding his arm.

"I thought you might stay near the museum, so I worked out from there, calling hotels."

"How many did you call?"

"Seventeen."

They did not talk much more until later, after he had taken off her blue suit and white silk blouse, after he had unclipped her stockings and rolled them down, divested her of her inner casing of girdle and bra and panties. He worked slowly and methodically, stopping her every time she tried to assist or hasten the process. When she was finally naked on the bed, her hair loose on her shoulders, he'd stepped back and looked at her. She'd stared back, and he'd closed his eyes, testing himself, summoning her image, willing himself to remember.

"My brother died," she said after, lying in the crook of his arm. "In the Pacific. I'd only just come out of the worst of it when I got your watercolor. I knew you'd gone, of course, but after Irving died I realized that if not for me, you might be tucked up safe somewhere. I'd actually tried to **shame** you. I suppose that's part of what drives this whole thing, isn't it? Everybody wants everybody else to suffer as they are. People wish things on others they never could have imagined. They **do** things they couldn't have imagined. When your painting arrived, all I could think was—what have I done?" She lifted her head to look at him. "If not for me, would you have gone?"

"I think so. You have power over me, but not that much. Don't feel responsible."

She dropped her forehead onto his chest. "I wish it were that simple."

"Me too."

"My husband's in the Mediterranean." She looked up again fiercely. "I **do** love him."

"I didn't think this meant you didn't."

She settled back down, tugged gently at his chest hair. "So blond," she said. "You turned out wooly. I wouldn't have expected."

"I'm as surprised as you."

"Did you know one of your Alaska paintings was in **Life** magazine?"

"Yes, they told me."

"Have you seen it?" Naked, unembarrassed, she got out of bed and extracted the magazine from her handbag. They leaned against the headboard together, and she flipped to an article about the Aleutians. His painting was of the airfield on Adak: a plane kicking up spray as it landed under an approaching storm.

He studied the reproduction. "I never thought I'd be a propagandist."

"Is that what they want from you?"

"No. Surprisingly, no. They've given me almost total freedom. Well, as much freedom as anyone has in the navy." He drew her close, rested his chin on top of her head. "This reminds me of when you'd come up to the attic to help me look through the art. It was the most alone I ever felt with you."

"We had clothes on then."

"I desperately wished we didn't."

"Me too."

"Really?"

"Sometimes. I didn't quite know what I wanted." She was still looking at the magazine. "You get used to thinking of the war happening in black and white because of the photos."

"Mmm." He thought of the Japanese soldiers blowing themselves apart. "There are colors."

"This painting does something different than a photograph because you've bent the perspective ever so slightly. It has a feeling that's informative in a different way than strict reality." Her foot moved against his calf. "It's still your work. It's still you."

He got out of bed, went to his satchel, came back with the sketchbook he'd had on Attu. He opened it to a page he'd filled with blotches and scribbles and handed it to her. "I made these during the banzai charge. I thought I was drawing what I was seeing."

She turned the pages. "Weren't you?"

"I mean, when I looked at the paper, I actually saw realistic images. Figures, you know. Scenes." She was quiet. "I killed three men," he said. He hadn't told anyone before. It would have been strange to tell anyone in the Aleutians. Superfluous. He churned with nerves, though he was not haunted by the memory of the three dead men; he was haunted by the medical tent, the shapes moving under the canvas.

"It's a war," Sarah said.

"Would you mail this to my sister for me?" he asked about the copy of **Life.** "I'd like her to see it. I don't know if I'll have a chance before I'm sent off again. I'll give you her address in England."

"She's in England?"

He told her, as best he knew, about the ATA and about Marian's years in Alaska and also, eventually, about Barclay.

After a hesitation, Sarah said, "I should say that my mother told me about when Marian came here. Not at the time but recently. After I last saw you.

Don't worry, she would never tell my father. He has no idea about most of what she does."

"It was a kindness. More than that. She gave Marian a new life."

"Yes, I think so, too, now that I understand. I'm embarrassed about how I reacted before, last time, when you said Marian didn't want to have children."

"It's all right. I'm embarrassed about some things I said, and also because I didn't find out anything really about your life. Will you tell me now?"

"I don't know where to start."

"Start anywhere."

She told him about her sons, her love for them but also her sense of being confined by motherhood. She told him she loved her husband but resented his assumption of her fealty. She told him about her sisters and their families, about Irving's death on Bataan. He told her about how he'd veered toward becoming a drunk, how Marian had taken him to Vancouver, about Judith Wexler and Sally Ayukawa, about going to the mountains and leaving again, about Wallace dying. The afternoon waned. The room grew dim, but they didn't turn on any lights. After they'd dressed, they held each other for a long time by the door, knowing that once they stepped outside, something would be over. He walked with her to the lobby, watched her go out into the evening, her hair still loose.

When he checked out of the hotel, before he boarded his train for San Francisco, he gave the clerk a paper-wrapped parcel and paid for it to be delivered by courier to Sarah's house. The note, which he'd written on hotel stationery and tucked inside the sketchbook, read:

Technically this belongs to the United States Navy, and it's not mine to give. But I don't want to send it to Washington, and I don't want to carry it around anymore. Would you keep it for me? Maybe I want to leave something with you so I have an excuse to see you again—yes, I do— but really the reason I'll come back is because I love you, and what I've left of myself can never be reclaimed.

**Stalag Luft I, near Barth, Germany
June 1943
Around the same time Jamie sailed
  from San Francisco**

Leo, when Eddie first saw him, a week after he arrived in camp, was onstage in a gauzy blue dress of dyed, stitched-together handkerchiefs and a brittle wig made from Red Cross packing material, two straw braids tied with twine. He was Gabby in **The Petrified Forest,** playing against a set made from Red Cross crates, with props bartered from the German guards, who had borrowed them from a theater company in town. Thousands of men desperate for distraction made good audiences. The guards came, too, sat in the front row.

"A lot of girls I know could learn a thing or two from **that,**" the guy next to Eddie whispered, gazing appreciatively at Leo.

That. Because what was he? He was obviously not a woman, but also, somehow, he could make himself indistinguishable from one. Some of the guys who played girls (not just in the plays, Eddie learned, but at the camp's oddly earnest dances and teas, too) fully embraced the rituals of womanhood and shaved their arms and legs and concocted homemade lipstick and blush, but Leo with his big beaky nose and hairy arms only had to put a bit of softness into his joints, a bit of sway into his spine and a careful flourish into his fingers, and he was a lonely, pretentious, impetuous girl tending a gas-station lunchroom in Arizona. Watching, Eddie could almost feel the desert heat, smell the grease of the deep fryer.

Eddie started looking for Leo after that, almost didn't recognize him when they wound up next to each other in the wash shed, despite the nose. "You were great in the play," he ventured. "Were you an actor before?"

"No, I was a bombardier."

"I mean before before."

"I knew what you meant. Only in my dreams. I never had the nerve even to audition in high school. But here—why not? What do I have to lose?"

"You were terrific. The guy next to me said real girls could learn something from you."

Leo pressed his lips together. "They like to say that."

"I suppose it's all in good fun," Eddie said, cautious.

Leo gave the same brief, polite smile. "Can be."

"Desperate times, desperate measures?"

"For some."

Eddie dropped his voice almost to a whisper. "Poor bastards," he said.

The plane had been shot up by a Messerschmitt; the engine caught fire. The copilot and the tail gunner were dead already, shot, when the pilot told the rest to hit the silk. The bombardier went out first, through the same bay from which he'd dropped so many bombs, then the radioman, then Eddie. Strange to plunge through the sky only in his body, without the encapsulation of the plane, falling among the flak and the bullets and the droning engines, the fire. He'd pulled the rip cord.

The radioman was shot dead while hanging from his parachute, and Eddie didn't know what happened to the pilot and the other guys. Eddie and the bombardier were taken to Frankfurt to be interrogated, and from there he was sent to the camp, on the Baltic. As the prisoners walked from the train to the gates, people gathered on the side of the road to jeer at them and mime nooses and firing squads.

. . .

"I don't understand why it has to be that I'm more a woman than a woman," Leo said to Eddie a month after they met. They were in Leo's barracks, Leo standing near the stove and Eddie wedged into a corner among the bunks, as there was nowhere else he could fit himself. The rooms were sixteen by twenty-four and housed fifteen men. Leo had a tin cup full of hot water from the laundry, a special favor from one of the guys there, and a sliver of Red Cross soap and was scrubbing at his makeup. "After the match, Lieutenant Bork or Brox or whatever it is, the religious one who won't shut up about being from Pittsburgh, told me there wouldn't have been any call for Eve—like Eve-in-the-garden Eve—if I'd been there! It would have been a different kind of original sin, no doubt, but I think he's confused. About a few things."

Leo had spent the afternoon sauntering around in a skirt and wig and shirt tied around his ribs, holding up scorecards for a boxing match while hundreds of kriegies hooted and hollered and shouted lewd suggestions.

Eddie said, "I hope someday someone tells Lieutenant Brock how babies are made."

"Guys just want to reassure themselves it doesn't mean anything if they think about me while they're spanking it. I'm more woman than a woman, after all! I'm femininity distilled down to its purest, tittiest essence."

"I think most of them just miss girls more than they know what to do with."

"Fine, but that's not **my** problem. Do I think they all want to suck my dick? No. Do I think most of them wouldn't turn down getting their dick sucked by me at this point? Well." He craned his face toward Eddie. "Did I get it all?"

Eddie dipped his thumb in the water and wiped at the corner of Leo's eye. "Just something here." He put his big hand around the back of Leo's head and kissed him.

Leo pulled away. "Someone will come in."

"Someone always comes in."

Leo was, to Eddie's mind, surprisingly shy about their relationship. There were one or two other couples in the camp—real couples—and they were generally tolerated as long as they maintained some semblance of discretion, which was a low bar in a place so crowded. There were other kinds of relationships, too: paired-off straight men as devoted and sexless as old spinsters, for example, or serious partnerships based entirely around food sharing. There were strictly sexual liaisons between camp queers, between queers and squares, between obliging squares. There were swapped favors of all kinds, all varieties of love. There were murky, confusing friendships that ended in bewilderment or hurt feelings or fistfights.

"After the war," Eddie said, "the first thing I

want to do is find a room, a clean room that doesn't smell like a latrine—"

"It's worse than ever right now, isn't it?" said Leo.

"—a clean room with a bed with clean sheets and a door that both locks and unlocks, and I want to spend a whole night with you. I want to be completely naked, and I want to take my time."

Leo patted his cheek. "Sounds great."

"And the next night, and the night after that."

Hamble, England
November 1943
Five months after Jamie sailed
  from San Francisco

A man came looking for you," one of the other pilots said as Marian sat down in the Hamble mess for lunch.

Marian took a bite of bubble and squeak. "What man?" She had gone to White Waltham for a few weeks in September to upgrade to heavy twin-engines, Class IV, and instead of being sent back to Ratcliffe, she'd been reassigned to Hamble, the all-female No. 15 ferry pool, not far from Southampton, near the Vickers Supermarine factories from which Spitfires and twin-engine bombers emerged as steadily as eggs from a henhouse. The town was pleasantly quaint. The airfield lay between the River Hamble and Southampton Water, blanketed by industrial smog and surrounded by balloon barrages.

"Couldn't say," said the girl. "I didn't see him. Nancy did and told me to pass on the message."

"Where's Nancy?"

"I think she was off for Belfast. Apparently he came by this morning. Must be keen, your fellow."

"I don't have a fellow. Did she say anything else? His name?"

"Let me think." The girl angled her eyes up to the ceiling, scouring her memory. "No, that's it."

Another pilot greeted them and sat. Marian ate pensively, letting the conversation pass her by. If Ruth were at the table, she would not have allowed Marian to be so unsociable, but Ruth had been summoned to White Waltham just as Marian finished there and, after her upgrade, had been sent back to Ratcliffe. They'd fallen out of sync again, mostly just logistically, though they were also handling their prolonged separation differently. Ruth wrote Marian long letters full of coded longing and more explicit reproach for what she called Marian's stoicism. Marian's replies were brief and unadorned, mostly about the flying. It wasn't that Marian didn't miss Ruth. Rather, she took her missing and sealed it away. Her natural inclination was to carry on, to think of other things. Of course, Ruth was also burdened by worry about Eddie. Word had come eventually that he was alive in a German prisoner-of-war camp. Then a Red Cross postcard had come from Eddie himself saying nothing more than that he was in Stalag Luft I.

After lunch, cloud came in, and around three the meteorological office washed them out for the day. Marian left on her motorbike. Most of the girls in Hamble were billeted in little brick cottages, but Marian preferred the Polygon Hotel in Southampton, seven miles away. She'd wanted space between herself and the ferry pool, some semblance of privacy.

Puttering along toward Southampton, dodging drab green jeeps and trucks full of the Americans who'd been arriving in greater and greater numbers, she wondered if the man who'd come looking for her could have been Jamie. She thought he was in the Pacific, but, on the other hand, she hadn't heard from him in more than a month. He'd been in Papua New Guinea when he mailed his last letter, being eaten alive by mosquitoes and rotted by mildew. **So much for paradise,** he'd written. He seemed to roam freely through the war. Maybe the navy had decided he was needed in the European theater, to chronicle the eventual invasion. All these Americans piling up in Britain, their camps sprawling along the south coast, were surely to be put to use before too long.

In midsummer she'd received Sarah Fahey Scott's manila envelope with the copy of **Life** inside, a paper bookmark stuck between the two pages taken up by Jamie's painting, and a card with a brief message:

> We've never met, but I'm an old friend of your brother's and have heard enough about you to wish we might be friends too. I was so grateful he looked me up when he passed through Seattle last month. He asked me to forward this on—that's his painting in there, being seen by millions, but I'm sure you'd know his work from a mile away. My mother sends her best wishes, by the way. She called you "a force," which is her highest praise.

Marian had wondered why Jamie had not told her he'd seen Sarah again and whether perhaps a letter had been lost. She'd studied the painting: a P-4 landing on some godforsaken speck in the Bering Sea. The subject wasn't his, but the execution was, the slight warp to the perspective and the sureness with which he'd suggested the clouds, the hovering white crown of a volcano, the reflections on the waterlogged runway. The airplane was well done—accurate without being fiddly. She didn't envy the pilot. When she'd been in Alaska there hadn't been many places to land in the Aleutians, certainly not as far out as Adak or Attu, and little reason to go. The weather was so murderous the sky there might as well have been a direct portal to the great beyond.

When she reached the outskirts of Southampton, it was only four but already sunset. She parked her motorbike and was making her way toward the Polygon Hotel's revolving door when someone caught her arm from behind.

Caleb. Caleb in an army uniform. She clutched at him. "What are you doing here?"

"I don't know if you've heard, but there's a war."

She pushed him back. "But **here.** It was **you** this morning. Why didn't you leave a note?"

"I left a message."

"The girl who took it couldn't even remember your name, just told someone to tell me 'a man' had come by. Oh!" she said, interrupting herself. "Your hair." Of course his braid would have been cut off, but she hadn't thought about it. She plucked his garrison cap from his head and reached up to touch his short hair, saying, "I thought it might be Jamie."

"Ah." He seemed to absorb her implied disappointment without offense. "Is he in England?"

"As far as I know he's in the Pacific. Before that he was in Alaska." She studied him. Besides the hair and a deep tan he looked remarkably unchanged from when she'd last seen him, when they'd clung to each other in the dirt behind his cabin. She said, "I'm so glad to see you."

"I couldn't remember which of us was mad at the other. I decided to chance it."

"Well, not me."

"Not me, either."

They smiled. The sound of an engine bulged in the sky. She craned to look. A Spit, barely discernible against the darkening sky. "Did you marry that girl? The teacher?"

"No."

She absorbed the news with a nod, less relieved than she would have expected. "Come inside." As they walked toward the hotel, she said, "Somehow I knew you were all right. Tell me where you've been."

"Algeria, Tunisia, Sicily. Now here."

"No wonder you're so brown. All those places?"

Caleb said, "What has Jamie been doing?"

"He's a combat artist. Did you know such a thing existed? He draws and paints for the navy."

They passed through the revolving door. Caleb steered her toward a leather Chesterfield. "He told me something about it when I last saw him. It almost gives me hope, that Uncle Sam wants paintings."

"You don't mind? Sometimes I don't tell people because I'm worried it seems unfair."

"Fair and unfair—none of that means anything anymore." He leaned toward her, his nearness lighting up her bones. "In the Med, I tried to never let myself wish to be anywhere else or even consider that anything else existed. It seemed for the best. Do you know what I mean?"

"Yes."

"But sometimes when I was waking up or falling asleep and had my guard down, I'd think of you.

I'd put you out of my mind, but now . . ." He hesitated. The back of one long finger rested discreetly against her thigh.

"What?" she said. "Now what?"

"Now I have twenty-four hours left on a thirty-six-hour pass. I'd like to spend as many as I can with you."

She wanted to climb into his lap. She wanted to strip him naked there in the Polygon's lobby and press against his skin. She said, "Let me change and we'll go for dinner."

"Can I spend the night?" There was nothing sardonic about him, nothing teasing. He was almost pleading.

If she went to bed with him, Ruth would see it as a betrayal, be devastated if she found out, but Marian couldn't summon any anticipatory shame. She hadn't stopped loving Caleb because she fell in love with Ruth. The two loves were like two disparate species coexisting obliviously in the same landscape: an elk and a butterfly, a willow tree and a trout. Neither diminished the other. Ruth had brought her back to life; she had never been infatuated with Caleb like she had been with Ruth, yet he was more essential. He was as inherent to Marian as one of her organs. "There's someone," she said.

"Does that matter? It's a genuine question. I'm not trying to be flip."

"That's what I'm asking myself."

"I told you how I would pretend there was nothing else. That's what I want tonight. Nothing else has to exist."

"But other things—other people—do exist." He waited. Lamely, wavering, she said, "I have to fly in the morning."

"I'll let you go in the morning. You know I will."

"It's as easy as that?"

"It doesn't matter what's easy," he said. "There's just what you do and what you don't do."

She stood in silence, galaxies of indecision whirling through her. Finally she said, "I can't."

He must have seen her anguish because he chucked her lightly on the shoulder. "Dinner, then. Good enough."

South Pacific
August 1943
Three months earlier

At first Jamie had asked the names of the islands, but usually the answer was that he didn't need to know. And, true, he didn't strictly **need** to know where he was: He was there regardless. But for that reason—that he was already there—how could it be a secret? To whom could he blab? Only to other men on the same ship, who were already there, too, in the same unnamed spot.

But he had discovered that the names didn't mean anything when he did manage to extract them, or didn't even exist, so he stopped asking, labeled his drawings and paintings with nothing more specific than **Solomon Islands.**

Most were protrusions of limestone or basalt, densely jungled, barricaded by shark-patrolled reefs, beyond which lay mangrove swamps and crocodiles and tall grass as sharp as scalpels and more mosquitoes than you could shake a stick at. Occasionally he glimpsed villages, people paddling dugout canoes, children playing on the beach. Sometimes they sailed past wrecked warships, a superstructure sticking out of the water or a hulk lying on its side like the bloated corpse of an animal. Some islands were nothing more than sandbars barely breaching the surface, a palm or two clinging on. He painted one of those, a cliché of paradise, and tried to invest it with the saturating bleakness he felt, the vulnerability of these little rafts of land in so much water. The fronds of his palm tree resembled, at first glance, a man hanging by his neck, blowing in the wind like a tattered kite.

They hid one night against the blackness of a long-extinct volcanic cone, waiting for a group of Japanese destroyers. When they came into range, Jamie felt his ship jolt as the fish launched. The Japanese didn't see the convoy, had no way of knowing torpedoes were speeding through the water until they hit. Jamie imagined a canvas, almost entirely black, the silhouette of a sinking destroyer lit by the yellow-white flash of exploding shells. But how to convey the hundreds of men in the water, their eerie silence? Almost all refused rescue, preferred to die. He saw their wet heads caught in the searchlights, some faces wild with silent fear, others defiantly blank.

He had no pity for the enemy anymore. In this place, compassion would be as superfluous as an overcoat, but he wondered if, when the war was over, it would come upon him all at once, strike him as stealthily as a torpedo.

Every time he was in port, changing ships in Cairns or Port Moresby, he sent paintings to Washington. There was no shortage of war to draw and paint, but, also, he was losing his ability to distinguish what was important. He spent hours painting a single oil drum, put that loving portrait of a rusty cylinder in the same crate as a painting of a full sea battle as though they were equals. He'd lost track, a bit, of his task: the essence or spirit of war. If such a thing existed, it couldn't be drawn or painted. You might as well paint a picture of the earth's molten core or of a starless corner of the night sky and say, **This is the earth, this is the sky.**

He painted the sea with nothing in it, just a blue horizon, sent that, too. No word came to him about whether or not his superiors were pleased with his work, his wandering chronicle, but neither did word come that he was to be reassigned.

In October, Jamie landed on an atoll recently reclaimed from the Japanese and stayed for a while in the tented camp there. He painted a row of Corsairs out on the baking-hot runway that had been made by crushing and smoothing coral, millions of years of work by tiny animals, into a flat, hard surface. When he swam in the sea, he wore sandals made from tires salvaged off crashed Japanese planes so the living, uncrushed coral didn't slice up his feet.

In November, he went to Brisbane, stayed in a vast camp of tents and huts set up in a public park, purple with blooming jacaranda and pungent with eucalypts. He sat in cinemas and bars and didn't draw or paint anything at all. Several letters from Marian found their way to him there, all from back in the summer. She had a friend. She liked London. She liked the flying. She wrote:

I'm ashamed to say I'm happier than I've ever been. I've always needed to feel I had a purpose, and now I have an undeniable one. Is this why people have wars? To give themselves something to do? To feel a part of something?

He thought he might eventually tell her about seeing Sarah in Seattle, but for now he preferred to keep their encounter inside a shell of privacy, away from judgment or any need to explain what it had meant, or not meant. He struggled to write anything meaningful at all to Marian. What could he tell her? That the war had crushed and smoothed him into a different substance entirely, something hard and flat? Apparently he was a person who could watch men drown and feel no pity. He'd been present for every minute, every second of his own life, and he hadn't known himself. He'd thought he could paint the war and not belong to the war. He'd fancied himself an observer, but there was no such thing here.

A few times he started a letter to Sarah but gave up. One evening, he went to a brothel, chose a small, redheaded girl. The next night he went back, chose a different girl, fleshy and blond. It didn't help. He didn't go back.

After the war, he thought, he would know what he wanted to tell Marian. After the war, he would find Sarah again.

A few days before Christmas, as dawn broke, he was asleep aboard a troop transport in a convoy, crowded in with Marines being sent to make a landing somewhere.

Six miles away, a man—the commander of a Japanese submarine—looked through a periscope. He had been following the American convoy for most of the night. Through the periscope he saw a disk of dim sky and black sea, the faint shapes of ships. He focused on a destroyer, relayed the bearing and angle to an officer. He must aim not at where the ship **was** but at where the ship **would be.** The trajectory of the destroyer was one line sketched across the blank indigo ocean. His submarine's course made another line; the torpedoes would connect the two with elegant yet unpredictable geometry.

Though dawn had broken, the water was still saturated with night when the three torpedoes passed through it. They all missed the destroyer (the captain's range was slightly off), but two hit Jamie's transport. The initial impact didn't kill him, nor did the explosion that broke through the hull, pulling up a geyser of water. He survived long enough to feel a sudden crush and violent churn of salt water, the other bodies against his, the pressure that squeezed his lungs, broke his eardrums. Heat billowed past like a wind. He thought he was swimming toward the surface, that the rippling pane of sunlight was almost within reach, that he was about to burst up into the air. And he did see light coming closer, but it was only the blooming glow from the exploding boilers. He didn't quite feel terror as he died—there wasn't enough time. Nor did he feel anything resembling acceptance, nothing like peace. He didn't think of Marian or Sarah or Caleb, or of his paintings or Missoula, though he might have, if he'd lived a few more seconds. No satisfaction came to him at having found, at last, the spirit or essence of war. He was almost as bewildered as if he were still an infant on the **Josephina,** plunged into an incomprehensible world of fire and water.

England
December 1943
A few days later

I s there still the someone?" Caleb asked Marian one night as they danced. It was an accidental London rendezvous, lucky timing. The dance hall was decorated for Christmas.

"Yes." In the month since Caleb's arrival, Marian's life would have been much simpler if she had seen a way to introduce him to Ruth, but she knew Caleb would intuit that Ruth was the **someone,** and Ruth would be jealous and territorial no matter how many assurances Marian offered. So the weeks had been dominated, in large part, by logistical concerns: how to spend time with each of them without alerting the other and how to avoid ATA gossip. The complexity of her schedule and the general wartime hecticness provided some cover, but there had been close calls. Caleb's camp was in Dorset, nearer to Marian than Ruth's posting at Ratcliffe, and so she saw him a bit more often, though occasionally Ruth got assigned a taxi flight to Hamble or a delivery to the Spitfire repair depot and showed up unexpectedly.

Only in the air did Marian ever fully relax. Flying, she was where she was supposed to be, doing what she was supposed to do. No one could reach her or ask anything of her.

On the other hand, she had made the unexpected discovery that the contrast of a present lover with a past one actually amplified her tenderness for each. What was the harm in being loved by both? Who was she to turn her back on such abundance after never before having quite enough love? Who knew how long any of them had to live, anyway. Caleb would go to Europe whenever the invasion happened, and ATA pilots died at about the same dismal rate as those in the RAF.

He found a pocket of space in the crowd to spin her out and pull her back. "If he's so important, why can't I meet him?"

The song ended, and a new one began, a swell of woodwinds, brass shimmering on top. They turned mostly in place, cocooned by other couples.

"Why do you want to?" she said.

"I'm curious."

"No, you're not. You think you'd look good in

comparison. You think no one could measure up to you."

She felt him smile against her temple. "That too."

When the song was over, she started to move away, but he pulled her back. He pulled her back, but she was the one who kissed him. Bound up in him, feeling his need through the strength of his grip, she had a sudden flash of Barclay, of being engulfed and erased, compressed down to nothing. The difference was that Caleb felt her panic, released her. She fled, pushing through the crowd. Caleb let her go.

On Boxing Day, some words came through the telephone in the ferry pool office, and after Marian had absorbed the sense of them, that Jamie had been killed, her first reaction was fear. What a terrifying idea that Jamie should be dead. Why had such a horrible hypothetical event been phrased as fact? **If** such a thing were to happen, **if** Jamie were to be killed, she would not be able to bear it. She recoiled from the idea.

But there was Jackie Cochran's voice again, all the way from across the Atlantic. "Marian? Marian? Did you hear me?"

"Why would you say that?" Marian said. "That's impossible. He's an artist, not a soldier. He's painting the war."

There was a silence in which Jackie must have been gathering her excuses for making such a bad joke, readying her apology. "I can't tell you how sorry I am," Jackie said, and for an instant Marian was relieved. "But I'm afraid it's true. His ship was sunk."

Marian set down the receiver.

Someone rapped on the phone-box door. Marian jumped, startled. A man was there, another ATA pilot. He drew back at the sight of her. "Sorry," he said. "I was only wondering if you were done in there."

She felt her lips move, but nothing came out. She pushed at the door, couldn't make it open because her body had turned to vapor.

"Are you all right?" the man said, opening the door.

She brushed past him, perhaps through him, like a ghost.

They'd been grounded all morning because of weather. She went to the ready room and pulled on her heavy flying suit and fur-lined boots anyway, picked up her bag and parachute. She drifted out to the Spit she was meant to deliver to Cosford, climbed in and took off without going through her checks, noticing in an abstract way that the lights at the end of the runway were red, not green. Immediately she was in cloud. The murk pulsed with circles of light like those that appeared when she pressed on her closed eyelids. Presently she noticed her eyes were indeed closed. She opened them. The air remained resolutely gray. Was she right side up or upside down? Did it matter? She had no sense of where she was, no interest in what she might be about to crash into. In another moment she punched through and was between a blue dome and an unbroken layer of fleecy white.

Jamie was dead. In the cockpit, she screamed. The plane did not fall out of the sky, back into the cloud, though it should have. Flight itself should have been revealed to be an illusion. But the plane continued on, its big Merlin engine droning indifferently. She turned hard to the west, the wings going perpendicular to the cloud, then flipped back level. She pushed up the throttle until a whine pierced the drone. The only impulse she could identify was to be drowned in the ocean. Before, when she had flown too high or too far, she had not really believed she **could** cause her own death, but now she sensed the presence of a border in the sky, a line over which she could pass and never return.

No gaps appeared in the cloud. She had no way of knowing if she was over land or water. It didn't matter. Eventually she would be over the Atlantic. Flying west had felt like the natural choice. Montana was west. Alaska was west. Jamie in the Pacific was west, almost exactly on the opposite side of the world. Then again, all those things were east, too. The water was what she sought, the expanse and oblivion. Maybe she would go down not too far from the **Josephina.** She and Jamie had always been meant to wind up in the ocean together.

Don't.

As clear as if there were no engine noise whatsoever, only the silence of the atmosphere. Jamie's voice, unmistakably.

Go back.

"I don't want to," she said aloud.

Turn around.

She was over the crevasse again. Her body condensed back into itself, surpassed her actual density, became heavy, full of dread. She was heavier than a mountain, heavier than all the water in the ocean. Though something so heavy should not be able to move, she pushed—so slowly—on the stick, pressed on the rudder as though her leg were the heaviest and slowest of pistons. The plane turned.

There was still the matter of finding a place to land. When her fuel gauge was showing nearly empty, a dark stain appeared on the northern horizon where the solid cloud had pulled apart like cotton wool. She dropped through into hillocked countryside, lightly dusted with snow. In the low sun, streams and ponds shone blinding yellow as though a sheet of gold leaf had been imperfectly torn away. She saw a farm with a flat open field, no cows or sheep in it, and she set the plane down, switched off the engine. She opened the canopy to the evening, and though there was only cold air above her, she felt the pressure of thousands of feet of water.

Glints

~

Seventeen

Adelaide Scott finally called. I'd just gotten cut off with Siobhan and assumed she was calling back from some other line, so when a voice said, "This is Adelaide Scott," I said, "Who?"

"We met at dinner at Redwood Feiffer's. I'm the artist. Apparently I didn't make much of an impression." She'd meant to call sooner, she said, but, well, she hadn't. She'd been uncertain. "But then my assistants told me about your . . . about your being in the news lately, and I decided to call."

"Right. Okay. Yeah, I was wondering why you wanted my number."

"Understandable. Well, here it is: I have some letters that belonged to Marian Graves, letters to her and also ones she wrote, and I thought you might be interested in them."

The moment when I'd been intrigued by the artist lady with intel about Marian Graves felt like a different life. "Honestly I'm not sure what I'd do with them," I said. "The movie is pretty set in stone at this point."

"I imagine so," she said. "That's not the point, though, I don't think. I'm not sure why I have an urge to show them to you. You—this will sound strange, but you represent something to me. I'm not sure what yet. You're a stand-in of some kind. Not for **her** but for something more abstract, something about the way people think about her."

After Adelaide had accosted me outside Redwood's powder room, I'd gone home and watched a grainy old documentary on YouTube about a sculptural series she'd made in the eighties of "boat-like objects," ramshackle wooden assemblages designed to sink, sometimes on their own, sometimes after she set them on fire. She'd launched them from different places along the California coast and every year for ten years she dove down and filmed them. Each object was titled just with a roman numeral, I through X. I watched the younger, wet-suited version of Adelaide heave on an air tank, plug her mouth with a regulator, roll backward into the water. She'd had long hair then. Gradually the wrecked objects were obscured by coral and sponges, encrusted with tiny creatures. Towers of kelp waved gently above VII and IX like the limbs of drowned monsters.

Were my parents bones? Or were their bones gone? Was their plane encrusted with tiny mussels, furred with algae? In the last scene of **Peregrine,** I was going to sit in the cockpit of a plane and gaze up at the receding light as I sank to the bottom of the ocean. I would make Marian be the way I needed to imagine my parents had been: not fearful, not struggling.

"What are the letters about?" I asked Adelaide.

"Different things. They span decades. I didn't show them to Carol Feiffer when she was researching her book because—well, Carol already seemed to know what story she wanted to tell, and I suppose I didn't want to derail her, or maybe, really, I didn't trust her to manage their complexities. She seems to want things to be always neatly tied up. The letters hint at some complex relationships . . ." She trailed off. Then: "Carol's a perfectly nice woman, but she's not Proust."

"I'm not Proust, either," I said.

"So you don't want to see them?"

Did I? Or was I just flattered she'd singled me out? I said, "I'm going to Alaska tomorrow for five weeks. Could you send them to me? Scan them or something?"

"I'd rather not. You couldn't come today, could you?"

"Today's nuts."

"Well. When you're back, then. You have my

number now." She still sounded imperious, though maybe a little deflated. "Will you be in Anchorage?"

"Off and on."

"A piece of mine is on display in the city museum. You could go see it."

I was about to say okay and goodbye and hang up with no real plans either to go see her art or to get in touch when I got back, but something odd occurred to me. I said, "Why do you have Marian's letters?"

"She left quite a few things to me. Paintings and family heirlooms. Some baker in Missoula had been storing stuff in his basement as a favor to her before she disappeared. The lawyers told him to ship it all to my mother. These were in the jumble. It might have been a mistake. She might not have meant to include them."

I was still missing something. "But why did she leave you anything?"

Adelaide was quiet for so long I checked to make sure we were still connected. Finally she said, "I'd ask you to keep this to yourself for now, although I suppose it doesn't matter so much, really, but Jamie Graves was my biological father."

The War

England
December 1943
The next day

The farmer's field where Marian had landed turned out to be only thirty miles from the No. 2 ferry pool at Whitchurch. She thought she had enough fuel. If not, she'd find another field. She spent the night on a chilly floor in the farmer's kitchen, regarded with suspicion by his wife, and in the morning managed to get the Spit off the ground, managed to get to Whitchurch to refuel and on to Cosford to deliver the plane. Weather, she told them in the ops office by way of explanation. The plane was in one piece, so she was scolded only perfunctorily, told she'd be written up. Fine, she said. By the time she got back to Hamble in a taxi Anson, twilight had fallen. Numbly she climbed astride her motorbike, groped for the

ignition. Without thinking, without quite knowing what she was doing, she rode toward Caleb's
camp, ran out of gas two miles out, walked the rest
of the way.

At the gate, she calmly repeated over and over
that she needed to see Caleb Bitterroot until the
MP gave up trying to tell her she couldn't just show
up, that the camp was closed, that whatever her
beef was with this Bitterroot person it wasn't the
United States Army's problem, that she was tres-
passing on military property, **miss,** and would be
prosecuted. Finally, he told her to sit and wait and
he'd see what he could do.

Time was behaving strangely. She seemed to step
out of it, only came back when Caleb was crouching beside her in the gatehouse. He understood
Jamie was dead. He'd only had to look at her. She
was grateful she wouldn't have to say the words.
Once she started crying, she couldn't stop.

Another man appeared—a medic, she thought.
He gave her two tablets and a paper cup of water.

After that, time stopped and started again, stut-
tered as though it were yet another machine running out of fuel. There were oncoming blinkered
headlights and shadowed stone walls between
moonlit fields and ancient trees making tunnels of
darkness over the road and the hard bounce of a
jeep. Somehow she directed the driver to her motorbike, and he and Caleb wedged it into the jeep's
little flatbed. Then there was the revolving door

of the Polygon, Caleb's arm around her shoulders, the yellow light of the lobby beyond the blackout curtains, and there was Ruth waiting slumped in a wingback chair in her ATA blues, standing as they came in, asking what had happened, asking Caleb who he was, demanding to be told what was going on. Marian wondered how Ruth could be so cruel as to ask, to make her say it. She remembered being in the elevator with each of them supporting one side of her. Ruth undressing her, Caleb putting her in bed. Her own voice, harsh, telling Ruth to leave, that she only wanted Caleb.

When she woke, Caleb was asleep in the armchair, and Ruth had gone. She wondered why he was in her room, and then she remembered, and she put out her arms first to ward off the knowledge and then for him to come to her.

The Celestial Wind

～

Eighteen

I climbed out of a plane and walked to where a man was waiting for me by a hangar: Barclay Macqueen, the bootlegger who would be my husband. I felt powerful and capable, in command of the whole fucking sky. He'd heard I could fly, he said. He needed a pilot.

Cut.

Hadley, go again, please.

We were filming in Alaska, which was playing not only itself in the movie but also Montana, like how theater actors play multiple parts both to save money and to show off.

I climbed out of a plane and walked to where a man was waiting for me by a hangar. He'd heard I could fly, he said. He needed a pilot. He had some—significant pause—goods needing to be picked up in Canada.

I knew he would change my life, and I was afraid. I let the fear into my eyes. There were mountains all around us, trees rusting away with autumn.

I'd thought if I played Marian Graves I'd get to be someone who wasn't afraid, but now I knew that wasn't the point at all. The point was to be someone who didn't treat fear like a god to be appeased.

Because movies get shot all out of order, it was like we'd taken Marian's life and dropped it from a great height onto something hard, and every day we picked up different pieces and pressed them into place, paving a path back to the beginning, which was Marian's death and so also the end. It was only because of coincidence and soundstage availability that we would film the last scene—the crash—last, but I was glad. I wanted a conclusion. I wanted the end to be the end. Bart was right when he said we don't always notice beginnings. Endings are usually easier to detect.

But the more of Marian I fit together, the more I felt the void on the other side, the empty space that held the truth but didn't contain it. Jamie Graves had fathered a daughter, and Marian had known. This was true, but nobody knew to believe it.

My dear, you are a revelation, Hugo texted one night after watching the dailies. **I can scarcely see you at all, not even when I squint.**

. . .

When I had a morning off, I went to the Anchorage Museum. Adelaide Scott's installation had a room to itself. A temporary exhibit, the sign said. Below was a list of patrons who had made it possible, including Carol Feiffer. In the middle of the pale wood floor under a skylight stood a huge white ceramic cylinder maybe ten feet high and twenty in diameter, its surface stippled with zillions of tiny black etched lines that, together, made an image of the sea, textured with light and current and wind. Toward the top was a horizon, gently scalloped, with suggestions of clouds and distant birds above it.

A smooth circular curtain of rigid pearly-white plastic hung suspended from the ceiling, encircling the drum, embossed with the same image, the same stippled sea. I walked around through the gap, passing between two versions of the same thing. I wanted to step back, get some vantage to take in the whole, but it was designed so you couldn't do that. You had to be trapped in it.

Redwood and I sat in the bar on the top floor of a hotel in Anchorage. It was all wood and brass and windows. Below, the city's ragged asphalt edge met a spreading broad flat of water, and on the far side of the water was a forested rise with Denali sticking up in the distance beyond, two hundred miles away but so gigantic its white top still peeped over the horizon.

"Adelaide Scott called me," I said.

"Really? Why?"

I felt a nagging trepidation, but I forged on. "She said she has some letters from Marian I might be interested in."

He seemed almost affronted. "**You?** Why you?"

Of course I'd asked myself the same question, but I bristled. "You'd have to ask her," I said.

"What's in them?"

"I don't know. She didn't get into details." I played with the skewer of olives in my drink.

"Sorry, I just— Did it seem like there's something in them that would change things? At dinner she was pretty adamant she didn't know anything helpful. And now it's a little late."

I'd been planning to tell him about Jamie Graves being Adelaide's father, but I found I couldn't. I'd only be doing it for the dopamine hit, to feel important, to create a bond. As soon as I'd spoken the words, the information would be as much Redwood's as mine and then, inevitably, Carol's and then **everyone's.** It made no sense to feel possessive about a fact that had nothing to do with me, but I did. Adelaide hadn't forbidden me from telling. She'd said she was tired of keeping secrets, didn't expect me to take on that role. She'd said she felt like she was playing Russian roulette by telling me, not in a bad way. I got what she meant.

I'd slapped that USB drive down right in front of Gwendolyn.

"I don't think my mother knows Adelaide has a stash of letters," Redwood said, agitated. "Does anyone know? We should know for the movie. Why didn't she tell us? She really didn't say **anything** about what's in them?"

"They might not be important."

"Or they could be really important. Shit. Would you be willing to ask her if I could read them? I mean, I can't help but feel a little hurt she didn't show them to my mom. What if there's some huge revelation in them, and she lets the cat out of the bag after the movie's finished? Would she do that? Could we ask her not to do that?"

"You can ask her whatever you want," I said.

"But she's chosen you to confide in. Apparently."

I shouldn't have told him anything. His keenness was making me turn away from him, clutching my little nugget of knowledge. **Mine, not yours.**

I'd figured out how to be Marian—and being Marian mattered to me—but every day we filmed I cared less about the movie. It didn't matter much to me anymore if it was good. I'd stopped imagining myself and my Oscar. This little flicker of truth, that Marian Graves had met her niece before she disappeared, had undermined everything, cracked through the artifice, like how in cartoons a building's whole facade might collapse forward, crushing everything except the hero, who is spared by a perfectly aligned window. I felt foolish but liberated, standing there amid the rubble.

"You know the movie's not true, right?" I said to Redwood.

"People will want it to be true," he said.

"I don't know if anyone will really **care.** People wanted **Archangel** to be true because they knew it wasn't. But this is already like a game of telephone. There's Marian's real life, and then there's her book, and then there's your mom's book, and then there's this movie. And so on, and so on."

"I just want less chaos," he said. He tapped his temple. "In here. I want to know what's going on."

"Yeah," I said. "I get that."

"I'm not sure love is something you find," I'd told the **Vanity Fair** reporter after she asked me if I was searching for love. "I think love is something you believe."

"Are you saying love is an illusion?"

"I had a shrink once," I said, "who told me to imagine a glowing tiger that ate all my doubts. The crazy thing is that it works if you believe it will. But does that mean the tiger is real? Or does it mean my doubts aren't?"

Then I told her how once I'd been in a cave and hadn't been able to tell glowworms from stars, and as far as a hatchling fly is concerned, the thing that devours it **is** a star.

Far out, she said, and I could tell she was going to make me sound like a huge flake.

I said that if you didn't believe you loved someone, then you didn't love them.

"Should we just sleep together and see what it's like?" Redwood said in the hotel bar, still rankled by Adelaide and her letters. His irritation with me was emboldening him; he wanted a sense of order, and he thought sleeping with me might get him that.

"What a delicate dance of seduction," I said.

"I'm being direct," he said. "I value directness. I like you. I'm attracted to you. I know you well enough now to feel like I wouldn't be going to bed with a stranger. Is it wrong to admit I'm also nervous?"

"You mean ambivalent."

"Are you **not** ambivalent about me?" he asked. "We both have reasons to be cautious. Neither of us claims to be a romantic. What if we entered into this deliberately, with radical honesty, following an experimental procedure?"

"You're right. That's not romantic."

"But it **could** yield romantic results. The big-leap thing hasn't worked for me. I want to try something else."

The sunset had turned Denali's summit the pink of strawberry ice cream. Some people at the bar were pretending to take a selfie but really taking a picture of us. I imagined inviting Redwood downstairs with me, going to bed in the fading light, our armor clanking together.

"Maybe," I said. "But not tonight." I pointed out the window. "I have Saturday free. Do you want to go see that mountain?"

"Makes you feel pretty small, doesn't it?" said the pilot through our headsets, talking in his clipped pilot voice over the engines.

The plane was red, with two propellers and two skis. Redwood and I were sitting behind the pilot. Beside him, a second yoke moved with his steering as though maneuvered by a phantom copilot. We'd passed over a braided river and flats of pine forest and clumps of autumnal cottonwoods turned such a bright, sweet tangerine it hurt my teeth to look at them. We'd entered a world of snow and rock. My eyes couldn't make sense of anything because everything was too big and also too simple, only ice, only snow, only rock, and we were dwarfed by the cliffs and ridges, the glacier's cracks and wrinkles, the sheer granite faces. Denali's summit was in cloud. There was no life in any of it.

"Do you know who Marian Graves was?" Redwood said into his headset.

"Can't say I do," said the pilot.

"She was a pilot in Alaska," I said. "Before the war."

"Best job there is," he said.

"My dad used to fly," I said. "As a hobby. He had a Cessna."

"Oh, yeah?" the pilot said.

"Yeah," I said.

"He doesn't fly anymore?"

"No." I said, "I took a flying lesson once. I didn't like it."

"What didn't you like?"

"The feeling, I guess?"

"Best feeling there is."

"That's what the other pilot said."

He laughed.

I said, "I felt like I would fuck it up."

"Nah," the pilot said. "You've got to trust the plane. The plane wants to fly."

He landed on a glacier in a bowl of ice and peaks, a frozen amphitheater he said was bigger than Anchorage. He shut off the engines, and we got out into the silence. The landscape was huge and beautiful in the way the concept of death is huge and beautiful—its beauty doesn't really apply to you. Stepping in the snow, I had a suspended, tentative feeling, like I might plunge through. **This,** I wanted to tell the pilot, **this is how it felt.** But he would just tell me to trust the glacier.

Redwood had walked away, but he came back, offered his hand. I took it. The landscape was the opposite of Adelaide Scott's sculpture. Here you could only see the whole thing. You couldn't pull it down to a scale that made sense. The silence felt as huge as the sky, and we were so tiny it couldn't possibly matter what we did. So we finally kissed there in the snow, and I closed my eyes and hid from what surrounded us.

D-Day

England
June 1944
Six months after the torpedo

May 15, 1944

Hi Kid

I bet you're surprised to hear from me, the way
we left things. I promise I'm not writing to mope
or scold, even if returning your letters seems
like an act of aggression. I just thought you'd
want them. I'm in ███████ towing targets for
gunnery trainees, if you hadn't already heard.
Cochran pretended like this job was some big
top-secret special deal, but it's about as much fun
as being a clay pigeon and half as glamorous. The
flight line is shit city. Red-lined ████ as far as
the eye can see and no spare parts or time to fix

them. ██████████████████████████████
███████

I don't know what the gunnery boys think about us being girls (seems like they're mostly confused about whether to aim at the target or the plane), but the pilots are pretty frosty. Here they are, bunch of hotshots fresh out of flight school, thinking they're on their way to combat and instead they got sent to tin can alley. Bad enough before we showed up and started doing the same job. Boo hoo is how I see it.

The girls say it's better than it was at the beginning, especially since the boys have realized that with us flying they can spend more time playing cards and less time getting shot at. We're always volunteering anyway because we've got something to prove. I've tried to make friends with the mechanics because, as I see it, having them on my side is my best chance for not packing it in. A girl named Mabel crashed before I got here. She would have made it, but her canopy wouldn't open and she burned up alive. The sticky latch had been marked on the form, but no one did anything about it.

There was another crash that killed a girl—the form said throttle problem, but ████████████ ████████████████████████████████████ ████████████ Jackie herself came down to investigate but kept her trap shut about whatever

she found. She worked pretty hard to get us this
gig, and if anyone important gets the idea we're
causing trouble, they'd be happy to get rid of us.

Some of the fellas have warmed up a little
too much. I've got an admirer. A persistent
one. I keep telling him I'm married, that my
husband's a POW, and he says, you know it's
wartime, don't you? Like because there's a war
I'm obliged to lust after someone with a face like
a rotten mushroom.

Maybe you mind that kind of attention
less than I do. I guess you did miss men, after
all. Funny story—a crew of our girls moving
bombers landed because of weather at some
hick town and got thrown into the local lockup
because women aren't allowed out in slacks after
dark there. The sheriff wouldn't believe they were
pilots. Guess it's not a funny story. You push
on men and eventually you get to the bedrock
of it all, which is that they think they're better
than us. And they're the ones who made this
war. I've been thinking about that. We get angry
and nothing happens. Men get angry, and the
whole world burns up. Then when we want to
do our part, they're always trying to keep us out
of danger. Because heaven forbid we should be
allowed to decide for ourselves. Their worst fear
is that one day we'll end up owning our lives
same as they do.

I'm ranting—sorry—partly because I'm trying to work myself up to say you hurt me awfully even though I know you were in a terrible state. I wanted to be the one you turned to, and when you went to him instead, scraps weren't going to be enough. Seems unfair I'd be the one to feel bad about leaving, but I do. Do you feel bad? It would mean a lot to me to know that you do. But, either way, I wanted to say this: In case anything happens to either of us, you should know that from my end anyway, we're okay. I don't know if I can say all's forgiven, but most is. I couldn't have stayed after what happened, but I still miss you and send my love.

Yours always,
Ruth

Marian hadn't seen Ruth again after that night in the Polygon, after she'd chosen Caleb, hadn't heard from her until the letter.

Thousands of ships clung to the south coast like a bloom of gray algae, choking the harbors. For weeks, Marian had watched the buildup. All of it seemed to push and strain against the Channel, threatening to overflow.

Caleb's camp had been sealed in preparation for the invasion.

At Hamble, she was given a Vultee Vengeance to take to Hawarden. From there she was to deliver a Wellington bomber to Melton Mowbray, but a gale came up before she could leave.

She found a room above a pub. In the morning, the rain still lashing down, she called Hamble and was told to stay put. The second evening, after a desultory day spent at the movies, she and another stranded ATA pilot, an Englishman too old for the RAF, had a drink. "I heard," he said, "that the invasion fleet set out this morning but turned back because of this." He cast an incriminating glance at the windows, the splattering rain. "I don't envy the poor sod responsible for forecasting."

Marian nodded. She could summon little interest in the invasion, though she knew it must be done if the war was ever going to end. She could not fear for Caleb. Jamie's death had muffled everything. Only in bed with Caleb had she felt any stirrings of life, and occasionally in the air, too, when she gazed on inanimate splendor: clouds furred on their bottoms by rain, a fat slug of pink light that thickened and yellowed on the horizon and became the moon, distant clouds full of lightning, things that would happen regardless of the war, would happen even if humans didn't exist. Of all the suffering in the past, the best she could say was that it was already over. At some point, the invasion would be, too.

"I flew in the Great War," her companion said. "I never would have imagined I'd live to see a greater one."

The description—great, greater—irritated Marian, though she knew he was only trying to say something about magnitude.

"I must seem terribly old to you," he said. Both forlorn and flirtatious. She glanced at his wedding ring.

"No," she said. Age had ceased to matter. The young lived nearer death than the old.

He turned his pint glass around and around on its cardboard coaster, and she thought he was working up his nerve to ask her up to his room. It was the war; they might as well. Maybe the sensation of life could be drawn from his body. "Do you want to come upstairs with me?" she said.

He looked up sharply. "I suppose I ought to? Something to mark the occasion?"

Already she felt weary, regretful of her invitation, but going to an empty room would be worse.

The following afternoon, the cloud ceiling lifted. After she finally delivered the Wellington, she caught a taxi Fairchild back to Hamble. Heading south, at every airfield they passed over, planes were lined up, rows and rows of them, their wings freshly painted with black-and-white stripes.

At the coast, lines of ships stretched into the

Channel, their wakes drawing arrows toward France. Tanks and trucks and jeeps filled the roads, went over gangways and were swallowed by ships.

In the night, for hours, came the droning of engines. In the morning, everything was gone.

Constellations

—

Nineteen

Adelaide Scott lived in Malibu, not in an aggressively beach house-y way but in a shabby-fancy country-living way, north up the Pacific Coast Highway, past the fishing pier and that restaurant Moonshadows where Mel Gibson had gotten drunk before he went off on a Nazi rant to the cop who pulled him over, past Nobu, past all the popular beaches, way uphill from the highway, above the hazy blue plain of ocean. The air smelled like sagebrush and dust and salt. Adelaide's three mottled mutt dogs came running out of her house when she opened the door and barked at me before sniffing around the bushes. "How was the drive?" Adelaide asked.

Commence ritual Los Angeles chitchat about routes and traffic.

"I used to have my studio in Santa Monica," she

said. "But the commute became unbearable, so I moved it to Oxnard, which has the advantage of being much cheaper and perfectly convenient from here. My assistants will never forgive me, but I have an entire warehouse now."

Inside, the house was all dark green tile and red-gold wood and many-paned windows looking out onto hillsides covered in the paper-dry California brush that wants nothing more than to burst into flame. "I'll make tea," she said, leading the way, the dogs following. "Wait here. I can't bear to have anyone watch me putter." She waved me into a big living room under red-gold beams.

Above the fireplace, a strange sort of spiraling horn was mounted diagonally, very sharp at one end and about seven feet long.

Adelaide reclined in an Eames chair, her feet up on the footstool. She'd hung some reading glasses around her neck, and there was a document box on the floor beside her that I assumed had Marian's letters in it. I sat on a leather couch facing the green tile fireplace, the spiraling horn. A dog jumped up beside me and immediately fell asleep with its butt against my thigh, apparently unaware I was a major motion picture star, an icon of the silver screen.

"What is that thing?" I said about the horn.

"A narwhal tusk," she said.

"What's a narwhal tusk?"

"If you don't know, it's better just to show a picture." She got up and pulled out a book of wildlife photography, flipped through to an image of what were apparently narwhals surfacing in a patch of open water surrounded by ice. "They're a kind of whale," she said. Their blunt heads were speckled brown and gray and smoothly featureless except for the insanely long single tusks that stuck up like jousting lances. They looked like unicorns crossbred with dirty thumbs.

"My understanding," Adelaide said about the tusk, "is that Addison Graves, Marian's father, acquired the tusk somewhere on his travels. I have other things, too—exotic souvenirs I think were his. The old books over there as well. And that painting"—she pointed to an oil of hazy dockyards—"was by Marian's uncle Wallace. I wound up with quite a few paintings by both Jamie and Wallace. Most of Jamie's better ones are in museums. Carol Feiffer was very interested in the tchotchkes, though I don't know any of the stories behind them."

She took a small sketchbook from the document box and handed it to me. "This might be of interest."

A piece of paper was folded inside the front cover. I opened it. **Technically this belongs to the United States Navy . . .**

Adelaide said, "That note is from Jamie to my mother." I kept reading.

. . . really the reason I'll come back is because I love you, and what I've left of myself can never be reclaimed.

I refolded the paper and flipped through the book. The pages were yellowed and crumbly and full of sketches in charcoal and pencil and occasionally watercolor. Mountains and ocean. Airplanes and ships. Soldiers' hands. Tents in a snowy valley. Then the drawings turned abstract: chaotic lines and blotches and scribbles. Maybe a dozen pages like that. The rest of the book was empty.

Adelaide was watching me. "Troubling, aren't they? Those last pages?"

"What are they?"

She ignored the question. "I was interested in what you said at that dinner, about how when we die everything evaporates. I think that was the word? It resonated with me. I try to pay attention to resonance."

I remembered saying that, but I didn't know what else I could add. "Honestly I think I was annoyed at that Leanne woman and trying to seem deep."

"Don't brush your thoughts off as imposture," she said sharply. "It's tiresome."

"Sorry," I said, taken aback.

"Don't apologize, either. Especially since you know from experience. Your parents. You aren't just blathering. You know exactly how much gets lost." One of the dogs was resting its head in her lap, and she stroked its ears. She looked at me slantwise with her glinty, mineral flicker. "It must be much worse for you, but people think they know about me because I've been around and have been written about and so on. Almost no one has more than a few scattered data points, but they connect the dots however they please."

"Oh my god, yes," I said, leaning forward. "And they come up with ideas about you that make sense to them and so seem true to them but are actually arbitrary."

"Yes, **exactly.** Like constellations. It's impossible to ever fully explain yourself while you're alive, and then once you're dead, forget about it—you're at the mercy of the living." She pointed at the sketchbook in my lap. "My mother said Jamie told her he filled those last pages during a battle. He thought he was making realistic sketches and only discovered later that they were scribbles." She sipped her tea. The mug was green ceramic, like the fireplace tiles. "I'm glad he didn't make the drawings he thought he did. They would have been lies. Art is distortion but a form of distortion that has the possibility of offering clarification, like a corrective lens."

"I don't completely follow," I said.

"All I'm saying is that it's good some things are lost. It's natural."

"But you still want to show me that," I said, indicating the document box, "rather than letting them be lost."

"Yee-ess." She stretched out the word, maybe

with uncertainty. "I don't know if it's so much that the letters fill in gaps as expose them."

"Well, like I said on the phone, I can't really change anything about the movie. Especially not now. We're almost done."

She waved a hand. "The movie is just another obfuscation. The truth is worthwhile in its own right."

"Totally," I said, oddly relieved. "It took me a long time to figure out that the movie doesn't really matter, but once I did, I could finally—I don't know—**act.**" I paused. "I should tell you," I said, "I told Redwood you have Marian's letters. He wants to read them."

"Do you want him to read them?"

"No."

"Then he doesn't need to," she said. "I've chosen to show them to you, specifically you, but, like I've said, my purpose isn't necessarily for them to be made public." She seemed to muse. "I wonder if I'm enacting a kind of installation." Then, mockingly: "Maybe this is my first stab at performance art."

I didn't know what to say, so I said, "I didn't tell Redwood about Jamie being your father, either."

"Biological father. No, I assumed I would have heard from Carol by now if you had. Why didn't you?"

Now I mused. Redwood and I had come back from Denali and gone to bed together, and it had been perfectly fine, perfectly nice, but I hadn't been able to shake that precarious feeling, like something was about to give way. "At first I thought I was just being possessive," I said, "but I think maybe it was more that I've had stuff about myself, information, get launched out into the world—or I've done the launching—and I'm not sure what difference it makes, how much strangers know about you. They still don't know anything. So it doesn't matter how much truth there is in **Peregrine.** Like maybe it's better if it's just a movie."

"Out of curiosity, what do you have left to film?"

"We're going to Hawaii with a skeleton crew to pick up a couple of location scenes, and then the plane crash is the last thing."

"It's almost like some kind of confrontational New Age therapy, you filming a scene where a plane crashes into water."

"Maybe it's performance art."

"Ha. Well, if you're going to Hawaii, you should look up the kid who was raised by Caleb Bitterroot. He's old now like me, but I'm pretty sure he still lives in the same house on Oahu where Marian stayed during the flight. We send Christmas cards." I had trouble imagining this woman sending a Christmas card. "His name's Joey Kamaka," she said. "I met him once, when I went to see Caleb."

Stupidly, I repeated, "You went to see Caleb? Marian's Caleb?"

"I went through a whole seeking phase in my twenties. I'd known my dad wasn't my biological father since I was fourteen, but I hadn't really tried to face it. So then I did try."

After my uncle Mitch died, I'd come home from New York to go through his house before selling it, and I'd found a folder of letters from my father. **We make each other miserable,** my father had written about my mother before I was born, **but we've decided we prefer our particular misery and the euphoria of our reconciliations to steady bovine contentment.**

The letters turned even bleaker after I was born, as my father realized a baby wasn't going to solve their problems. I don't know why anyone thinks babies will make literally anything easier. Reading his words—hearing his voice, in a way, for the first time—I'd started wondering if my father had crashed the plane on purpose. Later, when I hired that P.I. to look into the crash, I'd asked him if he thought a murder-suicide was possible, and he'd said, sure, anything was possible. But then he added that, in his opinion, if that's what my father had done, he'd have brought me along, too. These guys usually do the whole family, he said.

I said to Adelaide, "How did you find out that Jamie was your . . ."

"Biological father? My parents told me. My brothers were gone to college by then, and they just sat me down and came out with it. My dad was a doctor. He'd been a medic in Europe when

I was conceived. The story wasn't particularly dramatic. Jamie passed through Seattle during the war, and he and my mother reconnected, as they say. It was a fling. She wrote to my father as soon as she learned she was pregnant and told him everything. He was a very understanding man. He loved her, though I imagine my existence strained things. She wrote to Jamie, too, but he was already dead. So, eventually, she wrote to Marian, but the letter took a while to find her."

I said, "I watched that documentary about your project with the sunken boats—"

"Boat-like objects."

"Was that about Jamie?"

"I didn't want to think so at the time. I called it **Sea Change.** Do you know that verse, from **The Tempest**? 'Full fathom five thy father lies.'"

I didn't know.

"'Of his bones are coral made,'" she said. "'Those are pearls that were his eyes. Nothing of him that doth fade, but doth suffer a sea-change into something rich and strange.'" She smiled wryly. "You can't help being seduced by the image. I think it's less about the body and more about how our imagination does its best to contend with death, and fails."

I thought about holding the Cessna's yoke in my hands like it was a bomb. I thought about crashing a fake plane into a fake ocean, the fade to black. I asked, "What was Caleb like?"

"Charming, drank a little too much. I only spent a few days with him. He could be boisterous and then suddenly cloud over. He'd clearly loved Marian, but he didn't seem like the loss had devastated him. Sometimes he even talked about her in the present tense, which made me wonder if he'd ever really internalized her death. Or maybe he'd just known so many people who died. I don't know. He and I talked more about Jamie than Marian. Like I said, though, you should look up Joey Kamaka. He might know more."

"I still don't understand why me, though. Why don't **you** want to do it? Why do you think **I** should?"

"It's not the way I look for truth, personally, piecing information together. It depresses me. But that doesn't mean I'm not interested in the truth. As far as why you, I don't know that, either. It's just an idea that got into my head. The connections appeal to me. You playing Marian. Your parents." She lifted the document box onto her footstool, removed the lid. "Take a look."

"I might run to the bathroom first," I told her. "Where is it?"

I was thinking I'd pee and then just go right out the front door, not look back, not take on the responsibility of deciding what to do with whatever was in the letters, not continue on as some pawn in Adelaide's art installation, but when I came out of the bathroom, revving up for my escape, there on the wall staring back at me was Marian Graves, the original of the charcoal portrait I'd seen pinned up on the costume designer's inspiration wall. Strange that it was real, an actual object in the world, something that could be framed and hung up. Her brother's hand had made those lines, had summoned her face from a blank page.

I felt the abrupt onset of what can only be described as a hunch. There was something more that could be known, and I wanted to know it. There was something in Adelaide's document box, and there was something beyond that, out in the void. I felt this like I'd felt the presence of the gigantic snowy landscape while I'd kissed Redwood.

I went back to the living room.

There's some guy who surfaces every few years to say he's spotted what might be the **Peregrine** in satellite images of Antarctica or that he's found stuff on remote subantarctic islands that might be clues—bits of wreckage or an old lipstick tube he says is Marian's or some bit of bone he says might be human and might be Eddie's—and he promises that if people will just send him enough money he'll go down there and solve the mystery once and for all. He one hundred percent promises he will.

Maybe I was turning into that guy. Maybe I was like the handful of wannabe sleuths who post blurry old photos online they claim are of Marian and Eddie in Australia in the 1950s or of the **Peregrine** refitted as a cargo DC-3 in the Congo. Maybe I was like the flat-earthers who think Antarctica is an ice wall around the earth's perimeter and believe the **Peregrine** was shot down by the air force to stop Marian from discovering the truth. They all had hunches, too. They all desperately needed to feel like truth-tellers, to believe in their breakthroughs and revelations. Maybe I was a crackpot or a charlatan; maybe I was just trying to insert myself into an inscrutable, long-concluded drama.

Or maybe the past had something to tell me.

I sat on Adelaide's couch and wearily, almost against my will, reached for the box of letters.

The Flight

Where to begin? At the beginning, of course. But where is the beginning? I don't know where in the past to insert a marker that says: here. Here is where the flight began. Because the beginning is in memory, not on a map.

—MARIAN GRAVES*

New York City
40°45′ N, 73°58′ W
April 15, 1948
0 nautical miles flown

Matilda Feiffer, nearly seventy, ten years a widow, walks at a clip along Forty-Second Street. She wears all black, not

---

* From **The Sea, the Sky, the Birds Between: The Lost Logbook of Marian Graves.** Published by D. Wenceslas & Sons, New York, 1959.

to mark her widowhood but because she likes the severity. Narrow black skirt, nipped-in black jacket with an enamel brooch of a leopard on the lapel, black pumps, black beret over steel gray bob, enormous round glasses with heavy black frames. One bony hand, flashing with rings and bracelets, holds a tiny frothy white dog against her chest.

When Lloyd died, no one had been more surprised than Matilda to learn that her husband had left her not only the entirety of his fortune but also as much authority over his businesses as he could bequeath. **To freely do with as she sees fit.**

Clifford, her second son, an incompetent, had been the only one to rant and rage, perhaps because he knew he was the least deserving of the four living Feiffer boys. Lloyd, more sentimental than she, had let Clifford be at least nominally in charge of their shipping interests, which, even well insulated from real power, he'd made a hash of. So she had fired him as soon as she could. She hadn't put him out on the street, of course, but had given him a great deal of money, warned him there would be no more, and encouraged him to go abroad somewhere and embrace a life of relatively economical debauchery. (She suspected Lloyd had left her in charge partly because he'd known she would do the things he could not bear to.) Clifford had moved to St. Thomas and married a Caribbean girl and had three children with her, but Matilda refused to give him the satisfaction of being scandalized.

Henry, the oldest and brightest of her sons, had already been a vice president of Liberty Oil before Lloyd's death. This was by far their largest company, and she'd left well enough alone. Forty-six now, he was married to a woman Matilda didn't disdain and had four sons of his own.

Bless Henry.

Robert, third in line, also worked at Liberty Oil. He was neither brilliant nor burdensome, was polite in company but did not shine, had never married though he was forty-three. She suspected Robert might be a queer.

Next would have come Leander, whatever sort of man he might have been if not for diphtheria.

Then there was George, dear Georgie, the baby, grown from the dark soil of her grief for Leander, only twenty-four when Lloyd died, her only son to go to war, now finishing up his doctorate in geology at Columbia, married to a nice girl and with two children. Her gratitude he'd survived the Pacific felt as boundless as the cosmos. She could not have endured losing another son, and the war had killed Lloyd, she knew. Germany had invaded Poland in September 1939, and he'd died days later, at seventy-four, of a heart attack on his way to work. Matilda suspected his heart simply couldn't withstand the magnitude of fury he'd felt at his father's country.

So many women in black veils at his funeral.

Matilda had tried to sort out which had been her husband's mistresses but had given up in rueful exasperation.

It had taken some months for her to sort out Lloyd's complex financial interests, fighting off incursions by rivals as she went. When she felt she had a firm grasp, she'd sold off some assets and reorganized others, and then she'd gone out and bought herself a struggling publishing house, D. Wenceslas & Sons.

"Why books?" Henry had asked. "Why not philanthropy? I know plenty of boards that would love to have you."

"I like books," she'd said. "I don't care for boards." Furthermore, she'd given birth to five sons and spent nearly forty years with a philanderer and was now free to do whatever she liked. Maybe **that** was why Lloyd had left her in charge. Maybe he'd been making one of his oblique apologies.

After Pearl Harbor, it had been her idea to print thousands of cheap paperbacks off the Wenceslas backlist and donate them to the troops. The gesture was one of genuine goodwill, but, as she'd thought might happen, the boys hadn't stopped wanting books after they came home. Sales were strong. Thanks partly to her, paperbacks weren't considered trashy anymore, just affordable and convenient.

She lives in an apartment near Bryant Park, and it is from there she has come when she swings abruptly off Forty-Second Street and through the glass doors of the building that houses Wenceslas headquarters. From the elevator she marches directly to her office, ignoring the greetings from the secretaries and typists that rise up like cheeps from birds' nests. She'd chosen an office on the fifth floor with the editors, not the fourth floor with the sales and numbers types, and some of them can be glimpsed through their half-open doors, always reading, sometimes reading and talking on the telephone simultaneously.

"She hasn't canceled, has she?" Matilda asks her secretary, Shirley, who has followed her into her office. She tosses her beret onto a bookshelf and dumps the dog, Pigeon, unceremoniously onto the floor. On all available surfaces, piles of books rise above a general mess of paper: string-tied manuscripts, mock-ups of covers, clippings, correspondence.

Shirley sets down a silver bowl of water for Pigeon, retrieves the beret and places it carefully atop the hatstand. "No, not yet."

Not long after Lloyd died, Matilda had found herself wondering about Addison Graves. She had a vague memory of Lloyd telling her Addison had been released from Sing Sing, but after that . . . nothing.

There didn't seem to be anyone to ask. Even the

longest-serving employees at L&O had no idea, and the lawyer, Chester Fine, was dead. When Addison was in prison, Lloyd had gradually stopped mentioning him. Matilda had taken the end of their friendship as a natural, sorrowful consequence of the loss of the **Josephina** and the uncertainty surrounding the dispersal of blame. Perhaps the courageous thing would have been for Lloyd to defend Addison more vocally, but he'd had an entire company to think about, thousands of employees. And what of the passengers and crew who drowned? Certainly their families required a—not a scapegoat. Certainly they deserved justice. That Addison's odd young wife had perished was a tragedy, but at least the children had been saved.

"He never told you?" Henry said, inexplicably aghast. They were alone in the Liberty Oil offices, sitting opposite each other at a table heaped with files and ledgers.

"Told me what?"

And so Henry had relayed what his father had confessed about the smuggled crates of bullets and shells and nitrocellulose, about how Lloyd, almost beyond a shadow of a doubt, had been the one responsible for the ship's loss but had allowed Addison to take the fall. "He made little attempts to set things right," Henry said, "but he would never come clean publicly, which was probably the only thing that would have mattered to Addison Graves.

Sending that cargo was beyond foolish. It wouldn't even have made a real difference to the war effort, of course. It was a symbolic gesture. And then he had to be ashamed until he died."

Matilda stared at her son. After some time, she said, "What happened to the children? They were sent to their uncle, weren't they? In Wyoming?"

"Minnesota, I think."

"Do we have the address somewhere?"

"I suppose. Somewhere." A cautious glance. "Why?"

"I'd like to do something for them. I don't know what."

"We might not be able to find them. They're grown."

"I'd like to try."

"I'm not sure we want to dredge this back up."

"Henry," she said, hitting him with the full force of her reproof.

By the time an old address for Wallace Graves in Missoula, Montana, was turned up, 1939 had become 1940. Germany occupied Denmark, Norway, Holland, Belgium, France. Matilda wrote a letter, sent it off. No reply came, but neither was the letter returned. She wrote again. Throughout the war, she wrote every few months, always saying more or less the same thing: She was trying to locate the children of Addison and Annabel Graves because she would like to know what had become of them and to make some attempt to repay a debt. In 1945, she stopped writing.

In 1947, she received a reply.

And now Shirley is tapping on the door, showing in a tall, thin, blond, watchful woman in wool slacks and a long, unbelted cotton coat, and Pigeon is yapping and skittering around. "Hush!" Matilda says, scooping him up, offering her hand to Marian.

Marian has a strong grip. She appears older than she is, which must be thirty-three or thirty-four, a little older than Georgie. Her face shows lines made by squinting and worrying, and she has an aura of experience about her. The boniness of her father's face has survived in her, but, like her mother, she has unusually pale hair and eyes, both bleached like things left too long in the sun.

"Tea? Coffee?" Shirley says. "May I take your coat?"

"No, thank you," says Marian.

"You certainly look the part," says Matilda.

"What part?"

"Shut the door, please, Shirley," says Matilda. When they are alone, sitting on opposite sides of her desk, she says, "Well, here we are."

Marian looks around the office but does not speak. Matilda is not afraid of silence and waits until Marian says, "I'd never been on an airliner before."

"And?"

"It was all right. Strange to be cargo. Thank you for the ticket." She shifts in her chair, crossing her legs, which are so long Matilda wonders where she finds slacks that fit. "It wasn't necessary."

Matilda waves this away, and vigilant, dim-witted Pigeon barks at the clatter of her bracelets. To appease him, she takes an open tin of smoked mussels from a drawer and feeds him one off a fork.

In her letters, Marian is not given to elaboration, but they have been correspondents long enough that Matilda knows about the deaths of Jamie and Wallace and about the brief, long ago visit and subsequent disappearance of Addison. She feels no further need to discuss the past, though she has decided that, if the moment presents itself, she will tell the truth about the explosives in the **Josephina**'s belly. In her early letters, she'd simply asked questions. Later, she told Marian she had come to believe her family, the Feiffers, owed the Graves family a significant debt (she was vague about its nature, let Marian infer she simply felt bad about Addison's fate), and she intended to make some settlement. As the original form of the debt was not monetary, she wrote, its erasure was not possible, but money was what she had, what she could offer.

No, Marian had written back, she did not want money. **I learned the hard way that patronage can be dangerous.**

What then, Matilda asked, **do you want? You**

would be doing me a kindness to accept my offer. In allowing me to lessen my burden of guilt, you would be the benefactor, not I.

A month had passed before she received Marian's reply. **I've considered your question, and what I want is to fly around the world north-south, over the poles.** It had never been done. It would be very difficult and dangerous, perhaps impossible. She would need money, yes, enough to buy a suitable airplane and modify it and to pay a navigator to come with her, among other expenses. She would need fuel, a lot of it, which she imagined Liberty Oil would be in a position to supply, and she would need that fuel to be waiting for her in remote places, which she imagined Liberty Oil could reach. She would also need assistance in securing the necessary permissions and support.

Come to New York, Matilda had responded. **I would like to meet you. We can talk more.**

And here Marian is. Somehow this guarded woman is the same entity as one of the bundles in Addison's arms in the newspaper photos, being carried down the gangway from the rescue ship.

Matilda sees no point in small talk. "I've decided to help you with your flight, but I have a question."

Marian turns wary. "All right."

"Don't look so put out. Answering a question seems like a small concession."

"I thought you said you were the one who owes me." Not antagonistic but not playful, either.

Marian's body is relaxed, but the fact that she is still wearing her coat implies she might leave at any moment.

Matilda sets Pigeon on the floor, pushes aside the tin of mussels. "It might get tiresome to continually evaluate who owes whom. I was hoping we could be something more like collaborators." Marian gives a slight tilt of her head that Matilda decides to take as a nod. Matilda says, "I want to know why."

"Why what?"

"Why do this flight, of course." Matilda ticks off her fingers as she talks: "As you say yourself, it's very dangerous. Arguably, it's pointless, too. They've been to the poles. They've drawn all the maps. There's nothing left to discover. It's the most absurd idea, really. Even if you miraculously survive, you're buying a one-way ticket to exactly where you started." She sits back. "So. Why?"

Marian looks annoyed. "That question doesn't interest me."

"You mean you don't know the answer?"

"Not exactly."

"You don't know exactly, or that's not exactly what you mean?"

"Both. The second one."

"People will want to know why."

"What people?"

"If you do it, I thought you might write a book."

Marian laughs. "I couldn't write a book."

"Anyone can write a book with a little help."

"I wouldn't know what to say."

Matilda fetches a stack of hardbacks from a shelf, sets them on her desk in front of Marian. Antoine de Saint-Exupéry. Beryl Markham. Amelia Earhart. Charles Lindbergh, though he is included grudgingly as she has not forgiven his admiration of the Nazis. "You've read these?"

Marian turns her head sideways, reading the titles. "Yes."

"Then you know what to say. Write what you see, what you think, what happens. It's not terrifically complicated. The experience is the thing. You. Not some imaginary line on the globe. If the book catches on, other avenues will open up. Lecture tours. They might even make a film about you."

Marian looks caught between amusement and alarm. "Maybe I'd like to keep myself to myself."

Matilda made a **pfft** sound. "Don't pretend you're so modest and naïve. If you were, you wouldn't want to do a stunt like this."

Marian sits back. "I have a question for you, too."

"By all means."

"It's the same as yours: Why?"

"I've told you—I'm trying to atone."

"For what? What is this debt you talked about?"

Here is the moment, so conspicuous now it has arrived.

Matilda explains how Lloyd's dislike for his own father had fueled his hatred of Germany. In a steady voice she relays what Henry had told her about the crates on the **Josephina.** "Your father didn't know," she says. "Not explicitly. I didn't, either, but I think I should have guessed. I didn't want to know, that much is clear."

Marian's face has tightened in concentration. Matilda can imagine her wearing a similar expression while flying through a storm.

"I'm not sure what to think about this," Marian says. "I think mostly I'm relieved to know what happened."

"Aren't you angry? I was so angry."

"I might have been, at other times. But it was so long ago."

"Your life would have been very different."

"Yes. But I can't know how."

After a long pause, Matilda decides to return to the business at hand. "What would be the next step? For your flight?"

"Finding the right plane." Marian turns eager, leaning forward. "I think a surplus Dakota is the best possibility. They made thousands of them. They're almost indestructible. They can land anywhere, and it's not hard to put skis on them. In the war, they'd have a bigger crew, but I think I could do it with just a navigator. With auxiliary tanks, you'd have the range, too, though barely, and that's assuming I could refuel twice in Antarctica, which is a problem but, I think, not an insurmountable one. On the Ross Sea side there's cached fuel, but on the other . . . that I haven't figured out yet. It might make sense to look for a plane in Australia or New Zealand and start the flight down there. I've been thinking through different scenarios. It's a question of sneaking in between the seasons. The Arctic is less of a problem than the Antarctic." She has become animated, gesturing at an imaginary map, but catches herself, subsides warily. "There's still a lot to sort out."

Another silence, something carefully stretched between them to test its strength. Matilda nods. "All right."

Marian looks at her questioningly.

"Let's get a plane," Matilda says.

They talk for another hour, form the beginnings of a plan, poke around the edges of a formidable list of tasks. When Marian stands to leave, Matilda rises, too, hands her a canvas-bound book.

Marian flips through the blank pages. Yellow paper gridded with pale blue squares. "What's this?"

"It's for you to write in."

"Write what in?"

"Write about the flight."

Marian closes the book, holds it out. "I already have a logbook."

"Call it whatever you want. A journal, a diary. Call it **The Enchanted Chronicles of Marian Almighty** for all I care. Don't tie yourself in knots over it. Just write down what happens, and you can decide later what to do with it." She surprises herself with her own earnestness as she reaches up to grip Marian's shoulders, shakes her gently as she says, "You must do everything you can to remember. Not just what you see, but what it means. To **you.**"

Why go at all? I have no answer beyond my certainty that I must.

—MARIAN GRAVES

⌒

Long Beach, California
33°47′ N, 118°07′ W
June 30, 1949
0 nautical miles flown

The fleeting golden moment between afternoon and evening. The sun hanging peaceably in the western sky, warming the broad pale beach and the wooden roller coaster and palm-lined promenade, the tidy ranks of small houses stretching inland among green-crowned trees, the sprawled figure of Marian Graves lying on her back in the overgrown grass behind her rented bungalow. A book rests open and facedown on her belly; it is the blank journal Matilda Feiffer had given her a year ago. A breeze ruffles her close cap of hair, soft and fine and so pale it is almost greenish, like the fluff inside an artichoke.

She checks her watch, holding her wrist above her face. Six-seventeen. Eddie had said he would drive himself from Florida. He was in the mood for a journey. You'd **better** be, Marian had replied over the crackling long-distance line. The flight would be twenty-three thousand nautical miles, give or take.

In a letter now three weeks old, he'd told her that he would arrive on this day, June 30th, at six-thirty in the evening, and, as he is a navigator, she'd taken him at his word.

She rolls onto her side, smooths the book flat, takes up the pen. She writes only rarely, and tentatively when she does, letting stray thoughts catch in the pages like crumbs. She's surprised she writes at all. She can't imagine her little scribbles (and they are scribbles—her handwriting is awful) ever making a real book, but some inconsistent, unplumbable impulse keeps nudging her to pick up the pen.

I've thought more than I should about whether it would be possible to do the flight alone. It's an absurd idea, but I still pick at the question until reason puts its foot down and says, no, you cannot.

I mean no insult to Eddie; no person in the world would be fully welcome. The idea of going alone should terrify me, because going alone would mean death, but when I imagine it I feel no fear, only wistful longing. Does that mean I wish to die? I don't think I do. But the pure and absolute solitude in which we leave the world exerts a pull. I suppose I think a solo flight would be the purest possible attempt. But why? There is Matilda's question again. The reason sits there like a pebble just out of reach, inert and nondescript and insignificant, interesting only in its inaccessibility.

Or maybe the problem is that I want no navigator but Eddie, and also I never want to face Eddie.

A car horn sounds three times, quick and bright.

What had been her last words to Ruth at the Polygon Hotel? She doesn't remember clearly—the sedative pills from the medic at Caleb's camp had been powerful—but she has a horrible dread they had been **Go away.** Grief had made her cruel. She'd needed to hurt Ruth, to make her see she wanted Caleb instead, to drive her off. Jamie's death had seemed like direct punishment for her having been foolish and selfish enough to enjoy her corner of the war, her freedom in it, and Ruth could never be disentangled from that.

Marian had written back to Ruth's letter, but she'd taken too long. The envelope was returned. In

September 1944, in North Carolina, Ruth's plane had caught fire on takeoff and crashed. **She died,** Zip told Marian in Hamble. **I'm sorry. I know you two were close.**

Marian had stared at Zip, waiting to be overcome, but felt only pressure and heaviness, then nothing. Jamie's death had rent and torn her in such a way that she was no longer watertight; her emotions drained out, leaving her empty. So passed her grief for Ruth—she was too ruined to hold it. Guilt, though, lingered. For the first time since she'd started flying, she found no solace in being airborne. She picked up her chits, collected her planes, took them where she was told. Her own existence oppressed her.

After Caleb left with the invasion force, she had started saving money without knowing why. She took the bus instead of riding her motorbike. She left the Polygon Hotel for cheaper digs. Once the Germans began to retreat, she started getting ferry assignments to Europe and devised a minor smuggling operation. If she was flying to Belgium, she would leave her parachute behind and instead fill its bag with tins of cocoa, which wasn't rationed in England but was in short supply for the liberated Belgian bakers. She would sell the cocoa and buy things that were rationed or unavailable in England—sugar, clothes, leather goods—and then sell those on the black market in Britain.

After Ruth died, she understood why she was

saving up: She didn't want her old life, but she couldn't imagine a new one. The money was to buy time in between.

As soon as she opens the door, Eddie grabs her up and swings her like the pendulum of a gigantic bell, back and forth, tolling. When he sets her back on her feet, she squints against the sun's glare, trying to see if he's changed. It's been six years.

He touches her shorn head with a big, gentle hand. "Look at this."

"You're two minutes early."

"My watch much be fast."

"That's yours?" A royal blue convertible Cadillac coupe gleams at the curb, top down. Its buffed, elongated curves look like they've been formed by the wind.

"Homecoming present to myself. I got a deal from an old friend. I'm getting rid of it before we leave."

She catches a trace of sadness on his face. "No, don't! Put it in storage."

"No, I don't want her to get lonely. Here, let me get my bags."

In the house, they babble too brightly about things that have only just happened, the past so recently traversed it's still unsettled, as though by a wake. His square, horsey face and long, sturdy forearms are tan. He'd lingered on the drive, he says, followed whims and detours. He has his same old affable charm, but something is different, something nebulous but pervasive. He reminds her of a statue that has been broken and glued back together, its shape the same but its surface spider-webbed with cracks.

She talks about flying cargo to keep in practice. She's always at the bottom of the roster, has been told she can't fly passengers because the idea of a female pilot makes people nervous. None of it matters: not her thousands of hours, not the Spitfires and Hurricanes and Wellington bombers she'd flown, not her landings on high glaciers and frozen lakes and narrow sandbars. But so far the cargo hasn't complained that she's a woman. The engines and hydraulics she's worked on haven't minded. (She has her mechanic's license now, too.) Had he heard? Helen Richey killed herself back in January—pills. They say she did it because she couldn't get any flying work.

He hadn't heard. He remembered Ruth had liked Helen.

(The first mention of Ruth, made so casually.)

She shows him into the bedroom, tells him it's his. She will hear none of his protests. She herself will sleep on the couch. She insists. "You couldn't fit half yourself on that couch," she says.

"I don't want to displace you."

She is already moving away, down the hall. "Come see the war room."

. . .

It had been a small second bedroom when she moved in, and she'd enlisted the landlord to help her carry the bed out to the garage.

"What if your mother comes to visit?" the landlord had said from his end of the mattress, walking backward. "Or a friend?" He seemed like a nice man. Bushy eyebrows and heavy jowls, a Hawaiian shirt patterned with hula girls.

"I don't have a mother," she'd told him, and he left it alone.

Maps paper the walls and bury the small dining table her landlord had loaned her. Rolled charts stand dense as bamboo in crates and wastebaskets. There is a general shambles of heaped-up paper: checklists, invoices, aerial photos, notes on winds and weather, inventories, catalogs, letters of advice, survival manuals, correspondence with navy contacts, correspondence with Norwegian explorers and whalers, correspondence with the leaders of the Norwegian-British-Swedish Antarctic Expedition (which will carry fuel for her), lists of radio stations and beacons, correspondence and contracts with Liberty Oil, order forms for airplane parts, addresses and phone numbers of contacts in all the places where they might need contacts, paperwork for visas, scraps and scribbles, and on and on and on and on.

"Dear God," Eddie says.

"There's an underlying order."

"Chaos doesn't count as its own form of order."

A sea trunk resides in the near corner, and she clears papers from its lid, opens it to show him. Brown fur inside, like the humped back of an animal.

"Are we bringing a dead bear?"

She extracts a hooded parka, matching trousers, fur boots. "Reindeer. There's nothing better in the cold. We'll get you a set to match in Alaska."

"Nanook and Nanook take to the skies. By the way, I've been studying up on the high-latitude stuff. A guy I knew in the war is in Fairbanks with a recon squadron. He sent me a manual and some charts as long as I promised not to sell them to the Russians." Eddie wanders over to the largest map on the wall, a Mercator projection of the world with the Pacific centered, the Americas to the right and the rest of the continents hanging heavy to the left. On it Marian has penciled their route.

"I wanted to talk to you before I inked it in," she says, following him.

He makes a noncommittal noise, leans close to study the penciled line, the bits of land it connects. He touches the empty ocean below Cape Town. "They don't even bother including Antarctica."

"I don't know how you could, really, on a flat map."

"Sometimes there's a sliver of white, isn't there? Just to remind people it exists?"

From the mess on the table, she extracts a map of Antarctica, mostly blank, only a few scattered elevations marked, a few patches of mountains. "There's this." She swivels around, surveying the room. "I have some better charts somewhere."

"I thought you said there was an underlying order."

"Sometimes it underlies more deeply than I'd like."

Eddie studies the white shape. Finally, he says, "What have you got around here to drink?"

They take gin and tonics outside, brush leaves from the cushioned chaises at the edge of the grass. She pulls a lime from her neighbor's tree that hangs over the fence, carves slices from it with a pocketknife.

He clinks her glass. "To friends reunited."

They drink. The golden light has gone. She can't think what to say, where to start. They have never been together without Ruth, and her absence hangs between them, a void but also the thing that spans it.

"You know," he says, "I actually have the jitters. Don't you feel like we're newlyweds or something? In an arranged marriage?"

"I was nervous to see you. I didn't know . . ."

"If it would be the same? It won't be. Nothing is. But now you won't be rid of me for months and months. How's the plane?"

In the spring she had gone to Auckland. She'd

walked down a row of six superficially identical war surplus Dakotas, snub-nosed and jungle green, but one had stood out plainly and obviously. She'd recognized it immediately as hers.

"Some wear and tear," she says to Eddie, "but nothing major. It was in New Guinea, mostly."

"Have you named it?"

"I wanted to wait for you, but I was thinking **Peregrine**?"

He nods, satisfied. "I like it. An hour into our arranged marriage, and already we're parents."

The affection she feels for him is a relief, confirmation that not everything from before is gone or irreversibly damaged. She had not been sure she could trust her memory of how much she had liked him. "Eddie," she says, "I wanted to thank you."

"For what?"

"For agreeing to come."

"I'm flattered you asked."

"No, really. I'm grateful. There's no one else I could trust."

"I hope that's not misplaced. I haven't exactly been striking off into the unknown lately." In Florida, he's been a navigator for National Airlines, cycling between Miami, Jacksonville, Tallahassee, New Orleans, Havana. New York, once in a while.

"Part of it's that I trust you to trust me," she says. "We've never flown together, but I don't think you'll be the kind to try to take over or treat me like a novelty."

"No," he says quietly, "I wouldn't."

The marine layer is coming in. She is chilled, but she swirls the ice in her drink, sips. "Actually, I didn't think you'd say yes."

"To coming with you?"

She nods. "Why did you?"

"I didn't have anywhere better to be."

"Come on."

"It's the truth. First I tried going home to Michigan, then I tried Chicago, then I went down to Miami. Nothing's been quite right." He splashes more gin into her glass, then his. "Maybe I'm just restless. Don't tell me you got back from the war and settled right in."

"No, I wouldn't say so."

In a way, she had deserted. Two months after V-E Day, in the summer of 1945, she'd ferried a plane to France, and instead of hopping a taxi plane back to Britain, she'd hitched a ride into Paris, gone on from there. The ATA didn't need her anymore, anyway. She'd brought her little nest egg from saving and smuggling, the bills hidden in her rucksack and about her person. She drifted east into Germany, walked and hitched through pulverized areas populated by scarecrow people and the charred corpses of tanks and trucks, through towns and villages, even cities, that appeared untouched. Soldiers in tattered uniforms walked along roadsides and families carting all their possessions. The zones of occupation had yet to harden, and she went all the way to Berlin, watched kerchiefed women clearing rubble.

From Germany she'd gone to Switzerland, idyllic in its undisturbed neutrality, resplendent by then in autumn colors. She'd spent the winter in Italy, crossed the Mediterranean, spent a year making her way down the length of Africa through deserts and jungles, along wide, muddy rivers.

She took up with a man in Bechuanaland. One evening, in the Namib Desert, they watched a line of desert elephants walk along the rim of a sand dune. The animals and the sky behind them were red with dust. Marian found herself relishing the prospect of making camp, having a drink and a fire, going to bed with the man. From the sweetness that ran through her, she knew she had emerged from the war. She wasn't free of it, but she never would be.

She made her way to Cape Town, caught a ship for New York. When they sailed, she stood on deck looking to the south, in the direction of Antarctica, marveling that the only thing between it and her was water.

"It took me a long time to come back," she says to Eddie, "but that's another story. When I finally did, I went to Missoula to look for a friend, and instead I found Matilda's letters. They'd kept them at the post office." There had been a letter from Sarah in Seattle, too. After she'd read that Jamie had a daughter, she'd folded the papers up again and pushed them away, shocked by the force of her grief. She'd been in Caleb's cabin. He was, of course, the friend she'd come looking for, but he'd been gone to Hawaii for months. No one knew if he planned to return.

"So your body came back," Eddie said, "but your mind was already running away again."

"I don't know if I'd call this running away."

"What is it, then? Why do the flight?"

"Everyone wants to know why. I don't know."

"Come on."

If they are extraordinarily lucky and also don't make anything except the best possible decisions at all times, they will complete what they are setting out to do. Or they will fail. Or they will die, which is different from failure. There will be a last smashup against some mountain somewhere or a hard flat of sand or a cracked and jumbled glacier or, most likely, the surface of the ocean that kills with its hardness and then softens and swallows, hiding the evidence. Sometimes she thinks she has invented the flight as an elaborate suicide. Sometimes she thinks she is immortal.

She drinks. "All right. Here's the best I can do. When Matilda asked what I wanted, the first thing that came into my head was this . . . **vision** of flying over the poles. Every time I thought of it, I felt a burst of nerves, like there was a live wire I kept touching. But—and I'll only ever admit this to you—when I wrote and told her what I wanted, I never expected her to **agree.** And now I actually have to do it."

Carefully, he says, "You don't, though. Not really. You could change your mind."

"No, I can't. You could—and I would understand, truly. But I can't."

"You can. Matilda could sell the plane."

"I'm not worried about Matilda. It's the live wire. It's still there. Maybe it's more like a cattle prod. I **want** to do the flight, but I dread it. I'm always thinking about what could go wrong. So much could go wrong, and now I've roped you in, too."

"I have free will. I didn't have to come."

"But—" She doesn't know if she wants him to exonerate her or confirm her guilt. "After what happened to Ruth . . ."

She wants to say she couldn't bear it if something happened to him, too, but of course their fates will be hitched together. If something happens to him, she probably won't have to bear it because she will also be gone.

He sets down his drink. "Let's say this right now and then leave it as an established, mutually understood fact. We can't have it hanging over us, and, anyway, this is the truth. Marian, Ruth's death wasn't your fault. I'm not saying this to be kind.

I've given it a lot of thought. I've even let myself blame you at times, but the blame wouldn't stick."

"If she'd stayed in England—"

"She might have crashed a different plane or died in a car accident or gotten hit by a buzz bomb. Plenty of people did that last year. You can't know what would have happened. Look, she was a grown woman. She made her own choices. If you thought you might cause a death every time you disappointed another person, you'd be paralyzed. Do you know how many men accidentally got their friends killed in the war? How many people died because of random, casual choices?" She is looking across the patchy little lawn. Everything seems unnaturally still in the fog. Eddie says, "I'm going to make it a condition of my services as a navigator that you take my line on this. I loved her, too. And I'm telling you to let it go. Okay? Say okay, and we won't talk about this anymore."

Marian understands that no one can ever absolve her. She says okay.

It was a simple thing, in the end, to begin.
—MARIAN GRAVES

~

Whenuapai Aerodrome, Auckland,
 New Zealand, to Aitutaki, Cook Islands
36°48′ S, 174°38′ E to 18°49′ S, 159°45′ W
December 31, 1949
1,752 nautical miles flown

The slow predawn glug of fuel into the tanks, the walkaround, the checking of checklists, the coughing start of one engine and then the other, the roaring run-up, the heavy acceleration into lift. A circle over the aerodrome's intersecting triangles of runways and taxiways, dipping the wings. Matilda Feiffer on the hangar's apron, waving with both arms beside the gaggle of newspaper reporters and photographers she's summoned, shrinking to nothing. She'd appeared one day without warning as Marian and Eddie returned from a test flight, was waiting at the aerodrome with a cameraman to document their landing, drum up some newsreel publicity. They'd stood grinning awkwardly beside the plane while the camera rolled, then Matilda had taken them to dinner at her hotel in Auckland.

The city spreads to the south as they rise; bays and inlets eat away at the long northern finger of the North Island. Farms gridded off by belts of alders and eucalypts pass below, low green mountains, the shore with its wide ruffles of surf. Then water, only water.

They leave on New Year's Day, but they will cross the dateline on the way to the Cook Islands, returning them to 1949. They each bring only a small valise, soft-sided to save weight. Eddie will get winter things in Alaska, and additional Antarctic gear has been shipped ahead to South Africa. Marian's reindeer suit is stuffed behind one of the auxiliary fuel tanks that occupy the fuselage.

The plane is silver now, its jungle-green paint stripped away to save five hundred pounds of weight, its glass windows switched out for Plexi, its artificial rubber fittings swapped for natural, which won't crack as easily in the cold. A hundred other changes. ("It's really very chic," Matilda Feiffer had pronounced upon seeing the plane's polished silver skin.)

Light winds. Harmless clouds strewn loosely as

spilled popcorn. Eddie moves between his desk and the cockpit and the Plexiglas astrodome, taking his sights and making his calculations with the leisurely assurance of a tennis pro lobbing balls. He traps the sun in the sextant, hands up notes with course adjustments, plucking first Norfolk Island out of the empty blue, then Nadi in Fiji, then Apia in Samoa. Lagoons like turquoise amoebas. The bits of land scattered across the Pacific are so sparse that the existence of each island seems startling, perplexing, almost worrisome. **How did this wind up here all alone? What will become of it?**

They had done an earlier shake-out flight to the Cooks, and he knows this tract of ocean already, has a feel for it that runs deeper than the course plotted on his chart in pencil. He knows the airplane and its deafening drone and its gasoline reek. He knows the shape of Marian's elbow and knee visible through the cockpit doorway. He pencils his neat log of figures, updating the distance they've covered, the time they will arrive. Distance equals speed multiplied by time. Time equals distance divided by speed. He feels the lines of latitude sliding underneath like the rungs of a ladder, watches the whitecaps through the drift meter, measuring the difference between where they are going and where they mean to go. That's where life is, that wedge of discrepancy.

· · ·

The dealership, right in the middle of Raleigh, had been easy enough to find. HALLIDAY CADILLAC said the big revolving sign.

"I'd like to try the blue one," he'd said to Leo. "The coupe."

"Very well, sir," Leo said. "Please wait here, and I'll go get the keys." Bruce Halliday was Leo's father-in-law.

Everyone in Stalag Luft I had nearly starved in 1945, would have if not for the trickle of Red Cross parcels. As the boom of artillery lumbered closer and closer from the east, the Germans had made the kriegies dig trenches and foxholes. There had been rumors these would be their graves.

Then, an American voice over the loudspeaker one May morning before dawn: **How does it feel to be free, men?** The Germans were gone; the Russians were three miles away. They'd all rushed out of their barracks. Eddie had found Leo in the midst of the commotion, bear-hugged him and whispered that he loved him. Leo hadn't seemed to hear.

The Russians were wild and drunk and came in wagons piled high with looted linens and china and silver. They went from house to house, taking what they wanted, smashing portraits of Hitler with their rifle butts. They had girls with them who put on dancing shows for the kriegies.

"I'm out of a job," Leo had said, watching three Russian girls in short skirts spin and spin on a makeshift stage while a man played a concertina, clapping their hands, winding the kriegies' howl of longing around themselves like thread around spools.

"More for me," Eddie said.

Leo had given a perfunctory smile. "You don't think they'll let us keep this up, do you?"

"Who's they?"

Leo had looked perplexed, made a vague gesture encompassing the whole world beyond the partially torn-down prison fence and the demolished guard towers.

Eddie said, "I'd say we've earned the right to do whatever we want from here on out."

"That would be nice," Leo said, and dread had settled in Eddie.

They'd been airlifted to a transit camp outside Le Havre. Leo had turned distant, avoided Eddie. One day he just disappeared, presumably on a ship home. Soon enough Eddie got sent back, too.

How does it feel to be free, men?

A year later, when he was living in New York, Eddie had received a note in the mail. Leo was marrying his high-school sweetheart and going to work for her father. He was sorry he hadn't had a chance to say goodbye.

"Why would you come here?" Leo had said when they'd turned out of Halliday Cadillac in the blue coupe.

"I'm just passing through. I got a job in Florida with the airlines."

"I mean, what do you **want**? Turn left up here."

"I wish you would have told me this was what you were planning. The whole boring charade."

"**You** have a wife."

"Actually, she died. In a plane crash. I didn't find out until I came home. And you know that was different."

Leo touched his shoulder, just for a second. "I'm sorry. Eddie, I'm **so** sorry."

"We don't have to get into it."

"Pull over here. No one comes this way."

They were on a narrow road lined with forest. Eddie, too tall for the little car, swiveled as best he could to look at Leo in his unfashionable suit, his tie clip and wedding ring and short, almost military haircut. "Does your wife know?"

Leo looked out the window into the trees. "She's a good soldier. We have two little girls." He shifted, pulling his wallet from his back pocket and extracting a snapshot: two toddlers in dresses and sandals.

"They're beautiful," Eddie said, handing back the photo.

"Yeah."

"I guess I just wanted to see you again." Eddie slid his hand along the seat, stopped short of touching Leo. "You were right. Things haven't changed. Not in the way I'd hoped. Everyone's so desperate to pretend we weren't all just murdering each other five minutes ago that there's no room for anything but the picket fence and baby carriage. We're all going to grit our teeth and be happy."

"Pretty much."

"You're not surprised. I envy that. I wish I'd never hoped."

Leo put his hand on top of Eddie's. "Who would have thought I'd have the most fun of my life in a German prison camp?"

"You couldn't get away, could you? Just for a couple of days?"

Leo hesitated. Just when he seemed about to answer, a car passed, and he jerked his hand away. He said, "You aren't really looking to buy a car, are you?"

The coral runway on Aitutaki was built during the war and is plenty long and has a radio beacon. "Too easy," Eddie says when they've landed. "Maybe this won't be such an adventure."

"It won't be like this the whole way," Marian says.

"No," he agrees.

They have rooms at a thatched and stilted little inn on the lagoon where they'd stayed during their shake-out flight. "Going out tonight?" the inn-keeper asks them. "New Year's Eve? There's a pub down the road." He'd been a Seabee in the navy, had helped build the runway and come back after the war. **It's paradise,** he'd explained, incredulous anyone would ask why.

Eddie says no to the pub.

At sunset, he swims in the lagoon. The surface is glassy flat, mirroring the lurid pink-and-purple sky, the first few stars. He can see the distant white flutter of surf breaking on the reef and hear, muffled and delayed, the ocean roaring to be let in. The lagoon's sandy floor is pronged with dead coral and so densely populated with black sea cucumbers it is nearly impossible to take a step without feeling one squish underfoot.

He'd sold the blue coupe to some slick California lawyer who's now unwittingly zipping around Long Beach in a totem of lost love.

He stands waist-deep and closes his eyes. He'd had some rum before his swim. He thinks he can feel the planet turning. The immensity of the ocean troubles him. This is something he can't tell Marian. In the war, his worst fear, worse than burning, worse than a parachute failing, was drowning.

He tries to think what the next land would be in the direction he's facing, more or less due east. Maybe some tiny island, more likely South America, thousands of miles away.

An aerial navigator, the Army Air Corps manual had said, **directs an aircraft from place to place over the surface of the earth, an <u>art</u> called <u>aerial navigation</u>**. He'd liked the word **art,** how it had been underlined. He'd liked the idea of himself

directing the aircraft. Transplanted sullenly to a navigation classroom after he'd washed out of pilot training, he'd heard more words he liked. Celestial observation. Dead reckoning. Drift. Vector. Point of recognition.

Symbols had peppered the maps. Cities. Airfields. Railroads and abandoned railroads. Lakes and dry lakes. Ovals for racetracks and little oil derricks for oil derricks. Red stars for flashing beacons. Tidy reductions, pleasantly simple. Until he'd been shot down, he'd believed in his art, in a true relationship between three-dimensional space and printed maps, in the possibility of accurately saying **I am here.** But, after the war, no matter how far he traveled, he felt stuck, marooned, immobile. There must be another trajectory he hasn't yet found, more equations besides the ones he knows, another, more elusive dimension underlying the mappable world.

Inevitably we will omit almost everything. In flying the length of Africa, for instance, we will only cover one track as wide as our wings, glimpse only one set of horizons. Arabia and India and China will pass unseen to the east and the great stretched-out Soviet beast with its European snout and Asian tail. We will see nothing of South America, nothing of Australia or Greenland or Burma or Mongolia, nothing of Mexico or Indonesia. Mostly we will see water, liquid and frozen, because that is most of what there is.

—MARIAN GRAVES

Oahu, Hawaii
21°19′ N, 157°55′ W
January 3, 1950
4,141 nautical miles flown

Caleb has grown his hair long again but wears it in a ponytail at his nape now rather than a braid, loose strands flying around his face as he steers his truck up the windward coast, singing to himself. Marian can't catch the words. Out her window, jumbled black lava rock rambles into the sea, scraping the waves to white shreds. She sticks out her hand and the wind arches up under it like a cat's back. On Caleb's side: a fluted wall of rock, the island's steep green mountain spine.

Mauka. Toward the mountain. **Makai.** Toward the sea. Hawaiian words Caleb has taught her.

She and Eddie had thought they might fly the whole way from Aitutaki to Hawaii but decided instead to stop halfway at Christmas Island in the Line Islands, a huge flat T-bone of an atoll, nearly naked except for coconut palms, a few villages, an airstrip from the war. Land crabs skittered everywhere. They had spent the night, left before dawn. She's grateful Oahu has heft and height, a lush and shaggy green pelt.

Caleb is taking her to see the ranch where he works as a cowboy, a paniolo. When he'd first come, he'd worked on a taro plantation, but he prefers this. In his house she'd noticed a photo of him sitting on a horse, a garland of pink flowers wrapped around his hat.

He stops at a five-bar gate, and she gets out and opens it, closes it again behind the truck. When she's climbed back in, he says, "Eddie seems all right."

Eddie had claimed he wanted a nap, stayed behind at Caleb's place, a small blue house on stilts, almost at the water's edge. Marian thinks he is considerately giving them space but also supposes he's not anxious to spend time with the man Marian had chosen over Ruth.

Marian says, "I'd be lost without him." She smiles, pleased with herself.

"Navigator jokes. Is that what we've come to?" A man on a horse crosses the dirt road ahead of them, lifts a hand. His vaquero saddle is small and flat, cushioned by a wool blanket. "That guy was on Utah beach," Caleb tells Marian. "You can see his hat sits funny because his ear got shot off." All the other paniolos are native Hawaiian, he says, but they tolerate him because he's good with horses and only half white and because word of his war has gotten around.

The ranch house, low and long and built from blocks of coral and roofed with red tiles, sits beneath the mountains on an undulating lawn of vibrant, electric green. The branches of immense monkeypod trees hover in perfect domes.

Caleb drives past, into a narrow valley and through a maze of paddocks, stops at a barn.

Caleb puts rope bridles on the horses but no saddles. He takes off his boots before he mounts and makes Marian do the same. She understands why when, after they ride back the way they'd come, **makai,** and cross the road onto a beach, he rides straight into the sea. The roan shoulders of her short, willful mare move in front of Marian's knees. Her bare feet swing below the animal's belly as she breaks into a rushed, jolting jog, anxious not to be left behind, whinnying at Caleb's horse, chasing after it into the water. Marian hasn't been on a horse since she left Barclay. She bounces off-balance, rights herself. The mare wades through the low surf, straining against the drag, white spray breaking against her chest. When Marian is submerged to her waist, she feels the animal become buoyant. Her lower body lifts off, and she is stretched out along the horse's back, reins loose, clutching the coppery mane. The mare's head is high out of the water, and she snorts softly in rhythm with her churning legs.

"She's swimming!" Marian calls out to Caleb, giddy.

He turns. His same old amusement flashes from under his hat, his certainty that she loves him. "What tipped you off?"

She can feel the horse's ribs and muscle and beating heart, familiar since she was a child. She is still that child, still climbing mountains on old, dear, dead Fiddler, alone or with her body pressed against her brother's, his heart beating, too, his lungs working. Another self entirely is submerged in the cool Pacific Ocean, the water gently but persistently tugging at her, lifting her off the horse, separating her from the animal that is swimming so earnestly, so industriously. Where does the mare want to go? Wherever Caleb's horse is going. They swim parallel to the shore. Soon Caleb will turn back in.

Her body marks a junction. Toward the sea. Toward the mountain. Toward the sky. Toward the horse. Toward the man.

Caleb's bedroom is upstairs under a peaked roof, bare rafters. Outside, the palms toss their long, heavy fronds; the surf susurrates on the reef. The dark world curls around the little blue island house.

"Do you think I've gone soft?" Caleb says.

Marian has settled horizontally on the bed, up by the pillows, on her side, naked in the breeze that comes through the jalousie windows. His head rests in the crook of her hip. "Anything would seem soft after your war," she says.

Three years in the worst of it without a scratch—North Africa, Italy, D-Day, France, Germany. Good luck so miraculous it had taken on the weight and gloom of a curse. New guys would touch him in hopes that whatever spooky voodoo protection he had going on would rub off, then go out and get killed their first day, sometimes right beside him. He'd told her his intact body had started to feel shameful. At least if he'd been shot or blown up he could have stopped, alive or dead. But on and on he went, never even getting trench foot, waiting for some kind of end. He'd grown reckless, but it hadn't made any difference. The war refused either to swallow him or to spit him out.

She adds, "I think soft's all right."

"Sometimes I miss the war, and I hate myself for it."

"A lot of people miss things about it."

"Do you?"

"Sometimes."

Without the war, he tells her, he probably would have spent his whole life in Montana, hunting. It never would have occurred to him to leave. But when he came back, he found he didn't like walking in the mountains anymore. He didn't like being cold or sleeping outside or shooting things. He'd had enough of all that. He got confused sometimes.

"One minute I'd be out for elk," he says, "and the next I'd be hunkered down somewhere, hiding from the Germans, all mixed up about past and present."

"Time to go **makai**."

He laughs. "You're practically a local already. Yeah, I guess it was time. Did I tell you why I came here?"

"No."

"I was drinking a lot, that sort of thing, but I was also reading a lot because I had nothing else to do, and I happened to check a book out of the library that had these drawings of the islands, and all of a sudden I **had** to see Hawaii. I **had** to." His fingers trail along her ankle. "I packed a bag and got on a train, then a ship. That was it."

"I envy you," Marian says. "Finding a place where you can stay put. Being content somewhere."

"No, you don't. If you did, you'd find that place, too. You don't even let the possibility in."

She doesn't think he's strictly talking about geography anymore. "Maybe someday," she says.

The aurora occupies huge swathes of sky in a blink. One moment an arc of light hangs from horizon to horizon, bleeding up into the stars; the next it is gone. You feel you are receiving messages from an unknown sender, of indecipherable meaning but unquestionable authority.

—MARIAN GRAVES

Barrow, Alaska, to Longyearbyen, Svalbard
71°17′ N, 156°46′ W to 78°12′ N, 15°34′ E
January 31–February 1, 1950
9,102 nautical miles flown

They wait in Barrow for four days. When an auspicious forecast comes, they leave in the evening so as to arrive in Svalbard at midday, when the southern sky will glow with blue arctic twilight. The sun won't actually rise for two more weeks, but at least they won't have to land in pitch-darkness. This is an advantage to their delayed schedule, to the sixteen days they spent in

Hawaii instead of the planned-for two: more light in the north. On the other hand, Marian worries about the consequences of reaching Antarctica so late in the southern summer, assuming they reach the continent at all.

The **Norsel,** the ship bringing the Norwegian-British-Swedish Antarctic Expedition (and also the **Peregrine**'s fuel) to Queen Maud Land in East Antarctica, had suffered a delay, costing the expedition at least two weeks, probably more. A telegram had arrived for Marian at the Honolulu airport. The upshot: No hurry.

We might as well hunker down here for a bit, she and Eddie had said to each other, feigning more reluctance than they felt. Eddie had found his own lodgings in Honolulu rather than stay at Caleb's. He'd been the one to mention the waning Arctic night as reason to dally. They'd thought they would probably have to fly all the way from Barrow to the Norwegian mainland, at the outside edge of the **Peregrine**'s range, as there was no real airfield on Svalbard and few navigation aids, but with good weather and a bit of twilight they'd have a better chance. She'd seized on the idea, had told herself, as she lingered in Caleb's bed, that she had no choice but to stay.

As the **Peregrine** lifts off from Barrow, heavy with fuel, reluctant to climb, the edge of the frozen land is indistinguishable from the beginning of the frozen sea. To the north lies darkness, studded with stars. Green auroras ripple like shafts of light through moving water.

Extreme cold generally discourages overcast, but even so, they are lucky. For much of the flight the sky is not only free from cloud but so transparent there seems to be no air at all. At the pole, the stars hover against the black of the universe. Below, a frozen ocean is lit by starlight and the thinnest paring of moon, its platinum surface pushed up into broken dunes, shadow rippling in the trenches between. Where the tides have tugged rips in the ice, narrow channels of open water breathe fog as they freeze over. Never has Marian seen a landscape so suffused with hush, so monochromatic and devoid of life.

That woman marking up her map in Long Beach seems so distant, so silly, unrecognizable as herself, this other woman flying through an expanse of dark clarity. What did that map have to do with this place?

If they crash, survival will be impossible, but there are other perils, too. So far north, the compass wanders. Lines of longitude pinch together like bars at the top of a birdcage. To make sense of the place, the idea of true north must be banished, the ways in which they have previously oriented themselves against the planet forgotten. The birdcage must be lifted up and away, navigation done by specialized charts under a flattened grid where north is set artificially and lines of longitude wrenched parallel.

In Kodiak, they'd put skis on the plane. In Fairbanks, they had gotten Eddie a reindeer parka, and when she glances back, she sees his shaggy brown form hunched over his desk as though in this dream of polar night her only companion has been magically transformed into a beast. He'd had the remnants of a black eye when they left Hawaii, but it had faded to nothing, now seems as illusory and dreamlike as the rest of their tropical hiatus. She doesn't know how he'd gotten it. The Fairbanks recon boys, who fly high latitudes almost daily, had given Eddie some last-minute tips, but he had listened only casually, without concern. He seems unbothered by the Arctic's tricks and deceptions. He handles his charts and tables and astrocompass with the calm assurance of a priest readying communion.

As they near the Svalbard archipelago, long black crooked leads of open water fracture the ice into a sharp-edged silver jigsaw of drifting floes. Still the weather holds. It is almost noon; to the south the horizon is lit with a narrow band of weak dishwater light. The shapes of islands appear, shadows against shadows.

One afternoon in Hawaii, Caleb had convinced Marian to fly them to the Big Island. A friend of his, Honi, a younger guy who'd been in the Pacific and was also a paniolo, had picked them up at the little Kona airport, taken them out on his rusty old boat. In the evening, as they drifted offshore, drinking beer, Honi had given them masks and snorkels purloined from the navy.

"They like this spot," he'd said, gesturing at the inky water. She'd known she was supposed to ask who **they** were, but she resisted the bait, splashed in.

Emptiness below, cobalt fading to black. Caleb grasped her wrist, tethering her to him. A bright beam of light slanted down: Honi was shining a big flashlight into the water, attracting the floating sea motes. Some silvery fish glinted in the depths, like coins in a well. The first manta ray had appeared as an undulation in the murk, far below, barely perceptible. It curved upward, ascending, mouth opening, gills flexing, underside glowing white. As it arced under her, belly to belly, the water had shifted between them like wind. Descending, it became a winged shadow, briefly vanished before looping back up. Again and again it looped through the spotlight's slant, feeding, and she had fallen through a gap in time and felt the giddy weightlessness of spooling loops over Missoula in the Stearman biplane.

Eddie hands forward a note. **Might be in range Isfjord Radio. Will try.**

When she'd radioed their flight plan from Barrow, she had been promised all possible

Svalbardian assistance, and now the operator tells Eddie the sky is clear and everyone in Barentsburg and Longyearbyen has turned on lights for them.

The Nazis had taken Svalbard twice, wanting it for weather stations. Free Norwegians had glided over the glaciers on skis, chasing radio signals that came and went like will-o'-the-wisps, sometimes finding and killing the Germans at their source, sometimes not. Always more Germans came, deposited in the northern islands by submarine. The last Germans to surrender in the whole war had been in Svalbard. Four months after V-E Day. They would have surrendered sooner, but no one bothered to go get them.

Marian approaches from the west, low over the sea, passing through the frozen mouth of Isfjord, flanked by flattopped white mountains. They pass the lights of the Soviet mining settlement at Barentsburg. The fjord's frozen surface gleams patchily where the snow has blown thin. They will try to land up the valley from Longyearbyen, at Adventdalen, where the Luftwaffe had made an airstrip.

Caleb had given her the manta rays to tell her he loved her. He knew how to tell her so she would hear him. She and Eddie had left on January 20th, the day they received word the delayed **Norsel** had finally crossed the Antarctic circle, nearing the continent. Caleb was at work on the ranch when she'd gone to the airport. No goodbye, of course. Their love meant everything, changed nothing. Their trajectories would continue along, unbowed by it.

She turns down a small inlet off the Isfjord, passes over the clumped yellow lights of Longyearbyen and the rickety wooden structures and cables that support mining trams. Already the transit across the North Pole, the stars and auroras and ice, has taken on the disintegrating strangeness of a dream.

The narrow valley is hazy. A coal fire still burns in one of the mines, started by a shell from a German battleship. They land on smooth snow marked by burning flare pots. A crowd has gathered to greet them.

When you are truly afraid, you experience an urgent desire to split from your body. You want to remove yourself from the thing that will experience pain and horror, but you are that thing. You are aboard a sinking ship, and you are the ship itself. But, flying, fear can't be permitted. To inhabit yourself fully is your only hope and, beyond that, to make the airplane a part of yourself, also.

—MARIAN GRAVES

***

Malmö, Sweden
55°32′ N, 13°22′ E
February 2, 1950
10,471 nautical miles flown

Eddie is in bed, in a dark hotel room, under a plump white goose-down duvet. By some miracle, he is safe and warm and alive. Out the window, snow falls on a small city square, a smooth layer swelling upward, butter-yellow in the streetlights. The buildings are narrow, with steep roofs and tidy rows of windows, snow on their sills.

They had planned for Oslo, but a storm had made landing there impossible. "Where else?" Marian had shouted above the crash and rattle of the plane, and he had gone to his charts and set his fingertip on Malmö, at the southern tip of Sweden. At least they had not been over water. If they were to crash, he'd thought, please let it be into solid earth. By radio, through waves of static, he had pieced together that conditions at Malmö were poor but not murderous. Somehow he had found the airfield. Somehow Marian had landed the plane. Bulltofta Airport. He remembers hearing about damaged bombers making forced landings there in the war rather than flying all the way back to England.

The gently falling snowflakes, the tiny bits of frozen lace sifting through the streetlights, seem so delicate, so innocent, but they are emissaries from a black, blind fury that, even now, hangs over the orderly roofs, the pious steeples and meticulous clock towers. He'd seen the flakes streaking and swarming around the plane, darting at it maliciously, but now they waft peaceably down onto the square, accumulating like harmless dust knocked loose from the sky.

He thinks his body should bear some scar from the storm, some trace beyond the cold lingering in him. He'd sat for an hour in a near-scalding bath without dislodging it. How could that place and this one exist so closely, one stacked atop the other? All the things around him, the bed linens and hot water and light switches and radiators, are part of an elaborately constructed, pleasantly convincing, utterly inane illusion of safety, of consequence.

In Honolulu, he'd found a cheap hotel on the edge of Chinatown. Faded anchors and hula girls plastered the windows of tattoo parlors. Grocery stores and spice shops displayed gnarled roots and jars of unknown powders, signs in foreign characters. A fetid smell hung in the damp, tropical air: rotting fruit, a trace of sewage from the river.

A bartender told Eddie he should have seen the place during the war. Sailors six deep at the bar, lines down the street at all the brothels, everybody cutting loose in the full light of day. "Had to, because of the blackouts," he said. "Brothels got shut down, though. Now there's pimps out there, which don't seem any better to me, but I could introduce you to a nice girl if you wanted."

"No, thanks," Eddie said. He held the guy's eye. "Not my style."

The guy lowered his voice, leaned closer. "Try the Coconut Palm if you want something a little different."

The second time he went to the Nut, as people called it, he took a guy back to his hotel. The guy,

Andy, who'd lost his left hand on D-Day, was going to the University of Hawaii on the government's dime and offered to show Eddie around. They lay on powdery white beaches, climbed up red-earth hills to look at the pillboxes from the war, ate thick macadamia nut pancakes with passion-fruit sauce.

"Why are you doing this round-the-world thing again?" Andy said when they were sunning themselves atop one of the pillboxes, concrete hot under their bare backs. Andy had his arms up over his head. The sight of his bald stump still caught Eddie by surprise sometimes.

"She needed a navigator. I was bored."

"Bored. Sure. You can go to the movies if you're bored. Do you actually **want** to do it?"

Below, the ocean spread to the horizon. He dreaded the long overwater flights that remained: to Kodiak, to Norway, to Antarctica, to New Zealand. **Mankind lacks that sixth sense which seems to guide seabirds across thousands of miles of trackless ocean.** That had been the first sentence in the Army Air Corps manual. But there had been times when he privately suspected he might possess that missing instinct. In the air, he had a surety of where he was, even though he could not have proved it or explained how he knew.

"I wanted to do something that's really hard," he told Andy, "but in a practical-technical way, not a human-emotional way. You always **are** somewhere, you just have to figure out where. The place you want to go **exists.** You just have to find it."

One night after they'd come out of the Nut, a bunch of sailors had followed them. Eddie had told Andy not to turn around. He hadn't, but one of the sailors had thrown a bottle that hit him in the back, and then Eddie had been the one to turn. Andy had run away, not that Eddie really blamed him.

Eddie connected a few good swings, at least judging from his knuckles afterward, but one of the sailors got him in the head with something heavy, and he'd woken up sometime later, lying in a filthy alley between a Chinese bookshop and a fishmonger's. Opening his swollen eyelids, he'd seen a green blur that slowly resolved into the reflection of a neon parrot in a fish-reeking puddle, though he hadn't been able to think of the word **parrot** or to make sense of why one would be gleaming on the ground.

In the storm, coming from Svalbard, he had been afraid, but he doesn't think he will ever again be as afraid as he'd been waking up lost in that Chinatown alley. In the storm, he had kept hold of the net of longitude and latitude that held the planet together, but in the alley he had been so disoriented he might as well have been wrapped and chained and tossed into dark water, his lostness absolute. The storm, even if it had killed him, would never have had the power over him the alley did.

He begins to slide into sleep, wakes with a jolt from a dream of green lights that might be the aurora or might be the neon parrot.

In the morning, he will concern himself with his bath and his coffee and what kind of Swedish jam to put on his toast. He will remember in a detached, fading way how ice had grown over the plane like unwanted armor, a malicious crystalline straitjacket, how the **Peregrine** had grown sluggish and heavy, her engines labored. Their situation had been so precarious it had seemed like the weight of just one more snowflake might have tipped them into doom, but instead they had touched down in Bulltofta. Then the warm hotel, the white bed, the innocent snow.

He'd had a week to heal in his tatty room in Honolulu before he saw Marian, and by then he was mostly better, just a little bruised around one eye and bothered by headaches that rippled unpredictably through his brain. She'd looked at him with concern, asked if he was all right, then left it alone. He supposed she'd been preoccupied with Caleb. He hadn't gone back to the Nut, hadn't seen Andy again.

From Malmö they will fly to Rome, and from Rome across to Tripoli, then south into damp equatorial heat, ever-lengthening days.

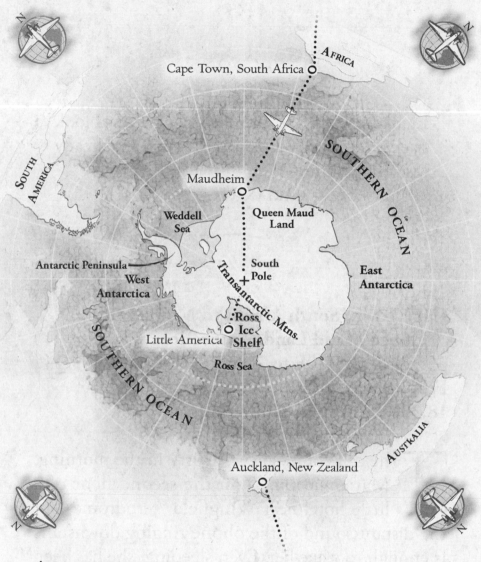

Antarctica

I look forward, and there is the horizon. I look
back. Horizon. What's past is lost. I am already
lost to my future.

—MARIAN GRAVES

⌒

Cape Town, South Africa, to Maudheim, Queen Maud Land, Antarctica
33°54′ S, 18°31′ E to 71°03′ S, 10°56′ W
February 13, 1950
18,331 nautical miles flown

The call comes at two-thirty in the morning.
Marian's room is on the second floor of a
little hotel near Wingfield Aerodrome, but
the distant sound of the phone ringing downstairs
is enough to wake her. Even sleeping, she has been
waiting. By the time the night clerk knocks on
her door, she is dressed. Out the window is a clear
summer night.

"The man from the aerodrome rang," the clerk
tells her. "He says—" He glances at a scrap of paper

in his hand. "He says the morsel radioed the weather's gone right." He looks up. "I hope you know what that's about because that's what he said."

"The **Norsel.** Anything else?"

"He said the morsel says it looks to stay all right, as best they can tell, which he wanted me to be sure to say was not well, and if you still wish to go, they recommend you leave as soon as possible. Though he said he personally wouldn't recommend going at all."

"Call back, please," Marian says, "and tell him we're on our way. Ask him, also, to try to raise any ships to the south and get a report on conditions."

His tongue poking from the corner of his mouth, the clerk makes a note and retreats down the stairs. Eddie's room is next door, and Marian presses her ear to the wall, listening for any activity. Surely he must have woken, but the silence is absolute. Please, she thinks, nearly prays, please be in there.

They had arrived in Cape Town on February 9th, and the Norwegian-British-Swedish Antarctic Expedition, after being repeatedly repelled by pack ice, had finally made landfall the next day. Before that, in Rome and Tripoli and Libreville and Windhoek, Eddie had taken to vanishing. She thinks that storm coming from Svalbard had shaken him, or maybe the change has something to do with whatever had happened in Honolulu to give him that black eye. He'd seemed fine in Alaska, had been in peak form navigating over the

North Pole, but since Malmö he's been slipping away from their lodgings, sometimes staying out all night. She's never quite sure if he'll return.

She had tried to engage him in the last planning tasks for Antarctica, sought his opinions on her endless nervous tinkering with calculations of load and fuel (the addition of the skis and their drag add a nagging unknown), but his answers were always perfunctory, indifferent, even terse, as though she were pestering him with frivolous and irrelevant concerns. He seemed to want nothing to do with her and her charts and scribbling pencil, but in Cape Town, she told him he had to stop wandering off. The season was waning. They needed to be ready to leave at any moment.

She knocks on his door. "Come in," he says at once. He is sitting on the bed, fully clothed. The bed doesn't look slept in.

"Did you sleep?" she asks from the doorway.

"I don't know. No. I haven't been, much. And tonight I had a feeling. Is it time?"

"The weather's gone right."

He looks down at the floor, clasps and twists his big hands. "Right for now. Three hours until we leave, probably. Maybe thirteen more in the air. It could be a whiteout when we get there. It could be anything."

She fights her impatience. Does he think she doesn't know this? "At some point we have to leap."

He looks up at her, wretched, supplicating. "I don't know if I can do it."

"You mean you don't want to go?" She is astonished.

He shakes his head. "I mean I don't know if I can find the way."

She comes into the room, sits beside him. "If anyone can, you can."

"That's not much of a guarantee."

"There never was any. Each of us had to accept that the other might fail."

"I've gotten shaken up."

"The storm?"

"That didn't help, but it's been more of an accumulation. I thought I'd get used to the long flights over water, but I haven't." He presses his fingertips gingerly to the side of his skull, and pain flickers across his face.

"Are you all right?"

"Just a headache. It'll pass." He takes a bottle of aspirin from his pocket, chews two.

"You did so well to Svalbard," she says as though reminding a recalcitrant child that he had liked a certain food just yesterday.

"That was different."

She can't deny this. Near the North Pole, the rules of navigation changed, but still they'd had decent charts, plenty of advice, radio beams from Barrow and Thule, people waiting in Longyearbyen. They'd had the good luck of clear skies, too, unobscured stars by which Eddie could take their bearings. In the south he will have woefully patchy charts, no beacons, and no stars except the sun, which is likely to be frequently occluded by vicious, fast-changing weather.

He says, "I've been thinking a lot about everything that could go wrong. But I've also been thinking about what will happen if nothing goes wrong. Do you think about after?"

"I'm trying to take it day by day. Each leg, each landing." She senses Eddie is in danger of coming apart but can't gauge the seriousness of the problem, as a structural weakness in a plane may or may not spell disaster, depending on the stresses exerted. He is bent forward, his elbows resting on his knees, his big head in his big hands. She says, "Have I dragged you into this?"

"No." He shakes his head again. "No, I chose it. I needed . . . I needed something, and I thought this might be it."

"We've come so far," she says quietly, pleading. "It's just more flying. Land, water, ice—it's all the same, really."

This is a lie, of course. They will be flying into severe danger. He knows this as well as she does—but she doesn't care. She almost couldn't conceive of caring. She has hardened inside. Only flying matters.

She knows he knows she is lying, but he says, "You're right."

She is impatient to get to the airfield. "Are you ready?"

He lifts his head. He looks exhausted. "Ready as I'll ever be."

They take off at dawn, arc to the south, catch one last glimpse of Table Mountain in the rosy sideways spill of the rising sun. A great migration of white-caps moves across the sea. The **Peregrine** bounces on the wind. Until they gain a bit of altitude, Marian is much too hot in her woolen clothes. She can't imagine needing the reindeer parka and finnesko boots and thick socks piled in the copilot's seat, but soon enough she won't be able to imagine not needing them.

After two hours, a thin veil of mist materializes below, broken in places. Ahead, a wall of cloud rises up, gray and solid, too tall to climb over. They pass into pale obscurity.

From time to time, Eddie hands up a note with a course correction. She can glean nothing from his impassive expression. She tries to send him a transmission of her own, a message of faith: He can find the way. Perhaps what's broken in him will be mended when they close the circle.

In the sixth hour, the cloud begins to lighten,

thinning from above, and there comes a white jostle and rattle, the magnificent pop into the open sky, the belly of the plane skimming the white. Eddie passes a note. **PNR -30.** Point of no return in thirty minutes.

He is not suggesting they turn back, only telling her, as is standard practice, that any opportunity to do so will soon be gone. But she is long past that point already. Their beginning and their end lie ahead.

The clouds clear. The PNR evaporates behind them. Below is a sheet of dark blue, ribbed with swell. In the plane, the temperature drops. Marian sits in comfortable boredom, the familiar trance of flying, watches the instruments and the engines, switching from one fuel tank to the next, following Eddie's recommendations. This is all she can do.

The first iceberg appears, a flattopped island the size of a city block, blue caves dug in its sides by waves. White birds wheel around. A glowing aqua lip of ice shows through from underwater. There is more of the berg down there, of course, much more, a huge frozen root.

The compass begins to wander, confused by the abundance of southerliness. The cold is getting the better of the **Peregrine**'s heaters. They put on heavy sweaters. Sometime in the eleventh hour, a bright white patch appears above the horizon: an iceblink, the overcast sky reflecting ice they can't yet see. The water is black now, glossy as obsidian, and soon enough a band of pack ice appears, a mess of slush and slabs and bergs. In places the water is mottled with translucent disks of ice like massed jellyfish. A group of seals lie clumped on one floe, and they stir and heave around, peering up at the noise. Another is speckled with penguins as though with poppy seeds.

The ceiling lowers, pushing them down to four hundred feet. Eddie is quiet, bent over his desk, recalculating and recalculating. Flecks of ice build up on the wings, clumping together like spitwads blown by the clouds. Marian inflates the boots on the wing edges to break off the crust. Twelve and a half hours.

Something strange appears between the black of the sea and the white of the clouds: a thin silver line, vertically striated like a stretched seam of glue, running as far as Marian can see in either direction. She calls to Eddie, thumps his shoulder when he comes up to see. The ice shelf. She hadn't expected him to look as he does, gazing out—like a man witnessing a holy miracle. His eyes well. She supposes he'd braced so violently against the fact of this flight that awe catches him by surprise.

They fly low, following the edge of the shelf. After twenty minutes, in answer to Eddie's repeated transmissions, radio contact is made with the expedition base, Maudheim. They've marked a landing strip with flags. After forty minutes: a ship docked against the ice, stacks of cargo and lines of chained dogs, trails in the snow from the ship to the site where the huts are being erected, small figures, arms waving. Flags and a wind sock mark a flat strip of snow. Marian circles, puts down the skis.

The sound of the wind has become my idea of silence. Real silence would sit heavily on my ears, like the pressure of the grave.

—MARIAN GRAVES

⌒

Maudheim, Queen Maud Land,
   to Little America III, Ross Ice Shelf
71°03′ S, 10°56′ W to 78°28′ S, 163°51′ W
February 13–March 4, 1950
20,123 nautical miles flown

They are offered accommodations on the **Norsel,** but the ship so stinks of whale meat and dogs and men that Marian and Eddie are glad to leave after dinner and pitch their tent near where the plane is anchored with cables, blocks of snow stacked on its skis for good measure. On Richard Byrd's first expedition in 1929, a Fokker was torn from its tethers by the wind, blown backward, and wrecked. If such a thing were to happen to the **Peregrine** after they've left

Maudheim, Marian thinks the best course of action will be to lie down in the snow and wait. Rescue doesn't figure into her plans. Rescue would be impossible. For the sake of weight, they are carrying only enough food to see them through one or two prolonged periods of bad weather.

Her bones still vibrate with the memory of the engines. Before plunging into sleep, she looks outside again. Daylight, of course, though it is late. The clouds have cleared, and a miasma of ice crystals shimmers around the plane. Antarctica had always seemed fantastical, but now it seems like the only possible place, the rest of the world fading away like an outlandishly lurid dream.

In the night, a sound like a burst of rifle fire wakes them. After a wide-eyed moment, Eddie says, "It's just the ice shifting." He had been lively at dinner, so much like the charming young man she'd known in London that she'd been disconcerted, almost fearful. Pilots who'd flown in Antarctica had warned her about fata morganas, phantom mountain ranges or icebergs that might hang above the horizon, doubling or magnifying some lesser feature of the landscape, and she wonders if this Eddie is another kind of mirage.

The sun is gone in the morning, the cloud too low. The meteorologist says to wait.

They help, as best they can, with the construction of Maudheim. The expedition members winch crates and equipment and Liberty Oil fuel drums off the ship and onto tank-treaded weasels that chug and grind a mile and a half over the ice to the site of the huts. Men are crafting ice foundations and putting up the timbering. Men are digging caves for storage and workshops, building passageways out of crates and tarps, stacking oil barrels as windbreaks. All of it will be buried in drifting snow soon enough. Dozens of sled dogs are tethered all around, keeping up a constant chorus of barks and howls.

The expedition leader tells Marian he'd never seen dogs so happy as theirs when they landed. On the sea voyage, the animals had been tied and kenneled on deck in the sea spray and the sluicing blood from the heaped-up whale meat and their own shit, but once they were finally on the ice they rolled themselves clean and dry in the snow and barked and frolicked and were new again. Perhaps Eddie is not a mirage; perhaps he is simply refreshed by the purity of the place.

After a day and night of cloud, the sky clears. The fuel barrels are brought, the **Peregrine**'s tanks filled. The engines are thawed under canvas hoods and fed a breakfast of warm oil.

Despite the heavy load and the throttle's stiffness in the cold, the skis lift cleanly from the hard-packed snow. Marian turns the plane away from the waving men and barking dogs, away from the sea, toward nothing.

In an hour, they pass over mountains that don't appear on their charts. Probably no one else has ever seen them. Steep ridges of black rock and lonely nunataks jut from the ice.

Then an astonishing infinity of white.

The surface of the ice has an ever-changing texture, like the sea. (Marian supposes it **is** a kind of free-standing sea, thousands of feet deep.) Sastrugi ripple like frozen waves; cracks run through like currents. Even with sun goggles, the glare bores into her skull. After four hours, a filmy haze forms, grows denser: a relief from the light but a problem in other ways. Ice speckles the wings. She climbs to twelve thousand feet, into clear air, only three thousand feet or so above the plateau, which has been rising steadily toward the pole. The sun casts the plane's shadow down on diaphanous cloud, a perfect miniature, ringed by a rainbow—a glory, it's called. By the book, they should be on oxygen, but she decides to conserve their supply. Who knows how long the fog will last, how much higher they will have to go.

South Pole now, reads the note Eddie passes up a bit later. **PNR -30.** He is smiling, radiating enthusiasm. He appears elated. The bottom of the world shows faintly through the haze, white and trackless, indistinguishable from the rest of the trackless white. Marian gazes on it without emotion. The only place she wants to go is onward, away. She understands now this place, vast and lifeless, might as well be death itself.

The oil pressure gauge has gone flat, but the instrument has probably just failed in the cold, as the engines still drone along. The heater has surrendered, too, and the metal in the cabin is cold enough to sear exposed skin.

She hesitates, thinking of the PNR. But why does she hesitate? Nothing is wrong.

She shouts to Eddie, "What do you think?"

He looks blank, bawls back, "About what?"

"Should we keep on?"

He peers at her from under the hood of his reindeer parka. "Why wouldn't we?"

"Just checking."

He grins and gives her a thumbs-up. "All good."

Was it possible she had dreamed the frightened man in the hotel in Cape Town, staring at her like she'd come to escort him to the gallows? How could that man be the same as this dauntless, ebullient one? But he is also being logical: There is no better reason to go back than forward. The visibility isn't perfect, but it could certainly be worse. Nothing is amiss with the plane. If they were to go back, assuming they made it to Maudheim, they would have no fuel to try again but would have to wait out the season, rely on the supplies and hospitality of the expeditioners, be retrieved by ship.

Another leap must be made. Go against your instincts, Trout had told her. Give in when you want to resist, she'd told Eddie in London. Resist when you want to give in. She flies on.

Sky and ice blend into a seamless shell, can't be prised apart. Like flying in a bowl of milk, pilots say. The horizon is gone. There is empty space around her, above and below, but she has no means of judging how much. The altimeter says they are at eleven thousand feet, but that's above sea level. She doesn't know how thick the ice is. They might be only a thousand feet above it. She can see nothing beyond a vague swirl of blowing snow. Eddie is leaning up beside her, peering out.

Once, in Alaska, she'd flown a man out to a copper mine, a city guy, an executive from San Francisco come to make an inspection. They'd gotten caught in cloud, couldn't get under or over, had to go through. After a while she noticed the guy kept pinching his earlobe between two fingers. When she asked him if his ears hurt, he admitted, in a dry whisper, that he was having the strangest feeling. He kept thinking they might have crashed and died and this shapeless droning white was purgatory. If he pinched himself, he said, he felt more confident he was still alive.

Now she understands. Where is the border

between life and oblivion? Why should anyone presume to recognize it?

She makes a shallow turn, retreating in hope of better visibility. She thinks she catches a faint glimpse of the ice below, and then it is gone. They need to land soon and without wasting fuel. Nearly blindly, playing close to stall speed, she brings the plane lower. Wind buffets. The engines whine. A gust, and she sees the ice, pulls up. A horrible scrape and jolt, the plane slewing sideways.

Their tent floats in nothingness. The wind shrieks without resting, might tear apart the rattling canvas at any moment. Marian wants to call it merciless, but, here, mercy is an alien concept, irrelevant.

Outside, the blowing drift blinds and suffocates. All is white. She seems to hang suspended, as there is no way to tell the snow she stands on from the air around her. She can't see the plane where it is dug in and tethered, can only hope it hasn't blown away. She can't go to it. If she were to take more than a few steps out into the white, she would never find her way back to the tent.

It is a miracle they'd survived the landing with only a bent prop blade and one damaged ski. She'd bent a million props in Alaska, knows how to whack them back with a sledgehammer and how to tape and tie and splint a ski. It is a miracle the blizzard had not yet reached full blast when they landed, that they'd been able (after a struggle) to secure the plane and erect their tent and light the stove so they might silently suffer the excruciating pain of thawing their feet and hands.

They sleep and wake inside their reindeer sleeping bags, sleep and wake, lie mostly in silence when they are awake. After two days, when the wind finally drops, Marian can think only of the plane. Quietly, trying not to wake Eddie, she crawls from the tent. There is only the faint shape of mounded snow where the plane had been. She begins to run, tromping in her heavy boots, and can't have taken more than a dozen steps when the snow does something strange under her right foot.

She has instinctively thrown her weight to the left and dropped to her knees before she understands what has happened.

Black space where she'd stepped, as though she had kicked a foot-size aperture from this white world into a subterranean void. A few feet of vertical ice glow blue in the crevasse; below that is a familiar darkness. It has been following her since she first flew to Canada, perhaps since the **Josephina** went down. She is sitting on a thin membrane between a white void and a black one. Two halves of a sphere, each made of absence: the absence of color, the absence of light.

She crawls back to the tent on hands and knees. Eddie stirs when she enters, murmurs that the

wind is dropping off. She can only make a gut-
tural sound she hopes he will take as agreement.
The chasm waits outside, submerged like a croco-
dile. The plane, assuming it's still there, might be
resting on a precipice. The tent might sit atop a
snow bridge that could collapse at any moment.
Thinking of the small black hole in the snow, she
feels terror but also pity for her body—its hapless, clumsy vulnerability, its smallness, the dumb
weight of it. She can do nothing for now. The wind
is rising again. She retreats into sleep.

Drifting snow buries the tent, insulating them.
They dig out the entrance every few hours to be
sure they aren't permanently entombed. Eddie,
when Marian told him about her discovery of the
crevasse, had remained the stalwart Antarctic version of himself. All they can do for now is be careful, he said, and when the storm abates, they will
see what they see. If the plane is gone, then it is
gone. He thinks, though, it is probably still there,
just buried.

The weather must break. Even in this most hostile place, the sun and sky must return. Marian
tells herself this but does not entirely believe it.
She thinks again of her passenger in Alaska trying to convince himself he was not already dead.
Could they be dead? Anything seems possible, but
also nothing seems possible except white and cold.

No, she thinks, oblivion must be pure, and their presence mars the purity of this place. They are the speck of imperfection that proves life.

There is still food and kerosene, but after a week, death has started to seem near, not a leap but a small sideways step. The cold is always nibbling at Marian's hands and feet, looking for a way in, a breach in her defenses. Numbness is not an absence of feeling but a felt absence. If they stay too long outside, frostbite turns their faces white as death masks. They rub at their cheeks and noses and toes, endure the pain of returning to life.

Condensation from their breathing accumulates as a flaky rime on the sleeping bags and tent walls that must be brushed off twice a day. Eddie leaves a damp sock on the floor of the tent, and when he picks it up, it breaks as crisply as chocolate.

The cold has found its way to the core of her and, once established, proves nearly impossible to evict. The crusted yellow patches on her nose and cheeks she can't get rid of, the fogginess of her mind—death is curled and waiting within her; death is massed along her borders. She has wild, colorful dreams that feel like small, vivid rebellions against the shrouding nothingness.

Sometimes she still finds herself thinking that she will visit Jamie after the flight. Remembering the truth brings a small detonation of grief.

"It doesn't make sense," she says to Eddie from inside her sleeping bag, "but sometimes my brother's death gives me courage. I catch myself thinking that if he could die, if he could endure it, so can I, though obviously I have no choice, and it's not something anyone **endures.** In fact it's the opposite."

"I think you should take courage from wherever you can find it," Eddie says. "What's the harm?"

Her gratitude to Eddie knows no bounds, and yet there are moments when she wishes him gone. To find the essence of Antarctica, she has an instinct it must be confronted alone. Or maybe the essence of the place is too large and empty for anyone to grasp, no matter how stark a confrontation is made. Maybe that is the appeal of Antarctica, the itch of it. She thinks of Jamie painting infinite space, knowing infinite space could not be painted.

When they go outside during lulls in the wind, Eddie stands with his back to her, staring out across the white disk, and doesn't seem to hear her when she speaks.

In the tent, he says he likes Antarctica because it hasn't been touched by the war. He likes that there is nothing to rebuild. "The rebuilding depresses me almost as much as the destruction did," he says. "At least the rubble was truthful."

She remembers cities reduced to flat patches of pink-gray dust and jumbled heaps of masonry. She thinks he means that no matter what earnest promises of peace are made, what fragments are hauled up and glued back together, the dead will not return. A return to the world as it was is impossible; the only choice is to make a new world. But making a new world seems dreary and exhausting.

The sky is clear and they are digging, exhuming the bloodless silver body of the plane from a mound of snow. They've exposed a wing and most of the tail. The inside is full of snow, too. Their hands are already raw inside their mitts, but they must keep digging. Eddie has made a careful survey of the crevasse, probing with a tent pole, and marked a safe path. He thinks the ice ahead of the plane is solid. They dig in a fever, hoping the weather holds.

Clouds close in, part, close again. They dig for a full day, can't stop without their sweaty clothes freezing solid. Once they get the body of the plane free, they dig out the inside, and they bang the propeller blade straight enough, patch the ski well enough.

Finally all that is left is to crack the last of the snow from the cowlings and wait, fearfully, while the engines warm under their hoods. They want nothing more than to sleep, but there is no reason another blizzard shouldn't come in and undo all their work.

The propellers spin feebly, stop. Marian tinkers with the booster. The fuel lines cough; the engines growl to life; the props spin, keep spinning. When the time comes, she has to throttle up hard to break the skis free of the ice, her weary arm aching just at that. The snow passes faster and faster out the cockpit windows. They bounce and jostle, and she prays not to hit any big sastrugi or a crevasse. They hover; they're ascending. The patch of ice that had held them and the hidden crevasse under it vanish immediately, indistinguishable from the rest of the white.

Eddie takes a sight, shows her on the chart where they had been. A blank spot, like all the others. Her adrenaline sputters as the flying lulls her. Sleep presses on her. Her head drops, snaps up.

The Transantarctic Mountains burst through the continent's white hide: pyramidal peaks and black serrated ridges and blue fields of shattered ice. Marian flies at thirteen thousand feet, steering among the passes. She tries to use oxygen, thinking it might wake her up, but a valve is frozen shut. Charles Lindbergh was awake for more than fifty hours when he flew across the Atlantic, she reminds herself. But, a self-pitying part of her counters, he hadn't had to dig a plane out of the snow.

The fuel is dropping too quickly. She peers around, spots an opalescent spray fanning out behind the wing. In her drowsiness, she had not noticed when it started, but now there is nothing to be done except hope the leak doesn't get worse.

Settling down to fix it is out of the question. Maybe some line had been wrenched loose in their hard landing or some seal had cracked in the cold.

They come to the Axel Heiberg glacier. Beyond, below, a layer of cloud extends to the horizon. Alarm revives her. Eddie passes her a course adjustment, and they exchange solemn glances. What can be said? Under the cloud, the glacier descends more than nine thousand feet from the mountains to the Ross Ice Shelf, a floating sheet of ice bigger than Spain. They see only a low blanket of gray.

To overshoot the ice edge is their best chance. They fly on and on, fuel draining down to nothing, until they must be over open water. At Eddie's signal, she drops into the cloud. Lower and lower through the blind white. Then, finally, a rapid darkening rising up from underneath, and they are in clear air, low over black water hazed with sea smoke. Not far away, a massive tabular iceberg reaches nearly to the bottom of the cloud. She turns the airplane, and there is the edge of the ice shelf, the barrier, a sheer blue wall emerging from the sea. Eddie has put them precisely on their target.

Here is where Roald Amundsen built his base Framheim before striking out on skis for the South Pole. Here is where Richard E. Byrd's camps, Little Americas I through IV, are sunken in the snow, subterranean mazes of living spaces and laboratories and workshops with caches of fuel and supplies. Marian had written to men who'd been on the expeditions; Eddie had made a map of the bases' relative locations. They'd formed guesses on what might still be protruding from the snow, what they should look for.

But the ice is always moving, pushed outward by the heaped-up mass of itself in the continent's interior, always sliding down to the sea, breaking off, floating away. She sees the remnants of Little America IV near the ice edge, closer than she expected, precipitously close, the tops of Quonset huts erected in 1947 for a navy operation of forty-seven hundred men, thirteen ships, seventeen airplanes. She aims instead for a cluster of ventilators and masts a few miles to the northeast: Little America III.

Strange to be warm. They had been so surprised when the generator came alive they had sprung back in terror and then laughed, teary and exhausted, collapsed on the floor of an ice tunnel. Eddie had cranked it as an experiment, almost a joke, but Admiral Byrd's men must have left kerosene in the hardy machine because it rattled and roared and set grumblingly to work. The main structure is designed so the generator blows warm air between two layers of a double floor, and quickly the chill had lost its harshness. Camped on the plateau, Marian had begun to regard even the slightest lessening of cold as warmth, but this, as she lies in a bunk after interminable sleep, is the real thing. There is no sense of struggle.

She had felt as vaporous as sea smoke while they anchored the plane and covered the engines, made their best guess at where to dig. She hopes never to dig snow again. Her hands resemble bloody beef, frozen then thawed. One veteran of the Byrd expeditions had sent her a sketched diagram of the base, and using that, they had dug and chiseled down into the subterranean lair of huts and ice tunnels, found the generator, melted snow for water, found bunks, collapsed in their sleeping bags.

She wakes in total darkness. Slowly, deprived of all other senses, she becomes aware first of the intense soreness in her arms and back and the stinging of her hands, then of her thirst and the fullness of her bladder, and then of a faint, nearly imperceptible rocking: the ice shelf flexing, floating on the swell. She lights a kerosene lantern. Her wristwatch reads four o'clock, but she doesn't know if it is night or day. "Good afternoon," Eddie says from somewhere nearby.

"Is it afternoon? What was it when we went to sleep?"

"I think it was yesterday evening," he says.

They are in a room tightly packed with bunks and jumbled supplies and gear, middens of discarded woolens and worn-out boots, the leavings of thirty-three men. Books lie open where they were left ten years ago. The walls and beams are carved with names and cryptic messages. Pinup girls laugh and point their toes. No catastrophe happened here, but there's a haunted feeling. It's the cold that does it, holds everything suspended, staves off decay. There's no water to corrode anything, no pests to nibble and gnaw, no rot, nothing to mark the passage of time. One of the ice tunnels has caved in, and the roof sags some, but otherwise the place might have been abandoned yesterday.

She goes up to the surface and for once is pleased to see low cloud. They are still so desperately tired she doubts they could endure the task of getting ready to leave.

Underground, ice tunnels lead to outlying huts and igloos. They find the machine shop, the ski room, the radio shack. In the blubber room, a pile of eviscerated seal carcasses await chopping up. Crates of food and cans of kerosene line the tunnels. In the dog tunnel, when her lantern first passes over them, Marian takes the frozen turds for enormous, glossy brown toads.

From an abundance of perfectly preserved, deep-frozen ingredients they cook a meal of ham and corn on the cob (grown in 1938, the package says). Eddie keeps venturing off down the tunnels, returning with unexpected treasures. He finds a cigar, then a Victrola, plays Benny Goodman and Bing Crosby. The music echoes off the beams, the bare walls, reverberates out into the ice, is heard by seals swimming underneath.

· · ·

The sky stays shut. Whenever she climbs up to check the weather, there is always cloud, sometimes blowing snow. It would be a lie to say she feels only disappointment. It is easy to forget, below, that this can't last, that they must leap again. The ice creaks to remind her.

They have found gasoline barrels and fueled the plane. Every day they dig away whatever snow has drifted against it. They have checked every hose and valve and gasket, should have eliminated any possible leaks, but doubt nags at Marian. And Eddie is behaving oddly again. He spends more time above than she does, wandering in contemplation, but when he comes below, he bustles with great purpose, tidying the huts and checking the supplies.

Antarctica has a trickster's spirit. In certain lights, a mountain a mile distant turns out to be a shoulder-high heap of snow fifty feet away. Dozens of tall, black figures marching toward them out of the fog turn out to be only five knee-high Adélie penguins, magnified and multiplied by some atmospheric illusion, stretched along an invisible horizon like an army.

They are inside the **Peregrine** when Eddie tells her he will not go with her. The weather has cleared, and they have just finished, again, shoveling out the snow that has blown in through the cracks. She isn't really listening, is thinking through everything that must be done, must be checked.

"The thing is," he says almost casually, "even if I did go, I don't think we'd make it, and I don't want to drown. The only thing I've ever been grateful for in the war was that I didn't drown."

Distracted, she thinks he is making a strange joke. "What?"

"I'm staying here," he says again.

Disbelieving, puzzled, she tells him, no, of course he isn't. She needs him. They will make it. There is no reason for them not to. They've patched the leak. They've come so far.

"No," he says, calmly, "I don't think we will. For me, it's not worth the risk."

"Are you talking about a **premonition**?"

"You could call it that."

Still looking for the prank, the joke, she asks him why he'd bothered shoveling out the plane if he wasn't going, and he says, still serene, that he thought she would still want to try, alone.

"But you don't think I'll make it. You think I'll drown."

"You could stay here."

"I can't. What are you talking about? Do you mean stay here and try to get a ship to rescue us? It's too late in the season. We'd have to wait a year, and there's no reason anyway."

"No, I don't mean that. I know you'll go. But I

don't want to. If I stay here, I know what will happen to me."

She is stunned, outraged, panicked. "You'll freeze or starve, or you'll fall in a crevasse and then freeze or starve."

"Maybe," he says. "Or I'll wait until winter and then go out in the night, on a clear night, and lie down under the aurora."

She shouts at him that he's being irrational, crazy, that he's breaking a promise, condemning her to death, and he lets her finish before he explains he doesn't like the mess of the rest of the world, wants no part of it anymore.

"Is this revenge?" she says. "For what happened to Ruth?"

"Please don't insult me," he says quietly.

She calms herself, speaks carefully. "There's a life for you after we finish," she tells him. "You'll find it. Antarctica isn't going to make you less lonely."

"But I'm not lonely here. That's the whole point. And there's not a life for me back there." He gestures at the water, the northern bulk of the planet. "Not one I want. I've tried. Really, I have. I can't find my way anymore."

"You **can.** You're a navigator."

"That's just a job," he says. "A task."

She tells him she can't fly and navigate at the same time. Not on a flight like this. She won't make it without him. "Is that what you want?" she asks.

"It doesn't make any difference what I want."

"What kind of thing is that to say?"

"We won't make it. The end is the same, but I don't want to be in the water."

"We **will** make it. We have to **try.** Why can't you finish this, think things over after? You could find a piece of land somewhere and live quietly, if it's isolation you want."

He looks at her with sympathy. "There won't be an after. I'm sorry, Marian, I know this is hard on you, but I'm choosing the way I go. You can choose, too. And I want to know what it's like, being here alone. I have a yearning for it."

This she understands—in fact, he is giving her what she thought she wanted, to fly alone—but she says, "That's the most selfish thing I've ever heard."

Maybe, he says. But in Antarctica he feels in possession of himself because there's nothing else. Or won't be, once Marian is gone. He's charted the route for her; she might be able to follow it alone. But, like he's said, he believes they are at the end of the road. She can die either in Antarctica or in the Southern Ocean. "What you do is your choice," he says, "but I've made up my mind."

She demands to know why he'd agreed to come on this trip if he was only going to abandon her, sabotage her.

Because until now, he says, he'd believed they would make it, but he'd been afraid. Now he knows they won't, and his fears are gone. Everything has been leading up to this. He'd had to be afraid so he would notice when he wasn't anymore.

She tells him he will get her killed with his superstitious obstinacy, that it's fine for him to have a death wish but she wants nothing to do with it. Ruth wouldn't want him to do this, she says. She says, her voice cracking, that he can't just abandon her.

"No," he says. "You're the one who's going to abandon me."

She writes one last entry in her logbook, breathless, scrawling. **I have made a promise to myself: My last descent won't be the tumbling helpless kind but a sharp gannet plunge.** If she makes it to New Zealand, having left Eddie on the ice, she will have nothing to say about the flight, the finished circle, will not be able to bear anyone reading the words of a person who would do something so shameful.

She tells herself he is leaving her no choice, but she wonders if she is simply not good enough with people to figure out how to persuade him. **I don't regret anything,** she writes, **but I will if I let myself. I can think only about the plane, the wind, and the shore, so far away, where land begins again.**

If she dies, though, she wants some version of the story to persist, fragmented and incomplete as it may be, even if the chances of anyone ever finding it are vanishingly small. **We've fixed the leak as best we can.** She hesitates, then finally writes an I, not a we. **I will go soon.**

Probably the ice will calve and carry Little America out to sea and her logbook with it.

What I have done is foolish; I had no choice but to do it.

Probably the snow will bury it too deeply to ever be found.

No one should ever read this. My life is my one possession.

Probably.

And yet, and yet, and yet.

She closes the book, wraps it in Eddie's life preserver, leaves it in the bunk room of Little America III.

Until she dies, she will wonder if she could have persuaded him to come with her. Until she dies, she will remember Eddie's small, dark figure on the ice, waving to her with both arms as she circles up. She will always be afraid that his valedictory gesture might have changed, at some moment when she was too far away to notice, into a plea for her to return.

Sitting-in-the-Water-Grizzly

Twenty

I knocked on the door of the blue house. Joey Kamaka opened it and burst out laughing. He laughed so hard he bent over with his hands on his thighs. "It's really you," he said when he'd recovered. "I thought for sure someone was messing with me."

He was wiry and barefoot, around sixty, in board shorts and a T-shirt, with a short gray ponytail. A small girl, maybe eight, also ponytailed, had her arms locked around his waist from behind and was peeping at me with giant cartoon bunny-rabbit eyes.

"This is my granddaughter Kalani," he said. "She's only seen the first **Archangel** movie because the others got too scary, but she has all the Katie McGee DVDs. She **loves** Katie McGee."

He waved me inside, and I stepped out of my flip-flops, added them to a pile by the door. The house was small but bright, with walls and ceilings of white-painted planks and beat-up dark ones for the floor. It was the first time I'd been in a room I knew Marian Graves had been in, too. Everywhere else had been sets and stand-ins. There was a toy-strewn living room with a braided rug and a sagging couch facing a big flat-screen TV, and through one door I glimpsed a bathroom and through another a chaotic den of pink and purple, presumably Kalani's room. Stairs led up through an open hatch, and a landscape painting hung slightly crooked on the wall: sharply angled mountains dense with trees and shadows. I moved to get a closer look.

"Is this . . . ?" I asked.

"It's by Jamie Graves," Joey said. "Caleb brought it with him from the mainland. I know it's worth a lot, and I should sell it or at least get a security system or something, but it's just kind of always been there. I still feel like it's Caleb's and not mine."

The night before, in a bigger, nicer version of this house some location scout had found, I'd filmed a scene where Marian and Eddie were staying with Caleb and there's a storm in the night, and Marian betrays Eddie by going to Caleb, and they fuck while Eddie's pretending to be asleep in the room below. So Actor Caleb and I, wearing little flesh-colored patches on our crotches, had feigned hot, hot passion while a bunch of people stood around holding booms and reflectors and the intimacy coordinator said things like **Hadley, would you be comfortable if he had his hands on your waist instead of your hips?** Bart had started to make noises about maybe the scene would be better, more authentic, if it showed my breasts, and I'd expected myself to say yes because that's what I've always done, but instead I said, "No one needs to see Marian's tits, Bart." And that was the end of it.

Thank god I hadn't read Adelaide Scott's box of letters until we were almost done shooting, because now I had to act on two levels: (1) like Marian, in a way that was consistent with everything else we'd shot, and (2) like I didn't know what I now knew, which was that Eddie had been gay and Marian had been in love with his wife.

In Adelaide's living room, I'd first set the letters out on the floor like a huge puzzle, and then I read late into the night, fell asleep on her couch. Some had been to Marian, some from her.

It seems an awful snare. I've told him I can scarcely imagine ever having one and absolutely not anytime soon, and I thought he understood, but—no, he does understand. It's that he doesn't care. He wants me snared.

Please keep writing, even if my replies are as anemic as this one. I'm not myself right now.

The doctor says I am doing well, and I haven't had a drink in a month. I know that counts for little, but I hope my small success is more than nothing.

I know you and Caleb had history, but I guess you did miss men, after all.

I am writing because it has come to my attention that my late husband, Lloyd Feiffer, allowed your father to suffer a great wrong.

Joey led me into a compact kitchen with plywood cabinets and an old beige refrigerator. "I'm just finishing making Kalani's lunch," he said, "and then we can talk. Can I get you anything?" He bent into the fridge. "Water, fruit punch, milk, beer?"

"I love day beers," I said. It wasn't really a joke, but he laughed as he handed me a can, cracked one for himself. His laugh seemed to be always bubbling just under the surface. Kalani's lunch was a compartmentalized plastic plate containing a sandwich cut into triangles, some baby carrots, and a dollop of something purple. Joey gave it to her and led me outside.

The lanai had rattan furniture with faded cushions printed with big green leaves. A ceiling fan turned languidly overhead. Their small and scrubby yard was bounded by a chain-link fence grown over with some kind of vine, and a pink bike with white tires lay on its side beside a child's playhouse in bleached pink plastic. In the corner a wet suit was draped over a hibiscus shrub. Beyond was a black rock shore, low foamy waves, an immensity of water.

"My wife, by the way, was so sure I was getting pranked that she went to Costco. She said she didn't want to witness my humiliation." Joey chuckled, a sort of rumbling warning tremor before an eruption, and plopped onto a love seat. "I hope she makes it back in time to meet you or she'll never believe me."

Kalani stood in the doorway, clutching her plate in two hands, still ogling me with mingled covetousness and fear, like she was Indiana Jones and I was a legendary, potentially cursed artifact. Joey patted the cushion next to him. "Kalani, come sit here by granddad. Hadley doesn't bite." To me, he said, "Not a lot of movie stars drop by."

I gave Kalani a little finger wave, and she bolted back into the house, a rain of baby carrots falling behind her. Joey nearly collapsed with mirth. "Oh man," he said eventually. "You know, that's probably the right response to meeting your heroes. Just run away."

"She lives with you?"

"For now." His expression turned somber. "Her parents have been having some issues."

"Sorry."

"That's life. But, so, you're in a movie about Marian Graves?"

"Nah, Caleb never got married," Joey said. "He wasn't really the type. He had some nice girlfriends, though. He was dating this hippie girl Cheryl for a while who was friends with my mom, and so when I was a sophomore in high school and my mom ran off with a guy to Arizona and I started getting in trouble—this was in like '70, '71—Caleb and Cheryl took me in and straightened me out. They broke up after a couple years, and Cheryl left but I stayed. I'd never really had a dad, so Caleb and I had our rocky patches, but we were always like this little team, you know? I didn't leave until I got married. Then when Caleb got sick, my wife and I and our kids moved back in with him to help out. Not like I could ever repay him." He pointed at the ocean. "I scattered his ashes just right there."

"You must miss him," I said.

"Yeah, sometimes, even though it's been twenty-one years. You don't really get it before it happens—how you always miss some people, you know?"

I thought of Mitch. "I do know."

He looked at me curiously. "So Adelaide Scott told you about her, um, **connection** to Jamie Graves."

I nodded. "She said she came here once."

"Yeah, a long time ago. She was on a big

family-discovery kick. She was trying to figure some stuff out for sure."

"Like what?"

"What you'd expect, I guess. Who am I? What should I do with my life? I was pretty young and not great at asking people, like, probing questions, so I didn't really interrogate her. Plus I had a huge crush because she was really hot and scary. She seemed like such a grown-up, but she would only have been in her twenties, I think. She's made a big success of herself, right? She's some big artist? It was Caleb she kept in touch with more, not me. What did we really have in common, you know?"

I couldn't think what to ask. I sipped from my beer to cover my awkwardness. Reading those letters at Adelaide's had felt good—exciting and re-velatory, almost like desire. I guess it was desire. I wanted to know more. But now the truth about Marian seemed too big, too amorphous for me to gather. She had spread out like debris from a wreck, drifting bits and pieces that didn't connect.

Joey didn't seem to notice how lost for words I was. He said, "Caleb was the best, though. Like he could be strict, and he wasn't the kind of guy to pre-tend he was in a good mood when he wasn't, but he was, you know, honorable. You could trust him. He partied a little too much sometimes, maybe, but I think he was like, I survived the war, so fuck it. He worked on a ranch until he got too old, and then he worked in the little library down the road. He liked to read. He didn't talk much about the war, but he said it had gotten him into books. When he got sick, he'd sit out here all day, reading. Then he got too sick to read, so he'd just hold a book in his lap and look at the ocean. He wasn't a spring chicken even back when he took me in. He must have been about the same age then that I am now." He looked into the house, in the direction Kalani had gone. "Life's full of surprises, though."

"Did he talk much about Marian Graves?"

"You know, honestly, he wasn't, like, chatty. He didn't really **share.** But she came up sometimes, yeah. He said she was really brave and a really good pilot. I watched a TV show about her once, and I tried to read her book, but I couldn't get into it. I'm not really a reader. Caleb was always trying to get me to read. So Marian left her personal stuff to Adelaide Scott, but she left her money—there wasn't much—to Caleb, and then he got royalties from her book after they found it at the South Pole or whatever. That money added up. I didn't even know how much until after he died. There was all this money in his will, and I was like, where did this **come** from? The lawyers told me it was the book, which I guess really had a moment back in the day. It came in handy because my son wanted to go to college on the mainland, and now we have Kalani."

"Did Caleb say if he and Marian were ever . . . involved?" I said. "Romantically?"

Thoughtful, he puffed out his cheeks and stared

up at the ceiling fan. "I don't think so, but I wouldn't be surprised. Why? Were they?"

I explained about Adelaide's letters. There hadn't been many from Caleb, certainly not love letters, but I knew he'd gone to see her in Alaska, and Ruth's letter suggested a man had come between them. Carol Feiffer had given Marian and Caleb a romance, and the Day brothers had run with it, but it seemed more like conjecture than anything. While I was talking, Kalani crept out and climbed up next to Joey without looking at me. She was fiddling with a plastic mermaid doll.

"No kidding," Joey said when I was done. A chuckle worked its way up from his belly. "That old dog. You know, thinking about him . . . he never seemed to be looking for, like, a partner. He had these relationships that went on for a year or two and were sort of casual but also sort of intense, and then they'd fall apart. He'd be alone for a while, and then he'd find a new woman when he felt like it. Almost to the end he had girlfriends. They'd come and hang out and cook him dinner. So maybe this thing with Marian was more of the same. Like, if their paths crossed, then great. They'd pick up where they left off." He pulled Kalani into his lap, said, "Or maybe she was the big one. Maybe he never settled down with anyone because he didn't want to replace her."

"Seems crazy to carry a torch for someone who's been dead for decades."

"I just mean maybe he didn't stop missing her. But I did always wonder why he never settled down."

"You never asked him why?"

"Nah. He would have just made some joke. I wish I could tell you more. I saved some of Caleb's stuff, though, if you want to see it. I got it out after you emailed." Setting Kalani on her feet, he got up and went inside, followed by the child, and came back out with an open cardboard box.

The top layer of Joey's box was a mess of photos in no particular order. I took them out one by one, making a stack. Sitting beside me, he pointed to a black-and-white photo of a dark-haired, vaguely Asian-looking man in an army uniform sitting on a stone wall. "That's Caleb," he said.

I turned the photo over. **Sicily** was penciled on the back.

"Go play, Kalani," Joey said, nudging the girl toward the yard, where she darted into the plastic playhouse like a gopher into a hole.

There were color photos, some faded: Caleb on a horse, his hat ringed with fuchsia flowers. Caleb with a woman at the beach, with another woman at what looked like a wedding reception, sitting with a third woman on a cement structure on a hillside, their legs dangling. "That's Cheryl, who I talked about," Joey said, pointing. She had long, wavy blond hair. "That's a pillbox lookout station from the war. It's still there." Caleb riding a horse up to its chest in the ocean. An ancient black-and-white studio photo of a pale girl with dark, tucked-up hair in a tarnished silver frame. She wore a dress with a lace collar, and the image was ghostly and washed out with age. "I think that was his mother," Joey said. "All he ever said about her was that she was a drunk and had bad luck." Three children sitting unsmiling on a fence, all in overalls: Caleb with Marian and Jamie Graves. Nothing on the back. Teenage Joey grinning in a striped T-shirt, tending something on a smoking BBQ while Caleb looked on, holding a beer. Another black-and-white photo of Caleb in uniform, cigarette in one hand, leaning back in a leather booth. Cocktail glasses glinted in the flash. Marian Graves, in her blue ATA uniform, was beside him, looking away. On the back: **London 1944.**

Under the photos was a bundle of letters, tied neatly together with a shoelace. Joey reached for them, embarrassed. "Those are from me, when Hanako and I did a road trip on the mainland. We were only gone for a month, but I wrote him every day."

Under the letters was a paper folder, soft with age. Inside were press clippings about Marian's flight, from both before and after she went missing, haphazardly folded. "Caleb collected those," Joey said. "I was surprised when I found them. Usually he wasn't into saving things."

I started unfolding the brittle paper. "I think sometimes people hope if they amass enough scraps eventually the whole picture will become clear."

"Is that what you're trying to do?"

"I don't know what I'm trying to do," I said.

The same photo appeared again and again in the newspapers: Marian and Eddie standing beside the **Peregrine** before they left Auckland, smiling, almost bashful, both with their arms folded across their chests. Later, after the reporters had dug around in Marian's past, they ran the old photo of Addison Graves carrying the twins down the gangway of the SS **Manaus.** There was one of Marian in her ATA uniform, climbing into a Spitfire. And there was her wedding photo next to some fluff piece about her "colorful" life.

I closed the folder. Underneath it in the box was a certificate of appreciation from the library where Caleb had worked and a program from his memorial service. Then came a magazine with a slip of paper marking an article about the ranch that included the photo of Caleb riding in the ocean.

At the very bottom of the box was a white envelope addressed to Caleb and bearing several foreign stamps. The return address was a post office box in New Zealand. "Mind if I . . ."

"Sure," he said. "I've never been able to make any sense of it. For some reason it was in the lockbox where he kept his birth certificate and important stuff like that. I don't even know why I kept it."

. . .

It was just a little bit of paper, another yellowed newspaper clipping, folded up small. I peeled its layers apart, pressed it flat. Bits flaked off around the edges. It was a photo from a newspaper called the **Queenstown Courier.** April 28, 1954. Four men in hats sat and sprawled on a grassy rise, each holding a beer bottle. In the background, sheep grazed. "High country shepherds enjoying well-earned refreshment after the muster," read the caption. In black pen, someone had drawn an arrow to one of the men and written something in the margin. The handwriting was nearly illegible, but the specific style of its illegibility was so familiar my insides fizzed like I'd swallowed a sparkler. I squinted at the words. **Sitting-in-the-Water-Grizzly.** When I set it down, the paper lifted up and curled slowly closed along its fold lines as though alive. I smoothed it out again.

"Sitting-in-the-Water-Grizzly," I said to Joey. "Does that mean anything to you?"

"No clue," he said. "I looked it up on the internet once, and all I got was some stuff about an Indian woman who lived as a man. I don't really remember specifics."

The man under the arrow was reclining on one elbow with his long thin legs stretched out, his face angled away from the camera and hidden by the shadow of his hat. I didn't know if I should tell

Joey anything, but I couldn't help it. I took out my phone and zoomed in on a photo I'd taken of one of the letters Marian had written to Ruth. I turned it so Marian's rows of crabbed and spiky words lined up with the scribbled note. "Check this out," I said.

Joey came around to stand behind me, leaned down to study my phone. "What is it?"

"It's a letter Marian Graves wrote."

"No way," he said, getting it. "No **way.**"

"It's the same handwriting, right?" I said. "I'm not imagining things?"

"It **really** looks like it."

"Did he get any more letters from New Zealand? Do you know?"

"Man, he **went** there! He went a bunch of times! I didn't mention it before because I thought he just liked New Zealand. People get really into that place." Joey flopped back onto the love seat, his hands gripping the top of his head. "No way," he said again.

The sparks in my gut spread outward. I felt like my skeleton should be visible, glowing through my skin. "When did he go there?"

"I don't remember specific dates or anything, but he'd kind of usually go after breakups? Not after all of them, but like maybe every five years or so? I know he'd been a couple of times before I moved in. He never took anyone with him. He said it was his thing he liked to do alone, and, yeah, he got other letters, too, but he didn't keep them. I think he might have actually **burned** them. I remember seeing bits in the coffee can he used as an ashtray and thinking it was sort of dramatic. It's not like he burned all the mail."

"Did you ever ask him who was writing to him or why he kept going?"

"He just said he had a buddy from the war down there."

"Do you remember anything else? Did he bring back photos?"

"No, no photos. Let me think for a second, though." He closed his eyes. I waited. The sun was white on the ocean. Kalani peeped at me from the playhouse window, retreated when she saw me looking back. Finally Joey opened his eyes and shook his head. "No. Sorry. Nothing else is coming to mind. I went through all his stuff when he died, and you've seen pretty much everything I saved. That was more than twenty years ago, anyway. Do you really think he might have been going to see **her**?"

What did I have? A photo of a faceless shepherd from sixty years ago, a scribbled reference to—maybe—a Native person who might never have existed. **I will go soon,** Marian had written at the end of her logbook. **I.** I'd never thought about how it was an I and not a we. What about Eddie? What about the plane? How could Marian have made it to New Zealand without anyone knowing?

Was it even possible to pass as a man? What about Adelaide Scott? If Marian had survived, she'd chosen never to see her niece again.

"I don't know what to think," I said.

The breeze in the palm trees and the sound of the waves gave the quiet a shifting, velvety texture.

"What will you do?" Joey said.

"What do you think I should do?"

"I don't know, man. Say you get out there and start telling people you have this crazy theory she survived, and then what? If you're **right,** and she **did,** she clearly didn't want anyone to know. If you're wrong, you look like a kook or like you just want attention or whatever. I guess my first impulse would be to let sleeping dogs lie."

Kalani burst from the playhouse, running to greet a small gray-haired woman in a big sun hat who was carrying a huge plastic bin of pretzels under one arm and a huge box of frozen waffles under the other. "Joey," she called, "can you help unload, please?"

"Okay," he called back, "but you'll have to entertain our guest."

She looked up and spotted me. Her mouth opened in shock, and I could see how truly and totally she had not believed I would be on her porch. But here I was. Joey fell apart with laughter.

The Flight

—

Our flight is in defiance of the sun and its daily traverse. Come west, the sun says. It tugs at us, runs off like a child trying to entice us to follow. But we must go north, leaving the light behind.

—MARIAN GRAVES

**Little America III, Ross Ice Shelf,
  to Campbell Island
78°28′ S, 163°51′ W to 52°34′ S 169°14′ E
March 4, 1950
21,785 nautical miles flown**

The worst of her agony, for the first hours, is that she thinks she will reach New Zealand. The day is blue and mostly clear. Eddie had given her charts he'd already marked up with bearings and angles for the sextant. He had hugged her tight and kissed her hard on the cheek, shaken her hand, sent her off to what he at least claimed to believe would be her death. He had made her promise not to send anyone for him in the unlikely event of her reaching land. He said there would be no point, that she should tell people he had fallen in a crevasse. She thinks of him lying in the snow on a clear night, waiting to die. She thinks of Barclay almost giving himself to the snow the night they met, of Caleb lost in the snowstorm as a boy. They had both almost surrendered themselves to the cold but had changed their minds. She finds herself hoping that Eddie will not change his, that the stars and the aurora will beckon him. Maybe she had left the logbook behind in order to abandon the truth along with Eddie.

She is past the PNR when her fuel begins to disappear too quickly. Vapor streams from under the left wing. At first she is aware only of relief. Eddie will avoid the fate he most feared.

A gannet plunge. She remembers what she'd written. She watches the fuel drop and decides to be true to her word. She decides, and yet she flies on. Does she understand then that she wishes to live? This memory will remain oddly blank, resisting her attempts to dredge the truth from it. Later she will conclude she'd had many contradictory wishes: to live, to die, to go back and live her life over and change everything, to live her life again and change nothing.

She doesn't know how much time passes before

she steels herself. She doesn't think but pushes down on the yoke, dives. The engines cry out. The water rises up to meet her.

When she had thought she was going to fly a Spitfire into the sea, Jamie, already dead, had told her not to. She'd listened then. She'd seen the end of the war because of it. She'd seen rubble and rivers and elephants on red dunes. She'd seen manta rays and the polar ice caps. She'd lain in bed with Caleb on Oahu, listening to the trade winds. No voice comes now, nothing but the whining engines, the rush of wind, but she pulls up. The plane levels off not far above the waves. The great gliding birds, the huge-winged albatrosses, carve the air. She doesn't belong among them. Up she goes, back into the sky. Her hands tremble. She pulls the charts onto her lap.

The fuel gauge doesn't care that she has changed her mind. The needle still drops. Vapor still streams from the wing. She searches Eddie's pencil marks on the gridded blue paper for a secret passage back into life. First she sees Macquarie Island, twenty miles long and oriented almost perfectly north-south. She knows there is a weather station there, manned year-round. But the island is well to the west, against the wind. She doesn't have the fuel. Farther north but farther east is another speck. Campbell Island.

South still tugs at her compass. Empty ocean surrounds her. Finding the island would be difficult even if her navigation skills weren't so rusty. Maybe she will fail, but she will try.

Of the next hours, she will remember capturing the sun in the sextant, scribbling calculations, churning with internal debates. The fear in her is smothered almost to nothing by the necessity of focus, of action. She will not remember how she comes to conclude that the plane itself must be lost, sacrificed, that she must try, if she can, to keep her survival a secret, that the only way she can contend with continued life is to make a new one. These decisions will become simple facts of her past, way points at which she turned, altering her destination. Any ambivalence she feels, any counterarguments she makes to herself will be lost, erased by the immutability of what has been done.

When, under a high overcast, the island's silhouette breaks the horizon, she sheds her reindeer parka, gets into her parachute and Mae West. The island grows steadily nearer. She braces the steering yoke as best she can. The plane only needs to be steady **enough,** and only for the few minutes she requires. When land is below, she goes to the back of the fuselage, heaves open the door, and jumps.

She has never done a parachute jump. Pridefully, she'd told herself she'd landed planes when other pilots would have jumped, but now, plummeting through space, she thinks some practice would have been useful. She pulls the rip cord. With a violent jerk, the chute opens.

The **Peregrine** flies on, oblivious to its new independence, the imminence of its watery end. A pang. She looks away. Between her feet sways a grassy, tussocked mountain.

Here is a truth: She prefers to hide, to cease being Marian Graves entirely rather than face what she has done to Eddie. She no longer cares the circle is unfinished. That causes her no shame. But she believes she brings death to those around her. Before she left, she had gone to Seattle to meet Jamie's child. She had thought she would visit the girl from time to time after the flight, know her as she grew up, but now she is certain she would bring only misfortune. Let Adelaide be something else entirely. Let her not be a Graves.

The wind pushes Marian out over a long and narrow inlet of black water. An albatross glides by with a whoosh, turning its head to inspect her. She had seen them nesting on the tussocked mountain as she descended: enormous, blindingly white birds settled among the windblown grass like dollops of snow. Glossy black water between her boots still. She pulls on the parachute's handles, trying to steer, but the wind ushers her firmly out toward the mouth of the inlet, out to sea. Just off a rocky beach, not wanting to be blown farther from shore, she unclips her harness and drops.

The cold of that water. The force of it. She makes her gannet plunge after all but feetfirst. She sees blurry darkness, a silver ceiling. Stunned as a

clubbed fish, she placidly watches the surface recede until she remembers she must pull the cords
of her Mae West to inflate it.

She will remember the air and waves, the heaviness of her boots and clothes, the numbing cold,
the startling nearby porpoise leap of a small penguin out of the water. Surf crashes. Black ropes of
kelp long and fat as fire hoses writhe in the surge as
she is dashed on the rocks—she keeps only a jagged
fragment of the event: a cascade of foam, a hard
impact. Her Mae West is punctured, her face badly
scraped, her nose broken. A last churning tumble,
and finally there is coarse sand under her fingers.

She drags herself from the water, permits herself to lie still for a moment in her sodden clothes
before her chattering teeth tell her she must walk.
Dense, brittle shrubs grab at her ankles, mud sucks
at her boots. (She's been lucky with the tide. Later,
when she has been on the island for a while and re-
traces this first walk, there will no beach at all, only
a cliff.) She sits and rests many times, is stumbling
and hypothermic when she reaches a hut marked
by a radio mast and spinning anemometer, smoke
rising from a chimney pipe. With the last of her
strength, she knocks on the door.

A Dive with Intent

Twenty-One

When I got back to L.A., before I had to film the crash, I took another flying lesson. This time the instructor was a woman, a no-nonsense sort of gal in Wrangler jeans with a strict bob of orange hair and aviator shades. "I took a lesson once before," I told her as she walked me around the plane, explaining its parts, "but I freaked out when it was my turn to fly."

"What do you mean freaked out?" she said.

"I just didn't want to fly it. I let go of the controls. Like this." I held up my hands as though someone were pointing a gun at me.

"Do you want to fly it now?"

"I might not," I said, "but I want to try."

"Cool," she said.

This time it was afternoon, and there was no

marine layer, just open sky dingy with smog. Catalina wallowed offshore; the ocean horizon was soft and hazy. In every other direction, the city sprawled and sprawled. The jets sailing up from LAX, noses in the air, almost made me feel sorry for our plucky little Cessna. "Okay," said the pilot as we churned effortfully toward Malibu, "go ahead and take the yoke. Just fly steady and level."

In Hawaii, when I left Joey Kamaka's house, I'd gone back to my hotel and flopped flat on my face on my bed and cried. I cried because Marian Graves hadn't drowned and, to one person, hadn't been lost. I cried because of Joey's kindness, because I was jealous of Kalani having a childhood, because I was the kind of asshole who could be jealous of a little kid whose parents couldn't take care of her. I cried for Mitch and for my parents. I cried because I'd gotten going and sometimes you just have to ride out the tears.

Beyond my balcony, beyond Waikiki Beach, out in the middle of the Pacific, the sun was easing down. Surfers dotted the water, sitting on their boards. Kids played in the shallows. In a movie, this would be the moment when I would rush outside and plunge cathartically into the sea. Newly whole, forever changed, I would float on my back, smiling beatifically at the sky.

Since I didn't have any better ideas, I put on my

bathing suit. I rode the mirrored elevator down to the tiki-chic lobby and jogged outside in my flip-flops and labored through the perfect, powdery sand. I dropped my hotel robe and walked into the water and dove under.

Down there, eyes closed, rocking with the swell, I imagined the sand sloping away into darkness, into submerged deserts and canyons and mountain ranges, rising again into the edges of all the continents. I thought of ships and airplanes and bones being eaten away to nothing by rust and by tiny nibbling things, grown over by coral and sponges, scuttled across by crabs. I thought of the **Peregrine** and how no one would ever find it. No one would ever know where to look. When I surfaced, a wave lifted me, pushed me back toward shore. I swam out again. I'd forgotten, somehow, that the sun was fire, that it was **molten,** until I watched it waver and redden as it slid, almost oozed, behind the sea.

The water dimmed; the clouds flushed. I didn't know what I would do after the movie was finished. It occurred to me that I could go to New Zealand or to Antarctica, keep playing detective, but, no, I didn't need to know the whole story. No story is ever whole. When I'd looked up Sitting-in-the-Water-Grizzly, I'd read that he died after someone reached inside him and cut off a piece of his heart, but then his body didn't decay, as though without his whole heart he couldn't transform anymore, not even into dust. I hoped Marian had kept her whole heart.

. . .

I put my hands on the yoke. The plastic was warm from the sun, and I could feel the vibration of the engine. The pilot showed which instruments to watch, showed me what was supposed to be the horizon and what was supposed to be the wings, how to line them up. "Doing okay?" she said.

"I think so," I said.

"If you pull back a little bit," she said, "the nose will go up."

I pulled back. The windshield filled slowly with sky.

Los Angeles, 2015

Twenty-Two

When the plane hits the water, the sound cuts out except for a faint ringing. Before, there'd been wind and the engines and my amplified breathing, but then, at the moment of impact, it all goes away. Seen from a distance: a massive, silent splash in an empty sea. The plane rocks in the waves. The nose dips under; the rest slides after. The ocean seals itself shut. Huge white birds glide along the waves, and you hear that high, sustained ringing, quiet enough to seem half imagined. Then we're underwater, looking at me and Eddie in the cockpit. Bubbles rise from my nose; my cropped Marian hair wafts around my head. Eddie is unconscious, his forehead bloody. I lean forward, looking up at the receding surface, wistful but resolute. I close my eyes. Then, as though to give me privacy while I drown, we cut away to a shot of the **Peregrine** from above, sub-merged, its shape sinking into blackness.

I expect a fade to black, but instead, light seeps in through the dark, eats through it like mold, fills the screen. "That was Bart's idea," Redwood says, whispering even though we are the only ones in the screening room. "The white." Music fades in. The end credits start.

Redwood's face is bright with reflected light. He points. "There!" His name is on the screen, and then it is gone.

I don't watch for mine. "Ready?" I say, and we get up and push out through a side door into the blinding afternoon.

It's not some big triumph, that I didn't freak out when I flew the Cessna, that I made it go up and down, left and right. Mostly I felt relief. And a little hit of amazement. And then I must have slipped back into being Marian Graves because, for a second, I felt free.

The End

~

She's in the ocean now, as she was always meant to be. Most of her has come to rest, scattered, on the cold southern seafloor, but some of her smallest, lightest fragments, floating dust, are still being carried along by the currents. Fish ate a few tiny motes of her, and a penguin ate one of those fish and regurgitated it to his chick, and some infinitesimal speck of her was back on Antarctica for a while, as guano on a nest of pebbles, until a storm washed her back out to sea.

She dies twice, the second time forty-six years after the first. She dies in the Southern Ocean; she dies on a sheep farm in the Fjordland region of New Zealand.

The man who opens the door to the hut on Campbell Island is called Harold, and he is, as he would say, being a practitioner of understatement, a bit surprised to find a sodden, semiconscious woman at his feet. She is mumbling, jabbering. As best he can make out, she is begging him not to tell anyone she's there. **But who are you?** he asks, heaving her to her feet, bringing her inside. By then she is past being able to respond.

There is another man on the island, John, and a border collie called Swift. The hut and a few small outbuildings had been constructed during the war to house coast-watchers, stationed there to alert the mainland if they saw enemy ships. They never did, but their meteorological observations proved so useful that, after the war, the station was kept going. A yearlong posting for a certain kind of man. A deliberate, meticulous kind of man who needed little society, who was content to perform the same tasks every day, take the same measurements, record the same data, translate that data to Morse code, and send it to some unseen recipient for use by people he will never meet, would prefer not to meet.

It is one of the most significant waypoints of Marian's life that Harold and John are two such men.

She spends several days in fevered delirium. When she first starts to regain her senses, she is afraid of the quiet, bearded figures she perceives around her, thinks of what so many men, sequestered on a desolate island for months, would be likely to do with a woman. But Harold and John only ever touch her with unobtrusive concern—a hand on her forehead, a changing of the bandage on her face where the rocks had cut her, support under her neck as she sips broth—and never leer or linger, even when they have to help her pee in a bucket beside the bed. Both have wives and children in Christchurch, but over time she comes to suspect they prefer the island, are content with their barometers and whirligigs and weather balloons. When she's regained some strength, she tells them a little bit of her story, and later all of it, because she thinks they'll be more likely to keep her secret if they can survey the entirety of its surrounding landscape, decide for themselves her right to it. The only thing she can't bear to tell them is that she left Eddie behind. She tells them her navigator fell into a crevasse, burns with shame instead of fever.

They listen gravely, without comment, and retreat outside to talk between themselves. When they return, they tell her they had received, a week before she arrived, a radio alert to report any sighting of a C-47 Dakota, feared lost. They ask who will miss her. She says, "No one." Caleb would forgive the lie. She says she has no husband, no children, no parents, no brother. They tell her they will respect her wishes, not report her, but also that the ship that brought them will not return until January, nearly ten months. She might change her mind before then. For now they have no objection to her remaining.

Shame again. She has invaded and disrupted

their little colony of two, spoiled their peaceful year. She promises to make herself useful, and they nod, unconcerned. When she asks about food, they say there ought to be enough, plus, if need be, there are seabirds and their eggs, some cabbages they are growing, and also sheep, left over from a failed experiment in which the government leased the island to farmers. She brings no hardship, they say.

Do they think she is wrong to try to leave herself behind? They exchange inscrutable glances. Finally, Harold says, "We reckon it's your business." But— she asks—what about the ship, when it comes? They will have to explain her; she will be found out, and all this trouble will be for nothing. They say that is something to be considered later. There is no hurry.

In shape, Campbell Island resembles an oak leaf eaten away by insects, its coast indented by inlets and bays and two long, narrow harbors: Perseverance, into the mouth of which Marian splashed, and Northeast. Its slopes appear gentle, but walking is hard going because of the tussock grass and the mud and that dense shrub that John, the more botanically inclined of her companions, teaches her to call **Dracophyllum longifolium.** Besides the beards, as she thinks of Harold and John, and the dog Swift and herself, the island is occupied by sheep, rats, feral cats, sea lions, fur seals, elephant seals, the occasional leopard seal, a number of species of albatross, other seabirds and land birds, and two kinds of small penguins: the abundant rockhopper, which nests in the rocks, and the more secretive yellow-eyed, which nests in the bush and is usually glimpsed hurrying furtively up the beach.

She wonders if Eddie could have changed his mind. If he had, he might hold out for quite a while, survive off the supplies in Little America and by hunting seals and penguins. She wonders if he might be hoping she will send help after all, if he had truly been so sure she would not make it. She wonders if he is already dead.

She regrets the sadness she will cause Matilda and Caleb, and perhaps Jamie's Sarah, but she thinks they might as well grieve, because she is gone.

The male sea lions have left for the year, Harold tells her. But the females have gone inland to pup, and she often encounters the animals. They burst roaring from the brush where they have hidden their babies, or they belly-toboggan down the hills on muddy trails, bound for the sea. Harold is conducting a survey of the southern royal albatrosses, and Marian goes with him to count nests and chicks and to hold the massive birds in her arms, one hand wrapped firmly around the bill, while he crimps identifying rings around their pinkish, leathery ankles.

They tramp all over the island, even in the

excoriating winter winds, recording, in total, nine hundred and thirty-eight birds in Harold's ledger. The birds are ungainly on the ground, easy to catch. The adults are magnificently white with good-humored black button eyes, thick pink bills, wingspans as long as two men set end-to-end.

When she first arrives, the birds are still sitting on their chicks, but gradually the young ones grow into hungry heaps of white fluff substantial enough to be left alone while the parents go to sea to feed. After their feathers come in, the chicks stand up and stretch their wings in the breeze, and, finally, around the time Marian leaves, the first ones fly away, making teetering, experimental leaps into the wind. Harold says once fledged they will not touch land for several years. They will fly around Antarctica, returning to Campbell from the opposite direction one day to breed.

Marian's special purview becomes the sheep. Before the war, farming on the island had been given up as hopelessly unprofitable and the sheep left behind to roam wild. They are hardy and wily, the ones who survived and bred, and she finds herself drawn to them. Swift the dog shares her interest in the sheep, and slowly, with many failures, the two begin to learn how to move them from place to place, just to see if they can.

In one of the abandoned farm structures, she finds old shearing blades. She patches up a falling-down corral, toils patiently with Swift for days before they actually manage to drive a single sheep into it. John had worked with sheep in his youth and offers suggestions in passing, mostly leaves her on her own. Shearing is hard work; she makes a hash of many a sheep before she gets the knack. There is no real reason to shear the incorrigibly wild Campbell sheep, but it has begun to dawn on her that she will need a skill other than flying airplanes if she is to become a new person.

After she has been on the island six months, the beards sit her down and say they might have a way to get her to the mainland undetected. "We would have told you sooner," John says, "but, begging your pardon, we weren't so sure about you at first." Harold's brother, it turns out, is a keen yachtsman and has talked about sailing to Campbell for a visit in early summer, before the annual ship comes in January to bring fresh beards and take away the old ones. She could, perhaps, if the brother is amenable, sail back with him. They hadn't wanted to ask him over the radio for lack of privacy, so they will have to wait and see what he thinks, if he comes at all. If he isn't amenable, or she isn't, well, then, they'll have another think. "But you're still sure," Harold asks, "that you don't want to be yourself anymore?"

She is sure, and the brother (who turns out to be even more taciturn than Harold) is amenable, and so after much silent valedictory hand-gripping with the beards, she leaves Campbell Island and reaches Invercargill at last, in January 1951, under sail.

. . .

After ten months wearing clothes borrowed from
the beards, it seems natural to continue dressing as
a man. She feels as she had as a teenager, skulking
around Missoula in overalls, hat pulled low, though
now her disguise is more convincing, with her broken nose and weathered skin, her rough hands and
her shoulders sturdy from shearing.

She goes north into the country around Mount
Cook and gets a job as a high-country shepherd.
She keeps to herself, which is easy to do, living in
a hut on the side of a mountain, tending to unruly
bleating masses of Merinos. They aren't as skittish
as the Campbell sheep, nor quite as hardy, but they
are by no means docile. She gets better with sheep-
dogs, better at shearing, though she is never especially quick. She speaks little, doesn't complain,
can hold her drink, and so is respected. From the
beards she'd picked up a passable Kiwi accent that
gradually becomes second nature; any oddnesses
she explains away by saying, truthfully, that her
mother had been American. Later, some people
will claim they'd had suspicions about her sex, but
at the time none are voiced, not directly. Certainly
she takes some ribbing for her slightness—Twig,
they call her in the shearing shed—but her broken
nose and her pilot's squint and the scars on her
face from frostbite and the rocky Campbell shore
give her a tough look. She's never had much in the

way of a chest, nothing a hard band of elastic and a couple layers of shirts can't hide. She calls herself Martin Wallace.

She believes she deserves to be isolated and unknown, that loneliness is a fitting punishment. But time weakens her resolve. Her self-recriminations grow softer. She has been a shepherd for three years when a photo of her (face obscured by shadow) happens to appear in a Queenstown newspaper, and on impulse she cuts it out and sends it to Caleb. **Sitting-in-the-Water-Grizzly,** she writes, wondering if he will remember the story he'd once told her. She can't bring herself to write down the bald truth, prefers to leave things up to chance. She has, in some ways, begun to lose any rigid idea about what constitutes truth. She catches herself remembering Eddie falling into a crevasse, though it had not happened. Or perhaps it had, later. What she is really remembering is her own foot popping through the snow, being balanced between a white nothingness and a black one.

Caleb comes to see her for Christmas in 1954, and an aperture is opened between her two lives. When she meets his ship in Auckland, it is her first trip to the city since she'd departed for Aitutaki with Eddie, and so the circle is finally closed, without fanfare, five years after she'd begun it. With Caleb, for two weeks, she returns to her body. There is no question, as there never has been, of him staying, but there is equal certainty he will return.

She'd told him, in Hawaii, that she envied how he'd found a place that quelled his restlessness. She had not thought she would ever find such a place for herself, but in New Zealand, she does. Perhaps her peace is inherent to the land, or perhaps she has simply exhausted herself. She longs to fly an airplane again, but she doesn't long to see over the horizon. And she feels she must make sacrifices in atonement for her survival, for leaving Eddie. She will not fly. She will not know Jamie's daughter.

The presence of her own book on her shelves is a dark joke. She had never quite intended to write it, and yet there it is, in its mustard dust jacket. If she had succeeded, if all had gone according to plan and they had landed triumphantly back in Auckland, she would never have let it be published as it was. She had left it behind in Antarctica as a gesture of defiance, a marker of her existence, like a stone cairn. But then she had neither succeeded nor died.

In the years before the logbook was found, she seldom thought of it. Then there it was in a newspaper photograph in 1958, in the gloved hands of an ice scientist doing research at Little America III. She'd been shocked and frightened by the prospect of stirred-up publicity, of her photo being printed and reprinted, of everyone being reminded that Marian Graves had once existed. For years she worried that someone might recognize her after all, but, as it turned out, no one did. She was greatly changed, and also she had settled in a corner of the world where people didn't pay much attention to things like lost American lady pilots.

When the book was found, she had wondered if Eddie would be, too. She'd wondered if there was any possibility at all he might still be alive after eight years, though surely even if he'd managed to feed and warm himself, he would have been broken by the solitude, the extremity. The question was irrelevant, though—he hadn't wanted to survive.

What were his last days like? How many of them had there been? Did he live until winter? Did he fall in a crevasse after all? His body wasn't inside Little America or the scientists would have found it. If it had been her, she would have done what he said he would do: walked in the winter night far away from camp and lain in the snow, under the stars and the aurora. Or maybe not—it is not lost on her she had twice failed to choose death. She'd written in her logbook that her life was her one possession. She had kept it; she had wanted it.

In 1963, the crew of a navy icebreaker will catch sight of buildings smushed like sandwich filling in the middle of a tabular iceberg drifting three hundred miles from the Ross Ice Shelf: Little America III, its bunks and Victrola and frozen dog turds and corn on the cob, all gone out to sea.

Eddie, too, wherever he was, would eventually